RENTED HEART

GARRETT LEIGH

RIPTIDE
PUBLISHING

Riptide Publishing
PO Box 1537
Burnsville, NC 28714
www.riptidepublishing.com

Rented Heart

Cover art: G.D. Leigh, blackjazzdesign.com
Editor: Carole-ann Galloway
Layout: L.C. Chase, lcchase.com/design.htm

ISBN: 978-1-62649-392-6

First edition
September, 2016

Also available in ebook:
ISBN: 978-1-62649-391-9

RENTED HEART

GARRETT LEIGH

RIPTIDE PUBLISHING

Hi Mum!
waves

TABLE OF CONTENTS

CHAPTER ONE

Tourist season was always a dodgy time for a rentboy in Norfolk, or, at least, Zac Payne assumed it was. He hadn't really been in town long enough to tell. In the city he'd left behind, every day had been dicey . . . and dirty. Even in high summer, the temperate British sun was no match for the noise and smog of the Big Smoke.

King's Lynn, Norfolk, was different—quieter, cleaner, and conversely less predictable. In London, he wouldn't have thought twice about approaching the miserable-looking hottie leaning against the front wall of the town's only gay bar, because one protracted stare would've told him all he needed to know: that the blond bloke was rich, lonely, and lost, and easy pickings for the faceless good time Zac had to offer. Here in King's Lynn though, Zac couldn't be sure the man was even gay, much less willing to put his hand in his pocket for the privilege of having Zac in his bed. Or that he didn't have a bunch of mates waiting around the corner, ready to give an audacious poof a kicking.

Not that Zac particularly minded a good kicking. In the right context, that shit was fun and the sick side of him enjoyed it.

Focus. Are you marking him, or not?

It was a fair question, because King's Lynn was a town that had a respectable bedtime. If he didn't pick up a job soon, he would be done for the night. *Fuck it.* Zac ducked behind a lamppost and lit up his last weed pipe. He sucked down a lungful of herbal smoke and closed his eyes as it filtered into his bloodstream, dulling what remained of his inhibitions and lighting his senses with a subtle fire. Reborn, he opened his eyes. Colours brightened, the stars sparkled, and across the street, the blond was more alluring than ever. With his high cheekbones, shaggy hair, and broad shoulders, all wrapped up in ripped jeans and a designer T-shirt, he was the kind of dude Zac dreamed of when he went to bed alone.

Zac crossed the road, weaving through the late-night revellers who were spilling from the club, searching for taxis to take them home. The blond saw him coming. His previously empty stare turned curious, and Zac's confidence took a boost. Perhaps he'd struck gold. "All right, mate?"

The blond smiled slightly, showing Zac a beautiful set of teeth. "Yes, thanks. You?"

Zac shrugged. "I'm bored. This club is shite."

The blond's grin widened. "That why you've been loitering outside all night?"

"How do you know what I've been doing all night?"

"Because I've seen you every time I've come out for a fag. Looked like you were waiting for someone."

Not someone. Anyone. But this bloke didn't need to know that. "Maybe I got stood up."

"Maybe we both did."

"Yeah?" Now Zac was the curious one. "What happened?"

"My mate dragged me out. Thinks I need to get laid."

"And do you?"

The blond shrugged. "Doesn't everyone?"

Zac couldn't argue with that. Fucking was like breathing to him, especially when he had a good partner, something he'd yet to find in the rural monotony of eastern England. *Shoulda gone to Newquay.*

"What's so funny?"

"Hmm?"

The blond raised an eyebrow. "You're smirking."

"Speculating, actually."

"Yeah? About what?"

"About how you need to get laid." It was a reckless move, but Zac didn't care. It had been a long night with no work, like the night before, and the night before that. No work tonight meant no food tomorrow, and he needed to eat almost as much as he needed to get fucked.

If the blond was taken aback by the bluntness, he didn't let it show. He took a moment to consider his response, before he treated Zac to another lopsided half grin. "If you'd said that a few hours ago, I'd have said I could live without it, but I've drunk my body weight in Jäger since then, and I reckon it might be the only thing that will sober me up."

It was as good a reason as any. "What's your name?"

"Liam. What's yours?"

"Zac. Wanna come back to mine?"

"Where do you live?"

"In town. The new flats on the high street."

Liam pulled the latest iPhone from his pocket and studied the screen before he seemed to make a snap decision. "Why the hell not? Looks like I've got nothing better to do."

"Then let's go." Zac held out his hand and wrapped his fingers around Liam's smooth, warm palm. "Oh, and by the way, it's a hundred for the fuck . . . three if you want to stay all night."

CHAPTER
TWO

Liam Mallaney dropped the beautiful man's hand like he'd been burned. *What the fuck? Have I seriously just been picked up by a hooker?* Nah, he'd heard him wrong. Shit like that didn't happen in Norfolk. Damn place was too bloody boring. *And that's why you're here.*

Shut up.

Liam silenced the devil on his shoulder and focused on the dark-haired man—on Zac—studying his intelligent, bottomless green eyes, searching for any sign that he was pulling Liam's leg, but Zac stared back at him, his gaze steady and expectant. *Jesus. He is a hooker.*

The realisation didn't horrify Liam as much as it should've done, because nothing truly horrified him anymore. Life had already played its trump card, and as he stood in the moonlight, a foot away from the hottest bloke he'd seen in years, there was no denying the spark of attraction—and arousal—creeping through him. He *did* need to get laid, really fucking laid, with no emotional strings to disentangle himself from in the morning, and no obligation to pretend he was still capable of giving a shit. Could he buy that freedom? Tonight, it seemed he could.

Liam checked his pocket for his wallet. "One hundred to fuck?"

"If you want. We can do other stuff if you don't have that much."

Liam snorted. "Trust me. I can afford you. Are we going, or what?"

Zac shrugged, his gaze slightly narrower than it had been before. "Whatever. It's this way."

Liam followed him down the side path that led to the high street. The alley was dank and dark, and it crossed his mind that following a rentboy home wasn't the cleverest move he'd ever made, but as he dodged murky puddles and the squashed remnants of discarded kebabs, he didn't much care. Whatever Zac had in store for him would be a relief, it had to be.

"Not going to drug me and kill me, are you?"

Liam glanced up, startled by the echo of his own fears. "Not likely, mate. What about you? Gonna handcuff and rob me blind?"

"If you want—the handcuffing, I mean. I won't need to rob you. I've told you my price."

Indeed he had. Liam's pulse quickened. He'd come to the club tonight sure he'd be home by ten, tucked up in bed with the dogs and his ever-overflowing inbox, harbouring no regrets save that he'd bothered to go out in the first place. Sex had been the last thing on his mind, until he'd spotted Zac across the road, dancing along the kerb, weaving to his own tune with a dubious-looking cigarette jammed in his mouth. He wondered if Zac knew he'd pictured them fucking long before he'd sauntered over and offered his services.

Not that it mattered. After all, Zac wasn't doing this for fun.

Liam tried to let the notion of paying someone to find him attractive seep into his self-esteem and shock him into calling time on the madness.

Nothing happened. He pulled a battered pack of Marlboro Lights from his back pocket and lit up, proffering the box to Zac, who took one and followed suit. "Am I your only client tonight?"

"Client?" Zac regarded Liam through a haze of smoke. "This ain't *Pretty Woman*, mate. In my world, you're called a john."

Liam didn't particularly care what he was called, but he was curious about his place in Zac's workday. Was he the first of many, or the last?

"This is me." Zac stopped outside a nondescript block of new-build flats. "Still wanna come in?"

"If you'll have me." The absurdity of his own answer made Liam snigger.

Zac grinned too and opened the exterior door to the flats. "Oh, I'll have you. Trust me, we're going to have a good time."

Liam didn't doubt it. Zac moved with a sensuous grace and the barest hint of a swagger, all signs of a man who knew he was dynamite in bed, though, he supposed Zac had probably had enough practice. Not like Liam, who hadn't touched a man in more than a year. Not since—

Stop it. Liam fought the cloud of misery as he climbed the steps behind Zac. Tonight, he'd drunk most of it away, but his Jäger-laced buzz had faded while he'd set himself up for an expensive night of fun with Zac, and he needed a distraction.

Arriving at Zac's flat provided one even faster than Liam had hoped for. Zac let them in and ushered Liam forward.

Liam stepped inside, glancing around nervously, though for what, he wasn't quite sure—*he's a hooker, not a serial killer.* If anything, Zac was taking the bigger risk. Liam had half a foot and a stone on him, maybe more. *Perhaps he's a ninja.* Liam sniggered again. Perhaps his buzz was still there after all.

"So . . ." Zac hovered in the doorway of what looked like a living room. "Do you want to come in and sit down?"

"What do you usually do with a john?"

Zac shrugged. "This and that. What do you want to do?"

"I want to fuck you." Liam hadn't known how true it was until he said it, but as he stared at Zac, taking in his slender frame and clear complexion, set off by the greenest eyes Liam had ever seen, he suddenly craved the very thing he'd left the club to avoid.

Zac smirked, like he'd known Liam was a good bet all along. "We need to go over some stuff first, so we both know what we're getting into."

"Okay." Liam chanced a surreptitious glance around what he could see of the flat, taking in the bare walls and basic furniture. "Do we need to sit down for that?"

"Not especially, but I could go for a whiskey. You want anything?"

More booze sounded like the worst idea Liam had ever heard, but he trailed Zac into the sparse living room anyway, and accepted an oversized shot of Grouse, perching on the arm of the couch while he waited for Zac to spit out whatever he needed to say before they got what they'd come here for.

Zac sat on the coffee table, relaxed and nonchalant, like he'd had a stranger over for sex a hundred times. "It's simple really. Cash up front and no sex without a condom—oh, and I don't do kissing and small talk."

"No kissing?" Liam couldn't suppress a laugh. "Thought this wasn't *Pretty Woman*?"

Zac scowled. "Them's the rules. Take them or leave them."

Okaaaaay. Liam retrieved his wallet and counted out five twenty-pound notes. He held them up, dangling them an inch from Zac's face. "I'll take it."

Zac took the money and stuffed it, without checking, in a drawer in the coffee table. "Do you have any questions?"

"Me? No."

"Sure? Don't want you freaking out halfway through."

Why not? Surely, if he bolted before they were done, Zac would get paid for half a job, but he kept that theory to himself and considered Zac's question while Zac topped up their glasses. A million responses sprung to mind, but none seemed appropriate, or anything less than stupid. Zac had covered most of the bases with his Edward Lewis rules: no barebacking, kissing, or talking. What else was there to say? It wasn't like those things had been high on Liam's agenda anyway. Jesus Christ, he just wanted—needed—to get laid.

He glanced around again, searching for the bedroom. "Do you live here alone?"

"Sometimes."

Liam raised an eyebrow. "'Sometimes'? What does that mean?"

"Exactly what I said. I share this place with a . . . colleague, but they're away at the moment. Don't worry. We're all alone."

Colleague. It took Liam a moment to catch on. Dear God, was this some kind of brothel? But the notion left him intrigued rather than perturbed, and as Zac rose from the coffee table and stepped forward, it was clear the time for talk had passed.

Zac spread his hands. "How do you want me?"

"Naked," Liam said without thinking. "Where's your bedroom?"

"Follow me."

Zac led Liam back into the hallway and to a closed door. On the other side was a room as utilitarian as the rest of the flat—a bed, a chest of drawers, and a large mirror.

The mirror stopped Liam in his tracks. "Is this the room you always use?"

"It's my room."

Fair enough. Liam ventured further into the room, then stopped as he realised he had no idea what to do next. This wasn't like fucking around with a friend—tumbling to the bed and kissing the hell out of each other until the chips fell as they may. This was something else.

Zac turned to face him. "Do you want me to take your clothes off?"

"What?"

"Your clothes," Zac repeated. "This works better if we're both naked."

"This works better." Zac's choice of words got under Liam's skin. *This is a job to him. Strip me, fuck me, then send me on my way.* For the first time, a flicker of doubt bloomed in his belly. Was he really going to do this? Fuck a stranger, a hooker, all in the name of distracting himself from old ghosts?

Liam's mind began to fragment, drifting to places he didn't want it to go, showing him faces he didn't want to see: Rosa, Mike, Dad. What the fuck would they think if they knew where he was? And what about Cory? Liam closed his eyes. *Till death do us part . . .*

"Hey." Zac appeared in front of Liam. "We don't have to do this, you know. I can give you your cash back and call you a cab."

"You'd do that?"

Zac shrugged. "I'm a hooker, not an arsehole. I don't want you to do something you're not comfortable with."

"It's not that."

"Yeah? Then what? Scared your wife might find out?"

"My what?"

Zac pointed at the ring Liam still wore on his left hand. "Married, ain't ya?"

"Yes, but there's no wife. Never was."

"You married a bloke?"

Liam rubbed the ring with the pad of his thumb, like he could magic up some perspective and get the hell out of here. "Why are you so surprised?"

"I'm not surprised. You've just got that guilty air that made me wonder if you were hiding from her indoors."

"I'm gay."

"Okay." Zac held out his hands in surrender. "You don't have to explain yourself. Man, woman, gay, straight, whatever. Makes no difference to me."

Liam frowned. "You do this with women too?"

"Not a crime, is it?"

"No, I—"

"What?"

It was Liam's turn to surrender. "Sorry, mate. I just assumed you were gay."

Zac's glare was brief, before it faded to an easy grin that softened the hard edges of his young face. "I'm not anything, but it's okay. I assumed you were stuck in the closet, so I guess we're even?"

"I guess so."

"Good." Zac closed his hands around Liam's wrists. "Now, are you in this, or not?"

"I'm in."

It was all the reassurance Zac seemed to need. He pushed Liam onto the bed and straddled him, tugging at his T-shirt. "Let's get this off."

Liam raised his arms and let Zac pull his T-shirt over his head, then quickly returned the favour, taking in Zac's lean, smooth torso as Zac lowered his face to Liam's chest and brushed an open-mouthed kiss to his nipple. *Dear God.* Liam's head spun. Was there anything hotter? If there was, he hadn't seen it in a long time.

Zac chuckled darkly, like he *knew* the effect he was having. "My no-kissing rule only applies to our lips. Feel free to put your mouth anywhere else."

"I'll bear that in mind." Liam lay back as Zac kissed a path down his chest and abdomen. The whiskey was beginning to kick in, but instead of the dizzying haze of too much booze, he found himself lost in Zac's diligent attention—his chapped lips and silky tongue, the dig of his teeth as he bit down on Liam's hip. Damn, he'd forgotten how good it felt to be touched.

Zac's teeth dug in harder, scraping bone. Liam jerked, his pelvis lifting from the bed, and his dick, still safely encased in his jeans, brushed Zac's face. Zac smirked, and Liam wondered why. *Are blowjobs extra?* He'd never thought to ask.

Like he'd read Liam's mind, Zac crawled up the bed and pressed his body against Liam's, chest to chest, groin to groin. "If you want head it's another fifty. Seventy-five if you want to blow me."

"It's more for *you* to get head?"

"Gotta get my perks somewhere."

Liam thrust up, grinding his dick into the bulge in Zac's jeans. "Is a good fuck not enough?"

"Not everyone's as hot as you, mate."

The thought of Zac doing this with countless men did odd things to Liam. He rolled over, taking Zac with him, and pushed him into the mattress. "Doesn't make any difference to me. I'm not here for a blowjob."

"Then you'd better get on with fucking me."

Zac's insolent defiance sapped what was left of Liam's nerves, or maybe it was that final shot of whiskey that drove him to stand up. Whatever. Liam roughly pulled Zac to his feet and undid his jeans, shoving them down Zac's slim legs and kicking them aside. He unbuttoned his own, but didn't remove them. Instead, he pointed at Zac's underwear. "Take them off."

Zac obliged, revealing that he was already hard. Liam stared and suddenly wanted more than anything to take Zac in his mouth. Too bad it wasn't the service he'd paid for.

"Do I get to see your dick too?" Zac closed the distance between them, cranking up the current.

Liam shivered, covering it with a shrug. "Do you want to?"

"Yes."

Okay then. Liam stepped out of his jeans, trying to forget how long it had been since he'd last been naked in front of someone. Cool air hit his dick, and he searched for Zac's gaze, but Zac's eyes were closed, a sly grin playing on his lips.

You will look at me. Liam shoved Zac, sending him stumbling into the bed.

Zac steadied himself and smirked. "Yeah. Get it out of your system. I like to play rough, blondie."

"Blondie?" Liam pushed Zac again, harder, leaving red marks on his chest. "You really wanna call me that when you're inviting me to get nasty?"

Zac widened his stance. "Try me."

The challenge dancing in his dark eyes lit Liam on fire. Liam lunged and sent him flying, leapt after him, and tumbled them both to the bed. They wrestled, but Liam had the edge in weight and height, and had Zac pinned in seconds. "This what you wanted? Me on top of you? Holding you down?"

"Yes." Zac reared up and sank his teeth briefly into Liam's chest. "Beat me. Bite me. I like that shit."

Rough play wasn't something Liam had ever been into, but the sting of Zac's bite seeped through him and went straight to his dick. *I want this*, and with kissing and blowjobs off the table, there was nothing left but to get right to it. "Condoms?"

"In the drawer."

Liam opened the bedside drawer. Inside were more condoms than he'd ever seen in his life. He picked one, and a bottle of lube, and tossed them on the bed. "Roll over."

"Make me." Zac's eyes gleamed.

Liam grabbed him and threw him onto his stomach. Zac resisted and tried to roll over, but Liam shoved a hand into his hair and bared his teeth at Zac's neck with a low growl. "Don't. Move."

He pushed Zac's face into the bed, and pulled his hips up, grinding Zac onto his cock. Zac moaned. Liam raised his hand and struck his thigh hard enough to sting. "Quiet."

It crossed his mind to whisper that Zac could make as much noise as he wanted, but he swallowed the words. If Zac wanted to stop playing, Liam reckoned he wouldn't be shy about saying so. Mind made up, he pulled back, dragging the tip of his cock over Zac's entrance. Zac shuddered and made no sound, but a flush broke out across his skin, so Liam did it again, and again, until Zac drove his fist into a pillow.

"Just fuck me, damn it."

Liam slapped him. "Say 'please.'"

"Please."

Once was enough for Liam. He sat on his heels and retrieved the condom and lube. Zac didn't move, and between his legs, his cock hung low, heavy and hard. Liam wanted to touch it, to squeeze it, lick it, and take it deep in his mouth, swallowing it down until Zac shot in his throat, but sucking Zac's cock was off-limits. Besides, as much as Liam craved Zac's dick sliding along his tongue, somehow it seemed too intimate, and he wasn't here for intimacy. Hell, no. He'd paid for a shag, a hard, fast, empty fuck, and Zac was there for the taking.

Liam tore open a condom and rolled it onto his cock, sucking in a breath as it encased him. He knew men who despised bagging up, but he'd always enjoyed the rubber squeezing him tight, like an extra fist around his dick. He coated himself with lube, then ran a slick finger over Zac, pressing and probing, testing himself as much as Zac. The tip of his finger slid inside, and when Zac tightened and made a strangled noise that could've been a groan, Liam twisted his finger and added a second. "Shh."

Zac fell silent again, neck strained, shoulders hunched, face pressed into a pillow. He pushed his hips back, fucking himself on Liam's fingers in a fluid motion that made Liam's head spin. *Jesus.* What the hell was going to happen when he finally put his cock in him?

He dug his teeth into his bottom lip and withdrew his fingers. In answer, Zac opened his legs wider and raised himself up onto all fours. Liam growled and pushed him down. "I told you to stay still."

Zac moved like a snake: rolling over, shoving Liam onto his back, and straddling him before Liam could protest. "So? Never said I would, did I? Now it's your turn to do as you're fucking told."

He cut off any argument Liam may have made by aligning himself with Liam's dick and easing down on it in a long, slow slide.

Liam groaned. The heady burn that had simmered between him and Zac since they'd struck their sordid deal increased tenfold, and his eyes fluttered closed. He thrust up, seeking friction. Zac met him in the middle, and their bodies collided over and over, flesh slapping flesh, grinding together, building to the brutal rhythm that Liam had craved so badly. The cheap IKEA bed shunted across the floor, and he braced himself on the frame, driving deeper inside Zac.

"Fuck!" Zac gasped, and his legs shook. Liam gripped his hips and flipped them over, pinning Zac once again, and pounding into him so hard he made his own eyes water as Zac cried out and arched his back. "Yeah, that's it. Don't stop, don't stop."

As if. Liam was on a one-way trip. He put his hands on Zac's chest and fucked him harder, clenching his eyes shut as Zac clamped down around him, digging his nails into Liam's skin. Orgasm roared through him like a wildfire, obliterating more than a year of abstinence, and he fought to hold his pace, but as he came with a gravelly yell, control abandoned him and he fell on top of Zac, mashing their bodies together, sweat merging with a sticky, wet warmth that suggested Zac had beaten him to the punch.

He came. For some reason, that surprised Liam as he lay in a sex-dazed stupor. Like he'd thought Zac's boner had all been for show. Like a man could fake a dick as hard as that.

"Open your eyes."

Liam shook his head. *Nope.* If he lay still in his self-imposed darkness, he could pretend the first stirrings of shame and disgust weren't brewing deep in his gut, and he wouldn't have to look at Zac and despise the both of them.

But the longer he lay there, the harder it became to block out reality. Guilt was relentless like that. He opened his eyes with a sigh. Zac stared back at him, his dark gaze . . . sad? No, that couldn't be right. This meant nothing to him. Liam was a client, a *john*, and Zac had completed the job he'd been paid for. The grief was all Liam's.

Liam rolled away and sat up, searching for his discarded clothes. Behind him, he heard Zac move too and open the bedside drawer. A rustling came next, and then the flinty flick of a lighter. Weed smoke filtered into Liam's senses, a smell he'd recognise anywhere, and the shield he'd cast around his heart in his haste to get Zac into bed began to crumble.

He found his jeans and yanked them up his legs, checking his pockets for his wallet, phone, and keys. His T-shirt was in the doorway. He retrieved it and pulled it over his head.

"Going already?"

Liam turned. Zac sat cross-legged on the bed, smoking a funky kaleidoscope pipe. With his sweat-sheened skin and tousled hair, he looked like one of those waifish models in the trendy cologne ads. "I've got to get home."

"To your husband?"

Liam snorted.

"It's okay," Zac said. "You're not the first to scarper with his tail between his legs."

"I can put my tail where I damn well please. There's no one around to notice."

"Ah." Zac nodded like he knew everything in the whole fucking world. "Divorced, eh? Is that the same for gays? All that legal bullshit?"

"Wouldn't know," Liam said flatly. "My husband's dead."

Zac blinked, missing a beat. "Sorry."

"Don't be." And Liam meant it. He'd long ago grown tired of hollow sympathy from people who didn't give a shit. "Have you seen my shoes?"

"Over there. You okay getting home?"

Liam followed Zac's direction to the foot of the bed and stamped into his shoes. "Think I can manage. I'll see you around, yeah? Thanks for . . . a good time."

"Pleasure was all mine." Zac regarded him a moment through a haze of smoke, then reached into his Aladdin's cave of a bedside drawer. He retrieved a card and passed it to Liam. "There's my number. Give me a call if you ever need another distraction."

CHAPTER
THREE

Two days later, Zac stubbed his cigarette out in the ashtray and blew the last precious lungful of smoke to the ceiling. He had no plans to buy any more. And that went for weed too . . . maybe. Of all his vices, it had proved the hardest to quit. Was there anything better than sharing the sunrise with a joint? Probably, but in recent months it had been his only way of winding down after an arduous night hooking.

Shame it didn't knock him out for long. Zac yawned and checked the time: 11 a.m. Still, four hours' kip was better than nothing, and it was better than pacing the small flat, waiting for a knock at the door that rarely came.

Speaking of which. Zac forced himself out of bed and padded across the hall, wincing as the sun hit his scratchy, sleep-deprived eyes. He opened the door to the second bedroom and found it deserted, like he'd known he would, the bed unslept in since he'd changed the sheets more than a week ago. *Fuck's sake.* It was the eighth morning straight he'd woken to an empty flat. Soon he'd have to catch a bus into Norwich and search the city centre—the squats, the alleys, the derelict warehouse behind the church. Jamie had a gift for winding up in the worst holes a city had to offer, a skill Zac had shared until circumstance had forced him to mend his ways . . . or at least sew a threadbare patch over them.

He tore himself away and drifted to the kitchen, despite knowing the fridge was empty. Staring at its bare shelves, he imagined what he'd eat if he didn't need the cash he'd made over the weekend for rent. A sausage sarnie maybe, with bacon, onions, and cheese. And brown sauce, loads of it. He'd pick up some HP next time he had money to burn. Which would be the next side of never.

Zac shut the fridge with a heavy sigh. Six months ago, the luxury of a roof over his head had seemed like a distant dream. To lust beyond that now felt wrong, so back to bed it was. He had another long night ahead of him tonight, servicing the most regular john he'd managed to find since moving to the arse end of nowhere—an old guy, with a penchant for spanking and a tiny cock. Still, he was clean and amiable, a perk of Zac picking his own johns. *No more grubby motherfuckers for me.*

Pondering, Zac took a piss and crawled into bed, burrowing under the covers that smelled of the last john he'd brought home. *The only john you've ever brought home.* He pulled a pillow over his head and let his mind meander back to his encounter with Liam two nights ago. It had been everything he'd imagined when he'd first laid eyes on him. *More.* And the tall, enigmatic blond had been on his mind ever since, much to his chagrin. After all, Liam hadn't struck him as the kind of bloke who called up hookers, begging for a repeat performance. *Yeah? So why did you give him your card?*

Zac snorted quietly. The stupid cards were a bloody joke. Some days, he could hardly believe he'd spent a precious tenner having them printed. It wasn't like they had anything on them, save the number for the pay-as-you-go budget smartphone he carried. The smartphone he'd checked religiously since he'd impulsively handed Liam his pathetic excuse for a business card. *Idiot.* He usually saved the cards for johns who looked rich, or desperate enough to want a regular arrangement, then forgot about them until they called, too caught up with the next job, or guarding an empty bed. Despite his designer clothes and surprising willingness to follow Zac home, Liam hadn't seemed rich *or* desperate, even with the wad of cash still stashed in his wallet at 3 a.m. *Perhaps he's tight.* The innuendo made Zac hot all over, but he didn't feel like wanking.

Didn't stop him brooding, though. He closed his eyes and pictured Liam, his strong body, wrapped up in smooth, tanned skin and shaggy blond hair. Arousal crept over Zac, but his mind brought him back to Liam's eyes. He didn't often notice the colour of a john's eyes, but Liam's chocolate-coloured gaze had been hypnotic, a molten mix of desire and an apathy Zac knew all too well. Liam had wanted Zac, had craved relief from the hurt simmering behind his eyes, but for the most part he'd seemed totally disconnected, like he'd been watching himself turn Zac inside out without giving a flying fuck.

Whether Liam knew it or not, he and Zac had that shit in common.

Zac shut the door of the seafront bungalow behind him and leaned briefly against the peeling paint, absorbing the entrancing sound of the waves hitting the nearby cliffs. The regular john—Frank—had been more work than usual, and Zac was tired and sore, but the cash in his pocket had made the bus ride to Snettisham worthwhile.

His bus home pulled up right on time at the stop across the road. Zac jogged down the driveway and jumped on, finding a seat next to an old lady who was engrossed in her knitting. Yawning, he settled in, closing his eyes as the small towns and villages flew by, and in no time at all, he was back in King's Lynn. He let himself into the flat and went straight for the whiskey bottle. With a full glass, he kicked off his shoes and tossed his keys on the coffee table while he checked his phone for missed calls and messages. There were none, and his heart sank. *Fuck's sake, Jamie. Where are you?* And what about Liam? Zac couldn't deny he was still holding out hope he'd call. Who wouldn't after a fuck like that?

He did the fucking, dickhead. You lay there and took it. Zac gave the devil on his shoulder the bird and pictured riding Liam, grinding down on his cock, though admittedly, it was the pounding Liam had given him after that stuck most in his mind. He'd slammed Zac like a pro and not left a mark on him, not a bruise or an ache. Not like Frank the Spanker, who'd rubbed Zac raw, despite his comical micropenis.

Recalling how he'd spent the last few hours was enough to pull Zac out of his Liam obsession. Shame had long ago deserted him, but he wouldn't be able to sleep without washing every trace of Frank from his skin.

In the windowless bathroom, he undressed and stepped under the puny electric shower. There wasn't much hot water, but enough to do the job, and with Fairy Liquid doubling as shower gel and shampoo, who could complain? And who'd listen?

Zac got out of the shower and hung his towel over the bathroom door. Though it was late September, the flat was still warm enough for him to walk around nude, something he'd miss when winter came. *Yeah, and the rest*, because there was no denying the drop-off in tourist trade would fuck with his shaky bottom line. Closeted gay boys passing through King's Lynn had made up a big part of Zac's pickups over the summer, leaving the need for regular johns less urgent. If he didn't find a few more soon, he'd have to join Jamie in Norwich, and that meant . . . No. Fuck that. *Over my dead body.*

The irony sent Zac back to the whiskey bottle. He took it to bed, craving the cigarettes he'd barely had the willpower not to buy, and passed out, still naked, and slept like a corpse until he woke some time later to cool arms sliding around his waist.

Relief washed over him, tinged with irritation as the smell of dirty clothes invaded his nose. "Fuck's sake. You stink."

An absentminded giggle was the only reply. Zac sighed and rolled over and met the bloodshot gaze he'd been searching for all week.

Jamie grinned back at him, pupils constricted, black hair sticking out in every direction. "Okay, mate?"

"Are you?" Stupid question. Jamie was fucked, either high as a kite, or coming down. In the years they'd known each other, Zac had rarely seen him any other way. "Come on. Let's get in the shower."

He got up and hauled Jamie to the bathroom, stripping his grubby clothes, and shoved him under the trickling hot spray.

Jamie leaned against the tiles. "Are you coming in?"

"In a minute." Zac scooped up Jamie's clothes and took them to the washing machine, loading them in with the wash he'd forgotten to turn on when he'd come home.

Back in the bathroom, he got into the shower with little conscious thought. He was still nude from when he'd gone to bed, and being naked with Jamie was his normal. They had nothing left to hide from each other.

Zac washed Jamie from head to toe, his lanky legs, protruding hips, and scarred back. His scruffy black hair and sharply angled face. "Are you hungry?"

Jamie opened his eyes. "Course I am, but don't get in a tizz, Zachy. I've got it sorted."

"Yeah?" Zac shut the shower off and reached for the towel he'd hung over the door. "Gonna break into Burger King again and steal all the buns?"

"Better than that."

Zac rolled his eyes and rubbed the towel over Jamie's body. High Jamie often had grand and fanciful ideas that came to nothing. Luckily, Zac had saved him a packet of Super Noodles and a few slices of bread, sustenance that, if Jamie's disappearing frame was anything to go by, he desperately needed.

"You don't believe me, do you?"

"Believe what?" Zac led Jamie back to his bedroom and found a soft pair of trackies for him to wear. "That you've got a master plan to end world hunger?"

Jamie sighed and pulled on Zac's too-big clothes. "Suit yourself. Guess I get all the pizza, then."

"Pizza? What pizza?"

"Well, it's stone-cold now, but we've got a microwave—"

Zac yanked his trousers on and pushed past Jamie and darted into the kitchen. On the counter lay two pizza boxes. "Dominos? Where did you twoc that?"

"I didn't." Jamie appeared in the kitchen doorway. With the hallway light shining across his face, he looked almost healthy. "I bought it."

"With what?"

"What do you think? You're not the only one who gets paid to fuck."

Yeah, but I'm the only one who has the cash long enough to do something useful with it . . . like buy food and pay the bloody rent. Any money Jamie made usually went straight back into the street economy, which in turn kept him out longer and longer, until he got too hungry and desperate to survive another night on his own. "Where'd you get the money, Jay?"

"I fucked a rich man."

"No, you didn't," Zac snapped. "Rich men don't cruise for toms down Clarence Road." Though that wasn't entirely true. Rich men *had* come cruising through every red-light district Zac had ever known, but they didn't pay over the going rate, especially when they picked up a junkie like Jamie. "Come on. Spill."

Jamie stepped around Zac and opened the top pizza box, snagging a cold slice and stuffing half of it in his mouth. "If you must know," he said when he'd swallowed, "I got myself a new pimp."

"You did what?"

"You heard." Jamie held out the box. "Decided I need a proper job, like you."

Zac took the box and dropped it on the counter. "I don't have a pimp. I'm not giving some cunt half my money."

"Yeah, well. If you worked where I work, you might think different. We needed one in King's Cross, didn't we?"

"That was different."

Jamie fixed Zac with a shrewd gaze. "Was it? It's a fucking ghetto out here too."

Zac didn't know much about the red-light district in Norwich—he'd done everything he could to avoid it—but if it was anything like London, Jamie had a point. Working without a pimp in the underbelly of the capital had been dangerous. They'd needed one for protection . . . and drugs.

The penny dropped. "Is that where you're getting the skag? From this pimp?"

"Need to get it from somewhere, and it's good stuff, Zac."

"Don't."

"Don't what? Tell you the fucking truth?"

Zac swallowed the age-old craving. Was it Jamie's fault it never really went away? That now they were both freshly showered and dressed in trackies, eating cold pizza from a box, they were one and the same? They were both hookers and addicts. Only difference was Zac hadn't fed his addiction since Jamie had peeled him from the pavement outside a grotty squat and bundled him into the nearest hospital. "What deal have you got with him?"

"Sixty-forty."

"In his favour?"

"Obviously. He gave me a bonus for signing up, though. Two hundred quid."

Zac sighed. He'd never come across a pimp who gave money away for fun, and his gut told him whoever Jamie had got involved with was bad news, but there was little he could do about it. Jamie was beautiful and wild, and no one would ever tame him.

"Do you want this or not?" Jamie waved a handful of notes under Zac's nose.

Zac took them. Seventy-five quid. "Where's the rest?" Silence. As if Zac had to ask. "Brilliant. So you got a bonus from your pimp and gave it straight back to him for junk?"

"I didn't bring it inside. It's in a bush up the road."

"Nice."

"Zac."

"*What?*"

Jamie stared hard at Zac. Zac sighed again and finally helped himself to a slice of pizza. They had an incarnation of this conversation every time Jamie crawled home, and each time Zac found himself backing down, constrained by hypocrisy. It wasn't so long ago that he'd have been doing everything Jamie was doing and more. Anything to stay alive . . . or not. Some days it hadn't seemed to matter.

They finished their pizza in silence. Zac jammed the remaining box in the fridge while Jamie took the empty one outside. As the door closed behind him, Zac wondered if he would sneak away to his stash in the bush, but Jamie let himself back in a few moments later.

"You found your key," Zac said. "Where was it?"

"In my pocket?"

"Seriously? It was there all along?"

"What are you talking about?"

Zac pictured the countless early mornings he'd found Jamie slumped in the street outside the flat, or been woken by his erratic thumping on the door. *Fuck it.* "I'm going back to bed."

"Can I come?"

"If you like." As if Zac could stop him. Jamie was irrepressible when he wasn't strung out on smack. Besides, Zac enjoyed his company on the rare nights he spent at the flat. A warm bed was a blessing, but no fun on his own.

They ditched their clothes—sometimes Zac felt like it was all he ever did—and crawled into bed, Zac on his back with Jamie curled against him. Jamie smelled good, now he was clean, almost as good as the fading scent on Zac's bed sheets.

A scent that wasn't lost on Jamie. He craned his neck and sniffed Zac's pillow. "You've been fucking in here."

"Have I?"

"I reckon so. What happened to your rule about bringing johns to the flat?"

"What makes you think it was a john?"

"So you have been fucking in here?"

Damn it. Jamie had always been quicker than Zac. "Piss off."

Jamie laughed. "No chance. Tell me. Did you hook up for fun? Pull some hottie at that lame club you've been loitering at?"

"Kind of. He *was* bloody hot, but I didn't pull him. I picked him up and brought him here because it was closest."

"It's always closest. Don't bullshit me. Why did you bring him here?"

Zac didn't have an answer for that, at least, not one he wanted to share with Jamie. How could he explain that he'd rushed Liam back to the flat—instead of talking his way into Liam's home—out of fear that Liam would come to his senses and realise he didn't want to fuck a skanky hooker after all? Sod that. "He was in a hurry."

Jamie didn't look convinced. "Well, he must've been pretty hot . . . and clean, if you haven't washed your sheets. You've been a total cleanaholic since we came here. Reckon I could eat my dinner off the bathroom floor."

"You probably would."

"True. So if you're not going to tell me why you brought him here, will you tell me what you did with him that's got you so misty-eyed? I've had to suck three dodgy dicks tonight. I could do with a happy ending."

"Misty-eyed? You sound like my nan."

"Wouldn't know."

Zac touched Jamie's face, tracing the dark circles under his petrol-blue eyes. They both had textbook tragic backstories—broken homes, evil foster parents, blah blah blah—but Jamie's was worse than most. Zac pictured the marbled scars on his back and shuddered.

Jamie was a shadow of the man he should've been, but Zac often found himself staring at him and marvelling that he'd made it this far at all.

Jamie scooted closer and kissed the tip of Zac's nose. "Tell me about him? Please?"

"Okay, okay." Zac let his hand drop from Jamie's face. "What do you want to know?"

"Everything. Especially the bits that have got your dick hard just thinking about him."

CHAPTER
FOUR

Liam sat back in his chair and turned his gaze to the window, watching the dogs chase each other around the garden as the business call droned on without him. They'd bought the house in this part of Norfolk because it was deserted. Despite the tourists that flocked to the nearby beach in the summer, there wasn't another house for nearly a mile around, and in the winter, they really would have been alone. Or, at least, that had been the plan before life had played its cruellest trick and forced Liam to finish building their dream home on his own.

And, ironically, with the office next to the kitchen and the phone ringing off the hook all day, he'd never felt so smothered. *Life's a bitch, and then you—*

"Liam? Are you there?"

Liam let loose an inaudible sigh. "I'm here, Mike. Sorry, what were you saying?"

"We were saying we're going to need you in London next week. We've got suppliers coming from China."

"China?" Liam sat up. "What are we talking to suppliers from China for? We manufacture in Sheffield."

"And it costs us three times what it would to import from the Far East. Liam, we've been over this."

They *had* been over it, more times than Liam cared to remember, and his answer was always the same. "We manufacture in the UK. I'm not making fifty people redundant just to save a few quid."

"Liam—"

"I said no, Mike. Outsourcing to China goes against everything we stand for. You want to pay a slave master to produce goods in a fucking sweatshop, go do it somewhere else. Funding child labour isn't in our ethos."

Silence. Liam got up and rounded the desk, but his blood simmered down a touch as he realised who he sounded like. *"The moment we give in to the number crunchers, we might as well open a bloody McDonald's..."*

Liam found himself eye to eye with the photograph he often had to turn around so he wouldn't feel its watchful gaze as he conducted these meetings with none of the flair or passion of the man before him. "It's not happening, Mike. I'll come to London to finalise the distribution for the summer line, but that's it. Don't even try pissing me about. Are we clear?"

"Clear."

Mike signed off with a frustrated sigh and Liam felt momentarily bad for him, but it faded fast. Mike, his best friend, brother-in-law, and second-in-command, had been with Sea Rave from the beginning and knew better than to tickle the beast with a capitalist agenda. At least, he should've done. Perhaps Liam hadn't reminded him, or anyone else, enough recently that everyone involved made more than enough money.

Liam drifted back to his desk and glanced at the flashing email icon on his laptop: fifty new messages in the last hour demanding his immediate attention. *Fuck that.* He couldn't put them off forever, but the conference call had done his head in and he needed some fresh air.

He closed the computer and went to the patio door, whistling for the two donkey-sized dogs destroying the garden. "Jazz! Dave! Come on."

Two labradoodles crashed into him, all woolly coats and drool. Liam clipped their leads to their harnesses and let them pull him outside, locking the door behind him.

They made their way to the secluded beach that lay a mile from the house. Safe on the sand, he let the dogs loose and followed them down to the ocean. In the distance he saw a horse and its rider, cantering through the gentle waves of the North Sea. It was a sight that warmed his brittle heart and reminded him why he'd stayed in Holkham when some days he longed for nothing more than a bag of clothes and a plane ticket to nowhere.

Stop it. Liam tore his gaze from the regal grey horse and instead let his mind meander to something else he'd been trying not to think about—that hedonistic night in King's Lynn ten days ago. To the utilitarian flat, the dark-haired devil, and the mind-blowing relief Liam had left with. He didn't dwell on the wad of cash he'd handed over for the privilege. Or the fact that it flew in the face of everything he'd chewed Mike out for. True, Zac had been younger than Liam, by a good few years at least, but he was no child, and he hadn't struck Liam as a bloke who was easily forced into anything, unless he wanted it.

Liam's thoughts took a darker, dirtier turn. *"Beat me. Bite me. I like that shit."* Zac had seemed so sure of what he liked—craved—but for Liam, the heady vortex of sex without love, of fucking for the sake of fucking, for wanton pleasure alone, had been a whole new world, a world he couldn't stop thinking about. Didn't want to stop thinking about, because Zac had become an obsession he couldn't ignore.

Dirty bastard. But Liam didn't care. He'd not thought of sex for so long, but his encounter with Zac had broken a dam, let a demon loose in his veins, and fantasising about the ecstasy money could buy was proving a welcome distraction. *Haven't called your hooker back, though, have you?* But Liam pushed that detail aside too. He hadn't called the number Zac had given him because he wasn't sure he had the balls to make his dirty dreams a reality. That he could face the shame and disgust he couldn't quite deny.

But that didn't stop him dreaming.

Half an hour later, he forced himself to call the dogs to heel and headed home to face his inbox. At the house, he found a battered four-by-four parked beside his own beloved VW Camper Van. He suppressed a heavy sigh and followed the dogs inside.

"Where've you been?"

"Nice to see you too, Rosa." Liam bypassed his sister's glare and went to the kettle. "Did you want something? Or are you here to annoy me?"

"Bit of both. I want you to eat the lasagne I brought you, and pissing you off is a bonus. Now answer my question. Where have you been?"

"Walking the dogs. Like I do every day."

"Four times a day, more like. You know they run me ragged when you're away, don't you? Can't have so much as a cuppa without them chewing a hole through my back door."

Liam grinned and placed a mug of tea on the kitchen table in front of her. "What can I say? They love their walks."

"Arsehole."

"Yup, but you love me anyway, and them . . . So, is there any chance you could have them next week?"

"Next week? Sure. It's half-term, so I could do with their help entertaining the boys. Going anywhere nice?"

"As if." Liam brought his own mug to the table and sat down, eyeing the homemade veggie lasagne Rosa had dumped by the fruit bowl. "Your husband's summoned me to HQ to blag my way through some corporate bullshit."

Rosa closed her hand around Liam's wrist and squeezed gently. "You're not blagging, Liam. You run the business as well as Cory ever did. Only difference is you don't want to."

Of course he didn't fucking want to. They'd founded Sea Rave with Liam as the head designer, not chief executive, and if he'd trusted anyone else with the business Cory had ploughed his heart and soul into, he'd have been long gone.

"What have you been up to, anyway?" Rosa's voice jolted him back to reality. "Sean said you crashed at his last weekend. I haven't heard from you since. Did you have a good time?"

An image of himself stumbling out of Zac's flat and a half mile down the road to Rosa's brother-in-law's bungalow hit Liam, but he wasn't about to share it with her. "Can I take the boys to Cromer when I get back? One more chance to go crabbing before it gets wet and shitty."

After a protracted glare, Rosa sighed, letting the subject of the nondate drop—for now. "Sure. They'd like that. They miss you when you're not around." *Which is all the time.*

She didn't say it, but she didn't have to. Liam was aware of his ability to ghost through the days like he was somewhere else entirely. That he could spend hours with people who'd once known and loved him—and Cory—and part ways knowing they barely recognised him. "Tell them I'm sorry. I'll make it up to them soon."

"They already know it. Don't worry about a thing. How long are you going to be in London for?"

"I don't know. Ask Mike."

"Are you staying at the apartment?"

"I'd imagine so. Why?"

Rosa shrugged. "The decorating's finished there now, isn't it?"

"Weeks ago. New floors, kitchen, bathroom. The furniture went in at the weekend."

"So, it's like a brand-new start?"

"If you say so." The London flat had been Cory's base when he'd worked away. Liam hadn't had much to do with it until circumstance had forced him to. Gutting the place had been cathartic, but in truth there'd been little of Cory to clean out. "Mike says it's looking good."

Rosa sighed again. "What Mike thinks isn't really important, Liam. The flat belongs to you, and I don't want you rotting in some faceless bachelor pad when you're in London."

"I'm fine, Rosa, honest. You worry too much."

"Do I? Seems to me that you hole yourself up here every chance you get. If it wasn't for the company dragging you to London, or my lot invading your personal space, you wouldn't speak to anyone."

Liam got up under the guise of chucking Rosa's lasagne in the oven. "I speak to plenty of people. I come to your house for lunch on Sundays, my phone rings off the hook all damn day, and I spent most of last week hanging from being out on the lash with Sean. What more do you want from me?"

"I want you to be happy."

"I *was* happy."

"I know, I just . . ." Rosa took a breath. "I can't bear you being so lonely, Liam. Why don't you try dating when you're in London? It's a big enough place that you wouldn't have to see someone again if they turned out to be a wanker. There's websites—"

"*Rosa.*"

"Okay, okay, but promise me you'll try?"

"Only if you promise to shut the hell up."

It was as close to a compromise as he ever got with the woman he'd shared a womb with. Rosa was relentless when she had something to say and Liam had rarely possessed the tenacity to argue with her, even before someone else's careless moment had robbed him of an idyllic life most people only dreamed of.

"Have you seen Dad today?"

It was Rosa's turn to look away. "This morning. That new woman from Croft House was taking him to the farmers' market."

"That's nice."

"Is it?" Rosa brushed imaginary dust from the kitchen table. "He told me he'd rather stick pins in his eyes."

Liam suppressed the vague humour he found in the image of his ailing father giving the battle-axe care worker a piece of his mind. "You don't think it's good that he's still with it enough to be a stubborn arse?"

Rosa shrugged, and her silence said everything. Len Mallaney's Alzheimer's diagnosis six months ago had rocked what was left of their close-knit family, and his slow descent into dementia was breaking their hearts all over again. "It won't be long now. He can't stay in the cottage forever."

"We'll cross that bridge when we come to it."

"But how will we know, Liam? What if something happens and—"

"Rosa." Liam cut her off before she could take them down a path of tragic speculation he didn't have the energy for. "We'll know, I promise. We'll know."

It seemed to be enough for her, for now. They ate Rosa's lasagne in a companionable silence while Liam tried to figure out a way to keep his word on being less of a hermit without subjecting himself to the meat market of online dating.

CHAPTER FIVE

"**Y**ou want me to meet you in London?" Zac sat up in bed and pressed his free hand over his speeding heart. He'd been waiting on this elusive call for nearly a fortnight. "And stay with you all night?"

There was a protracted pause before Liam answered, "If you like. I'm going to be there anyway, and I could do with the, er, company."

Company. That was a new word for it, if Liam was planning the same activity they'd practiced last time. "Whereabouts in London do you want me to come?"

"Farringdon."

Zac swallowed. Farringdon was closer to King's Cross than he wanted to be ever again. In fact, unless he took the world's most ridiculous detour, he'd have to pass through it to even reach Farringdon. *So? King's Cross is central to everywhere. Are you going to avoid the whole of London for the rest of your life?* Zac had half a mind to do just that if he could, but the stubborn edge to his heart, the pigheadedness that had given him the strength to leave the city—and the smack—behind in the first place, wouldn't let it happen. Besides, he couldn't deny how intrigued he was by Liam's vague invitation. "If you want me to come to London and stay the night, it's going to be expensive, and that's without, um, entertainment."

Liam chuckled. "I'd figured as much, but trust me, whatever price you name will be nothing compared to the crap I'll have to put up with every moment I'm not with you."

"Are you visiting your in-laws?" Zac caught his slip too late, but Liam didn't miss a beat.

"Nope. Worse. I'm working, which means being stuck in bullshit meetings all day long. I'll be climbing the walls by the time you get there, if I haven't killed anyone by then."

"How long do you reckon you'll hold out for?"

"I'll be home by eight."

"You want me to come to your house?"

"It's a flat, actually, but yeah, if you're cool with that. If not, we could go to a hotel?"

"No, no . . . your place is fine. What's the address?"

Liam recited a Farringdon address. "Listen," he said as Zac wrote it down. "I don't know how you usually do shit like this, but if at any time you're not happy, or comfortable with me, you're free to go. Seriously, take the money and go."

Zac swung his legs out of bed and ran his fingers through his hair. What was it about this bloke that made him hot all over when they were talking about something completely benign? "I doubt you could ever make me uncomfortable. You're the easiest john I've ever had."

"Easy?"

"As in, um, nicest, even when we got nasty." The glow that had ignited in Zac's belly when he'd first heard Liam's deep voice down the phone suddenly got brighter. Blood flooded his cheeks. "I mean—"

"I know what you mean, mate, though part of me managed to convince myself I'd dreamt all that."

"Was it that bad?"

"Only the good kind of bad."

Liam's cryptic answer made perfect sense. Zac grinned, and the heat in his veins spread to his dick. "What did you have in mind for next week? More of the same?"

"Maybe . . . Shit, hang on a sec." The line went quiet. Then Zac heard muffled voices and perhaps a door slamming before Liam came back. "I've gotta go. Um, this is my number. Call or text me if anything changes. If not, I'll see you Thursday?"

"Thursday," Zac said. "You'll be paying cash again, right?"

"Right. Don't worry about that, Zac. I'll have whatever you need."

Zac pondered the common sense of a man who'd tell a hooker he'd only met once that he'd have piles of cash at his home on a particular night, but then he pictured Liam and the steely stare that belied the flecked warmth in his gaze, and figured perhaps he wasn't a bloke to be messed with. Zac had come across men like that before.

"So, I'll see you soon?"

Zac blinked. "Erm, yeah. See you soon—Thursday."

"See you Thursday, Zac. Take care."

The line went dead. Zac lowered his phone, but something about the way Liam had said his name had him staring at the blank screen for a long time.

Zac stood at the end of Clarence Road and scanned the scrawny figures in the distance for the thousandth time, searching for Jamie's tatty leather jacket and inky hair. He'd waited all weekend for him to come home so he could tell him that he was going away, but by Wednesday—today—he'd been forced to admit defeat and come out looking, checking every side street and alley, the squats and underpasses. Clarence Road was his last stop, but so far he'd come up blank. There were hookers and junkies on every corner, but none were Jamie.

Damn it. Zac let out a frustrated sigh. His meeting with Liam was tomorrow, but there was no way he could go to London without seeing Jamie first. He was used to Jamie disappearing on him, but had long ago realised he was unable to do the same. What if Jamie came home and Zac wasn't there? What if he took Zac's absence to mean there was nothing left for him but the grimy world of hooking and smack he'd come home to escape? Not a chance. Zac owed Jamie more than that—a hell of a lot more.

Finally, he spied Jamie getting out of a car by the long-defunct phone box. In years gone by Zac might've whistled to get his attention, but not now. Not here. He'd spent enough time in Norwich's cruising district to notice the pimps and dealers in each window, tracking their toms, ready to pounce if they stepped out of line. Zac pondered which of the peeping eyes belonged to Jamie's pimp—the new guy who gave away money for free—then decided he didn't want to know. The less he knew about Jamie's day-to-day life, the better.

Zac walked nonchalantly up the road towards Jamie, trying to appear aimless and blend in. Luckily, with the worn jeans and T-shirts he preferred when he wasn't marking rich johns, he had the smackhead-chic vibe down, and no one glanced his way as he reached the corner where Jamie was clearly trying to score junk from some skank.

Twitchy, Zac forced himself to slow his pace, covering his move under the pretence of taking a phone call, eyes anywhere but at the foil packages and cash changing hands until he was sure the transaction was complete. Jamie glanced up. Zac met his gaze with a subtle nod, leaving the approach up to him.

Jamie scanned the road before pushing himself off the wall he'd been leaning against and falling into step beside Zac. "You shouldn't be here, unless you've come to procure my services."

Zac snorted softly. "Maybe I have. How much are you charging these days? We could go for lunch? Pretend we'd snuck off for a quickie in the park?"

"I wish." Jamie took another furtive glance around. "Don't spend your money on shit I'd give you for free any day of the week."

Zac thought back to the fuck-hot sixty-niner they'd indulged in last time Jamie had been home. It had started as a bet, and then descended into a flat-out race to see who could make the other come the fastest. Zac had won, naturally. He knew all Jamie's weak spots and had been sober enough to remember them. "Suit yourself. I came to tell you I'm going away tomorrow. Got an overnight with a john."

"An overnight?"

"Yup. At his place. I won't be back till Friday."

"Which john?"

Zac said nothing, knowing Jamie would work it out. *Five, four, three, two—*

"The hot dude from the other night?"

"It was nearly a month ago, Jay, but yeah, it's him. The surfer dude."

"Surfer, eh?" Jamie whistled. "So it was worth all that mooning over your phone?"

"I haven't been mooning, and even if I had, how the fuck would you know? You haven't been home in ages."

Jamie studied the pavement, guilt flashing in his bloodshot gaze. "I've been busy."

"I know."

"Where's his place? In King's Lynn?"

"No, London."

"London?" Jamie stopped walking. "Whereabouts?"

"Farringdon."

"Zac—"

"I know." Zac cut Jamie off before he could take the conversation down a path Zac had worn thin all by himself. "I'll be careful, I promise. It's not like I don't know where to avoid."

Jamie rubbed his grubby face with the heel of his hand. "It shouldn't matter. You wouldn't have to go if you didn't have me holding you back. I'd stop if I could, you know that, don't you?"

Zac nodded, though his heart knew Jamie was a long way from even wanting to be clean. "So I'll see you when I get home?"

"Sure." Jamie chewed on his lip like he wanted to say more, but something over Zac's shoulder caught his attention. "Shit. I've got to go. Can you give me a score so it looks like I sold you some skunk?"

Zac pulled his last twenty out of his pocket and handed it over without question, and without giving the stink eye to whoever was making Jamie so jumpy. "Is that enough? Or have you gone posh since your fairy godmother took over? Flogging Waitrose weed, eh?"

"Very funny. You'll be careful in London, won't you? You won't go near the station?"

"Mate, I'll have to pass through to get to Farringdon, but I won't get off there, I promise."

Jamie stuffed Zac's money in his pocket. "I'll pay you back."

Zac rolled his eyes. He'd heard that before. "Don't worry about it. Just don't make me come looking for you again, yeah? I fucking hate this place."

"All right, all right." Jamie started to turn away. "Fleece Mr. Rich for everything you can then, yeah? Then maybe we can both take some time off."

Zac climbed the steps to the swanky converted building and checked the address against the one he'd scribbled down when Liam had called nearly a week ago. *Seriously?* Liam lived *here?* Maybe Jamie had been right and he really was Mr. Rich. Either that or he was an axe murderer after all, luring Zac to the luxury apartments to fuck him, kill him, then stash his body in a suitcase in the basement car park.

Idiot. Zac snared his runaway nerves and pressed the intercom for flat six, wiping his sweaty palms on the jeans he'd swiped from River Island on his way home from Norwich the day before. On the train down to London he'd questioned his return to the bad old days of shoplifting at will, but he was glad he'd bothered now. Liam was probably going to answer the door wrapped in a gold sheet or some shit if he lived here.

The door buzzed. Zac took a deep breath and stepped inside the minimalist foyer. Liam had told him the stairs were quicker than the lift, which apparently took a week to figure out which floor you'd called it to, so he found the door Liam had described and jogged up two flights to the second floor.

Liam was waiting on the landing, dressed in ripped jeans and a white T-shirt with nothing on his feet. *So much for the gold sheet.* "You made it. Did you find it all right? Come in."

He disappeared down a corridor. Zac followed him until they came to the last door and Liam ushered him inside.

"Wow." The exclamation escaped Zac before he could stop it. "You live here?"

"Sometimes," Liam said. "Not if I can help it, though. The city isn't for me."

"Know the feeling," Zac muttered absently as he stared around Liam's flat. With its bare bricks, white floors, and chrome fixtures and fittings, it was probably the coolest place he'd ever seen. "This is lush."

"Yeah?" Liam gestured for Zac to follow him again and led him to an übermodern kitchen. "It was just redecorated. Today is the first time I've seen it in months."

"Where've you been?"

"At home in Holkham."

"You live in Holkham?" Zac stopped eye-fucking the décor and turned his attention to Liam, trying not to stare at the outline of his strong chest beneath his thin T-shirt.

"Why do you sound so surprised? Did you think I lived in King's Lynn?"

"No, I thought you were passing through. We didn't exactly make small talk."

"True." Liam's brown eyes flashed before he seemed to temper whatever emotion had ignited the reaction. "Well, I do live in Holkham, right near the beach. Do you know it?"

"Not really. I try to stay close to home."

"Why?"

Zac shrugged. How could he explain that the small Norfolk town he'd made his and Jamie's home was the safest place he'd been in years? That to stray too far from it felt like tempting the worst kind of fate? "Guess I've had no need to."

Liam shrugged and went to the fridge. He retrieved a couple of beers and slid one across the shiny marble counter to Zac. "So . . ."

"So," Zac echoed.

"Did you decide on your price? I'm assuming you want cash up front?"

"Erm, yeah." Zac thought quickly. He'd been so distracted, wondering what Liam had in mind for him, that he'd forgotten to hammer out a final number. *Some businessman you are.* "It's three hundred for the whole night, plus travel and any, um, extras so—"

"How about I give you five hundred now and we'll take it from there?"

"Five hundred?" Zac blinked. He'd been about to ask for three seven-five.

"Is that not enough?"

"No, no, it's fine."

"Good." Liam left the room briefly and came back with a neat roll of notes. "You can count it, you know. I won't be offended."

Zac shook his head and stuffed the money in his bag. Something—everything—told him that he didn't have to worry about Liam shortchanging him. "It's fine. I trust you."

"Yeah?" Liam seemed pleased, though the emotion was masked by the dullness Zac had noticed during their previous encounter. "So what do you want to do? Are you hungry?"

"Nope. I already ate." It was a lie. Zac had been too nervous to eat since the night before, but Liam didn't need to know that. "Besides, shouldn't I be asking what *you* want to do? I'm here for you, remember?"

"I want to make sure you're comfortable. That's allowed, isn't it?"

Zac had no idea. It had been quite some time since his comfort level had bothered anyone. Instead, he focused on Liam, taking in the little details he'd failed to notice the first time they'd met—his healthy tan and the natural highlights in his slightly too-long blond hair. Despite the luxury flat, he didn't look like a rich twat. Didn't much act like one either.

"What are you thinking so hard about?"

"Hmm?" In Zac's haze of staring at Liam, ironically, he hadn't noticed him stepping closer. "Oh, nothing really. Just trying to figure out who you are."

"Does it matter who I am?"

Did it? With any other john Zac couldn't have cared less, but Liam fascinated him. He closed the distance between them and laid a tentative hand on Liam's chest. The warmth of Liam's body seeped into his hand and up his arm, heating him from the inside out. Zac sucked in a sharp breath. He'd thought he'd remembered the electric effect touching Liam had on him, but the many—*many*—hours he'd spent reliving it had done the simmering current little justice.

Liam smirked and closed his hand around Zac's wrist. "How about we pick up where we left off and save the questions for after?"

He doesn't waste any time. But it was more than fine by Zac. His insane curiosity could wait . . . and hopefully fade, because it stood to reason that if he asked Liam too many questions, Liam would respond with some of his own, and that was something Zac could live without. "Show me your bedroom."

"This way."

Liam took Zac's hand and led him out of the kitchen. The bedroom was across the hall and looked like a five-star hotel room or, at least, how Zac imagined a five-star hotel room might be: low lighting; dark, thick carpets; and moody purple bedding. A far cry from Zac's own IKEA-basics bedroom back in King's Lynn. "I like this."

"Good." Liam stopped at the foot of the bed and grasped the hem of Zac's T-shirt. "Let's see what else you like."

Zac raised his arms as Liam pulled his T-shirt over his head. Cool air hit his skin and goose bumps broke out across his chest. Liam smirked again and trailed his fingertips down Zac's abdomen. Zac shivered. *What the fuck?* This wasn't how it was supposed to go.

But how *was* it supposed to go? Zac had never been attracted to a john before. In fact, he hadn't been attracted to anyone except Jamie in as long as he could remember, and that didn't really count. He fucked around with Jamie because they were hookers, and friends with benefits. Fucking Jamie was comfortable and familiar.

Simply touching Liam was beyond the fucking stratosphere.

Liam reached the button of Zac's jeans. He popped it and slid them over Zac's hips. "Commando?"

Zac grinned. "Didn't think I'd need my boxers much."

"You thought right." Liam pulled Zac's jeans all the way down his legs so Zac could step out of them, and his shoes and socks, then Liam dropped his own trousers, revealing that he'd forgone underwear too. His T-shirt quickly followed, and then they were naked, bare to the night, and staring like they'd never fucked before. Like that night, nearly a month ago, hadn't happened, and they were seeing each other for the first time.

Liam put his hands on Zac's face. For a moment, Zac thought he might kiss him, but he didn't. He slid a hand into Zac's hair and yanked his head to one side. The action was rough and caught Zac off guard. Another shiver ran through him, thrilling and raw. *Yes.* He wanted this. Craved Liam's teeth and tongue, his roaming hands. Being back in London had left him a little ragged—twitchy even— but Liam's electric touch was perversely calming and the shadowy city outside faded away.

Zac hardened. Liam saw it and raised an eyebrow, the question in his gaze clear. He wanted to touch Zac's cock, with his hands, perhaps his mouth. Zac licked his lips. "Do it."

"Sure?"

"Fuck yeah."

It was all the encouragement Liam seemed to need. He dropped to his knees and gripped Zac's thighs, his face inches away from where Zac wanted it most, and blew warm air over Zac's dick, smirking when it jumped. "Make sure you tell me when I run out of credit."

Zac took another sharp breath, but whatever reply he may have made was cut off by Liam's mouth closing around his cock. Zac bucked his hips, seeking out the heady depths of Liam's throat, but Liam tightened the grip on his thighs, stilling him as he grazed his teeth on the underside of Zac's dick just hard enough to make Zac's eyes roll. "Do that again."

Liam did it again, and again, and then turned up the heat. He pushed Zac onto the bed, sucking harder and moaning around Zac's cock. The vibration buzzed through his veins. *Jesus.* Since when had johns been so proficient at giving head? But then, Liam was no ordinary john; Zac's fast-approaching orgasm was testament to that.

Zac lay back on the bed and screwed his eyes shut, warring with the desperate urge to thrust into Liam's mouth and the knowledge that he needed to slow things down and get a grip on himself. He wasn't here for his own pleasure, though it appeared someone had forgotten to send Liam that memo. He used his teeth again, and Zac groaned, jamming his hand in his mouth. Jamie bit his dick sometimes, but he had nothing on the subtle scrape of Liam's teeth. Zac had never felt anything like it.

"Lift your legs."

"Wha—" Zac opened his eyes as Liam gripped his shoulders and heaved him further onto the bed, his lean muscles rippling beneath his tanned skin. "Fuck, you're strong."

"Not really. Lift your legs."

Zac obeyed, lifting his legs and spreading them wide, opening himself for Liam. He thought he was ready for the sensation of Liam's tongue sweeping over him, but he was sorely mistaken as Liam buried his face between Zac's legs, driving his tongue in and out of Zac, all the while keeping his hands busy on Zac's dick, pumping, squeezing, twisting. Zac fought for control—he was supposed to be the fucking professional—but Liam showed him no mercy and he abruptly found himself on the edge of a release he couldn't contain. "Suck me."

Liam pulled his tongue from inside Zac and swallowed Zac's dick, driving his fingers inside him and seeking Zac's prostate with a practiced touch that made him wonder how many men—or hookers—Liam had done this with before.

But he didn't have time to ponder it much as release rushed up on him. He shoved his hands into Liam's silky hair and pulled his head back. Cool air hit his dick and he came with a strangled yell. "*Fuck!*"

His orgasm seemed to go on forever as Liam tortured him with his fingertips, teasing every buck and groan out of Zac until he couldn't take anymore. "Stop, stop. Please stop."

Liam pulled away with a low chuckle. "Don't lose your head on me yet. I'm not done with you."

Zac didn't doubt it, but it was a few moments before coherent thought returned to him and he remembered that he'd had plans of his own, plans that involved Liam's cock. He lunged for Liam, sending him tumbling sideways. "Your turn."

Laughing, Liam propped himself on his elbows and eyed Zac with a gaze that was warmer than any Zac had seen from him so far. In another world, Zac could almost pretend they were lovers, making each other come simply because they wanted to, and perhaps even because they loved each other. But this wasn't the time for weed-laced daydreams. This was Liam's bed, they *were* hooker and john, and Zac had a job to do, albeit a job that made his mouth water.

He ran his tongue up and down the length of Liam's cock, taking in its size and thickness, and recalling how it had felt inside him the last time they'd fucked. How it had filled him to the point of combustion and left him sore, aching, and desperate for more, much, much more.

Easy. He's got all night to fuck you.

The thought of fucking all night made Zac's head spin. He squeezed Liam's dick and took it deep in his mouth, sliding it down his throat. Liam's cock throbbed in response, leaking and jumping against Zac's tongue.

"Damn." Liam's legs quivered. "Yeah, like that . . . deeper."

Zac was happy to oblige. He spent a *lot* of time giving head, but every sound Liam made went straight to his own sated cock. It wasn't long before he was rock-hard once more. He rutted against the mattress, desperate for friction.

Liam pulled on his shoulders. "Get up here."

The commanding tone shifted the air. Zac met Liam's gaze. It seemed darker than when they'd started, but that could've been the fading light.

"Don't make me say it again."

Zac crawled up the bed, sliding along Liam's sweat-sheened skin until they were face-to-face, lips inches apart. Zac had never been into kissing, especially not with johns—though in the old days he hadn't had much say in the matter—but as he stared at Liam and his lips tingled, he'd never wanted to kiss anyone more. Shame Liam rolled away before Zac could do something really fucking stupid.

Liam left the bed and went to a wardrobe on the other side of the room. He returned with a box of condoms and a bottle of expensive-looking lube, and tossed them on the bed.

Zac picked up the lube. "Is this the posh stuff?"

Liam snatched it out of his hands. "Get on your knees."

Zac got on his knees. He'd been with johns who took the dominant role to the extreme, shoving him face-first into a brick wall, wrapping an arm so tight around his throat that he passed out, but Liam wasn't like that. Instead Zac found himself rushing to obey his gentle commands, every instinct screaming at him to make Liam happy because pleasing Liam did amazing things to Zac's heart.

That, and he had a feeling Liam was going to fuck his brains out and he couldn't bloody wait.

Liam brought his hand down on Zac's thigh with a stinging slap. It hurt in just the right way, and Zac jumped in anticipation of the next blow, and the next and the next, until he saw stars and finally, *finally*, felt the blunt head of Liam's cock pressing into him, slicked by a healthy squeeze of designer lube.

Zac dropped his head and suppressed a moan, even though Liam hadn't instructed him to be quiet. He'd learned long ago that there was something insanely hot about keeping his rare sexual pleasure to himself, holding in every gasp and moan until he thought he'd combust. With Jamie, the game had the added bonus of driving each other half-mad, but Liam didn't seem to notice Zac's silence. He slid his dick all the way in and then held still, filling Zac, stretching him, and pulsing gently inside him while he rubbed soothing circles into the small of Zac's back.

That was a new one. The masochist in Zac often enjoyed the dry sear of a john's cock ramming inside him—unless it was someone too minging—but the sensation of Liam easing the pain away was out of this world. Zac's chest tightened and his eyes burned. His self-imposed suppression cracked and he let out a strangled groan.

Liam's hand stilled. "Want me to stop?"

"No."

"Sure? It's okay if you do. You can keep the money." Liam withdrew slightly.

Zac chased him down, slamming his hips back and making them both gasp. "I don't want to stop. I want you to fuck me."

"Yeah?" Liam sat on his heels, bringing Zac with him to sit, impaled, on his lap. "How much do you want it?"

Too much. "Enough to beg you, if that's what you want."

"Nah, I'm not into that slave shit. No begging. I want to watch you get off . . . fuck yourself on my cock."

It was a request Zac had heard a thousand times over, normally from fat old men too unfit to fuck him themselves, but coming from Liam it took on a whole new meaning. Zac involuntarily clenched as Liam leaned back on his hands. A bolt of heat shot through him. He dropped forward, widening his legs and raising his hips, then ground himself up and down, fucking himself on Liam's cock.

"That's it," Liam said. "Nice and slow."

Zac closed his eyes and drank it all in as pleasure built gradually in the base of his spine, radiating through him like creeping lava. He'd had slow sex with Jamie before, both of them too tired and strung out to do much else, but it had evoked nothing like the heady pressure building in him now. Nothing like the red-hot sensation of Liam's cock sliding in and out of him. Heat. Pressure. Heat. Pressure. Zac's control slipped, falling away and evaporating like it had never been there at all. He groaned long and loud, and slid further forward, stretching his arms out in front of him and fisting the expensive sheets. "Fuck me, Liam. Please."

Liam gripped Zac's hips, stopping his cock from withdrawing completely. "I told you not to beg. Why should I fuck you when you don't do as you're told?"

There was humour in his tone, like he found his own words slightly ridiculous, but Zac was too far gone to feel endeared. "Please. I need it."

Liam relented. He covered Zac with his body and pressed him into the mattress, reaching above Zac's head to grasp his hands. "You ran rings around me last time, playing me, making me fucking lose my head. I've been thinking about it ever since. Have you been thinking about me?"

"Yes."

"Liar."

"Am I?"

Silence, then Liam sank his teeth into Zac's shoulder and pushed himself deeper inside Zac, circling his hips, and fucking him into a fragment of the oblivion Zac craved so much.

"Harder . . . please."

Liam fucked him harder.

"Deeper."

Liam fucked him deeper and hit the tiny bundle of nerves that turned Zac's vision white. Zac cried out, so close to coming he couldn't think straight, couldn't speak as he fought to stem the wave of release as it rushed up on him. He yelled out again and tore a hole in the bed sheets. "I'm gonna come. I'm sorry, I'm sorry, *fuck*!"

"Do it." Liam slapped Zac's thigh. "Come for me and I'll come for you."

His dick swelling inside Zac, pulsing and throbbing, tipped Zac over the edge. He came with a loud groan that cut off as Liam joined him, warmth filling the crowded space where they were joined.

Zac gasped for breath, the air struggling to find purchase in his lungs. Black dots danced in front of his eyes. As he struggled to focus, only dimly aware of Liam pulling out and leaving the bed, he felt like he'd smoked a thousand spliffs, then run up the escalators at Angel Tube Station. *Damn it*, what was up with his chest? And why had his face gone numb?

Strong hands tugged him upright. Liam thrust a bottle of water into Zac's shaking hands. "Drink."

Zac obeyed, spilling water down his chin.

"That's it." Liam rubbed his arm. "Nice and slow."

The repetition of his earlier words broke through Zac's haze and he looked up to find Liam staring at him, his gaze an odd mix of desire and concern. Zac absorbed the mind-blowing shag still lingering in every facet of his being. *Jesus. What the fuck just happened?*

Liam took the water from Zac's hand. "Want to tell me what happened?"

Again with the echo. Zac shook his head. "Dunno. Guess it was my turn to lose my mind. Sorry."

"Don't be sorry, Zac. Shit happens. So long as you're okay."

"That's not what I'm here for though, is it? To be okay? I'm here to work."

For a brief moment—so brief Zac wondered if he'd imagined it—Liam appeared offended, then he shrugged. "Workers have rights. I don't expect anyone else I employ to work if they're not well, or something's going on that they need to deal with. Why should you be any different?"

The logic was sweet, but they both knew their arrangement wasn't quite the same as what Liam was talking about. It wasn't like Zac paid his taxes with the bundles of notes he hid in the toilet cistern. "I—I don't know what happened."

Liam sighed. "Suit yourself. Listen, I'm starving and there's nothing edible in this place, so I'm going to nip out and get some dinner. Why don't you take a shower and chill out, then, if you want to go when I get back, I'll call you a cab."

"What?" Zac started to sit up. "You want me to go?"

"No, I'm giving you the option. It's up to you, mate. I'll be back soon, okay?"

Liam stood and retrieved his clothes from the floor, much like he had in the aftermath of their first fuck. Zac hugged his knees to his chest. He hadn't wanted Liam to leave then, and he didn't want him to go now. "Are you sure you want to leave a dirty hooker alone in your flash pad? What if I nick everything?"

"I know where you live." Liam buttoned his jeans. "Besides, if that's really what you want to do, I'm not altogether sure I give a shit. There's nothing in this place I'd lose any sleep over. Take what you want."

Liam left the room and the front door slammed a minute later. Zac jumped and the unease he'd felt when he'd got off the train at Euston returned full force, merging with the disquiet from his postcoital meltdown. He put his hand on his chest, like he could slow his jumping pulse by rubbing it into submission. Nothing happened, so he let his hand drop and lay back against the marshmallow-like pillows. Liam had given him leave to take his money and run, but he made no move to get up. Despite the agitation fermenting in his nerves, he was suddenly profoundly tired, so tired he could hardly see straight. He closed his eyes, trying to forget that he was bollock naked and alone in a strange apartment. *I'll just rest my eyes, then maybe I'll take that shower . . .*

CHAPTER
SIX

L iam stood in the bedroom doorway, transfixed by the young man asleep on his bed. And young he was. Now, without a night on the Jäger bombs to cloud his judgement, or the haze of frenetic fucking blurring his vision, it was clear that Liam had ten years on Zac . . . maybe more, and Liam was thirty-four, which meant Zac was barely out of his teens.

Damn. Zac was clearly old enough to have taken Liam home, but it didn't take a genius to figure he must've lived beyond his years to wind up selling himself in the first place. Or did it? Liam had no idea. All he knew was he had a sleeping hooker in his bed who he couldn't stop staring at. And far too much Thai food that was going to get cold if he didn't put it in the oven to keep warm.

Liam tore himself from Zac's sleeping form and went to the kitchen, a room he rarely used at the London flat. He unpacked the bag of food and stashed it in the flashy cooker built into the wall, all the while missing the AGA he had at home, and the dogs sleeping in front of it, tangled together in a huge pile of muddy wool. With that done, he found himself at a loose end. Zac, still sprawled out naked on his bed, called to him like a siren, but he forced himself not to drift back to the bedroom and nudge Zac awake to make the most of their night together. Instead he went to the bathroom and turned the shower as hot as he could bear, a habit he'd got into over the past year, as though the stinging burn of the water could erase the grief-induced ache in his bones.

It worked, sometimes, but tonight he barely noticed the red-hot spray lancing his skin. His mind returned to Zac and his minor meltdown. Guilt tickled his gut. He'd been rough with Zac—like Zac had asked him to be—but was that what he'd truly desired, or had he danced to the tune he thought Liam played? Liam had no idea, and it was hard not to worry that he'd hurt Zac. Physically, Liam was a much bigger man, in all but cock.

Damn it. Liam leaned against the tiles and closed his eyes, trying to ignore his own cock as it rose slowly to meet the images of Zac in his mind. Zac's beautiful body, the perfect contradiction of slender and strong, wrapped up in flawless skin that smelled like fags, sweat, and the boyish deodorants Liam remembered from his teenage years. And he had a big cock—larger than his slim frame suggested, and Liam had enjoyed having it in his mouth.

Enjoyed. Ha. Liam allowed himself a smirk. He'd been dreaming of sucking Zac's cock since their first transaction had forbidden him from doing so, and fuck if it hadn't been worth the wait. Liam had always enjoyed giving head, but doing it for Zac had been something else—the taste of him, every sound he'd made, and the almost violent shudders that had wracked him when Liam rimmed him. He tried not to consider whether Zac's reactions had been real. He'd come, hadn't he? No man could fake that.

But as the comforting thought crossed Liam's mind, it collided with a thick wall of cynical doubt. Handing Zac his fee had taken mere moments, done and out of sight before he could blink, but he couldn't hide from the fact that he'd paid Zac for every gasp and moan, and nothing that passed between them was more than a brief respite from the real world.

A cool, dry hand closed around Liam's dick. "So this is where you're hiding, eh?"

Liam opened his eyes and took a breath, but Zac tapped his finger to his lips and pressed a condom into Liam's hand. "My turn to call the shots. No talking. Just fucking."

Who was Liam to argue? He turned Zac around and shoved him against the tiles, nudging his legs further apart. A gasp caught in his chest as he slid a finger into Zac and found him already slick and relaxed. *Jesus.* Liam's dick jumped. He braced himself on the tiles and gripped Zac's hip, aligning them, then he eased inside Zac, closing his eyes against the heat that enveloped him.

Zac groaned and pushed back, flexing and tightening around Liam's cock. "Yeah, that's it, that's it. Do it. You know you want to."

The dark mist Liam had come to expect from his encounters with Zac descended fast, eclipsing the pain and doubts holding him back. With his dick buried deep inside Zac, it was difficult to accept that it wasn't real, that Zac's drawn-out, gravelly moans meant nothing. In the heat of *this* moment, the carnal desire between them seemed undeniable.

Liam drew his hips back and thrust into Zac, hard enough to force a gasp from him and put himself right on the edge of orgasm already. "God, I love fucking you."

The declaration surprised him, but he meant it. Paid for or not, fucking Zac was bloody incredible. And this time it seemed destined to be over as abruptly as it had begun. Liam drove into Zac once, twice, three times before Zac cried out. "Shit, I'm going to come."

He tightened impossibly, and Liam was done too. A brutal release crashed over him, and he came hard, just beating Zac, who spilled without either one of them touching his dick.

For a long moment, Liam stood stock-still, panting, his forehead pressed between Zac's shoulder blades, as he held Zac up, fighting the trembling in both of their legs. Then Zac squirmed in his grip, so Liam let him go and straightened.

Zac turned and closed his hands around Liam's wrists, eyes briefly shut, like he was focussing, then a frown crossed his face and he blinked hard, staring at Liam's fingers. "Where's your ring?"

"What?"

"Your wedding ring. You're not wearing it."

Liam glanced at his bare left hand and reality forced its way into his post-fuck daze. "I took it off."

"Why?"

"What do you care?"

Zac shrugged. "Call me curious."

"I'd rather call you Zac."

"Oooh, deflection." Zac smirked. "Sorry. Didn't mean to sound like your mother. Haven't lost it, have you?"

The thought of losing the plain white-gold band he'd worn for more than a decade made Liam's blood run cold, despite the steamy heat of the shower. "No, no, nothing like that. I took it off to come here."

"Why? Didn't want to wear it to spend the night with a whore?"

"Whore? When have I ever called you a whore?" Liam didn't know why it mattered, *whore* was just a word like any other, but Zac's flat tone rankled him. "You're not a whore unless you want to be. You're Zac, regardless of how *you* see *me*."

"You deserve better than this."

"I decide what I deserve." Liam shut off the shower and got out, not looking to see if Zac followed, because he couldn't bring himself to admit that Zac was right about the ring. He *had* taken it off to spend the night with him, like locking it away in a box would make any of this right. Like it even fucking mattered.

Liam walked nude to the bedroom and scanned the floor for his clothes before he remembered they were still in the bathroom.

"I'm sorry."

He glanced over his shoulder. Zac was hovering in the doorway, holding Liam's clothes. "What are you sorry for?"

"Dunno. You don't seem very happy."

"Neither do you."

Zac grinned sardonically. "That better?"

"No." The cynical smile put years on Zac and echoed the apathy in Liam's heart. "Are you hungry?"

"Me?" Zac blinked. "Thought you went out for dinner?"

"No, I went out to *get* dinner. It's in the kitchen."

"Oh." Zac chewed on his bottom lip.

Liam took pity on him. It was impossible to guess how long Zac had been hooking, but it was obvious he wasn't used to clients— johns—or perhaps even anyone, giving a shit if he ate his dinner. "Come on. I'll show you."

They both pulled on jeans and went to the kitchen. Liam retrieved the food from the stove and laid it on the counter. Zac looked perplexed. "What is all this?"

"Thai. Never had it?"

"Nope. Is it like the curry from Jasmine House?"

Liam chuckled, picturing the dodgy Chinese takeaway on King's Lynn's high street that served dog food and rice when the pubs kicked out. "Not even close. Do you like spicy food?"

"I get chilli sauce on a kebab?"

Zac's bemusement was too endearing. Liam covered the fond smile threatening to break out by opening the cutlery drawer, except it wasn't the cutlery drawer, and it took him three tries to find the right one.

"I thought you lived here?"

"Not if I can help it." Liam finally found some forks and drew the nearest container towards them. "I told you. I only come here for work. Here, try this."

Zac peered into the container. "What is it?"

"Pad thai—rice noodles with eggs and tofu. It's got peanuts and chilli too."

"What's the lime for?"

"To squeeze over and stir in before you eat it."

Zac picked up a wedge of lime and squeezed it over the noodles, then loaded a fork and took a tentative bite. "Oh wow, that's lush."

"Isn't it?" Liam pointed to the remaining containers. "That's chilli tofu, a green fish curry, and coconut rice, oh, and prawn crackers."

"Prawn crackers? I've heard of them." Zac snagged a handful. "What's with the tofu? Are you vegetarian or some shit?"

"Some shit. I try not to eat a lot of meat. It isn't good for the planet, man, all those beef farms and battery chickens. It ain't right."

"But you eat fish?"

"Sometimes, and I do eat meat too, when I can't resist a roast or a bacon sarnie."

Zac nodded slowly, like he was filing it away for later, then stuck his fork in the tofu, the rice, and the green fish curry. "God, that's amazing too. Eat some, please, or I'll smash it all."

Liam picked up his own fork and for a while they ate in companionable silence, though Liam ate as little as he could get away with, leaving much of it for Zac, who put away enough food for three. "When did you last eat?"

"Hmm?" Zac looked up from scraping the pad thai container clean. "Oh, um, yesterday, maybe? I can't remember."

"Yesterday?"

"Probably."

Probably. Flipping heck. It was no wonder Zac was so bloody skinny. Liam got up and went to the fridge. Inside he found the cheesecake the cleaning lady always left him when she knew he was coming, bought from the Slovakian bakery down the road.

Zac peered curiously at it. "What's that?"

"Slovakian cheesecake."

"Slovakian? What's Slovakian about it?"

Liam shrugged. "Fuck knows. But it's nice. Here, try some."

He grabbed a clean fork and hacked a piece off, being sure to get all the layers of buttery pastry, vanilla, and blackberries. He held the fork to Zac's mouth, sliding it between his lips in a gesture that suddenly felt far too intimate.

Zac didn't seem to notice. He ate the cheesecake, and his eyes closed. "Damn, that's good."

"Isn't it?" Liam put the fork down and forced himself not to stare at Zac, not to gaze at him like the bloody moron he was clearly becoming. "Do you want a slice?"

Zac opened his eyes and shook his head with a regretful grin. "I want to eat the whole thing, but I reckon I'd probably puke. Man, I'm so stuffed. Thank you for dinner."

"No worries. What do you want to do now?"

"Isn't that up to you?"

Liam suppressed a sigh. Really? They were back to that? Part of him wanted to bend Zac over the kitchen counter and fuck his brains out again, but as hot as that would be, it didn't feel quite right, and an odd urge to take care of Zac swept over him, even if he could only do it for the short time they had together. "How about we get in bed and watch a film? I know it's late, but we've got all night, eh?"

"Right." If Zac was surprised Liam didn't want to fuck any more yet, he didn't show it. He put his fork in the sink, followed Liam back to the bedroom, and threw himself on the bed with the lithe recklessness of a teenage boy. "What are we watching?"

"Whatever you like." Liam opened a drawer under the huge TV unit in the bedroom. "I don't have a TV in my bedroom at home, but I like to have it here. Drowns out the noise."

"Yeah, London's like that, isn't it? Took me ages to get used to the quiet in King's Lynn. First morning there I thought I'd dropped off the face of the earth."

"You used to live in London?"

"Um . . . yeah." Zac slid abruptly from the bed and came to Liam's side. "What DVDs have you got?"

Liam knew a forced change of subject when he heard one. *He's not your friend, remember? He's not going to tell you his life story.* Shame, because Liam was far more curious than he cared to admit. There was much about Zac he didn't want to know, mostly relating to his choice of occupation, but there was no denying he found Zac himself fascinating. That he wanted to know what made him tick. Still, he knew better than to ask. Their professional relationship aside, Zac didn't seem much of a sharer, though his reticence was intriguing.

"Have you seen all these?" Zac asked.

Liam studied the neatly ordered drawer of DVDs. Most of them were Cory's. If they'd been Liam's, they would have been in a shameful mess, rubbing shoulders with stray socks and a random set of screwdrivers. "Not even close. I don't watch TV much. I'm more of a vinyl-and-chill kinda bloke."

"Vinyl? Like old records and shit?"

"Something like that. My dad and I collect them, so we have a good mix of the old and not so old."

"Do you have any here?"

Liam shook his head. "They're at the house in Holkham. Never needed them here."

"No?" Zac glanced around. "You could have an awesome rave in this place."

"Twenty years ago, maybe. It's been a while since I went raving, mate."

"You're not that old."

"Cheers."

Zac laughed. "You can't be. How old *are* you?"

Liam folded his arms across his bare chest. "Why should I tell you that? It's not like you'll return the favour."

"Wouldn't I?"

"I'm thirty-four."

"I'm twenty-three."

Thank fuck for that. Liam hadn't really worried Zac was underage, but the fact that he definitely wasn't settled the perpetual disquiet

Liam'd carried since Zac had arrived. A twenty-three-year-old was capable of making his own decisions. Christ, Liam had been practically married by then. "What do you want to watch?"

Zac selected a DVD and held it out.

"You want to watch *Young Guns*?"

"Sure."

Fair enough. Liam loaded the disc and turned on the TV while Zac retreated back to bed and sprawled out on his stomach again. Liam switched off the lights and hovered a moment before following him and mirroring his pose. It had been a while since he'd messed with the cantankerous DVD player, and it took him a moment to notice Zac fiddling with the half-dozen bracelets Liam wore on his arm.

"These are really cool. I thought they were all the same, but they're not."

Liam finally found the disc menu and hit Play, then glanced down at his arm and Zac's fingers tracing the worn leather. "I got them from the Sea Rave festivals in Newquay. One for every year I've gone."

"Never heard of it," Zac said. "Newquay is where the surfers go, isn't it?"

"Yup. Sea Rave is an eco festival for surfers and hippies. Kinda like Glastonbury with boards and waves."

"My mum went to Glastonbury. She told me once I was conceived there."

"Yeah? You should take her back. We took my dad last year. He loved it."

The spark in Zac's green gaze faded. "I don't know where she is. I haven't seen her in years."

"Oh." Liam had no words. His own mother was long dead, but he'd always known he was loved—that he and Rosa had been her whole world. "Sorry, mate."

"Not your fault, is it?"

Liam supposed not. The film's opening credits lit up the room, casting a shadow across Zac's face. On impulse, Liam untied the oldest bracelet on his wrist and held it out to him. "This is from the first festival eight years ago. I still have a bunch of them at the house in Holkham, so you can have this one if you like."

"Eight years ago?" Zac glanced at Liam's arm, clearly counting bracelets and doing the maths. "So you don't go every year?"

"Missed the last two. Shit happens."

That was one way of putting it, but Zac didn't seem interested in the details. He tied the bracelet around his own wrist and rolled over onto his back, staring at the ceiling. Liam let him be for a while, distracted by the firecracker gunfire from the film. He hadn't seen *Young Guns* in years, not since he'd taped over Rosa's favourite *Take That* video with it and had a remote control chucked in his face for the privilege. Had it been worth a black eye? Looking at it now, he wasn't sure.

"Do you want me to stay?"

Yes. "I do, actually, if you don't mind?"

"Of course I don't mind. You paid for the overnight."

"So? Doesn't mean you have to stay. Thought we'd covered this?"

Zac shrugged. "I don't understand you. I haven't worked for anyone like you before."

"Is that a bad thing?" Liam wasn't about to admit it was because he had no idea how he was *supposed* to behave with a hooker he'd hired for the whole night. Should they be fucking again already? Was it weird for them to sleep in the same bed? Or, indeed, sleep at all?

"It's not bad," Zac said. "I'm just not used to johns being so normal. Last one I stayed the night with left me tied up on the dining room table while he fell asleep on the couch."

A cold pang squeezed Liam's heart. He knew Zac had other clients—johns—probably loads of them, but imagining other men—and women—putting their hands on him, fucking him, making him gasp and moan, did odd things to Liam's gut.

"I don't even get to come, not properly, anyway, not like with you."

"Properly?" Liam felt slightly high.

Zac turned his head to look at him. "I can fake it well enough if they particularly want me to come. Most times they don't bother to check."

"Have you ever—" Liam stopped. Was he really about to ask if Zac had ever pretended to come with him? Did he even want to know?

Zac's hand on his face startled him. "I've never faked it with you. Chance would be a fine thing. You only have to look at me and I'm ready to bust."

Liam closed his eyes and pictured the last time he'd seen Zac come, in the shower, painting the tiles without either one of them touching his dick. He couldn't fake that . . . could he?

"Can I take my jeans off?"

Liam opened his eyes. "Um, sure. Should I take mine off too?"

Zac cast Liam a sideways glance. "If you want. I always sleep in the nude, don't you?"

So they *were* going to be sleeping. Liam wasn't sure if he was relieved or disappointed. He stripped his jeans and tossed them over the side of the bed, then crawled his way to the right end and got under the covers, gesturing for Zac to do the same.

Zac hesitated briefly before he did just that. Liam absorbed his presence and tried to pretend he wasn't there for cold, hard cash. This bed, like the one at the house, was brand-new, slept in only by Liam, but he'd missed the warmth of another body stretched out beside him so much his bones ached with the weight of it. He'd never known loneliness could hurt.

"Do you want to fuck me again?"

Liam studied Zac's face, taking in his barely dry hair flopped over his forehead and the subtle shadows under his dark-green eyes. The crisp white bedsheets stood out against his brown hair, and in the dim light of the room he was utterly beautiful.

And, despite his catnap earlier, clearly exhausted. Liam tugged the duvet further up Zac's slim body and shook his head. "Get some sleep, mate. I'll bank that one for the morning."

CHAPTER
SEVEN

It was light when Zac woke to Liam gently shaking him.

"I wanna suck you. That cool?"

Hell yeah. Zac nodded sleepily, then jerked awake again to the earth-moving sensation of Liam's mouth on his cock, and his dick hitting the back of Liam's throat. "Fuck!"

Liam chuckled, and true to form, had Zac on the edge before Zac could comprehend that he was happy to be awake. He clenched his eyes shut and fought the inevitable, but lost—like he cared—and it was over before it had really begun.

"Bastard," Zac grumbled sleepily.

"Am I?" Liam crawled up the bed, dragging his hard cock over Zac's stomach. "How about if I let you choose where I shoot my load? That do ya?"

Of course it would. Jamie aside, Liam was the only person who ever let him make such decisions. Zac deliberated briefly, then pointed to his chest. "I want you to come on me."

Liam straddled Zac and jacked himself off, his bottom lip between his teeth and his gaze locked with Zac's. "Like this?"

"*Yeah*. Like that."

Liam groaned, like he had a hundred times over when they'd fucked around, but this time the gravelly sound seemed to travel through Zac and reverberate in his bones. Christ, Liam was gorgeous. Jamie was hot—beautiful in his own way—but Zac knew him too well, saw the flaws that were too close to his own. It was different with Liam. Despite the cash burning a hole in Zac's pocket, somehow this seemed more real.

"*Shit.*" Liam came abruptly, shooting all over Zac's chest. "God *damn*, you fuck me up."

Zac grinned, relieved it wasn't only him having issues with stamina, and caught Liam as he lurched forward and collapsed on Zac's chest. He wrapped his arms around Liam and it felt good. *Too good.* He buried his face in Liam's silky sun-streaked hair and breathed in a scent so fresh and clean that he closed his eyes to it, pretending for a moment that this was a life they shared, and he didn't have to let go and return to the drudgery of hooking by the sea.

Still, there was some comfort in knowing he wouldn't be leaving Liam behind entirely. Liam hadn't given any indication that he spent a lot of time in King's Lynn, but Holkham was only twenty miles away. No distance at all if Liam wanted his services again.

Liam raised his head. His grin was like the sun filtering through the posh curtains they'd neglected to close the night before. "Breakfast?"

"Um, sure."

Liam rolled away and slid off the bed, disappearing from the room before Zac could protest. Zac mourned the loss of his soothing weight warming his bones. He'd never much cared for men lying on top of him in any context, but with Liam, it was okay. More than that. With Liam, it was so fucking perfect it frightened him.

In an effort to distract himself from the odd brooding mood he'd woken up with, he got up and searched out his phone. It was dead, and he'd forgotten his charger. Not that it mattered. It wasn't like anyone he truly wanted to speak to ever called. He shoved the phone back in his bag and drifted to the bathroom that was bigger than his bedroom. He took a piss and splashed water on his face, trying not to smirk at the shower where they'd had so much fun the night before. Fun that, despite being the one to initiate it, had caught Zac off guard. In truth, he'd tracked Liam to the bathroom because he'd woken alone in a dark, strange room and panicked, which had led him into Liam's arms, if getting bent over in the shower counted as a rescuing embrace.

"You okay?"

Zac spun around. Liam stood in the doorway balancing a couple of plates in one hand. "I'm good. What you got there?"

"Croissants. I found them in the freezer." Liam ventured further into the room and set the plates down, producing a jam jar from under his arm. "Fuck knows how long they've been there, but this hasn't been opened, and it's in date."

"Winner." Zac was suddenly ravenous. He followed Liam's example and crawled back into bed, accepting a plate loaded with warm pastries. Liam served him a big dollop of some weird kind of orange jam, and for a while they ate in companionable silence. Then Liam switched on the TV, flipping to the news channel, and Zac saw the time. "Fuck. It's eleven o'clock."

"Got somewhere to be?"

"No . . ."

"Ah, I see. Have I run out of credit?"

It hadn't occurred to Zac to watch the clock. He usually had an alarm on his phone that he pretended was his driver calling to pick him up, so johns wouldn't know he was alone, but, like the first night they'd met, Zac had forgotten about the need for caution. "I guess I should get going soon."

Liam said nothing. Zac swallowed the last of his breakfast and tried to pretend he wasn't hanging out for Liam to ask him to stay, like the idea of pulling his clothes on and trudging home didn't seem like the worst thing in the world.

He'll want to fuck me again, though, won't he? But Liam made no move to tug Zac back into bed. Instead, he watched Zac dress with an inscrutable gaze, then got up himself and pulled his own clothes on. "Will you be okay getting home?"

"Hmm?" Zac glanced up from stamping into his tatty trainers. "Oh . . . yeah. I bought a return ticket."

"From King's Cross?"

"No, from Liverpool Street." Silence. Zac wondered if Liam could hear the thud of his pounding heart. "What? Why are you looking at me like that?"

Liam shrugged. "Just seems a bit weird to be heading in the same direction on different paths. And I feel a bit bad for dragging you all the way here, especially when we didn't leave the flat. I probably shoulda taken you out for dinner or some shit."

"I'm a whore, not an escort." Zac pushed past Liam and headed for the door.

Liam followed and shoved his way in front of him, blocking him again. "Will you stop calling yourself a fucking whore?"

It was the first time he'd raised his voice in anything other than coming like a train. Zac stopped short, though he couldn't contain his anger. "Why? For your benefit? Fuck that. Don't try and make me something I'm not to make yourself feel better."

"Make myself— What the fuck?" Liam's usually kind brown eyes darkened. "I don't want you to call yourself a whore because I reckon there's far more to you than that, not because I'm under any delusion that I haven't paid you to pretend you enjoy fucking me."

"I do enjoy it."

"Yeah?" Liam stepped closer, so close Zac could feel the warmth radiating from him. "And does that make you feel like a whore? Do I? Do I treat you like one?"

"No," Zac said sullenly. "Doesn't change who I am, though, does it? You can call me what you want. I'm still a fucking hooker."

"I'm going to call you Zac," Liam said. "I don't care if it's not even your real name, I'm never going to call you a bloody whore."

It was probably the nicest thing anyone had ever said to Zac, but it didn't change the fact that he had to leave, or that their night together was ending on a strained note. Zac stepped around Liam and put his hand on the solid front door, but something—everything— made him turn and face Liam's steady gaze. He had no more words, no explanation for yet another emotional shit-storm, so he just grasped Liam's T-shirt and pulled him closer until their faces were inches apart.

He pressed his lips to the corner of Liam's mouth with the barest brush of a forbidden kiss. "Thank you for treating me like I matter. I won't forget it."

It took Zac nearly four hours to get home. A fallen tree delayed Zac's already late train, and it was five o'clock by the time he reached his own front door. He rummaged in his pockets for his key, but the door flew open before he found it.

Jamie's furious glare greeted him. "Where the fuck have you been?"

"Hello to you too." Zac shoved him out of the way and went inside. "You know where I've been. I came and told you, remember?"

"Of course I remember," Jamie snapped. "Why else would I be here checking you hadn't been bloody murdered or some shit?"

"What?"

"You said it was an overnight. I thought you'd be back this morning."

"Why? What do you need? I'm not giving you my money."

"That's why you think I'm here?" Jamie's gaze narrowed, eclipsing the crazy-blue eyes that made him so strikingly attractive. "I told you, I came to make sure you got home okay. Why are you being such a dick?"

Zac stared hard at Jamie, searching for any sign that he was being played, but all he saw was concern, mixed in with the fatigue of someone who clearly hadn't slept in days. "Sorry. I'm okay, mate. I promise."

"Really? 'Cause I bloody lost my shit when your phone was switched off. Thought you were fucking brown bread and buried in some weirdo's back garden. I was ready to dig you up and feed you to the swans . . . set you free in the river."

Zac laughed, he couldn't help it. Jamie's way of thinking had always been an odd, sadistic poetry, even when his fierce intelligence was dulled by the junk. "Can you chuck me off a bridge instead? I'd rather fly than swim. I don't like the cold."

"Good." Jamie's gaze turned guilty. "'Cause I turned the heating on."

"The heating? Dude, it's barely October."

"So? I'm freezing."

That made sense. Jamie was coming down from what was likely a week-long junk binge, and nothing was colder than withdrawing from a bellyful of smack. Zac tried not to notice the other signs that Jamie had been kicking around the flat for a while: the sofa cushions scattered on the floor, half-empty glasses of water on every surface. "Have you eaten?"

Jamie shook his head. "Nope."

"Okay." Zac went to the kitchen and opened the cupboard where he kept their paltry provisions. Inside were their trusty Super Noodles and a tired packet of crumpets. It wasn't exactly authentic Thai, but it would do. Like it always did.

He cooked them up a couple of blocks of instant noodles and toasted the crumpets. They didn't have any butter, but neither of them cared, used to going without. They took their feast to the couch and inhaled their food. When they were done, Jamie took the plates to the kitchen, then reclaimed his space beside Zac, stretching out and dumping his head in Zac's lap.

"So . . . how was it? Did you have to fuck all night? I can run you a bath if you want?"

Zac played absently with Jamie's grubby hair, repressing the urge to tell him he was the one who needed a wash. "I'm okay, honest. We fucked a lot, but nothing too heavy."

Jamie didn't look convinced, and before Liam, Zac had thought the same: that hooking, whatever way you dressed it up, was just about sex. The john wanted as much as possible for his money, and the tom as much cash as he could get away with asking for. But it hadn't been like that with Liam. Not even close. They'd had a lot of sex, but not as much as Zac had imagined they would. On paper, without the cash, their night together could've been a date if Zac had been anything close to the kind of bloke Liam deserved.

"You like him, don't you?"

"Hmm?"

Jamie wriggled around so Zac could see his face. "Don't get emotional, man. It'll fuck you up."

"I'm not getting emotional."

"Bollocks. I can see it in your eyes. You've connected with him and you think it means something. It doesn't, Zac. Don't forget who you are."

Zac sighed. "I'm not anybody."

"Not to him, maybe. You're my best mate, though, if it's any consolation."

"I'm your only mate."

"True."

Jamie closed his eyes and shivered. Zac pressed his hand to Jamie's clammy forehead and his heart sank a little more. If Jamie had been here all day waiting for him, he'd missed his afternoon fix, the extra-large hit he needed to get him through a long night on the street. Which meant he'd be feeling it now, craving it, clinging to his addiction like an obsessive lover, knowing it was wrong, but too far gone to let go.

Don't write him off. You beat it. So will he . . . eventually. But it was the *eventually* that was so terrifying. Jamie was fading fast, and Zac knew too well that he was only a strong hit away from his last high. He stroked Jamie's hair back from his face with a heavy soul. If the worst happened, would Zac ever know? Or would Jamie just be another anonymous dead junkie? A statistic that meant nothing to anyone but Zac?

Jamie shuddered again and curled in on himself, a sure sign that it wouldn't be long before he gathered his few possessions and left Zac to make the two-hour bus journey back to Norwich. It was on the tip of Zac's tongue to beg him to stay, but it would only fall on deaf ears. Jamie loved him, as much as an addict could love anyone, but he needed the junk more.

"I need to go." Jamie rolled off the couch, lurching unsteadily to his feet. "Can I borrow some money for the bus?"

"Borrow?"

Jamie scowled. "Don't be tight. It's only a score."

A score was twenty quid. It cost less than a tenner to get the bus to Norwich, and there were no prizes for guessing where the change would end up. Still, Zac supposed he was lucky Jamie hadn't waited for him to fall asleep and simply helped himself to the roll of cash Zac had added to the stash in the cistern. It wasn't like he hadn't stolen from Zac before.

Zac went to the kitchen and found the jar he kept a few quid in for moments like these. He retrieved the last two tenners and took them back to Jamie. "Do you need anything else?"

Jamie shook his head and kept his gaze averted. Zac could almost see the guilt creeping into his soul, merging with the pain only a fellow addict would understand. He relented, knowing his good intentions were making things worse, and went to the hallway, grabbing the coat he'd stowed away in the cupboard, saving it for when the weather turned and Jamie's ruined jacket was no longer enough to keep him warm at night. "Here, take this, but don't sell it, got it?"

Jamie rolled his eyes, but took the coat and immediately put it on, wrapping it around himself like a water-tank insulation jacket. He didn't say thank you, but Zac didn't need it, didn't *want* it, because saying it would acknowledge how skewed their relationship had become, how moments like these were getting less frequent and each good-bye could be their last.

The buzz of a phone that wasn't Zac's shattered the silence. Jamie pulled a phone Zac had never seen before from his back pocket and squinted at it, like the light from its tiny screen hurt his weary eyes. His expression hardened, but not in time to hide the flash of apprehension in his bloodshot gaze.

"Nice phone," Zac said. "Where'd you get it?"

"The market. Irvine said I had to have one."

"Irvine?" It took Zac a moment to compute. "That your pimp?"

"He's the boss's pit bull. What do you care?"

"Are you fucking serious?"

Jamie flinched. Zac rarely raised his voice, even when things went horribly wrong. "Don't bitch at me."

"I'm not—" Zac caught his temper before it boiled over. He didn't want to row with Jamie when he had a foot out the door. "Listen, be careful, okay? I don't like worrying about you. It makes me twitchy."

Jamie closed the distance between them and pressed his forehead to Zac's. "No, it doesn't. Nothing makes you twitchy because you're better than that. You're better than *this*, Zac. Now let me go . . . please? I don't want you to see me like this."

Zac could have pointed out that they'd seen each other in plenty worse states than simply jonesing for a fix, but he let Jamie go all the same.

Jamie spared him a last tired grin before he left, shutting the door with a quiet click behind him. Zac listened to his soft tread on the stairs and the thud of the exterior door. He pictured Jamie on the bus to Norwich, and then heading out into the city centre to score the brown that would take the pain away. For a moment, Zac was jealous, still tied to that first euphoric high, even though the hundreds that had come after had paled in comparison, but then he recalled the bright January morning he'd woken alone in a utilitarian London hospital, strung out in a bed with the world's meanest methadone prescription coursing through his veins. *Fuck that shit.*

Zac waited by the bar for the woman to come back. She'd told him her name, but buoyed by a long evening of drinking sugary alcopops in the crappy club, he'd forgotten it. All he knew was that she was nice, willing, and ripe for a mark. He hadn't broached the subject of payment yet, but reckoned one more drink would give him the balls.

The woman returned. She handed Zac a drink with a pretty smile. "They didn't have any WKD left, so I got you a Jäger bomb."

Zac took the drink, noting that she'd got herself a coke. Good. He wanted a punter who knew their own mind, not one who came to their senses at the last minute and kicked him to the kerb.

It was harder with women, though. A mile off, Zac could spot a closeted gay, a married man desperate for a bit of cock, but the kind of woman willing to pay for sex wasn't like that. They craved conversation rather than an orgasm, and Zac often found that more arduous. At least with sex he was certain of his role. Huddled in the corner of the bar, hoping the woman was enjoying his company enough to pay for more of it, he felt a little lost. And bored. Picking up women was a long game, and he found himself perversely wishing he'd simply turned a trick on the streets and gone home.

But you don't do that anymore. And fuck if that didn't feel like a burden tonight. He'd come out scouting for women on purpose, but despite being miles away from the gay bar where he'd met Liam last month, he still caught himself looking for him around every corner, searching for the broad shoulders and shaggy blond hair that weren't there.

Hmm. Perhaps that explained why he'd zeroed in on the pale-skinned, dark-haired woman who was a world away from everything he was missing. He swirled the ice in his drink. It had been two weeks since his London encounter with Liam and he hadn't heard a thing—despite checking his phone every ten seconds—and the silence had left him antsy. He'd serviced all his usual johns, and picked up a few on top, but he couldn't get Liam out of his mind. Getting fucked by strangers had always felt perverse, but he'd been hooking so long he'd perfected the art of disconnection—even without the junk. But Liam had undone that. Zac had turned a dozen tricks since his trip to London, but each one had proved more difficult than the last. He'd never had any trouble getting—or staying—hard, but the last few days had been . . . awkward, and it seemed Zac's dick was craving Liam's touch as much as Zac was.

"Um . . ." The woman laid a hand on Zac's arm. "Do you want to get a drink at my house?"

Bingo. Zac raised a smile from somewhere and plastered it on his face. "Sure. Let's go."

The taxi ride to the woman's house provided the ideal opportunity for Zac to spin his usual sales pitch. He moved closer to the woman as she fumbled in her purse for the cab fare. Her debit card popped up—Emily Pines. Zac filed the information and put his hand on her leg. "So, Emily . . . after we've had that drink, is there anything else I can help you with?"

It was almost too easy. The woman—Emily—didn't even seem that surprised when Zac revealed his motives.

"Should've known," she said. "I knew you were too fit for the likes of me."

He felt bad then. Emily was pretty—pale and alluring—but more than that, despite Zac's preoccupation with the phone call that would likely never come, she was actually rather nice and he felt comfortable in her presence, and in her bed. He flipped her over onto her belly and took her from behind, gentle and slow, almost sweet, resolving to give her the attention she deserved, and push all thoughts of Liam aside, which, with Emily's soft, rounded body, wasn't as hard as it might've been if he'd picked up a bloke.

He left her sleeping in the early hours, creeping down the stairs and letting himself out. Halfway down her drive, he spun on his heel and jogged to the front door, and impulsively posted the money she'd given him back through her letterbox.

What the fuck are you doing? He had no idea, but was gone and away before he could give it much thought.

At the flat, he plugged his phone in to charge, then searched for any sign Jamie had been home. But he found none. There was no mess or trail of destruction, and, more importantly, Zac's wad of cash was still safe in the back of the toilet.

He took a shower, washing with the bodywash he'd bought with the money left over from paying the rent. It smelled like Liam—like mint and the sea, though it was nothing like the expensive toiletries he'd had in his bathroom—and it wasn't long before Zac's hand drifted to his cock. He closed his eyes and fought the images of Liam that bombarded him, picturing Jamie, and Emily, and even a few johns who hadn't been as vile as most of the others, anything to stop his obsession with Liam bleeding into every private moment of his life.

But it was no good. He'd enjoyed his time with Emily, and he *always* enjoyed fucking Jamie—teasing his familiar body, baiting him until they both tumbled over the edge—but none of it had anything on the crazy heat he'd found with Liam. It had been two weeks since they'd laid a hand on each other, and despite all that had happened since, Zac could still feel the burn of his cock digging inside him, and the sting of teeth sinking into his back.

"Fuck!" Zac pushed his swollen dick aside and slapped the wet tiles, growling in frustration. Couldn't he have a wank without his obsession with Liam spoiling it? *Idiot.* Like he needed a fucking wank. Like he even wanted one.

Grumbling, he turned off the shower and dried himself with the towel that was still damp from before he'd gone out. Perhaps Jamie had been right and it was time to turn the central heating on after all. At least then he wouldn't have to put clothes on to walk around the flat—clothes it took him a while to find, as it had been a week since he'd done any washing. For the first time in days, he checked his phone as an afterthought instead of the manic compulsion he'd developed over the past fortnight. A message flashed up, and his first thought was Jamie. Two weeks was a long time, even for him.

But it wasn't Jamie, it was Liam, and his short, ten-word message warmed Zac's soul from the inside out.

Call me in the morning. Got something to ask you. — L

CHAPTER
EIGHT

"I've got to take the van up to Sheffield for the day and it doesn't go faster than fifty miles an hour, so I could use the company." Liam drummed his fingers on the van's bonnet as he waited for Zac to reply. He'd sent the text in the early hours after a maudlin night on the beer, half expecting Zac not to respond, so the 9 a.m. phone call had caught him on the hop.

"What's in Sheffield?" Zac asked.

"Work, and a specialist garage for the van. She needs some TLC."

"'She'?" Zac sounded amused. "Don't tell me your van has a name?"

"Hettie. Don't take the piss. It'll make sense when you see her."

Zac said nothing. Liam wondered if he was calculating how much a day trip would earn him and if it was worth the hassle. "I'll pay you five hundred again."

"Five hundred? How long are we going for? A week?"

Liam chuckled. "No, just the day, but I reckon you'll have earned it by the time you've spent a day bouncing around in Hettie."

Another dose of silence, then Zac sighed. "I didn't think I was going to hear from you."

"Why not?" Liam pushed himself off the van and wandered to the cliff edge, lighting his first cigarette in weeks and peering over the barrier to the crashing sea below. "Wasn't that bad in London, was it?"

"Not for me. Just figured I might've scared you off by freaking out on you. Wasn't exactly what you paid for."

Liam studied the waves as they rolled inland and hit the rocks. The resulting mess of froth and foam felt much like the chaos in his brain, chaos that only seemed to fade when he had Zac in his arms.

Who am I to judge him? "Worse things happen at sea, mate. I'm all right with it if you are."

"When do you want to go?"

"When are you free?"

"Thursday?" Zac said. "I've got, er, some stuff to do before then."

By *stuff*, Liam assumed Zac meant other clients—*johns*—and the thought of him with someone else still made Liam feel slightly sick. Sometimes, it was all too easy to convince himself he was the only one and try not to ponder why it even mattered. "Thursday is good for me. I need to leave early, though. Around half seven?"

Zac whistled. "Probably not worth going to bed, then."

"If you say so. Where should I pick you up? The flat?"

"That works. I'll wait for you outside."

Liam searched for a way to end the conversation, but saying good-bye and hanging up suddenly seemed impossible. Shame he couldn't think of an intelligent reason to keep Zac on the line.

Zac cleared his throat. "So I'll see you on Thursday? Bright and early?"

"Er . . . I guess so."

"Bye, then."

"Bye."

Zac hung up, leaving Liam still staring at the sea and wondering how these rare, stilted conversations had become the highlight of his day. But the waves held no answers and he had a million things to do between now and Thursday. With a heavy sigh, he tore himself away from the cliffs and climbed into the van. He turned the key, and she rumbled to life with a tired splutter.

Liam patted the dashboard. "Easy, girl. Gonna get you sorted out soon."

Hettie made no reply, and Liam questioned his sanity, but he wasn't in the mood to lose that game today. Zac's call had distracted him from something he'd been putting off for weeks, and he needed Hettie's asthmatic purr to keep him grounded, just as he'd need her on Thursday when he drove to King's Lynn and introduced her to the beautiful young hooker who'd claimed every thought Liam couldn't fill with work, hassle, and plain old grief.

Liam eased the van out of the cliffside lay-by he'd pulled into when Zac had called. The sign for Fakenham came into view not long after. Liam followed the road inland until the turn for the cemetery popped up on the left, half hidden by the giant oak tree he'd slept against one dark night after he'd buried Cory within the graveyard's walls. He parked in the deserted car park and got out, drifting to the shiny headstone that stood out like a new penny. *Cory.* Liam knelt and touched the fresh flowers Rosa left every week. The grave was neat and tidy, unlike some of the older plots nearby—the one next to Cory hadn't been touched in years.

"If anything ever happens to me, just chuck me on the compost heap..."

Liam allowed himself a watery smile. He'd been tempted to follow Cory's wish to the letter, but the world didn't work quite like that. A biodegradable coffin had been the best he could do.

And look at you now, eh? Fucking hookers for therapy. Liam closed his eyes against the mocking inner voice, but without the stark reality of Cory's grave to ground him, Zac filled his mind, dancing through his consciousness from that first heady night in King's Lynn to their last encounter in London—Zac with his long, slender body and sharp, green eyes, his smooth skin and slim hips. Everything about him so entrenched in Liam's brain it was hard to believe they'd only met twice.

Liam opened his eyes and took a deep breath of the cool October air. He rarely came to the cemetery. Its calm tranquillity was so unlike Cory that there seemed to be no connection between the bleak grave and the riotous, colourful man Liam remembered, even with Rosa's weekly flower drop. He brushed some dirt off the shiny stone and wondered what Cory would think if he could see him now—the business, the house, the dogs...Zac. Most folk would probably hazard a guess that Cory wouldn't be too pleased to know Liam had been paying a hooker to keep him company, but they didn't know—hadn't known—Cory. If there was anyone who'd understand, it would've been him.

"Don't ever be lonely, dude. There's someone worth knowing in every smile you see."

They'd used that catchphrase on the festival ad campaign the first year they'd put it on. Liam had laughed and humoured Cory, even as he'd painted it on yards and yards of up-cycled fencing, but the words haunted him now. Zac's smiles were rare, and Liam was still so lonely that his soul ached for the man who'd taught him how to love, so what the fuck was the point?

There were no answers in the cemetery, so he left Cory behind and drove home to Holkham. On his desk, he found a stack of updated employment contracts for the designers Sea Rave had commissioned to take his place when he'd been forced to take over Cory's CEO role, exactly where he'd tossed them the day before. Rosa's husband, Mike, had drawn up the contracts, setting out the terms and conditions, and the expectations from both sides. Liam ran an absent eye over them, checking for discrepancies and anything Mike had missed. One section stood out:

Sea Rave will provide fringe benefits, including health insurance, paid holiday and parental leave, and discounted clothing, regardless of the employee's role within the company.

This meant that everyone from business director Mike to the teenager who swept the factory floors on a Saturday was treated as equally as they could be without bankrupting the business. The policy, dreamed up by Cory at a surf festival in France years ago, buoyed by too much beer and a foggy cloud of local weed, and reinvented and tweaked by Mike since, meant that Sea Rave's employee turnover was next to nil. People came to work for them and never left. Liam couldn't count the number of times he'd been told Sea Rave had become someone's family.

It was a legacy Cory would've died five times over for. Liam approved the enhancements Mike had drafted, but as he finished up, he thought again of Zac and his heart sank a little further into his stomach. Sea Rave took care of their employees because they gave a shit. Who cared about Zac? Who made sure he was treated fairly? Supported him when he was ill and couldn't work?

Dave walked into his leg, reminding him in her clumsy way that he hadn't taken her and Jazz to the beach yet. Liam looked down and made a feeble attempt to tame the mud-streaked wild wool framing her face. Whose idea had it been to get labradoodles again?

Damn things were dirt magnets. *It was your idea, dickhead.* Of course it was. The stupid ideas had always been his.

Liam rounded up the dogs and gathered their leads. Dave didn't really need one, but Jazz had a tendency to bound away, a habit that had worsened since Cory had gone. Liam wasn't brave enough to wonder if he was searching for his master, so he clipped the leads on and headed out to the beach, loosing the dogs once they were off the beaten path. He was halfway to the sea when he saw a familiar figure by the water, limping along the wet sand.

The dogs spotted him too, racing across the sand to greet his father, fairly knocking him off his feet. Liam hurried to rescue him. "Dave! Jazz! Down! Dad, what are you doing here? Rosa said she was taking you to Hunstanton today."

"Aye, and she did. Tried taking me to the bloody bingo hall too. Whose fecking idea was that?"

Despite his obvious vexation, Len Mallaney's gentle Derry accent washed over Liam like an old friend, bringing with it soft memories of his childhood. "Not mine, Dad. I swear. I told her you'd rather go to the bookies. She said bingo was pretty much the same thing."

Len grunted. "Let her go, then. See how she likes it."

"You know she means well."

Len let him have that one and blew cigar smoke into the wind. Liam regarded him for a moment, taking in his lined face and stature that was becoming more stooped by the day. His weathered hand wrapped around the walking stick he'd once threatened to burn in the fireplace of his tiny cottage, a mile up the road from Liam's converted barn. His faded brown corduroy trousers and battered— "Dad, where's your shoes?"

"Hmm?"

"Your shoes. You're wearing your slippers."

"Am I?" Len glanced absently down at his feet. "Oh yes. Silly me. I had half an eye on the races when I left. Must've slipped my old mind."

Liam tried to smile, but it was hard, and Rosa's ominous warning echoed in his mind. *"It won't be long now. He can't stay in the cottage forever . . ."*

"Come on, Dad. Let's get you home."

Len came willingly enough. Liam and the dogs walked him to his cottage and settled him by the fire with the *Racing Post* and a warm dram of his favourite Irish whiskey. The dogs fell asleep at his feet while Liam took his customary place on the old, threadbare couch—the one Len refused to let him replace.

"You okay there, son?"

Liam tore his gaze away from the flickering flames. "What's that, Dad? Oh yeah, I'm fine."

"Sure about that? You look a little peaky."

"You always say that."

Len raised a greyed eyebrow. "Then it must be true. Get some whiskey down you. Warm you up."

"I'm plenty warm enough, thanks." Liam made a mental note to make sure Len wasn't just having Celtic Cask for his dinner.

"You know your sister's worried about you?" Len returned his gaze to his betting paper. "She thinks you're keeping to yourself too much."

"Chance would be a fine thing."

"Wouldn't it just?" Len fixed Liam with intelligent blue eyes that were as bright as they'd ever been. "Your boy wouldn't like it."

He said no more, but he didn't have to. Len Mallaney had always been a man of few words, and Liam heard his message loud and clear: *Don't be lonely.*

Ha. If it was only that easy.

Thursday morning found Liam pulling up outside Zac's King's Lynn flat fifteen minutes early. For some reason, he wasn't surprised to see Zac already waiting for him, slouching on a wall by the pavement, hood up and smoking a joint.

Liam stopped the van and wound down the window. "Herbal breakfast?"

"What if it is?" Zac regarded him from the depths of his hood, his green eyes glinting moodily. "Not my mother, are ya?"

"I'm not anyone's mother. Just wondering if you're off your tits on something more than a spliff."

"Like what?"

Liam shrugged. "Crack? Smack? Whatever you kids are calling it these days."

"Do I look like a junkie?"

"What does a junkie look like?"

Zac stared. Liam inwardly cringed. *Nice one, idiot. Do you want him to think you're a complete knob?* "Er, never mind. You getting in or what?"

Zac flicked his smoke away and opened the passenger door. "When you said van, I kinda thought you meant a Transit, like a works van."

"Hettie is a works van." Liam patted the dashboard. "I've been driving her since I was seventeen."

Zac whistled. "Damn, so she's nearly as old as you are?"

"Piss off and get in."

Zac got in and pushed his hood back, revealing bloodshot eyes that suggested he probably hadn't been to bed.

"Long night?" Liam asked, though he really didn't want to hear Zac's answer.

Zac shrugged. "Aren't they all?"

He had Liam there. It had been long past midnight before he'd found rest himself and he'd been up again at five, walking the dogs and getting them sufficiently tired to spend the day with Rosa, tidying the shameful mess he'd let his bedroom become, and generally doing anything he could to keep his mind off his bizarre "date" with Zac. "Are you going to be warm enough in that hoodie? It's blowing a gale."

"Van's got heating, hasn't it?"

"She," Liam corrected. "Hang on a sec."

He killed the engine and got out of the van, moving to the back to open the tailgate.

"Damn, you're such a dude."

Liam jumped. He hadn't expected Zac to follow him. "A dude?"

Zac peered around Liam and into the van. "You never said she was a camper van. This is the coolest thing I've ever seen. Is that a barbecue?"

"Fire pit, actually, but it's got a grill."

"Ah, and you're veggie, aren't ya? So it's not much good to you, is it?"

"You'd be surprised, and I can't resist the occasional banger, so it gets plenty of use. Here, take this to the front." Liam handed Zac the thin, rolled-up duvet he kept in the van for the rare winter nights he slept out with Hettie. "She's got heating, but it fucks with the engine. This'll keep you warm."

Zac looked at Liam like he'd grown horns, but took the duvet anyway. Liam grabbed a couple of pillows and shut the tailgate, and they both got back in the front.

Liam started the engine and eased into the flow of traffic heading north out of the town. In his peripheral vision, he saw Zac awkwardly fumbling with the duvet. "Put your feet up on the dashboard if you want. Get comfy."

"You're obsessed with me being comfy."

"So?" Liam wasn't in the mood to have that conversation again. "There's something in the glove box for you, by the way."

Zac leaned forward and opened the dashboard. He took the roll of notes Liam had left in there for him and frowned. "This is more than five hundred."

"I know."

"Have you got something in mind I don't know about?"

Liam didn't know quite how to explain the impulse he'd had when he'd withdrawn Zac's cash from the bank the day before. The truth made him sound like a bit of a weirdo, but it was all he had. "I figured you could do with a bonus—call it holiday pay, whatever."

"Holiday pay?" Zac looked mystified.

Liam shrugged. "I don't know how often you, er, work, or what you need the money for, but I reckon it's been a while since you took some time off. Am I right?"

Zac opened his mouth. Shut it again. "I don't really take time off. I just work."

"I know that feeling," Liam said. "It happens when you work for yourself. There's no one to tell you when you've done enough, so you keep going until you run yourself into the ground."

"Is that what you do?"

"Sometimes, but my sister's pretty good at reining me in."

"I still don't understand why you gave me eight hundred quid."

Liam shot Zac a curious glance. He hadn't seen Zac count the money. "I gave it to you so you can afford to take a night off, from me, or anyone else. Eat, sleep, er, rest . . ."

Jesus Christ. Why couldn't you give him the money and shut the fuck up? Liam had no idea, and by the puzzled frown on Zac's face, it was clear he didn't either.

"I'm just saying you should have some time for yourself too."

"I don't know what else I'd do if I wasn't working."

"No? You don't have anything else you'd rather be doing? People you'd rather be with? Family? Friends?"

Zac shook his head. "Don't really have any."

"No boyfriend?"

"No."

"Girlfriend?"

Zac rolled his eyes. "Flippin' heck. When did you get so nosy?"

Liam couldn't think of a sensible answer, so he said nothing, and for a while, neither did Zac. Three miles had passed before either of them spoke again.

"Thank you," Zac said finally.

Liam raised an eyebrow. "What for?"

"For the money. Being with you doesn't feel like working. I'd do it for free if I could afford it."

Liam grinned. "Yeah? Well that's nice, though I reckon there's not much I wouldn't pay for the privilege of spending a few hours with you."

CHAPTER
NINE

"**...t**here's not much I wouldn't pay for the privilege of spending a few hours with you."

Zac almost pinched himself to check he was really awake, before the inevitable cynicism set in. Why on earth would Liam want to spend time with Zac? With his luxury flat and übercool camper van, it was clear he had the whole world at his feet. Nah, this was about the sex. It had to be.

Liam had fallen silent again, his eyes on the road. Zac pocketed the cash he'd been paid and settled back in his seat, slumping down on the pillows Liam had tossed to him. The duvet called his name, but he didn't dare retreat beneath it. Warm and comfy was one thing, sleeping all the way to wherever they were going was something else altogether.

He let you sleep last time. Zac couldn't deny that, but Liam seemed different today, more intense—if that were possible—and every glance he sent Zac pierced his soul. "Where are we going?"

"Sheffield."

"I know that," Zac said. "And I know you're taking the van— Hettie—to the garage. What else is in Sheffield for you?"

"Work. My company has a factory there. I've not been up in a long while, so it's time I showed my face."

Zac couldn't think why Liam would need a hooker with him for that, but he wasn't about to question it. Perhaps he had an office he wanted to get naughty in, a desk to bend him over, a filing cabinet to push him against and fuck his brains out. Liam wouldn't be the first john to pay him to perform a long-held fantasy. "What does your company make in the factory?"

"Clothes, mainly, and a few accessories. We make the boards in Newquay."

"Boards . . . you mean surfboards?"

"Yep."

Liam kept his eyes trained on the road, but something in his tone made Zac sit up and take in the tightness around his eyes and his white knuckles around Hettie's steering wheel. "Why don't you like Newquay?"

"What makes you think I don't like Newquay?"

"Okay," Zac countered. "Why don't you like talking about Newquay?"

Liam sucked in a deep breath and let it go slowly without meeting Zac's gaze. "It's not Newquay I don't like, it's everything it represents. Me and Cory—my partner—we lived there before he died, and we were happy, you know? It never occurred to me that there was anything else."

"Happy?" Zac stretched his legs out and dumped his feet on the dashboard. "You'll have to tell me what that's like."

"Are you not happy, Zac?"

"Wouldn't know."

"Oh, I think you would. I reckon you've seen the dark side, mate, and you can't see light without the dark." Liam grinned in a slightly manic way. "Got that nugget in a Christmas cracker. Good, eh?"

"If you say so."

Liam snorted. "I do today. But I should warn you, I haven't been up there since Cory died either, so people might be surprised to see us."

"Is that why you needed company? To distract them?"

"More to distract me, actually. I'd have fucked off home by now if you weren't here."

"Why?"

"Why what?"

Zac sat up a little more. "Why me? Don't you have anyone else who could've come with you?"

Liam appeared to consider the question, then he shook his head. "Plenty of people would've come with me if I'd asked them, but the only folk I can handle most days are my dogs, and they're not allowed in the factory."

Fair enough. Zac let it go and settled back into his nest of pillows. He watched the road whizz by and fought the heaviness in his eyelids, but after a while, when Liam flicked a switch that blew wonderfully warm air across his face, the hypnotic rumble of the van—Hettie—overtook him and he fell asleep.

They were in Sheffield by the time he woke sometime later. At least, he assumed they were, as the van was parked outside a large white building with a vaguely familiar logo splashed across the front. "Is this your factory?"

Liam looked up from his phone. "Ah, there you are. I was about to wake you. Yep, this is it. Welcome to SRP."

"SRP?"

"Sea Rave Productions."

Zac frowned and fingered the leather bracelet he still wore on his right arm. "Sea Rave? As in the festival? You never said you worked for them."

"I don't work for them. I own them. Technically, I'm the CEO, but I try and avoid that shit as much as possible."

"Oh." And it was a big "oh." Zac knew fuck-all about fuck-all, and he'd never heard of Sea Rave before Liam, but it didn't take a genius to work out that his suspicions about Liam being a big deal in the world had been bang on. Owned the company? Surfboards, clothes, festivals . . . damn. Was Liam the Norfolk equivalent of Richard bloody Branson? "Are you going inside?"

"If you'll come with me." Liam seemed apprehensive.

Zac frowned and nudged his arm. "I'll do whatever you want me to. Anything."

"Yeah?" Liam smirked, and the disquiet in his gaze was gone like it had never been there at all. "Maybe later. I would like you to come in with me, though, if you don't mind. I'll be stuck there for hours otherwise, and I can't be arsed."

That was good enough for Zac. He sat up and made an attempt to tame his hair. "Do I look okay?"

"Hmm?" Liam had gone back to his phone. "Look okay? Course you do. Sorry, I was trying to figure something out before we went in. Take a butcher's at these . . . which is better?"

Liam held up a phone that had a bigger screen than the tiny TV Zac had at home. He pointed at the two T-shirts on display. Zac squinted at them, his eyes still scratchy from his impromptu nap. "What am I butchering at?"

"Whatever you see. Don't think about it, just pick one."

"The one on the left."

"Why?"

"It's cleaner."

Liam brought the screen back into his line of vision. "Cleaner? That makes sense. Thanks."

"You're welcome. Did I get it right?"

"There was no right answer, mate. Just opinion, and I needed a fresh one. I've been staring at that for weeks. It's the first piece I've done in months and I'm totally freaking out that it's shite."

"Piece?"

"Design," Liam said. "I used to design most of the clothes, back when we just did T-shirts, but I had to quit when the corporate bullshit took over. Pretty sure I've lost my mojo."

Zac reached out and turned the phone screen towards him, studying the sea-blue T-shirts with the cartoon-style fish-shaped surfboard printed on the front and the slogan *Battered* beneath it. The one on the left—the one he'd picked—was perfect. If Zac closed his eyes, he could easily picture it hugging Liam's strong frame as he sat behind the wheel of his cherry-red camper. "I like it."

"Good. Hopefully you're not the only one. The art director who took my place is a fucking dragon. If it's shit, we'll soon know."

Liam got out of the van. Zac followed suit, stretching his stiff legs. He hadn't meant to fall asleep, but fuck if he hadn't needed it. He'd spent the night with another regular john, trying to avoid anything heavy so he'd be ready for Liam, but dodging the john's drunken advances had been as exhausting as getting slammed all night, and he was more drained than he had been in a long time.

He bent in front of the wing mirror and fiddled with his hair again. Had those bags beneath his eyes always been there? Next to Liam with his tanned skin and muscles, Zac felt like a scrawny sack of pale bones. The heroin chic incarnation of the Milkybar Kid—

Liam gripped his shoulders and tugged him upright. "Leave it alone. You look fine, better than fine. You're fucking gorgeous."

"Pull the other one."

Liam's gaze darkened. "I mean it."

"Yeah?" Zac swallowed the inevitable thrill that came with Liam's electrifying touch. "And is that what you need with you in there? Who the fuck do these people think I am, anyway?"

"No one yet. I was gonna tell them we were friends. That okay with you?"

Friends. Zac nodded slowly as he turned the word over in his mind. *Friends.* "Yeah, I like that."

Liam grinned. "Then friends we are."

Turned out the inner workings of a clothes factory were pretty boring. The giant sewing machines and rolls of fabric were of little interest to Zac until they came to the printing section and everything changed. Zac stared around at the kaleidoscope of colours and huge screens. "This is so fucking cool."

"Yeah?" Liam smiled. "It's probably my favourite part too. I don't get to play much anymore, though. Too many bullshit meetings and conference calls."

He rolled his eyes in a way that took ten years off him. If it hadn't been for the staff around them, Zac would've jumped him there and then. Not that Liam's age bothered him. Why would it when he was by far his youngest client?

"What's that?" Zac pointed to an intriguing black stencil being applied to white fabric at the back of the room.

"That's our flagship T-shirt range. It's coming out in the spring."

"Can I see?"

"Sure." Liam approached the young woman operating the screen press. She stopped what she was doing and exchanged a few quiet words with Liam, before giving him a big hug and leaving the room with her lunch bag.

Zac had noticed that everyone in the building had a hug for Liam, like he was a long-lost friend rather than their boss. It was like they all owned a piece of him, and Zac found himself more than a little jealous. He wanted to put his arms around Liam, wanted to hold him and whisper in his ear, though what he would say, he had no clue. Perhaps he wouldn't say anything. Perhaps he'd just hold Liam and hope it would be enough to ease the subtle pain clouding his gaze.

"Zac?"

Liam was staring at Zac like he'd called his name a hundred times. *Oops.* "Sorry, what?"

"I was saying . . ." Liam cuffed his shoulder. "That these are the templates for the shirts."

Zac studied the templates, trying not to dwell on the fact that Liam's affectionate punch was the first physical contact they'd had all day, and read the various slogans. They were all clever plays on words or graphics, delivering a subtle eco-warrior message, and the last one was his favourite. The font was made of dying trees and the slogan simply read, *think.* "Who comes up with the words?"

"The designers, mainly, sometimes our marketing team. This one's mine though, actually. A vintage one from years ago that we've relaunched."

"It's awesome."

"Thank you."

They grinned at each other for a long moment before a factory worker called Liam's name and the spell was broken.

A little while later, Liam's business at the factory was done. They took Hettie to a nearby garage. Whatever she was having done would take a few hours, so they decamped to the pub across the road.

Liam left Zac at a table and went to the bar. He came back with a Pepsi and a pint of ale that he passed across the table.

Zac took a tentative sip. He'd never drunk cask beer before and the concept was something of a mystery to him. Lager had always made more sense, until he tasted the ale and it slid down his throat into his belly like a warm, beery hug. "Wow. I like that. What is it?"

"Fuggle Bunny. They brew it up the road. It's strong stuff, though, so go easy."

"Trust me, I can handle it." Zac took another gulp, ignoring the quizzical frown Liam shot him. "What are we doing now?"

"Not much. I ordered some lunch. Pie and chips okay with you?"

Hell, yeah. Liam had blown his mind with the Thai feast in London, but there was nothing Zac craved more when he was tired and hungry than a heaping plate of pie and chips. Not that he often had the means to indulge. A Pukka Pie from the chippie was as good as it got, and that was rare. And a far cry from the gigantic pie that appeared in front of him ten minutes later. "Fuck me."

Liam snorted. "Not in here, mate."

Zac hardly heard him, too caught up in the huge dome of pastry towering over his plate. "What's in the pie?"

"Lentils and ale."

"Fuggle Bunny ale?"

"Maybe." Liam grinned and passed Zac a bottle of ketchup and a fork. "Dig in and see."

He didn't have to say it twice. Zac hadn't eaten since the dodgy sausage roll he'd picked up on the cab ride home that morning. The pie was stuffed full of lentils and onion gravy, and accompanied by a pile of thick-cut chips, but it didn't take Zac long to devour it. When his plate was clean, he sat back in his seat, rubbing his stomach, and found Liam watching him, amusement lightening his chiselled features.

"Hungry, were we?"

Zac shrugged. "I'm always hungry. My mum used to say I had hollow legs."

"What does she say now?"

"No idea."

"No? You're not close?"

Zac rolled his eyes. "What do you think? I told you before, I haven't seen her in years."

Liam stuffed his last chip in his mouth and wiped his hands on a paper napkin. "I think I don't know the first thing about you, other than how to make you come, so I have no idea how to respond when you say shit like that."

Zac couldn't argue with the fact that Liam knew how to make him come, and something about Liam's evident annoyance was insanely hot. Heat bloomed in his veins and merged with the already entrenched warmth from the second pint of ale Liam had fetched for him. He gazed at Liam, wondering if he felt it too, but Liam's eyes held nothing but a sad fascination. *Oh.* Maybe Zac couldn't make him happy, but he had plenty to ease his curiosity. "I haven't seen my mum since I was fifteen and her boyfriend kicked me out. The council put me in a foster home, but it was shit, so I sofa-surfed my way to London."

"What did you do in London?"

"Same thing I do in King's Lynn."

Liam took a protracted gulp of Pepsi. "So you've been doing . . . this for eight years?"

"If you say so." The numbers meant little to Zac. In his mind, he'd never been anything more than a dirtbag hooker and the fifteen years he'd lived before belonged to someone else. "It hasn't always been quite like this, though."

"Like this?"

"Not so, what's the word? Civilised?"

Liam frowned. "Jesus, really? I know I'm probably not the most exciting john you see, but I don't remember anything particularly *civilised* about the last few times we've seen each other."

Again with the heat, but Liam was missing the point. Zac drained the last of his second pint and wiped his mouth with the back of his hand. "I picked you up at the club because I wanted to, you let me because you wanted to, and then we fucked in my bed in my nice warm flat. Trust me, it's a world away from the way shit has been in the past."

Liam's frown deepened before he seemed to make a conscious effort to school his features. "A new world is a wonderful thing."

"Sometimes, but that's enough about me. I want to know how someone builds something like you have in that factory. You're like Bill Gates or some shit. How does that happen?"

Liam chuckled. "I wish I knew. Most days it feels like I was dropped into this life upside down. I got a job straight from art school designing surf-wear for Nike in California. Until I realised how fucked up global clothes production was, I kinda thought I'd be there forever."

"You lived in California?"

"For three years. Sea Rave has an office there."

"What made you come home?"

"Lots of things really," Liam said. "But mainly Cory. I met him in India when I was visiting a factory in Mumbai. He was consulting for a charity promoting better conditions for low-paid workers and we both reckoned there had to be a way to produce affordable clothing without killing and maiming children. In the end, we figured we'd come home and try."

"Cory is your husband?"

"Yes, he was."

Was. Shit. Zac wanted to drop through the floor, but Liam didn't react to his slip. In fact, by the way his eyes had glazed over, he might have forgotten Zac was there at all.

"We came back to live in Newquay because that's where the waves were. We set up a tiny shop selling custom T-shirts and boards. It never occurred to us that it could become something as big as Sea Rave is now."

"What brought you to Norfolk after Cory died?"

"Family," Liam said. "I grew up in Holkham, and we'd been building a house there anyway so we could be closer when my dad started needing a bit of looking after. When Cory died, it made sense to leave Newquay behind and go back there."

"Do you miss him?"

"Who? Cory?"

Zac bit his lip. "Yeah. I knew someone whose girlfriend died. He seemed okay after a while. Said being without her became normal."

He didn't add that the bloke in question had dulled every feeling he'd ever had with a bucketload of heroin. Liam didn't need to know that shit. Besides, it was clear by the tightness in Liam's jaw and his bright eyes that he *did* miss Cory, more than anything.

Dick. What the fuck did you have to say that for? Zac wished he knew, but something about Liam made him lose all his filters, and he doubted it would be the last time he put his foot in his mouth. *If he even wants to see you again. Not like he's asked to fuck you, is it?*

Zac silenced the devil on his shoulder and reached for Liam's hand. "I'm sorry."

"What for?"

"Dunno. Upsetting you? You probably don't want to talk about your dead husband."

"He wasn't technically my husband; we called each other that because we wanted to."

"You didn't get married?"

"Oh, we did, but the ceremony we had in Thailand wasn't recognised over here, and we couldn't be arsed to do it again. We were married in our eyes and that was all that mattered."

"It's all that matters still," Zac said. "Who gives a fuck about the technicalities?"

Liam grinned. "Not me. Shit like that has never bothered me, and it bothered Cory even less. And, in answer to your question, yes, I do miss him, every day, but your friend was right about time. It doesn't make it better, but some days it's not as hard."

Zac needed another drink. He squeezed Liam's hand, then stood and went to the bar.

After surreptitiously downing a vodka, he took another pint and a coke back to the table, but instead of reclaiming his seat opposite Liam, he drifted with little conscious thought to the bench where Liam sat and dropped down beside him. "Where does Hettie come into this? Was she yours and Cory's?"

"Oh God, no. Cory was a bit of a hippie, but he liked to go home at night to his own bed. Hettie was mine. I've had her since before I met him."

For some reason, Zac was relieved that every part of Liam didn't belong to Cory. *Yeah, 'cause you can't even hold a candle to a dead man.* "Have you travelled a lot with her?"

"Back in the day, I drove her all around Europe, chasing the waves and the parties, but it's been a while. She hasn't gone further than Cornwall since we founded the Sea Rave festivals."

"And you stopped going to those because Cory died."

It wasn't a question, but Liam nodded anyway. "I've missed the last two. My sister runs them now."

He looked tired, like the burden of talking about Cory was draining the life from him. Zac wanted to let it go, but the primal fascination he had for Liam was too strong to ignore. "How long have you been surfing? I've only seen it on the telly."

"Surfing's in my blood. My dad had me out at Cromer before I could walk. I don't get in the water much these days, though. Fucked my back up a few years ago."

Zac gave an involuntary shudder. "I can't imagine wanting to do it. You must freeze your balls off."

"That's part of the magic. Besides, you don't really feel it once you've caught a wave. You don't feel much of anything except the buzz of the ride."

"What about sharks?"

Liam choked on a mouthful of coke. "In the North Sea? Ain't many great whites about, mate. The driftwood will get you first."

Zac let Liam's humour seep into him. It was good to see him smile again. He absently shifted closer and nudged Liam's shoulder with his head. "Still reckon it sounds horrible. I've always been scared of the sea."

"Why'd you move to the coast, then?"

"London tried to kill me." The words were out before he could stop them, stark and blunt, and laced with the deadbeat sardonicism he usually saved for Jamie.

The laughter in Liam's gaze faded. "You're not even joking, are you?"

Zac shrugged and picked up his glass. In some ways, Liam seemed to see right through him, but in others he clearly didn't have a clue who he'd chosen to share his bed with. "What time did they say Hettie would be ready?"

"Um . . ." Liam checked his phone. "Around now, actually. Are you ready to go?"

Zac drained his glass. "Let's roll."

They picked up Hettie and hit the road, heading southeast towards home. Liam was quiet as they left the north behind, and that suited Zac fine. He'd spent years keeping himself detached from every john and trick he turned—the rare not-so-bad and the awful—but give him Liam and a few pints of sleepy ale, and he was ready to cough up his life story. How the fuck did that happen?

And it wasn't just that. As the van joined the A road and rumbled along in the slow lane, the heat Zac had felt in the pub returned full force, merging with a healthy dose of confusion he hadn't known was there. *He hasn't touched me all day.* "What are we doing when we get back?"

"Hmm?" Liam shot him a distracted glance.

"I said, 'What are we doing when we get back?' Have you got something else in mind?"

"Not really. I figured I'd take you home so you could get on with the rest of your night."

"Are you taking the piss?"

"Excuse me?"

Zac turned to face Liam, even though Liam had returned his gaze to the road. "You paid me eight hundred quid. Are you seriously trying to tell me *this* is all you wanted?"

"This?" Liam frowned. "I told you I wanted you to come to Sheffield with me. We went to Sheffield. What else were you expecting?"

"Er, I don't know, maybe that you'd pull over and fuck me? Or get me to give you a bit of roadhead? I'm a hooker, Liam. You pay me to do that shit."

The fury in Zac's tone surprised even him, but Liam appeared unmoved, like raging toms shouted at him all the time. Perhaps they did. He'd never said Zac was the only one. "I thought I was paying you for your company."

"But why? You have loads of people in your life who want to spend time with you. Why me?"

"Does it matter? I thought you'd enjoy the time off."

"Why the hell would you think that? I like fucking you. Why else would I be here?"

"Er, I don't know? Perhaps for the money?"

Technically, Liam wasn't wrong, but then, he didn't know that Zac had been looking forward to this encounter so much he'd been climbing the walls when he hadn't been occupied with other johns. Didn't know that the scant few hours of sleep he'd managed had been filled with dreams of how today might go, and none of those dreams had involved yelling at each other in a cramped camper van.

Zac slumped back in his seat, his irrational anger all but gone. The beer he'd drunk sloshed around in his belly and he felt a little sick, and cold too. Hettie's heaters were whirring, but they didn't seem to kick out much warmth. He closed his eyes, shivered, and rested his head against the window, wishing it was Liam's shoulder. Sometime later, the duvet was tossed over him, covering everything except his left knee, which was taking most of the draft from Hettie's rattling doors, but the stubborn streak that had got him this far in life kept him from stirring. From admitting he was awake and facing the puzzled disappointment he knew he'd find in Liam's gaze.

From admitting that being so close to Liam and not touching him, exploring him . . . perhaps even kissing him, was driving him fucking insane. The cacophony of bullshit turned somersaults in his brain, but exhaustion crept over him like a snake in the grass, and, lulled by Hettie's purring engine, he fell into a restless doze.

The cold blast of air to his face sometime later took his breath away.

Zac opened his eyes as the passenger-side door opened all the way and Liam released his seat belt. "Get out."

"No."

"Do it."

Zac got out. "What the—"

Liam silenced him by pushing him into Hettie's side panel and caging him with his arms. "What do you want from me?"

"What?"

"You heard me," Liam growled. "I've paid you for your time—paid you well, by all accounts—but you're not happy. Why? What do you need?"

"Need?"

"Need, want, whatever. Just fucking tell me."

"I want you."

Liam blinked. "What?"

"I want *you*." Zac shoved Liam hard in the chest, making him stumble backwards. "I want you to fuck me. I want you to *want* to fuck me, and I want—"

"What?" Liam closed the distance between them again. "What else do you want, Zac?"

Fuck it. Zac seized Liam's face and threw himself forward, catching Liam's lips in a brutal kiss. Liam let out a grunt of surprise and froze, but then his arms came around Zac in a suffocating embrace and he returned Zac's kiss, responding with his whole body, like kissing Zac was all he'd ever wanted.

Zac hit the van for a second time, jarring what breath he had left from his lungs. He gasped. Liam took advantage of it and swept his tongue into Zac's mouth as Zac shoved his hands into Liam's hair, twisting and tugging, searching for any kind of purchase with the world. His heart quickened, stampeding in his chest, and his blood roared in his ears. He'd had Liam's tongue in places far more intimate than his mouth, but not like this. Kissing Liam was mind-blowing, and if he died right now, he wouldn't give a flying fuck.

But he didn't die, far from it. He hooked his leg over Liam's hip and pressed his dick into Liam's bulging crotch, moaning as the friction hit him, too much and not enough all at once until, too soon, Liam pulled away.

"Shit, shit, shit. I'm so sorry."

"What? Why?'" Zac made a grab for Liam's hands. "Why are you sorry?"

"You don't do kissing."

"I don't kiss *johns*."

"And that's what I am, remember? I'm a dirty old john, like the others."

Zac yanked Liam back into his personal space and took Liam's face in his hands. "You're not a dirty fucking john."

"No? Then what am I, Zac?"

"My friend."

Liam laughed, but it was bitter and cold, and nothing like the warm chuckles Zac dreamed of when he was alone. "Then why do I feel like I'm taking advantage of you every time we touch?"

"You don't feel like that."

"Don't I?"

Zac pulled Liam to him and kissed him again, slow and sweet, as if they'd kissed a thousand times before and had never been apart. "Does this really feel wrong? Does it feel wrong when we fuck? When we hold hands and fall asleep together?"

Liam held Zac's stare for a long moment, his forehead pressed tightly against Zac's, then he sighed like a man with the weight of the world on his shoulders. "It never feels wrong at the time, it's just after, you know? You deserve so much better than this."

"What makes you think that—"

"Don't. Don't call yourself a whore and tell me you're a fucking scumbag, Zac, because I won't believe it. If you are what you say you are, then so am I."

There was nothing dirty about Liam—except the good kind of dirty—and the shame in his gaze broke Zac's heart. He fumbled in his pocket and held out the roll of notes Liam had given him that morning. "You're not a john."

Liam pushed the money back. "Then you'll never be my whore."

CHAPTER
TEN

A lifetime seemed to pass before Zac relented and stuffed the money back in his pocket. Liam blew out a long sigh, though the relief was laced with an emotion he couldn't quite name. There was no doubt in his mind that Zac needed the money, but knowing next to nothing about why he needed it so badly was still unnerving, especially with Zac's forbidden kiss still bruising his lips.

Liam swallowed and stepped back, trying to put some much-needed distance between them, and this time Zac let him be, his own gaze distant and lost.

"I should go," Liam said.

"Why?"

Liam shrugged. "Are you working tonight?"

"I have to. You gave me a lot of money, but rent, electric, gas, water . . . there's so much to pay for." The flash of guilt in Zac's face broke Liam's heart, and he couldn't live with the shame he saw next. He had his own cross to bear, but his woes weren't Zac's.

He pulled Zac close, wrapping him in the kind of embrace he'd never thought he'd find again, kissing Zac's hair and breathing him in. "I'm gonna go before this gets out of hand. I can call you later, though, if you like?"

Zac blinked and looked around him, peering beyond Liam to the block of flats behind him. "I hadn't even realised we were home."

Liam forced a smile. Zac had been away with the fairies for most of the day, and it wasn't hard to see that he hadn't slept much recently. *Unless it's something else.* But Liam killed the thought before it took hold. Society taught that prostitution and drugs came hand in hand, but he'd yet to see much in Zac that led him to believe that was true. "Do you need anything before I go?"

Zac shook his head. "You'll call me later?"

"If you want me to."

"I do."

It was all he needed to say. Liam held Zac a little tighter, then let him go. He desperately wanted to kiss Zac again, kiss him like *Zac* had kissed *him* that first time, and the second, brutal and hard . . . then slow and sweet, stealing Liam's breath with every brush of his lips and sweep of his tongue.

Leaving felt so fucking wrong. But he had to. His brain was about to explode, and the last year had taught him that he was better off alone when shit like that went down.

He left Zac by the roadside and drove away, forcing himself not to glance back as his heart began a stampeding tattoo in his chest, throbbing up his throat and into his ears. He'd known today would be tough: visiting the factory, facing all the people who'd worked so hard for them—for Cory—to make their dreams a reality. Just taking Hettie further than Hunstanton had felt like a nosedive into the past, until Zac had slid into the van with his heavy eyes and grubby jeans, looking for all the world like he'd just rolled in from a big night out.

Perhaps he had. *'Cept he wasn't having fun with his mates, was he?*

Liam rummaged in the van door for his cigarettes and lit up with shaking hands, blowing the smoke out the window. He didn't often smoke in Hettie, but fuck if he didn't need a fag right now. Zac's kiss alone would've been enough to drive him to it, even without the bullshit that came before . . . and after, and would probably never go away.

Another rush of anguish swept over him as he turned towards Holkham. The desperate need to get home and lock himself away was consuming and merged with the crippling sensation of leaving the battered remnants of his heart with a man Liam couldn't be sure wanted them. Oh yeah, Zac kissed him first, but why? Because he wanted to? Liam had meant it when he told Zac he'd never be his whore, but that didn't mean he understood Zac's motivations any more than he did his own.

He crossed the boundary into Holkham. The house was at the other end of the village, and he remembered just in time that he needed to fetch the dogs from Rosa before he could go home. Great. He loved his twin to death, but he wasn't in the mood to have her see straight through him—or think she did—and give him the look that reminded him far too much of their long-dead mother.

Thankfully Rosa's car wasn't on the drive. Liam let himself into their cottage to find Mike asleep in front of the TV—when he should've been revising advertising budgets—with Jazz pinning him to the couch.

Dave met Liam at the living room door, greeting him with a lick and low whine, letting him know she didn't, however much she'd no doubt enjoyed her day with Uncle Mike, approve of being left for so long. Liam scratched her ears and whistled softly for Jazz, hoping for a quick getaway, but no such luck. Jazz used Mike as a springboard to leap from the couch, and Mike woke with a groan.

"Bloody brute!"

Liam had to laugh. At six foot four and fifteen stone, Mike was a bit of a brute himself. "You shouldn't let him on the couch. I warned you it was asking for trouble."

"Dick." Mike brushed himself down and sat up. "Like you don't have them in your bed."

He had Liam there. Even before Cory died, they'd spent most nights jostling for space in the bed Liam had chucked on the bonfire with Cory's fishing boat.

"You all right, bud?"

Liam came back to earth to find Mike had hauled himself from the sofa and come to stand in front of him. "Hmm?"

"You're on another planet. How did today go?"

For a brief, heart-stopping moment, Liam thought he was asking about his day with Zac, then he remembered Mike was the only soul who'd known he was braving the trip up to Sheffield, and that had been because Mike was the only person who wouldn't have given him shit if he'd bottled it and stayed at home. "It was fine. Nice to see everyone, and Carol-Anne accepted my design for the summer line. Winner."

"Bosh." Mike raised his hand for a high five. "Told you she'd love it."

Liam snorted, remembering the jovial disdain of SRP's new creative director. "She said it would be good in the winter sales."

Mike laughed, a real, deep belly laugh that sounded unnaturally loud in the airy living room. "Not everyone's got the gift of the gab, mate."

And how well did Liam know that? One of the reasons Cory had become the face of the company instead of Liam was because he'd possessed all the charm and patience Liam lacked, the ability to sit through endless bullshit meetings without calling a twat a twat.

"You look like you need a beer," Mike said. "Come on."

In that moment, there was nothing Liam wanted more than a cold can of whatever Mike had stashed in his fridge.

He followed Mike to the kitchen and accepted a beer. Mike stared at him, then pulled a bottle from a nearby cupboard too. "Fuck it. Let's get on the whiskey."

Liam hadn't drunk whiskey since that first charged night with Zac, spent throwing each other around Zac's bed. Had the booze been behind the madness that had seen him take Zac's hand and follow him home? Did it matter? Liam had loved Cory with all his heart, but there was no denying Zac had stamped his own place in his soul. Even if he never saw Zac again, he'd never forget him. Never. *But you don't know jack shit about him—*

"Liam?"

"*What?*"

Mike raised a good-natured eyebrow. "What the fuck's up with you? I know you're not Mr. Chatty, but you're taking the piss today."

Liam opened his mouth. Shut it. Mike had been the closest he'd had to a best friend for more than a decade, but he was Rosa's husband first, always had been. Liam couldn't put this on him and expect him to keep it to himself.

"Right." Mike filled two glasses with healthy shots of whiskey and passed one to Liam. "Get that in yer, then we're going down the juicer."

Liam necked the whiskey, then rounded up the dogs to slope off to the quiet village pub at the end of the road. Except it wasn't that quiet when they got there. The Hope and Anchor was playing their rival pub at darts and the place was packed with old-school, ale-swilling locals, the kind who'd never quite come to terms with the local lad and his dreadlocked husband. Burly, ruddy-faced men who still eyed Liam like he was going to shag their damned sheep. And it didn't help that Jazz had no manners when it came to pub etiquette. As far as he was concerned, an unattended glass was fair game.

Liam had rescued three pints from Jazz's slobbery nose by the time they found a couple of seats in the back corner, away from the rowdy darts game.

"Come on, then," Mike said when they were settled. "And don't go giving me those big cow eyes either. I know you're my boss and I knocked up your sister, but I'm still your mate. Spill."

Liam could hardly complain about Mike getting Rosa pregnant when she'd been twenty-eight at the time. "I slept with a hooker."

Mike froze in the process of swallowing a gulp of beer. His eyes bulged and his face turned red, and it seemed an age before he figured out how to stop himself from spraying a mouthful of Old Speckled Hen all over the dogs.

He put his glass down and wiped his mouth. "I'd ask if you're taking the piss, but I don't reckon you are."

"I'm not." Liam reached for his own beer and downed half of it. "Say what you like about me, but I've never been a bloody comedian."

"True that. So . . ."

"So?"

"You slept with a woman?"

"What? No! Why would you think that?"

Mike shrugged. "I don't know. The only hookers I've ever seen are women. Is it the same for blokes? Standing on street corners and whatnot?"

"Probably, but it wasn't quite like that. I met him at The Stables."

Mike pulled a face. "What were you doing in there?"

"Your brother made me go."

"Sounds about right." Mike rolled his eyes. "Don't tell me Sean talked you into this hooker thing?"

"Course he didn't. I was on my way out when I met Zac."

"Zac?"

Oops. If he'd had any hope of keeping the story vague, he'd buggered it now. "That's his name."

"His real name?"

Liam shrugged. "I think so."

Mike blinked a few times, then took another long gulp of his drink. "Let me get this, er, straight. You, the bloke who married the first dude who asked, went up town and came home with a hooker?"

"We went to his place, actually, and leave Cory out of it, but yeah, that's about the size of it." Liam didn't need reminding that, until Zac, Cory had been the only man he'd ever laid a hand on.

"And you slept with him . . . and paid him? Is that what I'm hearing?"

"Something like that. To be honest, I was pretty wasted, but I knew what I was doing. He told me what he was before we got to his place, and shit, it kinda made sense at the time."

"Does it make sense now?"

"Some days."

Mike blew out a gusty sigh. "Listen, I'm not going to pretend I understand what you've been through. I can't imagine losing Rosa or the boys, but I don't think there's any shame in blowing off some steam. So you banged a hooker? It's no big deal, right? It was only that once. It's not like you'll ever see him again . . ."

Mike's voice fell away as he met Liam's gaze and comprehension dawned in his face. "Oh shit. That's the problem, isn't it? You've been back for more."

Liam nodded. "A few times, but not only for sex. I took him with me to Sheffield today."

"Why?"

"Why not? I needed the company, and that's what he offered me."

"Company? Is that what they call it these days?"

"Piss off, Mike. Don't sit there and judge me. Do you think I didn't see you with those strippers on your stag do? You might not have fucked them, but you wanted to, and that makes you no better than me."

The hurt in Mike's gaze was instant. The guilt in Liam's gut came a few seconds later. He closed his eyes briefly, then closed his hand around Mike's wrist. "Sorry, mate. I didn't mean that."

And even if he had, who the hell was he to judge anyone when he'd been so bloody reckless? Damn, he'd had Zac's cock in his mouth, rimmed him, swallowed his cum—

Stop it. Zac's risked himself just as much as you have.

"Liam?" Mike laid his hand over Liam's. "You *know* I'd never cheat on Rosa. I might've taken a pissed-up glance at a pretty girl, but that's nothing I'd hide from her. She's not beyond having a glance herself."

Of course she wasn't. Rosa liked a hot girl as much as Mike did. "I'm sorry."

"Don't be sorry, just tell me what's really going on. Have you got feelings for this bloke? Is that what's fucking you up? How does he feel about you?"

If only Liam knew, though it had been hard to doubt the intensity of Zac's kiss. He'd pulled Zac from the van with little consideration of what would come next, just a wild notion that if he didn't say something—do something—he'd fucking combust. It had never crossed his mind that Zac would kiss him. "I need beer."

Liam got up and went to the bar. He bought two more beers and a couple of whiskey chasers, trying not to think about how much time he'd spent buying or drinking booze that day. A heart-to-heart with Mike was always the same. Liam would be lucky if he didn't wind up sleeping in the van, too tanked to make it home. He'd already had too much to drive any time soon.

He went back to the table and pushed Dave out of his seat. "I can't have feelings for him. I hardly know him. Christ, I've only met him three times."

"So? Me and Rosa got engaged after a month."

"I don't want to marry him, Mike." Liam suppressed a shudder and rubbed the blank space on his finger where he'd yet to put Cory's ring back on.

"Then what do you want? An expensive fuck buddy? Or something more?"

"I just want to know him, I guess. He intrigues me and he's beautiful."

Mike knocked his whiskey back. "I'll have to take your word for that, mate. I suppose you have to figure out if what you're feeling, whatever it is, is real, or you're trying to replace what you've lost. I know you've always been a bit of a lone ranger, but it's not hard to see you're lonely as fuck now."

Liam had no answer to that, and Mike didn't seem to want one. He shuffled off to take a piss and when he came back, he launched into his usual rant about the woes of Hull City Football Club, who were languishing at the bottom of the Premier League. The conversation seemed to be over, but much—*much*—later, as they stumbled to Mike and Rosa's cottage, dogs in tow, Mike put his hand on Liam's shoulder.

"I can't make sense of this shit for you, but not understanding it isn't a reason for you to be alone for the rest of your life. If you really see something with this . . . bloke, take it, roll with it. Don't rent your heart out for nothing when I reckon you've both been through enough to deserve a hell of a lot more."

It was moments like these that reminded Liam how lucky he was to have his family. It would've been easy for Mike to take Liam's odd friendship with Zac at face value and write Zac off as the whore he believed himself to be, but Mike hadn't questioned Zac's motives, or Liam's. He'd seen beyond the word "hooker" and applied his own very human way of thinking to the clusterfuck Liam's life had become.

Shame he didn't stick around when they reached the cottage for Liam to tell him he loved him like the brother he'd never had.

Liam heard the front door slam and winced. Rosa would kill Mike if he woke the boys. He listened for any sign of her opening the bathroom window and giving him what for too, but none came. With a sigh of relief, he rummaged in his pocket for the van keys. There was a bed for him in Rosa's house, but he'd always preferred roughing it, kicking back under the stars with the dogs for company. Only the weather, like tonight's drizzle, forced him into the rock-and-roll bed in the back of Hettie.

Yawning, he settled down in the van, leaning on the pillows with his favourite sleeping bag, and his phone in his hand. He purposely hadn't looked at it all night, but with Mike's beer-fuelled words of wisdom echoing in his head, the time to call Zac seemed to be now or never.

Squinting through his drunken haze, he swiped the screen, expecting to see nothing more than the usual barrage of work emails. The text message delivered ten minutes ago made his breath catch.

Call me. I'll be waiting. – Z

Liam's thumb hit redial. He put the phone to his ear and Zac answered on the second ring.

"Liam?"

"I'm here."

"Where's here?"

Liam chuckled. "Half-pissed in the back of the van on my sister's driveway. Not gonna make it home tonight."

Zac laughed too. "Where does your sister live?"

"A mile away from me. I could walk home, but I don't want to leave Hettie, so . . ."

"So you're sleeping in the van by yourself?"

"Not quite." Liam eyed Jazz and Dave, who'd settled in their customary place at the foot of the bed. "I've got the dogs with me. Besides, it's no different to being alone in bed."

"True." The humour in Zac's tone faded. "I quite like my bed, though. It's the first one I've had in a while."

Liam's chest tightened. "You didn't have a bed in London?"

"Not exactly. I didn't have much of anything. It was a strange time."

"I've had my fair share of those."

Zac hummed, and Liam sucked in a breath. *He gets me.* Zac didn't know him any better than he knew Zac, but the empathy in that low hum said far more than any words ever could.

"So . . ." Liam sat up and looked out of the van's window, searching for the stars to remind him that the whole world was out there waiting for him. *Here goes nothing.* "Are you working tomorrow?"

"Why?"

"Because I'd like to see you, if you're not busy."

Silence, then a barely audible sigh. "I have to go into Norwich in the morning, but I'm free in the afternoon. What did you have in mind?"

"I was thinking you could maybe come over? Spend the night if you wanted to?"

"Spend the night? At your house?"

"If you like. I could show you the beach, cook you some dinner, let you catch up on your sleep . . ."

"Are you making fun of me for falling asleep every time I see you?"

"Maybe." Liam actually found it pretty fucking endearing that Zac had trusted him enough to take a nap in his presence. After all, what would have stopped Liam taking his money back and kicking him to the kerb? Liam didn't know much about the kind of men who used Zac's services, but he was willing to bet they cared a hell of lot less about Zac's welfare than he did.

"Where's your house?"

Liam caught his imagination before it could conjure up images of Zac being robbed, beaten, and left in a dirty alley by an unscrupulous john. "Holkham."

"I know that, duh, but where? Is there a bus stop nearby?"

It was on the tip of Liam's tongue to offer to pick Zac up, but the thought of opening the front door to find him on the doorstep was too tempting to deny.

He gave Zac directions to the house. "So, I'll see you tomorrow? Come over whenever you like. I'll be in."

"See you tomorrow. And, Liam?"

"Yeah?

"I can't fucking wait."

CHAPTER
ELEVEN

Zac woke with a jump, excitement churning in his belly. He felt like a kid at Christmas, and was up and in the shower before he thought to check the time: 6 a.m. *Damn.* He'd only been asleep a few hours. Though when he'd curled up in bed, clutching his phone, he'd been certain he wouldn't find sleep at all.

He pressed his hand over his chest and his heart quickened as he recalled Liam's late-night phone call and how his soft, slightly slurred voice had warmed Zac from the inside out. He'd waited all night for the phone to ring and had almost given up hope when it had finally buzzed under his pillow.

Zac washed himself from head to toe, lingering under the hot water, a luxury he could afford now Liam had paid his bills for the next month, maybe longer if he was careful. After that he'd have to think of something else, because for the first time in as long as he could remember, the numbness he'd carried had faded to nothing, and turning tricks felt like it really would kill him. *I only want Liam to touch me.*

The notion stayed with Zac as he got out of the shower. Liam's touch had been indelibly imprinted on his soul from the beginning, but hooking was all he knew, and there probably weren't many jobs for retired whores—

A noise somewhere in the flat stopped Zac in his tracks, his hand on the bathroom door, his imagination already in Liam's arms. It sounded like it had come from the living room, but that couldn't be right. Zac had been alone since Liam had left him on the doorstep, and the landlord wasn't due to inspect the flat until the end of the month.

So why the fuck could he hear voices?

Zac yanked on a pair of damp trackies and left the bathroom, fists clenched, ready for whatever he found. He'd lived in too many squats to imagine it would be anything pleasant.

He opened the living room door. Jamie was sitting on the couch, grubby shoes still on and his hood up, partially obscuring his face. The scene seemed normal—for them, at least—until Zac sensed they weren't alone.

A glance around revealed a scrawny girl crouched in the corner, with dirty hair and bad teeth, like every smackhead tramp Zac had ever seen. He turned back to Jamie and saw the powder and syringes covering the coffee table. *My coffee table.* "What the fuck are you doing?"

Jamie didn't look up, engrossed in chopping and scraping the powder on the table. "What do you think?"

"I think you've brought a load of skag and a crack whore to my place."

"Your place? Thought this was home for both of us?"

Jamie seemed amused, but Zac was far from it. His blood boiled with rage, and worse than that, his soul—which moments ago had been only for Liam—wept for the sticky brown powder he'd fought so hard to escape. He stared at it, knowing how easy it would be to swipe a handful and cook it up, load a syringe and fire it into his veins. The euphoria would be instant and all-consuming, and it would likely be days, weeks, months before regret caught up with him.

Zac's hands twitched and his skin prickled. He took a step towards the table, but when Liam's voice echoed in his brain again, instead of reaching for the smack, he lunged at Jamie, knocked the razor blade from his hand, and sent the powder flying. "Get out."

Jamie blinked, his bloodshot gaze only mildly surprised, like he'd already jacked so much junk he barely felt Zac's bruising grip on his wrist. "Easy, mate. I'm cutting it . . . you know, like we did back home, stirring in a bit of talc so we can flog it, yeah? Make some dosh. Kelly's going to get—"

Zac lifted Jamie from the couch and threw him across the room, scattering the contents of the coffee table and the mud from Jamie's shoes all over the floor. "Get the fuck out!"

Jamie landed in a heap by the girl's feet. She got up and backed towards the door, eyeing Zac like he was an unexploded bomb, but Jamie didn't move. Just stared as though Zac was the one who'd lost his fucking mind. "What's wrong with you? Thought you'd be pleased I'd brought cash home."

"But you haven't brought cash home, have you? It's a bucketload of fucking smack, and I don't want it. I don't want it in my place. Take it and go, Jamie. Before I fuck you up."

Zac's fury finally registered in Jamie's long-dead eyes. He stood and faced Zac down, a cold sneer marring his wrecked face. "Fuck me up? Watcha gonna do? Stab me or some shit?"

"Get out!" Zac sprang at Jamie again, shoving him back. Jamie was taller than him, but his once-athletic frame had shrunk and shrunk over the past few months, leaving him nothing but bone and sinister ink that clung to his pale skin like broken barbed wire.

Jamie stumbled, saved from losing his feet only by the living room door. "Don't be a dick, Zac. I'm not going anywhere."

For a brief, foolish moment, guilt-tinged second thoughts clouded Zac's brain, then he remembered the drugs on the table and knew without doubt that there was only one reason Jamie wouldn't leave.

He spun around and grabbed a handful of Jamie's stash from the floor. "This what you want? Go fucking get it."

Zac opened the window and tossed the powder into the dim early-morning air, then grabbed another handful and another and another until Jamie jumped on him, but by then it was too late. There wasn't much left of his haul save a few bags, some syringes, and a sprinkling of brown powder on the cream carpet that looked like sugar on porridge.

"You fucking arsehole!" Jamie lashed out, catching Zac with a clumsy punch and a swipe of his grimy, too-long nails. "What have you done?"

Zac growled and threw Jamie off him. "Chucked your junk on the street where it belongs. You're next."

Jamie wiped his nose with the back of his hand. In the scuffle, his hood had slipped, revealing his unshaved face and sunken eyes, his cracked, sore lips and chattering teeth. Zac's heart ached for him, but he had too much to lose to let Jamie's plight break them both. As much as he owed Jamie, he couldn't save him. Not from this.

"Please, Jay, just go. You can't be here right now."

"Don't want to fucking be here anyway. You're a cunt, and I should've left you to rot when I had the chance."

It would've hurt less if Jamie had kicked him in the face, but there was little Zac could do but watch him stumble out of the living room and wait for the thud that would surely come next.

The front door slammed a few moments later. Zac closed his eyes as his fury left him, mentally following Jamie wherever he was headed, like his own imagination could cocoon Jamie and shield him from whatever life held for him now. Would he ever come back? Perhaps when he was hungry . . . or desperate. Shit. Zac knew addiction well enough to know he'd have to change the locks.

He sank to the floor and put his head in his hands. The light and air he'd woken up with was long gone, leaving in its place the dark suffocation that came from the world he truly belonged in. *Damn it, Jamie. Why today?* Not that it mattered. With junk and syringes scattered over the living room floor, calling to him like a long-lost child, Zac was no better than Jamie. Never had been, and never would be unless he found the strength to scrape the remaining heroin from the carpet and let it join the rest on the pavement below.

With a heavy sigh, Zac opened his eyes and crawled across the floor, picking up syringes and bags as he went, until he got to the cupboard where he kept the cheap Hoover he'd bought with the money from his first night with Liam. He hoovered up the mess, being sure to get every last speck, but knowing it was languishing in the Hoover bag still did his head in.

Cursing Jamie, he wrestled the bag from the Hoover and took it outside, bypassing the wheelie bin assigned to the flat and traipsing barefoot down the road until he came to the bin that belonged to the three-bed semi with a gaggle of young children. It felt a little wrong to be stuffing a heroin-laced bag in with family rubbish, but addict or not, there was no way he'd be revisiting the rotting nappies of *that* bin.

Back at the flat, he noted that there was no sign of Jamie or his pal scrabbling around on the pavement, which was just as well. It had been dark when Zac had got up, but the sun was rising now, revealing the first frost of the year, a light, sparkling sprinkle that bit into his bare feet. As angry as he was with Jamie, he didn't want to think of him down on his knees in this, not that there was much hope that Jamie wouldn't end up on his knees somewhere that night.

Zac shut the front door with a heavy heart. He'd always known he'd lose Jamie at some point, had even prepared himself for the possibility that the very worst could happen, but he'd honestly believed they had more time. That the inevitable was far enough away that he could take comfort in an unhealthy dose of denial. But it wasn't to be. Even if Jamie made it through the winter, he'd likely not forgive Zac this side of Christmas. Besides, as Zac checked his stash of cash behind the toilet and found it significantly lighter than it had been before Jamie's clusterfuck of a homecoming, Zac was still angry enough for the both of them. Fuck Jamie. And fuck his junk.

The flat had been warm and cosy when Zac had got out of the shower, but it had cooled while he'd fought with Jamie and made his sad dash to the neighbour's bins. And an empty bag and syringe wedged halfway under the sofa chilled his bones even more. Zac scooped them up and stuffed them in his pocket. He couldn't face trudging back to the nappy pit just yet, but there was no way they could stay in the flat. Fuck no. *I'll deal with them later.* He shut the window shivering, and picked up his phone as an afterthought. Seeing a message from Liam stilled his heart, and he was almost afraid to open it. It would top off his already shit day if Liam had changed his mind overnight.

Zac opened the message, squinting with one eye like it might blow up in his face at any moment, but Liam's three words, punctuated by a kiss, quieted the demons dancing in his soul and made him smile so hard his face ached.

See you soon X

Zac bounded off the bus in Holkham and gazed around at the quaint village. There didn't seem to be much here, save the bus stop and a few cottages, none of which were anything like the house Liam had described. Zac glanced at the directions he'd scrawled on a page of the free paper that got stuffed through the letterbox every week, and turned left, following the signs for the beach. For what seemed like miles and miles, he saw nothing but trees and fields, and wondered if he'd cocked it up, and then he saw the sign for the car park and turned right. In the distance there was a single building that looked like a barn . . . the converted barn that was Liam's house.

Liam's house. Zac's heart skipped a beat. He'd been to the homes of dozens of johns over the past six months, kidding himself that it was better than hooking on the streets, but this felt like a strange new world that he had a teeny tiny place in, if only for today.

He followed the road until it turned into a dusty lane that led to a sweeping drive. Hettie was waiting for him by the garage, and then the front door opened, and two camel-sized dogs burst out of the house, tearing down the driveway like giant manic sheep.

"Jesus!" Zac steeled himself as the dogs leapt up at him, barging each other to lick his face. "Easy, easy."

"Jazz. Dave. Down."

The quiet authority in Liam's tone had an instant effect. The dogs calmed and scampered to his side. Zac searched for his gaze and their eyes locked, and the clusterfuck of his morning with Jamie faded away. "Hey."

Liam smiled. "All right?"

"I am now your sheep have stopped trying to eat me."

"Eat you? Fat chance. These two would bring a burglar a cuddly toy and show him where I kept the sausages."

Zac laughed, and it felt so fucking good he couldn't stop. Liam chuckled too, though by his puzzled grin, it was clear Zac's uncharacteristic humour bemused him.

"Are you coming in?"

Zac got ahold of his hysteria and nodded. "Lead the way."

He followed Liam inside, shutting the heavy wooden door behind them. The heat from the open fire hit him like a warm hug and his face-splitting smile returned full force. "Wow. This place is amazing."

And it was. The flat in London had been so luxurious it hadn't seemed real, but even from the open-plan ground floor, it was obvious the converted barn was something else. Warm, homely, and as comforting as the smouldering fire, it was beautiful.

"Glad you like it," Liam said. "I don't have many people over, so it's nice to hear that from someone other than my sister."

"How long have you lived here?"

"Nine months."

"Nine months? So you didn't live here with—"

"Cory? No. We planned the building work together, but he died before it was finished."

"Oh. So he never got to see it?"

"No, but that's probably a good thing, because it's nothing like how he wanted it."

Zac didn't know what to say to that. "Do you like it?"

"Actually, yeah . . . I do. If Cory had got his way, the whole place would be painted orange or some shit, and organised within an inch of its life. I prefer some mild chaos. . ." Liam gestured at the pale, neutral walls stacked with vinyl records, and the piles of books and clutter that made the house seem so wonderfully lived in. "A little bit of mess calms me. Helps me feel human. Can I take your coat?"

Zac shrugged out of his jacket. "Would you like me better if I dropped it on the floor?"

"Only if you dropped your jeans too." Liam took Zac's jacket with a devilish grin and draped it over a nearby bench. "Come through and sit down. Are you hungry?"

Of course Zac was hungry. Nerves and the lingering disquiet from his fight with Jamie had kept him from eating breakfast. He followed Liam's direction to what was clearly the living room and took a seat on a couch that was covered in throws and blankets. One of the dogs came with him. Zac read his name tag—Jazz—and scratched his ears. "Hello, boy."

Jazz grunted and tilted his head. Somewhere behind Zac, Liam chuckled. "You've got yourself a pal there. Jazz won't share his couch with many folk."

"He's not on the— Oh." Zac looked back to find Jazz had taken advantage of his momentary distraction and jumped on the couch beside him. "Oops. Is he allowed up here?"

"Sure he is." Liam ventured further into the room from where Zac assumed the kitchen was and set a plate of giant sandwiches on the table. "Having a donkey sit on your head when you're watching TV is part of the fun."

Liam's tone was droll, and on cue, the other dog—Dave—stepped clumsily onto the sofa and trod on Zac's balls.

"Shit!" Zac sucked in a breath and tried to gently push Dave off. He didn't budge. It was like pushing a horse.

Liam took pity on him and tugged Dave away by his collar. "Sorry. Shoulda warned she's a stamper. It's her favourite way to wake me up."

"She?"

Liam cringed. "Yeah. Don't ever choose a puppy's name when you're stoned. You won't be as funny as you thought you were the next day."

"You smoke weed?" Zac didn't know why that surprised him so much. He'd seen Liam smoke fags, and he hadn't blinked when he'd caught Zac, joint in hand.

"Not really. Cory used to, though. I like the smell."

That made sense. Zac's efforts to quit had been hampered by his fondness of the comforting scent. "Well, Dave weighs a ton," Zac said. "Surprised your dick still works."

"Oh, it works."

Zac grinned. "Oh, I know."

For a moment, they stared at each other, heat rising, and Zac debated whether to ask Liam for a guided tour of the upstairs, or jump him right here, then his stomach rumbled so loud Jazz barked, and the spell was broken.

Liam reached for the plate. "Eat."

Zac didn't need telling twice. He picked up one of the huge sandwiches. "I can see chicken. What's the green stuff?"

"Avocado."

Fair enough. It looked like jade-green clay, but Zac wasn't about to argue, and anyway, he was too hungry to much care what he shoved in his mouth.

Lucky for him, the sandwich was fucking delicious, avocado and all. It disappeared in ten seconds flat. Liam pressed another into his hand. "Eat up. You're gonna need your energy."

"Yeah?" Zac was entranced by the glint in Liam's gaze. He made short work of his second sandwich and inhaled the can of weird fizzy herbal drink Liam passed his way, and then waited for Liam to finish.

The moment he was done, Zac grabbed his arm. "Show me upstairs."

"Upstairs?" Liam wiped his mouth with the back of his hand. "Tired already?"

"Very funny. Let's go."

Liam let Zac drag him to the staircase, then stepped in front of Zac, guiding him up the stairs to a landing the size of Zac's entire flat. "Where do you want to see first?"

"Don't care. Show me what you got."

Liam appeared to deliberate, then he spun around and pushed Zac up against a nearby wall. The air between them shifted, grew heavier, thicker, and suddenly they were right back where they'd started all those weeks ago. "I had so many plans," Liam said. "I was gonna throw you down and have my way with you the moment you arrived."

Zac licked his lips. "Why didn't you?"

"It didn't seem so important once you were actually here. I mean, I still want to do that, but then I just needed to . . . I don't know, be with you?"

Liam's shy grin was unsure, but Zac understood him perfectly. There was almost nothing he wanted more than to physically reconnect with Liam right now, but the quiet half hour they'd spent downstairs meant the world to him. Zac stretched up and kissed Liam lightly on the lips. "Show me around?"

The landing was huge, but there weren't as many doors as Zac had imagined, only three, and the closest one was ajar. Liam led Zac to it and pushed it open. "This is my room."

It wasn't as gigantic as Zac had expected, but every bit as lovely, and with its cosy blankets, piles of books, and distinct lack of TV—so, so, so Liam. The bed was odd, though, and it took Zac a moment to work out why. "Is that made of trees?"

"Yup. Made it myself."

"Wow. That's pretty cool."

"Not especially. I didn't have a bed for ages, and I needed a reason to stop my sister buying me one, so I told her I was making my own. Eventually, I had to actually do it."

"Why didn't you have a bed?"

"Burned the old one."

"Oh." Zac didn't have to ask why. What else would you do with the bed you'd shared with your dead husband? "I like this one. Is it solid?"

"See for yourself."

Zac padded into the room and ran his hand over the rustic tree trunks that made up the bedframe. They felt sturdy enough—*sturdy enough for fucking*—and the finish was incredible. "I can't believe you made this. I bet you knocked it up in an afternoon, didn't you?"

Liam grinned guiltily. "Two, but it really wasn't that hard. I hacked the trees down, sanded them, then bolted them together. Nothing epic."

Zac rolled his eyes. "You're talking to someone who can barely tie his shoelaces."

"I don't believe that." Liam held out his hand and pulled Zac back to the door. "I reckon you can do amazing things. You just don't know it yet."

Zac would have to take Liam's word for that, though he was pretty sure Liam had seen most of his skills already, unless he had a hankering for a Super Noodle sandwich. "What's in there?"

Liam opened the second door, revealing a room that stopped Zac in his tracks. *Jesus.* If Zac had been fifteen—fuck it, ten—years younger, it would've been the coolest room in the world. Football wallpaper, Star Wars curtains, radio-controlled cars. Even the bunk beds had slides instead of ladders.

"My nephews," Liam said by way of explanation. "They're a bit wild, so I built this to stop them trashing the place when they're here."

Zac eyed the slide, ruing the fact that he was, alas, far too big for it. "It'd work for me."

"Come with me, then. I've got another room you can play in."

Zac was intrigued. There was only one door left on the landing, and he'd yet to see a bathroom. He wasn't disappointed when Liam kicked open the final door, revealing a charcoal-grey wet room, complete with a double shower and a tub the size of a small swimming pool. "*This* is your bathroom?"

Liam shrugged, like it was nothing—though perhaps to him it was. "It actually came, in part, with the house. Some dude had already started renovating it when we bought it. Think he was some kind of playboy. We thought it was funny, so we kept it."

The flashy bathroom was more like the Farringdon flat than the cosy barn, and didn't feel like Liam at all, but Zac couldn't deny the lure of that double shower.

He let go of Liam's hand and pulled his T-shirt over his head. Liam raised a curious eyebrow but was silent as Zac stripped the rest of his clothes, though he did lick his lips when Zac hooked his thumbs into Liam's belt loops and tugged him closer.

"I want to play," Zac said. "Take your clothes off... please?"

"You do it."

Fine by me. Zac unbuckled the canvas belt Liam wore around his trademark ripped jeans, belatedly noting that he was barefoot, like he had been at the flat, and that his toenails were spotlessly clean. *How have I not noticed that before?* Dirty feet were one of the worst parts of turning a trick for a grimy john.

Zac wanted to suck Liam's toes, but he had other priorities and getting Liam naked was at the top. He stripped away Liam's clothes and tossed them over his shoulder, then eased him back until Liam hit the tiled wall beneath the dinner plate–sized showerheads. "Turn it on."

Liam smirked and reached behind him, pressing a button in the control panel built into the tiled wall. Cold water blasted them, but the temperature rose before Zac could react, warming until it was just right. "Hot enough?"

"It'll do," Zac said. "The rest is up to us."

Without warning, he dropped to his knees and took Liam's half-hard cock in his mouth. Liam gasped, and Zac grinned around his dick. Too often, he'd let Liam have the upper hand, tying him in knots before they'd truly got started, and pushing him embarrassingly close to the edge. Not this time.

He swallowed Liam whole, swirling his tongue around Liam's dick as he worked his mouth up and down, cupping and squeezing Liam's balls for good measure, all the while resisting the urge to touch his own cock. And it was a strong urge. He'd loved giving Liam head from that night in London, and the feeling hadn't lessened since.

Liam's legs tensed, and his breath quickened, and Zac lost himself in every gasp and groan until Liam's fingers tightened in Zac's hair.

"Jesus, if you don't stop now, I'm going to shoot my load before I fuck you."

It was probably the only thing he could've said to persuade Zac to let Liam's dick slide from his mouth with a wet *pop*. Giving Liam head was amazing, but getting fucked by him?

Yeah. No contest.

He got to his feet, wiping his mouth with the back of his hand. "Where do you want me?"

Liam seized Zac's shoulders and spun him round, pressing him face-first against the slick tiles. "Here will do nicely. Don't move."

As ever, the playful command lit Zac on fire. He braced himself on the tiles and widened his stance. "Whatever you want."

Liam grabbed Zac's hair and yanked his head to one side. "I want to kiss you. Is that okay?"

It was more than okay. Zac leaned into Liam's kiss and lost himself in the gentle sweep of his tongue until Zac's legs shook and he had to pull back for air. Damn. He'd thought he'd remembered what kissing Liam was like, but the wobble in his legs was new. *Holy shit.*

Liam grinned and released Zac's hair, then stepped back. "I'm gonna grab some rubbers."

Zac nodded, mourning the loss of Liam's solid presence behind him, but Liam was there again in a flash. He nudged Zac's legs still further apart and slid his hand between them, grazing his fingertips over where Zac wanted him most.

"Want me to rim you? Or shall we get straight to it?"

The temptation of having Liam's tongue dancing inside him was overwhelming, but the no-contest rule won out. "Fuck me. Please, just fuck me."

Liam kissed Zac's shoulder, biting down as he fiddled around, then his fingers returned, slick and wet, and pressed inside Zac, probing and stretching. His touch was gentle, sweet and searching, and so fucking good that Zac banged his head against the tiles and cried out.

"Easy." Liam rubbed a soothing circle into the base of Zac's spine. "Breathe deep, I'm gonna fuck you now."

He withdrew his fingers and replaced them with his cock, sliding in slowly until his toned stomach touched Zac's spine. The hot spray continued to batter them, filling Zac's lungs with steam, but he felt none of it, felt nothing at all, except the addictive sting of Liam's cock filling him to the brim. God, he'd missed this.

Liam wrapped his arms around Zac's chest and bit his earlobe. "Okay?"

In answer, Zac pushed his hips back, chasing the burn. "Fuck me."

"Oh, I'm gonna." Liam braced one hand on the wall and withdrew, easing his cock out of Zac with a sweet slide that belied the heat between them. Zac steeled himself for him slamming back in, but it never came. Instead, Liam pushed inside him again as slowly as he'd pulled out, and Zac wobbled, his legs betraying the coil of fire in his belly.

Liam steadied him, but not for long. He squeezed Zac's hip, then preceded to fuck him at a pace that could've felt almost leisurely were it not for the electric jolts each gentle push and slide sent through Zac. He'd stripped his clothes craving a good, hard fuck, the kind of fuck he dreamed of when his memories of Liam weren't enough, but this? There was nothing like it. There couldn't be.

His fingers scrabbling for purchase on the wall, Zac cried out, and Liam's body pressed tighter against his own with every thrust until they were melded together, fused by sweat, skin, and bone, despite the steaming water cascading over them.

And it seemed Liam felt the same. He came without warning, slamming his fist into the wall, and groaning low and long. His cock swelled inside Zac, and the warmth pulsing where they were joined tipped Zac over the edge.

"Fuck!" Zac lost his precarious control of his legs and stumbled sideways.

Liam caught him. "Easy. I got you."

"*I got you.*" Zac liked the sound of that, and he liked the steadying cage of Liam's arms even more. He fell back into Liam's chest and stretched, searching for Liam's lips, his scruffy jawline, and strong neck, clinging to Liam like he was the only thing tying him down to this strange new world.

Liam broke the spell, pulling back with a soft smile. "I've got a pretty massive boiler, but we should probably get out in case we need a hose down later."

"Hose down?" Zac giggled, slightly loopy, high without the nagging guilt of having loaded junk into his veins. "How dirty are we going to get?"

"I reckon not knowing is part of the fun. Come on, let's get you dry."

Liam shut the shower off and reached for the towels stacked neatly on a nearby shelf. He wrapped one around Zac's neck and playfully rubbed it over his hair, a joke that turned into a full rubdown.

"My turn." Zac took the towel and scrubbed it down Liam's body, taking his time over the areas that entranced him most until Liam put an end to his game.

"Dude, I'm dry. Let's go. I'm fucking starving."

Zac was still pretty stuffed from the super-sized sandwiches, but he let Liam drag him, still naked, downstairs all the same, and then he watched, fascinated as ever, as Liam threw ingredients in a pan and turned them into something a galaxy away from a packet of instant noodles. Zac inhaled every bite, despite the sandwiches, and when he was done, sat back on the kitchen stool at the breakfast bar and rubbed his distended stomach. "You're going to make me chubby."

"Don't think there's much chance of that. Wouldn't mind putting some colour in your cheeks, though."

"Colour?"

Liam touched Zac's cheek, tracing under his eye with the pad of his thumb. "You look like you haven't seen the sun in years."

"I don't see it often. I work the night shift."

Liam's thumb faltered so briefly Zac was almost sure he'd imagined it, until Liam reclaimed his hand and got up, dumping dirty plates and cutlery in the sink. Zac watched him carefully, taking in the tense set of his shoulders. He didn't like it and reckoned he knew what had put it there, but Liam was back before he could think of a way to fix it, bringing with him a familiar roll of notes.

"What's that?"

"What does it look like?" Liam tossed the money on the counter. "Did you think I'd forgotten?"

"I hadn't thought about it at all." It was true. When he'd taken Liam's call the night before, money had been the last thing on his mind. "I . . ."

Liam frowned. "What?"

"Um." Zac bit his lip. Was he really about to admit he'd somehow imagined Liam had asked him over for anything other than a casual trick? "I . . ."

The power of speech seemed to have deserted him.

Liam stared hard at him for a long moment, and then comprehension dawned in his face. "I don't think of us like that anymore, I'm not sure I ever really did, but I'm offering you the money because I figure you probably need it."

Zac shook his head. "I don't need anything as much as I needed to come here today and not be a hooker."

CHAPTER
TWELVE

"**I** *needed to come here today and not be a hooker.*" Liam had never felt like a bigger wanker. The roll of notes between him and Zac seemed to burn a hole in the kitchen counter and the uncertainty in Zac's face, a crater in his heart. "I'm sorry."

Zac shrugged. "Don't be. I'm the idiot here."

"How so? Because you sensed something had changed between us, and you didn't know what it meant? Jesus, Zac. I got that money out of the safe six times before I settled on giving it to you."

"Why?"

"Why did it take me so long to decide?"

Zac nodded.

"Because I don't want to feel like a john any more than you want to feel like a hooker. I don't give a shit about the money— I have more than I'll ever need—but I don't want to pay you to be here . . . I want— Shit, I just want you."

Zac said nothing, as he picked up the roll of notes and spun it between his fingers. "Are you really that rich?"

"Define 'rich.' I have money, but it doesn't mean much without the things that matter."

"You say that because you have it."

"I had fuck-all ten years ago, and I reckon I was much happier."

"Let's burn it, then."

"What?"

"Burn it." Zac slid off his stool and padded to the couch, hopping lithely over it to the fireplace. He dangled the money over the smouldering logs. "We could argue about this shit all night, but what's the point? I don't want your money and you don't want to give it to me."

"That's not entirely true," Liam protested. "I don't want you to be with me for the money, but I want you to have it if you need it."

"Why? The fact that I've only got a fiver to my name isn't your problem."

"A fiver?" Liam couldn't contain his surprise. He'd given Zac eight hundred quid just a few days ago. Where the fuck had it gone?

But Liam didn't quite have the balls to ask. What Zac did with his money was no business of Liam's, unless . . . But he didn't have the guts to finish that thought. Zac wasn't one of the junkie hookers he'd seen drifting around Norwich—he wasn't a hooker at all, he was *Zac*.

Liam was as sure as he could manage. The idea of Zac with other men turned his stomach, but it wasn't a woe he owned. Zac had sold his body, but his soul was his to keep. "You can fire it to the moon for all I care. Keep it or burn it, and come upstairs when you're done, yeah? I've got something to show you."

He knew Zac would follow. His heart remembered every touch and kiss, every shy grin and heated stare, and when he heard footsteps on the stairs behind him, he glanced over his shoulder and smiled. Zac had tiny flecks of soot on his face. *So he did burn it.* A faint beacon of hope broke through the grey cloud Liam had lived with for so long. Friends, lovers . . . Liam couldn't find the right word to define what they'd become, but they were hooker and john no more, and for now, that was enough.

Zac raised a curious eyebrow. "What do you have to show me? Is it good?"

"Come and see." Liam opened the bedroom door and pointed to the bed. "Jump on that."

"Jump on it?"

"Well, flop on it, whatever. There's something I didn't tell you about it."

Zac shot Liam a look that made it clear he thought Liam was off his rocker, but approached the bed anyway. He sat tentatively on the edge and lurched backwards. "What the fuck?"

Liam chuckled. "Water bed. My nephews caught me at a weak moment and convinced me there was no place in this house for normal beds. Conventional mattresses are banned."

"Bloody hell." Zac lay back and rolled over, letting the sloshing mattress propel him to the end of the bed. "This is awesome. It's warm too. Is it heated?"

"Yup, it runs off the solar panels in the roof."

"The what?"

Liam shook his head. "I'll give you the lecture on renewable energy tomorrow, if you're staying?"

"Do you want me to?"

"Yes, but it's up to you. I can run you home anytime—"

"Fuck that." Zac bounced on the bed. "I want to stay."

Hope flared inside him again. Liam tried to switch it off, to contain the grin that threatened to split his face in half, but he failed spectacularly, and Zac's answering smile was mesmerising.

Liam forced himself to break the spell and moved to the window to close the curtains, to shut the cold, windy late afternoon out of the warmth simmering between them. At some point he'd have to go down and walk the dogs, but for now, his world was all about Zac. He took one last look at the beach path beyond his garden wall, the trees, the sand, the emergency phone box, and the lone figure in the distance, heading towards the sea in nothing but a pair of shorts. *What the fuck?* Liam stared harder, squinting in the fast fading light. The man was far away, but the set of his shoulders seemed familiar, his gait, and the slight limp. "Jesus fucking Christ!"

"What? What is it?"

Zac shot upright, but Liam hardly heard him as he scrabbled around the room for clothes, yanking on the first jeans he found. He dashed from the room and down the stairs, throwing the front door open and racing out into the night barefoot, the gravel on the driveway biting into his toes.

Heart in his mouth, he sprinted to the beach path, barely aware of Dave hot on his heels, her bark disappearing into the howling wind. His feet hit sand. He cupped his hands around his mouth. "Dad! Dad! Stop!"

Len didn't look around, set on his wavering path to the sea. Panic surged in Liam's veins. The North Sea was nippy at the best of times, but with winter approaching it was cold enough to give a man hypothermia in moments, and that was without the deadly tides and rip currents.

Liam yelled for his father again, desperation spilling over as he realised he wasn't going to reach him in time, but the dogs were faster than Liam, and they overtook him, crashing into Len just a foot from the rolling waves.

Like she'd read Liam's mind, Dave dodged around Len and jumped up at him, pushing him away from the sea, sending him stumbling into Liam.

"Dad?" Liam steadied Len, gripping his ice-cold shoulders. "What the hell are you doing out here?"

Len smiled, beaming at Liam like he'd just opened the door to him on a Sunday afternoon, his tiny cottage full of the scent of his famous lamb stew. "Hello, son. How are ya, lad?"

"Never mind me. Let's get you inside."

Liam grasped Len's arm and tried to pull him back up the beach. Len resisted, wrenching his arm free. "Not today, son. I've got things to do."

"*Dad*, you've got no bloody clothes on."

"No clothes on? Wash your mouth out, boy. That's no way to talk to your father. Go and get dressed and help your mother."

Liam gazed at his father and the faint light in his soul faded like it had never been there at all. Dear God, they'd known this was coming, but now? Really? Did this shit train never stop?

"Liam?" Liam turned his head. Zac was behind him, holding both dogs on their leads and clutching Liam's old winter coat. "Put this on him."

Dazed, Liam took the coat and held it out to Len, who stared at him like he'd grown horns. "Dad, please. Put it on. It's freezing."

Silence. Len's gaze drifted away, returning to the sea, a soft smile forming on his weathered face. An overwhelming urge to shake him swept over Liam, and then the age-old desire to run and keep running until he'd left everything behind hit him so hard he took a step back. *Fuck this.*

Zac's hand on his arm stayed him, and then the dogs' leads were being pressed into his grasp as Zac took the coat and moved between Liam and Len. "Fancy a walk, mate?"

Len blinked. "Who are you?"

"Zac. You're Len, yeah?"

"Are you from Croft House?"

"Nope. I'm from Liam's house. Where do you live?"

Len turned back in the direction he must have come from. Zac took advantage of his distraction to slip the coat around his shoulders. If Len noticed, he didn't react. "I live up there. Rachlen Cottage. Been there fifteen years now."

"Yeah? Can you show me?" Zac glanced at Liam. "That okay?"

Liam considered their options. This close to the beach, Len's house probably wasn't much further than his own, and it was clear Len was headed there with or without him. "Let's go."

He trailed Zac and Len over the wet sand and back to the path. They took a right at the fork towards Len's part of the village. On the way, Zac spoke gently to Len in a way Liam had never heard him talk before, his voice so soft it was impossible to make out the words. Liam drifted behind, leading the dogs and shivering in the cold wind as evening began to fall around them.

They reached Len's home. Thankfully, he'd left the door wide open, his clothes folded neatly by the roaring fire. Without looking at Liam, Zac set about dressing Len, who was fully clothed again before Liam thought to find himself a pair of Len's thick fisherman's socks for his own feet.

Zac settled Len in his chair and, following Len's direction, fetched his pipe from the mantelpiece, stuffing it and lighting it, taking a lungful of smoke himself before handing it over to Len. He clicked the tiny TV on, somehow knowing to find the racing channel, then patted Len's arm and stood. "Tea?"

Len grunted and sucked on his pipe. "I like you. Tell them to send you next time instead of that daft woman with the apron."

Zac grinned and left Len to his pipe and horses, coming to Liam and touching his arm. "Show me the kettle?"

Liam beckoned Zac into the cottage's cramped kitchen. Once out of Len's sight, he seized Zac and pushed him against the counter, taking his face in his hands and kissing him senseless. "Thank you."

Zac smiled against Liam's lips. "For what? Letting you snog me in your dad's kitchen? Because that's all I'm going to let you thank me for."

Liam kissed Zac again, then pressed their foreheads together. "He's my dad."

"I know."

For a long moment, silence cocooned them, heavy and comforting, and for the hundredth time since they'd met, it seemed like he'd known Zac forever. "I should call my sister."

"Okay. Do you want me to take the dogs outside?"

Liam leaned back and looked into the living room. Both dogs were taking advantage of the fire, Dave doing her best to sit on Jazz's head, all the while keeping a watchful gaze on Len. "Nah. They're good. Shit, I haven't got my phone. I'll have to use the landline."

Zac nodded and reached for the kettle. Liam trudged upstairs to Len's ancient handset. He dialled Rosa's house, hoping there was someone home. Mike answered on the third ring and fetched Rosa straight away.

Liam explained himself, leaving out the part about his ex-hooker-slash-new-best-friend saving the day. "I don't know what to do with him now. He's watching TV like nothing's happened."

"It hasn't for him, Liam. And it's better like that. Can you imagine how he'd feel if he knew how much he'd upset you?"

"I'm not upset."

"Of course you're not. Either way, I'm getting in my car."

"Rosa, don't. It's fine. I'll stay here with him. The boys need you at home."

"For a FIFA marathon?" Rosa scoffed. "I don't think so. You're doing me a favour. Stoke the fire and get the spare pillows down, okay? I'll be there in ten."

She let herself in twenty minutes later, clutching a casserole dish of Len's favourite haddock pie. "I thought you said Dad was naked?" she asked after she'd greeted Len. "Where are *your* clothes?"

Liam looked down at his bare chest. Being half-dressed around Zac was so normal he'd forgotten to put some clothes on. "I, er, ran out of the house."

"Uh-huh. Who's your cute friend?"

"Zac," Zac helpfully supplied from his position on the rug, poking the fire and scratching Jazz's ears.

"Hello, Zac." Rosa raised a curious eyebrow. "I'm going to drag my brother into the kitchen now and ask him all kinds of inappropriate questions. Will you be okay out here by yourself?"

"I reckon so."

Zac seemed a little bemused. Liam absorbed it, throwing him what he hoped was a reassuring smile, then gave in to Rosa's insistent tugging on his arm.

In the kitchen, Rosa lit the stove, then rounded on Liam with a smirk of her own. "*Zac*, eh? He's pretty. What's the story?"

As if he could ever tell her. As if he had any other option but to play the childish sibling card. "None of your bloody business."

Rosa's grin widened. "I'll bet. Guess there's no explaining why you were half-naked with a *friend* in our darling father's hour of need."

"That's not fair."

"None of this is fair, Liam. That's why I'm taking the piss out of you instead of dealing with the fact that our dad is about to spend the last days in his own home. Work with me, will you?"

Liam relented, trying to ignore the sad wave of defeat that washed over him. The precious hours he'd spent with Zac felt like a lifetime ago, the tentative joy they'd nurtured obliterated by reality, despite the fact that Zac was but a few feet away. *He's still here.* Liam held on to the warmth that notion brought and fixed Rosa with a watery smile. "He really is a friend, and he's awesome. That's all you need to know."

"It's all I want to know. Now take him home. Dad and I are going to have our dinner and watch *Last of the Summer Wine*."

Liam had learned long ago that there was little point arguing with Rosa when she had a plan. "Do you want me to leave the dogs? Keep you warm on that couch?"

"Yeah, leave me Dave. Her snoring reminds me of Mike, so I won't have to miss him."

"I'll be back first thing."

"If not before, no doubt. Now piss off."

Fair enough. Liam rounded up Zac and Jazz, and bid Len good-bye for the evening. It wasn't lost on him that Len seemed more affected by Zac's departure than his, but that didn't hurt as much as it might've done a year or so ago, back in that hazy time when happiness had been too normal to appreciate.

Outside, he shivered, and Zac's slim arm around his waist felt all the warmer.

"Come on," Zac said. "Let's get you home."

"I like the sound of that."

"Good, then stop feeling bad about leaving your dad."

When had he fallen into a world where the people he loved read him so easily? Liam considered the crazy idea that he did indeed love Zac, a man he still hardly knew. It didn't seem possible, but he didn't have the energy to ponder it much, not tonight. Tonight he wanted to go home and shut the world away, lose himself in Zac, and then sleep until it was time to adult again.

He let Zac lead him home, noting that Zac had possessed the presence of mind to snatch his keys from the dish by the door and lock the house behind him. Inside, it felt natural to go straight upstairs, strip, and crawl into bed, Zac on his back, cradling Liam's head on his chest in a gesture so intimate Liam would've cried if his brain slowed down enough to allow it. "You were so calm. I wanted to deck him."

Zac's sigh was barely audible. "It's difficult to handle someone when they're not really there. I don't know how many times I've wished there was someone around to do it for me."

"Your dad?"

"No."

"Your mum?"

"No."

"You're not going to tell me, are you?"

"No, but if it's any consolation, you wouldn't have decked him. You never will. You'll just get on with it, like you always have."

Zac's voice sounded too far away for Liam's liking. He raised his head and touched Zac's cheek, drawing Zac's eyes from the ceiling. "Thank you. I might've managed to do it myself if you hadn't been here, but I'm glad you were."

"I like being here."

Liam wanted to ask him to stay forever, but pride and common sense kept him quiet. Instead he kissed Zac, trying to remember a time when Zac's lips had been forbidden. Trying and failing as Zac pulled back and fixed Liam with a gaze that seemed too shrewd for his young face.

"What is it about your dad that makes it so hard to see him like this?"

If the question had come from anyone else, Liam would've dodged it—changed the subject and moved on—but somehow he knew that whatever answer he gave, Zac would understand. "My mum died when I was nine. Breast cancer. Before that, my dad wasn't around much. He worked on the crab boats out of Cromer, and the mackerel ones. He worked all night, sometimes all day too."

"Fisherman?" Zac nodded. "Makes sense. He looks like one."

"Smelled like one too, back in the day. Until mum died, we never saw him without salt crusted all over his hands."

"What changed?"

"Everything . . . and nothing. He still worked the boats, but he had to do everything else too—the cooking, cleaning, even shit like sewing Rosa's country-dancing costume. There were women in the village who'd have helped him, but he insisted on doing it himself."

"Strong man."

Liam sighed and put his chin on Zac's chest. "The strongest, in every way. He coped with everything me and Rosa ever threw at him. Didn't bat an eye when I came out, when Rosa got herself married and knocked up in ten seconds flat."

"And that's why it's so hard, eh? Because he doesn't seem like your dad anymore?"

"I guess."

Zac wove his fingers into Liam's hair and fiddled with the strands. "I have a friend who lives a different life to me these days. I don't like seeing him weak when he used to be so much stronger than me. Makes me feel like there's no hope for anyone."

Liam couldn't handle the sadness in Zac's gaze. He crawled over him and kissed him deeply, grinding into Zac as Zac lifted his legs and wrapped them around his waist. They fucked again later that night, more than once. Zac slept in between, waking without protest each time Liam nudged him, smiling and opening his arms, and holding Liam's eyes as Liam pushed inside him again and again, until they both trembled and groaned.

In the morning, Liam watched the sun rise to a clear sky that had no doubt brought a bitter frost with it. Beside him, Zac slept on, sprawled on his stomach with his arm flung out, his hand resting in Liam's lap. During the night, Liam had held it from time to time, learning the web of veins and scars, his bitten-down nails, and in the glistening light of the early morning, he took it once more, counting the warm pulse in Zac's wrist and willing him to wake up.

It didn't happen, and before long, it was time for Liam to get ready to take Rosa's place with Len, and prepare for a long day of decisions they'd hoped against hope they'd never have to make.

Reluctantly, Liam left Zac and hauled himself into the shower. Alone, the hot water held little allure for him, so he didn't linger. He dried off, then padded back to the bedroom, picking up his stray clothes as he went and tossing them into the neglected hamper in the cupboard.

He hung Zac's clothes on the end of the bed: his socks, T-shirt, and jeans—sometime during the night, his boxers had disappeared. As he hung Zac's jeans, something fell out the pocket.

Liam bent to retrieve it, feeling about under the bed. His fingers closed around a plastic tube, and what felt like a bag. He pulled his hand back. In his palm lay a syringe and powder-dusted plastic bag, and the small beacon of hope he'd found the previous day crumbled into the grey despair he'd been stupid enough to ignore.

He stood up slowly, blinking and hoping each time that the hard undeniable truth would disappear.

But it didn't, and the perspective he'd obviously lacked for the last month crashed into him like a freight train. How the fuck could he have been so bloody naïve? Prostitution and drugs came hand in hand. Everyone knew that. And now Zac had brought drugs into Liam's home, perhaps even used them, shooting up in the bathroom each time he'd told Liam he was taking a piss.

Liam fingered the empty bag. What if he hadn't taken the drugs? What if, instead, the bag had leaked, scattering who-the-fuck-knew-what all over the place? Len's house? On the couch for the dogs to find? In the boys' bedroom?

Fury swept over Liam, so swift and sudden that he was standing over Zac before he could take a breath. He lashed out, waking Zac with a sharp kick to his legs. "Get up."

Zac gasped, sucking in a harsh breath that made him splutter and cough in a way that would've broken Liam's heart five minutes before. But it was already broken now, the pain masked by rage, and an all-consuming need to get Zac out of his house.

"Get. Up."

Zac rolled over, rubbing his shin where Liam had struck him, and shooting Liam a confused, dozy grin. "Hey, hey, easy. I'll do anything you want. You don't have to boot me."

Liam wanted to do more than thump him. He wanted to scoop him up and chuck him through the damned window. Instead, he threw the bag and syringe in Zac's face. "You dropped something. I'm going to see my dad. I suggest you find anything else you've misplaced and get the fuck out of my house."

CHAPTER
THIRTEEN

Zac lay on the couch and stared at the tiny flat-screen TV that was built into the wall of this particular john's living room. He should've got up and gone home hours ago, but he couldn't make himself move. It hurt, and he was tired, so fucking tired. He'd worked every night since Liam had kicked him to the kerb, and tonight had been particularly brutal. Not that he'd noticed the pain much, or, at least, he hadn't until the tenth night in a row he'd cruised the club and gone home with whichever grubby dude took his bait first.

Wincing, Zac shifted, and a dull ache spread up his spine and down into the tops of his thighs. The last john—now passed out on the sofa opposite—had done a real number on him and it hurt like hell, but . . . *"Get the fuck out of my house."* Nah. The pain in his heart was worse.

Sometime later, after talking himself out of filching any of the tramadol he'd seen piled up in the bathroom, Zac forced himself to leave the grotty bedsit and shuffled home to his own flat—a space that had seemed more cold and bare than ever since he'd crawled home in disgrace from Liam's house.

He let himself in and kicked his shoes against the wall, trying to care that they left a mark big enough to take a chunk out of his deposit. He failed and abandoned them where they lay, hauling himself into the shower to wash away the grime of a long night's work.

Under the spray, he fiddled with Liam's leather bracelet, contemplating for the thousandth time how it would feel to take it off, bury it, chuck it in the bin like Liam had never existed, but he couldn't do it. Liam's fury still felt like a knife to his chest, his ignored phone calls like acid lacing his blood, but it was a pain Zac clung to grimly, afraid to let it fade in case it took all that was left of him with it.

Dude, no one died. Zac shut off the shower with a heavy sigh, eyes closed, head bowed. The pain lancing his heart was tough to bear, but the knowledge that Liam knew an agony far worse was unbearable, because someone *had* died for Liam, someone whom Zac had been a fool to believe he could ever replace. Liam had founded a business with Cory, built a house, married him. Syringe or no syringe, hooker or not, Zac had never had a hope of being anything other than an empty fuck.

At least, that's what he'd told himself every day since Liam had so furiously thrown him out, the rage in his eyes second only to the overwhelming sadness that had hurt Zac far more than his anger ever would. *You hurt him.* Zac didn't know much, but of that he was certain. Stuffing that fucking syringe in his pocket had been the worst mistake of his whole miserable life.

And miserable Zac was. So miserable it was all he could do to pull on some unwashed trackies and crawl into his bed. He stared at his phone, willing it to light up, but of course it didn't. Aside from a few regular johns' calls, his phone had remained as dark and desolate as the fog that clouded every moment he was unfortunate enough to be awake.

Zac closed his eyes and chased sleep, running down the blank nothingness that had become his only relief. He found it more quickly than he had of late, drifting into a deep sleep, worn out from days and days of gazing at the ceiling, and night after night of turning tricks.

It was midmorning when he woke with a jump, sitting bolt upright, cold sweat streaming down his face and chest, heart racing, feeling for all the world like he'd been dropped back into the hell pit of withdrawal.

He laid his palm over his thundering heart. What had woken him? Most mornings this week he'd slept past noon. Then he heard it: a light knocking at the front door that had him scrambling from the bed like a cat on roller skates. He stumbled out of the bedroom and into the hall, shoulder-barging the doorframe in his hurry.

He threw the door open, slamming it into the wall behind. His heart searched for Liam, and for a moment he almost convinced himself that the stooped figure on the doorstep was tall and strong, wild-haired and bright-eyed, but then the halo of golden hair dulled to an inky, greasy black, and the eyes darkened, revealing a repentant-looking Jamie.

"All right, mate?"

Zac blinked. Though history had taught him Jamie would eventually return, he was, for some reason, the last person Zac had expected to see. *Seriously? You thought Liam was going to come running back and beg you for one more night?* The absurdity of the notion hit Zac hard. He laughed, manic and loud, a crazed burst of laughter that sounded like it had come from someone else.

Jamie clearly thought the same. His red-rimmed eyes widened, and he caught Zac's arms. "What the fuck's up with you? Are you trashed?"

If only. Zac had a bottle of corner-shop whiskey stashed in the cupboard and four cans of Stella in the fridge, but he hadn't dared touch them for fear of where the bottom of a bottle would lead. He'd learned the hard way that binge-drinking alone was the toughest test of his resistance. Even this far from London, it wasn't like he didn't know how to get junk. Christ, Jamie was right here. Chances were he had a pocket full—

"Zac?"

In his haze, Zac hadn't noticed Jamie getting his foot in the door. "What?"

Jamie stared at him, holding his arms in a death grip. "What's the matter? You look fucking awful."

Coming from Jamie, it was all Zac could do not to laugh again, but perspective returned in time for him to remember that Jamie was an unwelcome visitor.

He wrenched his arms free and found the remnants of his equilibrium. "What are you doing here?"

"What do you think?" Jamie dropped his hands, but didn't step back. "I came to say sorry for being a cunt, if you'll let me."

"For being a cunt?"

"Yep . . . yep, that's me. I'm a cunt."

"Why's that?"

Jamie frowned. "You know why."

"I want to hear you say it."

"Fine . . . for bringing skag into the flat and nicking your dosh. Are you going to let me in?"

"No." And for a brief moment, Zac truly meant it. His anger with Jamie had faded as time had gone by, overwhelmed by a yearning for Liam so strong he could hardly hold himself up, but staying close to Jamie was still a bad idea, especially now, when it wouldn't take much to persuade himself that there was little point resisting all Jamie had to offer.

But the longer Jamie stared at him, his familiar gaze and hesitant smile seeping into him, the harder it became to push Jamie away. Jamie's mistake had cost him the only thing he'd felt good about in as long as he could remember, but did that make it Jamie's fault? It wasn't Jamie who'd shoved the syringe in his pocket, and it wasn't Jamie who'd convinced him he was worthy of anything other than the misery he had for company now. No. He'd done that shit all by himself.

He stood back and let Jamie pass. "Don't steal my stuff."

"Don't look like you have anything." Jamie had already drifted past him and opened the empty Super Noodle cupboard, and then the barren fridge. "Seriously. I know we're crap at this domestic bollocks, but you always buy milk and bread. And what's with the beer? That was here when I left. You stuck in a time warp, or something?"

It sure felt like it. "Don't pretend you give a rat's arse."

Jamie shut the fridge and stood up. "That's not fair."

"Isn't it?"

"No. I might be a deadbeat junkie, Zac, but I'm still your mate. What's going on? Have you slipped?"

"No."

Zac turned on his heel and stomped to the living room, unwilling to let Jamie see how close to the mark he was. To let him smell his weakness. He threw himself onto the couch, only dimly aware of Jamie standing over him, until Jamie grabbed hold of him and yanked him upright again.

"If it's not the junk, what is it? A bad trick? Come on, mate. You can tell me. It can't be anything I haven't ballsed up myself."

Zac snorted, though he had no idea if Jamie had ever felt about anyone the way he'd felt—still felt—about Liam. They were the closest to a best friend either one of them had ever had, but Jamie endured a life of his own away from the flat, a life Zac spent most of his time trying to hide from. For all he knew, Jamie had a junkie lover out there waiting on him right now.

'Cause you and Liam were lovers? Zac snorted again, though there was no humour in it. He'd never been sure what love was, but he knew enough to know that Liam was more than a naïve infatuation for him.

"*Zac.*"

"*What?*"

Jamie sighed, for a moment assuming the air of an overworked mental health nurse. "Have you got a quid? I think you need a bag of chips."

"I'm not giving you money."

"Suit yourself." Jamie dug around in his pockets and came up with some loose change. "Might have enough anyway."

He got up and left the flat. Zac didn't expect to see him again, so he was a little taken aback when Jamie reappeared ten minutes later, brandishing a bag of chips from the greasy spoon down the road, a tub of gravy, and a wide grin even Zac couldn't ignore.

"I found a two-pound coin outside the post office."

"Bonza. And you bought gravy with it? Looks like you're the one on the turn."

Jamie held out his bounty. "I got it for you."

Zac could've cried, but he didn't. He sat up and took the chips, scooting over to make room for Jamie on the couch. "Share them?"

"If you want."

In answer, Zac unwrapped the chips and shoved a handful in Jamie's mouth, and then his own, realising for the first time in days how hungry he was. The chips were good, the gravy better, and he and Jamie made short work of both.

Zac contemplated dashing out for some more, but the ache in his back kept him still. In his hurry to answer the front door, he'd forgotten about his war wounds.

Jamie noticed him shifting and raised an eyebrow. "Wanna shower?"

"Me? You're the one who stinks." Zac couldn't remember a time when Jamie hadn't smelt of dirty pavements and unwashed clothes.

"So come with me."

Jamie stood and held out his hand. After a brief second of deliberation, Zac found himself powerless to refuse. This was his role in life, right? Get fucked by the johns and keep Jamie from rotting? What else was there?

A few minutes later, Jamie turned the shower on in the windowless bathroom. The extractor fan whirred to life and he reached for the light.

"Don't," Zac said. "Leave it off."

Jamie left it off, leaving them at the mercy of the bare lightbulb in the hallway. Steam filled the room. Zac leaned against the tiled wall and closed his eyes, recalling the last time he'd shared a shower with someone, and then steeling himself against the tidal wave of Liam-fuelled arousal that swept over him.

The sound of Jamie's clothes hitting the floor stirred him. Damn. Zac usually did that bit, because Jamie was often so strung out he forgot. But not today. Today, Jamie ditched his own clothes, then came to Zac, his gaze curious and more heated than Zac had seen it in a very long while.

Jamie nudged Zac's waistband down over his hips, letting his cock spring back and bounce, hard and heavy. "Someone's horny."

Zac rolled his eyes. "I'm not horny. Got turned inside out yesterday."

"So? Doesn't mean your dick is broke."

True. Despite the aches and pains of the night before, Zac's cock seemed A-OK, jumping and twitching as Jamie brushed his fingers over it, much to Jamie's obvious amusement.

He took Zac's hand and tugged on it. "Come on. Let's get you clean before we get dirty all over again."

Zac refrained from pointing out that he'd washed himself just fine the night before, as Jamie pulled the shower curtain back and guided him under the spray. Instead, he focused on Jamie's lean body, taking in his scraped skin and visible ribs, his bony chest and protruding hips, all sure signs that he'd lost more of Jamie since they'd last done this.

And when had that been? Zac recalled washing Jamie a few days after he'd met Liam, but he couldn't remember a time when being naked together had felt so intense. He gazed at Jamie as the water beat down around them. With his black hair and stormy eyes, Jamie was his own brand of beautiful, and fucking him had always been good. The kind of good that had, in the past, kept them both alive. And fuck, if Zac didn't need to feel alive right now, to lose himself in the frail warmth of Jamie and forget that he'd briefly known what it was like to live for the sake of someone else.

"Jay?"

"Yeah?"

"Can I fuck you?"

Jamie shrugged. "Of course. Have you got rubbers in here—"

"No . . . Jay, I mean, really fuck you?"

Confusion coloured Jamie's sunken features, before comprehension seemed to dawn and he moved closer . . . close enough that Zac could count the drops of water on his cheek. "I'm your friend, Zac. You can fuck me however you want and it will always be okay."

That was enough for Zac—for now at least, until the inevitable high wore off—so he pushed the fruitlessness of what he was about to do aside, reaching for Jamie and crushing them together in an embrace that was as empty as it was familiar. He shoved Jamie against the wall and kissed him, biting and bruising, searching for the magic he knew was missing, and when he didn't find it, he spun Jamie around, for once ignoring the odd pattern of marbled skin on Jamie's back. "Wait here."

The dash for condoms and lube seemed surreal, and easing inside Jamie even more so. It wasn't until he was fucking Jamie, far slower than he'd ever fucked him before, that he felt a whisper of the oblivion he craved so much.

Jamie cried out and shook, clenching his hands into fists, clearly frustrated by this side of Zac he'd never seen before. He punched the wall. "Goddamn it, you're better than junk, don't stop, don't stop."

As if Zac could. Jamie was the only man he'd ever fucked, and it had been so long he'd forgotten how good it felt, how good Jamie felt, and why they'd been doing this since they'd rolled into each other on the floor of a scummy London squat.

Zac drove into Jamie, picking up the pace as the coil of pleasure in his belly expanded, threatening the edges of the shadows. He fucked Jamie harder, and harder still, but it wasn't until Jamie screamed his name and came, tipping Zac over the edge, that release gave him a few moments of peace.

He recovered his senses with his face buried between Jamie's shoulder blades, his lungs burning and his eyes clenched shut, fighting to keep reality at bay. But it was a battle he couldn't win, and his gloom returned as the hot water gave out.

Jamie squirmed, reminding Zac that they were still connected. Zac laid a hand on his back and withdrew, then turned him around, checking he was okay, like he always did after they fucked. Like no one else ever did for Jamie. "All right?"

"Yeah. You?"

Lacking the energy to lie, Zac shut the shower off and pushed the curtain aside, grabbing the towel and handing it to Jamie first while he disposed of the condom.

Jamie was silent as he dried off, but his stare was quizzical. He handed Zac the towel with a frown. "Why are you being so weird?"

"I'm not."

Zac left the bathroom, knowing Jamie would follow, and drifted to his bedroom, crawling into bed and pulling the duvet over his head.

Jamie joined him moments later, smelling distinctly better than he had before their shower-time adventures. "Please tell me what's wrong. Is it that special john you had the hots for? Did he turn out to be a wanker?"

"He's not a wanker."

"So it is him?"

Zac scowled. "I never said that."

"Didn't have to." In the dim light under the duvet, Jamie's eyes seemed to gleam. "You've been different ever since you met him."

Zac couldn't deny it, though he didn't see how Jamie could be so certain. They'd hardly seen each other in recent months. "Well, you don't have to worry about that anymore. He's gone."

"Gone where?"

"Nowhere. I meant figuratively."

"Oh. Don't use big words like that. You know they confuse me."

"Liar." Jamie was fiercely intelligent and more articulate than Zac could ever dream of being. "I only know what it means because you told me."

"Whatever. Okay, so what happened to Hot Stuff? Did he get a better offer?"

"No, he found one of your syringes in my pocket and threw me out of his house."

Silence. Jamie bit his lip and guilt like Zac had never seen in him before softened his sharp features. "He thought it was yours?"

"I reckon so. He didn't really say much apart from 'get the fuck out.'"

"Why didn't you tell him it was mine?"

"Because it didn't matter by then. He'd already come to his senses."

Jamie frowned. "I don't understand."

Zac recounted the whole sorry turn of events, filling Jamie in on all he'd missed, right up until the moment Liam had stormed out of his own house, slamming the front door so hard behind him that the whole building had shaken.

"Why didn't you wait for him to come back?" Jamie asked. "Or follow him out?"

Zac sighed. He'd asked himself that a few times over the last ten days. "Because it wouldn't have changed anything. I saw his face, Jay . . . when he was holding the rig. It was like he'd finally remembered what I was, and what a fucking idiot he'd been to ever forget. I might've convinced him I wasn't shooting up in his bathroom, but I'll always be a whore."

"And what's wrong with that? We're not killing anyone, mate."

Zac didn't entirely agree, but kept the sentiment to himself. Who was he to lecture Jamie? "Just forget it. It's over now, anyway."

"Doesn't mean you didn't deserve it, whatever it was. I can't stop you blaming yourself, but don't start believing it's because he's better than you, because that's bollocks, Zac. He was the one using hookers for kicks."

"It wasn't like that."

"Then what was it like? This ain't no *Pretty Woman* fable. Johns are johns."

Zac shook his head and sat up, letting the duvet fall away. "Not Liam. He's *not* like that. He never made me feel like a whore. He's just—"

"What? A rich dude with more money than sense?"

"No, he was lonely. His husband died and he was lonely, Jay. He was so fucking lonely."

"You've said it three times, Zac. I get the point." Jamie sat up too, eyeing Zac warily. "But being lonely doesn't make him nice. Rich twats are never nice. How do you think they make their money?"

"*No.*" Zac shook his head so hard it was a wonder it didn't fall off. "He didn't mean to make so much money. He gives most of his profits back to the company to run their eco festivals."

"Eco festivals? Thought you said he was a surfer?"

"He used to surf. He makes T-shirts now . . . or, at least, his company does."

Jamie frowned. "What did you say his name was?"

"Liam."

"Liam what?"

"Erm . . ." Shit. Zac didn't actually know. There had been no reason for Liam to share his surname, or Zac to share his. "I know the company's called Sea Rave. He took me to the factory."

Jamie's dark brows shot up so fast that his face morphed into a slightly frightening expression. "Dear God, are you seriously telling me you've been shagging Liam Mallaney all this time and you haven't had a fucking clue?"

"Who?"

"Give me your phone."

Zac handed it over. Jamie furiously swiped and tapped at the screen until he brought up an image that showed Liam in all his beautiful glory, posing in the colourful chaos of a beachside festival, the Sea Rave logo behind him, and his arms around a wiry black man with the biggest smile Zac had ever seen. "Oh."

"Yeah . . . *oh.*" Jamie tapped the phone. "Your sugar daddy is like the Mark Zuckerberg of surf clothes, only way cooler."

"Mark who? Is that like Richard Branson?"

Jamie rolled his eyes. "Yeah, if you're stuck in the nineties. Do you never read?"

"Piss off." Zac shoved Jamie away. "How do you know so much shit when you spend your whole life loaded? I've been clean for six months and I don't know fuck-all about anything."

"Yeah, but you're clean, Zac. That makes you twice the man I am, whatever way you look at it."

The sadness in Jamie's gaze broke Zac's heart. He reached for his only friend and pulled him into a tight hug, burying his face in hair that was so silky now it was clean. "You can do it too. It's not easy, but you can do it, I know you can."

Jamie shook his head. "I can't. I'm not like you. I'm not strong. I can't turn tricks and live in this shit without it. I need it, Zac . . . I wish I didn't. And I don't even want to be clean."

And there was the problem. Recovery had been forced on Zac, but as horrific as withdrawal had been, he'd embraced it, welcoming the pain, knowing each day spent writhing on his back, shivering, moaning, screaming, was a day closer to becoming human. The light at the end of the tunnel had been small, a pinprick in the distance, but Zac had seen it, wanted it, and chased it down until he had it.

For Jamie, any light he could see was still a train coming, a train that could only be stopped by a sweet hit of heroin.

Zac lay back down, taking Jamie with him, making the most of this time together before Jamie left him. A few months ago, they would've fucked some more, perhaps fucked till the night came to take Jamie away, but something—perhaps everything—had changed between them. Right then, all Zac wanted was to hold Jamie close until the shadows called them both home.

Speaking of which. "Are you going to tell me where you got that junk from? And don't tell me you bought it, unless you robbed the bookies again."

"I don't go robbing anymore, you know that."

It was true. To the best of Zac's knowledge, Jamie had given up on the fake armed robberies—a pretend gun under a tea towel—he'd perfected in London, mainly because he was too fucked up to make a decent getaway. Didn't mean he'd stopped doing daft things, though. Jamie had the brains of Britain, and the common sense of a rocking horse. "So where did it come from?"

Jamie raised his head and cupped Zac's face with his callused palm, stroking his cheek with a bony fingertip. "I'll tell you tomorrow. Can we sleep now? I want to lie on top of you and dream of the sun."

Damn you. Jamie's poetic way with words had always rendered Zac mute until it was too late for him to argue, and true to form, Jamie was snoring before he found his tongue again, leaving Zac with little choice but to shut his eyes and join him. He wrapped his arms around Jamie and fell asleep, dreaming of Liam, the sea, and the sunshine Jamie craved.

An earsplitting crash woke him late in the evening. He bolted upright, letting Jamie slip from his arms and fall to the side. "What the fuck was that?"

Jamie mumbled, but didn't wake, even as footsteps sounded in the hallway.

Zac pushed him away and swung his legs out of bed. His feet hit carpet as the bedroom door was smashed open and three black-clad figures burst into the room, each one brandishing a baseball bat.

The first figure was on Zac before he could stand, throwing him to the floor and kicking him in the ribs so hard his bones crunched.

Pain ricocheted through him, driving the air from his lungs. He coughed and spluttered, curling in on himself, like he could hide from the steel-capped boot that was heading his way again, kicking him over and over until white spots danced in his eyes. "What do you want?"

"We want the money," the man growled. "Or the product. Don't really give a fuck. Give us what's ours, you thieving faggot."

The second man advanced on Zac and pulled him upright. "Where is it?"

"Where's what?"

"The junk you stole."

"I didn't steal any junk. I don't know what the fuck you're talking about."

The man crouched. For the first time, Zac noticed he was masked, like the two behind him. "Yes, you did. My guvnor said the little poof in this flat stole a kilo of skag from his car, and I don't see anyone else here, do you?"

Zac glanced at the bed. It was empty. Somehow, Jamie had vanished into thin air. "It wasn't me."

The masked man punched him hard in the chest, jarring the ribs that already felt broken. "Yes, it was."

"No, it wasn't. I haven't lived here long. Must've been the tenant before me. Or you've got the wrong place."

"Nice try." The man seized Zac's hair and jerked his head up, forcing Zac to meet his gaze. "Do you think I haven't heard all this shit before? Do you think my mates didn't hear it when they came looking for you last week?"

"Ask them. They'll tell you it wasn't me."

"Suit yerself." The man let Zac go and stood, then strode to the open doorway. "Oi! Get down here and tell this jammy bender what you told him before. Then I can kick his head in for telling porkies."

Another masked man appeared. He peered into the room, fixed his gaze on Zac, then shook his head. "Weren't him. I told you. It was that skinny kid from the corner."

Skinny kid. Jamie. Of course it fucking was. And that solved the mystery of how he'd acquired enough heroin to sustain a small army of junkies. "Told you it wasn't me."

"Shut it." The masked man came back from the door and stamped on Zac's leg. "You talk when I say you talk."

Zac gasped, steeling himself for more blows as the man crouched in front of him again, but they never came. Instead, the man pulled a knife from his sleeve and trailed it down Zac's bare chest.

"So you're not the scroat we came for, but I reckon he's a pal of yours, am I right?"

Zac shuddered, forcing himself not to look at the empty bed. The man, whose accent betrayed him as a Scot, grinned, showing Zac a set of blackened teeth, and pushed the knife in a little harder.

"You can't protect him, you know. I'll find him eventually. At least if you tell me how to find your pal, I won't be quite as vexed when I get my hands on him."

"I don't know who you're talking about."

"Liar."

"I don't. I told you, I haven't lived here long."

"Have it your way."

The man pounced, lifting Zac from the floor before he could blink and tossing him on the bed like a rag doll. The impact jolted

Zac's already battered body and he retched, rolling to one side, dry-heaving, until the man pulled him onto his back.

"You're not going to convince me you don't know the wee prick who owes my guvnor twenty grand, so you can give him a message for me. That all right with you?"

Despite the pain, Zac fought the man's hold on him. "I don't know who you're talking about."

"Aye, you do. I know it, you know it, so you just lie still and let me do the talking, eh?" The masked man drew the knife slowly and deliberately down Zac's forearm, slicing the skin from his elbow to his hand.

Zac screamed. The man sneered and wiped the knife on the carpet. "You're going to bleed from your artery now, so if your friend makes it home before you snuff it, you tell him from me there's a lot worse waiting for him if he doesn't bring me the money by tomorrow."

CHAPTER
FOURTEEN

Rosa folded her arms across her chest and glared at Liam in a way that made him feel nine years old again, like he had the morning after their mother died when Rosa'd turned to him and told him she wasn't going to let him treat her like a little girl anymore, even if he was eight minutes older than her. "You can't pay for everything, Liam. It's too much. Let me and Mike pay half."

Liam shut his chequebook with a heavy sigh. "Paying for stuff is what I'm good at. Least I can do when you set all this up. Besides, this is only the down payment. There'll be plenty of bills to settle for however long . . ." His voice fell away. He didn't need to remind Rosa that whatever happened, they wouldn't be paying Len's care home bills forever. "Leave it to me, okay? We've got it— *I've* got it covered."

Rosa frowned. Clearly, it had been a long while since Liam had last referred to himself as more than the pathetic loner he was. "Listen, I know this is hard, but we've done the right thing."

Liam sighed again. "I know. It's just so fucking unfair. He'd do his nut if he really knew what we'd done. He always told us to shoot him if he lost his marbles."

"Doesn't mean he expected us to actually do it." Rosa took the cheque Liam had written and tucked it in the ever-expanding folder of paperwork that chronicled Len's move into a residential care home. "Now eat your dinner, or I'll get you more salad."

Liam knew better than to argue. He cleared his plate of lentil stew and took it to the sink, following the house rules of washing it, drying it, and putting it away.

He was staring at a drawer of clean tea towels when Rosa came up behind him and pushed it shut. "What on earth is going on with you?

And don't say 'nothing,' because I'll bloody deck you. I know you've got Mike in your pocket."

"In my pocket?"

"On your side, whatever. I always know when he's hiding stuff because he goes off sex."

Liam cringed. "Seriously? I didn't need to know that."

"Then you shouldn't keep things from me. I'll tell you how my last period was if you don't cough up."

"Rosa!"

Rosa shrugged. "I'm beyond giving a shit. Moving Dad has been hard, but I know there's something else going on. Are you upset because you've got a boyfriend?"

"A what?"

"That cutie from the other week. It's okay, you know. Cory wouldn't mind; he'd want you to be happy."

"Zac's not my boyfriend."

"No? Then why are you blushing?"

"I'm not." Liam subconsciously rubbed the back of his neck. "Why do you have to be such a pain in my arse?"

"Because Mum's not here to do it. Now cut the crap and spill."

"No."

"Liam."

"Trust me, you don't want to know."

"And who gives you the right to decide—"

"Because he's a fucking rentboy. Not Prince Charming the Second come to sweep me off my goddamned feet."

Rosa absorbed Liam's explosion with little more than a blink, and it took seconds for Liam to realise that she'd intended to provoke him all along. She was well-versed enough in Liam's personality to irk him revealing everything he'd tried so hard to keep from her. "You've been sleeping with hookers?"

"Hooker, singular. Just Zac."

"I see. Did you know he was a hooker?"

"Yes."

"Did you pay him to sleep with you?"

"Yes."

"Why?"

Now there was a question, and one he'd yet to find an answer for, despite the eleven long days since the fateful morning he'd slammed the door on the tentative new world he'd found with Zac. "He didn't feel like a hooker . . . never did."

Rosa pointed at the kitchen table. "Sit."

Liam sat.

"Tell me from the beginning. How long has this been going on?"

Dear God, did the torture never end? But now he'd started, Liam felt unable to stop, because despite Rosa's suspicions that Mike knew all about it, he hadn't mentioned Zac to Mike since his drunken confession in the pub, and suddenly, the weight in his heart was too much to bear.

He took a deep breath and returned to the start, back to that heady night outside the club, and told Rosa everything, right up to when he'd picked up that damn fucking syringe and the bubble he'd imagined around him and Zac had burst into a thousand pieces.

Rosa listened in silence until Liam's sorry tale was done, and then she sat back and folded her arms, a sure sign she was about to say something Liam wouldn't like. Not that she could say much that would make him feel worse. Recounting it all out loud had cast a different light on the anger he'd been so quick to assume. And even if the worst had been true, if only he'd stopped to listen, he could, perhaps, have even helped Zac—

"Have you considered the possibility that the syringe wasn't his? Or at least, that he didn't have it for the reasons you thought?"

Despite Liam's train of thought, it was the last thing he'd expected Rosa to say. "That's what you want to talk about here? Not the fact that I hired a hooker to keep me company?"

"The fact that Zac's a hooker is kind of irrelevant now, don't you think? It's obvious that you were drawn to him because you're lonely."

"Lonely?"

Rosa rolled her eyes. "Don't. Your husband died. You're lonely. Deal with it."

"By banging a hooker?"

"No, by accepting that you did it for a reason, and that reason won't go away just because you bloody want it to. How did you feel when you were with him?"

Liam shrugged. "I felt alive."

"And?"

"For fuck's sake, Rosa— Okay, I felt alive when I was with Zac, like nothing else existed. I didn't care how many others he'd been with. I only cared about him."

"And now? Do you miss him?"

Liam snorted. "Do I have any right to miss him? I only knew him five minutes."

"So?" Rosa plucked an orange from the fruit bowl, though she made no move to peel it. "Those five minutes changed you. Surely that's worth something?"

"Even if he's a fucking junkie?"

"You don't know that he is, or why he had the syringe. For all you know, he could've found it in the park and pocketed it to stop a kid from doing the same. Don't let losing Cory make you believe the worst is inevitable."

Liam parked Hettie in the library car park behind Norwich High Street and shut the engine off, resisting the urge to rest his pounding head on the steering wheel. Jesus, he hadn't had a hangover this bad in years, but that was what he got for spilling his guts to his sister, then hitting the Hope and Anchor for a night of solitary heavy drinking.

And it hadn't helped his wayward sense of perspective either. Rosa's parting words were echoing in his head, and more than that, he *missed* Zac. He'd been on his mind from the moment they met, but thinking about him now felt all wrong, like he'd lost the right to remember their short time together and didn't deserve the memories.

That's what you get for being a dick. And Liam couldn't deny that, when it had taken a lecture from Rosa for him to realise he'd assumed only the worst before he'd torn Zac apart. He'd ripped Zac's head off, then left him high and dry, blocking his number and changing the locks on the house. *Yeah, 'cause it wasn't enough to assume him a junkie, was it? Gotta be a thief too.*

Liam got out of the van and drifted to the car park's ticket machine, digging in his pocket for change. The urge to hang his head in shame was strong, but there was little point. Rosa's riot act might've led to an epiphany, but her words of wisdom had come too late. Short of hammering on Zac's door and begging forgiveness, there wasn't much he could do—though what was stopping him from doing just that?

"Because you're a stubborn arsehole, like Dad, unless, of course, you're worried Zac's gonna send you packing..."

Rosa was right, but he'd had enough of her voice in his head for the time being. Arsehole or not, he had shit to do; shit that made up the mile-long to-do list that had brought him to Norwich in the first place.

He navigated his way through the crowds of lunchtime shoppers on the high street, searching out the minimalist window display of Sea Rave's only UK store outside of London and Cornwall. As was his habit, he paused when it came into view, observing it for a few moments, as if he'd never seen it before. Usually, he arrived at the store as the friendly grim reaper, bearing a list of things they'd fucked up since his last impromptu visit, and a box of doughnuts to ease the pain, but today, as he stared at the window, he couldn't find it in him to care that the mannequins weren't perpendicular with the signage. Because really, what the fuck did it matter? He was only there because a long-serving staffer was leaving the family to go travelling in Oz.

Liam crossed the street and entered the shop, head down, hiding beneath the baseball cap he'd jammed over his wayward hair, hoping to take a surreptitious look around before he caught the staff's attention, but as the glass door swished shut behind him, a commotion at the tills caught his attention. Sammy, a duty manager, was remonstrating with one of the many homeless men who hung around the city centre.

Fuck's sake. Liam moved quickly to intervene. He stayed out of the day-to-day running of Sea Rave's stores, trusting the retail teams they had in place, but he wouldn't tolerate this crap.

He stepped in front of the man, who slammed his hand down on the counter beside him.

"I don't give a fuck where he is. I need to see him now!"

"All right, mate." Liam pushed the grubby hand off the white counter. "That's enough shouting. What's your problem?"

The scrawny man's haunted, bloodshot gaze flickered over Liam. "Who are you?"

"Doesn't matter who I am. What do you want? Are you buying something? Or hanging around? Because if you're after somewhere to chill out, there's a shelter down the road in the crypt under the church."

"What the fuck would I want to go to church for?"

Liam shrugged. "They do soup and sandwiches at lunchtime if you take a voucher from the Red Cross. I can call them if you want. Get you a meal and a bed for the night?"

"I don't need a bed. I'm looking for someone."

From behind Liam, Sammy tugged on his arm. "Liam, he said he was looking for you."

"What?" Liam glanced over his shoulder.

Sammy shook her head, clearly as bewildered as he was. "He burst in here ten minutes ago, shouting your name. He said something happened to Zac."

Liam's heart stilled, like it had more than a year ago for Cory. He turned back to the man, Sammy and the store instantly forgotten. "Who the hell are you?"

"I'm Jamie—Zac's best friend."

The name meant nothing to Liam, but the fact that Jamie had come to the shop to seek him out filled him with dread. "Tell me what's happened. Now."

"He got hurt," Jamie said. "Hurt bad. You need to come with me and take care of him."

Liam took a step forward, already halfway to wherever Zac was. "Where is he? At the flat?"

Jamie shook his head. "He's at the hospital in King's Lynn. They won't let me see him."

"Why not?"

"Would you?"

Good point. Liam grabbed Jamie's arm and propelled him to the door. "Let's go. You can tell me what happened on the way."

He dragged Jamie out of the shop, ignoring Sammy's alarmed stare. Jamie came willingly enough. They were halfway to the van before he began to squirm. "You don't have to yank me. I'm coming with you."

Liam didn't loosen his hold. "Start talking and I'll stop yanking. What the hell's going on?"

"He got stabbed."

"*What*?" Liam came to an abrupt standstill. "How the fuck did that happen? Did you do it?"

"No!" But the guilt colouring Jamie's eyes was unmistakable.

Liam tightened his grip on Jamie's arm, fury sweeping through him. "Tell me who did."

"I will, I promise, but we need to hurry. They said they might transfer him and they won't tell me where."

The thought of reaching the hospital to find Zac gone got Liam moving again. He dragged Jamie to the van and threw him into the passenger seat. "Don't fucking breathe unless I say so. If I find out this was you, I'll kill you. Do you understand?"

Jamie said nothing, shrinking down in his seat as Liam rounded the front of the van and climbed into the driver's seat, gunning the engine hard enough for Hettie to whine in protest, but he didn't have time to placate her. The hospital in King's Lynn was forty miles away and as far as Liam was concerned, it might as well have been a hundred.

He peeled out of the car park and joined the road that would take them to King's Lynn. With a sharp eye on the speed dial, he turned briefly to Jamie. "Talk."

Jamie shifted in his seat, bringing his knees to his chest. "It was my fault, but I didn't do it—I didn't stab him. You have to believe me."

"How bad is it?"

"Bad. The ambulance guys said it was his artery."

"Which one?"

"His arm."

"Was he conscious?"

Jamie bit his chapped bottom lip. "For a while. He wasn't when they took him away, though. They said they had to operate or he'd die."

"Jesus." Liam shook his head to clear it, swerving around a slow-moving people carrier. "When did this happen?"

"Yesterday. I've been hanging around the hospital all day, but they won't let me near him. Said they'd get the police to kick me out if I kept asking."

Jamie's voice wavered, and his fear was palpable. Liam let him be for a few miles while he mulled over what he knew so far. Liam was no doctor, but he had enough general knowledge to know a wound to a major artery was bad news. What if he got to the hospital to find Zac dead? He gripped the steering wheel tighter, turning his knuckles white. No. Fuck that. He couldn't go through that again.

He cast a glance at Jamie, who appeared to have fallen asleep. "Wake up. You're not done."

Jamie opened his eyes. "What else do you want to know?"

"I want to know why he got stabbed. What went down? And where the hell were you?"

The guilt in Jamie's expression deepened, exposing anguish almost as painful as Liam's own. "They didn't see me. I rolled under the bed and let them go for Zac, because I thought once they realised he wasn't me, they'd leave him alone."

"Who would?"

"I can't tell you that."

"Why were they after for you?"

Jamie tore his broken stare from Liam's and stared out the window, his eyes fixed on the light rain that had begun to fall. "Because I stole their gear."

"Gear?" And then the penny dropped. *Gear* meant *drugs* and even without Liam's propensity to assume the worst, Jamie couldn't have looked more like a junkie if he'd tattooed it on his damned head. "What was it? Heroin?"

"Yes."

"How much?"

"Does it matter?"

"Probably not." Liam steeled himself for the next question. "How was Zac involved in this? Is he a junkie too?"

"Fuck no." The vehemence in Jamie's tone was unnaturally loud in the cramped van. "I mean . . . he used to be, but he's been clean since we moved from London. Six months."

Clean. Somewhere in the terrified chaos that Liam's mind had become, he knew what that meant. "He doesn't take drugs anymore?"

"No. And the syringe you found in his pocket was mine."

Liam couldn't speak for the rest of the journey. Rosa's prophecy was playing on a loop in his brain and he was so angry with himself he could barely breathe.

He threw the van into a space in the hospital car park and jumped out, dashing for the front entrance, leaving Jamie to shuffle behind him. The information desk was straight ahead, manned by a young woman who seemed engrossed in her computer screen. Liam slowed and pulled Jamie to one side. "What's his name?"

"What?"

"Zac. Is that his real name?"

"Of course it is. We're hookers, not MI5."

So Jamie was a hooker too. A dim memory of Zac mentioning a "colleague" flashed into Liam's mind, but they didn't have time for specifics. "Tell me everything you know about him, and leave the rest to me. If they ask you anything, just agree with what I've said."

Jamie rambled off a barrage of information, most of it useless. Liam stopped him. "Okay, okay." He shrugged out of his jacket. "Put this on and tell me Zac's name and date of birth."

Jamie obeyed, and once he appeared a little less like a tramp, they approached the front desk, Liam sporting his best impression of Cory in full charm mode.

The receptionist glanced up with a yawn. "Can I help you?"

Liam smiled. "Hope so. I'm looking for Zac Payne? He was brought in yesterday."

"Date of birth?"

Liam repeated the date Jamie had told him. The receptionist typed it in, then frowned at her computer screen. "Are you a relative?"

"No, I'm his employer, and this is Jamie, his next of kin."

Beside him, Jamie squirmed. Liam trod on his foot, and he stilled with a startled yelp, but the receptionist didn't seem to notice. She tapped her keyboard a few more times, then pointed to a sign above a nearby set of double doors. "He's on the HDU ward. Go through those doors and turn left. Give your details to the desk there and they'll help you."

They went through the doors and braved another reception desk, where a stern-faced nurse directed them to a waiting room. Then they were alone briefly until a doctor and a female police officer joined them.

The policewoman acknowledged Jamie. "Is this the man you were talking about?"

Jamie nodded. "Zac works for him. He's going to help us."

Liam extended his hand. "I'm Liam Mallaney. Zac is doing some work experience with my company. Do you need to see ID?"

It was obvious the woman recognised him from God-knew-where, but she nodded anyway. Liam produced his driving license and the tense atmosphere in the small room faded a touch. "Jamie said you won't let him see Zac. Is there a reason he can't have visitors?"

The doctor and policewoman exchanged a glance before the doctor met Liam's gaze. "Zac has been in surgery overnight. We wanted to stabilise him before we let anyone in."

"Is he stable now?"

"He lost a lot of blood. We gave him a transfusion and repaired the artery, but he has shown some signs of hypovolemic shock. We're going to need to keep an eye on him for a few days, check his kidney function and electrolyte balance."

Jamie leaned forward. "But he's okay, right? He's not going to die?"

"He's better than he was this morning, but he's still quite unwell," the doctor said. "We'll know more in the next twenty-four hours."

"Is he awake?" Liam asked.

The doctor shook his head. "No. I wouldn't expect him to come round until the morning at least."

There wasn't much else to say. The doctor agreed to move Zac to a side room reserved for private patients so that Liam and Jamie could sit with him, and, after handing Liam the paperwork to pay for the privilege, left them in the care of the severe-looking nurse.

The policewoman lingered, eyeing Jamie. "If I leave you with Mr. Mallaney, are you going to behave yourself? No more shouting at nurses or disturbing the other patients?"

Jamie's brooding frown turned sullen. "I only shouted because you wouldn't let me see Zac."

"The doctor explained why you couldn't see Zac. And I kept you at the flat initially because I needed your statement. We're on your side here, Jamie. We just want to know what happened to Zac so we can ensure whoever was responsible is caught. You understand that, don't you?"

Jamie grunted, and the policewoman admitted defeat. She gestured for Liam to follow her out of the room. In the corridor, she turned her probing gaze on him. "How well do you know Jamie?"

Liam shrugged, choosing his words carefully. "Enough to know he's close to Zac. Don't know much else."

"How long has Zac worked for you?"

"A month or so."

"Seems a little overboard for you to come down here for an employee you've only known a month. Your company must keep you busy."

So she had recognised him, and now she was trying to rattle him. *Fuck you, lady.* "Zac's been doing work experience at my home office. We'll be offering him a permanent contract soon. And anyway, we treat our employees as family. Google us. You'll see."

She was clearly far from convinced, but as a nurse appeared in the corridor, Liam ran out of patience. He called Jamie forward and left the policewoman behind, following the nurse to Zac's new room.

"Here he is," she said. "We'll be in and out to check on him through the night. Don't worry. We'll tell you if there's anything to worry about."

She left the room. Jamie appeared about ready to drop, so Liam directed him to a chair before he found the balls to take a proper look at Zac.

What he saw horrified him. Zac on the hospital bed, an IV jammed in his hand and tubes in his nose. It was hard to see where the pillow ended and his deathly white face began. Only his slightly blue lips stood out—them, and the massive bandage wrapped around his left wrist, grotesquely contrasting the delicate leather bracelet he still wore on his right.

Liam wanted to kiss those blue lips, stroke Zac's hair, and whisper in his ear that he was safe now, that whatever happened, Liam would take care of it, take care of *him*, for as long as Zac let him, but with Jamie trembling in the seat beside him, Liam remained silent. This wasn't about him. Besides, there was no guarantee Zac would even wake up, let alone accept his help.

"When did they say he'd wake up?"

The echo in Jamie's shaky voice startled Liam. "Erm, the morning, I think? He's had surgery, remember, as well as losing a lot of blood from the original injury."

"I can't handle this." Jamie rubbed his eyes. "I thought he'd wake up when you came in."

"Why'd you think that?"

Jamie shrugged. "He likes you."

Liam's heart twisted painfully. "I like him too."

"I figured. You wouldn't have come with me otherwise. Or given that copper what for."

"I didn't do that. She was only doing her job. All I asked her for was an explanation."

Jamie grunted, reminding Liam that their views of the police were likely worlds apart. "Zac's going to need you."

"He'll need us both," Liam said absently, giving in to the urge to lay his hand on Zac's cool forehead. "Recovering from any operation is rough. He's going to be tired and in pain." *And likely fucking traumatised.*

"He doesn't need me. He'll be better off without me."

"Why? Where are you going?"

"Where do you think?" Jamie glared at Liam like he was the world's biggest idiot. "They won't stop coming for us until they get their money, or we're both dead. I've gotta give myself up. I can't let Zac live with my shit anymore."

"Zac wouldn't want you to let them kill you. Why don't you just give back what you stole?"

"The gear?" Jamie snorted. "I shot most of it, then Zac chucked what I had left out of the window. Didn't want it in his flat."

Liam closed his eyes and tried to picture Zac flinging piles of heroin out of an open window. Perversely, the image didn't come to him as easily as the one of him shooting up in Liam's bathroom. "Why the hell did you nick it in the first place?"

"'Cause I needed it."

The answer seemed obvious, but as Liam reached over Zac's prone form and found his good hand, he felt like he'd missed something. "But you always need it, right? What made this so tempting?"

"My pimp kept fucking me over, sending me out to work all night, then keeping my money, and my shit. One day I saw Irvine, his guy, put a bag in the boot of his car. I knew what it was, so I took it. I—I thought I'd cut it and sell it. Make crap-loads of money and give it to Zac so he didn't have to hook anymore. He didn't like it after he met you. He never said, but I could tell. He wanted you."

"He had me." The words were said before Liam realised he'd spoken aloud. "He had me, Jamie, and he can have me again, if that's what he wants."

"I don't think Zac's ever had what he wants."

Liam sighed. "And what do *you* want? I can give you the money to pay your debt, but I don't reckon it will make your life any better. You're shaking like a bloody leaf. You need a hit, don't you?"

Jamie's teeth chattered as he sucked in a clearly painful breath. "Don't matter what I need."

"Why not?"

"Because I fucked everything up. I'd have offed meself if Zac had died."

Liam didn't doubt it. He couldn't quite get a handle on the relationship Jamie had with Zac, but it was obvious he cared for Zac a great deal, and if Liam knew anything, it was how it felt to have the person you cared about most snatched away.

An idea began to take shape in his fragmented mind. "I need to make some calls. Will you be okay by yourself for a bit?"

"No, but I won't leave him, if that's what you're asking."

And the rest, but Liam took Jamie at his word anyway, and left the room, though each step away from Zac was like a kick to the gut.

He'd only gone a little way down the corridor before he couldn't bring himself to go any further. Phone in hand, he found a quiet corner and called Rosa, blurting out the vaguest explanation in the world before asking her to go to the house and take the dogs for the night. He hung up before she found the words to respond.

Next he left Mike a voice mail, telling him he'd be out of the office until further notice and the business was in his hands, and then, after warning Mike he'd likely need a monumental favour from him sometime soon, he made the call that had driven him from Zac's side in the first place.

It took a while for Sea Rave's California office to pick up, and even longer for the girl who answered the phone to find Marv, the company's US director . . . and Cory's youngest brother.

"Hey, dude," Liam said when he finally came on the line. "What was the name of that rehab retreat we sponsored last year?"

CHAPTER
FIFTEEN

Sleep wrapped itself around Zac like a comforting quicksand, sucking him under every time the flicker of light stinging his eyes grew too bright to bear, but like most pleasant things he'd experienced, too soon the comfort of oblivion began to fade.

Groaning, Zac rolled over, reaching for Jamie, who was bound to be sleeping like a corpse, whatever time it was, making the most of being tucked up safe in Zac's bed, but a jolt of pain stilled him before he found Jamie's bony ribs. "*Shit.*"

"Easy." Warm hands that definitely weren't Jamie's gripped Zac's shoulders and rolled him back the way he'd come. "Don't move too much yet."

Zac's brain was sluggish, like he'd loaded himself with junk cut with Valium, but as he opened his eyes, it rebooted, replaying his last memories at rocket speed, dizzying and terrifying him in equal measure.

He bolted upright, ignoring the agony in his left arm and the sharp scratch in his right. Where the hell was Jamie? And the men who'd come for him? Had they found him? Killed him—

"*Zac.*" The warm hands on his shoulders tightened their hold. "Calm down. It's okay, I promise. You're safe here. Jamie's safe. Everything's going to be okay."

His eyes found the hands, struggling to focus enough to see who they belonged to. He looked up as his vision cleared and as kind brown eyes stared back at him, there was no doubt in Zac's mind that he was fucking dreaming. "Liam?"

"It's me."

It couldn't be. Zac didn't believe it. Liam had chucked him out of his house, cast him aside as the no-good junkie he was. Why the hell would he be here, in a hospital room, smiling and holding Zac so tenderly that Zac would've cried if it had been real?

Go back to sleep, idiot. Zac closed his eyes, but his head was spinning too hard for him to stand it for long. Nausea surged through him. He opened his eyes again, but found his tongue too late to warn imaginary Liam that he was about to puke all over his vintage Vans.

Zac heaved painfully over the side of the bed, fearing with each retch that the hallucination would evaporate and perspective would return, confirming that Jamie was indeed dead, and Zac had honoured his memory by diving back into the junk. But it didn't happen. As his stomach emptied itself on the shiny hospital floor, the hands rubbing his neck and stroking his hair from his face only became more vivid.

The sickness finally eased.

"Come on now," Liam said gently. "I know you're confused, but I need you to trust me for a moment and lie down, okay? Then I can tell you everything that's happened while you've been sleeping."

"How long have I been out? Where's Jamie?"

"He's safe. And you've been in and out since he brought you in a couple of days ago."

Zac shook his head. "No . . . that's already happened. I've already done this. Jamie brought me here months ago, but that's over. I'm clean. I don't do that shit anymore."

"I know. And I'm sorry I didn't give you a chance to tell me that before, but this isn't about the drugs. You got hurt, remember? In the flat? Someone was looking for Jamie and they found you instead."

Zac's brain whirred too fast to match Liam's words with what his brain already knew. "I don't understand. Why— How are you here?"

"Lie down, Zac."

Dazed, Zac obeyed, allowing Liam to arrange him in a way that was instantly less painful. "I've done this before, you know that, right? I OD'd and Jamie brought me to a hospital. He saved my life."

Liam smiled tightly. "No wonder you're so close. He's probably saved you again. From what I can tell, it was him who called the ambulance."

"He shoulda left me on the floor of that squat. Saved you all the trouble."

"Don't say that. I know you've had it hard, but you're still here for a reason."

Guilt hit Zac in a dizzying wave. Life had been shit for him at almost every turn, but Liam hadn't had it easy either. "I'm sorry."

"What for? It's not like you stabbed yourself."

"Stabbed?"

Liam wiped Zac's mouth with something wet that smelled of lemon. "I told you, Jamie got in some trouble and you got caught up in it. Someone looking for him found you, stabbed you in the arm, and cut your artery. You lost a *lot* of blood. You've had surgery to repair it, but you're still in a little bit of shock. Put that with the anaesthetic and it's no wonder you feel fucked."

Fucked wasn't the word. Zac stared at his bandaged arm. He couldn't picture the event . . . the knife, the blood, but somehow the sound of the blade piercing his skin was deafening. His stomach rolled again. "Where's Jamie?"

"Um . . ." Liam let his hands fall from Zac and moved to the end of the bed, grabbing a roll of blue paper and using it to blot up the mess Zac had made on the floor. "I kind of sent him away."

"What?" Zac struggled to sit up. "You said he was safe, not back out there for—"

Liam held up his hands. "He *is* safe, I promise. My brother-in-law has him. He got him a passport and an ESTA, and took him to California."

Zac stilled in his feeble attempts to swing his legs out of bed. "California? As in . . . America?"

Liam nodded. Zac opened his mouth. Shut it. "I think I'm missing something. Did you seriously just tell me Jamie's gone to *California* with your brother-in-law?"

"Er . . . yeah. It seemed like a good idea at the time, and I'm hoping you're not going to be too mad about it."

"What's in California?"

"Rehab."

"Rehab?"

Liam nodded. "He didn't believe he could do it alone, so I offered him some help. Sounds like it wouldn't hurt for him to disappear for a while either."

"Rehab." Zac repeated like Liam hadn't spoken. "I didn't think he was ready."

"Perhaps he's not. Doesn't mean it's not worth trying, though."

"I don't know what to say."

"Don't say anything, then. We can talk more later."

"You're going to stay? Even though you know I'm a junkie as well as a hooker?"

Liam sighed. "No, I'm staying because I want to. I don't care about any of that stuff, Zac, and I'm sorry I ever made you feel like crap because of it. I should've given you a chance to tell me that syringe was Jamie's. Perhaps if I had, we could've helped him sooner and none of this would've happened."

The rational part of Zac's brain could hardly believe Liam knew so much about him now, but the other less logical part didn't care. Liam knew he was a junkie and had accepted him as a whore long ago. With Jamie safely on his way to who knew where on the other side of the world, nothing else seemed to matter, save the desire to learn more about the man who'd made it happen. "Will you tell me how your husband died?"

"Why do you want to know that?"

"Because you're still here."

Liam smiled softly, seeming to understand Zac's cryptic answer, which was lucky, because Zac barely understood it himself. Liam pulled a chair close to the bed, absently taking Zac's good hand. "There's not much to it, really. He was cycling home from work one day, and he didn't make it. Farm truck backed out of a lane. He never stood a chance."

"Where did it happen? In Newquay?"

"Yes. If Holkham is my spiritual home, Newquay was Cory's. Only reason I didn't bury him there was because he'd once specifically told me not to. Said he wanted to be by the North Sea because it had the best fish." Liam shook his head slightly, his tight expression growing fond before it tensed again. "You want me to tell you how he died, but I reckon it would make more sense if I told you how he lived."

"I'm listening," Zac said softly.

"I told you we met in India, right?"

Zac nodded.

"We followed each other around the world for a while after that, California, Bali, Mexico. I thought we were travelling for fun. I didn't realise Cory was searching for his next big idea until he dreamed up Sea Rave. He was the brains behind it, you know. I just drew a couple of T-shirts."

"I doubt that's true." Zac reluctantly relinquished Liam's hand as Liam got up from his chair and drifted to the window, staring out at whatever lay beyond. "You're the brains behind it now."

Liam snorted. "Hardly. He had a ten-year plan to save the world. I'm merely seeing it through."

"He sounds amazing."

"He was. Cory taught me so much—before you, he was the only bloke I'd ever slept with. But after he'd gone, I looked back on the time I had with him and wondered if I'd always known I wouldn't have him forever, like it had been too good to be true, you know?"

Zac didn't. As he absorbed the fact that Liam had slept with just two men in all the years Zac had spent being fucked by more than he could count, Liam's life seemed like another world to him, the kind of world he'd never have even thought to dream of if they hadn't met. "You must miss him."

"Course I do, but I've come to accept that we weren't meant to grow old together. Perhaps he was sent to guide me. I wouldn't have done half as much with my life if I hadn't met him, and I'll always love him for that."

Zac absorbed the quiet conclusion of Liam's story. He'd expected to be jealous again of the bond Liam had shared with Cory, but he was only overwhelmed with sadness at what Liam had endured on his path to Zac's bed. He'd give Liam back to Cory in a heartbeat if he could, if it eased his grief... grief that was likely no longer reserved for his lost love. "How's your dad?"

Liam shook his head. "Honestly? I don't know. Rosa and I were always terrified that putting him into a home would finish him off, but we moved him a few days ago, and if anything, I think he's happier."

"Perhaps he understands that he's in a different place, rather than staring at his own house and wondering why he doesn't know it."

"You're probably right."

Liam reclaimed Zac's hand, though his liquid gaze was a million miles away. It felt selfish to pull him back, but Zac missed him, damn it, even for the few short moments he was gone.

He squeezed Liam's fingers. "Are you okay?"

"Hmm?" Liam looked up, blinking. "Oh, yeah. I don't talk about this shit very often, though. Until you came along, everyone I cared about had lived it with me, so I didn't have to."

"I'm sorry. I shouldn't have—"

Liam silenced Zac with a brief kiss to his knuckles. "It's okay. Perhaps if I'd talked about it more, I wouldn't be such a wreck."

"Are you? A wreck, I mean. You seem pretty together to me."

"Why? 'Cause I've got money? It's all bullshit, Zac. None of it means much when you're so lonely you can't get out of bed in the morning."

Zac's heart ached, eclipsing the pain in his bandaged arm. "I don't want you to be lonely."

"Well, maybe we can work on that together, eh?"

Zac couldn't think of anything he'd rather do. He tugged on Liam's hand, drawing him down until their faces were inches apart and they were milliseconds from sharing the kisses Zac had missed so much. "I'd like that."

Liam rewarded Zac with a kiss that lifted him from the bed and cocooned him in the gentle warmth he'd always found with Liam, the comforting fog that was better than any high he'd chased before. Then Liam pulled away with a comical grin.

"What's so funny?"

"You know what we've just done, don't you?"

Zac frowned. "Um . . . kissed?"

"Yeah, and had one of those cheesy reconciliations you see in crap films, you know, where the hero gets shot or some shit and his lover, who he pissed off at the tipping point of the film, comes rushing to his hospital bedside and they live happily ever after?"

"Are you saying I've pissed you off?" *'Cause it's highly unlikely he's calling you a hero.*

Liam laughed. "No! I'm saying we've become a little bit mainstream . . . normal, and I like it."

Zac was officially mystified, but the rare sight of Liam laughing proved too distracting for him to ponder his confusion much. With his wide smile and sparkling eyes, Liam was fucking beautiful, and he was all Zac would ever need.

EPILOGUE

Zac pressed the Stop button on the portable CD player in Len's room. The calming tones of the older man's favourite Vaughan Williams album shut off with a quiet click. Zac waited a moment to see if he'd stir, but Liam's father remained peacefully asleep; a sight that warmed Zac's ever-growing heart.

He left Len to rest and made his way out of the nursing home, waving good-bye to the nurse on the front desk. "Bye, Jan."

She smiled. "See you soon, Zac. Be safe."

Zac timed his exit to perfection and caught the next bus back to Holkham.

The journey took forty-five long, rumbling minutes. To pass the time, he pulled out his battered smartphone and engrossed himself in his new favourite pastime: scrolling through pictures of Liam, of him and Liam, the dogs, the nephews, and the rest of the family who'd welcomed him with open arms, asking no questions of his past, or why he'd stumbled into their lives six months ago, broken and scarred, and entirely dependent on Liam. He came to an image of them all together, taken on Christmas Day at Liam's house, Zac's face half-hidden by Jazz's woolly coat, and he couldn't recall ever being so happy as he had been then.

A message flashed up on his phone screen. He opened it with little thought, assuming it was from Liam. Jamie's profile caught him off guard, and then he remembered the date: May fourth. It was Jamie's birthday and Zac had forgotten.

Not that Jamie was complaining. His message simply read: *Skype?*

Zac chewed on his bottom lip. Aside from text messages, it had been months since they'd last talked, and even longer since they'd laid eyes on each other. With Jamie far away in California, Zac had relied on Liam for updates on his well-being, and though he'd missed him, without his drama, Zac felt more free than he had in years.

Free. The word chewed its way into Zac's conscience. Jamie was clean now, by all accounts, and living on the coast with some friends of Liam's, working in the company canteen, and attending night school in his spare time. It sounded amazing, but as hard as Zac tried, he couldn't see it, couldn't picture Jamie as anything other than the shambolic junkie who'd twice saved his life.

Think you can manage a video call on his birthday, don't you?

Zac got off the bus in Holkham and hurried home, hoping Liam would be there to help him reason his way to the right path, but as he jogged up the driveway, he saw Hettie was gone from her space and the porch door was shut. *Damn it.*

Still brooding, Zac let himself in, bending down to greet the dogs before they knocked him over. A barrage of paws and licks later, he scrambled to his feet and went to Liam's office, both dogs trotting behind him, bumping his legs with their wet noses. He powered up the iMac and logged into the Skype application, searching out the profile Jamie used to talk to Liam when Zac wasn't around. He hovered over it a moment, before biting the bullet and placing the call.

The weird, bubbling dial tone filled the silent room. Zac sat in Liam's chair and whistled Jazz to him, seeking solace in his dark, shaggy coat, a tic that had become a habit since he'd come to live with Liam in Holkham. Jazz was every bit as nuts as Dave, but he always seemed to know when Zac needed a comforting bulk on his lap.

"Zac?"

Zac jumped. For all that he'd placed the call, Jamie's tentative voice had scared the bejesus out of him. He peered through the wispy tufts on Jazz's head. A grainy face had filled the widescreen monitor, but it took Zac a few moments to match it with his last memories of Jamie. "Shit. You're blond."

Jamie laughed. "Hello to you too."

"You're blond," Zac repeated. "How the fuck did that happen?"

"Same way it happens to anyone else. I bleached it, it turned orange, and then the sun did the rest. What do you think? Am I as cool as Liam? Could I pass for a surfer?"

Zac snorted, because whatever Jamie did to himself, he'd never be as cool as Liam—*no one* was as cool as Liam. How could they be, when Liam didn't even have to try? "I think you look well."

And it was true. With his bleached blond hair and tanned skin, and the extra stone in weight he'd gained, Jamie looked fucking amazing.

"Thanks," Jamie said sincerely. "You look good too. How's things going? Liam told me about the, er, dead guy."

Zac swallowed as bile bubbled in his throat. With Jamie off the scene, Liam had encouraged Zac to talk to the police, telling them the truth about the attack, that he really had been an innocent victim of his mysterious assailant's brutal attempt to kill him. He'd claimed not to know the motives behind it, and believing him, the police had linked his statement with information they'd already had and launched a series of raids across the city, but the action had come too late to catch the man who'd left his mark on Zac's arm. Police divers had found his body in the canal a few weeks later, riddled with stab wounds. It seemed karma had caught him first.

"You don't feel bad about it, do you?" Jamie asked when Zac didn't speak.

Zac shrugged. "Do you?"

"No. Irvine was a cunt. I saw him kick the shit out of a pregnant girl because she was a fiver short. You'd think I'd have known better than to—" Jamie stopped and took a deep breath. "I do feel bad, Zac. I feel bad about what happened to *you*. I know that was my fault, and I'll never forgive myself, but I can't spend the rest of my life obsessing about shit I can't change."

"When did you get so wise?"

"When your boyfriend put me through five months of hippie therapy. I swear down, I seriously came out of that place wanting to wrap myself in hessian and eat quinoa for the rest of my life."

Zac was lost, and his face hurt. It took him a moment to realise it was because he was smiling so hard. "What the hell is quinoa?"

Jamie grinned too. "I'm still trying to find out. I'll let you know."

"How long are you going to stay? In America, I mean?"

Jamie sobered. "Um, that's kinda what I wanted to talk to you about. Marv's offered me a better job, running the factory canteen. I said no at first because I thought it would be crappy school dinners or some shit, but it's actually pretty fucking cool. It's like Wagamama's on acid."

Zac could've done without the drug reference, but having seen how Sea Rave operated on this side of the pond, he could well believe that their staff canteen in California was awesome. "So you're going to stay?"

"I might as well. You're in love with Liam, aren't you?"

Zac frowned. "What's that got to do with it?"

"Mate, if you don't know, then I really should stay here. Be far easier on both of us than me making a complete arse of myself."

It took far longer than it should've for the penny to drop, and even when it did, it made little sense to Zac. He hadn't been through the therapy Jamie had, but he knew enough about addiction to be sure that neither one of them had been capable of loving the other as much as they'd loved the junk. "You don't love me like that. You think you do because you don't know any better, but you'll meet someone soon and you'll see I'm right. You're going to love someone else, Jay, and love them hard, and you'll never look at the world the same way again."

"Is that what happened to you with Liam?"

"Yes."

"You love him?"

"Yes." It felt good to say it, even tinged by the brief hurt in Jamie's now clear-blue gaze. "I do. I love him."

"Then I'm going to stay here and cook poshed-up ramen for American hipsters, and keep searching for my cool-dude Prince Charming."

"Okay."

"So I'm staying."

"Okay."

"I'm going to go now . . . I have to work."

"Okay."

"Is that all you're going to say to me?"

Zac shook his head. "No. There's one more thing."

"Shoot."

"Happy birthday, mate. I miss you."

Liam let himself into the house to find Zac lying on the living room floor, tossing a rubber ball into the kitchen for Dave to charge after, knocking over everything in her path. By the destruction already wreaked, it looked like they'd been at their game for a while. "Where's Jazz?"

Zac turned his head to the left. "In his bed. He's got the hump."

Liam grinned. Jazz often got jealous if Zac played with Dave, skulking to his bed to sulk until Zac went to get him. "What about Dad? Did he have the hump too?"

Zac finally treated Liam to one of his favourite grins. "Not at all. We played poker for a bit, then watched the Towcester races. It was fun."

"Yeah? I'll come with you tomorrow, if you want?"

"It's not about what I want. It's about you and your dad enjoying each other."

Easy for Zac to say: he'd never known Len as anything more than the skatty, bumbling old man he was now. For Liam, visiting Len was devastating, even on his good days.

"You might wish you were anywhere else on earth when you're there," Zac said when Liam failed to respond. "But if you don't spend this time with him, you'll regret it forever after he's gone."

Shame rippled briefly through Liam's veins. Zac had been his rock as he'd tried to confront the reality of Len's illness, and despite the heavy dose of denial that often kept him from Len's side, his heart knew Zac's wise words to be true. "I'm in. Remind me to bring Dad's bridge set. The nurse said it would be good for him to play, right?"

"Right."

Zac's gaze turned absent. Liam frowned. "Okay, so if Dad had a good day, what's got you chewing a wasp?"

"I talked to Jamie."

Ah. Liam had wondered when that would happen, and when Jamie would tell Zac of the job Marv had offered him now that he'd completed the rehab stage of his recovery and proved himself serious about staying clean. "How did it go?"

"You know, don't you?"

"About the job? Yes. Marv ran it by me, but I let him decide. It's none of my business. He runs Cali."

"That's not what I meant. I know you don't interfere with the overseas operations."

Liam frowned. Zac often bemused him, but never more so than when he slipped back into the guarded persona he'd had when they'd first met. "What did you mean, then?"

"Jamie loves me."

Oh. Liam had suspected that to be the case, but he'd kind of assumed Zac knew. "Is that a bad thing? You love him too, don't you?"

"Not like that. Not like I love you."

Warmth flooded Liam's veins. He knew Zac loved him, it was in every gentle touch and soft smile, every bruising kiss and clash of teeth, but Zac didn't often say it. "You really love me?"

Zac peered up at Liam. "Of course I do."

"Good. I suppose I should tell you I love you too, eh?"

"Only if it's true."

Liam dropped to the floor, covering Zac with his body and capturing his lips in a searching kiss, before he found Zac's gaze and held it firm. "You know it's bloody true. Told you enough, haven't I?"

Zac's eyes blazed and he licked his lips, then his expression sobered. "I don't expect you to love me like you did him."

Liam wished he had the words to explain to Zac that there was nothing Cory would've wanted more than for him to love someone the way he loved Zac. Instead, he smiled and mussed Zac's hair. "And I don't love you the way I loved Cory. It's totally different because I love *you*, and it's fucking amazing."

"Even though I'm an unemployed junkie hooker?"

"You're not unemployed. You're part of the family like everyone else. And as far as I know, you've been clean since long before I met you. At most, you're a retired hooker, and that's the reason we found each other, so it ain't all bad."

Zac didn't seem convinced, but Liam had come to accept it would take a long time for Zac to believe he was worthy of the new life he'd worked so hard for. Zac's past did haunt Liam sometimes, but only because it had nearly taken Zac from him before they'd had a chance to be who they were now. Judgement was for other folk. Not Liam.

"So . . ." Liam pushed Zac's longer hair out of his eyes. "Has Jamie made a decision?"

"He's staying."

"And how do you feel about that?"

Zac shrugged. "Dunno. I mean, it's not like I've seen him in months, is it? What right have I got to feel bad about it?"

"Every right. He's your friend."

Zac looked up at Liam. "He was more than a friend for a long time, but you already know that, don't you?"

Liam couldn't deny it. He'd spent so long knowing little about what made Zac tick, but that fateful night in the hospital with Jamie, and the weeks that followed, watching Zac recover from his horrific injury and adjust to life in Liam's world, had given him some clues to the things he might've missed otherwise. "I know your relationship is complex."

"And you don't mind?"

"Why would I? You are who you are, Zac. We both are."

"I really do love you."

Liam smiled. "I know. Now stop chucking that ball around and come to bed with me."

He led Zac upstairs, tugging him into the bedroom and shutting the door behind them, leaving the dogs to their own devices. He pushed Zac onto the bed and straddled him, unbuttoning his jeans, taking control the way Zac often seemed to want him to, especially when he'd had a challenging day. "What do you want?"

Zac licked his lips. "You know what I want."

"Say it." Liam freed his cock and rubbed it on Zac's lips. "I want to hear you say it."

"I wanna fuck you."

Heat surged through Liam. He'd started bottoming for Zac when he'd come home from the hospital, unable to bring himself to fuck him, fearing he'd lose control, hurt Zac even more than he'd been hurt already. He'd got over it—*they'd* got over it—but the new dynamic in their physical relationship had remained, hot and heady, like a good addiction, if there was such a thing.

Liam pushed all thoughts of the past aside and stripped, making short work of his own, and then Zac's. With them both bare to the seaside chill, he lubed up, rolled a condom onto Zac, then sank down on his cock, taking Zac inside with a long, slow slide.

Zac gasped and threw his head back, digging his nails into Liam's hips. "You do something to me. Never felt anything—*fuck*—like it."

Liam grinned. It was good news if Zac was incoherent already. He ground down a little harder, losing himself in Zac's throaty moans and desperate, grasping hands. He'd had great sex before—with Cory— but nothing like the inferno he and Zac had been building from the start, the unpredictable coil of pleasure that fluctuated between them fucking all night long, or coming in ten seconds flat.

This time they seemed destined to collapse in a sweaty heap of limbs before they'd truly got started. Zac tightened his hold on Liam's hips and drove up into him, once, twice, three times, growling with every thrust. Liam's head spun, and he came without warning, painting Zac's chest, only dimly aware of Zac following suit.

When it was over and they'd cleaned up, Liam lay on his back, holding Zac close as they watched the sun set over the beach. "Would you like to visit Jamie in California? Now you've bullied me into designing again, I'll have to go over there eventually."

"I did not bully you."

"I know." Liam met Zac's mock glare with a shrug. "I'm messing with you because I want you to know how much you've inspired me."

"Be easier to just tell me, wouldn't it?"

Zac had him there. "I couldn't draw before I met you. Was too fucking lonely and morbid. Sea Rave was founded on life. You gave me mine back."

For a long moment, Zac's eyes blazed with a heat that had nothing to do with the scent of sweat and sex lingering in the air, then he bit his lip and shyly looked away. "I was the one that needed saving, mate."

"We're not going to agree on this, are we?"

"Probably not."

Liam let it go. "So what about Cali? Wanna go?"

Zac's shrug was barely detectable. "Maybe one day. You'd come with me, wouldn't you?"

"I'd go anywhere with you."

Zac smiled. "Really?"

"Of course. Name your place. We can be there by tomorrow."

Zac thought on it a moment, then shook his head. "You know what? I'm fine right here, and I think I will be for a long time . . . at least until the Sea Rave Festival next month."

Liam's grin suddenly matched Zac's, breaking his face in half. Given Zac's addiction history, he hadn't thought a festival—even one as tame as Sea Rave—would've been possible, but he couldn't have been more wrong. Zac wanted to learn to surf, sit around the fire pits, and eat vegan burgers, and better than that, he wanted to do it with Liam. Which meant for the first time since Cory had died, Liam couldn't think of a better way to spend a summer that every beat of his heart told him was going to be magical. He kissed Zac fiercely, lost in his blazing eyes. "I can't wait, but if it's gonna happen, we'd better get up. Rosa says we're not going anywhere until we move Dad's vinyl from her dining room."

"And Rosa's in charge, right?"

"Right." Liam kissed Zac again. "Trust me, babe, as far as our family's concerned, that's all you ever need to know."

Dear Reader,

Thank you for reading Garrett Leigh's *Rented Heart*!

We know your time is precious and you have many, many entertainment options, so it means a lot that you've chosen to spend your time reading. We really hope you enjoyed it.

We'd be honored if you'd consider posting a review—good or bad—on sites like **Amazon, Barnes & Noble, Kobo, Goodreads, Twitter, Facebook, Tumblr,** and your blog or website. We'd also be honored if you told your friends and family about this book. Word of mouth is a book's lifeblood!

For more information on upcoming releases, author interviews, blog tours, contests, giveaways, and more, please sign up for our weekly, spam-free newsletter and visit us around the web:

Newsletter: tinyurl.com/RiptideSignup
Twitter: twitter.com/RiptideBooks
Facebook: facebook.com/RiptidePublishing
Goodreads: tinyurl.com/RiptideOnGoodreads
Tumblr: riptidepublishing.tumblr.com

Thank you so much for Reading the Rainbow!

RiptidePublishing.com

ALSO BY
GARRETT LEIGH

Misfits
Between Ghosts
What Remains
Slide
Marked
Rare
Freed
Bullet
Bones
Bold
Only Love
Awake and Alive
Heart
My Mate Jack
Lucky Man
More than Life
Shadow Bound

ABOUT
THE AUTHOR

Garrett Leigh is an award-winning British writer and book designer, currently working for Dreamspinner Press, Loose Id, Riptide Publishing, and Fox Love Press.

Garrett's debut novel, Slide, won Best Bisexual Debut at the 2014 Rainbow Book Awards, and her polyamorous novel, Misfits is a finalist in the 2016 Lambda Literary awards.

When not writing, Garrett can generally be found procrastinating on Twitter, cooking up a storm, or sitting on her behind doing as little as possible, all the while shouting at her menagerie of children and animals and attempting to tame her unruly and wonderful FOX.

Garrett is also an award winning cover artist, taking the silver medal at the Benjamin Franklin Book Awards in 2016. She designs for various publishing houses and independent authors at blackjazzdesign.com.

Enjoy more stories like
Rented Heart
at RiptidePublishing.com!

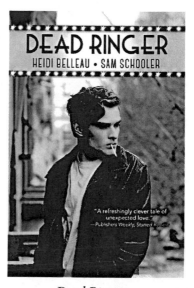

Starting New
ISBN: 978-1-62649-431-2

Dead Ringer
ISBN: 978-1-62649-338-4

Earn Bonus Bucks!

Earn 1 Bonus Buck for each dollar you spend. Find out how at
RiptidePublishing.com/news/bonus-bucks.

Win Free Ebooks for a Year!

Pre-order coming soon titles directly through our site and you'll
receive one entry into a drawing for a chance to win free books for
a year! Get the details at RiptidePublishing.com/contests.

Devolution in the United Kingdom

Vernon Bogdanor FBA

OXFORD
UNIVERSITY PRESS

OXFORD
UNIVERSITY PRESS

Great Clarendon Street, Oxford ox2 6DP

Oxford University Press is a department of the University of Oxford.
It furthers the University's objective of excellence in research, scholarship,
and education by publishing worldwide in

Oxford New York

Athens Auckland Bangkok Bogotá Buenos Aires Calcutta
Cape Town Chennai Dar es Salaam Delhi Florence Hong Kong Istanbul
Karachi Kuala Lumpur Madrid Melbourne Mexico City Mumbai
Nairobi Paris São Paulo Singapore Taipei Tokyo Toronto Warsaw

with associated companies in Berlin Ibadan

Oxford is a registered trade mark of Oxford University Press
in the UK and in certain other countries

Published in the United States
by Oxford University Press Inc., New York

© Oxford University Press 1999

The moral rights of the author have been asserted

First published 1999

British Library Cataloguing in Publication Data

Data available

Library of Congress Cataloging in Publication Data

Data available

ISBN 0-19-289310-6

1 3 5 7 9 10 8 6 4 2

Typeset in Times
by Cambrian Typesetters, Frimley, Surrey

Printed in Great Britain by
Cox & Wyman Ltd,
Reading, Berkshire

For Judy, Paul, and Adam
with thanks

Preface

In 1979, at the time of the referendums, I published a book entitled *Devolution*. This book is based on that earlier work, but it has been almost completely rewritten. Part of the reason for this is obvious. I have had to take account of the legislation of 1998 which, unlike all previous legislation on Home Rule or devolution, with the partial exceptions of the Government of Ireland Act of 1920, and of devolution in Northern Ireland in the years 1974 and 1982-6, will actually come into effect. The years since 1979, moreover, have spawned a large literature on the history and politics of devolution which I have tried to take into account. In addition, although my basic attitudes towards devolution have not changed, I have altered my mind on some important matters. I now feel that, in *Devolution*, I tended to underestimate the scope and depth of Gladstone's attempted resolution of the Irish problem, the problem of holding together a multinational state, as difficult today as it was in the nineteenth century. In writing *Devolution in the United Kingdom*, I have become aware of how much current approaches to devolution owe to Gladstonian precedents. It is a nice coincidence that the third reading of the Scotland Bill in the House of Commons took place on the centenary of Gladstone's death.

Devolution in the United Kingdom seeks to analyse the political and constitutional aspects of Home Rule and devolution from the time of Gladstone's espousal of Irish Home Rule in 1886 to the present day. I hope that, in doing so, it succeeds in casting some light both on how we are governed, and on how constitutional ideas are affected by political realities.

The book was read in draft by Brigid Hadfield and Kenneth Morgan, to its very great advantage. I am grateful also to the following for reading and commenting on various chapters: Nick Barber, Sir Kenneth Bloomfield, Tony Bradley, James Campbell, Sir John Chilcot, Ian Dewar, Sir Nicholas Fenn, Valerie Flint, Sir John Garlick, Sir Michael Quinlan, John Robertson, Conrad Russell, Kevin Sharpe, Michael Steed, Anthony Teasdale, Richard Tur, Brian Walker, Sir Michael Wheeler-Booth, Lord Windlesham, and Patrick Wormald. I am particularly grateful to Michael Steed and Anthony Teasdale for conversations over many years from which I have learnt much about devolution. I should also like to thank Oonagh Gay and David Heald for helping me in various ways. But these kind friends are not to be implicated in my arguments, still less my errors.

I am deeply indebted to the Principal and Fellows of Brasenose College for providing, over a very long period, so stimulating an intellectual atmosphere. I am fortunate indeed to be a member of such a convivial and lively society.

I am grateful also to George Miller of Oxford University Press for being so patient and helpful a publisher, to Shelley Cox, and to Belinda Baker for her skilful copy-editing.

But my greatest debt is to my wife and to my sons, Paul and Adam, for encouraging me to complete this book and for tolerating my constant absences at the word processor.

This book was completed in September 1998 and takes no account of developments since then.

V.B.

Oxford, 1998

Contents

The Making of the United Kingdom

What know they of England
Who only England know?

(Rudyard Kipling, 'The English Flag')

I

Devolution is the most radical constitutional change this country has seen since the Great Reform Act of 1832. This is because it seeks to reconcile two seemingly conflicting principles, the sovereignty or supremacy of Parliament and the grant of self-government in domestic affairs to Scotland, Wales, and Northern Ireland.

The supremacy of Parliament, our central, perhaps our only constitutional doctrine, is of course primarily a legal principle, but its influence resonates throughout our political system, influencing the thought even of those who would seek to escape from it. If the principle has, as some believe, become a fiction, it is, nevertheless, a fiction which remains highly potent.

The principle implies that power is centralized in one supreme and omnicompetent parliament. Westminster, under the British Constitution, is the sun around which every planet revolves. We do not find it easy to think in terms of a separation of powers, nor to understand government as a series of interdependent layers, each with its own rights and responsibilities. We have remained a highly centralized country, more so even than France, traditionally the paradigm of centralized government, which, since 1982, has adopted a policy of regionalism and decentralization. Britain has been, amongst stable democracies, the largest of the unitary states, apart from Japan; no other democracy seeks to manage the affairs of so large a population through a single parliament. Our conception of parliamentary supremacy, moreover, makes it difficult for us to accommodate ourselves to structures of government, such as that of the European Union, whose raison d'être is that of power-sharing. It will make it difficult also for us to accommodate ourselves to the devolution of power downwards to a parliament in Edinburgh, a national assembly in Cardiff, and an assembly in Belfast. European Union and devolution offer complementary challenges to the profoundly unitary nature of the British state. This unitariness, as expressed in the supremacy of Parliament, has been one of the strongest of the tacit understandings which underpin our Constitution.

Our Constitution rests of course on certain defining features of British society. One authority has referred to:

the overwhelming unitariness of British political culture, especially in the great trunk of England, which works against all forms of territorial politics. This anti-territorial dimension is doubtless partly derived from the extraordinary continuity and stability of the British state. ... Equally, too, the extent of cultural homogenization of British society following two hundred years of industrialization must also be taken into account in identifying the components of the anti-territorial bias. Finally, some recognition would need to be given to the relatively low status of sub-national government, to what one observer has called the centre's 'culture of disdain' for it.[1]

The challenge of altering this culture through devolution was first posed in the late nineteenth century when Irish nationalists began to demand Home Rule, an Irish parliament in Dublin. But Westminster refused to concede Home Rule until it was too late to satisfy Irish nationalists. Nevertheless, the Home Rule controversy, which racked British politics between 1885 and 1921, raised the question, which still remains unresolved, of whether Home Rule or devolution, the concession of a local and subordinate parliament in one part of the United Kingdom, is compatible with the supremacy of Westminster and the maintenance of the United Kingdom. The purpose of this book is to answer these questions. First, however, it is necessary to define what we mean by devolution.

Devolution involves the transfer of powers from a superior to an inferior political authority. More precisely, devolution may be defined as consisting of three elements: *the transfer to a subordinate elected body, on a geographical basis, of functions at present exercised by ministers and Parliament.* These functions may be either legislative, the power to make laws, or executive, the power to make secondary laws—statutory instruments, orders, and the like—within a primary legal framework still determined at Westminster.

Devolution involves the creation of an elected body, subordinate to Parliament. It therefore seeks to preserve intact that central feature of the British Constitution, the supremacy of Parliament. Devolution is to be distinguished from federalism, which would divide, not devolve, supreme power between Westminster and various regional or provincial parliaments. In a federal state, the authority of the central or federal government and the provincial governments is co-ordinate and shared, the respective scope of the federal and provincial governments being defined by an enacted constitution as, for example, in the United States or the Federal Republic of Germany. Devolution, by contrast, does not require the introduction of an enacted constitution.

Admittedly, 'federalism' is a term used rather loosely in current discourse in Britain on constitutional change; and in most of the proposals for a 'federal solution' in Britain, 'federal' is intended to mean not a division of power between Westminster and provincial units of government, but rather a policy of devolution applied to the whole country, and not just to parts of it such as Scotland and Wales. Such a policy in the nineteenth and early twentieth centuries was known as 'Home Rule All Round', and such proposals might now be termed 'federal devolution', to avoid confusion with a strictly federal system of government.

Devolution has profound implications for the way in which we are governed, and for the kind of society in which we are to live. One of the main purposes of what follows is to show how the issue has arisen in British politics, and then to spell out the implications of devolving power from Westminster. But to understand the implications of devolution, we need first to understand how the United Kingdom came about, and how it has been held together.

II

The United Kingdom was formed through the coming-together of four nations, England, Wales, Scotland, and Ireland. Wales, Scotland,

and Ireland were joined to England by very different means. Wales was incorporated into England by two Acts of Parliament, in 1536 and 1543; Scotland was made part of the kingdom by means of a treaty signed between two independent states in 1706, and then ratified by the English and Scottish parliaments, thereby creating, in 1707, the new kingdom of Great Britain; while Ireland was made part of the kingdom through Acts of Union passed by Westminster and Dublin in 1800, following resolutions passed in the British and Irish parliaments. These Acts created the United Kingdom of Great Britain and Ireland. The union with Ireland, however, was the only one that did not succeed, being dissolved in 1921 under the terms of the Anglo-Irish Treaty, which provided for the granting to Ireland of dominion status as the Irish Free State with an independent parliament of her own. The six counties which now comprise Northern Ireland were, however, allowed to exclude themselves from the new Irish Free State, and promptly did so, thus remaining part of the United Kingdom under the 1800 Act of Union. Thus the United Kingdom is no longer that of Great Britain and Ireland, but of Great Britain and Northern Ireland.

The United Kingdom came into existence, not through the growth of a single national or linguistic consciousness, but as the outcome of a series of historical contingencies. It was created by ordinary Acts of Parliament, and not by a constitutional document. The United Kingdom, in the words of Richard Rose, was 'not the product of a compact, drafted and signed by its constituents, as is usually the case in a country with a written constitution. It is an agglomeration created by the expansion and contraction of territorial power in the course of a thousand years.'² Union was achieved by placing England, Wales, Scotland, and Ireland under a common and supreme parliament, and by abolishing the parliaments of England, Scotland, and Ireland. It is representation in a common and supreme parliament that has been the crucial feature, the very essence of the process of union. Westminster had begun, however, as the English parliament, and the constitution of the United Kingdom was marked by the dominance of the institutions of the English state, the largest and most powerful of the components of the United Kingdom. Thus the formation of the United Kingdom came about through the expansion of

England which, through a process of conquest, treaty, and negotiation, played by far the major role in the creation of the state.

England itself was formed through the expansion of Wessex, which, during the reign of Alfred the Great between AD 871 and 899, began the absorption of central England. Alfred's grandson Aethelstan, who reigned from 924 to 939, extended control over the whole of England south of the Humber–Mersey line and west of Offa's Dyke. By the middle of the tenth century, the contours of an English state could be seen, although its northern borders were to remain ill defined for many years.

England came to be permanently unified far earlier than any Continental state, and there was already a powerful English consciousness and sense of national identity before the Norman Conquest. The dominance of England meant that notions of Scottishness and Welshness were to be formed in opposition to that of Englishness. The idea of Englishness, however, came to be an integrating one, binding the other parts of the United Kingdom to the centre. Yet the heart of England lay in London and the south-east, and it is there that power was centralized. England came to be ruled by a strong central government which left little room for provincial loyalties, although this was not of course inconsistent with regional diversity and a firmly rooted shire-system of local government which, created in the tenth century, lasted substantially unchanged until local government reorganization in 1974.[3]

It is not possible to give a precise date for the formation of the English state. 'England', Conrad Russell has argued, 'is unique among the states of Western Europe in that it cannot claim a recorded foundation. We can say that England became a state sometime between 899 and 956, but the English omitted to make any record of the fact.'[4] This is of fundamental importance for British constitutional development. The English state has no document recording its foundation, and therefore no source of authority, such as a constitution, capable of limiting its power. The English state never began. Rather, it evolved. Thus it had no place for any fully agreed and defined constitutional principle limiting the supremacy of the king, nor, following the establishment of parliamentary government, of the king in parliament. The principle of supremacy was retained when the

English parliament expanded to include the representatives of Wales, Scotland, and Ireland.

The parliament of the United Kingdom took on the characteristics of the parliament of England; in particular, it was, as the English parliament had been, a supreme parliament. In Britain, as Maitland once argued, we have substituted the authority of Parliament for a theory of the state. In the sixteenth century, Thomas Cromwell sought a strong central administration as a means of extirpating competing powers. In the seventeenth century, Thomas Hobbes lamented the dangers of the absence of a supreme authority. 'If there had not been an opinion received of the greater part of England that these powers were divided, the people had never been divided and fallen into this civil war.'5 The doctrine of parliamentary supremacy, however, proved inadequate to meet the challenge from the American colonies in the eighteenth century, and from the Irish Home Rulers in the latter part of the nineteenth century. As the twentieth century comes to an end, the doctrine may have become, once again, a threat to the unity of the United Kingdom, rather than a means of holding it together.

In the twelfth century, England began to acquire lands in Wales. During the reign of Edward I between 1272 and 1307, the conquest of Wales was completed, and in 1277 Welsh independence was ended by the Treaty of Aberconwy. In 1284, lands in the north and in the west of Wales were annexed by the Crown, but these were separated from England by quasi-independent buffer lands owned by great feudal families known as the lords marchers.

Royal authority was defined over the whole of Wales in the reign of Henry VIII by two Acts, in 1536 and 1543. The first of these Acts is commonly but misleadingly known as the Act of Union. It was in fact entitled 'An Act for laws and justice to be ministered in Wales in like form as it is in this realm', and claimed that Wales was already part of England, declaring that 'as it rightfully is and ever hath been', Wales was 'a very member and joint of the English realm'. It has been held therefore that this Act confirmed the union with England rather than creating it.6 The Act of 1536 laid down the general terms of union. It provided for Wales to return Members to Parliament, and in 1542 elections were held in Wales for the House of Commons. Representatives from Wales were thus present in the Commons for the Act of 1543, which was entitled 'An Act for certain ordinances in the King's dominions and principality of Wales'. This Act complemented that of 1536 by laying down the details of union. Its 130 clauses provided for the legal and political assimilation of Wales into England. The Tudors sought to eliminate competing sovereignties and to construct a powerful administrative system with a single system of law in place of the separate jurisdictions of the lords marchers. It was for this reason, and not out of an intent to suppress the Welsh language, that the Tudors insisted that English and not Welsh be the official language of Wales. In 1563, Elizabeth I ordered the translation of the Bible and Prayer Book into Welsh to secure Welsh allegiance to the state Protestant religion, and this exerted a profound impact on Welsh life by ensuring the survival of the language.

Although the Tudors established a strong central administration, they were content for this to remain in the hands of local Welsh élites, and separate Welsh courts were to survive until 1830. It has indeed been the characteristic technique of the state to insist upon political unity but to rely upon local interlocutors and the mechanisms of indirect rule for the administration of the peripheries. This meant, in the case of Wales, that union was not incompatible with the retention of Welsh cultural identity and a sense of Welshness. Moreover, the Tudors themselves were in origin a Welsh dynasty. Thus nationalism, when it arose in Wales at the end of the nineteenth century, was motivated not, as in Ireland, by a desire to break the British connection; nor, as in Scotland, by a desire to refashion government so as to guarantee her distinctive institutions. Welsh nationalism was concerned less with political independence than with the defence and preservation of a culture and way of life which seemed under threat. Thus, since the sixteenth century, the union with Wales has been seen as a success, and in 1775 Burke, in his great speech on conciliation with America, was to invoke its beneficial consequences as an illustration of wise and generous statecraft.[7]

III

Scotland emerged as a kingdom during the ninth and tenth centuries and, unlike Wales or Ireland, was never conquered by

England. The attempts by Edward I, 'the hammer of the Scots', to subjugate the country at the end of the thirteenth century were unsuccessful, and England recognized Scottish independence in the Treaty of Northampton in 1328. During medieval times Scotland became a monarchy uniting together its Celtic and non-Celtic population. The Celts in Scotland, by contrast with their Irish counterparts, were, from early times, treated not as second-class citizens, but as a part of the Scottish nation.

Scotland came to be constitutionally linked to England in 1603 when James VI of Scotland succeeded to the English throne, after the death of Elizabeth I, as James I of England. James called himself 'Emperor of the whole island of Britain', and claimed to govern Scotland from London: 'Here I sit and govern it with my pen—I write and it is done, and by a Clerk of the Council I govern Scotland now—which others could not do by the sword.'[8] The Union of Crowns did not create a new state, nor did it create a new British nation. It was a purely dynastic union. England and Scotland retained their separate laws, and the rules for succession to the throne remained different in the two countries.

A union of this kind could work only so long as the king remained the true source of authority in both kingdoms. By the terms of the Bill of Rights, however, William III became, in 1689, responsible to the English parliament. It was difficult to see how the Union of Crowns could survive a constitutional monarchy. The king could not easily be responsible to two different parliaments following different policies. Because the actions of the king were falling under the control of the English parliament, Scottish independence was becoming illusory. Of William III, it has been said:

The more helpless he found himself to defy the wishes of the wealthier and stronger nation, the more completely was the weaker nation entangled in his claims and dragged with him at the heels of the English Parliament. The growth of parliamentary government in England crushed out all possibility of parliamentary government in Scotland.[9]

The Crown came to be tied to the English parliament by the need for regular, annual meetings of Parliament to grant taxation, an unanticipated result of the war against Louis XIV.

If the Scots were not prepared to be governed by an English ministry, then 'either the monarchies must be separated or the parliaments must unite.'[10] Thus, the Treaty of Union was, in a sense, nothing but a logical corollary of the restoration of constitutional government in England in 1689.

In 1701, by the Act of Settlement, the English parliament unilaterally altered the line of succession to the throne. The Act provided for the throne to pass to the Electress of Hanover and her descendants, on condition that they were Protestant. Scotland, however, threatened not to accept the Hanoverian succession, and England, in retaliation, passed the Aliens Act of 1705, declaring all Scots in England to be aliens and prohibiting Scottish imports of cattle, linen, and coal. The Aliens Act implicitly threatened war with Scotland if she did not make provision for a closer union.

Scotland, however, also had much to gain from union. She would gain access to England's expanding markets and to those of her colonies; and she would be able to avoid the threat of a Stuart and Catholic restoration. Above all, she would ensure peace with her southern neighbour. In the words of Lord Roxburgh, 'if Union fail, War will never be avoided; and for my part the more I think of Union, the more I like it, seeing no security anywhere else.'[11] For the Scots, the loss of their parliament was not quite so high a price to pay for Union as might seem the case today, for until 1690, the Scottish parliament had not assumed the dominant position in Scottish life which the English parliament had long claimed. It was, even after 1690, 'only one of a number of rivals for the exercise of executive, and even of legislative authority';[12] and 'In 1707 ... a free Scottish Parliament was not a time-hallowed institution but a novelty (though highly appreciated) of seventeen years standing.'[13] The kirk lay far more at the centre of Scottish national life than parliament. If, therefore, a settlement with England could preserve the kirk together with other Scottish institutions, then the Scots might be able to co-exist with the English in a unitary state with a common parliament, while at the same time maintaining their national identity.

The precise constitutional status and significance of the Treaty of Union have been a subject of much dispute. Scottish nationalists argue that the Scottish parliament was abolished against the wishes of the Scottish people, and that the vote for union was secured solely through bribery and the promise of high office in the new state. Thoroughgoing unionists, on the other hand, claim that the new state of Great Britain created by the Treaty was to be so firmly unitary that Scotland's position in it would be no different from that of Cornwall or Yorkshire.

Both of these two extreme interpretations—the nationalist and the unionist—serve but to obscure the reality of what happened in 1707. The nationalist interpretation is not accepted by serious historians, since it entirely ignores the concrete arguments which persuaded the Scottish negotiators to accede to Westminster's demand for union; and yet, contrary to the unionist interpretation, the Scots never intended Scotland's status to be that of a mere province or region of England. The Scottish negotiators accepted union not only because they were political realists, but also because they came to be convinced that even an incorporating union could safeguard Scotland's vital interests.

There can, admittedly, be no doubt that bribery and the promise of high office in the new state were important factors in persuading the Scottish parliament to ratify the Treaty of Union. Indeed, the Scottish Act of Union was, in the words of one historian, 'probably the greatest political job of the eighteenth century'.[14] Perhaps, however, in the circumstances of the time, it would have been more surprising if bribery had not been involved; and Scottish acquiescence to the Treaty is not to be explained by bribery alone. For the Scots drove a hard bargain. They secured the preservation of the Scottish legal system, in Articles 18 and 19 of the Treaty. Article 18 guaranteed Scots private law, distinguishing between 'public right', i.e. public law, which would be regulated by the new parliament of Great Britain, and 'private right', which was to remain unaltered 'except for evident utility of the subjects within Scotland'. Article 19 laid down that the Scottish Court of Session would 'after the Union and notwithstanding thereof, remain in all time coming within Scotland as it is now constituted by the Laws of that Kingdom, and with the same Authority and Privileges as before the Union'. Other Scottish courts were similarly guaranteed. No Scottish lawsuit was to be tried before an English judge; and English judges were explicitly debarred from 'recognising, reviewing, or altering the acts or sentences of the judicature within Scotland, or stopping the execution of the same'. Admission to English markets was of equal importance to the Scots, and the Treaty provided for free trade and a common fiscal system— indeed fourteen of the twenty-five articles of the Treaty deal with economic issues.

Finally, the Scots gained recognition for their state church. The Treaty was accompanied in 1706 by, in England, an Act of Security for Securing the Church of England as by law established; and in Scotland by a Scottish Act of Security, for securing the Protestant Religion and Presbyterian Church Government in Scotland. The Scottish Act provided that this form of church government was to be 'held and observed in all time coming as a fundamental and essential condition of any Treaty of Union to be concluded between the two Kingdoms without any alteration thereof, or derogation thereto in any sort for ever'. This Act has been held to represent 'a real concession by England',[15] and without it the Scots would almost certainly have refused to agree to the Treaty.

It is the first three articles of the Treaty of Union that define its essential purpose. The first declares that there will be union between the two countries for ever, the second that the rule of succession to the throne in Scotland is in future to be the same as in England, and the third that both kingdoms are to be represented by a single parliament. Thus the Treaty created a new state with one parliament, but two systems of law and two established churches.

The Scots agreed to an incorporating union because they believed that it was not incompatible with the preservation of their nationality, but also because there seemed no realistic alternative. One authority on the Treaty has expressed 'regret that the Scots Parliament, largely as a result of its new-found vigour and vitality, had to be abolished, and that the federal solution was not tried.'[16] But the regret is anachronistic. The first federal constitution was not established until 1787, in the United States, eighty years after the Treaty of Union. It is true that some of the Scottish negotiators, and in particular the Scots patriot, Andrew Fletcher of Saltoun, called for a federal solution. But by 'federal', they meant not a division of powers between a federal government, with a common parliament, and provincial units, but something more like a *confederal* arrangement, such as that in existence in the Dutch confederation, the United Provinces, or eighteenth-century Switzerland before she became a federal state in 1848— a league of states without any constitutional provisions for unity of action. By 1707, however, the United Provinces had become weak and had fallen prey to Louis XIV. The constitution, once lauded, was now discredited. A confederation, therefore, an association of two equally sovereign parliaments, would be subject to just those quarrels and disagreements which had bedevilled Anglo-Scottish relations in the period leading up to the Union; and it would have been unacceptable to England.

The Scottish negotiators of union regarded Fletcher's 'federal' proposal as, in the words of Sir John Clerk of Penicuik, 'ridiculous and impracticable' and it seems to have been 'no more than a gesture for the benefit of the Scottish public, something to show that at least an attempt had been made to save their Parliament'. 'Federation', however, was 'not worth the paines . . . and will be a mother of future dangers and discords at some unhappy occasion'.[17] Seton of Pitmedden declared in November 1706 that 'Federal Union . . . may be handsomely fitted to delude unthinking people'.[18]

Fletcher of Saltoun, however, appreciated that a confederation might prove unworkable because of the dominant position of England. Fletcher took the view that a workable confederation required a rough equality between the units composing it. He therefore suggested breaking up both England and Scotland, dividing the two kingdoms into separate regions. Fletcher's proposal would thus have secured the sovereignty, not so much of Scotland, as of regions within Scotland. The new kingdom would have contained a number of regional capitals—London, Bristol, Exeter, York, Norwich, Edinburgh, Stirling, Dublin, Cork, and Londonderry. Fletcher in fact accepted the English argument that a parliament had to be sovereign, and that its powers could not be divided. He sought not to *divide* power, something he believed impossible, but to *distribute* it amongst a number of different sovereign authorities, rather than have it concentrated in just one sovereign parliament of Great Britain.

Fletcher was thus not so much a precursor of Madison, but rather a footnote to the Greeks. Far from looking forward to the United

States of America, he was looking backwards to the city-states of the ancient world; or perhaps he was an early prophet of a Europe of the Regions. But, in the Scotland of the early eighteenth century, his proposals were completely unrealistic.

However, the absence of the federal idea from the Treaty meant that there was a crucial weakness in the settlement from the Scottish point of view; for there was no machinery through which Scottish interests could be defended in the face of a permanent English majority. The Treaty could thus make no political or juridical provision by which Scotland's wishes could be ascertained, other than through her representatives at Westminster. The referendum and the convention were unknown to the constitution at this time, and there was no overall system of public law to which both England and Scotland could appeal. In general, judicial review of legislation had to await the United States Supreme Court decision in *Marbury* v. *Madison* (1803), before being admitted to the armoury of instruments of constitutional protection.

The new state of Great Britain would have a new parliament which, although located in Westminster as the English parliament had been, was, nevertheless, the parliament of a new state. The English parliament was a sovereign parliament, but the Scottish parliament was not. It is by no means clear why the new parliament of Great Britain should have been expected to take on the characteristics of the English parliament, rather than those of the Scottish parliament. Yet, there was little doubt, even amongst the Scottish negotiators of union, that the new parliament would in fact take on the characteristics of the English parliament, and that, in particular, it would be a sovereign parliament. How, then, could the Scots have held with any confidence that the provisions of the Treaty would be respected by a parliament in which Scottish members would be but a small minority? It remains a puzzle that the Scots could believe that words such as 'for ever' and 'in all time' could constrain a sovereign parliament. While, from time to time, Scottish judges and commentators have declared that the Treaty is a form of fundamental law, constraining the British parliament, that argument has never been accepted by the courts. The 1706 Act preserving the Scottish form of church government was in fact amended as early as 1712 in the

Toleration and Patronage Acts whereby Westminster altered the powers of lay patrons within the Scottish church. Westminster could hardly have affirmed its sovereignty more explicitly, but no court suggested that it was acting *ultra vires*. Later, in 1800, the Act of Union with Ireland was to declare that the established position of the Church of Ireland was unalterable, but when Gladstone disestablished this Church in 1869, the courts, in *Ex parte Canon Selwyn* (1872) 36 JP 54, refused to rule that it was unconstitutional. The Union with Ireland Act of 1800 which was also declared to be 'for ever' was in effect repealed by Parliament, except with regard to the six counties of Northern Ireland, in 1921.

The Treaty of Union with Scotland has undergone considerable modification since it was signed. Almost every one of its articles has been amended or repealed, including provisions which were intended to be binding.[19] Yet no court has ever struck down legislation emanating from Westminster on the ground that it breached the Treaty; and, in a Scottish case *Murray* v. *Rogers* 1992 SLT 221, in which defaulting poll-tax payers argued that the Scottish legislation providing for the poll tax was contrary to the Scottish Act of Union, Lord Kirkwood stated that 'there is, so far as I am aware, no machinery whereby the validity of an Act of Parliament can be brought under review by the courts'.[20]

What, then, was the point of phrases such as 'for ever' and 'in all time'? Dicey argued that, although such phrases could not bind, they had a purpose, and that:

the enactment of laws which are described as unchangeable, immutable, or the like, is not necessarily futile . . . A sovereign Parliament . . . although it cannot be logically bound to abstain from changing any given law, may, by the fact that an Act when it was passed had been declared to be unchangeable, receive a warning that it cannot be changed without grave danger to the Constitution of the country.[21]

Thus the bald statement that the Treaty created an incorporating union fails to capture its full flavour. It would be better to say that the state of Great Britain which resulted was not a unitary state, but a union state. The distinction between the two has been drawn in the following way:

The unitary state [is] built up around one unambiguous political centre which enjoys economic dominance and pursues a more or less undeviating policy of administrative standardisation. All areas of the state are treated alike, and all institutions are directly under the control of the centre. The union state [is] not the result of straightforward dynastic conquest. Incorporation of at least parts of its territory . . . [is] through personal dynastic union, for example by treaty, marriage or inheritance. Integration is less than perfect. While administrative standardisation prevails over most of the territory, the consequences of personal union entail survival of pre-union rights and institutional infrastructures which preserve some degree of regional autonomy and serve as agencies of indigenous elite recruitment.[22]

The spirit in which political transactions are carried out can be as important as their outcome. The Treaty had been freely negotiated on a footing of equality, and it had the character of a contract between two equal consenting parties. For nearly 300 years, it seemed to have achieved its purpose of enabling the Scots to reconcile their national identity with membership of a United Kingdom.

Devolution revises the terms of the Treaty of Union. But it does not signify a return to the pre-1707 condition in which Scotland possessed a parliament co-ordinate with that of England. That policy, the policy of re-establishing the Union of the Crowns, is favoured by the Scottish National Party, but it is far from the purpose of the Labour government which has legislated for devolution. Devolution instead provides for a parliament which is constitutionally *subordinate* to Westminster. Devolution seeks to revise the Union, not to destroy it.

IV

From earliest times, Ireland had been culturally unified, but had found it difficult to attain political unity. Following the defeat of the Viking invaders in 1002, Brian Boru became, in effect, king of Ireland, styling himself emperor of the Irish. But when Henry II invaded Ireland in 1169 the kingship rapidly collapsed, and since that time, Ireland has enjoyed political unity only under English rule.

Henry II did not, however, complete the subjugation of Ireland and it was not until 1534 that England assumed direct rule over the country, Henry VIII being accepted in 1541 as 'king of Ireland'. By the end of the reign of Elizabeth I in 1603, Ireland had become constitutionally subordinate. In the seventeenth century, following the plantation of Ulster by Protestants, primarily from Scotland, the Celtic, Catholic population of Ireland came to be treated as second-class citizens, being excluded from the Irish parliament in 1692 and disfranchised in 1727. Largely for this reason, the Irish Celts were never assimilated as the Scottish Celts had been. Moreover, there were, in Ireland, no dynastic links with the throne as there were in Wales, through the Tudors, and in Scotland, through the Stuarts. In Ireland, the king and the English state were associated not with local aspirations, but with alien Protestant settlers, and the Catholic majority came to develop a separatist ideology.

The Irish parliament, unlike the Scottish, lay at the centre of the nation's political life; but in Ireland the political nation was the Protestant nation. Until 1782, the Irish parliament was subordinate to Westminster. In that year, however, with the repeal of Poynings' Law, it became a parliament with co-ordinate powers to those of Westminster, although, like the Scottish parliament but unlike the British, it had no control over the executive. It was not, moreover, a representative parliament, since it contained no Catholic members; indeed, until 1793, no Catholic could vote in Ireland.

This arrangement, of co-ordinate parliaments, proved unsatisfactory to British interests, especially after the rebellion of 1798 which led the British government to fear that Ireland could become a base for a hostile landing by the forces of Bonaparte. The government therefore proposed union with Ireland; and, in 1800, Acts of Union were passed by Westminster and Dublin following resolutions by the two parliaments, providing for a permanent union between the two countries under one parliament. Although, as with Scotland, there is no doubt that bribery played a role in securing the assent of the Irish parliament to union, it would, again, be mistaken to ascribe union solely to corruption. The Irish parliament was moderately responsive to public opinion in Ireland, and the British government had to modify some of the provisions of union in order to secure its passage through the Irish parliament.[23]

Yet, in any case, the methods by which union was secured were not responsible for its failure. The Catholic population of Ireland was induced to support union by the promise of Catholic emancipation. Indeed, those Irish parliamentarians who opposed union did so precisely because they feared that it would destroy the Protestant ascendancy. But, when Pitt sought to implement his promise, George III vetoed it, arguing that it would be contrary to the coronation oath requiring him to maintain the Protestant religion. Thus, whereas in Scotland, the Scottish Act of Security safeguarded the church of the majority of the Scottish people, in Ireland, by contrast, the Union guaranteed the Anglican church in Ireland, the Church of Ireland, which was the church of a minority. Many Catholics came to believe that their disabilities would be removed only by agitation, and the Catholic cause came to be identified with Irish nationalism. Catholic emancipation indeed was not secured until 1829, after a long struggle led by Daniel O'Connell.

The Union also failed to resolve Ireland's economic and social problems, and indeed, in the view of nationalists, exacerbated them when Britain displayed an indifference amounting to callousness during the great famine of the 1840s. The bulk of the Catholic population, therefore, came to believe that Ireland's problems could be resolved only by separation from Britain; or, if that were not possible, by a revision of the terms of the Union allowing Ireland her own parliament, so that Irishmen could at least be in control of their own domestic affairs. In 1885, in the first general election in which the majority of Irish males could vote, 85 out of the 103 Irish seats were won by nationalists. This was a challenge which Gladstone, as Liberal leader, could not ignore, representing as it did the fixed desire of a nation, constitutionally expressed. In 1886, therefore, Gladstone proposed Home Rule, the restoration of a legislature in Ireland.

Many liberal-minded people, however, took issue with Gladstone's approach. For them, the Union of 1800, by whatever methods it had come about, was the consummation of a long historical process which had united the British Isles under one parliament. To undo this process by conceding Home Rule was, they believed, contrary to the course of British history, and would, in Dicey's words, 'undo the work not only of Pitt, but of Somers, of Henry VII and of Edward I'.[24] Unionists believed that the times were unpropitious for small states.

The future, as the victory of the North in the American civil war and the recent unification of Germany and Italy had shown, lay with large states. Thus the Irish nationalist movement was not to be equated with Continental nationalisms such as those in Germany, Italy, or Poland. For, whereas those movements had created new nations, the Irish nationalists were intent on destroying an already existing nation, the British nation, in the creation of which the Act of 1800 was but the final stage in a long and irreversible process of historical evolution. Opponents of Home Rule thus saw it as a threat to the building of a new homogeneous British national identity. Gladstone and his supporters, by contrast, saw Britain not as the country of a single nation, but as 'a partnership of three kingdoms, a partnership of four nations'.[25] Unity was to be achieved not by absorbing the identity of these different nations into one undifferentiated whole, but by explicitly recognizing that Britain was a multinational state, and devising institutions which allowed the various identities of her component nations to be expressed. The conflict between these two standpoints lies at the heart of the debate on devolution, and it remains unresolved.

Irish Home Rule

The Channel forbids union, the ocean forbids separation.

(Henry Grattan)

I

'The long, vexed, and troubled relations between Great Britain and Ireland', claimed Gladstone in 1886, 'exhibit to us the one and only conspicuous failure of the political genius of our race to confront and master difficulty, and to obtain in a reasonable degree the main ends of civilized life'.[1] Irish Home Rule sought to secure those 'main ends of civilized life' by allowing Ireland to govern herself in her domestic affairs within the framework of the United Kingdom, and it proved the most convulsive issue in British politics between 1886 and 1914.

During this period, three Home Rule Bills were introduced into Parliament. The first, in 1886, was defeated in the Commons by 343 votes to 313, as the result of a split in the ruling Liberal party, 93 Liberals voting against it. The second, in 1893, passed the Commons, but was defeated in the Lords by the overwhelming majority of 419 votes to 41. The third bill, introduced in 1912, was again rejected by the Lords, but, under the provisions of the 1911 Parliament Act, limiting the delaying power of the Lords to three sessions, it became law in 1914. With the outbreak of war, however, the Act was suspended, and in fact it never came into effect. Its passage was accompanied by threats of direct action on the part of Ulster Unionists and Conservatives of a kind not seen in British politics since the seventeenth century, threats which led many to believe that Britain was on the verge of civil war in 1914.

Perhaps the best definition of Home Rule was that given by John Redmond, the Irish nationalist leader, in a lecture delivered at Melbourne in 1883. 'What do I mean by Home Rule?' Redmond asked.

I mean by Home Rule the restoration to Ireland of representative government, and I define representative government to mean government with the
constitutionally expressed will of a majority of the people, and carried out
by a ministry constitutionally responsible to those whom they govern. In
other words, I mean that the internal affairs of Ireland shall be regulated by
an Irish Parliament—that all Imperial affairs and all that relates to the
colonies, foreign states and common interests of the Empire, shall continue
to be regulated by the Imperial Parliament [i.e. Westminster], as at present
constituted. The idea at the bottom of this proposal is the desirability of finding some middle course between separation on the one hand and over-cen-
tralisation of government on the other.[2]

Home Rule thus entailed the establishment of a legislature in Dublin
responsible for Ireland's domestic affairs—the term 'parliament' was
deliberately avoided, since that was seen to imply a challenge to
Westminster's sovereignty—with an Irish executive responsible to
that legislature. The sovereignty of Westminster would remain.

The policy of Home Rule, then, was designed to modify, though
not to repeal, the Act of Union of 1800. Under the union, Ireland's
governmental arrangements were distinct from those of other parts of
the kingdom. There remained a separate Irish administration in
Dublin, headed by the Lord Lieutenant, representing the sovereign,
and the Chief Secretary, normally a member of the British Cabinet.
There was a separate Irish Privy Council and a separate judiciary and
law officers. Thus Ireland had an executive and a judiciary of its own
but no legislature of its own, while the Chief Secretary, the political
head of the Irish government would spend around nine months of the
year in Westminster. The constitutional implication of the union
between Ireland and Great Britain had been the legal equality of
Ireland with Great Britain; in practice, however, Ireland was governed under a system which seemed to the majority of her population
to put her in a position of inferiority. For she was ruled not by
Irishmen but by the British. Scotland had been treated as a partner
after the union, but Ireland seemed a dependency.

In 1884, the third Reform Act extended the franchise to the agricultural labourer, giving Ireland for the first time popular if not yet
universal suffrage, and increasing the Irish electorate fivefold. In the
1885 elections, the first held under the new system, eighty-five of

Ireland's 103 MPs were members of the Irish parliamentary party, and committed to Home Rule. In consequence, whether Liberals or Conservatives were in power at Westminster, the Chief Secretary and the Irish administration were bound to be in the hands of a party which enjoyed only minority support in Ireland. Thus, although Ireland was, in Gladstone's words, 'nominally under a free Constitution',[3] her representatives would no longer be able to play a part in the government of their country.

When expansion of the franchise was being planned, Gladstone's Home Secretary, Sir William Harcourt, feared that:

there will be declared to the world in larger print what we all know to be the case, that we hold Ireland by *force and by force alone* as in the days of Cromwell, only that we are obliged to hold it by a force ten times larger than he found necessary . . . We have never governed and we never shall govern Ireland by the good will of its people.[4]

This was because, for all but two years since the first Reform Act of 1832, Ireland had been administered through special coercive legislation which had no counterpart in the rest of Britain. Despite such special legislation, however, agrarian crime had not been rooted out, but had become more habitual. Indeed, Gladstone believed that agrarian crime was 'at times threatening to break up the foundation of social order, and bring us to touch upon a state of things essentially belonging to civil war'. The prevalence of agrarian crime was, however, Gladstone believed, 'not so much the cause as the symptom of a yet more deeply rooted evil, that is to say, a want of sympathy with the criminal law in all that relates to or bears upon the holding of land'.

Repressive legislation had, in Gladstone's view, failed. It was 'morally worn out'. The success of further coercion required 'two essential conditions, and these are the autocracy of Government and the secrecy of public transactions'. Neither of these conditions could be met for long under a liberal political system. Indeed, Gladstone believed that the British public would not admit the case for further coercion until all other alternatives had been exhausted. Coercion, moreover, had been unsuccessful because it bore the character of an imposition by a foreign authority, and 'stamped on the

Executive Government in Ireland' there was 'the aspect of a Government essentially foreign'. The 'inevitable consequence' was 'to produce in Great Britain not only disparaging and hostile judgment but estrangement of feeling from Ireland and thus to widen the breach between the countries'. Government in Ireland, however, could succeed, only if 'as in England the law is felt to be indigenous'.[5]

It was essentially these practical considerations rather than any idealistic view of the rights of small nations which turned Gladstone's mind towards Home Rule. Gladstone followed Burke in opposing 'the opening of abstract questions respecting the indefeasibility of natural rights; questions which are . . . capable of introducing confusion into affairs'.[6] He was concerned less with the supposed right of the Irish to self-government than with the practical question of whether the Irish demand for self-government could be reconciled with the central principle of the British Constitution, the supremacy of Parliament.

That it could be so reconciled flowed, in Gladstone's mind, from three separate considerations. The first was his understanding of the nature of Irish nationalism; the second his belief that the insights of Edmund Burke could be applied to the Irish problem; and the third was the practical experience both of other European countries and of the self-governing colonies, which showed 'that the concession of local self-government is not the way to sap or impair, but the way to strengthen and consolidate unity'.

Irish nationalism was, for Gladstone, not a demand for separation or for independent statehood, but a 'local patriotism . . . The Irishman is more profoundly Irish, but it does not follow that because his local patriotism is keen he is incapable of Imperial patriotism.'[7] Gladstone was accustomed to speak not of Irish nationalism, but of Irish 'nationality', which was similar to Scottish or Welsh nationality. Thus, just as a Scot's loyalty to Scotland was compatible with his loyalty to the United Kingdom as a whole, so also the loyalty of an Irishman to Ireland could be made compatible with loyalty to the United Kingdom. For separate Irish nationality 'does not mean disunion with England. It means closer union with England.'[8] Irish nationality, Gladstone believed, was 'a nationality which has regard to circumstances and traditions . . . a reasonable and reasoning, not . . . a blind and headstrong nationality',[9] which 'vents itself in the demand for local autonomy, or separate and complete self-government in Irish, not in Imperial affairs'.[10] The sense of Irish nationality could be satisfied, therefore, through a judicious policy of Home Rule, placing Irish government on the firm foundations of consent and representative institutions.

While preparing the first Home Rule Bill, Gladstone studied the writings of Edmund Burke on Ireland, and his speeches on conciliation with America. He found them 'a mine of gold for the political wisdom with which they are charged',[11] for Burke, the theorist of responsible government in the colonies, had shown how the imperial connection could accommodate a sense of nationality in the colonial communities.

Burke had noticed that the imperial parliament at Westminster performed two functions; it was not only 'the local legislature of this island', but also possessed an 'imperial character, in which as from the throne of heaven, she superintends all the several legislatures, and guides and controls them all without annihilating any'. These functions were, for Burke, separable, and, in the case of the colonies ought to be separated by devolving to the colonies responsibility for local legislation. Such devolution would prove that the imperial rights of Britain and the privileges of the colonists could be reconciled; they were 'just the most reconcilable things in the world'.[12] Imperial supremacy, therefore, and the supremacy of Parliament were not dependent upon the centralization of all local functions in the imperial parliament. What Burke had shown was the possibility of two political communities, the one supreme and the other subordinate, with the subordinate enjoying practical autonomy in its own affairs.

It was not, however, necessary to rely on the beliefs of political philosophers for a solution to the problem of reconciling Irish demands with the supremacy of Parliament and the maintenance of the United Kingdom. Nor was it necessary to look for the solution in terms of abstract principles of government. For other countries had attempted to resolve a similar problem: indeed, Gladstone, citing the union between Sweden and Norway and the dual monarchy of

Austria–Hungary as examples of countries which remained united but with separate legislatures, believed that the 'last half-century [is] rich in lessons', whereby, 'unity not only preserved but strengthened'.[13]

If such a solution had been adopted in these cases, then, *a fortiori*, it would be possible in Britain which had '*greater advantages*'. For 'if two independent and nearly equal States can, by the expedient of autonomy, be made to work as an organic unity, how much slighter must be the strain, where there is no question of constitutional independence, and where in the last resort the superior Parliament retains the power to solve any and every controversy between them in such manner as it may think fit?'[14]

These advantages had been exploited by granting responsible government in the colonies, in Canada and in the Australian and South African states, where the concession of local parliaments had, as Burke would have predicted, served to preserve the imperial connection and to remove grievances. The British North America Act of 1867 establishing the Confederation of Canada yielded, for Gladstone, an example 'not parallel', but 'analogous'.[15] It is strictly and substantially 'analogous', and the great lesson of imperial history was that 'forcing uniformity and centralizing authority have caused severance', while 'local independence and legislative severance' had maintained union.[16]

Gladstone's policy of Home Rule was based, then, upon principles that had already, in his view, been applied in imperial relations; it offered the same remedy as had been successfully adopted in Canada. It was a policy, moreover, which, owing much to Burke, was 'especially founded on history and tradition'; a policy which aimed 'in the main at restoring, not altering the Empire';[17] for it was an undoubted fact that 'the creation of such legislatures had in certain cases been an instrument, not of dismembering, but of consolidating Empire'.[18] Home Rule was, for these reasons, the policy of an enlightened imperialist, and most emphatically not a Little England policy. It was, moreover, a policy which 'Surely . . . has high title to a conservative character', for:

it is a policy which, instead of innovating, restores; which builds upon the ancient foundations of Irish history and tradition; which by making power local, makes it congenial, where hitherto it has been unfamiliar, almost alien;

and strong, where hitherto it has been weak. Let us extricate the question from the low mist of the hour, let us raise the banner clear of the smoke of battle, and we shall see that such a policy is eminently a conservative policy.[19]

It represented conservatism of the kind that Gladstone had noticed in his mentor, Peel, 'the conviction that it is possible to adjust the noble and ancient institutions of this country to the wants and necessities of this unquiet time, without departure from the fundamental principles, not which theory, but which history ascribes to them.'[20]

However, although these principles had already been applied elsewhere, modifications were necessary when applying them to Ireland. Because Ireland was so much nearer Britain than Canada or Australia, an Irish legislature would inevitably lie in a relationship to Westminster which differed from that of a legislature in Canada or New South Wales. Moreover, in view of the danger that would be posed by a hostile Ireland in time of war, Britain would have to retain some powers, such as control of defence, which had been devolved to the self-governing colonies.

There were, therefore, precedents for Home Rule, but they were not exact precedents, and a measure had to be devised which took into account Ireland's specific circumstances. In establishing an Irish legislature, Parliament, moreover, would be assuming obligations of honour not to interfere with its working under normal conditions. Parliament had done something similar when it had promised to respect Scottish legal and ecclesiastical institutions in the Treaty of Union. Gladstone believed that the 'same care should be exercised in constituting such obligation of *honour* as if we gave away *powers*'.[21]

The method of the legislation providing for colonial self-government had been to devolve power on a plenary basis to the colonies. Imperial supremacy was preserved not through the exercise of reserve powers, but by means of the Governor-General's veto, and by the Judicial Committee of the Privy Council, which acted as a final Court of Appeal on the jurisdiction of the colonial government. Gladstone, however, sought to give Ireland self-government only in domestic affairs, reserving imperial matters to Westminster. Home Rule, therefore, involved a contract by means of which the Irish were pledged 'to an express admission of that supremacy by the same vote which accepted Local powers'. Gladstone thus required the Irish 'to accept as a satisfactory charter of Irish liberty a document which contained an express submission to Imperial power and a direct acknowledgment of Imperial unity'.[22] But, in addition to the weapons of veto and reservation of powers, each of the Home Rule Bills added further prohibitions on the exercise of devolved powers, the primary prohibition being on laws interfering with religious equality. In this way, Gladstone sought to undermine the unionist contention that Home Rule was incompatible with parliamentary supremacy. For, if, he argued, devolution had worked in subordinate communities such as the Canadian provinces, communities which had been given wider powers than those to be granted to Ireland, then, *a fortiori*, Home Rule would work in Ireland; for if supremacy was compatible with a weaker degree of subordination, it could more easily be maintained with a greater degree of subordination to Westminster.

The problem remained of defining those imperial rights which would need to be retained at Westminster. There had to be, Gladstone believed, a 'strict and thorough severance of Imperial from Local affairs', with a 'reservation of the first', and 'transference of the second'. And this should be based 'on the principle of Trust—which is adverse to Exceptions'.[23] But, what ought to be the extent of the reserved powers? Here, too, Gladstone looked at the historical precedents. There were indeed two examples of constitutions based on a division of powers which would have naturally presented themselves to him. The first, the Constitution of the United States, was unsuitable for his purposes, because it did not secure sufficient power for the federal government; this had been a prime cause of the American Civil War, which had begun in 1861, just twenty-five years before the first Home Rule Bill was presented to Parliament. But the second example, the division of powers between the federal government in Canada and its constituent provinces, was of far more relevance, since the aim of those who had drawn up the Canadian Constitution, in contrast with that of the United States, had been to maintain the power of the centre at the expense of the provinces.

Gladstone, therefore, decided to reserve to the imperial parliament at Westminster those powers which the British North America

Act of 1867, the Act establishing the Canadian Constitution, had reserved to the Dominion Parliament in Canada. Clause 3 of the 1886 Government of Ireland Bill is in fact taken from clause 90 of the British North America Act, enumerating the reserved powers of the Dominion Parliament. These reserved powers were of four kinds. First, there were matters relating to the Crown and defence; second, foreign and colonial relations; third, 'subjects reserved on practical grounds',[24] such as patents, copyright law, and contracts; and finally 'all power of protection and differential duties'.[25] Gladstone's original intention had been to allow the Irish legislature the power to vary revenue duties, but he changed his mind on this matter during the preparation of the bill, and, in its final version, all indirect taxation was reserved to Westminster.

The structure of the first Home Rule Bill, presented to Parliament in 1886, formed the basis for all later Home Rule measures. It blended two different constitutional models into a hybrid that was entirely *sui generis*. The idea of a devolution of power to satisfy the principle of nationality was, as we have seen, based on the model of colonial self-government, and especially upon the model of responsible government in Canada. The particular division of powers between Parliament and the Irish legislature, however, was based upon the federal division of powers between the Canadian provinces and the Dominion Parliament.

The complexity of the first Home Rule Bill, however, meant that it was widely misunderstood, both by supporters and by opponents of the measure. John Morley, one of Gladstone's closest colleagues, wrote to him in January 1887 that the object of the first Home Rule Bill had been 'to bestow on the Irish body the functions of provincial legislatures in Canada'.[26] Yet the Irish legislature would have enjoyed wider powers than those legislatures, and it would in fact have enjoyed all the powers not specifically reserved to Westminster. In the Canadian provinces, by contrast, the powers of the provinces were specifically enumerated and the Dominion Parliament was given all residuary powers.

The opposite criticism was made by Joseph Chamberlain, a leading Liberal opponent of Home Rule, when he argued that the bill, instead of being based on the federal principle, which, he claimed, he could have supported, was based instead on the relationship of Canada to Britain, a relationship which in his view was fundamentally different from that of Ireland to Britain. But, as we have seen, this criticism was misconceived because the Irish legislature, in contrast to the Dominion Parliament of Canada, was not to have control of taxation, trade, and commerce or military or defence matters. The scope of the powers of the Irish legislature, therefore, lay between those of the Dominion Parliament of Canada, and the powers of the provincial parliaments such as Ontario.

The hybrid nature of Home Rule laid it open to damaging criticisms that might perhaps have been avoided if a clear-cut choice between the two models—the colonial and the federal—had been made. On the other hand, it could plausibly be argued that neither of the two pure models would have been as appropriate to the particular circumstances of Ireland as the Home Rule Bill actually produced by Gladstone.

The central distinction between the two models is clear enough, for the colonial model is marked by two features which distinguish it from the federal model. The first is that the colony had never been represented at Westminster, the second—seemingly a logical corollary—is that the colony was not taxed by Westminster. In a federal relationship, by contrast, the different units continue to be represented in, and contribute their share of taxation to, a federal parliament.

Since, under Home Rule, Ireland would continue to receive the benefits of the reserved services, she would be required to contribute her share of the costs of these services. She would, therefore, unlike the colonies, have to pay what was called an Imperial Contribution, and this was to be a first charge on her expenditure. Thus the colonial solution for Irish finance could not be applied.

On the other hand, Gladstone proposed, in the first Home Rule Bill, that Irish members be removed from Westminster, as in the colonial model. It was at this point that the hybrid scheme of Home Rule began to present difficulties; for Ireland was to be taxed by Westminster, but no longer represented there. Thus, the first Home Rule Bill raised the spectre of taxation without representation, the very constitutional contradiction which had led to the loss of the American colonies.

In considering the reasons for the defeat of Home Rule, it is of course important not to exaggerate the importance of defects in the legislation itself. A full historical account would have to give considerable and perhaps preponderant weight to wider factors, and especially to changes in the intellectual climate at the end of the nineteenth century, as Gladstonian imperialism came to be superseded by a very different sort of imperialism, based on *Realpolitik*; nor should the factor of anti-Irish prejudice be minimized, for there is ample evidence to confirm the view of one commentator that 'what really killed Home Rule . . . was the Anglo-Saxon stereotype of the Irish Celt'.[27]

There is little doubt, however, that all the Home Rule Bills, and the first Home Rule Bill in particular, displayed considerable faults of constitutional logic, faults which may well have played some part in their defeat, and which must also cast some doubt on the contention that Home Rule would have yielded a permanent settlement of the Irish question.

The Home Rule legislation had three central deficiencies. The first was the failure to find a solution to the conundrum of how Ireland was to be represented at Westminster after Home Rule. The second was the failure to divide taxation-powers in a way which would combine equity between the different parts of the United Kingdom with the financial independence of Ireland. The third was the failure to show that the supremacy of Parliament would remain a real supremacy rather than a merely symbolic one.

II

The exclusion of Irish members from Westminster in the first Home Rule Bill was, according to Joseph Chamberlain, 'not a technical point, but the symbol and flag of the controversy'.[28] For Ireland would not long tolerate a situation whereby her foreign and tariff policy were decided at Westminster without Irish representation there. Sooner or later, Ireland would demand control of these functions, and that would imply national independence. Thus taxation without representation would lead, inevitably, to separation, as had been the case with the American colonies.

So Gladstone had to face what in his notes for the second reading speech on the Home Rule Bill in 1886, he called 'the double dilemma'. The first horn of the dilemma was:

Ireland is to have a domestic legislature for Irish affairs.
   Cannot come here for English or Scotch affairs . . . [29]

'The one thing', Gladstone told the House of Commons, 'follows from the other. There cannot be a domestic legislature in Ireland dealing with Irish affairs, and Irish Peers and Representatives sitting in Parliament at Westminster to take part in English and Scotch affairs.'[30]

Could Irish MPs be recalled, then, solely for reserved matters, such as foreign policy and defence? This, the so-called 'in and out' proposal, was ruled out by Gladstone in 1886. He did, however, consider it for the second Home Rule Bill, in 1893, but the final version of the Bill, as presented to Parliament, provided for continued but reduced Irish representation at Westminster. There would, under the final 1893 proposal, have been eighty Irish MPs at Westminster, instead of 103.

In 1886, Gladstone decided against the 'in and out' proposal for two reasons. First he argued that the distinction between imperial and non-imperial affairs, 'cannot be drawn. I believe it passes the wit of man.'[31] Yet, in dividing powers in the Home Rule Bill, Gladstone seems to have made that very distinction. The problem was perhaps rather different: it was that the distinction, once drawn, would not in fact be of much assistance, since any proposal to spend money, whether on English, Scottish, or Welsh matters, or on Irish matters, would compete in terms of priorities with any other proposal. The amount of money which accrued to Ireland would remain dependent upon the amount which English, Scottish, and Welsh MPs decided to spend upon their own priorities. Therefore, the standard of living of the Irish would depend upon decisions made at a forum from which they would have been excluded.

There was, however, a second and even more fundamental objection to the 'in and out' proposal. In his notes, Gladstone wrote that it was 'impossible (because opinion touches responsibility)'.[32] The 'in and out' proposal would bifurcate the government of

Britain since there might be one government with the Irish MPs present—a Liberal-Irish government—on foreign and colonial affairs, and a government of an opposite political colour—a Conservative government—with the Irish absent, for domestic English, Welsh, and Scottish affairs. The 'in and out' proposal would thus undermine the principle of collective responsibility according to which a government must stand or fall as a whole, and therefore command a majority on all the issues that come before Parliament, not just a selection of them.

Gladstone, therefore, came to the conclusion that 'Irish members *cannot ordinarily* sit in the Imperial Parliament'. Moreover, so he believed, 'Painful Parly relations of later years recommend a period of intermission.'[33] Many Liberals were anxious to bring an end to the parliamentary obstruction which Irish MPs had practised since 1880, and ensure that the government in London was no longer dependent on Irish votes. Lord Granville, to be colonial secretary in Gladstone's third government, told Harcourt, who was to become the Chancellor, in December 1885, 'The great bribe to me and I expect to England and Scotland would be to get rid of the Irish MPs here, who are introducing the dry rot into our institutions.'[34] If the Irish were to remain at Westminster, then, John Morley believed, 'there is no power on earth that can prevent the Irish members in such circumstances from being . . . the arbiters and the masters of English policy, of English legislative business and of the rise and fall of British Administration.'[35]

To exclude the Irish from Westminster, however, impaled Gladstone on the other horn of the dilemma:

How then is Ireland to be taxed?[36]

The powers reserved to Westminster under the Home Rule Bill were primarily the Crown and defence, foreign and colonial relations, and indirect taxation. It was the last which caused Gladstone the greatest difficulty.

With regard to the Crown and defence, Gladstone was forced to confess that he did 'not see how to modify the Bill with any advantage'. Concerning foreign and colonial relations, 'the "sentiment" presses for a change. But how could Irish members, unless always here, be enabled to participate in dealing with a class of subjects which are mainly in the hands of private members (at least I should say in proportion of twenty occasions against one) and perfectly uncertain as to the time and method of handling?' To deal with this problem, Gladstone made two suggestions, the first a series of 'regular communications between the British and Irish executives . . . Foreign policy is thus managed as between Sweden and Norway'. The second suggestion was the Austro-Hungarian model of a joint delegation or standing committee from the two legislatures, with Ireland being represented 'in some reasonable proportion such as perhaps one third'.[37]

But this still left the difficulty that changes in indirect taxation which would affect Ireland could be made without the participation of the Irish themselves. It could perhaps be argued, as it was by Lord Thring, the parliamentary draftsman, that 'Ireland could not be said to be taxed without representation when her representatives agreed' to the provisions of the Home Rule Bill.[38] Gladstone, however, was willing to go further and to concede that 'When the Government makes a proposal for the alteration or repeal of any tax now levied in Ireland by the authority of Parliament, or for the imposition of any new tax', the Irish members would be granted the right to return. They would also be granted the right to return in the case of any proposed amendment to the Home Rule settlement.

It might seem as if Gladstone had now reached by a rather roundabout route the 'in and out' proposal which he had earlier repudiated as impossible, but in fact his scheme was subtly different. The 'in and out' solution provided that the Irish would remain at Westminster as of right, and with the right, therefore, to participate in parliamentary votes on which issues were to count as reserved and which as transferred. Gladstone's provisions of 1886, however, would make it much more difficult for Irish leverage to be applied to every single reserved issue at Westminster.

There might, Gladstone admitted, be 'some inconvenience in this, as there might be intrigues with the Irish to overthrow a ministry through its Budget'. But this inconvenience would probably not be very great: 'we know the worst of this inconvenience now. Since the Act of Union, I think that only two Ministries (one of them already in a minority) have been overthrown, i.e. driven out, on Budgets. These cases were in 1852 and 1885.'[39] Further, it could be argued that on what Gladstone called a 'question of class', the Irish members might be just as divided as the English, Scottish, and Welsh, and that 'on any question of national interests, . . . they would still require over 260 British MPs to win a majority'. Moreover, 'It would not seem very unjust that they should gain their point when Ireland was unanimous on a matter primarily affecting her or was supported by more than 5/12 of the British representatives.'[40]

In this way, Gladstone sought to escape from his 'double dilemma'. But he did so only at the cost of bringing over the members of the Irish legislature to Westminster on what the jurist Anson called 'a sort of imperial or financial excursion'.[41] A solution of this kind would have required a good deal of tolerance and mutual forbearance if it were to be made to work.

The alternative to exclusion or to the 'in and out' solution, and one which was adopted in the 1893 bill and the 1912 bill, was to allow the Irish to continue to attend at Westminster, and to be able to vote on all matters, but in reduced numbers. Indeed, Gladstone was to come to the conclusion, after 1886, that such retention was necessary as an outward and visible sign of the supremacy of Parliament. Retention, however, raised the objection that Irish members would be voting on English, Scottish, and Welsh domestic affairs, although English, Scottish, and Welsh MPs would have no say in the domestic affairs of Ireland. Moreover, to reduce the number of Irish MPs at Westminster was of little help in terms of constitutional logic, since, as Harcourt pointed out to Gladstone in 1889, 'though it may lessen the *amount* it does not really touch the *principle* of the objection. When parties are pretty equally divided fifty Irish votes may be as decisive as 100 . . . and when you have once conceded the objection to Irish interference you don't get rid of it any more than the young woman did of the baby by saying it's such a little one.'[42]

Retention of the Irish MPs would also deprive Britain of one of the principal advantages which she hoped to gain from Home Rule, the opportunity to devote more parliamentary time to the discussion of English, Scottish, and Welsh affairs, and the removal of the Irish question from Westminster. In fact, Irish MPs might have proved just as unreasonable, from the point of view of the English, in a post-Home Rule Westminster, as they had been in the early 1880s. For they might well have come to see themselves as agents or delegates of the Irish legislature. Thus Irish issues would have to be fought out first in Dublin, and then once again at Westminster.

It is hardly surprising, then, that Gladstone told Parnell, the Irish leader, in 1889, that 'the real difficulty' still lay 'in determining the particular form in which an Irish representation may have to be retained at Westminster'.43 For each of the answers to the problem of Irish representation—exclusion, 'in and out', and retention with reduced representation—suffered from crucial weaknesses in constitutional logic. These weaknesses were unavoidable in principle, resulting as they did from the attempt to devolve power to one part of the kingdom, while retaining a fundamentally unitary constitution elsewhere. Thus, the failure to find a solution to the problem of how Ireland was to be represented at Westminster after Home Rule was logically unavoidable. This does not, however, mean that a solution to the problem was not *practically* possible; for the success of a constitutional arrangement does not depend only, or even perhaps mainly, upon its logical coherence. What it does mean, however, is that the Gladstonian settlement had within it the seeds of friction.

Gladstone had been grappling, with great intensity, with a fundamental problem that was to resurface in the 1970s, when British governments came once again to propose asymmetrical devolution, this time for Scotland and Wales. The problem of parliamentary representation for an area with legislative devolution was to prove as insoluble in the 1970s as it had been for Gladstone. It was resurrected by Tam Dalyell, MP for West Lothian, as the West Lothian Question. Dalyell asked why it was that, after legislative devolution to Scotland, Scottish MPs would be able to vote on English domestic matters such as education and health in West Bromwich, while English and Welsh MPs would no longer be able to vote on education and health in West Lothian. Gladstone had struggled to find an answer to a question which, as he came to realize, had no answer. Tam Dalyell, ninety years later, sought to embarrass supporters of devolution by demanding an answer to the same question. The key issue is whether the logical impossibility of finding an answer of itself condemns asymmetrical Home Rule or devolution. To that issue we shall return in Chapters 7 and 8.

III

The attempt to discover workable and fair financial arrangements for Ireland led to difficulties as serious as those involved in resolving the problem of representation.

Gladstone laid down as one of the conditions of a good plan of Home Rule that there be a fair and equitable division of the financial burden. But what was Ireland's fair contribution to total British revenue, and how was it to be assessed? All three Home Rule Bills proposed a payment from Ireland to the British exchequer in the form of an 'Imperial Contribution' to cover the cost of Ireland's share of reserved services. It was vital, therefore, to form some estimate of what the value of this share might be.

Unfortunately, however, there seemed to be no objective method of determining the correct amount, and the Irish were disposed to argue that the sums being required of them by the Exchequer were excessive. The Irish argument was that the Imperial Contribution should 'be measured by the only genuine test—how much can Ireland spare?'[44] This meant that the Imperial Contribution should be not a first charge, as Gladstone proposed, but a residual, to be paid after Ireland's local needs had been met. The trouble was, however, that the Irish legislature would, understandably, seek to use its financial resources for the purposes of economic development, rather than paying what it might regard as tribute to Britain. Thus, as a residual element, the Imperial Contribution would sink to nothing.

Some members of the Irish parliamentary party went even further, suggesting that Ireland be granted special consideration on account of alleged over-taxation in the past. One MP, Tim Healy, suggested that Britain should make reparation for her past ill-treatment of Ireland by not seeking an Imperial Contribution at all, a proposal which the *Economist* on 7 January 1893, dubbed 'an impudent request'.

These problems of relative taxable capacity and historical obligation were, in the words of a government committee on Irish finance, chaired by Sir Henry Primrose in 1912, almost certainly 'insoluble, not in the sense that no answer to them is possible, but because so many plausible answers are possible that the number of solutions threatens to equal the number of solvers'.[45] Nevertheless, the need for Ireland to pay the Imperial Contribution as a first charge meant that Irish revenue would probably be insufficient to meet her basic requirements; and as Healy said, again in *The Economist* of 7 January 1893, if the Irish legislature began by saying, 'We will have to impose a new tax', then, 'he would say that the members of that Parliament would deserve to be hissed out of the country.'

Gladstone was by temperament on the side of financial retrenchment. For him, one of the advantages of Home Rule was that it would stimulate economies in public expenditure. He would have agreed with the comments made by his former secretary, Sir Edward Hamilton, in 1893, that, after Home Rule, 'Great Britain being rid of an expensive partner will be no longer subject to the constantly growing demands of Ireland on the common purse'.[46] Gladstone was ill disposed to any request from the Irish for additional revenue to improve the condition of the education system in Ireland or the Irish railways. 'If the Irishmen don't like my proposals,' he told Hamilton in 1893, 'they must lump it.' It is hardly surprising that Hamilton wrote of Home Rule in his diary as 'the dissolution of a partnership in which the partner with no capital and most spendthrift habits was leaving the firm'.[47]

In addition, however, it was not clear how the taxing power should be divided so as to reconcile Irish autonomy with the freedom of the Chancellor of the Exchequer in London to manage Britain's financial affairs. Three-quarters of the Irish revenue was derived from customs and excise duties. Some Irish nationalists believed that a tariff policy would be necessary to stimulate economic development in Ireland. Britain, however, was a Free Trade country, and on ideological as well as material grounds would hardly be willing to countenance a protectionist Irish legislature which might use its power to impose tariffs against Britain or to make commercial treaties with foreign countries.

Surprisingly perhaps, Gladstone, in 1886, was at first perfectly prepared to devolve the power to vary customs and excise to the Irish legislature. But his Cabinet overruled him. 'I feel confident', Gladstone's

Home Secretary, Hugh Childers, argued, 'that English and Scottish public opinion will never tolerate any plan which gives to an Irish Legislature power to impose Customs duties, to make Ireland a "Foreign country" and trade with Ireland "Foreign trade" '.[48] Thus, in all three Home Rule Bills, customs and excise duties were retained by Westminster.

This meant, however, that the Irish legislature had control of just one-quarter of total Irish revenue. Of this quarter, one-quarter came from the Post Office, and it was difficult to alter postal rates to any significant extent; of the remainder, roughly half was derived from income tax. While it might be possible to raise income tax in Britain, one could not easily do it in Ireland without, as Healy put it, being 'hissed out of the country'. Thus the system of finance proposed seemed devised for English and not for Irish conditions.

The financial arrangements attached to Home Rule would have imposed strict limitations upon the extent of the autonomy which Ireland would enjoy. Moreover, on both of the contentious issues bedevilling the financial relationship—the value of the Imperial Contribution and the division of the taxing power—Gladstone and the Liberal Party found themselves at odds with their Irish allies.

As with the issue of parliamentary representation, Gladstone strove hard to overcome the financial difficulties. In the 1886 bill, he sought to circumvent the problem of ascertaining Ireland's true revenue with all the ammunition for discord which that search involved. Instead, he proposed that Ireland pay a fixed proportion of a specific sum as the Imperial Contribution. This was assessed, in clause 15 of the Government of Ireland Bill, as one-fifteenth of total imperial expenditure, that is, expenditure on the reserved services, and was to be a first charge on the Irish Exchequer. All other revenue collected in Ireland was to be the property of the Irish Exchequer. Moreover, the sum of one-fifteenth of total imperial expenditure in 1886 was to remain fixed for thirty years—it was not to alter with variations in British revenue, and it could be changed only by agreement between London and Dublin. This would ensure that it could not be altered to Ireland's disadvantage by the Westminster Parliament in which the Irish would no longer be represented, and would, it was hoped, provide Ireland with a surplus on her domestic account of £404,000, sufficient to allow her to begin self-government with a margin for domestic expenditure.

Parnell, however, regarded a surplus of this size as inadequate, believing that at least £1¼ m was necessary. More importantly, however, the 1886 arrangement would have meant that the Chancellor of the Exchequer in London could make no change in indirect taxation without disrupting Irish financial arrangements. For, if the Chancellor in his budget raised customs duties, Ireland would enjoy a windfall benefit, while if he lowered duties, she would suffer an unexpected loss.

If the Chancellor reduced duties, Irish revenue would fall but she would still have to meet a fixed Imperial Contribution. The Irish administration, therefore, would either have to reduce its spending, or budget for a sharp rise in Irish direct taxation which, it will be remembered, constituted less than one-quarter of Ireland's total revenue. Some idea of the magnitude of the sums involved can be gained by considering that it would have required a 40 per cent rise in Irish direct taxation to compensate for the repeal of the tea duties.

To Ireland, therefore, it would seem as if Britain was compelling the payment of a tribute through the Imperial Contribution while at the same time disrupting Ireland's budget through her fiscal policy. Britain and Ireland would be 'brought into direct hostile collision. The rich English [*sic*] government appears in the light of an imperious creditor, the Irish government stands in the position of a poverty-stricken debtor.'[49]

If, on the other hand, Britain were to raise customs duties, Ireland would gain a windfall benefit. Were she to lower direct taxation in compensation, this would have socially regressive consequences, since the poor would be paying higher taxes on consumption goods, while the rich would be relieved of part of their burden of income tax. Ireland would, therefore, have forced upon her a change in her financial arrangements which she might not want, and, moreover, 'a ratio between direct and indirect taxation which might be both financially unsound and socially harmful'.[50] Direct taxation, which appeared to be under Irish control, would not in fact be so, because it would vary inversely with variations in indirect taxation, determined by decisions made in London. Thus the Irish government would be dependent upon a British budget which could at any moment upset all its calculations of revenue.

Nor would the British budget be in a healthier situation. Suppose that an increase in the cost of imperial services meant that Britain required additional revenue. If this revenue were to be obtained through increasing direct taxation, Ireland would be making no contribution towards it. The Irish might well not respond to a patriotic appeal from the British government to raise direct taxation given, as Harcourt rather delicately put it, 'the ethical and patriotic temperament of the men with whom we have to deal'.[51] Therefore, to ensure that Ireland made a proportionate contribution to any increase in revenue, Britain would have to raise her customs duties, a difficult option for a Liberal and Free Trade government to accept.

The financial scheme of 1886, therefore, might well not have worked successfully. The finances of Britain and Ireland would have become hopelessly intertwined. The arrangements would both have restricted the freedom of the Chancellor of the Exchequer, and eroded the financial autonomy of the Irish legislature almost to non-existence.

Such a dilemma was inevitable in any financial scheme unless it either gave to Ireland control of customs—something ruled out in 1886—or, alternatively, credited Britain with Irish customs duties, treating a proportion of the sum raised through customs as the Imperial Contribution. This second solution was adopted in 1893, when it was proposed that one-third of Irish customs and excise be credited to Britain, leaving Ireland with a surplus of £½m. This proposal enjoyed the considerable advantage of being easy to comprehend, and it meant that a proportion of customs duties, attribution of which it was difficult to assign precisely, would be retained as British taxes. For these reasons, the proposal appeared to the Primrose Committee on Irish finance, in 1912, as the best available, since 'it would have provided a clear-cut line of demarcation between Imperial and Irish finance', and it did not require any reference to the insoluble problems of relative taxable capacity or historic obligation.[52]

Unfortunately, this scheme too had its defects, for it made the size of the Imperial Contribution entirely dependent upon the fiscal policy of the British government. Under a Free Trade Chancellor, such as Harcourt, Ireland would enjoy an uncovenanted gain. Harcourt's aim was a 'free breakfast table', a reduction of the duty on commodities such as tea, and a recouping of the revenue through death duties. Ireland would then obtain the entire benefit of the reduction of the tea duty while contributing nothing via death duties, since direct taxes had been devolved, towards increased taxation in the rest of the country. The Irish would thus enjoy cheaper tea at the expense of the British taxpayer. It is little wonder that Harcourt told Gladstone: 'I plainly foresee that either the Budget will kill the Irish finance, or the Irish finance will kill the Budget'.53 Here too the policy of the Irish administration would depend upon the vagaries of the British budget, which could at any moment upset its calculations of revenue. It would, however, be futile to speculate on how this problem might have been resolved, since the scheme had to be withdrawn, after 'an enormous error' was discovered 'in the computation of the Excise revenue due to Ireland and Great Britain respectively'.54 The effect of this error was to reduce the Irish surplus from £½ m. to £140,000, a sum insufficient for Ireland's domestic expenditure. The scheme was dropped in committee in 1893.

The government's response was to establish an advisory commission under Hugh Childers, which reported that Ireland's taxable capacity was only one-twentieth of Britain's and that an Imperial Contribution could not be fixed, but would have to be variable, and imposed only after Irish local needs had been satisfied. The implication of the Childers report was that the scheme of 1886 and the original scheme of 1893, both of which required a fixed Imperial Contribution, would not have been workable. The new scheme was, however, open to the objection that it required an objective estimate of Ireland's true revenue, a problem which, as we have seen, was likely to prove insoluble.

By the time of the third Home Rule Bill in 1912, the introduction of measures of state welfare, such as old-age pensions in 1908 and the National Insurance Act of 1911, was placing considerable strains upon the Irish domestic accounts, which were now in deficit. This deficit could be expected to increase with the further development of the welfare state. Had Ireland been an independent country, compelled to finance her expenditure from her own revenue, she would not have been able to afford old-age pensions at the British level.

If the Irish account were in deficit, then, so it would seem, there could be no question of requiring an Imperial Contribution from her. Under the 1912 bill, the British taxpayer would find it necessary to subsidize Irish domestic services, as well as the Irish Imperial Contribution, her share of the reserved services, for some years to come. Otherwise, the first act of an Irish legislature would have had to be a drastic increase in direct taxation. The 1912 bill, however, had it been implemented, might have caused, 'a material change in the attitude of the British taxpayer towards the question'.55 For the British taxpayer might find it anomalous that Ireland would enjoy self-government within the United Kingdom at his expense. In those circumstances, how could Ireland enjoy autonomy when her domestic account was in deficit?

The Irish nationalists did not accept any of the Liberal financial proposals as a final settlement. In 1886, Parnell declared that he would strongly oppose the financial clauses in committee, while in 1893, Redmond declared on the third reading of the Home Rule Bill:

I maintain that no man in his senses can any longer regard it either as a full, a final or a satisfactory settlement of the Irish nationalist question. . . . With regard to the financial part of the bill, if in every other detail the Bill were satisfactory, that part of the Bill is so grave and faulty that it would be impossible for me to allow the third reading to go without uttering a protest and making it clear that my vote cannot be held as approving that part of the scheme. It is not merely that Nationalists regard the financial clauses as ungenerous . . . it is the practical ground that they believe it to be impossible to govern Ireland successfully under these financial clauses.56

The 1893 bill, Redmond declared, was a 'toad, ugly and venomous, yet wearing a precious jewel in its head'.57 The Irish nationalists also condemned the financial clauses of the 1912 bill, and refused to accept them as a final settlement.

Liberal statesmen did not succeed in discovering a financial settlement which could both underwrite Irish autonomy and avoid conflict between the two legislatures. What militated against such a solution was, as we have seen, the peculiar structure of the Irish economy, in particular her dependence upon customs and excise duties for the bulk of her income. This meant that probably the only way to give Ireland financial autonomy was to give her control of customs, as Gladstone had originally proposed. But, as we have seen, such a proposal was unacceptable to the Liberal Cabinet, and probably to Liberal MPs and Liberals in the country as well. Moreover, an Ireland with control of customs, able to impose a protective tariff on British goods, and to sign commercial treaties with other countries, would have been well on the way to a break with Britain. From this point of view, Home Rule, rather than binding Ireland more closely within the United Kingdom, as Gladstone hoped, would have put her on the slippery slope to separatism.

IV

For Home Rulers and unionists alike, the supremacy of Parliament was the keystone of the constitution, the cement which held the country together. There was, however, considerable ambiguity in what the doctrine entailed. It might, at that time, have meant the exercise of real political authority which Parliament enjoyed in relation to the United Kingdom; or it might have meant the more nominal, although not wholly nominal, supremacy that Parliament enjoyed over the self-governing colonies such as Canada.

This ambiguity reflected the different interpretations of Home Rule offered by British Liberals and Irish nationalists. For the Irish nationalists, the supremacy which Westminster should enjoy over Ireland after Home Rule should be a dormant supremacy, very like that which Parliament exercised over Canada. Were it to be a real supremacy, implying the regular intervention of Westminster in Ireland's affairs, that, in the eyes of Irish nationalists, would diminish Irish autonomy to zero.

Liberals, however, did not intend to allow the Irish so great a degree of autonomy. That, indeed, is why the Home Rule Bills reserved certain matters to Westminster and required of Ireland an Imperial Contribution. Nevertheless, once an Irish legislature sat in Dublin, Britain would be under a moral, although not a legal, obligation not to legislate for Ireland in her domestic affairs. For as long as Home Rule worked normally, the Irish parliament would, in Irish domestic affairs, be in practical terms a co-ordinate and not a subordinate body.

Even in an emergency, however, difficulties would arise if Westminster sought to exercise its supremacy. It would not be easy for Parliament to use its veto, for it might prove impossible to secure an Irish administration, resting on a majority in the legislature, except one which insisted on ignoring the veto. The difficulty was that use of the veto would depend in effect upon the consent of the Irish administration. This was a problem which, as we shall see, the British government was to face when it tried to overrule a friendly administration in Belfast, in 1922 (see pp. 74–5). How much more difficult it would have been with an unfriendly administration in Dublin. It was for this reason that a Conservative opponent of Home Rule, Sir Michael Hicks-Beach, argued of the 1893 bill that 'the safeguards in the bill are absolutely unreal. There is not one of them that is not at the complete mercy of the very persons against whom they are devised.'[58] After Home Rule, there would be only two ways in which the British government would be able to secure compliance with its wishes from an Irish government—agreement and force. Agreement, although more necessary after Home Rule, would, however, become more difficult, since the Irish legislature could legitimately claim to represent the Irish nation. Nothing would mobilize that nation more effectively than a British demand which the Irish legislature was determined to resist. It was for this reason that the Primrose Committee declared that 'there is no means, short of the employment of force in the last resort, by which an independent legislature or executive can be compelled to do something positive against its will'.[59] It was, then, not clear how the British government could in practice make the supremacy of Parliament effective once the judiciary and the police were in Irish hands.

Self-government had worked in the colonies, which were generally content with their constitutions; peopled mainly with settlers of British descent, they were in no sense hostile to Britain. Moreover, they knew that if they genuinely sought separation, it would not be refused. With the Irish, by contrast, these conditions did not apply. They were by no means content with the limited degree of autonomy which Home Rule offered them; they sought revision of the financial clauses; and they might well seek to use their political leverage to extract further concessions. The Irish, therefore, were in a stronger position than the colonists to enforce their demands, but Westminster was far less likely to countenance separation.

V

The seemingly insuperable difficulties involved in any scheme of Irish Home Rule led some politicians and opinion-formers to argue that only a 'federal solution' could reconcile the demands of Irish nationalists with the requirements of parliamentary supremacy. The term 'federal' was, however, used with considerable imprecision. It was not intended to imply a juridical division of sovereignty on the model of the American Constitution. Rather, it implied a policy of general devolution or 'Home-Rule-All-Round', by which Scotland and Wales, as well as Ireland, together with either England or the English regions, would be given legislatures of their own. The supremacy of Parliament would be retained, since each of these legislatures would be subordinate to Westminster. Federalism was, admittedly, a misnomer, declared Philip Kerr in August 1910, 'But it is a good fighting word to begin with. Devolution has noisome associations. Home Rule all round, worse. Federalism has been a success everywhere and people will therefore not be inclined to fight shy of the word.'[60]

A federal solution in this sense seemed to offer answers to the three constitutional problems which bedevilled Home Rule. The creation of subordinate legislatures in England, Scotland, and Wales would resolve the problem of representation, since Westminster would become a federal parliament, and the Irish would be represented in it on precisely the same terms as the other nationalities in the United Kingdom. Thus federalism would provide for the equal treatment of the different portions of the United Kingdom. Federalism might also help to secure a more equitable division of revenues between the various parts of the state, since each of the legislatures would enjoy the same taxing powers.

Above all, however, federalism could preserve the unity of the kingdom and ward off separatism, since it would give to Ireland nothing which was not also to be given to other parts of the United Kingdom. Speaking in the House of Commons debate on devolution in 1919, the geographer Halford Mackinder claimed that Joseph Chamberlain, in putting forward the federal idea,

saw that there was safety in numbers. In the number of subordinate Parliaments there is safety, for the majority of subordinate Parliaments will be able to exercise restraint on the recalcitrant Parliament that would cut itself adrift or otherwise misbehave.[61]

Moreover, federalism held out the possibility of resolving the Ulster problem, if it led to the creation of a separate legislature for that province. Under those circumstances, Home Rule would confirm Ulster's membership of the United Kingdom instead of undermining it. By 1919, Sir Edward Carson, leader of the Ulster Unionists, was thus able to declare, 'I do not believe that devolution is a step towards separation. Indeed, I am not sure that devolution, if properly carried out, may not lead to closer union'.[62]

Federalism had been proposed by the former Liberal Prime Minister, Earl Russell, in 1872, as a means of relieving parliamentary congestion. Also in the 1870s, the leader of the Irish parliamentary party, Isaac Butt, advocated it as a solution to the Irish question. Later, leading Liberals such as Lloyd George and Churchill came to espouse it, and the second draft of the 1912 Home Rule Bill included a scheme proposed by Lloyd George for Grand Committees in England, Scotland, and Wales, with wide legislative powers of the same scope as those to be offered to Ireland. The title of the bill was to be Government of Ireland and House of Commons (Devolution of Business) Bill. This scheme was dropped from the final draft of the bill, but all the same, in introducing it, Asquith declared that it was 'the first step and only the first step in a larger and more comprehensive policy'.[63]

Federalism was attractive not only to Liberals, as a means of meeting the claims of the Scots and the Welsh, but also to unionists who, if they could not avoid Home Rule, were determined to ensure that it should not lead to separatism. Disraeli in 1880 was, apparently, 'prepared to consider some sort of federal constitution for Ireland'.[64] Joseph Chamberlain argued in his second reading speech on the 1886 Home Rule Bill that the solution should be found 'in the direction of federalism' as an alternative to Home Rule. For, under federalism, Ireland might 'really remain an integral portion of the Empire. The action of such a scheme is centripetal and not centrifugal, and it is in the direction of federation that the Democratic movement has made most advances in the present century'.[65] However, on other occasions, Chamberlain declared that federalism would involve a massive and unwanted constitutional upheaval, and so it may be that his espousal of federalism was merely tactical. In the years before the First World War, however, Chamberlain's son, Austen, came to be attracted by the federal solution and sought to convert other unionists to it; and he was supported by imperialists of the Round Table school who believed that a federal United Kingdom could be a preliminary to a federation of the self-governing colonies of the Empire—an imperial federation.

Yet the federalist solution remained a constitutionalist's creation. It never became part of the practical agenda of politics. 'The question', declared Gladstone in 1886, 'seems to imply that the wants and wishes of England, Scotland, Wales and Ireland are the same. I have no evidence before me which would lead me to assume that this is the case.'[66] The most obvious objection to federalism was that it gave to England a constitution which she did not want in order to retain Ireland within the United Kingdom. Lord Curzon told the War Cabinet in July 1918 that 'he was not prepared to pull up the British Constitution by the roots in order to get Ireland out of her difficulties'.[67]

There was no popular pressure in England for a federal solution involving the creation of an English legislature. 'After all,' argued Lloyd George, when the federal option was put to him after the First World War, 'here is a population of 34,000,000 out of 45,000,000, and unless you have got a substantial majority of the English representatives in favour of it, it is idle to attempt it.'[68]

Moreover, there was considerable doubt whether a federal constitution would actually succeed in placating the Irish nationalists. Neither Parnell nor Redmond showed much sympathy with federalism, which they saw as an attempt to deny the urgency of the Irish problem by linking it to the far less urgent problems of nationalism in Scotland and Wales. In 1886, Parnell sought, for the Irish legislature, the power to tax imports, declaring that 'An Irish custom-house is really of more importance to Ireland than an Irish parliament.'[69] Such a demand was hardly compatible with a federal constitution. The Irish nationalists were, in any case, not prepared to wait while governments drew up large and complex schemes of federalism. They demanded Home Rule as the solution to what they saw as an immediate and pressing problem.

A federal constitution would require from the Irish at least as much loyalty to the imperial parliament as a policy of Irish Home Rule. For, as Dicey put it,

A Federal Government is, of all constitutions, the most artificial. If such a government is to be worked with anything like success, there must exist among the citizens of the confederacy a spirit of genuine loyalty to the Union. The 'Unitarian' feeling of the people must distinctly predominate over the sentiment in favour of 'state rights'.[70]

England, however, the largest state in the Union, did not seek 'state rights', while Ireland was not particularly enamoured of union. Under these circumstances, federalism would increase, not reduce, the possibilities of conflict between Britain and Ireland.

For Ireland, moreover, the federal parliament might well appear as the English parliament writ large, since England would enjoy such a powerful preponderance within it. In addition, a federal arrangement would allow Irish MPs to employ the same tactics of obstruction that they had used in the 1880–5 parliament, and government could easily become paralysed as a result. 'A sick man fears to lose a limb', Dicey declared. 'He will not be greatly consoled by the assurance that his arm may be retained at the risk of his suffering general paralysis.'[71]

The federal solution thus suffered from the double drawback that the Home Rulers thought it a diversion, while most unionists believed that it would weaken the government of the United Kingdom without resolving the Irish problem. Moreover, although Carson made favourable noises, many Ulster Unionists were suspicious of a federal system based on the principle of nationality, for they came to regard themselves neither as part of the Irish nation, nor as a separate nation of their own. Instead, they saw themselves as an integral part of the

United Kingdom, like Yorkshire or Sussex. Therefore, the only type of federalism which they would countenance would have to be based on regions, not on nations. Yet the Irish nationalists did not regard Ireland as a region, and a regional form of government would not, they believed, satisfy the national aspirations of the Irish people; and the English were not prepared to restore the heptarchy solely to help resolve the Irish problem.

These difficulties were graphically illustrated when, after the First World War, in 1919, a conference on devolution was established, with thirty-two members, sixteen from each House, under the chairmanship of the Speaker of the Commons, James Lowther. The task of this conference was not to consider whether devolution was desirable, but rather to propose a practical scheme. The war and the immediate post-war years saw numerous grandiose schemes for social and economic reconstruction, and the first Speaker's Conference of 1917 had achieved agreement between the parties on universal male suffrage and female suffrage. Federalists, therefore, hoped that a second Speaker's Conference, on devolution, could achieve similar agreement under the auspices of a coalition government under which party divisions seemed, for a time, in abeyance. Unfortunately for the Conference, however, Lloyd George decided, during the course of its sittings, to deal separately with Ireland, and a Government of Ireland Bill was introduced into Parliament. The Conference, therefore, decided to exclude Ireland from further consideration, and nationalist Ireland was not represented on it. But, in any case, Ireland outside Ulster had moved well beyond devolution, and the Sinn Féin landslide in the 1918 general election presaged a more violent phase in Ireland's struggle for independence.

The Conference did indeed reach agreement on four of the crucial matters which it had to consider: the division of powers; the division of financial powers; the territorial organization of the judiciary; and the areas in which subordinate legislatures should be set up. The Conference decided that the principle of nationality should be fundamental, and that, therefore, England ought not to be divided, although the Ulster members continued to argue for a divided England so that they could more easily press for a divided Ireland.

The Conference failed, however, to agree on whether the subordinate legislatures should be directly elected. Murray Macdonald, a federalist MP, argued for direct election, but the Speaker felt that this proposal was unrealistic.

The more I considered the proposal of one supreme and four independent legislatures, the less I liked it. The confusions which might arise, the multiplicity of elections, the novelty of five (possibly even more) Prime Ministers and Cabinets of probably divergent political views, the enormous expense of building four new sets of Parliamentary buildings and Government offices and providing all the paraphernalia of administration, frightened my economical soul.[72]

Moreover, the Speaker felt that the Conference 'was hardly numerous or representative enough to be qualified to undertake the very serious task of drawing up what might in effect be a new Constitution for the component parts of Great Britain'.[73] One of the members of the Conference, Lord Gladstone, son of the former Prime Minister, was more forthright in declaring 'the personnel of the Conference with few exceptions' to be 'incompetent'.[74] Lowther, therefore, proposed, as an alternative to direct election, a system of national Grand Councils, composed of the MPs of England, Scotland, and Wales. These Grand Councils would be an extension of the idea embodied in the proposal for a Scottish Grand Committee, first established in 1894, that bills affecting the different nations comprising the United Kingdom should originate and have their legislative stages in their respective national parliamentary committees. Perhaps these committees might sit not only in London, but also in Edinburgh and Cardiff. A scheme of this kind could perhaps evolve into the larger scheme of directly elected bodies should the demand arise. It could be supported therefore by federalists as a transitional device. The trouble was, however, that the Speaker's scheme would make no contribution to the relief of parliamentary congestion, which was one of the main motives behind the federalist movement.

Each of the two schemes—Murray Macdonald's and the Speaker's—had the support of thirteen members of the Conference. Five members supported both schemes, the Speaker's scheme on an interim basis, and the Murray Macdonald scheme as the desirable terminus. Faced with this deadlock, it is hardly surprising that the deliberations of the Conference were stillborn. 'It may be said', reported the Speaker ruefully to the Prime Minister, 'that the Conference has been more successful in bringing into the open, than in solving, the doubts and difficulties that surround the task of recasting the British Constitution with the aid of imperfect analogies supplied by other countries, which under totally dissimilar conditions have adopted federal principles of government for the purpose of uniting previously separate states.'[75]

In any case, the mood of the country was hardly sympathetic to a grand reconstruction of the Constitution, and the government had no mandate for so radical a change. As Lord Birkenhead, the Lord Chancellor, had said of the federalists, 'It is now actually proposed that an immense revolution of the Constitution of these Islands is to be carried through after a General Election at which it is not possible to pretend even that one constituency voted with this question before them. To attempt to do so would, in my humble judgement be a national scandal.'[76] When Lloyd George's government decided to deal separately with the Irish question, the political dynamic which might have led to federalism disappeared entirely. 'The discussions', declared Lowther in his memoirs, 'had been of great interest, as they often raised recondite and sometimes difficult questions of Constitutional lore and law, but all along I felt that the driving force of necessity which had been so active a factor in the Electoral Reform Conference was absent.'[77]

Lord Salisbury was perhaps being too dismissive when he replied in 1889 to a correspondent who was urging the federal solution upon him: 'As to Home Rule in your sense—which is Federation—I do not see in it any elements of practicability. Nations do not change their political nature like that except through blood.'[78] Federalism might have been made acceptable to the electorate if it had been presented as a remedy for deeply felt and immediate grievances. In the absence of that, however, it was bound to appear as remote and impractical.

VI

Liberal statesmen did not succeed in reconciling Ireland to membership of the United Kingdom by their policy of Home Rule. Gladstone had believed that Irish nationality was a purely local patriotism, like that of Scotland and Wales, and therefore perfectly compatible with the British connection. Had that been the case, then the consensus and goodwill needed to work Home Rule might well have been present. But, if Irish nationality was rather different from Scottish and Welsh nationality, if it was instead a nationalism fuelled by 'a thirst for revenge . . . that hatred, that undying hatred for what they could not but regard as the cause and symbol of their misfortunes—English rule in Ireland',[79] then the attempt to corral it through Home Rule was doomed to failure. It was, to change the metaphor, an attempt to mix oil and water.

The truth is that the Liberals no less than the Conservatives, were unionist, in that they sought to find a method by which Ireland could be kept within the Union. They differed from their opponents not on the necessity of maintaining the Union, but on the subsidiary issue of whether the existing relationship of Ireland within the Union was a tolerable one.

Yet any scheme of Home Rule which a Liberal government proposed, or which the British people could be persuaded to accept, was bound to fall short of what Irish nationalists demanded, even if only in symbolic terms—and of course symbolic issues are often of the utmost importance in relationships between governments. For any scheme of Home Rule was bound to display and indeed make explicit Ireland's practical subordination to the United Kingdom, a subordination from which Irish nationalists wished to escape. The real issue at the heart of the Home Rule controversy was perhaps not so much the conflict between Home Rulers and unionists, but whether any relationship could be devised which retained Ireland within the Union as a subordinate community and yet which the Irish could be persuaded to accept; the resolution of this issue would depend on whether the fundamental attitude of the Irish people to Britain was one of hostility or friendship. For Home Rule, or devolution, 'suggests only a means whereby better government may be secured within a single State. Its value disappears once the unity of the State is questioned'.[80]

However, even if it is accepted that Home Rule would not have satisfied Irish aspirations, the argument does not end there. For after all, if the Home Rulers did not succeed, nor did the unionists. 'All resistance to this measure', Gladstone declared in April 1886, 'is a contribution to the cause of separatism, and those who offer it are not Unionists but Separatists.'[81] The unionists did not achieve their aim of maintaining the Union, which was dissolved by force between the years 1918 and 1921, in an atmosphere of mistrust and hostility which was to poison relations between Britain and Ireland for many years.

Unionism had comprised two elements. The first, that represented by the Conservatives and by the Whig leader Lord Hartington, had declared that any form of Home Rule was a threat to national unity. This element believed that a self-governing Ireland could not remain part of the United Kingdom, unless the United Kingdom were to be transformed into a federation, which was hardly possible. Otherwise, Home Rule was inherently separatist.

Home Rule, however, might not have been defeated if the opposition to it had been constitutionalist alone. In 1886, as in the 1970s, devolution was defeated because opponents from the Right received additional support from defections on the Left. In 1886, the second element in unionism was a radical unionism, led by Joseph Chamberlain, and it depended for its vitality less upon constitutional propositions than upon the view that the problems of Ireland were not at bottom constitutional at all, but fundamentally social and economic in nature. For Chamberlain, the difficulties faced by the Irish peasant were no different in kind from those faced by the Scottish crofter, the Welsh peasant, or the English agricultural labourer. The answer to these problems was not to dilute the forces of radicalism by establishing separate legislatures, but to mobilize them so that a strong radical government could be formed at Westminster to make a serious attack on economic and social grievances. A similar answer was given by many on the Labour Left in the 1970s when devolution once more came to the fore. MPs such as Eric Heffer and Neil Kinnock were to declare that the problems of the Scottish working class and the problems of the Welsh working class were similar to those of the English working class, and were to be resolved not by devolution, but through the installation of a strong socialist government at Westminster. That argument is less an argument about *sovereignty* than about *power*. On both occasions, in 1886 and in the 1970s, the Left chronically underestimated the force of nationalism, treating it as a surrogate for something else, which it was not.

Gladstone, speaking just before the defeat of Home Rule in the Commons in 1886, asked MPs to 'think, I beseech you, think well, think wisely, think not for the moment, but for the years to come before you reject this Bill.'[82] In rejecting Home Rule, the unionists did not settle the question. They had to face the problem of how Ireland was to be governed in the face of the near-unanimous demand of her representatives, outside Ulster, for Home Rule. It was a problem they were unable to resolve.

The Irish parliamentary leaders were ambiguous, perhaps deliberately so, as to whether they would have accepted Home Rule as a final settlement. 'We cannot, under the British Constitution,' declared Parnell at Cork in 1885, 'ask for more than the restitution of Grattan's Parliament. But no man has the right to fix the boundary to the march of a nation. No man has a right to say to his country, "Thus far shalt thou go and no further", and we have never attempted to fix a *ne plus ultra* to the progress of Ireland's nationhood and we never shall.'[83]

Gladstone sought, through Home Rule, to create a 'Union of Hearts' with Ireland, to reconcile her to the British connection. Home Rule, he told Queen Victoria, was 'a proposal eminently Conservative in the highest sense of the term, as tending to the union of the three countries . . . and to the stability of the Imperial throne and institutions'.[84] It is impossible to tell whether Gladstone would have succeeded in his aim. Even if he had been unsuccessful, however, and Home Rule had proved to be a step on the slippery slope to independence, this would have occurred in a far happier atmosphere than in fact it did. From 1886, right up to the Second World War, Ireland, whether part of the United Kingdom or independent, was to prove a perpetual irritant. 'What fools we were', George V told Ramsay MacDonald in 1930, 'not to have accepted Gladstone's Home Rule Bill. The Empire would not have had the Irish Free State giving us so much trouble and pulling us to pieces.'[85]

The apparent triumph of the Irish nationalists in 1921, however, turned out to be as illusory as that of the unionists in 1886. The 1921 settlement had the effect of entrenching the partition of the island, but the greater the distance between Britain and Ireland, the more difficult it became to resolve the position of the Catholic minority in Northern Ireland, since the Protestant majority feared that the Catholics, by seeking to join with the rest of Ireland, were displaying a lack of loyalty to the United Kingdom. The manifold links between Britain and Ireland and their common interest in finding a stable constitutional settlement in Northern Ireland could not be contained within a formal framework of total separation, which, theoretically at least, made Britain and Ireland as foreign to one another as Poland and Chile. In 1998, the Belfast Agreement provided for the establishment of a British–Irish Council, at which the British and Irish governments, together with the devolved governments in Britain, could meet, agree to delegate functions, and decide also on common policies. In the long road towards the Belfast Agreement, both the British and Irish governments had painfully rediscovered the essential truth of the Gladstonian proposition that neither separation nor partition could yield a solution to the Irish problem. A permanent solution, it became apparent, could be achieved only through a process which both recognized and yet also transcended nationalism, through institutions which expressed not only the separate national identities of the various parts of Britain and Ireland, but also the fundamental unity of these islands.

Northern Ireland

If we believe that the sovereign national state is the best form that national sentiment can take and the almost unavoidable form of human government in the modern world, there is probably no lasting acceptable framework of government for Northern Ireland.

(Bernard Crick)

I

Northern Ireland is the only part of the United Kingdom with practical experience of devolution. For just over fifty years—from 1921, when the Northern Ireland Parliament was opened by George V, to 1972, when it was prorogued by the British government, prior to abolition in 1973—six of the nine counties of Ulster enjoyed Home Rule, the form of government which Ulster had taken the lead in resisting since 1886. Any study of devolution in Britain must, therefore, take account of the experience of Northern Ireland in operating devolved institutions.

There are, however, two interconnected factors which limit the value of Northern Ireland as a case-study of devolution. The first is that her parliament was not established, as devolved legislatures generally are, to meet a nationalist or separatist threat. Indeed, a separate parliament was not sought by the Ulster Unionists at all, but was pressed upon them by the British government as a means of ending British rule in Ireland and so resolving the Irish problem. The Ulster Unionists accepted a parliament, not because they sought separation, but for the opposite reason, to ensure that Northern Ireland remained part of the United Kingdom. The circumstances surrounding the birth of the Northern Ireland Parliament conditioned the whole experience of devolution in the province.

The second factor which makes the experience of Northern Ireland atypical of devolution is the community problem, which is not replicated anywhere else in Britain—the antagonism between the unionist community, primarily Protestant, which seeks to maintain the link with Britain, and the nationalist community, primarily Catholic, which seeks union with the rest of Ireland. An analysis of devolution in Northern Ireland must ask whether Home Rule exacerbated the community problem and whether alternative political arrangements might have helped lessen the antagonism which erupted into open violence in 1968 and led to the suspension of devolution in the province.

The community conflict in Northern Ireland has deep historical roots. There was, from earliest times, a significant Scottish presence in Ireland, the Scots referring to themselves as 'the Britons in Ireland'.[1] But the Reformation was firmly resisted by the vast majority of the Irish population, who retained their Catholic religion. In the early seventeenth century, however, the Protestant presence was massively reinforced by the 'Plantation', the colonization of Ulster with immigrants primarily from Scotland but also from England, whose ascendancy was assured after the Battle of the Boyne in 1690. Since that time, the Protestants have tended to regard the Catholics as both disloyal to the Crown and as a threat to religious freedom. Ulster, moreover, developed along different lines from the rest of Ireland, being more orientated towards industry than agriculture and with a different system of land tenure. Already, by the 1830s, Ulster seemed to be separate from the rest of Ireland, and a Protestant preserve.[2]

The rise of Irish nationalism and the growth of a modern sense of Irish identity from the end of the eighteenth century exacerbated the differences between Protestants and Catholics. For, although a number of the leaders of the Irish nationalist movement—Wolfe Tone and Parnell, for example—were Protestant, nevertheless Irish nationalism came to be identified with the Catholic majority. In 1886, the vast majority of Protestants opposed Home Rule and demanded continuation of the union with Britain, so that the terms Protestant and unionist came to be almost interchangeable. It is indeed this superimposition of a nationalist conflict upon a religious one which largely explains the persistence and depth of the Irish problem. There is an unresolved conflict of national identities within a context of incompatible national claims. As a conquered country, Ireland generated a nationalism which sought independence from Britain. As a 'planted' country, Ireland generated a distinct community which sought to retain the link with Britain.

In 1886, the Protestants were a scattered minority in Ireland as a whole, but a concentrated majority in the north-east. They constituted majorities in four counties of the province of Ulster—Antrim, Armagh, Down, and Londonderry; nearly 50 per cent of the population in two other counties in the province—Fermanagh and Tyrone; and a significant minority in the other three counties—Cavan, Donegal, and Monaghan—which are now part of the Irish Republic. In 1886, Joseph Chamberlain declared that Ireland: 'is not a homogeneous community . . . it consists of two nations . . . it is a nation which comprises two races and two religions.'[3]

There is an inconsistency in this claim, which suggests on the one hand that the Protestants were a separate nation, and on the other that Ireland was one nation, but a divided one. In fact, the Ulster Unionists rejected Home Rule not because they wished to claim an alternative nationhood of their own, but because they wished to remain part of the British nation. It is therefore misleading to regard the conflict in Ireland as one between two nations. For the Ulster Unionists did not see themselves as a separate nation, and saw no reason why their Irishness should conflict with their membership of the United Kingdom. What the Unionists sought was, in the words of Ulster's Solemn League and Covenant of 1912, to preserve 'for ourselves and our children our cherished position of equal citizenship in the United Kingdom'. The fact that Ulster Unionists sought nothing more than 'equal citizenship' made it difficult for Britain to ignore their claims. For they were not seeking, as the Irish nationalists were, privileges denied to others, such as a separate parliament. All they desired was to retain a position which was under threat from those who, so they believed, sought to undermine, if not break completely, the link with Britain. Thus Ulster Unionism was not an assertion of a separate Ulster nationhood, but a reaction against the claim made by Irish nationalists that the assertion of Irish nationhood was separatist in nature. There is therefore no symmetry between Irish nationalism and Ulster unionism. The one is a claim based on nationality, the other a claim based on citizenship.

The partition of Ireland had first been suggested by Macaulay in response to O'Connell's campaign for repeal of the Union. 'If a root-ed difference in religion, and the existence of the worst conse-quences of that difference would justify the separation of the English [*sic*] and Irish legislatures, the same difference and still more, the same baleful consequences, would warrant the separation of Protestant Ulster from Catholic Munster'.4 When Gladstone intro-duced his first Home Rule Bill, however, he made no provision for special treatment for Ulster, whose Protestant population he saw as part of a minority in Ireland, rather than as a majority in the north-east part of the island. It seems, however, from the diary of Lewis Harcourt, the son of Gladstone's Chancellor of the Exchequer, that Gladstone might, in fact, have been 'prepared to except Ulster from the Act as a compromise'.5 There was, perhaps, no inherent reason why he might not have considered special arrangements for Ulster. At that time, however, Ulster made no such claim. Ulster Unionists, together with their counterparts in the rest of Ireland and in Britain, were confident that they could defeat Home Rule for the whole of Ireland. Therefore there was no reason for them to consider exclu-sion.

By the time of the third Home Rule Bill in 1912, it was becoming apparent that special consideration would have to be given to Ulster. In the first reading debate on the 1912 bill, Sir Edward Carson, the leader of the Irish unionists, claimed that the argument for self-deter-mination used by the Irish nationalists could also be used by the Ulster Unionists, and that every argument for giving Home Rule to Ireland, was also an argument for giving Home Rule to the north-eastern part of Ulster. But the central aim of Irish unionists, in both north and south, was still to kill Home Rule, rather than to establish a separate Ulster. For this purpose, the 'Orange card', first used by Lord Randolph Churchill in 1886, was an indispensable weapon. 'If Ulster succeeds,' Carson had claimed in 1911, 'Home Rule is dead.'6 At that time it was widely believed that an independent Ireland, which unionists regarded as the inevitable consequence of Home Rule, would not be viable without the industrial wealth and strength of Belfast and its environs. This assumption was shared by the vast majority of Home Rulers, who agreed with the Irish nationalist view that Ireland was a single political unit. One could no more divide

Ireland, Asquith told the House of Commons in June 1912, than one could divide England or Scotland.[7]

The Ulster Covenant of 1912 pledged its signatories to use 'all means which may be found necessary to defeat the present conspiracy to set up a Home Rule Parliament in Ireland'. The unionists could not, however, prevent Home Rule in any part of Ireland except the north-east. What they proposed, once Home Rule was passed, was to refuse to accept the authority of a Dublin parliament, and to take over for themselves the responsibility for government in that part of Ireland which they could effectively control. Thus, the Northern unionists 'would vote against Home Rule for Ireland to the end of time, but they would only *fight* for the exclusion of Ulster'.[8] In that fight, moreover, they would enjoy considerable support from British public opinion, which could not understand why a loyal part of the kingdom should be extruded from it; and, after the Curragh incident of 1914, it seemed that leading army officers would not be a party to forcing Ulster to accept the jurisdiction of a Home Rule parliament in Dublin. Thus, if the Liberals wished to avoid civil war, special arrangements would have to be made for Ulster. That seemed to mean the exclusion of Ulster from Home Rule, and therefore the partition of Ireland, a position which Ulster Unionists and British Conservatives were willing to accept as a second-best if they could not prevent Home Rule. The original unionist position had been that the whole Irish nation was part of the larger British state. When that position became untenable, unionists retreated to a fall-back position, insisting that Ulster had the right to opt out of the proposed new Irish state.

The partition of Ireland had indeed been discussed in Cabinet in February 1912 before the third Home Rule Bill was introduced into the Commons. It was advocated by Lloyd George and Churchill, but the government decided to wait upon events. Partition was first proposed in Parliament by T. Agar-Robartes, a Liberal back-bencher, in an amendment to the third Home Rule Bill in 1912. Arguing that 'I have never heard that orange bitters will mix with Irish whisky',[9] Agar-Robartes proposed the exclusion of the four counties with Protestant majorities. His amendment was defeated by sixty-one votes, but two Cabinet ministers, Lloyd George and Churchill, absented themselves on the vote. That was not the end of proposals for partition, however. In January 1913, Carson proposed a 'clean cut' exclusion of the nine Ulster counties, and in March 1914, Asquith, as Prime Minister, proposed an amending bill according to which, on a basis of county option, any county could opt out of Home Rule for six years. Carson, however, rejected what he called 'sentence of death with a stay of execution for six years',[10] and the bill was amended by the Lords to nine-county exclusion on a permanent basis. This in turn was unacceptable to the Liberals and Irish nationalists. At the Buckingham Palace Conference, held in July 1914, the exclusion of six counties was suggested for the first time, but the Conference ended in deadlock, and the issue remained unresolved when Britain declared war on Germany in August 1914.

The third Home Rule Bill finally received the Royal Assent in September 1914, some six weeks after the outbreak of war. It was, however, put on the statute book together with a Suspensory Act providing that it would not come into effect until the end of the war; and Asquith promised that it would not be allowed to come into force until special provision had been made for Ulster. The size of the area to be excluded remained, however, to be settled, as did the question of whether exclusion was to be temporary or permanent.

In 1916, Lloyd George proposed to Irish nationalists and unionists that a six-county area be excluded. Both nationalists and unionists accepted this but could not agree on whether exclusion should be temporary or permanent. Six-county exclusion was also proposed at the ill-fated Irish Convention of 1918. The presumption was, however, that the excluded area would continue to be governed directly from Westminster, rather than be provided with a parliament of its own.

By 1918, Lloyd George faced a 'situation in regard to Ireland' which was 'governed by two fundamental facts: the first that the Home Rule Act of 1914 is upon the statute book; the second that in accordance with the pledge which has been given by me in the past, and indeed by all Party leaders, I can support no settlement which would involve the forcible coercion of Ulster.'[11] Home Rule for Ireland combined with exclusion seemed the only policy that was compatible with these 'two fundamental facts'.

Partition, however, did not necessarily imply that the excluded area should have its own parliament. The unionists, indeed, did not seek a parliament of their own. Their main aim had been, as we have seen, to resist Home Rule for the whole of Ireland. Failing that, they demanded the exclusion of the Protestant areas from the jurisdiction of the Home Rule parliament. The excluded areas should, they believed, be ruled from Westminster, just as the rest of Britain was ruled from Westminster. Consequently, proposals for exclusion from 1912 onwards had provided, not for a Northern Ireland Parliament, but for direct rule from Westminster.

In 1919, Sir Edward Carson told the House of Commons that:

Ulster has never asked for a separate Parliament. Ulster's claim has always been of this simple character: 'We have thrived under the Union; we are in sympathy with you, we are part of yourselves. We are prepared to make any sacrifice that you make, and are prepared to bear any burden that is equally put upon us with the other parts of the United Kingdom. In these circumstances keep us with you.' They have never made any other demand than that, and . . . I appeal to the Government . . . to keep Ulster in this united Parliament. I cannot understand why we should ask them to take a Parliament which they have never demanded, and which they do not want.[12]

The Ulster Unionist Council, when presented with the proposal in the Government of Ireland Bill for a parliament for Northern Ireland, rejected it. In March 1920, it passed a resolution declaring that:

Inasmuch as the new Bill is based on the principle of Home Rule and would deprive us of our equal citizenship in the Parliament of the United Kingdom, this Council cannot recommend the Parliamentary representatives of Ulster to accept any responsibility for it.[13]

When, however, in 1919–20, a Cabinet committee came to draw up proposals for exclusion, it decided to require Northern Ireland to accept a parliament. Its reason for doing so was that:

the policy of exclusion is open to one general objection of the most serious kind. It involves the retention of British rule in some part of Ireland. There is good reason to doubt whether it would ever be possible to convince Irishmen themselves or Dominion or American opinion that Great Britain was sincere in its policy of Home Rule unless it withdrew its control from the domestic affairs of Ireland altogether. British rule in the domestic affairs of Ireland has been the root of the Home Rule movement from start to finish. If it is retained anywhere in Ireland the opponents of Great Britain will be able to say either that Great Britain is ruling nationalist majorities against her will, or that it is giving active support to Ulster in its refusal to unite with the rest of Ireland.

A separate parliament for Northern Ireland, however, 'gets rid of the taproot of the Irish difficulty by providing for the complete withdrawal of British rule from the whole island. It thus meets the fundamental demand of the overwhelming majority of Irishmen ever since the days of O'Connell'. Moreover, it would 'enormously minimise the partition issue. The division of Ireland becomes a far less serious matter if Home Rule is established for both parts of Ireland than if the excluded part is retained as part of Great Britain. No nationalists would then be retained under British rule'.[14]

Partition was intended to be temporary. In November 1921, Lloyd George wrote to Sir James Craig, the first Prime Minister of Northern Ireland, that dominion status for the North was impossible since it:

would stereotype a frontier based neither upon natural features nor broad geographical considerations by giving it the character of an international boundary. Partition on these lines the majority of the Irish people will never accept, nor could we conscientiously attempt to enforce it. It would be fatal to that purpose of a lasting settlement on which these negotiations from the very outset have been steadily directed.[15]

The 1920 Act provided for machinery to terminate partition, in the form of a Council of Ireland, to be composed of an equal number of representatives from each of the two parliaments in Ireland. This Council was to have power 'by mutual agreement and joint action to terminate partition and to set up one Parliament and one Government for the whole of Ireland'. The unification of Ireland could thus in theory be achieved by mutual agreement, without further reference to Westminster. In the words of Walter Long, chairman of the Cabinet Committee which drew up the Government of Ireland Bill, the bill would provide for:

one Parliament for the three Southern provinces and a second parliament for Ulster, together with a Council of Ireland composed of members of the two

Irish Parliaments to discharge certain immediate functions, but mainly to promote as rapidly as possibly and *without further reference to the Imperial Parliament* the Union of the whole of Ireland under a single legislature'.[16]

Establishing a parliament in Northern Ireland was thus defended on the ground that it would make the eventual unification of Ireland easier to attain. Macpherson, the Chief Secretary for Ireland, told the Commons during the second reading of the Government of Ireland Bill: 'The division of Ireland, I need hardly tell the House, is distasteful to the Government, just as it is distasteful to all Irishmen . . . All of us are aware that the division may be temporary only.'[17]

The conclusion of a Cabinet meeting on 10 December 1919 at which the bill was discussed was the strikingly Gladstonian one that 'a united Ireland with a separate Parliament of its own, bound by the closest ties with Great Britain' was 'the ultimate aim'.[18] Lloyd George himself 'developed the parallel of S. E. Wales which when he began his public life was out of sympathy with Welsh aspirations but which had been won over largely by a policy of persuasion and Cardiff today was the home of several of the chief national institutions.' Moreover, every dominion except New Zealand had begun with partition. In particular, Natal had, in 1910, taken up Ulster's attitude and refused to join the Union of South Africa, but had come in at the last moment.[19]

The fallacy behind this viewpoint was well exposed by the Foreign Secretary, Arthur Balfour:

The doctrine assumed throughout the Committee's Report, and more than once explicitly proclaimed, is that Ireland, *all* Ireland, has a separate national existence, and should naturally and properly be organised as a single undivided unit. The Committee admits, of course, that, so long as Ulster remains the Ulster we know, such an ideal cannot be realised. Hence their very artificial scheme of two Home Rule Parliaments and an Irish Council. But they regard this division of Ireland as a misfortune; and evidently think it rather perverse of Ulster to throw obstacles in the way of complete unification. In their recommendations they carry this view to such length that while, on the one hand, they make it as easy as possible for Ulster to join itself with the rest of Ireland . . . on the other hand they give it no power whatever to remain what it is, and as I think, it ought to be,—an integral part of the United Kingdom. This they call . . . 'respecting the principle of self-determination . . . [20]

In practice, the parity between Northern and Southern Ireland in the Council of Ireland gave the North a veto on Irish unity. Yet, even if Ireland remained divided, the British government would still have washed its hands of the Irish problem. British politics would henceforth, it was hoped, be free of Irish quarrels. Violence and conflict on the island of Ireland would have to be resolved by those who lived there. This perhaps cynical prognostication turned out to be true for nearly fifty years, until in 1969, the civil rights movement and the eruption of sectarian conflict in Northern Ireland forced the incursion of British troops into the province.

Thus the fourth Home Rule Bill, which became the Government of Ireland Act of 1920, proposed that two Home Rule parliaments be established in Ireland, one in Dublin and one in Belfast. This Act, which institutionalized partition in Ireland, was passed without any representatives of the majority in Ireland being present. For Sinn Féin, which won seventy-two of the 103 Irish seats in the general election of 1918, had refused to take its seats at Westminster. It is difficult to believe that the outcome would have been as adverse to Irish nationalist interests if the Sinn Féin MPs had not boycotted Parliament.

The absence of Sinn Féin, however, and the decision to establish a parliament in Northern Ireland, gave the unionists a crucial veto on the size of the excluded area. The British government, until shortly before the Government of Ireland Bill was introduced, favoured nine-county exclusion. In the nine counties, the Protestants, enjoying only a narrow majority overall, would, it was thought, be more likely to treat the Catholics fairly; and, moreover, with a small change in the demographic balance between Protestants and Catholics, the excluded area could be expected to vote to join the Dublin Parliament. But, precisely because of the narrow demographic balance, the Ulster Unionists had come to be suspicious of this proposal. Captain Charles Craig, an Ulster Unionist MP and brother of the first Northern Ireland Prime Minister, Sir James Craig, told the House of Commons in March 1920 that the counties of Cavan, Donegal, and Monaghan contained 70,000 unionists and 260,000 'Sinn Féiners and Nationalists', and would thus reduce 'our majority to such a level that no sane man would undertake to carry on a Parliament with it'.[21] The Ulster

Unionists were determined to be responsible only for an area which they could firmly control, and they therefore insisted on six-county exclusion. The decision to establish a parliament for the six counties was therefore not based on any considered view of good government in Ireland, but was rather the by-product of an attempt by the British government to extricate itself completely from Irish affairs.

The Lloyd George government made three crucial decisions in the years 1919–20: that Ireland was to be partitioned, that the excluded area was to comprise six counties rather than nine, and that the excluded area should have its own parliament. The second and third decisions were dependent upon each other, but they were by no means necessary consequences of the first, which was perhaps inevitable. Partition, it may be argued, was in accordance with the realities of Ulster Unionist opposition to Home Rule, and flowed from the principle of self-determination. But the application of this principle was made subject to two important qualifications. The first was that self-determination would be applied to the six counties as a single unit, and not on a county basis, which would have meant that Fermanagh and Tyrone, with their small Catholic majorities, would have joined the Irish Free State. 'In order to persuade Ulster to come in,' Lloyd George told Sinn Féin, 'there is an advantage in her having a Catholic population.'[22] With Irish unity as the aim, as Lloyd George put it to his Cabinet on 10 November 1921, the 'position of Tyrone and Fermanagh [is] not so important'.[23] The border so created had little logic, for it partitioned Ulster as well as Northern Ireland. It might well not have been chosen had the Lloyd George government believed that it would be permanent.

The second qualification was that the excluded area was not allowed to decide that it did not want a parliament of its own, but would continue to be ruled directly from Westminster. The Ulster Unionists were thus granted the right to self-determination, but, as Balfour had pointed out, not the right to remain an integral part of the United Kingdom, with direct rule from Westminster. The decision to partition Ireland on the basis of six counties and the decision to give the six counties a parliament were, however, in no way a necessary consequence of the decision to partition Ireland. The three decisions together did much to determine the unhappy future of the excluded area.

The Government of Ireland Act was intended to apply to the whole of Ireland. It came into effect, however, only in one part of Ireland, the North. Elsewhere, Sinn Féin demanded not Home Rule, but independence, which was in effect secured by the Anglo-Irish Treaty of 1921. Ireland was to become a self-governing dominion within the British Empire, to be called the Irish Free State. Northern Ireland, however, comprising the six counties, was given the option of seceding from the Free State, and retaining her own Home Rule legislature subordinate to Westminster, an option which she immediately took. The Council of Ireland never came into operation, and its powers in relation to Northern Ireland were transferred to the government of Northern Ireland in 1925. Home Rule for Northern Ireland remained as the relic of a failed attempt to resolve the Irish problem.

The rejection of Home Rule by Ireland outside the six counties was, by 1920, predictable. The long title of the 1920 Government of Ireland Act stated, ironically, that it was an Act 'for the better government of Ireland'; yet, as Asquith wrote in his memoirs, Northern Ireland was to be given a parliament it did not want, and which, arguably, would not provide better government for the province, while the rest of Ireland was to be given a parliament it would not accept.[24] The Act was, it has been said, an Act to govern Ireland with the dissent of the governed. Lord Robert Cecil told the House of Commons in 1920:

we shall have this astounding position, that the only form of Home Rule which will exist in Ireland will be that which exists in Ulster. . . . Home Rule is to be established effectively only in that part of Ireland which hates and loathes the whole idea of Home Rule and where they are only accepting this, as I understand it, through fear of having something worse . . . No one wants Home Rule there, and there is no reason for it.[25]

Carson's case against creating a separate Northern Ireland Parliament had been prescient. He feared that it would isolate Northern Ireland from the mainstream of British politics, and that it would identify unionism, which, for him, meant equal citizenship in the United Kingdom, with sectarianism and Protestant supremacism. He declared in the Commons:

We have never asked to govern any Catholic . . . We are perfectly satisfied that all of them, Protestant and Catholic, should be governed from this Parliament, and we have always said that it was the fact that this Parliament [i.e. Westminster] was aloof entirely from these racial distinctions and religious distinctions which was the strongest foundation for the government of Ulster. Therefore, not only have we never asked to get an opportunity of dealing in a hostile way with the minority, but we have sought from beginning to end of this controversy to be left alone, and to go on hand in hand with Great Britain as one nation with Great Britain.

. . . She [Ulster] has always made the simple appeal to you to leave her alone and to treat her as you treat your own people and she would be perfectly satisfied. And I am bound to say that this breaking up and the giving to Ulster a Parliament may lead to many unforeseen consequences. . . .

. . . Therefore I say try to look ahead, and looking ahead, I believe the policy which we have urged from the beginning of retaining Ulster as she is now as part of the United Kingdom, and treating the people of Ulster exactly as you treat the people of Great Britain, is the truest and surest policy for His Majesty's Government to pursue.[26]

Northern Ireland, in the words of her first Prime Minister, Sir James Craig, accepted 'as a *final settlement* and supreme sacrifice in the interests of peace' a separate parliament, 'although not asked for by her representatives'(my emphasis).[27] Once, however, the Northern Ireland Parliament had been established, the Ulster Unionists began to appreciate its advantages. In 1936, the Ulster Unionist Council declared that:

Had we refused to accept a Parliament for Northern Ireland and remained at Westminster there can be little doubt but that now we would be either inside the Free State or fighting desperately against incorporation. Northern Ireland without a Parliament of her own would be a standing temptation to certain British politicians to make another bid for a final settlement with Irish Republicans.[28]

Northern Ireland returned but a small number of MPs to Westminster. Under direct rule, it would be easy for her to be outvoted and handed over to Dublin against her wishes. During the debates on the 1920 bill, Captain Charles Craig explained what advantages Northern Ireland could expect from a parliament of her own:

we feel that an Ulster without a parliament of her own would not be in nearly as strong a position as one in which a parliament had been set up . . . We
believe that so long as we were without a parliament of our own constant
attacks would be made . . . to draw us into a Dublin parliament . . . We
believe that if either of these parties [Labour or the Liberals] or the two in
combination, were once more in power our chances of remaining a part of
the United Kingdom would be very small indeed.[29]

With a parliament in Northern Ireland, however, it would be difficult
for any Westminster government to hand over Northern Ireland to her
enemies without her consent. This would institutionalize Ulster's
veto and so the Northern Ireland Parliament could prove the means
by which her continued membership of the United Kingdom would
be assured. The parliament would be a bulwark against secession.

After Ireland became a Republic in 1949, the position of Northern
Ireland was formalized in section 1(2) of the Ireland Act of 1949,
which declared that neither Northern Ireland nor any part if it would
cease to be a part of the United Kingdom without the consent of the
Northern Ireland Parliament.

So it was that by accepting a separate parliament, Northern Ireland
ensured that she could determine her own future, even in the face of
a hostile majority at Westminster. So also was vindicated the claim,
first made by Lord Randolph Churchill and Joseph Chamberlain in
1886, that Ireland was not a political unity. By a striking paradox, it
was that part of Ireland which most strenuously resisted Home Rule
that came to accept and indeed to welcome it.

The circumstances attending the birth of Northern Ireland offered
a strong inducement to the success of devolution, since failure might
mean not independence but absorption into the hated Irish Free State.
The Northern Ireland government could not, therefore, use the threat
of nationalism or secession in order to get its own way with London.
The British government, for its part, came to feel a moral obligation
to ensure that citizens of the United Kingdom living in Northern
Ireland enjoyed a similar standard of living to that enjoyed by those
living elsewhere in the country, although, unfortunately, there was no
similar commitment to ensure that standards of civil rights should be
the same as those in different parts of the country. The British government was willing to contribute the financial resources needed to

make devolution succeed. Precisely because the pressures which led
to devolution in Northern Ireland were not, as is usually the case,
centrifugal, but centripetal, there was a strong incentive, both in
Belfast and in Westminster, to minimize conflict and to make devolution work. In other circumstances, devolved administrations would
be unlikely to be so passive *vis-à-vis* the centre as Northern Ireland
was. Moreover, owing to the centrality of community conflict in the
province, Northern Ireland became a one-party state. The Unionists
were a permanent majority party, and none of the nationalist or anti-
partitionist parties had any hope of displacing them. This was bound
to affect the working of devolved government. An administration
which faces the continual threat of replacement by a lively opposition acts very differently from one which knows that, whatever it
does, it can never be defeated. For these reasons, Northern Ireland
can be said to have 'evaded rather than refuted the Unionist thesis
that Home Rule is impracticable'. For 'That thesis rested on the natural assumption that a regional legislature would insist on making
full use of its powers.'[30]

II

The 1921 Treaty between the British government and the provision-
al government of Ireland, which led to the setting-up of the Irish
Free State, was embodied in legislation in Westminster in the Irish
Free State (Agreement) Act of 1922. This Act amended the Act of
Union by excluding the twenty-six counties of the Irish Free State
from its jurisdiction. When Northern Ireland exercised her right not
to join the Free State, she retained her position under the Act of
Union of 1800. Northern Ireland's status as part of the United
Kingdom derived from the creation of the United Kingdom in 1801,
but it was the 1920 Government of Ireland Act which became the
Constitution of Northern Ireland.

The Act laid down the division of legislative and financial powers
between Westminster and Belfast and provided for machinery by
which Belfast could be prevented from acting in breach of the
Constitution. Section 1 of the Act set up a parliament which reproduced, so far as was possible, Westminster in Belfast, and consisted

of the king—represented until 1922 by the Lord Lieutenant, and after that by the Governor—and two legislative chambers. Section 4 of the Act conferred on the parliament a general grant of legislative power to make laws for the 'peace, order and good government' of the inhabitants of Northern Ireland. This general grant of power was, however, made subject to certain specific limitations. Section 4(1), paragraphs 1–14, enumerated excepted matters on which it was necessary to secure uniformity throughout the United Kingdom. Responsibility for these excepted matters would remain with Westminster; they included the Crown, the Navy, Army, and Air Force, relations with foreign countries, and external trade. Because she enjoyed, unlike any other part of the United Kingdom, a separate parliament, it was provided that Northern Ireland be under-represented in proportion to population, and she was allocated just thirteen seats (reduced to twelve after the university seat at Queen's, Belfast, was abolished in 1948) instead of the seventeen to which she was entitled on a population basis. These MPs tended to see themselves as representatives of the Northern Ireland Parliament, however, rather than of their constituencies; and on the whole the ablest unionists in Northern Ireland tended to gravitate to the Northern Ireland Parliament, where they could expect to obtain ministerial office, rather than Westminster. All this had the effect of increasing the isolation of Northern Ireland from the rest of the United Kingdom.

Because the number of MPs returned from Northern Ireland was so small, devolution did not in practice raise the problems of representation with which Gladstone had grappled. It was perhaps fortunate that, during the period from 1921 to 1972, there was no occasion on which a Conservative government was elected to power in London with a majority of less than thirteen. In May 1965, however, Harold Wilson found himself leading a Labour government with a majority of only two. In a debate on steel nationalization, he warned the MPs from Northern Ireland, all of whom sat on the Conservative benches:

I am sure the House will agree that there is an apparent lack of logic, for example, about steel, when Northern Ireland members can, and presumably will, swell the Tory ranks tonight, when we have no power to vote on questions about steel in Northern Ireland because of the fact that the Stormont Parliament has concurrent jurisdiction in these matters.

Wilson asked the House of Commons 'to look at the question of why he [the leader of the Conservative Party] gets the support of his honourable Friends beside him—for example, on matters affecting housing discrimination in London—when we English, Scottish and Welsh Members cannot express our views about housing conditions in Belfast.'

I would hope that Northern Ireland Members, who are here, and who are welcomed here, for the duties they have to perform on behalf of the United Kingdom in many matters affecting Northern Ireland, would consider their position in matters where we have no equivalent right in Northern Ireland . . . It is certainly the case that Northern Ireland Members have great duties to perform here in the sense of foreign affairs, defence, and matters affecting Northern Ireland, involving taxation and expenditure. What was not envisaged, I am sure, in 1920 was that those who came here, with that responsibility for representing Northern Ireland interests, should just become hacks supporting the English Tory Party.[31]

Section 5(1) of the Act, like the First Amendment in the United States, sought to entrench religious freedom by prohibiting laws interfering with religious equality; while section 8(6) extended this prohibition to the executive acts of government. Sections 21 and 22 reserved to Westminster the power to levy certain taxes, including income tax, surtax, customs and excise duties on goods manufactured or produced, business profits tax, and any general taxes on capital. The transferred taxes, to be under the authority of the Northern Ireland Parliament were, by contrast, of minor significance, the most important of them being the motor vehicle licence tax. Section 25 of the Act gave the Northern Ireland Parliament the power to grant Northern Ireland taxpayers a rebate on income tax or surtax; but, for reasons that will be explained, this power was never used.

The Act also provided for machinery by which the validity of Northern Ireland legislation could be tested and the supremacy of Westminster enforced. Sections 49 and 50 allowed for appeal to the Northern Irish courts, with a right of ultimate appeal to the House of Lords, while section 51 provided for a reference to the Judicial

Committee of the Privy Council on constitutional matters. These sections provided for statutes of the Northern Ireland Parliament being declared *ultra vires* by the courts, a conception which was regarded by one authority as 'novel in our constitutional law',[32] since it allowed the courts to declare Acts of Parliament, albeit acts of a subordinate parliament, invalid.

Section 12 of the Government of Ireland Act required the Lord Lieutenant, and later the Governor, to withhold assent to legislation of the Northern Ireland Parliament when so instructed by the king, acting of course on the advice of his United Kingdom government. Section 6 prevented the Northern Ireland Parliament from amending or altering the Act; and finally section 75 of the Act, with great emphasis, reiterated that the parliament of Northern Ireland was subordinate, through the declaration that:

Notwithstanding the establishment of the Parliament of Northern Ireland . . . or anything contained in this Act, the supreme authority of the Parliament of the United Kingdom shall remain unaffected and undiminished over all persons, matters and things in Northern Ireland and every part thereof.

Because Westminster remained supreme, it retained the right to legislate for Northern Ireland even within the transferred sphere, if it so wished. The constitution was thus a rigid one from the point of view of Northern Ireland, imposing seemingly powerful constraints upon the Northern Ireland Parliament, but a flexible one from the point of view of Westminster.

Precisely because sections 6 (providing that in cases of conflict between Northern Ireland and Westminster, Westminster would prevail), 12, and 75 preserved Westminster's supremacy, Northern Ireland lay in a subordinate, rather than in a federal, relationship with Westminster. In practice, however, Northern Ireland came to enjoy a degree of autonomy more appropriate to that of a provincial unit in a federal system. This was so for two reasons.

The first was that, by convention, Westminster did not attempt to legislate on matters for which responsibility had been transferred. Sir Ivor Jennings, indeed, argued in successive editions of his book *The Law and the Constitution*, that it would have been 'unconstitutional' so to legislate.[33] Moreover, in 1923, the Speaker of the House of

Commons ruled that parliamentary questions could not be asked on matters for which responsibility had been transferred to Northern Ireland, since no British minister could be held responsible for transferred matters. The Speaker's ruling was as follows:

the fact that Northern Ireland sends Members to this House does not affect this question. With regard to those subjects which have been delegated to the Government of Northern Ireland, questions must be asked of Ministers in Northern Ireland, and not in this House.[34]

This ruling had the effect of stultifying discussions of alleged injustices in Northern Ireland. In 1965, when a back-bench MP sought to raise the issue of the property-vote in local government elections in Northern Ireland, the Deputy Speaker ruled him out of order, saying, 'We are now going into the details of local government in Northern Ireland, which is a matter for Northern Ireland . . . he must show what the House of Commons can do about it and what some responsible Minister can do about it.'[35]

In July 1964, Henry Brooke, the Home Secretary, went so far as to suggest that alleged religious discrimination in Northern Ireland could not be debated at Westminster, since 'the reserve powers in the Government of Ireland Act do not enable the United Kingdom Government to intervene in matters which under Section 4 are the *sole* responsibility of the Northern Ireland Parliament and Government'(my emphasis).[36] This was a curious argument since, the Northern Ireland Parliament being a subordinate body, there were, as emphasized by section 75, *no* issues that were the *sole* responsibility of the Northern Ireland Parliament or government. In 1965, however, the Deputy Speaker seemed to endorse Brooke's argument, by claiming that it was out of order for the Commons to discuss religious discrimination in Northern Ireland: 'discrimination in housing in Northern Ireland is not a matter for the United Kingdom Government; it is a matter for the Northern Ireland Government . . . Any question of religious discrimination in Northern Ireland is not a matter for the United Kingdom Government . . . Boundaries for local government and Parliament in Ireland are matters for Stormont'.[37] One result of this, according to an MP who became chairman of the Campaign for Democracy in Ulster, was that it proved impossible 'to penetrate the blank wall of incomprehension and ignorance about Ulster. Members who knew about Saigon or Salisbury seemed to know nothing of Stormont.'[38] It was not until 1967 that Roy Jenkins, as Home Secretary, put forward a new doctrine that, while 'successive Governments had refused to take steps which would inevitably cut away the authority of the Northern Ireland Government', nevertheless the British government had to work towards 'common standards of political tolerance and non-discrimination on both sides of the Irish Sea'.[39]

The second reason why Westminster's supremacy proved to be more theoretical than real was that the constitutional safeguards embodied in sections 5(1), 8(6), and 12 proved ineffective. Neither section 5 nor section 8 was ever invoked to deal with allegations of discrimination against the Catholic minority.[40] Section 51 appeared to give the Judicial Committee of the Privy Council power to rule on whether the executive, as well as the legislative, acts of the Northern Ireland government were within its lawful authority, but it was used only once. The failure to use the courts was in part due to a feeling on the part of the Catholic minority that the courts were a part of the unionist establishment, and would not deliver a verdict hostile to the instincts of that establishment. It was alleged in 1973 that of the twenty High Court judges appointed in Northern Ireland since the Northern Ireland courts were established, fifteen 'have been openly associated with the Unionist Party', while in the late 1960s, two out of five County Court judges were former Unionist MPs, and another was the son of a Unionist MP.[41] Moreover, the property qualification for jurors seemed biased against the Catholic community. It is a chastening reminder of the ineffectiveness of what has been called 'an embryonic form of a legally enforceable Bill of Rights', that the only area of the United Kingdom where there were constitutionally entrenched safeguards against religious discrimination was also the only area in which discrimination was prevalent and unchecked.

Section 12 was invoked just once, by the Lord Lieutenant in 1922, when the Northern Ireland government proposed to abolish proportional representation in local government elections, which had been prescribed for all local authorities in Ireland by a Westminster Act of 1919 so as to ensure fair representation for minorities. Proportional representation in local government had yielded nationalist majorities in the counties of Fermanagh and Tyrone. These county councils, together with other nationalist-controlled local authorities, had proceeded to vote to join the Irish Free State. [42] The bill to abolish proportional representation in local elections lay within the competence of the Northern Ireland Parliament, but assent was, nevertheless, withheld for two months at the request of the British government. The Prime Minister of the provisional government of the Irish Free State, W. T. Cosgrave, told the British government that the bill was a breach of the spirit of the Anglo-Irish Treaty of 1921; and the British government did not dissent from this view. Sir James Craig, however, the Prime Minister of Northern Ireland, argued that 'The Bill was clearly within the powers of the Northern Parliament, and either they must make some patched-up arrangement or his Government must resign.'[43] Faced with this threat, the British government was forced to give way, and Winston Churchill, the Colonial Secretary, wrote to Cosgrave, 'I have come, though most unwillingly, to the conclusion that the Local Government (N.I.) Bill could not be vetoed . . . I have never concealed from Sir James Craig my opinion that the measure was inopportune.'[44] The British government considered reserving legislation on only one other occasion, in 1925, when the Governor was worried lest a provision in the Education Act (Northern Ireland) concerning religious instruction in state schools violated section 5 of the 1920 Act. He wrote to the Home Secretary proposing to reserve the legislation. The Home Secretary replied that, but for the impending dissolution of the Northern Ireland Parliament, he would have advised the king to instruct the Governor to reserve the bill so as to consider its constitutionality. [45]

On no occasion until 1969 did Westminster legislate for Northern Ireland within the sphere of transferred matters against the wishes of the Northern Ireland government. Westminster did, however, apparently threaten to intervene on a number of occasions. One example occurred in 1965 when the Northern Ireland Parliament seemed unwilling to introduce capital gains and corporation taxes, which had been introduced in the rest of the United Kingdom through the budget, into the province. On this occasion the Northern Ireland Minister of Finance advised the Northern Ireland House of Commons: 'we must pass this measure in this Parliament, or have it forced upon us at Westminster.'[46]

Nevertheless, the broad picture, after the failed attempt to reserve legislation in 1922, was one of non-interference.

Reintroduction of the first-past-the-post system in local government was followed by the rearrangement of local government boundaries in the interests of the unionists. The consequence was that despite Catholic majorities in Fermanagh, Tyrone, and Londonderry city, their local councils came to enjoy unionist majorities. In 1969, the Cameron Commission was appointed by the government of Northern Ireland to analyse the causes of the disorders that had arisen in the province. It concluded that amongst the causes were:

(1) a rising sense of continuing injustice and grievance among large sections of the Catholic population in Northern Ireland, in particular in Londonderry and Dungannon, in respect of . . . unfair methods of allocation of houses . . . misuse in certain cases of discretionary powers of allocation of houses in order to perpetuate Unionist control of the local authority . . .
(2) Complaints, now well documented in fact, of discrimination in the making of local government appointments, at all levels but especially in senior posts, to the prejudice of non-Unionists and especially Catholic members of the community, in some Unionist controlled authorities . . .
(3) Complaints, again well documented, in some cases of deliberate manipulation of local government electoral boundaries and in others a refusal to apply for their necessary extension, in order to achieve and maintain Unionist control of local authorities and so to deny to Catholics influence in local government proportionate to their numbers.[47]

These evils were made possible by devolution and by Westminster's failure to scrutinize what was happening in the province. Under direct rule, by contrast, Westminster would have had clear and unequivocal responsibility for the electoral system for local government. Even if Westminster had decided to restore the first-past-the-post system for local government elections, it would have been more likely to have ensured that ward boundaries were drawn fairly and the rights of minorities respected.

The failure of the British government to overrule Craig on the abolition of proportional representation in local government elections

doubtless encouraged him, in 1929, to abolish proportional representation for elections to the Northern Ireland Parliament itself, something which had been provided for in the 1920 Government of Ireland
Act. The Northern Ireland Labour Party sent a delegation of MPs in
1928 to protest to the British government at this proposed measure.
The Home Secretary, Joynson-Hicks, reported the protest to Sir James
Craig:

> I told them, of course, that this was a matter for the Ulster Parliament, and
> not for myself, but that I should feel in duty bound to tell you of the
> Deputation. I don't know whether you would care at any time to discuss the
> matter with me; of course I am always at your disposal. But beyond that I
> 'know my place' and don't propose to interfere.[48]

Craig's aim in abolishing proportional representation was not the
crude one of increasing unionist representation at the expense of the
nationalists. Indeed, first past the post did not greatly increase the
number of unionists nor decrease the total number of anti-partition-
ists in the Northern Ireland House of Commons. Craig sought, rather,
to prevent any fragmentation of the unionists which would, he
believed, weaken Northern Ireland's leverage *vis-à-vis* Westminster.
It was, moreover, in Craig's interests that the main opponent of the
unionists should be the nationalists, rather than a non-sectarian
Labour Party, campaigning on economic and social issues. For Craig
and the unionists, proportional representation, by fragmenting unionist strength, had proved a distraction from the constitutional issue.
There was, in Craig's view, room for only two parties in Northern
Ireland, a unionist party and a Republican party, and the unionists
would of course always constitute the majority. His aim, he told the
Northern Ireland House of Commons in 1927, was 'to get in this
House, and what I believe we will get very much better in this House
under the old-fashioned plain and simple system, . . . men who are
for the Union on the one hand or who are against it and want to go
into a Dublin Parliament on the other.'[49]

The abolition of proportional representation for elections to
Stormont consolidated unionist strength, leading to the disappearance
of Independent unionist members, and it also strengthened various
anti-partitionist parties at the expense of the Northern Ireland Labour

Party, which might have succeeded in polarizing Northern Irish politics around issues of social and economic policy rather than the border. It served to reinforce the siege mentality of the unionists, of which it was itself an expression.

Under proportional representation, the Catholic minority had secured representation in every part of the province. With the introduction of first past the post, however, election results came to be a foregone conclusion, depending as they did upon the sectarian composition of the constituency, and there was a considerable increase in the number of uncontested seats, from none in the Northern Ireland Parliament elections of 1923, to eight in 1925, twenty-two in 1929 and an average of twenty in the post-war years. The abolition of proportional representation led, therefore, to 'the stagnation of political life in Northern Ireland'.[50] It put an end also to a brief period of hope in the politics of the province, which had occurred in the aftermath of the 1925 election, when the leader of the nationalist minority in Northern Ireland, Joe Devlin, took his seat in the Parliament and declared that he and his party were willing to act as a constructive opposition and work its institutions. In the debate on the address in 1926, Devlin went so far as to declare that:

We are all Ulstermen and proud to be Ulstermen. [*Hon. Members*: Hear, Hear]. We want to further the welfare of our Province. We are all Irishmen and want to see North and South working harmoniously together. The causes that divided them have largely disappeared. We rejoice at that, because we do not believe that unity can ever spring out of conflict.

This interlude of 'voluntary consociationalism' was, however, ended by the abolition of proportional representation in 1929, which was interpreted by the minority as a symbol of unionist triumphalism.[51] It was an action which 'revealed a complete lack of sympathy with the minority outlook. At the worst, it was a party manoeuvre; at the best a psychological mistake.'[52] It meant that every issue would be forced into the mould of the community conflict. As Joe Devlin told the Northern Ireland House of Commons in October 1927 in the debate on the abolition of proportional representation:

when there are too many workers out of employment and you come along to this House and say 'What are you doing for the unemployed', the reply will be 'We are doing what we can for the unemployed, but if you listen to this man it may be that the Pope will be again supreme in Ulster.'[53]

It is just possible that the retention of proportional representation could have prevented the congealing of Northern Ireland politics into a sectarian mode and assisted in the formation of a more inclusive state in which the Catholic minority would have gained legitimacy. In 1934, Devlin told the House of Commons of Northern Ireland:

You had opponents willing to serve. We did not seek office. We sought service. We were willing to help. But you rejected all friendly offers . . . You went on the old political lines, fostering hatreds, keeping one third of the population as if they were pariahs in the community.[54] •

Further alienation of the Catholic minority occurred with the passage of the Civil Authorities (Special Powers) Act of 1922, which remained in existence until the Northern Ireland Parliament was suspended in 1972. This gave the executive wide powers to frame regulations to provide, *inter alia*, for detention and internment. Admittedly, these powers were little used, once devolved government had been firmly established in the province. Nevertheless, not enough was done to assuage the fears of the minority that special powers were in fact being used to buttress unionist rule, and the Cameron Committee reported that the Act had led to 'widespread resentment among Catholics in particular'.[55]

Westminster, then, proved unwilling to assert its supremacy over Northern Ireland until its problems spilled over into violent protest in 1968. Through the years of devolved government, Westminster devoted on average two hours a year to Northern Ireland.[56] This lack of attention corresponded with ignorance in Great Britain about the province. A commercial survey conducted in 1957 by a Northern Ireland firm in England showed that 45 per cent of the population did not know what Ulster was, while 56 per cent were unaware that it had its own government. Many thought that it was 'part of Eire', of Scotland, or a British colony or independent state.[57] When James Callaghan arrived at the Home Office in 1967, he was offered, in his first full day as Home Secretary, a briefing which included nothing on Northern Ireland.[58] From 1968, however, the British government pressed reforms upon Stormont. Captain O'Neill, Prime Minister of

Northern Ireland between 1963 and 1969, in a radio broadcast in December 1968, warned the people of Northern Ireland that 'Mr Wilson made it absolutely clear to us that if we did not face up to our problems the Westminster Parliament might well decide to act over our heads'.59 In August 1969, the Downing Street Declaration was issued, stating that:

The Northern Ireland Government have reaffirmed their intention to take into the fullest account at all times the views of Her Majesty's Government in the United Kingdom, especially in relation to matters affecting the status of citizens of that part of the United Kingdom and their equal rights and protection under the law.

This was the first time that the Northern Ireland government had acknowledged that it must take account of the views of the British government on matters of civil rights.

Westminster, then, was able to bring its supremacy into play only under pathological conditions when the normal working of devolution had been disrupted by sectarian protest. It did not use its powers before that, in the years between 1921 and 1968, to secure the civil rights of the population of part of the United Kingdom. What James Callaghan called the 'supreme authority to withdraw such power as it had delegated' was a very different thing from the 'unaffected and undiminished supremacy over all persons, matters and things' of section 75 of the Government of Ireland Act. In practice, then, the system of government in Northern Ireland between 1921 and 1968, although not, of course, the legal relationship, may be classified as quasi-federal. For the relationship was much more like that characteristic of a federal state, in which power is divided, rather than devolution, where power is delegated. Indeed, the canons of constitutional interpretation adopted by the courts when dealing with the legislative competence of the parliament of Northern Ireland came to be very similar to those applied in federal systems.

The British government found it difficult to ensure that common standards of civil rights were observed in Northern Ireland. After 1968, the government could threaten action on the basis of section 75, but if that failed, the only weapon left was a threat to repeal the Act or to prorogue Stormont, a step finally taken by the Heath government in 1972.

Thus, the political consequence of the establishment of a separate parliament in Northern Ireland was to sever the six counties from common United Kingdom principles of equity and fairness, and to take away from the Catholic minority in Northern Ireland the redress which they could have expected from Parliament at Westminster.

The constitutional problems faced by Westminster proved very different from what had been expected in 1920. The 1920 Act had been drafted in the expectation that the main problems would arise over the division of legislative powers and the attempt of *Southern* Ireland to circumvent it. Northern Ireland, however, sought not to circumvent the Constitution, but to use it so as to secure unionist supremacy, a supremacy which was in effect a challenge to the supremacy of Westminster. Successive British governments before 1968 proved unwilling to meet that challenge. Indeed, the violent history of Northern Ireland since 1968 is in part a consequence of the failure of British governments to take more effective action in the field of civil rights in the years before 1968.

III

It was paradoxical that Northern Ireland enjoyed a great deal of autonomy in the area of civil liberties and electoral matters, where a common United Kingdom policy would seem to have been justifiable, while enjoying little autonomy in the development of public services—an advantage which devolution is supposed to confer. This failure arose not, however, because the British government intervened in Northern Ireland's affairs, but because Northern Ireland lacked sufficient financial independence to pursue an autonomous policy.

The framers of the 1920 Act aimed to render the two parts of Ireland distinct and self-sufficient fiscal units. They believed that this could be achieved by providing Ireland with her own revenue, and requiring her to use that revenue to pay for transferred services. The taxing power would be divided between reserved and transferred taxes, but Ireland would not be expected to pay for transferred services entirely through transferred taxation.

The British government was determined, however, that Ireland, despite being fiscally distinct and self-sufficient, should not enjoy autonomy at Britain's expense: she would be required to pay an Imperial Contribution. Because, by 1920, the imposition of war taxation had led to a surplus from 1915–16, the Imperial Contribution could be a first charge on the Northern Ireland Exchequer, as Gladstone had intended in his own Home Rule legislation. The size of the Imperial Contribution was to be determined by a Joint Exchequer Board, composed of members drawn equally from the Treasury in London and the Ministry of Finance in Belfast.

The 1920 Act was, however, framed, as we have seen, primarily with Southern Ireland in mind, and the British government sought to retain as many taxes as possible so as to ensure that Southern Ireland could not evade her Imperial Contribution. Transferred taxation, therefore, included only minor taxes, the most important of which were the motor-vehicle licensing tax, entertainment duties, and stamp duties; these were responsible for at most 20 per cent of total taxation in Northern Ireland, and often a much smaller proportion. Thus, raising transferred taxation would yield comparatively little extra revenue, since these taxes produced so small a proportion of Northern Ireland's total revenue. The power to offer income-tax rebates or rebates on surtax was never used. The reason for this was that, since tax relief could not be given at the expense of the Imperial Contribution, the rebates would have meant cuts in public services. Otherwise, major taxes, which included income tax, surtax, customs and excise, and profits tax, remained with Westminster. Thus Northern Ireland would not be able to finance her transferred services entirely from transferred taxation, but would have to rely on a portion of reserved taxation as well. This meant that some estimate would have to be made of the share of total UK taxation which was properly attributable to Northern Ireland as her share of reserved revenue. Northern Ireland was thus to find herself in the anomalous position of being treated as a separate financial region from the point of view of expenditure, in that revenue attributable to Northern Ireland could not be spent in any other part of the United Kingdom, but as a part of the United Kingdom from the point of view of taxation.

From the beginning, however, these arrangements proved unworkable. Northern Ireland found it impossible to finance, from her revenue, a level of services equal to that in the rest of the United Kingdom. In the first financial year of devolution, 1921–2, Northern Ireland was unable to make her accounts balance, and in June 1922, Sir Robert Horne, the British Chancellor of the Exchequer, complained that 'We have already gone far beyond what was contemplated in the Act'.[60] The position worsened with the depression of the 1920s, when revenue fell so far that it reached just one-half of the anticipated level, while expenses proved far greater than foreseen, because of the costs of paying benefit to the large number of unemployed, and of policing the province against the IRA.

If the Imperial Contribution were to remain a first charge upon the revenue of Northern Ireland, the standard of public services there would be very low. Yet the citizens of Northern Ireland were paying the same rate of income tax, surtax, and so on as citizens in the rest of the United Kingdom. Surely they were entitled to the same level of services, especially as they had accepted devolution not because they wanted it, but because it had been pressed upon them by the British government. Had Northern Ireland remained under direct rule, there would have been no doubt that she would have been entitled to the same standard of social services as the rest of the United Kingdom. 'It would be a very sad day for us', Sir James Craig declared, 'if at any time it became known that it is better to live in Norfolk, or Suffolk, or Essex, or in any other county in England, than in the Province of Ulster.'[61] One way of dealing with this problem would have been to increase the share of her revenue which Northern Ireland could finance out of her own resources, by transferring further taxes from Westminster to Northern Ireland. This, however, would have meant that Northern Ireland taxpayers would have to pay higher rates of tax than everyone else in the United Kingdom in order to enjoy a similar standard of service. So, after 'long and irritating controversies', between the Northern Ireland Ministry of Finance and the Treasury, a Northern Ireland Special Arbitration Committee was set up under Lord Colwyn.[62] In its second report in 1925, the Colwyn Committee proposed a drastic modification to the initial financial settlement. It argued that *per capita* spending on services in Northern Ireland ought to increase at the same rate as *per capita* expenditure on services in the rest of the United Kingdom, and the sum required to secure such a rate of increase should constitute Northern Ireland's necessary expenditure. The Imperial Contribution should not be paid until this necessary expenditure had been financed. Thus, the Imperial Contribution would become not a first charge upon Northern Ireland's Exchequer, but a residual. The Colwyn Committee offered to Northern Ireland a guarantee that, if her level of transferred taxation were equal to that in the rest of the United Kingdom, her services would be improved at the same rate as services in the rest of the United Kingdom. A consequence, however, was that Northern Ireland lost much of the limited fiscal autonomy that the Act of 1920 had given her. For, were she to raise the rate of her transferred taxes, she would not be able to secure a level of service beyond her necessary expenditure, but would simply pay the additional amount in the form of a higher Imperial Contribution.

The Colwyn formula did not, however, imply that public services in Northern Ireland would be of the same standard as those in the rest of the UK, since Northern Ireland had a disproportionate number of claimants on her public services. To help meet the cost of payments for unemployment insurance, the Colwyn formula was supplemented by an Unemployment Insurance Agreement in 1926. This Agreement provided that if in any year the payment by the Northern Ireland Exchequer to the Unemployment Fund per head of population exceeded the corresponding payment by the UK government to the fund in Great Britain, then the UK government would meet three-quarters of the difference; and it was the first of a series of agreements through which funds were transferred from the United Kingdom Exchequer to Northern Ireland for specific purposes, thus further subverting the financial arrangements embodied in the 1920 Act.

However, neither the Colwyn formula nor the Unemployment Insurance Agreement resolved the financial problems facing Northern Ireland. By 1931, she was receiving far more under the Unemployment Insurance Agreement than she was paying through the Imperial Contribution, which had dwindled almost to nothing. The prospect arose of the Imperial Contribution becoming a negative amount, i.e. of Northern Ireland being unable to finance even her transferred services to an acceptable level from her revenue. In 1932, therefore, the Colwyn formula was abandoned.

It was becoming clear that Northern Ireland could not hope to finance herself as a self-sufficient revenue unit so as to provide services at a level equivalent to those in the rest of the United Kingdom. This difficulty had not been foreseen in 1920 when the Northern Ireland budget showed a surplus, in a year of limited government and high employment. But 1920 was to prove a highly untypical year. It was becoming obvious by the 1930s that the UK government would have to offer much more help to Northern Ireland.

In 1938, therefore, Sir John Simon, the Chancellor of the Exchequer, laid down the principle of parity, which was to govern future financial relations between the UK and Northern Ireland. This principle provided that, in the event of 'a deficit on the Northern Ireland Budget which was not the result of a standard of social expenditure higher than that of Great Britain nor the result of a standard of taxation lower than that of Great Britain', the UK government would 'make good this deficit in such a way as to ensure that Northern Ireland should be in a financial position to continue to enjoy the same social services and have the same standards as Britain'.[63] This meant, of course, that Northern Ireland's very limited degree of fiscal autonomy was now completely eliminated, since if she lowered taxes, parity would be lost, while if she cut public expenditure, Northern Ireland taxpayers, paying at the same rate as taxpayers in the rest of the United Kingdom, would simply receive worse services.

The parity principle was supplemented in 1942 by another principle, the principle of 'leeway'. Sir Kingsley Wood, the Chancellor of the Exchequer, told the Prime Minister of Northern Ireland in September:

I recognise that in certain spheres Northern Ireland has considerable leeway to make up in order to attain equality of standard with the United Kingdom, and you can confidently rely on the Treasury always considering such a case sympathetically, as indeed the principle of parity requires us to do.[64]

This principle committed the British government to additional expenditure in Northern Ireland to make up the leeway in housing, schools, and hospitals, as well as additional expenditure to offset Northern Ireland's economic disadvantage. In addition, there were further agreements by which the UK government assisted Northern Ireland with the cost of specific services such as, in 1948, national insurance, national assistance, family allowances, pensions, and the health service; in 1966, the regional employment premium; and finally in 1971, supplementary benefits and the new family income supplement.

By this time of course the financial settlement of 1920 had been transformed beyond recognition. The finances of Northern Ireland were now to be determined not by her revenue, but by her needs. The financial arrangements which had begun by being revenue-based, had now become expenditure-based. The sample budget for Northern Ireland for the last year before direct rule, shown in Table 3.1, makes it clear that the Imperial Contribution had become a mere book-keeping item.

The crucial element in the Northern Ireland budget had now become the determination of the size of the funds which were to be transferred to her Exchequer from London. This was, from 1938, to be determined by the parity principle. But what precisely did parity mean? 'It is tempting to conclude', the Royal Commission on the Constitution declared in 1973, 'that "parity" was simply what could be secured by negotiation.'[65]

The central consequence of parity was that the Northern Ireland budget in effect needed to be approved in advance by London. From 1946, the amount to be transferred to Northern Ireland was decided by negotiations between the Northern Ireland Ministry of Finance and the Treasury. London did not, however, give to Northern Ireland a block grant to spend as she pleased. Instead, the principle of parity involved highly detailed scrutiny so as to ensure that it was not being used by Northern Ireland to secure for herself a higher level of service than that to which she was entitled. Moreover, policies with substantial spending implications required Treasury approval.

In theory, disputes about the parity principle could have led to serious conflict between London and Belfast. 'To a large extent,' Terence O'Neill wrote, 'Northern Ireland's income rested on attributions of revenue. How, for instance, does one accurately assess Northern Ireland's fair share of Tobacco Revenue? The answer is that

Table 3.1 Northern Ireland budget, 1971–2

		£m
Revenue		
Share of UK reserved taxes		269
Less: Imperial Contribution	1	
Cost of reserved services in Northern Ireland	4	
		5
Residuary share of reserved taxes		264
Revenue from transferred taxes		45
Total revenue accruing to Northern Ireland under the Government of Ireland Act, 1920		309
Receipts from the United Kingdom Government		
Health Service Agreement	20	
Social Services payments	37	
Remoteness grant payable under the Agriculture Act, 1957	2	
Additional selective employment premiums payable under Finance Act, 1967	11	
		70
Other revenue (mainly interest from local authorities)		39
TOTAL		418

In addition, Northern Ireland received £30m from the United Kingdom Government to pay for agricultural subsidies in Northern Ireland, and £15m for the Northern Ireland National Insurance Fund. The total amount she received from the United Kingdom Govern-ment was therefore £70m—the sum transferred for specific services— + £30m + 15m = £115m, as well as the true value of the Imperial Contribution. Expenditure, in the form of the cost of Northern Ireland services, was £418m.

Source: Report of the Royal Commission on the Constitution, Cmnd. 5460, 1973, para. 1295.

if you put your case well and establish a good rapport you will get a generous attribution.'[66] That more conflict did not occur was not solely because the system was, as the Royal Commission on the

Constitution thought, 'a monument to British pragmatism',[67] but because London and Belfast were predisposed from the start to achieve agreement. That might not have been the case had the Treasury been negotiating with an Irish nationalist administration in Dublin or a Scottish administration in Edinburgh.

Even so, there were serious weaknesses in the financial arrangements from the standpoints of both efficiency and democracy. The authors of the 1920 Act had sought to establish a system which would enable the Northern Ireland Minister of Finance to predict his revenue in advance, so that he could plan a realistic spending programme. Yet, because the transferred taxes were so meagre, he was in practice dependent upon the decisions of the Chancellor of the Exchequer with regard to reserved taxation. This made it difficult for the Northern Ireland Minister of Finance to plan expenditure in advance. 'Our problem', Sir Cecil Bateman, the Permanent Head of the Department of the Prime Minister of Northern Ireland, and of the Northern Ireland Finance Department, told the Royal Commission on the Constitution in 1971, 'is that . . . we find it very difficult to plan our expenditure a long time in advance because we are at the mercy of the economic policy of the United Kingdom. The Chancellor may change taxation, which could drastically reduce our revenue.'[68]

The Northern Ireland government was, then, in practice accountable for its financial decisions not to its own electors, but to the Treasury in London. The Northern Ireland budget was decided each year in private negotiations between Belfast and London, negotiations from which the Northern Ireland parliament and people were excluded. In the words of one commentator:

Parliament has effectively ceded power to the executive; the outcome is that neither Parliament exercises sufficient scrutiny over the financial relations between the two governments. Westminster exercises no oversight on the Treasury's role in the negotiations to fix each year's Ulster budget; the Ulster Parliament, faced in recent years with generosity from the Treasury, is glad to take what it can get without stirring up questions of principle.[69]

The result was that 'financial questions of great public interest and importance were shrouded in secrecy . . . it is apparently taken for granted that the public have no right to know, except in purely general terms, how Ulster's revenue and permissible expenditure are fixed'. In 1968, when the British Cabinet was approving a subsidy to Short's of Belfast, Richard Crossman asked:

'May I be told what is the exact financial arrangement?' Nobody could say. Neither Jack Diamond [the Chief Secretary of the Treasury] nor the Chancellor knew the formula according to which the Northern Ireland Government gets its money. In all these years it has never been revealed to the politicians and I am longing to see whether now we shall get to the bottom of this very large, expensive secret.[70]

Thus, the financial arrangements between London and Belfast came to violate the canons both of efficiency and of democracy. They violated also a fundamental principle of good government, that the spending power and the taxing power ought, so far as possible, to be in the same hands, for, since spending is generally popular and taxation unpopular, it is only right that government should have to balance expenditure and taxation at the margin. The Northern Ireland government, however, while responsible for around 90 per cent of public expenditure in Northern Ireland, enjoyed transferred revenue which, by 1972, amounted to just 15 per cent of total Northern Ireland revenue. So nine-tenths of Northern Ireland's expenditure was decided in Northern Ireland, while seventeen-twentieths of her revenue came from London. The settlement with Northern Ireland thus came to dissociate the spending power, which remained with Belfast, from the taxing power, which lay primarily in London. Parity had stabilized the financial position of Northern Ireland, but at the cost of drastically undermining her financial autonomy and destroying the connection between expenditure and revenue.

IV

What scope then was left for autonomy in Northern Ireland? Parity did not entirely inhibit the development of different policies, for not all legislation is concerned with finance. On matters of mores, Northern Ireland took her own path, declining to follow the rest of the United

Kingdom in modifying her divorce, abortion, or homosexuality laws in the 1960s. She also declined to abolish capital punishment when Westminster did so in 1965, and decided not to adopt the Industrial Relations Act of 1971.

The Northern Ireland government produced, for the Royal Commission on the Constitution, figures showing the proportion of her legislation and statutory orders determined by the parity requirement. It turned out to be surprisingly small (Table 3.2).

Table 3.2 Proportion of legislation and statutory orders determined by parity requirement

Acts of Parliament	1965	1966	1967	1968	1969
A. Parity legislation	6	13	5	3	9
B. Legislation falling between categories A and C	8	11	15	14	12
C. Legislation peculiar to Northern Ireland	8	17	16	14	15
Technical Acts	3	3	4	3	3
TOTALS	25	44	40	34	39
Statutory Rules and Orders					
A	65	88	92	70	85
B	110	98	109	94	138
C	102	124	143	115	129
Miscellaneous	12	9	5	5	9
TOTALS	289	319	349	284	361

The Northern Ireland government added the comment:

It is estimated that, if legislation is divided into two categories only—parity and non-parity matters—about two-thirds of both administrative and legislative time is spent on purely Northern Ireland matters. This is, however, a rough estimate only and the proportions vary from department to department; in the Ministry of Heath and Social Security, for example, the proportion of time spent on parity matters would be much higher.[71]

This comment draws attention to the fact that devolution made much less sense in health and social security than in other areas of government. The framers of the 1920 Act did not consider how the development of the Welfare State might affect devolution, and where the proportion of time spent on parity matters was very high, as in health and social security, it might have been better if responsibility for the service had been retained in London. Where there was little scope for divergence of policy, devolution seemed not to make much sense. Even in these areas, however, there were some successes. A Tuberculosis Authority was set up which 'worked so vigorously as to undermine its own existence', while in mental health, Northern Ireland's 'post-war legislation leapt at a bound from darkness into light'.[72] In other areas, so it was said, 'The task which faces the Parliamentary Draftsman is to polish the jewel of parity and to put it in an appropriate Northern Ireland setting.'[73]

In agriculture and industrial development, where the problems faced by Northern Ireland were quite different from those experienced in the rest of the United Kingdom, the advantages of devolved government were manifest. The administration of both agriculture and industrial policy underwent an evolution characteristic of that in many federal states in which powers, once divided, come to be shared between the provincial unit and the centre.

Under the 1920 Act, agriculture was a transferred subject, except with regard to exports; yet Northern Ireland could not sustain from her own resources the UK system of agricultural support. The Northern Ireland Ministry of Agriculture acted as an agent for the Ministry of Agriculture, Fisheries and Food in London, so that the agricultural support system could be uniform throughout the United Kingdom. Joint action was taken on agricultural marketing also.

Other aspects of agricultural development, however, remained the responsibility of the Northern Ireland government. This gave Northern Ireland greater freedom of variation and adaptation than Scotland, which had only administrative devolution: where legislation was required, the Northern Ireland government could pass it rapidly, whereas, in the case of Scotland, it could often take two or three years before time could be found in the crowded Westminster timetable. Northern Ireland faced particular problems in agriculture because of the high proportion of her produce which was sent across the Irish Sea. For produce from Northern Ireland to be genuinely competitive, it would need a guarantee of quality. The government of Northern Ireland took early steps to regulate the quality of eggs, by introducing a system of compulsory grading in 1924, and then extending it to other products such as fruit, potatoes, dairy produce, and meat. A system of this kind was not introduced into the rest of the United Kingdom until some years afterwards, and when it was brought in elsewhere, the grading was entirely voluntary. Legislation of this kind, therefore, would probably not have been introduced had there not been a local parliament in Northern Ireland. Giving evidence to the Royal Commission on the Constitution, the Assistant Secretary to the Northern Ireland Ministry of Agriculture was able to speak of the quality-conscious produce of Northern Ireland and to claim that 'we have led the field in this respect'.[74]

In industrial policy also, power came to be shared between London and Belfast. After 1945, London gradually came to assume responsibility for regional policy, seeking, through the use of industrial development certificates, to hold the balance between the depressed regions of the United Kingdom. Moreover, Northern Ireland was bound to be affected by the macro-economic policies followed by the British government.

Northern Ireland, however, remained responsible for industrial development and regional planning, and the record of her government on aid to industry was, on the whole, imaginative. Indeed, the Northern Ireland government can claim to have been a pioneer of regional policy, and many of the measures adopted by Northern Ireland in the immediate post-war years were later to be used in the rest of the United Kingdom by the 1964 Labour government.

Northern Ireland confronted a similar problem to that faced by other depressed areas in the United Kingdom—an outdated industrial structure and heavy regional unemployment. She also faced the extra problem of a cost disadvantage, since her goods had to be transported across the Irish Sea. The government of Northern Ireland established a generous system of capital grants to industry, and pioneered the building of factories for rent or sale. The government also offered grants towards the operating costs of factories situated in areas of particularly high unemployment. To deal with the differential in transport costs, the government provided a cost subsidy on fuels and used the powers to vary road taxes to assist industry by reducing the cost of the licence for heavy vehicles.[75] Northern Ireland opened an industrial development office in the United States two years before the United Kingdom did so.

The government of Northern Ireland also adopted a manpower policy geared to the special requirements of the province, pioneering a manpower survey to identify the particular needs of industry and to develop training facilities in accordance with these needs. The government encouraged the diversification of industry, building upon the particular skills of the labour force. In textiles, for example, the government succeeded in attracting synthetic textile firms to help replace declining textile industries. Its success in this area can be quantified. Between the years 1961 and 1967, the value of the net output of 'miscellaneous textiles'—a category which includes synthetic textiles—increased almost sevenfold from £4m to £27m—and the share of 'miscellaneous textiles' in Northern Ireland's total output of textiles increased from 14 per cent to 47 per cent.[76]

These developments probably owed most to the 'immense intangible advantage of regional government—accessibility of the decision-makers and consequent speed of decision. Red tape tends to be a result of sheer scale.'[77] The Ombudsman for Northern Ireland declared that the standard of administrative performance in Northern Ireland ministries 'compares well with my experience of government departments in the United Kingdom', and that 'The individual citizen frequently gets a better service from a Northern Ireland ministry than he would get from a United Kingdom department in similar circumstances, owing to the easier access to central government that is both feasible and customary in a territory the size of Northern Ireland.'[78]

When the Royal Commission on the Constitution held its hearings in Northern Ireland, the following exchange took place:

Sir Geoffrey Crowther: I have been told that when a member of the public has a grievance or a matter on which he seeks information, his natural and more usual course in Northern Ireland would be to walk into the appropriate Ministry and ask the question himself rather than use the channel of the Parliamentary question: is that so?

Sir Cecil Bateman: Yes, that is correct.[79]

The Royal Commission on the Constitution summed up this advantage of devolution in the following way:

Even the most severe critic of home rule amongst our witnesses . . . considered the devolution of administrative and executive powers to have been an outstanding success. [One witness] argued . . . a dissatisfied farmer anywhere within its boundaries ought to be able (and is able) to travel by public transport to the administrative capital, horse-whip the responsible official and get home again (in time to milk the cow).[80]

The close relationship which the administration was able to build with individual firms was also of great importance in economic policy. In its evidence to the Royal Commission of the Constitution, the Northern Ireland Council of the CBI argued: 'that such steps as have been taken are greater than would have been the case had we depended solely on the activities of a central legislature. The problems of Northern Ireland are pertinent, real and close to an indigenous government, but would be less urgent and pressing if merely those of one of a number of similar areas.' The Council was 'convinced that the existence of the Parliament at Stormont has been, over the years, a major factor in the economic development of the Province'.[81]

Even more striking was the evidence of the Northern Ireland Labour Party, since it was politically opposed to the Unionist administration. The party nevertheless admitted that 'the machinery of regional autonomy, even under a Unionist Government, can be a means of readjusting of regional differences . . . The result . . . has been a better economic performance than the other regions of the United Kingdom which had basically similar economic problems— remoteness, and decline of the major traditional industries.'[82] The party presented the index of the growth of personal incomes in different regions of the UK to prove its point (Table 3.3).

Table 3.3 Index of growth of personal incomes in different regions of the United Kingdom

	1964–5 (1954–5: 100)
Northern Region	174
North West	182
South West	204
Wales	188
Scotland	182
Northern Ireland	204
UK as a whole	194

Of course, these gains might not have been as great if other parts of the United Kingdom had enjoyed devolved government. 'Young man, you must never again make a suggestion like that,' Terence O'Neill was told when he advocated devolution for Scotland, 'we do not want any more provincial calves pulling at the one cow.'[83]

A corollary to the intimacy of regional administration in Northern Ireland, however, was the weaker role of local government in the province. Since Northern Ireland covered a relatively small geographical area, ministers were not compelled to delegate to the same extent as ministers in Whitehall departments. Services such as fire and the police, which in the rest of the United Kingdom were the responsibility of local authorities, were in Northern Ireland the responsibility of the government. Given that the British government was committed to parity in the provision of public services in Northern Ireland, it was of course to the advantage of Northern Ireland ratepayers to be able to transfer responsibility for these services to the British taxpayer. Moreover, the Northern Ireland government took powers in housing and education from local government, which had proved itself weak and unimaginative in these areas.

The poor house-building record in Northern Ireland between the wars led to the creation of the Northern Ireland Housing Trust in 1945 to supplement the efforts of local authorities. This body gained 'a world-wide reputation for the provision of well-planned and competently administered housing estates', and Northern Ireland was the only part of the United Kingdom to enjoy subsidies for private house-building.[84] The Housing Trust, however, was, inevitably, a step towards housing being located entirely with the regional government rather than with local authorities, and in October 1969, the governments of the United Kingdom and Northern Ireland issued a joint communiqué declaring that they had 'reluctantly decided that local authorities are not geared—and cannot be geared—to handle such a task and that the best hope of success lies in the creation of a single-purpose, efficient and streamlined central housing authority . . . to tackle this most urgent problem.'[85]

In some areas of education, too, powers which in the rest of the United Kingdom were exercised by local authorities gravitated to the centre. The salaries of teachers in schools and colleges of further education under the control of the local education authority were, except for those in voluntary grammar schools, paid centrally. The Exchequer, however, limited its liability under this head, and a levy was exacted from local authorities to contribute towards the cost. There was little scope for practical initiative on the part of local education authorities, and, moreover, some of them displayed sectarian attitudes, seeking to discover the denomination of candidates applying for teaching posts, and so arousing the suspicion that Catholic candidates were discriminated against in appointments to maintained schools. There was, therefore, a strong case for a central education authority in Northern Ireland.[86]

Local authorities in Northern Ireland were weakened still further by the restrictive financial arrangements established by the government of the province. The share of local authority finance falling on the Exchequer was greater in Northern Ireland than in the rest of the United Kingdom and it was met to a greater extent than in other parts of the country from percentage or specific grants, rather than the block grant introduced in England in 1958. This led inevitably to close scrutiny of local-authority projects. Moreover, since local authorities had to contribute to the cost of the fire service and the police force, which were run from Belfast, and also to pay the education levy, there came to be a disconnection between local expenditure and local taxation. Devolution in Northern Ireland thus led to a restriction of local autonomy. The dispersal of power from London to Belfast was accompanied by a centralization of power within Northern Ireland itself.

V

The communal disturbances which broke out in Northern Ireland in 1968 brought the problems of Northern Ireland to the attention of ministers and MPs in London and put the relationship between Westminster and Belfast under serious strain. British ministers and Members of Parliament demanded the application of British standards of citizenship in Northern Ireland and pressed ministers in the province to implement reforms rapidly. Behind the formal machinery of devolution, the British government increasingly came to assume control of Northern Ireland's affairs. Joint working parties of officials were established in which London was dominant, and an official from the Foreign Office was attached to the Northern Ireland Cabinet Office, to sit in a room next to the Prime Minister of Northern Ireland, and to 'explain British policy . . . and warn [the Northern Ireland Prime Minister] where he was likely to get into difficulties with us'.[87] In 1972, Westminster demanded the transfer of powers over law and order from Stormont to London, a proposal which was unacceptable to the unionists. The government accordingly prorogued the Northern Ireland Parliament in the Northern Ireland (Temporary Provisions) Act, 1972, and abolished it the year afterwards in the Northern Ireland Constitution Act of 1973.

Between 1972 and 1998, with the exception of the five months between January and May 1974, Northern Ireland was governed under a system of direct rule.[88] The functions of the government of Northern Ireland were taken over by the Northern Ireland Office, headed by the Secretary of State for Northern Ireland, a senior minister in the British Cabinet, who was assisted by various junior ministers. While Acts of Parliament could be enacted for or extended to Northern Ireland, the

Northern Ireland Act of 1974 provided for power to undertake primary legislation for Northern Ireland by means of Orders in Council, subject to resolutions of both Houses of Parliament.

In compensation for the abolition of the Northern Ireland Parliament, the under-representation of Northern Ireland in Westminster was ended, and the number of Northern Ireland MPs was increased, following the report of a Speaker's Conference in 1978,[89] from twelve to seventeen in 1979, and eighteen in 1997. In 1975, a standing committee for Northern Ireland was established in the House of Commons and in 1994 it was renamed the Northern Ireland Grand Committee. It comprises all the MPs from Northern Ireland constituencies and not more than twenty-five other MPs, and now enjoys deliberative and scrutiny powers over proposals for draft Orders in Council; also in 1994, a select committee, the Northern Ireland Committee, was established.

Following the suspension of the Northern Ireland Parliament, it was necessary to replace the guarantee in the Ireland Act of 1949 which provided that neither Northern Ireland nor any part of it would cease to be a part of the United Kingdom without the consent of the Northern Ireland Parliament. Accordingly, section 1 of the Northern Ireland Constitution Act of 1973 provided that neither Northern Ireland nor any part of it would cease to be a part of the United Kingdom 'without the consent of the majority of the people of Northern Ireland voting in a poll'. The consent principle was reiterated in the Belfast Agreement of 1998. Provision was made in 1973 for polls to be held at intervals of not less than ten years to ascertain the views of the population of the province. A poll was accordingly held in March 1973, but its value was considerably lessened by the decision of the nationalist parties to advise their supporters to boycott it. On a 58.1 per cent turnout, 591,820 (98.9 per cent of those voting) supported Northern Ireland remaining part of the United Kingdom, while just 6,463 (1.1 per cent of those voting) supported Northern Ireland being joined with the Republic of Ireland. No further polls have been held.

Direct rule has been regarded by British governments, whether Labour or Conservative, as a temporary expedient rather than a permanent method of rule, for it is subject to considerable weaknesses from the point of view of democratic accountability. Laws, which in other parts of the United Kingdom are made by primary legislation, by Acts of Parliament, are, in Northern Ireland, made largely by Orders in Council. During the period of direct rule, between 1972 and 1997, there were thirty-three Acts passed applying wholly or mainly to Northern Ireland, but 557 Orders in Council. These Orders are not, and cannot be, effectively scrutinized by Parliament. Unlike bills, they cannot be amended, but must be either approved or rejected. They are in fact generally considered late at night, and often approved with little debate, for MPs, other than those representing Northern Ireland constituencies, cannot be expected to be familiar with the details and implications of proposals contained in draft Orders. In consequence, there has been less parliamentary control of Northern Ireland legislation than there has of legislation for the rest of the United Kingdom.

'Scrutiny of Northern Ireland at Westminster was lamentable,' James Prior, a former Northern Ireland Secretary, has written; 'the usual ration, year-in, year-out, was monthly forty-five minute question time on the floor of the Commons, a few poorly attended debates usually held late at night, and the occasional statement to the House following some particularly awful atrocity'.[90]

This lack of accountability was exacerbated by the fact that local authorities in Northern Ireland have far more limited powers than in Britain, the bulk of local powers being located in non-elected and nominated boards such as the Housing Executive and the Education and Library Boards.

However, the most serious defect of direct rule as it operated since 1972 was that, as James Prior said when Secretary of State, it gave the political parties in Northern Ireland 'all the advantages of political activity with none of the disadvantages of responsibility'.[91] Direct rule left a political vacuum in Northern Ireland which extremists were able to fill more easily than responsible political leaders, who found it difficult to display the concrete advantages of moderation in the absence of a political forum. In particular, Sinn Féin, the extreme wing of the nationalist movement, was able to portray the problems of Northern Ireland as a conflict between an indigenous nationalist movement in Northern Ireland and a colonial government in London, thus obscuring the reality of conflicting identities and allegiances inside the province.

Direct rule, then, was intended as a temporary expedient. It could have been replaced either by devolution or by full integration of Northern Ireland within the United Kingdom. Direct rule, it should be noted, is the opposite of integration in that it implicitly recognizes the distinctiveness of a particular area of the country. No one claims, for example, that Scotland or Yorkshire is under direct rule. The option of integration, on the other hand, proposes that Northern Ireland be governed, if not like Yorkshire, then like Scotland. It has at times been advocated by a number of commentators, primarily Conservative or unionist. The main purpose of integration would be to submerge the Northern Ireland conflict in United Kingdom-wide issues, to replace communal conflict with conflict over socio-economic issues more familiar to those living in other parts of the United Kingdom. There are, after all, tensions between Protestants and Catholics in Liverpool and in Glasgow, but these have not led to disturbances and terrorism of the kind that has disfigured Northern Ireland since 1968.

No British government, however, has been prepared to espouse integration, and for very good reasons. A significant difficulty is that the party system in Northern Ireland is now so very different from that in the rest of the United Kingdom. While in the 1920s, integration might well have been successful in assimilating the party system in Northern Ireland to that in the rest of the United Kingdom, by the 1970s, communal divisions had become so congealed that this was no longer possible. Indeed, no United Kingdom party has been able to win a Westminster seat in Northern Ireland. The Labour Party has never contested an election in Northern Ireland, nor does it accept membership from those living in the province. It rejected the approach of the Northern Ireland Labour Party for affiliation both in 1924 and in 1970, treating the NILP not as an affiliated party but as a 'fraternal' one, like, for example, the French or German Socialist parties. The Conservatives maintained, until 1974, a formal relationship with the Ulster Unionists, whose MPs sat and voted with Conservative MPs in the House of Commons. But the Conservatives did not, until 1989, contest elections in Northern Ireland, nor set up constituency associations in the province, nor accept membership applications from those residing in Northern Ireland. Since 1989, they have indeed formed constituency associations in the province and contested elections there, but they have secured only a derisory vote. The Liberals fought very occasional elections in Northern Ireland from the 1950s, but their Gladstonian tradition deprived them of Protestant votes, while the nationalist parties were more success-ful in winning the anti-partitionist vote. The Liberal Democrats do not contest elections in Northern Ireland so as to avoid splitting the vote with their sister party in the Liberal International, the non-sec-tarian Alliance Party of Northern Ireland.

None of the major British parties, then, offer a serious electoral alternative in Northern Ireland. Conversely, none of the Northern Ireland parties represented at Westminster compete in Great Britain. This has the consequence that, because the government of the United Kingdom is formed by British parties, the Secretary of State for Northern Ireland can never be a representative of the area for which he is responsible. This is in contrast to the Secretaries of State for Scotland and Wales who generally represent Scottish or Welsh con-stituencies, and political parties which enjoy electoral support in Scotland and Wales. The parties which represent Northern Ireland, by contrast, have no representation at all in the government of the United Kingdom and the Secretary of State for Northern Ireland is electorally disconnected from the province. He or she represents MPs from any part of the country excepting only Northern Ireland. James Prior felt, as Northern Ireland Secretary, 'as though I was a foreigner in another land',[92] while Tom King declared that 'The longer I have had the wide powers that a Secretary of State exercis-es, the more it has convinced me that people in the province and elected representatives in the province should take a greater share of those powers and responsibilities.'[93] Under direct rule, Northern Ireland came to assume the aspect of a dependency incapable of self-government.

The voter in Northern Ireland has been unable to play a direct role in choosing the government of the United Kingdom. The communal conflict in the province means that Westminster elections in Northern Ireland are not about whether the Conservatives, Labour, or the

Liberal Democrats should form the government, but rather about the balance of representation between and within essentially communal parties.

The main objection, however, to integration now is that it would make the prospect of agreement between the two communities more remote, since it would take away from the people of Northern Ireland responsibility for their own affairs. By preserving the political vacuum left by direct rule, integration would thereby prolong its most serious defect. Moreover, integration would be seen by the nationalist community in Northern Ireland as a sign that the aspirations of the unionists were being preferred to their own, that the British identity of the unionists was being given a privileged status as compared with the Irish identity of the nationalists. 'I rejected integration', James Prior wrote, 'because it would have made a bad situation worse. It offered as a permanent solution an approach favoured by only a minority of the Unionists—one section of the Official Unionists. It would have made the position of moderate democratic Nationalists impossible, and played into the hands of the terrorists. It would have scuppered any hope of institutional co-operation with Dublin.'94

Successive governments have insisted, however, that any new system of devolution must, unlike the parliament which existed from 1921 to 1972, be such as to be acceptable to both communities in the province. This has been interpreted to mean both that the government of Northern Ireland should contain representatives of both communities, and that the aspirations of the nationalist minority should be recognized through the Irish Dimension, some form of institutionalized connection with the Irish Republic.

Such an approach involves a striking departure from the Westminster model of government, which is based on the possibility of alternating governments. This model, it is clear, is unsuitable for societies divided by religion, language, or ethnicity. Societies of this kind must be governed by a different principle of democracy, the principle of power-sharing. That is the principle which operates, with more or less success, in other divided societies such as Belgium and Switzerland. Indeed, one commentator on the politics of Northern Ireland has declared as a political scientist who has specialised in the study of divided societies, that some kind of power-sharing has *always* been a feature of government in such societies which have successfully overcome their internal divisions. I do not claim that power-sharing will succeed—it broke down in Cyprus and Lebanon. But I know of *no* case where a divided society has been stable without power-sharing. As cases where it has been successful, I would point to Switzerland, the Netherlands, Belgium, South Tyrol, certain provinces of Canada, Malaysia, Fiji. The detailed arrangements in these countries differ . . . But in all of them there is some set of arrangements whereby the different segments of the population share power roughly in proportion to their numerical strengths, so that no segment feels permanently left out in the cold.[95]

Before the Belfast Agreement of 1998, British governments legislated for devolution on three occasions as part of their long-term objective of securing government by agreement in Northern Ireland—1973, 1975, and 1982. In 1973, the Northern Ireland Constitution Act provided for an assembly—not a parliament as in the 1920 Government of Ireland Act—of seventy-eight members to be elected by the single transferable-vote method of proportional representation. Devolution, however, was to be dependent upon the formation of a broadly based executive which appeared to the Secretary of State for Northern Ireland to be widely accepted throughout the province. He was required to ensure that the government of Northern Ireland included representatives of both communities. In addition, the Assembly would be required to establish consultative committees which reflected the balance of parties in the Assembly. The new Assembly and Executive would thus be very different from the former Northern Ireland Parliament, whose central principle had been majority rule.

The 1973 Act, by contrast with the Act of 1920, excepted franchise and anti-terrorist powers for Westminster, and reserved powers over law and order. There was provision, however, for these latter powers to be transferred to the Assembly at a later date with the agreement of the British government. The main powers transferred were health and social services, housing, education, environment, and agriculture.

Elections to the new Assembly were held in June 1973, and the leading unionist and nationalist parties agreed on a power-sharing executive, which took office in January 1974. In December 1973, at Sunningdale, agreement was reached between the British and Irish governments and the members of the new Northern Ireland executive-designate on the creation of a Council of Ireland with some executive functions, to comprise seven ministers from the Republic of Ireland and seven from the Northern Ireland Executive.

The Council of Ireland was, however, unacceptable to the majority of the Ulster Unionist Council, which repudiated the Unionist leader Brian Faulkner, who in consequence resigned from the Ulster Unionist Party. In February 1974, before Faulkner had a chance to regroup his forces, a British general election was held. In that election, eleven out of the twelve Northern Ireland seats were won by the United Ulster Unionist Coalition, a grouping pledged to oppose the Sunningdale Agreement. This helped to deprive the Assembly of democratic legitimacy. In May 1974, the Ulster Workers Council, supported by loyalist paramilitaries and by other unionists opposed to the Assembly, called a general strike. This led at the end of the month to the resignation of Faulkner as leader of the Executive and the prorogation of the Assembly. The Northern Ireland Act of 1974 dissolved the Assembly and restored direct rule in the province. It also proposed the election of a Northern Ireland Convention, elected by the single transferable vote, to produce new proposals for devolution. However, this failed to reach agreement and was dissolved in 1976.

In 1982, a new Northern Ireland Act provided for another assembly, once again elected by the single transferable vote.[96] The functions of this assembly, by contrast with those of the assembly of 1974, were to be those of scrutiny, consultation, and deliberation. It would in particular be able to scrutinize proposals for draft legislation and make reports and recommendations to the Secretary of State for Northern Ireland. Provision was, however, made for the 'rolling' devolution of functions, on either a partial or a total basis, to the Assembly if at least 70 per cent of its members were to agree on it, or if the Secretary of State were satisfied that particular proposals were acceptable to both communities. Full devolution would have to contain recommendations for the composition of an executive acceptable to both communities, and that almost certainly meant a power-sharing executive. An Order would then be laid at Westminster to provide for devolution. It would, therefore, be up to the Assembly whether devolution took place; but the actual decision to transfer powers would be taken by Parliament and not, as in 1974, by the Secretary of State.

In 1982, the SDLP and the other parties representing the nationalist community refused to participate in the Assembly because insufficient recognition was given, in their view, to the Irish Dimension, i.e. the creation of links between the minority community and the Irish Republic. There was, therefore, no chance of the cross-community requirement being met, and it proved impossible to devolve any functions to the Assembly. In consequence, 'Rather than rolling along the road to devolution and power-sharing, the Assembly ran into the sands of unionist factionalism and nationalist abstentionism and was dissolved in June 1986, four months before the expiry of its statutory term.'[97]

A crucial step forward in achieving devolution occurred when the IRA announced a ceasefire in August 1994, thus allowing for the representation of Sinn Féin, its political wing, in all-party talks. In 1996 multi-party talks began in Northern Ireland between the elected representatives of the parties in the province, under three independent chairmen led by Senator George Mitchell, a former majority leader of the United States Senate. These talks culminated in the Belfast or Good Friday Agreement of 1998.[98]

The Agreement provides for a 108-member assembly to be elected by the single transferable vote for a four-year fixed term. The Assembly enjoys specific powers devolved in finance, personnel, agriculture, education, health, social services, economic development, and the environment. The Agreement also states that the British government is ready in principle to consider devolving responsibility for policing and justice in due course. The Assembly is to have no tax-raising powers. As in the 1998 Scotland Act, the question of whether the provision of an Assembly bill is within its legislative competence can be referred by a government minister to the Judicial Committee of the Privy Council. By contrast with the 1920 legislation, however, there will be no Lord Lieutenant or Governor of Northern Ireland, an office which ceased to exist in 1972.

The crucial features of the Agreement, however, relate to the proposals for power-sharing. By contrast with 1973, the appointment of the executive is not to be made by the Secretary of State, nor is the coming of devolution to be dependent on a 70 per cent vote in the Assembly as it was in 1982. Instead, the executive is to be formed through a novel cross-community voting mechanism. At the first meeting of the Assembly, members are required to register a declaration of identity—unionist, nationalist, or other. For key decisions, which are to be designated in advance, instead of majority voting, cross-community consent will be required. This is to be achieved either by parallel consent, i.e. a majority of those members present and voting, including a majority of the unionists and nationalists present and voting; or, alternatively, a weighted majority of 60 per cent members present and voting, including at least 40 per cent of unionists present and voting and 40 per cent of nationalists present and voting. Those designating themselves as 'Others'—in 1998 only the Alliance Party of Northern Ireland and the Women's Coalition—do not count in either case.

By contrast with the arrangements in 1973, the First Minister and Deputy First Minister are to be elected jointly by the Assembly by means of a particular form of cross-community support, namely a majority of the members voting, a majority of the designated unionists voting, and a majority of the designated nationalists voting. This system provides an incentive for each community to nominate a candidate acceptable to members of the other community. Thus, even if Sinn Féin were to gain more votes than the SDLP in an Assembly election, it might not be wise for the nationalists to nominate Gerry Adams, since his nomination could be blocked by the unionists. In fact, the First Minister elected in 1998 was David Trimble, leader of the Ulster Unionist Party, and his Deputy was Seamus Mallon of the SDLP. The First Minister and the Deputy First Minister hold office jointly as a dyarchy and if one resigns the other also loses office. They are semi-presidential figures in the sense that they cannot be removed by the Assembly. But they do not, unlike most chief executives, appoint the other ministers, who take office in proportion to party strengths in the Assembly.

The requirement that members of the Assembly declare their identity had not been present in 1973 nor in 1982, and the former Irish Taoiseach John Bruton, in a debate in the Dáil in April 1998, while accepting that the requirement was 'necessary', added:

I hope it does not entrench division by defining parties on the basis of ultimate aspirations, which conflict with one another, rather than short-term aspirations which may coincide with one another. The rules may aggravate this by making it disadvantageous for a member to designate himself or herself in the 'other' category, where his or her vote will only count in initial votes but not in determining a minimum level of support in either community. I am worried that this new institutionalisation of two labels will also institutionalise old divisions.[99]

Although a novel requirement in the United Kingdom context, however, similar provisions have been put forward in other divided societies. Under the new Belgian Constitution of 1994, for example, Article 43 (1) provides that, for certain issues affecting the two communities, the elected members of each legislative chamber are divided into a French language group and a Flemish language group. Under Article 55, a motion signed by at least three-quarters of the members of one of the linguistic groups can delay legislation which would affect community relations. In Northern Ireland, in addition to the requirement for cross-community support, every minister is required, on the assumption of office, to take a Pledge of Office in place of the Oath of Allegiance to the Crown, which requires him or her, *inter alia*, to promise to abstain from violence and to act in accordance with the general obligation to avoid discrimination.

The Agreement, however, provides for more than devolution within the United Kingdom. For it also recognizes the Irish dimension in the politics of Northern Ireland and a confederal relationship between the United Kingdom and the Irish Republic. The Assembly is required, before powers are transferred to it, to make proper arrangements for the effective working of two new bodies established by the Agreement. The first is a North–South Ministerial Council to bring together representatives of the Irish government and the executive of the Northern Ireland Assembly to develop co-operation on matters of common interest in the island of Ireland, all decisions to be by agreement between the two sides. It is noticeable that the new body is not to be called 'Council of Ireland', a term with unfortunate overtones for unionists who refused to activate the 1920 Council, and whose opposition to the 1973 Council was largely responsible for the failure of the power-sharing experiment the following year.

The Agreement provides, under Article 1 (vi) for both the British and Irish identities of the people of Northern Ireland to be respected. Accordingly, anyone living in Northern Ireland is allowed to hold Irish citizenship, as well as British citizenship if he or she should so choose. Were Northern Ireland ever to be joined, by consent, with the Irish Republic, those living in Northern Ireland would be allowed to retain their British citizenship if they so chose.

The second new body is the British–Irish Council. This will bring together representatives of the British and Irish governments, and of devolved institutions in Northern Ireland, Scotland, and Wales (and in England, if devolved institutions are established there), as well as representatives of the Isle of Man and the Channel Isles, to consider matters of mutual interest. Because it links the Northern Ireland Assembly with other devolved institutions in Britain, the British–Irish Council might well succeed in defusing fears amongst unionists that the North–South Council is a step towards a united Ireland. For the unionists are more likely to countenance closer links with the Republic if both parts of Ireland are in turn linked together in an organization which includes the rest of the United Kingdom.[100]

The Belfast Agreement was approved in a referendum held on 22 May 1998 when, on a turnout of 81.1 per cent, 71.1 per cent voted 'Yes' and 28.9 per cent 'No'. The size of the 'Yes' majority indicated that the Agreement enjoyed majority support in both communities in Northern Ireland, the unionist and the nationalist. In a referendum held in the Irish Republic on the same day, the Agreement was endorsed by 94 per cent of those voting on a 56 per cent turnout. Elections, accordingly, were held for the new Assembly in June 1998, as provided for in the Northern Ireland (Elections) Act 1998, and Parliament implemented the Belfast Agreement in the new Northern Ireland Act 1998. This Act reiterates the constitutional guarantee to Northern Ireland, as in the Northern Ireland Constitution Act of 1973, with plebiscites to be held whenever the Secretary of State considers that a majority for change exists, but at intervals of not less than seven years, by contrast with the minimum ten-year period specified in the 1973 Act. The Act, however, repeals the Government of Ireland Act of 1920, most of the Northern Ireland Constitution Act of 1973, and the whole of the Northern Ireland Acts of 1974 and 1982. It provides for the final end of direct rule in Northern Ireland.

The Belfast Agreement offers, by contrast with previous attempts to secure devolution in Northern Ireland, a novel scheme of power-sharing designed to overcome the deep-seated communal conflict in the province; and also provisions designed to minimize the scope for boycott and obstruction by determined minorities. The Agreement has a double significance for the government of the United Kingdom since it proposes not only a solution to the Irish problem, but also recognition of the process of devolution to the non-English parts of the United Kingdom. It offers, in essence, a return to the original Gladstonian conception of Home Rule in a form suited to modern conditions. Gladstone's particular conception of the British–Irish relationship—a united Ireland enjoying Home Rule within a United Kingdom of Great Britain and Ireland—was breached in 1920 and 1921 by partition and by secession, and cannot of course be restored. But the proposals for devolution, together with the North–South Council and the confederal implications of the British–Irish Council, offer a chance of realizing the underlying theme of Gladstonian thinking—recognition both of the various and distinctive national identities within these islands, but also of the close and complex links between them.

Scotland

Up to date the Scottish Nationalist movement seems to have gone almost unnoticed in England. . . . It is true that it is a small movement, but it could grow, because there is a basis for it.

(George Orwell, 1947)

I

The Union brought political stability and economic progress to Scotland, and this helped to ensure its acceptance. Scotland was at first administered by a Scottish Secretary, but this post was abolished after the Jacobite revolt of 1745, and between 1782 and 1885 the Home Secretary was the minister nominally responsible for Scottish affairs, although the actual administration of Scotland was still undertaken by Scots. Nevertheless, assimilationist feeling probably reached its peak after the suppression of the Jacobites, at a time when Scotland was making considerable economic advances. During these years, it was coming to be believed that union might imply assimilation after all. In 1754, Lord Chancellor Hardwicke wrote to Lord Kames:

I am extremely obliged to your Lordship for . . . that zeal which you express for improving and perfecting the union of the two Kingdoms, to which nothing can contribute more than an uniformity of laws. Those great men who conceived and framed the plan of the Union [had sought uniformity] . . . but found it impracticable in the outset; but I have reason to think that they never imagined near half a century would have passed after their articles were established, without a greater advance being made towards it than has hitherto been attempted—an evil which I have often lamented, and should rejoice to see remedied, because, without it, an incorporating union must be very defective.[1]

Hardwicke and Kames, both lawyers, seem to have taken it for granted that an incorporating union implied assimilation. During the nineteenth century, Scotland was often referred to as North Britain, and it was by no means clear that she would be able to retain her separate identity, rather than becoming a mere province of England. That this did not happen may be ascribed to two factors: first, Scotland's separate legal and administrative system which compelled government and Parliament to take account of her particular needs; and second, the influence of the Irish Home Rule agitation which stirred national feeling in both Scotland and Wales.

In the 1880s, Scotland's claims were championed at Westminster by Lord Rosebery, a young Liberal peer who was a favourite of Gladstone's. Rosebery was not a Home Ruler but he urged the establishment of a separate minister for Scotland, and, partly as a result of his efforts, the Scottish Office was resurrected in 1885. 'The whole object', Lord Salisbury told its first holder, the Duke of Richmond and Gordon, 'is to redress the wounded dignities of the Scotch people—or a section of them—who think that enough is not made of Scotland.'[2] Gladstone, in the 1886 Irish Home Rule debate, called the recreation of this post, 'a little mouthful of Home Rule'.[3]

At its inception, the Scottish Office was seen as something of a sinecure. 'The work is not heavy,' Salisbury had told the Duke. 'It really is a matter where the effulgence of two Dukedoms and the best salmon river in Scotland will go a long way.'[4] From 1892, however, the Scottish Secretary was always to be in the Cabinet except in wartime; and in 1926, he was made a Secretary of State. In 1939, the office was moved to Edinburgh, although a branch office remains in London.

The Scottish Office began, in 1885, with hardly any functional responsibilities; but from then on it saw a continual accretion of functions until, by the 1960s, the Secretary of State was expected to take an interest in all matters affecting Scotland and to put the case for Scotland in the Cabinet. Before devolution, he was responsible for a wide range of statutory functions which in England are the responsibility of nine or ten departmental ministers. These statutory functions were, until 1999, administered by five main departments within the Scottish Office: the Agriculture, Environment and Fisheries Department; the Development Department; the Education and Industry Department; the Department of Health; and the Home Department. The Scottish Office thus became the department of government administering Scotland's domestic affairs and the real heart of executive government in Scotland. Moreover, the Secretary of State became the focus of Scotland's political identity. He came to be seen in a wider sense as 'Scotland's minister' and thus held accountable for all government decisions affecting Scotland, whether or not they lay within his area of statutory responsibility.

In 1954, the Royal Commission on Scottish Affairs, the Balfour Commission, laid down two criteria to assess the effectiveness of governmental arrangements in Scotland. The first was that 'the machinery of government should be designed to dispose of Scottish business in Scotland', and the second that Scottish needs and the Scottish point of view should be borne in mind 'at all stages in the formation and execution of policy'.[5]

The wide range of statutory powers conferred on the Secretary of State undoubtedly satisfied the first criterion. Indeed, it is difficult to think of any specifically Scottish matter which had not already been transferred to the Scottish Office. It seems likely, therefore, that the limits of administrative decentralization had been reached.

The second requirement laid down by the Balfour Commission was met by governmental arrangements which allowed Scotland to be formally represented on any policy-making committee whose decisions might affect her, even where those decisions lay outside the Secretary of State's area of statutory responsibility. When the membership of Cabinet committees was first published by John Major's government in 1992, it became apparent that the Secretary of State was a member of all of the key economic and social committees of the Cabinet. Secretaries of State of both major political parties have used this influence to further Scotland's interests. Perhaps the first Secretary of State to make full use of his position was Thomas Johnston, the Labour Secretary of State in the wartime coalition government between 1941 and 1945. Johnston was, in the words of Herbert Morrison:

One of the most able men in the technique of getting his own way at cabinet committees . . . He would impress on the committee that there was a strong nationalist movement in Scotland and it could be a potential danger if it grew through lack of attention to Scottish interests . . . by dint of cajoing, persuasion, plus some slight exaggeration of the grievances fertilising the Scottish

Nationalist movement, he got his schemes through after three or so committee meetings.[6]

Johnston was by no means the last Secretary of State to adopt this
tactic and it may be for this reason that public expenditure in
Scotland appears in the post-war years to have been higher than its
needs would warrant. This important issue is further discussed in
Chapter 7, in the section 'Financing devolution'.

Yet the very effectiveness of the system of Scottish administration
only brought into greater prominence the conflict between the
Secretary of State's role as 'Scotland's minister', and the convention
of collective Cabinet responsibility. For this convention made it difficult for the Secretary of State to initiate policies creating new
precedents which might be unwelcome in England. Any new depar-
tures would be noticed by other ministers, who would be very conscious that they might have implications for their own 'English'
departments. The Cabinet did not, under these circumstances, find it
difficult to overrule one not very senior minister in a Cabinet of
around twenty.

The Secretary of State's autonomy thus tended to be limited to
matters, such as the reform of local government, where English ministers did not particularly care what happened in Scotland, and where
there seemed no implications for policy across the border. Many of
the differences in administration between Scotland and England are
in fact probably more the result of the legacy of history than of deliberate governmental decisions to legislate specifically for Scottish
conditions.

The consequences of this system have been well summed up by a
former Scottish Office civil servant:

It was therefore possible to create a semblance of Scottish distinctiveness
and autonomy which went beyond the reality. The same process made it possible to enforce uniformity, or near uniformity, beyond what was necessary
or desirable, when there seemed a risk that a distinctive Scottish line might
raise embarrassing questions for another Minister concerned with the same
field of policy elsewhere.[7]

In recent years, however, the main objective of the Scottish Secretary
was less to take separate Scottish initiatives than to extract more

resources for Scotland from the government. But the Barnett formula, introduced in 1980 to regulate the shares of increments in identifiable public expenditure between England and Scotland, reduced the extent to which the Secretary of State could negotiate to Scotland's advantage. (This formula is discussed in detail in Chapter 7, in the section 'Financing devolution'.) This made it more difficult for the Secretary of State to defend his position. He seemed to be able to provide neither distinctive attention to Scotland's needs, nor extra money for Scotland. His position became particularly embarrassing during the years of Conservative government between 1979 and 1997, when he enjoyed the support of only a minority in Scotland. It was hard for him to represent Scottish opinion effectively in Westminster, and he became, in reality, more like the ambassador of a hostile power than Scotland's spokesman in the Cabinet.

It is sometimes argued that the Scottish Office suffered from an especial lack of accountability in comparison with other Whitehall departments. The crucial difference, however, is that, when Parliament is sitting, the Secretary of State is unable to spend more than half of the week in Scotland, and he has to include in this period his constituency business and meetings with Scottish Office officials as well as the numerous interest groups which demand an audience with him. It was because the minister was 400 miles away from Edinburgh for much of the time that the degree of control he could exercise on the *implementation* of decisions and on day-to-day administration was bound to be very limited.

Moreover, the wide range of responsibilities enjoyed by the Scottish Office, covering matters for which nine or ten Whitehall departments were responsible, led to the overloading of the executive in Scotland. Education, for example, which in England is the responsibility of five ministers, was in Scotland just one of the responsibilities of the Secretary of State, aided by a Minister of State whose responsibilities included industry as well as education. This meant that fewer decisions were taken by ministers and more by civil servants than would have been the case in England. It also made it difficult for the House of Commons to hold the Scottish Office accountable, since Questions over this wide range of functions were held just once a month. Thus the arrangements for disposing of government business in Scotland did not meet the canons of accountability which were taken for granted in other government departments. The Scottish Office, it has been held, 'stimulates rather than satisfies the appetite for self-government. It has made Scottish government at once more Scottish and less subject to parliamentary control.'[8] It was in a sense the very success of the Scottish Office that made so powerful a case for devolution.

Just as it has long been recognized that Scotland is a separate unit for executive purposes, so also special arrangements have been made for the conduct of Scottish business in the House of Commons. The committee stage of bills certified by the Speaker as relating exclusively to Scotland is taken by one of two Scottish standing committees. These committees comprise between sixteen and fifty MPs and must include at least sixteen Scottish MPs. They are constituted, like other standing committees, to reflect the party balance in the House. Until 1987, only Scottish MPs could be members, but since 1987, there have never been more than eleven Conservative MPs returned in Scotland, so that, during the remaining period of Conservative government until 1997, it was found necessary to include MPs from English constituencies in order to give the government a majority. There is also a Scottish Grand Committee, comprising all of Scotland's seventy-two MPs. In contrast to other legislative committees and to select committees, the government does not necessarily enjoy a majority on the Scottish Grand Committee, and did not do so in the years of Conservative government between 1979 and 1997. The Grand Committee often meets in Scotland, and has power to take the second and third reading debates and the report stage of non-controversial Scottish bills. It also holds debates on secondary legislation for Scotland, and a question time at which it can question Scottish ministers. As with the Scottish standing committees, however, it is difficult to refer controversial matters to the Grand Committee, since such a reference can be blocked if ten MPs indicate their objection in the House. Moreover, the Grand Committee does not vote on legislation and has no legislative powers. It is an arena for discussion, not for scrutiny. Finally, there is a Select Committee on Scottish Affairs, one of the departmentally related select committees established in 1979 to scrutinize government departments. The Select Committee's remit is to enquire into the expenditure, administration, and policy of the Scottish Office and other public bodies in Scotland. After 1987, however, the Conservative government found it impossible to find sufficient Scottish MPs to serve on this Committee and it fell into abeyance until 1992, when it was reconstituted with eleven members and an opposition MP as chairman. As there were only ten Conservative MPs, five of whom were ministers, the problem of Conservative representation was resolved by appointing Conservatives from south of the border to serve. The Select Committee has performed a valuable inquisitorial and deliberative function in questioning Scottish Office ministers, and in scrutinizing projections of public expenditure in Scotland and the activities of the various non-departmental public bodies in Scotland under the authority of the Secretary of State.

The arrangements for considering Scottish legislation in the Commons have served to separate Scottish legislation and administration from non-Scottish MPs, most of whom are quite uninterested in it, and expected not to interfere. In 1968, Richard Crossman had it in mind to attend a second reading debate on the Social Work (Scotland) Bill, but

Just as we were going in we realised that the Scots would suspect some poisonous English conspiracy so we would have to keep out, come what may. I quote this to show how deep is the separation which already exists between England and Scotland. Willie Ross [the Scottish Secretary] and his friends accuse the Scot. Nats. of separatism but what Willie Ross himself actually likes is to keep Scottish business absolutely privy from English business. I am not sure this system isn't one that gets the worst of both worlds which is why I'm in favour of a Scottish Parliament.[9]

There was then already a Scottish subsystem in the House of Commons. Devolution transfers that subsystem to Edinburgh and places it under direct electoral control.

It is clear, then, that the distinctiveness of Scotland as a political unit was recognized, both at the executive level of government and in the arrangements for the dispatch of parliamentary business. But the conventions of the Constitution were bound to limit the extent to which Scotland could be treated as a distinctive unit even within the framework of the union state.

Collective Cabinet responsibility, as we have seen, limited the extent to which the Secretary of State for Scotland could act as a genuine minister for Scotland; while, in the Commons, the unwillingness of the House of Commons, which is jealous of its authority, to delegate that authority to committees, restricted Scottish control over Scottish business to relatively uncontroversial matters. For the working of Scottish committees has been conditioned by the principles on which the House of Commons operates. These committees cannot approve legislation without the agreement of the whole House; and while ministers took part in the debates of the Grand Committee and could be questioned there, they could not be required by the committee to change their policies. When, in November 1995, MPs asked whether the Scottish Grand Committee could block the imposition of nursery vouchers in Scotland, the Secretary of State, Michael Forsyth, declared that 'the absolute Westminster veto over Scottish business remains', adding that 'the Scottish Grand Committee is not a Scottish Parliament'.[10] That was a correct statement of the constitutional position.

Thus Scotland was in the anomalous if not unique position of having a separate legal system, together with separate arrangements for the handling of executive business, but no separate legislature to which the Scottish executive could be held responsible. 'It would be hard throughout the familiar world', Lord Kilbrandon, the Chairman of the Royal Commission on the Constitution, argued, 'to find a parallel for a country which had its own judicature and legal system, its own executive and administration, but no legislature, its laws being made within another and technically foreign jurisdiction, by an assembly in which it had only a small minority of members, but to which its executive was democratically responsible.'[11]

This anomaly might not have mattered when the party system transcended the border, as it did between 1945 and 1959, the party with a majority in the United Kingdom also enjoying a majority in Scotland (except in 1951 when the two major parties were level north of the border). Since 1959, however, Labour has won the majority of Scottish seats. This has meant that in years of Conservative government—the years between 1959 and 1964, 1970 and 1974, and 1979 and 1997—government was even less willing to devolve important business to Scottish parliamentary committees; while the Secretary of State for Scotland was handicapped in acting as Scotland's minister by the fact that the majority of Scots had indicated that they did not want him or the policies of the government of which he was a member. The distinctive arrangements for the handling of Scottish business, both at executive and at parliamentary level, could, it might be argued, work only within a very limited range of election results. That limit was breached between 1979 and 1997.

Thus the mainspring of the case for devolution was a democratic one, the need to repair a relationship which had been seriously undermined. The arrangements for handling Scottish business, both at executive and at parliamentary level, had become unsatisfactory and could hardly have been improved within the unitary framework. The Treaty of Union between England and Scotland had envisaged Scottish identity being preserved through her legal system and system of church government. These institutions, however, have long been displaced from their central position as guarantors of Scottish identity. In the modern world, Scottish identity is determined far more by the institutions of government than by the legal system or the church. Thus, it could be argued that it was only possible to preserve the spirit of the Union if the government of Scotland were able to reflect Scottish interests and needs more effectively.

Yet the machinery of government in Scotland proved unable to resist the centralizing pressures of modern government, since the machinery of Whitehall is inevitably geared towards standardization; the pressures towards uniformity could be resisted only by providing constitutional protection for Scotland in the form of a directly elected legislature. Part of the case for a devolved legislature in Scotland was that it would provide a corrective to the pressures of Whitehall. The great increase in the functions of government since 1945, only partially reversed by the Conservative governments of Margaret Thatcher and John Major, made the maladjusted arrangements for the government of Scotland of greater consequence than they had been before. When the scope of government was limited, it mattered less whether government was situated in London or in Edinburgh, since its decisions did not affect the individual as much as those of indigenous Scottish non-governmental institutions. Today, however, it is the institutions of government which, for good or ill, affect the lives of individuals. The need was to make the governmental arrangements providing for Scottish distinctiveness real rather than merely symbolic. Scottish devolution may be seen, from this perspective, as a means of renegotiating the terms of the Union so as to make them more palatable to Scottish opinion in the conditions of the late twentieth century. Such a renegotiation may be the only way to re-establish the kind of relationship between England and Scotland envisaged in 1707, a relationship which has been eroded by developments in government and in electoral behaviour in the latter part of the twentieth century. Seen in this light, Scottish devolution may be regarded analogously to Gladstonian Home Rule in the nineteenth century, as a policy of a strikingly conservative character.

II

Without the rise and electoral success in the 1970s of the Scottish National Party, the SNP, it is doubtful whether devolution would have assumed as prominent a place on the political agenda of the United Kingdom as in fact it has done. But nationalism in Scotland has not displayed the emotional hostility to the British connection which animated the Irish nationalists, and it has adhered strictly to constitutional methods.

The first distinctively modern political nationalist movement in Scotland, the Scottish Home Rule Association, was set up in May 1886, just one month after Gladstone introduced the Irish Home Rule bill into the Commons. It emphasized not the injustice of British rule, after the fashion of the Irish, but 'the legislative neglect of Scotland' and the need to reform the licensing laws and the land, game and fishery laws.[12] The emphasis was thus not separatist but integrationist, the securing of national equality with England. At the end of the nineteenth century, Home Rule was supported by such future Labour leaders as Keir Hardie and Ramsay MacDonald, and it also enjoyed the support of many Liberals. Between 1890 and 1914, measures proposing Scottish Home Rule appeared thirteen times before the House of Commons, being accepted in principle by the House on eight occasions and securing the support of a majority of Scottish

MPs on eleven occasions. But none of the bills was successful in reaching the committee stage, and this reflected the low priority attached to Scottish Home Rule even amongst MPs sympathetic to the cause.

Moreover, it would be wrong to suppose that the frequency of appearance of Scottish Home Rule bills corresponded to any great degree of popular feeling in Scotland at the time. They seem rather to have been introduced as ritual gestures on the part of Liberal and Labour MPs who felt duty-bound to argue that Scotland had claims no less important than those of Ireland. There was, however, no Parnell in Scotland, nor even a Tom Ellis, since Scottish grievances did not seem powerful enough to form the basis of a larger political programme. Before 1914, indeed, Scottish nationalism had the character of an imitative and rather artificial movement.

The founder of modern political nationalism in Scotland was John MacCormick who, while a student at Glasgow University, left the Labour Party to form a university Nationalist Society. He was the first leader of the SNP, which was born in 1934, but his aim was to secure Home Rule, a Scottish parliament within the United Kingdom rather than independence. He sought, moreover, to work in collaboration with other parties rather than in electoral competition with them, and so the SNP did not at first contest elections. MacCormick, however, was ousted from the leadership during the war and the SNP then became an explicitly separatist party committed to contesting elections against the other parties. It succeeded in winning Motherwell in a by-election in April 1945, during the period of the wartime electoral truce between the major parties, but the seat was lost in the general election just three months later when party politics was resumed. The SNP achieved little success in the immediate post-war years, and seemed to many to be little more than a merely picturesque grouping of cranks and faddists.

From 1955, however, the SNP's electoral performance improved steadily if unspectacularly until, in the general election of 1966, its twenty-three candidates secured 5 per cent of the Scottish vote, an average of 14 per cent per opposed candidate (Table 4.1).

After the 1966 general election, in the atmosphere of disillusion with Harold Wilson's Labour government, the SNP began to make

Table 4.1 SNP results in the elections of 1955–66

Election	Candidates	Total votes	% of Scottish total
1955	2	12,112	0.5
1959	5	21,738	0.8
1964	15	64,044	2.4
1966	23	128,474	5.0

spectacular progress. In March 1967, in a by-election in Glasgow, Pollok, the SNP gained 28 per cent of the vote in a marginal seat gained by the Conservatives from Labour. Then, in November 1967, the party won a by-election in Hamilton, hitherto a Labour stronghold. In the municipal elections of 1968, the SNP became a major force in local government, winning nearly a hundred seats, and gaining the balance of power in Glasgow, depriving Labour of overall control for the first time since 1952; and its average performance in the four parliamentary Scottish by-elections of the 1966–70 Parliament was 29 per cent of the vote.

In the general election of 1970, the SNP fought on a broader front that ever before, contesting sixty-five out of the seventy-one Scottish seats. Since then, the SNP has contested at least seventy seats in every election in Scotland. Its progress between 1970 and 1974 is shown in Table 4.2.

In February 1974, the SNP gained six seats, four from the Conservatives and two from Labour. In October, it gained a further four

Table 4.2 SNP results in the elections of 1970–4

Election	Candidates	Seats	Total votes	% of Scottish total
1970	65	1	306,802	11
February 1974	70	7	633,180	22
October 1974	71	11	839,617	30

seats, all from the Conservatives. The October 1974 election made the SNP the second largest party after Labour, overtaking the Conservatives, in terms of its percentage of the vote in Scotland. The SNP's percentage of the vote in October 1974 made it, indeed, the second strongest ethnic minority party in Western Europe.[13] It had by this time eleven seats, and was second in a further forty-two constituencies, including thirty-five of Labour's forty-one seats. A further swing of 5 per cent to the SNP from the sitting incumbent would give it sixteen more seats. The SNP, then, threatened not only the hegemony of Labour in Scotland, but also Labour's chances of continuing to be a governing party in the United Kingdom. But the rise of a strong nationalist party in Scotland posed a challenge, not only to Labour, but to all of the parties which sought to preserve the United Kingdom.

III

The spectacular growth of support for the SNP in the early 1970s not only caused problems for the British parties; it also posed difficult questions for those whose task it was to explain electoral behaviour, forcing them to readjust many of their preconceptions. The conclusions of psephology had, until that time, very much reflected the social democratic consensus of the immediate post-war years; and the social sciences had given little attention to those historical and geographical factors which made one part of the United Kingdom different from another. 'Class', it had been said in 1967, 'is the basis of British politics: all else is embellishment and detail'.[14] Regional differences in electoral behaviour, declared Butler and Stokes in the first professional analysis of British voting behaviour in 1969, were but 'variations upon the central theme of class'.[15] Paradoxically, class, being a nationwide factor, made for national unity. Such an analysis made it difficult, however, to explain the advance of the SNP as being anything other than a 'protest vote' against the two major parties, a temporary departure perhaps, from a stable political norm. The modicum of truth in the 'protest' explanation was that, until the late 1960s, the SNP performed well only in years such as 1961 and 1962, when disillusionment with government was strong enough for the Liberals to do well in England also. In the 1966–70 parliament, however, disillusionment with government led, in England, not to support for the Liberals, but to massive Labour abstentions and very large swings to the Conservatives. The Liberals were unable to attract Labour abstainers in England, but in Scotland, and also in Wales, disillusioned Labour supporters had an alternative to abstention; they could vote instead for a nationalist party.

In the 1970–4 parliament, the SNP did not perform well until after the Liberal breakthrough at Rochdale in October 1972. From then until the general election in February 1974, the Liberals gained five seats in England, four from the Conservatives and one from Labour. In addition, a Labour defector, Dick Taverne, succeeded in holding his seat at Lincoln, standing as a Democratic Labour candidate against official Labour opposition. During the same period, the SNP gained 30 per cent of the vote in Dundee East, 42 per cent of the vote in Glasgow, Govan, winning the seat from Labour; and 19 per cent of the vote in Edinburgh North. In February 1974, the SNP gained 21.9 per cent of the Scottish vote as compared with the Liberals' 23.6 per cent average share of the vote per opposed candidate in Britain as a whole; in October 1974, however, the SNP made further gains, its vote going up to 30.4 per cent while the Liberal vote declined to 18.9 per cent per opposed candidate. At this election, the advance of the SNP could no longer be explained by the mobilization of those who had previously not voted, since turnout was 4.2 per cent lower than it had been in February. Nor did it seem plausible any longer to describe the vote simply as a 'protest'. For the concept of a 'protest' vote did not seem to explain why it was that support for the SNP continued to increase while support for the Liberals in England and Plaid Cymru in Wales had begun to fall.

It seemed that the SNP was about to break the constraints of the two-party system in Scotland, something that the Liberals had never succeeded in doing. What might perhaps originally have been a protest vote appeared to be solidifying into something much deeper. It seemed that a new alignment was developing in Scottish politics, something that could be explained only by the powerful sense of Scottish nationality, strongly buttressed by history, which gave to economic and other grievances a shape unmatched in other parts of Britain. It was this strong sense of Scottish identity which provided the basis for the electoral success of the SNP. Indeed, the potential for nationalist revival in Scotland had perhaps existed for some time. In 1966, just before the SNP upsurge, Budge and Urwin in their study of Scottish political behaviour, perceptively put 'one awkward question' which 'has not been faced by our discussion'. The question was: 'If Scottish feeling is so widespread through all groups and both classes, why have the Conservative and Labour parties not lost more ground to the SNP and the Liberals who have promised to implement Home Rule?'[16]

The answer seems to be that, until the late 1960s, when the age of affluence ended, it had appeared that the major British parties—Conservative and Labour—would be able to secure Scotland's interests. Although Harold Wilson's Labour government, which came to power in 1964, showed little interest in Scotland's national claims, this might not have mattered if centralized government had been accompanied, as it had been in the 1940s, by economic progress. During the late 1960s, however, the combination of centralized government and economic failure led to disillusion in Scotland with Labour, as it did also in England. In Labour seats in England, voters found it difficult to cross class lines and support the Conservatives. But in Scotland, disillusioned Labour voters sympathetic to self-government could turn to the SNP which seems not to have been perceived, as the Conservatives were, as a class party.

Thus nationwide economic grievances were beginning to break up traditional party allegiances. But the strong sense of nationality in Scotland meant that the reaction to economic failure when it came would take a different form from that in England. The SNP gained support, not so much perhaps as the party of independence or separatism, but as the party that could speak for Scotland against the London parties, the party of Scottish identity. The SNP came to be seen as a pressure group for Scottish interests. In its Scottish general election manifesto in October 1974, Labour proclaimed how much it had done for Scotland in its seven months of office. It had doubled the

Regional Employment Premium, bringing Scotland an extra £40m. a year in revenue; it had given Edinburgh and Leith development-area status, bringing in a further £8m. a year; it had moved the Offshore Supplies Office to Glasgow; it had agreed to establish the British National Oil Corporation in Scotland; it had promised to move 7,000 civil service jobs to Scotland by the early 1980s; and it had tightened the limit for industrial development certificates, so improving Scotland's chances of attracting new industry. There were also further promises—to establish a Scottish Development Agency and a Centre for Oil Drilling Technology in Scotland, to halt rail closures in Scotland, and to modernize the Glasgow underground system at a cost of £11.8m. In addition, Labour promised to create a directly elected Scottish assembly. It does not require very much cynicism to ask how many of these reforms and promises would have been made in so short a time without the electoral threat posed by the SNP.

During the early 1970s, there were two developments which increased still further the credibility of the SNP and seemed to shift the balance of the argument significantly in the direction of Scottish independence. The first was the discovery and commercial exploitation of oil in the North Sea. This seemed to destroy the central unionist argument that the union was essential to Scotland's economic health. The choice could now be presented by the SNP as one between rich Scotland and poor England. It could now be argued that the union in fact placed Scotland under an economic handicap, for Scots could claim that their interests required a slower rate of extraction than was demanded by the British government, so as not to exhaust the country's resources too rapidly. The priority of the British government, on the other hand, seemed to be to use the oil revenues to pay off its debts as quickly as possible. Moreover, a rapid rate of extraction of the oil might have serious effects on the environment in the north-east of Scotland. Admittedly, a slower rate of extraction would lessen the immediate benefits of North Sea oil to Scotland, and would, in particular, mean a slower increase in employment. Nevertheless, it could be argued that the British balance of priorities, as between British energy needs and Scottish environmental needs, was not necessarily the right one for Scotland.

A further problem was the use to which the oil revenues would be put. The long-term benefits of oil lay in the gain to the balance of payments and the revenues accruing to government, rather than the immediate effects on incomes and employment, which were likely to be small. An independent Scotland, the SNP argued, if her legal claim to ownership of the oil fields was conceded—and this itself was a highly contentious point, most international lawyers being hostile to the SNP claim—could herself enjoy the benefits of the revenues. But, remaining in the United Kingdom, Scotland might not benefit at all unless the British government were to make a positive attempt to use the revenues to revive Scotland's industrial structure.

It would, however, be a mistake to put too much weight upon the discovery of oil as an explanation for the rise of Scottish nationalism. The increase in support for the SNP in the late 1960s pre-dated the discovery of oil, and surveys showed that support for Scottish independence remained fairly stable at about 20 per cent from around 1968 to the end of the 1970s, there being no dramatic increase in support for this option after the commercial exploitation of oil began. One account of support for the SNP found that 'attitude to self-government was clearly much more influential than attitude to oil revenues', for 'oil and, by extension, the feeling that Scotland could "go it alone economically" cannot be seen as more than a constraint breaking influence that reduced the perceived costs of an already desirable objective'.[17] Voting choices between 1974 and 1979 were determined much more by attitudes to devolution than by attitudes to oil. The feeling that Scotland should have a major share of the oil revenues inclined voters to support the SNP only if they were already favourable to devolution or independence.[18] Thus oil reinforced electoral support for the SNP; it did not create it.

The second factor which altered the nature of the political argument in Scotland was Britain's entry into the European Community in 1973, which both emphasized the disadvantages for Scotland of remote government, but also seemed to lessen the benefits to be derived from remaining in the United Kingdom. With important areas of decision-making being removed from London to Brussels, Edinburgh would become even more remote from the centres of power. Scotland was already part of the British periphery; how much more peripheral it would be when viewed from Brussels.

Economically, Scotland was at some distance from the European 'golden triangle', centred on the Rühr. High transport costs would make it more difficult for industry located in Scotland to penetrate European markets, and Scotland might find it hard to attract a skilled supply of labour or to persuade new industries to locate there. Thus Britain's entry into the European Community was likely to accentuate even further the economic advantages of the south-east core of the UK to the disadvantage of Scotland.

But if Scotland gained her independence, all this might be changed. An independent country would still retain the prime advantage which membership of the United Kingdom gave her: access to a duty-free market. Scotland could now avoid what had hitherto been seen as the main disadvantage of independence, namely that England would be able to ruin Scottish industry by imposing a tariff on Scottish goods. Such a policy would now be forbidden by the rules of the European Community. The very limits which the Community placed upon independence ensured that England could no longer threaten Scotland with disruption of markets and loss of trade in the event of independence. The Community, therefore, seemed to offer Scotland the economic advantages of union even in the absence of union. Moreover, an independent Scotland would, through its representation in the institutions of the Community, be able to argue powerfully for her interests and perhaps secure more favourable treatment for Scotland than the British government had been able to do. During the 1970s, the European Community was dominated by the so-called Luxembourg Compromise of 1965–6, according to which member states enjoyed a veto on matters essential to their national interest. This meant that Scotland could not be outvoted by the larger member states. She would enjoy a veto in the Community, and, so it could be argued, be in a stronger position to protect her interests than by remaining part of the United Kingdom.

IV

The rise of the SNP confronted the major parties with a dilemma: should they resist nationalist pressures, or, by offering devolution, appear to be appeasing them? How would the parties react? Their attitudes would reflect a complex mixture of tactical consideration and principled commitment, with conceptions of party self-interest jostling with ideologies inherited from long ago. Labour's philosophy of social democracy presented it with the problem that devolution might undermine the centralized allocation of economic resources, to be decided upon grounds of need rather than regional or national pressures. The Conservatives—who had called themselves Unionists between 1886 and 1921—had a long tradition of resisting national claims within the United Kingdom. Moreover, they were becoming increasingly an English party, and therefore more susceptible to the prejudices of their English members. Neither the Labour nor the Conservative party in Scotland enjoyed much autonomy; the Labour Party's Scottish Council was merely a regional branch of the Labour Party, possessing little more autonomy than, for example, the East Midlands Labour Party; while the Scottish Conservatives' role in policy-making was entirely subordinate to that of the leader of the party as a whole.

The Liberals would seem to have been in the most favourable position to take the nationalist tide at the flood. For devolution had, since the time of Gladstone, lain at the very forefront of Liberal policy. The Liberals had been strong supporters of Home Rule for Scotland and Wales, and had advocated parliaments in Edinburgh and Cardiff at every general election since 1950. Since surveys of Scottish opinion during the 1960s and 1970s showed that the majority of Scottish voters preferred devolution or federalism to either the separatism of the SNP or the status quo, the Liberals would seem to have been well placed to capitalize upon the politics of locality as the basis for a new Liberal breakthrough.

The difficulty was, however, that the Liberals found it difficult to decide upon the relative priority of Scottish claims. For the Liberal commitment to Home Rule for Scotland and Wales was within the context of a federal United Kingdom. Did this mean, however, that Scotland was to be equated with an English region and would she have to wait for devolution until the English regions also wanted it? The Scottish Liberal Party regarded Scotland as a nation and favoured a federal system of government for the United Kingdom, which included an English parliament with similar powers to the Scottish one. Some English Liberals, primarily from the south of England, shared that view. Most English Liberals, however, and especially Liberals from the north of England, took the view that a federal system should comprise regional assemblies in England with roughly similar powers to those of a Scottish parliament. In 1976, in a desperate attempt to reconcile these conflicting views, the Liberal Assembly committed itself to a federal United Kingdom which comprised both subordinate English provincial assemblies as well as an English assembly.

During Jo Grimond's period of leadership—between 1956 and 1967—the Liberals had sought the support of 'the new middle class' and the affluent worker, in the hope that these groups might be willing to support a radical, non-socialist alternative to the Conservatives. So, although the Liberals were trying to break up the two-party system in British politics, they were still relying upon the traditional assumption that class was the central motivating factor in voting behaviour. They were unwilling to commit themselves to a strategy based upon exploiting locality. The Grimond strategy, however, failed to yield a breakthrough for the Liberal Party. The 'new middle class', evenly spread as it was in the south-east, did not constitute a sufficiently concentrated grouping of support to enable the Liberals to win seats. There was, however, according to the historian John Vincent, writing in 1967, room in Britain, 'for a party which puts locality before party conflict',[19] a party which focused the resentments of provincial England, Scotland, and Wales against the metropolis. That had, Vincent believed, been a large part of the *raison d'être* of the Liberal Party from the time of its formation in the 1850s.[20] The early Labour Party had assumed this role also. In the 1960s, the Liberals might well have been able to secure a new electoral base in the peripheral areas of Britain, areas reacting against excessive centralization. In 1964, they had gained three seats in the Scottish Highlands—Caithness and Sutherland, Ross and Cromarty, and Inverness; and in a by-election in 1965, they gained Roxburgh, Selkirk, and Peebles, a border constituency, 'to some extent a second Scottish periphery',[21] suffering from many of the same problems as the Highlands—remoteness, poor communications, migration, and disruption of community values. By 1966, of the twelve Liberal seats, five were in Scotland, one in Wales, two in Cornwall and one in Devon—that is, six in the 'Celtic fringe' and three in the south-west, leaving just three seats in English suburbia.

In Scotland, the Liberals faced competition from the SNP. Should they seek, at the cost of a few deposits, to destroy the SNP? Or should they, alternatively, ally themselves with the SNP on a Scottish self-government platform? The Liberals might well have been able to destroy the SNP had they put forward Scottish Home Rule as an absolute priority from the 1960s. An alliance with the SNP, however, was probably never possible because liberalism and nationalism were such different philosophies. The basic cause of lack of agreement remained that, during the 1960s, the SNP was nationalist while the Liberals were not. The SNP took the view that it was not logical to seek federalism as an initial goal, and that it was for the Scottish people, and not Westminster, to decide what kind of constitution they wanted for Scotland. The Liberal Democrats, together with Labour, had come round to this view by the time of the Scottish Convention in 1989, which argued that the Scottish people, and not Westminster, were sovereign; but by then it was too late for the Liberal Democrats to present themselves as a specifically Scottish party.

Thus the Liberals failed to make an electoral breakthrough by championing the peripheral areas of the United Kingdom. Indeed, despite their longstanding commitment to devolution, they had given so little attention to the details of the subject that during the period of the Lib–Lab pact in 1977–8, when they were invited to produce proposals for resurrecting the legislation, they were forced to rely upon an outside policy unit, the Outer Circle Policy Unit, for their ideas.

'The Liberals', John Vincent commented in 1967, 'have been obsessed for ten years with the belief that they, like the Congregational Church, have a vocation to serve the "new" middle class. . . . The Liberals set their cap at the London commuter and ended up with the Ross and Cromarty crofter. They tried to win by spotlighting a particular social group. They should have spotlighted place.'[22] It is difficult to quarrel with this verdict.

V

Neither of the other two United Kingdom parties would appear to have been in as strong a position as the Liberals to meet the SNP challenge. The Scottish Conservative Party had called itself the Unionist Party between 1912 and 1965. It had opposed Scottish as well as Irish Home Rule. The Conservatives therefore seemed much less likely than Labour or the Liberals to prove sympathetic to Scottish aspirations. But there was another tradition in Scottish conservatism, which had become unionist to defend Pitt's union with Ireland, rather than the 1707 settlement with Scotland. This latter settlement was, after all, not under challenge, and was in any case a triumph of Whig rather than Tory statesmanship. If conservatism meant reverence for tradition, then Conservatives could well regard themselves as guardians of that sense of Scottish identity which Scotland's institutions sustained. Indeed, in Scotland, it had been the Tories who had in a sense been the nationalists, and the Whigs who appeared as the anglicizers and assimilationists. Sir Walter Scott has been called 'the outstanding example of what Scottish nationalism meant both in its depth of feeling and in its practical good sense'.[23] In 1808, after a debate in which he had fiercely opposed alterations in the procedure of the Scottish judicial system, his companions began to joke about it: ' "No, no," cried Scott, " 'tis no laughing matter; little by little, whatever your wishes may be, you will destroy and undermine until nothing of what makes Scotland Scotland shall remain." And so saying, he turned round to conceal his agitation— but not until Mr. Jeffrey saw tears gushing down his cheek.'[24]

Conservatives could thus respect the feelings which animated the national movement in Scotland, and they supported reforms designed to decentralize administration to Scotland. In the twentieth century, the expansion of the role of the Scottish Office, in 1926 and 1939, took place under Conservative governments. In opposition in the late 1940s, the Conservatives sought to harness Scottish feelings against the Attlee government, and the Churchill administration, in office from 1951, pursued a programme of further administrative devolution to Edinburgh.

By the late 1960s, however, the Conservatives were a sharply declining electoral force in Scotland. In 1955, they had secured a majority of Scottish seats and a majority of the Scottish vote—the only time that this result has been achieved by either major party since the war. But, by 1966, the Conservatives had been reduced to twenty seats in Scotland and 37.7 per cent of the vote. Within eleven years, they had lost sixteen seats and one-eighth of their vote. The traditionalist approach of the Scottish party appeared deeply unattractive to an electorate becoming increasingly concerned at the economic difficulties facing Scotland. The Scottish Conservatives were therefore eager to inject some element of Scottish awareness into their policies, and in the summer of 1967 they set up a committee under the chairmanship of Sir William McEwan Younger to consider how the structure of government could be made more responsive to Scottish needs. At the same time, a parallel investigation into Scottish government was being carried out by a new Conservative 'ginger group' called the Thistle Group, which was to become identified as a pro-devolution pressure group.

Both of these investigations were begun some time before the Hamilton by-election of 1967 and were motivated more by a concern for the reform of Scottish government than by fear of the SNP. The two groups came to strikingly similar conclusions, agreeing that the existing structure of government in Scotland was inefficient, because the range of functions for which the Scottish Office was responsible was too wide to be scrutinized properly either by Parliament or by ministers. As a result, too much power rested in the hands of civil servants.

Edward Heath, the Conservative leader, was not unresponsive to the argument for devolution in Scotland. He told Richard Crossman, leader of the House of Commons, a week before the Hamilton by-election, that 'nationalism is the biggest single factor in our politics today'.[25] Moreover, devolution would allow Heath to contrast Conservative sensitivities to different parts of the country with the centralizing tendencies of the socialists and the separatism of the SNP. The Conservatives, therefore, became the first of the two major parties to commit themselves to devolution.

At the Conference of the Scottish Conservatives in 1968, Heath, in a speech known somewhat grandiloquently as the Declaration of

Perth, proposed a directly elected Scottish assembly. He explicitly recognized the need for devolution as a counterweight to the central-izing tendencies of the European Community, and his speech dis-played a far-sightedness which, in different circumstances, might have done much to pre-empt the rise of the SNP in Scotland. Heath emphasized the contrast between the Conservative Party's stand for diversity and a 'world of mass industrialisation, mass communica-tions, and increasingly complex organisation' in which the strongest influences were those of 'uniformity and centralisation'. These pres-sures had led many to feel that they were losing control over their lives and there was, as a result, frustration and resentment with gov-ernment. The Labour Party, being the party of state control, was, Heath argued, unable to understand this new source of discontent. The SNP understood it, but proposed a wholly inappropriate remedy which involved sacrificing the gains Scotland derived from member-ship of the United Kingdom. 'The art of government', however, was 'to reconcile these divergent needs. The need to modernise our insti-tutions so as to cope with our complex changing society. And the need to give each citizen a greater opportunity to participate in the decisions that affect him, his family, and the community in which he lives.' The reconciliation of these needs involved finding a balance between two contrasting principles—the one being the unity of the United Kingdom, and the other being 'our belief in the devolution of power'. Heath ended his speech with a quotation from Quintin Hogg's *Case for Conservatism*. 'Political liberty is nothing else but the diffusion of power. If power is not to be abused, it must be spread as widely as possible throughout the community.'

Heath set up a Scottish Constitutional Committee under Sir Alec Douglas-Home, the function of which was to consider whether, while preserving 'the essential principle of the sovereignty of Parliament', it was possible to meet the desire of the majority of the people of Scotland to have a greater say in the conduct of their own affairs.[26] The Constitutional Committee reported in March 1970, and advocat-ed a directly elected Scottish assembly, a Convention, to take those bills certified by the Speaker as exclusively Scottish measures and considered by the Scottish Grand Committee and a Scottish standing committee. The Convention would thus consider the second reading, committee, and report stages of Scottish bills, leaving only the third reading and House of Lords stages to be taken at Westminster. The Secretary of State for Scotland, however, would remain responsible to Westminster and not to the Convention.

The great advantage of this scheme was that it could be presented as 'a natural evolution and extension of parliamentary practice as we know it'.[27] The Scottish Convention would take its place as a part of the Westminster machinery. Awkward questions, such as the future of Scottish representation at Westminster under devolution, could be entirely avoided. The Douglas-Home proposals offered the maximum degree of devolution possible within the existing parliamentary framework. The proposals were also constitutionally innovative in that they provided for legislation to be scrutinized by those who were not members of either House of Parliament.

It was not difficult of course for critics to find weaknesses in the Douglas-Home report. The proposed Convention, critics claimed, would do little to make the Scottish Office more accountable, since the Scottish Office would remain responsible to Parliament, not to the Convention. Moreover, decisions of the Convention could still be overturned at Westminster, and difficulties would arise when a Scottish majority, represented at the Convention, came into conflict with a majority of a different political colour at Westminster. The Douglas-Home committee denied that the Convention would cause conflict, since it would discuss only Scottish legislation which 'in the main consists of legislation which is not unduly controversial'. But, if controversial legislation were to be kept from the Convention, it was difficult to see what value it could have, and in particular whether it would have enough powers to deal with the serious weaknesses in Scottish government which the Douglas-Home committee had diagnosed. The committee, for example, had deplored the slow pace of decision-making on Scottish industrial matters. 'Long delays in deciding on matters which seriously affect the level of Scottish employment and generally influence the Scottish standard of living cannot be tolerated', the committee declared; and it found itself 'particularly impressed by the working of the Northern Ireland Ministry of Commerce—and especially by the speed of its decision-making'.[28] Yet what was proposed fell far short of the Northern Ireland model and the Convention, since it would lack executive powers, would be able to do nothing to speed up the process of administration.

These criticisms, however, were, in a sense, beside the point. For the Convention proposal would, it was hoped, be seen by the Scots as a signal that Westminster would henceforward take more notice of the Scottish point of view. It would give Scotland a political forum within which her problems would be discussed; and it would not be easy for Westminster to overrule the settled wish of the Scottish people as expressed in the Convention. Even if it did not provide the final answer, therefore, to the problems of Scottish government, the Convention might serve as a practical point of departure for further evolutionary development. Politically, moreover, the report isolated Labour, now the only major party opposed to devolution.

The Douglas-Home report was accepted by the Conservative leadership, and the Conservative election manifesto of 1970 promised that its recommendations, including the Scottish Convention sitting in Edinburgh, 'will form a basis for the proposals we will place before Parliament, taking account of the impending re-organisation of local government'. The Queen's Speech of 1970 promised that measures would be produced 'for giving the Scottish people a greater say in their own affairs'. Yet the Heath government made no move to establish a Scottish assembly. For this omission, two explanations have been given.

The first is that the Heath government did not want to legislate in advance of the report of the Royal Commission on the Constitution, which had been established by the Labour government in 1969, and did not in fact report until October 1973, when Britain was in the grip of the rise in oil prices which followed the Yom Kippur War. Had the Conservatives simply gone ahead with devolution in 1970, some at least of the members of the Royal Commission would have resigned, and this would have been an embarrassment for the government. Possibly the Heath government could have pressed the Commission to issue an interim report, as a basis for rapid action, but it did not do so.

The second explanation is that the Conservatives decided, without waiting for the report of the Royal Commission, to proceed with local government reform in Scotland, and this was hardly compatible with establishing an assembly in Scotland as well. Heath in fact argued that local government reform was a more important priority than devolution, writing to John Mackintosh, a pro-devolution Labour MP, in May 1973:

We for our part have always held that reform of local government is a matter of importance and urgency for the people of Scotland and that there should be no avoidable delay in putting in hand the complex arrangements needed to implement it. The question of devolution, while clearly a related matter, has always seemed to us one which should be pursued separately, and *later*, in a United Kingdom context ... [emphasis added.][29]

The government appears to have believed that local government reorganization might defuse Scottish grievances so that devolution would be unnecessary. Reorganization, however, created a cumbrous two-tier structure in Scotland, the upper tier of which consisted of regions, with the largest—Strathclyde—containing over half of the population of Scotland. This meant that if ever a Scottish assembly was set up, local government would have to be reorganized again, since the assembly would not easily be able to coexist with Strathclyde. It would have been better, if devolution had been in prospect, to have created a unitary system in Scotland; better still to have established an assembly first, and to have allowed it, as the representative body of Scotland, to put forward its own proposals for local government reform. The future shape of government in Scotland should have been decided first, and the new local government system could then have taken its place within that framework. For devolution was hardly, as Heath suggested in his letter to Mackintosh, an issue 'which should be pursued separately', after local government reform.

The probability is that devolution had ceased to be an important priority for Heath after 1970. The nationalist threat seemed, until 1973, to have evaporated and the energies of the Heath government were exercised elsewhere, on matters such as industrial relations legislation, incomes policy, and the European Community, itself a major constitutional issue. Thus, while the formal commitment to devolution remained, nothing was done about it. Nor were Scottish Conservatives particularly enamoured of devolution. Indeed, the Scottish Conservative Conference rejected the Douglas-Home proposals in 1973 and the only reference to devolution in the February 1974 election manifesto declared that the Conservatives were studying the report of the Royal Commission, although the Scottish manifesto declared that 'We are preparing proposals taking into account the different recommendations' made by the Royal Commission on the Constitution and that 'Our commitment to present proposals still stands.'

In the two elections of 1974, the Conservatives lost eight seats, all of them to the SNP, and 13 per cent of their vote. In twenty years they had lost no less than twenty seats in Scotland and a quarter of their vote. Following the success of the SNP in the elections of 1974, the Conservatives reiterated their support for devolution, but the election of Margaret Thatcher to the leadership of the party in 1975, as successor to Heath, replaced a supporter of devolution by someone whose instincts were hostile to it. 'Ted', she wrote, 'had impaled the Party on an extremely painful hook from which it would be my unenviable task to set it free. As an instinctive Unionist, I disliked the Devolution commitment.'[30]

Thus, when the Labour government presented its devolution proposals, in the form of a Scotland and Wales Bill, to Parliament in December 1976, the Conservatives, against the advice of the majority of Scottish Conservative MPs, opposed it. In May 1977, the Conservative spokesman on devolution, Francis Pym, announced that the party's commitment to a directly elected assembly was now 'inoperative'. The Conservatives had become the party of the Union again. The decline of the Conservatives in Scotland continued until, in the general election of 1997, they were completely wiped out, failing to return a single MP for a Scottish constituency.

VI

In the 1960s, however, it seemed as if it was the Labour Party which was in the most danger from the rise of Scottish nationalism. For

Labour had only twice in its history—in 1945 and 1966—succeeded in securing a majority of English seats. Not only, therefore, was Labour's industrial heartland in Scotland threatened by the SNP, but separatism foreshadowed the possibility of Labour becoming a permanent minority at Westminster.

It has been said of the Independent Labour Party, forerunner of the Labour Party, that it was 'in many respects a rebellion of the provinces and intrinsically regional in character'.[31] The Scottish Labour Party, founded in 1888, and influenced by men such as Keir Hardie and Cunninghame Graham, inherited the radical mantle of Scottish Home Rule. At Scottish Labour Party conferences between 1916 and 1923, Home Rule for Scotland was regularly passed without dissent, and the Scottish party helped to draft a Home Rule Bill in 1924. Indeed, many Scottish socialists wished to go further. For by 1922 Labour had become the largest party in Scotland. Why should it wait for the rest of the United Kingdom to be converted to socialism? Could not Labour establish a socialist bridgehead of its own in Scotland? Such were the thoughts of a number of Scottish socialists, amongst whom John Maclean was the most prominent, in the early 1920s.

With the onset of mass unemployment, however, socialists came to believe that economic progress depended upon a strong central government. The search in the 1930s was for measures of state control to cure the slump. National ownership by the state would be better than ownership by the capitalists of Scotland. Tom Johnston, Secretary of State for Scotland during the years of Churchill's wartime coalition, and a former Home Ruler, warned, after the Second World War, that a Scottish parliament might have nothing to administer but 'an emigration system, a glorified Poor Law and a graveyard'.[32] During his tenure as Secretary of State between 1941 and 1945, moreover, Johnston had shown what could be done for Scotland by using the machinery of a powerful centralized state to lobby for Scotland's interests.

In the years between the wars, the trade-union wing of the Labour Party had also come to be hostile to devolution because of its belief that national wage bargaining was needed to maintain wage levels in Scotland. Indeed, even as they claimed to support Home Rule, the

Scottish trade unions pressed for national bargaining, prompting
J. H. Thomas, Labour's minister in charge of policy for unemploy-
ment in 1929, to remark that 'Scotsmen are far-reaching people.
They want Home Rule in everything that does not cost anything'.33

In the immediate post-war years, Scotland benefited from the
Attlee government's regional policies and it was natural that the
Scottish Labour Party should be unwilling to put this at risk by a policy of Home Rule. In 1945 the Scottish Council for Labour rejected
by 113 votes to five a motion by the nationalist, Douglas Young, calling for Home Rule; and Arthur Woodburn, a future Secretary of State
for Scotland, argued that agitation for a Scottish parliament would
drive industry away from Scotland. Home Rule suffered a further setback in the Labour Party when it came to be used by the
Conservatives in their campaign against the Attlee government. For
the Conservatives, 'London government' became a euphemism for
the Labour government. In Scotland, Walter Elliot, a former
Conservative Scottish Secretary, declared nationalization meant
denationalization.34 John MacCormick, standing in 1948 as a Liberal
candidate at Paisley, with Conservative support, went even further,
declaring that the issue was 'one between freedom and totalitarian-
ism. If the Government is allowed to pursue its present course our
retrogression towards State tyranny is inevitable.'35 Such overheated
rhetoric did not endear Labour to the nationalist cause.

The interventionist state seemed to be yielding benefits to
Scotland in the form of social welfare and economic aid, and yet, by
integrating her more closely into Britain, it perhaps meant that
Scotland was coming to lose something of herself. In reaction to
this centralization, MacCormick launched, in 1949, the Scottish
Covenant, and it attracted over two million signatures in favour of a
Scottish parliament. Attlee, understandably, regarded the Covenant
as a move to embarrass Labour, and refused to meet a delegation
from the Convention. Churchill, however, during the 1950 general
election, sought to draw the connection between interventionist government and Scottish nationalism and to harness the new Scottish
mood to the Tory cause.

The principle of centralisation of government in Whitehall and Westminster
is emphasised in a manner not hitherto experienced or contemplated in the

Act of Union. The supervision, interference and control in the ordinary
details of Scottish life and business by the Parliament at Westminster has not
hitherto been foreseen, and I frankly admit that it raises new issues between
the two nations. . . . If England became an absolute Socialist state, owning
all the means of production, distribution and exchange, ruled only by politicians and their officials in the London offices, I personally cannot feel that
Scotland would be bound to accept such a dispensation. . . . I would never
accept the view that Scotland should be forced into the serfdom of Socialism
as the result of a vote in the House of Commons. It is an alteration so fundamental in our way of life that it would require a searching review of our
historical relations.[36]

Attlee himself 'was not inclined to give much time to Scottish problems' and he 'was intolerant of any regional variations that might
impede progress'.[37] What might be called the ideology of the welfare state was to conflict sharply with the view that Scotland enjoyed
a special status within the United Kingdom, which was guaranteed
by the Treaty of Union. Thus, the traditional unionism of the
Conservatives which attacked Home Rule as a threat to national
unity came to be complemented by a unionism of the Left which
stressed that only a strong central government in London could
secure equity of treatment between the different parts of the United
Kingdom.

The centralist approach continued through the 1960s, and whereas in the Conservative Party grass-roots pressure had created a
favourable climate for devolution proposals, in the Labour Party
pressure came from the top. For the instinct of Labour, as shown by
the opposition of Left-wing MPs such as Eric Heffer and Neil
Kinnock to the devolution legislation in the 1970s, was that devolution would make the task of socialists more difficult. They were concerned less perhaps with the loss of *sovereignty* involved than with
loss of the *power* of central government, a power which was needed,
amongst other reasons, to remedy the very territorial disparities and
inequalities which so concerned advocates of devolution.

The first reaction of the Labour Party's Scottish Council to the
rise of Scottish nationalism in the 1960s was that it was a product of
economic setbacks, and that with the return of prosperity, nationalism would disappear. Devolution, the Council held, would threaten

the position of the Secretary of State for Scotland, and also Scotland's over-representation at Westminster, both of which enabled Scotland to gain advantages when it came to the allocation of public expenditure. In 1968, therefore, the Scottish Labour Party Conference rejected devolution by a large majority, and in its evidence to the Royal Commission on the Constitution, the Scottish Council declared, 'We think that legislative devolution would damage Scotland's economic development. Labour's record in this respect . . . is something we cannot afford to lose.' And the secretary to the Scottish Labour Party told the Commission that 'There is . . . no such thing as a separate political will for Scotland.'[38] These attitudes were reinforced in the Cabinet by the determination of William Ross, Secretary of State for Scotland, who, in the 1960s, was adamantly opposed to devolution. Ross, Richard Crossman believed, was 'determined to treat nationalism as a mere emotional attitude which can be cured by economic policies alone'.[39]

The Labour election manifesto of February 1974 said nothing about devolution, although its Welsh manifesto promised a directly elected council for Wales. After the election, however, in which the SNP had gained six seats, two of them from Labour, the issue of devolution was one which the party could no longer ignore, especially since, in office as a minority government, it would be forced to go to the polls again shortly. At its conference in March 1974, the Scottish Council came out in favour of a directly elected assembly. In June, however, the executive of the Scottish Council, meeting with one-third of its members absent watching a World Cup football match, rejected devolution by six votes to five as 'irrelevant to the real needs of the people of Scotland', because:

The essential strategy for the Labour Party is to bring about a fundamental and irreversible shift in the balance of power and wealth in favour of working people. Public ownership and control of North Sea oil is a vital element . . . constitutional tinkering does not make a meaningful contribution towards achieving our socialist objectives.

This decision caused considerable embarrassment to Labour's National Executive in London, which was preparing the party's programme for the next general election, and was convinced that, unless

Labour committed itself to devolution, it would suffer further losses to the SNP.

The Scottish organizer of the Labour Party was therefore summoned to London and pressure was put on constituency parties and trade unions in Scotland to call a special conference to reverse the decision of the Scottish Executive. At this special conference on 16 September 1974, two days before the general election was announced, 'the devolutionists', in the words of one commentator, 'got their way by arm-twisting', the union block vote being swung to the government's policy on devolution as a quid pro quo for the social contract on wages.[40] Tam Dalyell, the leading Labour opponent of devolution in Scotland, wondered how one union leader, 'believing what he does about the assembly will be able to look at himself in his shaving mirror'.[41] In the general election of October 1974, Labour made an official commitment to devolution, and published, for the first time, a separate manifesto for Scotland, although 'there were complaints, nonetheless, that the Scottish manifesto had been written in London and shown to the Scottish Executive only when it was too late to make any major changes.'[42]

It is ironic that Labour became a devolutionist party under pressure from London. The parties indeed had reversed their positions, the Conservatives beginning as devolutionists and ending as supporters of the status quo, Labour beginning as supporters of the status quo, and ending as devolutionists. In each case, the shifts were made on grounds of tactics rather than principle. All the same, these tergiversations of the 1960s and 1970s were to prove of vital importance for the future not only of Scottish, but also of British politics. For they were to determine party positions on devolution for many years to come. The parties were to become frozen in the positions of the mid- and late 1970s. The Conservatives would be the party of the constitutional status quo and Labour the party of constitutional change.

From the late 1970s, Labour began to recover its electoral position in Scotland, even while it was losing support in the rest of the country. In 1979, although defeated in the general election, Labour actually improved its performance in Scotland, while the SNP lost nine of its eleven seats (Table 4.3).

Table 4.3 Labour results in Scotland, October 1974 and 1979

Election	% of Labour vote	Labour seats in Scotland
Oct. 1974	36.3	41
1979	41.6	44

During the long years of opposition, between 1979 and 1997, Labour retained its position as the majority party in Scotland. Labour, whose support for devolution had begun by being halting and uncertain, would become the strongest political force arguing that only devolution could keep Scotland within the United Kingdom.

Wales

Britain is the creation of the state. Wales the creation of providence.

(Gwynfor Evans, *Wales Can Win*)

I

Following the incorporation of Wales with England in the sixteenth century, the Welsh people did not find it easy to maintain their identity. For governmental purposes, indeed, Wales came to be treated as if it were part of England. Section 3 of the Wales and Berwick Act of 1746, provided that 'in all cases where the Kingdom of England, or that part of Great Britain called England, hath been or shall be mentioned in any Act of Parliament, the same has been and shall from henceforth be deemed and taken to comprehend and include the Dominion of Wales.'[1] This Act remained in force until 1967. By the nineteenth century, Gladstone could claim that 'The distinction between England and Wales ... is totally unknown to our constitution.'[2] For Wales, unlike Scotland, did not enjoy those independent institutions which not only ensured separate treatment, but, more crucially, preserved the memory of independent statehood.

Thus Welsh nationalism, lacking an institutional focus, had to build on less concrete factors—language, religion, and culture. It was left to writers, poets, and preachers to create 'the cultural form, the tracery of a nation where no state had existed'.[3] The Welsh faced the same uphill task as other ethnic minorities in Europe—the Corsicans and the Bretons, for example; they were seeking to create a national movement on the basis of symbols such as language and religion whose importance was declining in the modern world.

The crucial difference between Scotland and Wales has been summed up by Marxists in the distinction between a 'historic' nation and a 'non-historic' nation, between a nation which had succeeded in retaining the institutions of statehood and one which had not. For nations of the latter sort, Engels at least had little sympathy. They were merely:

remnant people, left over from an earlier population, forced back and subjugated by the nation which later became the repository of historical development. These remnants of a nation, mercilessly crushed, as Hegel said, by the course of history, this *national refuse*, is always the fanatical representative of the counter-revolution, and remains so until it is completely exterminated or de-nationalised, as its whole existence is in itself a protest against a great historical revolution.[4]

Wales, however, has always been very far from being a 'fanatical representative of the counter-revolution'. Indeed, the politics of Wales in modern times has been characterized by its consistent and powerful support for the Left, first for the Liberals and then for Labour. Before the First World War, Wales was the most anti-Conservative area in Britain; during the years 1885–1914, there were only two Welsh constituencies where the average Conservative vote was higher than the average Liberal vote, and the Conservatives performed appreciably worse than the Liberals in rural constituencies, 'at a time when in Britain as a whole the Conservatives were regarded as the party representing most effectively the interests of both landlord and farmer'. Indeed, during the six elections between 1885 and 1914, the average vote for the Conservatives was 38.6 per cent in Wales, but 52.7 per cent in the predominantly working-class constituencies of inner London. There can be little doubt therefore that, during these years, 'nationalism contributed something to political feeling which went beyond the mere sense of economic grievance'.[5] The prime reason for the minority position of the Conservatives in Wales was that they were seen as the political representatives of the Anglican church, the church of a minority in Wales, and the landowner—influences which seemed hostile to the national as well as the social aspirations of Wales. 'A Welsh nonconformist who is a Conservative in politics', it was said in 1914, 'is considered by his co-religionists a traitor to his sect, and almost a traitor to his country.'[6]

The Liberal ascendancy began with the general election of 1857, and coincided with a remarkable reawakening of Welsh national consciousness. The Liberals sought to have this consciousness recognized. Their first success came in 1881 with the Sunday Closing (Wales) Act, the first time that a legislative principle was applied to Wales but not to England. For many Welsh Liberals, indeed, radicalism and nationalism were indistinguishable. Tom Ellis declared in his election address at Merioneth in 1886, 'I solicit your suffrages as a WELSH NATIONALIST'; and Lloyd George characterized himself in Dod's Parliamentary Companion until 1923 as a Radical and Welsh Nationalist.

In 1866, the *Cymru Fydd* (Wales of the Future) movement was founded. It began as a cultural movement, but became nationalist in the 1880s. Its nationalism, however, entailed not separation from England, but equality with England. This was because, in the words of one account of *Cymru Fydd*, it was

recognised, not only that union with England is inevitable, but that it provides the best opportunity that Wales could have to deliver her mission . . . to the world. The closer the connection the better it will be for the purposes of *Cymru Fydd*; for it is by influencing England that Wales can influence the world. The one condition which is insisted upon is that the connection shall not be closer at the expense of Welsh nationality or at the sacrifice of some national qualities. The voices of England and of Wales should be joined, not in unison, but in harmony.[7]

Home Rule was in no way crucial to the Welsh claim for equality. Indeed it was, as we shall see, a divisive issue in Wales; and for Tom Ellis, 'it was the nonconformity of Wales that created the unity of Wales, rather than any spontaneous demand for Home Rule.'[8]

The agitation for Irish Home Rule gave an impetus to national sentiment in Wales, but there are a number of reasons why Home Rule did not play as crucial a role in Welsh politics as it did in Ireland. Wales, it is true, shared with Ireland an agrarian problem and resentment at English domination; but its experience of English rule had been very different, and there was no equivalent in Welsh history to the Irish famine and emigration which had so embittered Irish attitudes.

In Wales, unlike Ireland, the agrarian problem was not complicated by the existence of an alien and absentee landlord class belonging to the dominant nation. However much the landlords had become anglicized, they were still either Welsh or linked in marriage to the native Welsh, and many of them were nonconformist and Welsh-speaking. It was impossible to feel for them the same depth of antagonism which the Irish peasant felt for his English landlord. Moreover, Wales, unlike Ireland, had not been a colony of settlement, nor had it been 'planted' with those of an alien religion. There was, furthermore, no agrarian violence or crime in Wales. Altogether, therefore, conditions in Ireland and Wales were very different.

In addition, the effects of the gradual democratization of life were felt more tangibly in Wales than they had been in Ireland. In the first elections to the Welsh county councils in 1889, 'the Welsh national feeling' was 'very strongly brought out' and the Liberals succeeded in winning every county except Brecknock. Precisely because these new local authorities succeeded in undermining the rule of the landowner and the gentry, it was apparent that reform in Wales did not depend upon Home Rule. Indeed, the results of the elections 'created a social transformation more striking even than the extension of democracy at the national level'. 'It is not', Gladstone told his friend Stuart Rendel, MP for Montgomery, in 1892, 'the Irish case over again.'9 In Wales, unlike Ireland, there was no desire for separation and little doubt that Home Rule could be killed by kindness.

Home Rule, moreover, was a divisive issue in Wales, and schemes for establishing Welsh national institutions were continually to founder 'on the same rock, the balance of representation between Glamorgan and Monmouth and the rest of the country'.10 In 1892, for example, a proposal for a Welsh national body to take over the powers of the Local Government Board, the Board of Guardians, Commissioners for Works, and the Charity Commissioners for Wales, was considered. But Welsh opinion failed to agree on what the basis of representation on this new national body should be. Glamorgan favoured representation on a population basis under which it would secure twenty-five of the fifty-nine seats. This meant, however, that Merioneth and Radnor would secure only two seats each. Radnor therefore sought equal representation by county on the lines of the American Senate. But to this Glamorgan would not agree; so the proposal came to nothing.

Shortly afterwards, Lloyd George attempted to create a centralized democratic political leadership in Wales. This involved the abolition of the North and South Wales Liberal Federations and their replacement by one central body. Lloyd George was defeated, however, by opposition from the South Wales Liberal Federation which refused to merge its powers, one English-speaking Liberal from Cardiff, Alderman Bird, declaring that 'a cosmopolitan population from Swansea to Newport' would 'never bow to the domination of Welsh ideas'.[11] Nationalism in Wales proved, as it was to do in 1979 and in 1997, divisive, not integrative as it was in Scotland. The Liberal Party, therefore, concentrated on measures designed to secure 'equality for Wales within the British and imperial framework, not exclusion from it'.[12]

The development of industrialism in south Wales served further to weaken the pressure for Home Rule. It did so in two ways. First, it helped to relieve the growing pressure on the land, and thus provided an alternative to migration of a kind not available to the Irish peasant. Second, industrialization introduced a new element into Welsh politics, threatening not only the Liberal Party, but that radical nonconformist nationalism which had first triumphed in 1857. For class conflict was to cut across the old Liberal–Conservative and Welsh–English cleavages. This meant that a Welsh nonconformist industrialist such as D. A. Thomas, later Lord Rhondda, who had found himself on the progressive side of politics when the cleavage had been a religious and cultural one, came to be branded as a class enemy by the Labour Party. Moreover, industrialism, by tying the economy of south Wales more tightly to the English economy, made nationalism appear not only sociologically irrelevant, but also economically foolish.

It was for these reasons that the collapse of the *Cymru Fydd* movement in 1896 proved to be the end of political nationalism in Wales for seventy years until the Welsh nationalist party, Plaid Cymru, together with changes in political culture in Wales, once more put Home Rule onto the political agenda.

II

The failure of *Cymru Fydd* made it seem as if the sentiment of nationality in Wales was not powerful or unified enough to sustain a strong Home Rule movement. Accordingly, Welsh Liberals concentrated their efforts upon winning recognition for Welsh cultural aspirations and religious distinctiveness. Rather than a Welsh parliament, they sought national educational institutions and the disestablishment of the Welsh church. The first of these aims proved easier to achieve than the second. In 1889 the Intermediate Education Act made Welsh county councils the first local education authorities in Britain. They were empowered to raise a halfpenny rate for secondary education, with a Treasury grant being made available to the local authorities equivalent to the sum raised in the rates. This was the system later adopted in England in A. J. Balfour's Education Act of 1902. In 1893, a charter was granted to the University of Wales, and in 1896, a Central Welsh Board was established to administer examinations. The Welsh educational system was thus in the process of becoming 'a national system, the first and most striking expression in institutional terms of the reawakened consciousness of nationhood'.[13]

But Welsh Liberals sought, above all, disestablishment of the Welsh church, the church of a minority of the Welsh people, to which no Welsh-speaking bishop had been appointed between 1715 and 1870, and yet a church to which Welsh tenant-farmers were compelled to pay tithes. The 'tithe war', under which tithes were withheld, linked together the issues of land and church, class and religion, powerfully strengthening the Welsh Liberals; and in Wales it was disestablishment rather than Home Rule which served to unify national opinion.

Welsh disestablishment, however, was a highly contentious issue in British politics, and when Gladstone embarked on his Home Rule crusade, it took second place to the Irish demand. For this reason, Gladstone, in his final ministry of 1892-4, failed to carry disestablishment, while the short-lived Rosebery government of 1894-5 fell before a Welsh disestablishment bill could complete its passage through Parliament. Welsh Liberals could, in theory, have reacted to this setback by forming an independent party on the Parnellite model, threatening to withhold support from any government which did not meet their wishes. But it never occurred to them to do so. They well appreciated that liberalism could not survive in Wales

merely as a vehicle for Celtic claims. They sought primarily not separation but recognition. 'The ideal of Wales was to be recognised as
a part of the British political and social structure: the ideal of Ireland
was to be severed from it. The object of the one was equality: the aim
of the other was exclusion.'[14]

But if Welsh Liberalism was a political instrument fashioned to
meet the challenge of recognition, it was less well equipped to meet
the challenge of industrialism. Too many of its policies assumed a
social homogeneity that was rapidly disappearing in Wales. Indeed,
both Welsh Liberalism and Welsh nationalism came to be tied to symbols—the land, religion, and the language—whose importance in
Welsh life was diminishing. In 1895, the *Cymru Fydd* programme had
placed 'labour and industrial' questions seventh, well behind such nos-
trums as Home Rule for Wales, temperance reform, and security for
the tenant-farmer. Lloyd George himself 'remained an Old Liberal in
Wales, although a "New Liberal" in England', and for Wales he argued
that 'the land question, the temperance question and the question of
disestablishment were equally matters of interest to labourers as an
Eight Hours bill'.[15] National claims came increasingly to be focused
on the limited aim of disestablishment, and when that was achieved in
1914—although it did not come into effect until 1920—the movement
faded and Welsh Liberalism lost much of its vitality. Disestablishment
in Wales was an end in itself and not, as it was in Ireland, a prelude to
the demand for political change. There was to be no Welsh Parnell.

In 1918, most Welsh Liberals allied themselves with Lloyd
George and the Conservatives in the 'coupon election', and this
proved fatal to the claims of the Liberal Party to be the radical party
in Wales. By 1922, Labour had replaced the Liberals as the dominant
party in Wales, and by 1951 there were only three Liberal MPs left
in the principality, all of whom held their seats through tacit
Conservative support. The Liberals had ceased to be the party of
Welsh aspirations. That title now went to Labour.

III

Labour always held an ambivalent attitude to Welsh national claims.
It inherited the mantle of Liberalism as the party of the provinces and

the periphery, but it was also a British-wide movement which saw class rather than community as the basis of political action. Thus, 'To the old pattern of Welsh solidarity, expressed in the Liberal Party and closely allied to Nonconformity, [Labour] opposed a new philosophy—one of secular Socialism, British rather than Welsh in content.'[16] The trade unions, the industrial wing of the Labour movement, saw themselves as national bodies, and feared that if they allowed themselves to be divided by geography, employers would have an excuse to cut wages in the less prosperous parts of the country. The trade unions, therefore, protested when, as a concession to national sentiment, Lloyd George, in his National Insurance Act of 1911, agreed to set up separate administrations for National Health insurance in Scotland and Wales as well as in Ireland.

During the early years of the century, however, Labour proved a unifying force in Welsh politics. Like the Liberals, Labour enjoyed a broad cultural appeal, based as much upon the chapel and the Sunday school as upon class-consciousness. Labour, in the words of Tom Jones, was 'not bound by a narrow economic doctrine; our approach was ethical or rather we were striving to bring the economic and religious factors into a right relation ... we wanted a classless society but not a class war'.[17] This cultural dimension, much influenced by Keir Hardie, implied recognition of ethnic diversity in the fashioning of the state, and Labour, in its early years, espoused the Liberal doctrine of 'Home Rule All Round', which of course implied a Welsh parliament.

But, as we have seen, Home Rule and the redress of nonconformist grievances were becoming more peripheral to Welsh politics. After the First World War there was a brief flurry of interest in regionalism and nationalism, but this soon died away. A conference on devolution in Wales held at Shrewsbury in 1922 failed disastrously, the industrial counties of Glamorgan and Monmouth not even bothering to send representatives.

During the inter-war years, faced with mass unemployment and migration from south Wales to the Midlands and London, nationalism seemed to have nothing to offer. Instead, the unemployed looked 'fixedly, if resentfully, to the government in London, apparently seeing no prospect of salvation under a separate system of government in Wales'.[18] The solution to the problems of Wales was to be found in a Labour government, able to plan the economy from the centre, not in a Welsh parliament.

In office from 1945, Labour's main concerns lay with economic policy and social reform, and this tended to reinforce its centralist outlook. On the first Welsh Day debate in the House of Commons in 1944, Aneurin Bevan declared that 'My colleagues, all of them members of the Miners' Federation of Great Britain, have no special solution for the Welsh coal industry which is not a solution for the whole of the mining industry of Great Britain. There is no Welsh problem.'[19] On devolution, Bevan said in 1946:

Is it not rather cruel to give the impression to the 50,000 unemployed men and women in Wales that their plight would be relieved and their distress removed by this constitutional change? It is not socialism. It is escapism. This is exactly the way in which nation after nation has been ruined in the last 25 to 50 years, trying to pretend that deep-seated economic difficulties can be removed by constitutional changes.[20]

Bevan in the 1940s, like Eric Heffer and Neil Kinnock in the 1970s, saw socialism as a doctrine which required control of the levers of economic power. It would be madness for socialists, having after so many years achieved power at Westminster, to dissipate it by dividing it up between subnational units. In the 1960s, Labour was to become even more committed to central planning of the economy and to a regional policy run from London. Thus, with Labour the dominant party in Wales in the post-war years, 'Welsh nationalism seemed as dead as the druids.'[21]

Yet Labour was still electorally dependent on the peripheries, and, in 1964 and 1974, would not have been able to form a government without support from Wales. It is not surprising, then, that Labour's approach to Wales should have been so ambivalent, its centralist philosophy clashing with its traditional role as the party of peripheral protest, and with its electoral self-interest.

IV

The Welsh nationalist party, Plaid Cymru, was born in 1925 in the midst of an era of disillusion and depression in the principality. As with the SNP, so also with Plaid Cymru—its birth was a sign not of the strength of peripheral nationalism but of its weakness. For both movements were founded on a recognition that neither national self-government nor even devolution were to be obtained from the other parties. The Conservatives had always opposed Welsh Home Rule, the Liberals were no longer in a position to offer it, while Labour seemed uninterested.

Plaid Cymru, however, faced problems far more daunting than those of the SNP. For in Scotland, nationalism was a unifying and integrative force, the institutions of nationhood eliciting feelings of sympathy from nearly every Scot. In Wales, by contrast, the symbols of nationality—the land, religion, and the church—seemed symbols of a dying culture, while the language, the most obvious badge of Welsh identity, was for many years to prove a deeply divisive force, tending to confine Plaid Cymru to 'Welsh' Wales in the north-west, as opposed to the industrial south-east.

In the twentieth century the Welsh language was in steady retreat until, by 1981, only 21 per cent of Welsh people spoke Welsh. By 1991, the figure had fallen to 18 per cent, but there were signs of a revival in Welsh-speaking amongst young people, on whom the future of the language depends. Nevertheless, if language were to be the criterion of Welshness, around 80 per cent of the inhabitants of Wales would have to be dismissed as not truly Welsh. The English-speaking majority could hardly be expected to vote for a party whose main platform was the promotion of a language which they could not speak. If, on the other hand, Plaid Cymru were to underplay the language issue, it might lose its central core of support from those who saw the preservation of the language as the main purpose of self-government. The party was placed, therefore, in a cruel dilemma and it has never succeeded in resolving it.

Plaid Cymru began as a movement to preserve the language, and it was originally more of a 'cultural conservationist society' than a political party.[22] Admittedly Saunders Lewis, its president from 1926 to 1939, believed that only self-government could save the language; but, in a radio broadcast in 1962 he modified his position, proclaiming that the language 'is the only political question deserving of a Welshman's attention at the present time', and that it was:

more important than self-government . . . if we were to have any sort of self-government for Wales before the Welsh language is recognised and used as an official language in all the administration of State and local authority in the Welsh areas of our country, it would never attain official status, and the doom of the language would come more quickly than it will come under English government.[23]

Saunders Lewis hoped that just as English was the official language of England, so also Welsh would become the sole official language of Wales. However, a later generation of Plaid Cymru's leaders adopted a more moderate stance on the language problem. In his book, *Plaid Cymru and Wales*, published in 1950, Gwynfor Evans, president of the party, insisted that: 'since common membership of the Welsh community rather than language or descent is the test of nationality in Wales, nationalists are proud to know them [English-speaking Welshmen] as fellow-Welshmen. Wales has no finer patriots than some who have no knowledge of the national tongue'.[24]

The party dissociated itself from the extremists of the Welsh Language Society, which one of Plaid Cymru's leaders, Dr Phil Williams, accused of 'alienating increasing numbers of the population' and creating 'hostility to the Welsh language'.[25] In 1968, Plaid Cymru adopted a policy of bilingualism, but it did so somewhat reluctantly. Since then, however, it has moved further in the direction of seeking to accommodate English-speaking Wales, and in 1998, it decided to change its name to Plaid Cymru the Party of Wales. Its electoral successes, however, have remained largely confined to the Welsh-speaking north-west of the principality.

In its early years, Plaid Cymru was so preoccupied with the language question that it devoted little attention to the economic changes which were visibly altering the face of Wales. Since the early 1960s, however, there has been 'a campaign of attrition by a growing band of Modernists to bring the party into the world of modern Wales, to drag the movement, however reluctantly, away from total preoccupation with the cultural strongholds of the north and west'.[26] The party has put forward ideas based on the thought of E. F. Schumacher, author of *Small is Beautiful*, and Leopold Kohr, an *émigré* social scientist at Aberystwyth University College, who sought to put some of Schumacher's prescriptions into concrete form. Crucial to Plaid Cymru's vision is a means of strengthening the identification of the individual with his ethnic community. This, according to Gwynfor Evans, means preserving the heritage of the Welsh past:

Adaptation requires a hold of the past, of traditional life. The past lives in the tradition of the national community; if it is destroyed no adaptation is possible. Therefore, although they are a radical party which seeks fundamental changes in Wales, nationalists have been conscious of the necessity for roots and continuity in human society and of the importance of identity and community in human life.[27]

During the parliamentary debates on devolution in the 1970s, Evans argued for a federal system within which Wales would take its place, rather than for separatism, although he was not clear whether England or the English regions should be the units in the system. Plaid Cymru's concern seemed to lie less in setting up a classic nine-teenth-century nation state as the SNP was seeking to do, than in transcending the notion of sovereignty altogether. Plaid Cymru was and is as much a communalist and decentralist party as a separatist one, and, whereas the debate in Scotland has been primarily one about nationalism, in Wales it has been about how to restore the lost spirit of community.

As with the SNP, Plaid Cymru found itself unsuccessful at the hustings for many years, although in by-elections in Ogmore and Aberdare in 1946, it was able to secure 29 per cent and 20 per cent of the vote. Between 1950 and 1956, Plaid Cymru took part in an abortive all-party campaign to press for a Welsh parliament. A petition was drawn up which received a quarter of a million signatures, equal to 14 per cent of the Welsh electorate, but it was ignored both by the government and by the Labour opposition, while the Labour MPs who were associated with the campaign—including Cledwyn Hughes, a future Secretary of State for Wales—were carpeted by Labour's National Executive Committee for defying official party policy on the issue.

Until 1959, Plaid Cymru concentrated its electoral forces on the Welsh-speaking areas. As late as 1969, seven constituencies in Glamorgan and Monmouth had never seen a Plaid Cymru candidate.

Yet, ironically, Plaid Cymru's breakthrough, when it came, occurred not in the rural Welsh-speaking areas of Merioneth or Carnarvon, but in the areas of industrial decline in the valleys—Rhondda and Caerphilly—and in Carmarthen, where in a by-election in July 1966 Gwynfor Evans overturned a Labour majority of 9,233 to win the party's first seat. In a by-election in Rhondda West, one of the safest Labour seats in the country, in March 1967, Plaid almost won, slashing a Labour majority of 16,888 to 2,306. In the third and last by-election in Wales in the 1966–70 parliament, in Caerphilly in July 1968, Plaid Cymru also ran a close second. 'In the Midlands', the journalist David McKie commented, 'the slump in the Labour vote looked merely like the collapse of a habit: in South Wales, it looks like the death of a religion.'[28]

In the two general elections of 1974, however, Plaid Cymru failed to emulate the SNP and its percentage of the vote remained static (Table 5.1).

In October 1974, although Plaid Cymru won three seats, there were only five seats where its vote exceeded 20 per cent, and the party succeeded in saving only four deposits outside the six predominantly Welsh-speaking constituencies. In Wales, by contrast with Scotland, the demand for a third force in Welsh politics found its outlet not in the nationalists, but in the Liberal Party, whose share of the vote increased from 6.8 per cent in 1970 to 15.5 per cent in October 1974.

However, because Plaid Cymru gained *seats* in both of the two elections in 1974, Westminster politicians and commentators believed that there was increasing support for nationalism in Wales

Table 5.1 General election results in Wales, 1970 and 1974

Election	Total votes in Wales	% of vote in Wales	Candidates	Elected
1970	175,016	11.5	36	0
February 1974	171,374	10.7	36	2
October 1974	166,321	10.8	36	3

as well as in Scotland. It was common for politicians and commentators in the mid-1970s to speak of 'the rise of nationalism in Scotland and Wales', ignoring the fact that Plaid Cymru's support had fallen from its high point in 1970; and this mistaken diagnosis was to play its part in the events that led to the débâcle of the 1979 referendum.

V

Welsh nationality, however, did not depend primarily upon a nationalist party for its expression. During the twentieth century, Welsh distinctiveness came to be underlined, in an almost unnoticed way, by a series of reforms whose effect was to decentralize administration from London to Cardiff. Whereas Scotland already had its own institutions and distinctiveness which the establishment of the Scottish Secretary in 1885 merely recognized, in Wales, by contrast, governmental institutions were established by Westminster and Whitehall, not so much to meet national claims as to meet the needs of central government itself.

The first recognition by any government department that separate treatment was necessary for Wales occurred in 1907, when a Welsh Department of the Board of Education was established. This innovation showed that administrative devolution in education could yield valuable benefits, for the Welsh Department was able to secure 'a unified approach to the educational problems of each individual authority so that, at any one time, officials of the Welsh Department were able to see the whole range of educational services provided in a particular area'. The Department, unlike the Board of Education in London, was able to shift funds from primary to secondary education and vice versa, and it had the added advantage that 'it was possible for the officers of the local authorities to establish a close personal relationship with the Department's officials'.[29] The Department was also given a free hand to encourage education in the Welsh language, and the outstanding feature of the Board's work in its first two years was 'the definite recognition of the Welsh language and Welsh literature in the curriculum of the schools and training colleges of Wales'.[30]

The next instalment of administrative decentralization in Wales occurred in 1911 with Lloyd George's National Insurance Act. The Irish demanded a separate national commission, and Scotland and Wales then sought a similar concession. Lloyd George, who had originally hoped for a unified system of administration, gave way, saying 'you have got to defer to sentiment'.[31] The Welsh commissioners came to exercise 'an influence and authority which nobody sitting in and operating from London could have hoped to exercise'.[32] The Act, therefore, proved, 'not only a necessary but a very successful experiment in applied home rule'.[33]

The third area of administrative decentralization was in agriculture. In 1912, a year after the Scottish Board of Agriculture had been set up, the office of Agricultural Commissioner for Wales was established, together with an advisory Agricultural Council for Wales. However, as the Welsh Land Enquiry Commission reported in 1914, 'the problem of land in its varied features is so vast and complicated that it is impossible to deal effectively with Wales by a department located in Whitehall and staffed by men out of touch, and more often than not, out of sympathy with the special needs of Wales'. In consequence, a Welsh office of the Board of Agriculture and Fisheries was set up in 1919.[34]

This process of administrative decentralization continued until, by the 1950s, no fewer than seventeen departments had established administrative units in Wales.[35] This did not, however, reflect any overall plan of devolution. The process of decentralization was entirely pragmatic, and the extent of decentralization differed from department to department. There was no obvious reason, for example, why the Welsh Board of Health, the successor to the insurance commissioners, which, by 1950, was exercising most of the major powers of the Ministry of Health in Wales, should have come to enjoy more autonomy than the Welsh Department of the Ministry of Agriculture. Were there, however, to be a minister whose responsibility it was to concern himself specifically with Wales, then, it could be argued, it might be possible to shape policy more effectively to meet Welsh needs. There would then be an overall approach towards administrative devolution to Wales as there had been in Scotland, in place of the piecemeal approach of earlier years. The logical next step seemed to be a Minister for Wales. This proposal was rejected in the 1930s by Neville Chamberlain and in the 1940s by Attlee, but in 1951, Winston Churchill appointed his Home Secretary, Sir David Maxwell-Fyfe, as also the first Minister for Welsh Affairs. Sir David was to be answerable to the Commons for the general effect of government policy in Wales and for the annual White Paper on government action in Wales, and he was also to lead in Welsh Day debates. But he was given no executive powers and, as he lacked a departmental machine, his effectiveness was bound to depend upon the degree of influence which he could secure over his Cabinet colleagues. Moreover, Sir David suffered from the handicap of sitting for an English constituency.

In 1957, Harold Macmillan announced that the Minister of Housing and Local Government, Henry Brooke, would in future also be the Minister for Welsh Affairs, since this Minister, unlike the Home Secretary, had executive responsibility for a wide range of matters affecting Wales. He would therefore be in a position to take the initiative through the use of his own departmental powers. But Brooke too sat for an English constituency, and his credibility was shattered when he approved the acquisition of water in the Tryweryn Valley in Merioneth by Liverpool, even though it was opposed by twenty-seven of the thirty-six MPs in the principality.[36] Macmillan refused, however, to consider the appointment of a Secretary of State for Wales, and from this point on, the initiative in the process of administrative decentralization passed to Labour, which had advocated a full-time Minister for Welsh Affairs since 1954. When in 1956 James Griffiths, MP for Llanelli, was elected deputy leader of the party, Welsh interests were given greater prominence in Labour's policy-making; and in its 1959 and 1964 election manifestos, the party promised to create a Secretary of State for Wales. Griffiths duly became the first Secretary of State when this commitment was honoured following Labour's election victory in October 1964. At a meeting of the Welsh Grand Committee on 16 December 1964, Griffiths declared that the establishment of the Welsh Office was 'recognition of our nationhood'.

Nevertheless, the Secretary of State's powers were at first extremely limited; he was given executive powers only over the functions of the Ministry of Housing and Local Government in Wales, and responsibility for roads. In addition to these powers, however, the Secretary of State was to participate in the process of policy-formulation in the economic plan for Wales in conjunction with the newly established Department for Economic Affairs, and he was given powers of 'oversight within Wales of the execution of national policy' by other domestic departments in Wales, which in Harold Wilson's view would enable him 'to express the voice of Wales'.[37] Gradually, the responsibilities of the Office were extended. In 1968, the Secretary of State was given powers over health functions in Wales, and in 1970 powers with respect to primary and secondary education. Since that time, the responsibilities of the Welsh Office have been further extended so that its responsibilities have become nearly as great as those of the Scottish Office.

The establishment of the Welsh Office gave to Wales advantages not enjoyed by the regions of England; for not only did Wales have a representative in the Cabinet, but she was also represented at the crucial interdepartmental committees involved in policy-formation. However, the scope of the Welsh Office was limited, as was that of the Scottish Office, by the conventions of British government, and in particular by the convention of ministerial responsibility. Any divergence in policy in Wales might create unwelcome precedents in England, and so there were limits to the discretion which civil servants could exercise as they strove to meet Welsh needs. The Welsh Secretary, moreover, is far junior in rank in the Cabinet to his predecessors, the Home Secretary and the Minister for Housing and Local Government. It was for this reason that Sir Keith Joseph opposed the setting up of the Welsh Office, arguing that 'a minister who speaks for a large department has slightly more of a chance of getting his case put or heard, than a minister who speaks for a smaller department'.[38] In general, moreover, the Welsh Office, since Wales lacks a separate system of law, which has allowed the Scottish Office to argue for distinctively Scottish legislation, has tended to follow the policies laid down by the London-based departments. It has not played a large part in creating policy, but has, at best, been able to modify agreed policies to ensure that the interests of Wales are taken into account. There are very few instances where the Welsh Secretary has challenged an important policy presumption or worked out a major policy from basic principles dictated by specifically Welsh patterns of need.

Devolution to Wales, as we shall see, divorces the execution of policy from law-making in Wales. Yet it might be argued that such a divorce existed before devolution if the role of the Secretary of State in the formulation of laws for Wales was in practice minimal, since law-making normally emanated from the 'English' departments. Of course, putting the legislative and executive responsibilities in separate elected bodies raises new and important problems. But the divorce between law-making and execution in Wales is perhaps in itself nothing new.

As with the Scottish Secretary, there was some danger that the more responsibilities the Welsh Secretary accumulated, the more, in the words of Sir Goronwy Daniel, the first Permanent Secretary at the Welsh Office, Wales would come to be governed 'by an élite civil service'. There were, Sir Goronwy believed, two ways in which this might happen: 'One might be that if accountability is only to Westminster, the amount of parliamentary time which can be made available is limited. The other factor would be that as the functions of the Secretary of State grow it becomes more necessary to delegate more and more work to officials.'[39] The powers of the Welsh Office have expanded greatly since Sir Goronwy issued his warning, and before devolution it had the responsibilities of seven English departments.

The position of the Welsh Secretary became particularly difficult under Conservative governments, since the Conservatives have never, in modern times, gained a majority in Wales. Indeed, only one of the six Conservative Secretaries of State for Wales—Nicholas Edwards, Welsh Secretary between 1979 and 1987—actually sat for a Welsh constituency. Under Margaret Thatcher, the Welsh Secretaryship was used as a form of internal exile for Tory dissidents—Peter Walker, Welsh Secretary between 1987 and 1990, and David Hunt, Welsh Secretary between 1990 and 1993; while John Redwood, Welsh Secretary between 1993 and 1995, appeared to be using Wales as a laboratory for his particular form of free-market economics, a doctrine which enjoyed very little support in the principality.

The distinctive parliamentary arrangements devised for Wales by no means overcame the dangers to which Sir Goronwy Daniel had drawn attention in his evidence to the Royal Commission on the Constitution. Welsh question time lasts for a little over an hour every month, and the Welsh Grand Committee, established in 1960, is a far weaker body than its Scottish counterpart, since there is so little legislation which relates exclusively to Wales. It was given new standing orders in 1996 allowing it to hold question time, second reading debates, and various other debates, but met only twice in the 1996–7 parliamentary session. It has, admittedly, enjoyed a revival since the 1997 election since, under a Labour government, the majority in Wales is of the same political colour as the majority at Westminster. Nevertheless, the Welsh Office, like the Scottish Office, came to be seen as unaccountable. Thus, once the principle had been accepted of a separate minister with responsibility for Wales, it naturally came to be asked why Wales should still be accountable for her domestic affairs to Westminster, rather than to an assembly directly elected by her own voters.

VI

Because Labour has been the dominant party in Wales for so long, the recent history of devolution in Wales is very largely the history of an internal Labour Party debate. But the debate has had a very different flavour from that in Scotland. In contrast to the Scottish Labour Party's gradual yet grudging concessions on devolution, the Welsh Council of Labour committed itself to an assembly in the mid-1960s; but it had to fight hard to maintain this commitment against increasingly recalcitrant MPs and constituency parties, especially in the south-east of Wales.

The initial response in Wales was more enthusiastic than in Scotland for two reasons. The first was that the plethora of non-departmental public bodies or quangos in Wales gave the Conservatives a means of retaining a hold over Welsh public life even though they remained very much a minority in Wales. An assembly would be able to render these quangos democratically accountable. A more important reason, however, was that in Wales, unlike Scotland, devolution could be linked to local government reform, and the case for devolution was first presented in the mid-1960s as part of a broader argument for the reform of Welsh local government on a two-tier basis—a lower tier of district bodies and an upper, all-Wales tier. This was first proposed by the Executive Committee of the Welsh Council of Labour in 1965, and also, at the same time, by an interdepartmental working party set up by the Welsh Office to advise the Secretary of State on local government reform. Thus, the idea of an all-Wales body was put forward some time before Plaid Cymru appeared to threaten Labour. It is best understood perhaps, together with the rise of Plaid Cymru, as an illustration of the revival of feelings of Welsh identity in the late 1960s. Whereas in Scotland, local government reform and devolution seemed conflicting priorities, in Wales they seemed complementary. Indeed, as originally conceived, the all-Wales body would not have been a devolved admin-istration at all, but rather an upper tier of local government which would not have assumed any of the functions of central government in Wales. It would, however, have been able to control Welsh-nominated bodies.

The first two Welsh Secretaries, James Griffiths and Cledwyn Hughes, were sympathetic to an elected Welsh Council, and they had an ally in the Labour Cabinet of the late 1960s in Richard Crossman, who asked, 'Why not accept this local government reorganisation as a political necessity and then go for a really ambitious plan for a Welsh Council or Parliament?'[40] When, however, the proposal for an elected council reached the Cabinet, it met, ironically, the deter-mined opposition of William Ross, the Scottish Secretary, who feared that it would become impossible to resist the demand for a Scottish parliament if an all-Wales body were to be set up; it was also opposed—a further irony—by James Callaghan, the Home Secretary, who sat for a Cardiff constituency and believed that the Welsh Council would provide a powerful forum for Plaid Cymru. The proposal was thus watered down in Cabinet, and the Welsh Council was converted into a nominated body with purely advisory and promotional powers. This prompted the *Western Mail* to make the tart comment that Cledwyn Hughes 'had been placed in charge of a Government department which though set up to deal with Wales's unique problems is forbidden to propose uniquely Welsh solutions, because of the repercussions in England and in Scot-land.'[41]

If Labour in Wales was more sympathetic to devolution than its Scottish counterpart, it was desperately anxious to avoid the taint of separatism. MPs who might be perfectly prepared to vote for a new local government structure would not support proposals which appeared as a concession to separatist feeling. That was why the rise of Plaid Cymru in Wales in the late 1960s undermined Welsh Labour's commitment to devolution. In Scotland, by contrast, where there appeared a real threat to the Union in the 1970s, the SNP helped push Labour into a devolution commitment. The advocates of an all-Wales body were placed in an even more difficult position when, in 1968, Cledwyn Hughes was replaced as Welsh Secretary by George Thomas, a strong anti-devolutionist who, in Crossman's words, 'regards Cledwyn's views as sheer treason',[42] and did his best to frustrate the devolutionists.

In retrospect, it is clear that an excellent chance to secure an all-Wales body was lost in the 1960s through a specifically Welsh reform of local government. The Conservative government which came to power in 1970 reorganized local government in Wales, in an Act which applied both to England and Wales, establishing a two-tier structure in Wales. But the top tier consisted not of an all-Wales council, but of eight county authorities, and this was bound to make devolution more difficult, since an elected council for Wales on top of two tiers of local government would, in the Welsh Council of Labour's view, be 'like a jellyfish on a bed of nails'.[43] 'No responsible government', declared Dr Phil Williams of Plaid Cymru, 'would totally reorganise local government in Wales without first deciding the pattern of devolution. Unfortunately we underestimated the total irresponsibility of the Heath government.'[44]

Labour moved an amendment to the 1972 Local Government Bill calling for an elected Welsh Council; it was moved by George Thomas, who had undergone what one Conservative member called a conversion 'faster than recent conversions to North Sea Gas'. Thomas, however, declared that Labour were '100 per cent in support of this motion ... that there shall be established from 1 April 1976 an elected Council for Wales'.[45]

Just as the commitment to an elected all-Wales body arose from an internal Labour Party debate, so also did the particular form which devolution was to take. When preparing its evidence for the Royal Commission on the Constitution in 1969, a Labour research group had argued for a legislative Welsh assembly. George Thomas, however, as Welsh Secretary, pressed for an indirectly elected body. Labour in Wales compromised by committing itself to a directly elected assembly, but without tax-raising or legislative powers. Its evidence to the Royal Commission in 1970 declared: 'We anticipate that the Assembly would work within the legislative decisions of the House of Commons.'[46] The Welsh Council's evidence to the Royal Commission, therefore, contains the germ of the notion of executive devolution for Wales: an assembly with powers to alter only secondary legislation, an innovation in British constitutional experience which was nevertheless to be the central principle of the abortive Wales Act of 1978 and the Government of Wales Act of 1998. The commitment was made when it appeared that Labour in Scotland was not interested in devolution at all. When, in a panic, Labour offered legislative devolution to Scotland in 1974, Labour in Wales pressed for her devolution commitment to be upgraded to parity with Scotland (legislative devolution), to be met with the argument that they had not originally asked for it. 'Labour's decision to grant legislative powers to its proposed Scottish Assembly but only executive powers to a Welsh Assembly, had as much to do with political compromise and accident as with any rational argument.'[47]

Yet even the limited form of devolution on offer came to be opposed by many in the Welsh Labour Party. During the 1970s, the anti-devolutionists in the Welsh Labour Party, led by Neil Kinnock, conducted a powerful rearguard action against devolution, demanding a referendum before it was implemented. The political climate in Wales was also changing from the optimistic years of the 1960s when institutional reform had been seen as the remedy for so many ills. Thus Labour entered the Welsh devolution debate unhappy and divided. Wales, having lost the opportunity of establishing an all-Wales body in the 1960s, would have to wait thirty years for the establishment of an assembly; and when it came, it did so with a narrow and half-hearted mandate given by a bare majority of the 50 per cent of Welsh electors who had taken the trouble to vote.

Devolution
Challenge, Defeat, and Renewal

England is not governed by logic but by Parliament.

(Benjamin Disraeli)

I

After the settlement of the Irish problem in 1920–1, devolution disappeared from the British political agenda. Indeed, it had seemed to be an important issue in the years between 1885 and 1921 largely because it appeared to offer an equitable method of dealing with the Irish problem. Once Lloyd George had decided to deal with Ireland separately from the remainder of the United Kingdom, the impetus behind the movement for devolution elsewhere collapsed. Moreover, the decline of the Liberal Party not only removed from the centre of politics a party for which devolution and constitutional reform were vital issues; it also corresponded with an important change in political alignments.

Before 1914, politics was based as much upon locality as it was upon class. The Conservatives were the party of the nation-builders, of the established church, and of the land; the Liberals the party of the periphery, of the dissenting churches, and of the urban middle class. The politics of locality had most force where the grievances of peripheral areas of the United Kingdom could be linked with nationality. That was most obviously the case with Ireland; but it was true also for Scotland and Wales where, as we have seen, the strength of the party of the Left, the Liberals, is difficult to explain merely in socio-economic terms. The two general elections of 1910, for example, were dominated not only by reform of the House of Lords, but also by Irish Home Rule and the disestablishment of the Welsh church. These were explicitly core-periphery issues, Welsh disestablishment pitting the core religion, Anglicanism, against the beliefs, practices, and languages of the periphery. These core-periphery issues had been at the very heart of politics since 1886, when Gladstone had first espoused Home Rule.

After the First World War, however, the democratization of the franchise and the growth of class feeling turned national and regional resentments into class politics, and the Liberal Party, the party of the provinces against the metropolis, was eclipsed by Labour, the party of the working class; and the working class, as Marx and Engels had declared in *The Communist Manifesto*, had no country. The transition is symbolized by changing perceptions of the mine-owners of south Wales, some of whom were Welsh-speaking non-conformists. From being perceived as on the progressive side of politics as nonconformists, they now came to be perceived as being on the reactionary side because they belonged to a hostile class. Representing the organized working class, Labour came to adopt the same centralized structures as the trade unions:

Like the unions the Labour Party was national in its organisation and centralised in its institutions. It deliberately over-rode regional boundaries and local interests ... In its formal organisation, the Party had consistently imitated the great unions. With its national executive secretariat and pyramidal structure it was (and is) quite unlike any other British party.[1]

But Labour, as well as representing the politics of class, also represented, as the Liberals had done, the periphery, and articulated the old radical grievances against the centre, thus inheriting Liberal strength in Wales and in Scotland. There had been a powerful decentralist tradition in the early Labour Party, symbolized by the commitment of Keir Hardie to Scottish and Welsh Home Rule. Indeed, Hardie saw socialism, as 'at bottom ... emerging from a rooted local culture'.[2] The Webbs and Laski had also displayed much sympathy with decentralist ideas during the Labour Party's early years. Nevertheless, Labour, while continuing to represent the interests of the periphery, had become, by the mid-1920s, a centralizing party, because the periphery wanted policies which, so it was thought, could only be achieved by central government. Thus, while the Liberals had emphasized the dispersal of power, Labour came to emphasize nationalization and centralized economic planning. This meant that Labour in office might well come to disappoint those who still looked upon it as the party which would return power to the peripheries. In the late 1940s, there was, as we have seen, a mild nationalist revolt in Scotland; but its support, although wide, was not deep, because Labour's policies of full employment and social welfare contrasted so markedly with Scotland's experience in the inter-war years of mass unemployment and depression. In the late 1960s, however, the centralization of power under Labour was combined not with economic success, but with economic failure, and the politics of class came once again to be complemented by the politics of locality. Labour was, however, ideologically ill equipped to deal with the revival of nationalism.

It has been argued that 'European socialists inherited the tradition, deriving from Louis XIV but reinforced by the French Revolution and Napoleon, that large centralised states were progressive and small regional autonomies reactionary.'[3] Labour had proved an exception to this generalization in its early years, but it gradually came to conform to it, for it came to see peripheral nationalism as a force splitting the working-class movement. It was reinforced in this view by the trade unions who, even when they supported Home Rule, demanded national wage bargaining and were fearful lest decentralized bargaining allowed employers to lower wages in the less prosperous areas of the country. In a devolution debate in 1975, Neil Kinnock gave powerful expression to this outlook:

If I had to use a label of any kind, I should have to call myself a 'unionist'. However, I am a unionist entirely for reasons of expediency. I believe that the emancipation of the class which I have come to this House to represent, unapologetically, can best be achieved in a single nation and in a single economic unit, by which I mean a unit where we can have a brotherhood of all nations, and have the combined strength of working-class people throughout the whole of the United Kingdom brought to bear against any bully, any Executive, any foreign power, any bureaucratic arrangement, be it in Brussels or in Washington, and any would be coloniser, either an industrial or a political coloniser. I believe that the organised strength of the working-class people has brought the only benefits to have been secured by those whom I came here to represent. Their misfortunes are not the result of being British, Welsh or Scottish.[4]

Here too, as with Joseph Chamberlain and Aneurin Bevan, there is the anti-Home Rule, anti-devolution motif from the Left, based not on Conservative fears concerning the undermining of sovereignty, but on radical or socialist fears about the dissipation of power.

From the 1920s, Labour came to believe that economic efficiency required centralization. The unemployment of the inter-war years could be cured only if the state retained control of the instruments of economic management. To devolve economic functions, therefore, would threaten centralized planning and was inconsistent with Keynesian demand management, an orthodoxy in British politics until the mid-1970s.

But in addition an effective social policy also required centralization. For it would be inequitable if benefit rates varied in different parts of the country as a result of political vicissitudes in a decentralized state. Benefits should depend on need, not on geography. 'The underprivileged child in Eastbourne is as important as the child in Glasgow', declared one Labour MP, Colin Phipps, in the devolution debates.[5] It would be inequitable if the deprived child in Glasgow received a higher level of benefit simply because he or she lived in a part of the country which had a strong parliament able to press for higher standards. The devolution of social policy, however, implied just that—different standards of social welfare in different parts of the country, and it threatened, therefore, the very foundations of the Welfare State.

Thus devolution would undermine the twin pillars of Labour's programme, full employment and the Welfare State. Social democracy, therefore, was only to be achieved through centralized government. During the debates on devolution, Colin Phipps once again gave eloquent voice to this attitude: 'Any Labour Government who gave up central power to decide on matters such as comprehensive education and the moving of money around the United Kingdom would be foolish . . . If comprehensive education is right in Glasgow, it is right in the South of England'.[6] During the inter-war and immediate post-war years, socialists in Scotland and Wales shared this perspective. Like their counterparts in the industrial areas of England, they demanded not autonomy, but a government which took more notice of their grievances. They sought to strengthen the government in London, not to undermine it.

By the time of the general election of 1951, the issues had become overwhelmingly class based—nationalization, the future of the welfare state, and so on. The manifestos of the two major parties said nothing about Scotland or Wales, while the now shrunken Liberal Party offered just one paragraph promising Scottish and Welsh parliaments.

From the late 1960s, however, core-periphery issues were to spring up once more. This was a result of the gradual and steady emergence of a new cleavage between the parties, with the Conservatives gaining strength in the south-eastern core, while Labour increased its strength in Scotland and Wales as well as in the north-west. From the time of the two general elections of 1974, core-periphery issues began to play an important if still subordinate part in general election campaigns. But this, by contrast with the period before the First World War, was occurring *as the result of* a change in voting behaviour. It was not itself a cause of that change. And, in the four general elections of 1979 to 1992, the victorious Conservatives fought on the basis that the core-periphery cleavage was fundamentally irrelevant to British politics. Nevertheless, a major issue in the general elections of the past twenty-five years has been the geographical distribution of political power. The overwhelming Labour victory in the general election of 1997, therefore, would decide the future shape of the polity as well as which party would win power at Westminster. It would decide the issue in favour of the non-English parts of the United Kingdom, whose power would increase at the expense of that of England.[7]

II

In the late 1960s, Labour's ideological inheritance meant that it would respond with considerable caution to the rise of nationalism. For concessions to nationalism would threaten Labour's economic and also its social philosophy. Moreover, devolution might also threaten the position at Westminster of Labour MPs from Scotland and Wales, and also the Secretaries of State for Scotland and Wales. Labour had far more to lose than the Conservatives from a weakening of the Scottish and Welsh presence in London.

It would, however, have been foolish to dismiss the claims of

Scotland or Wales out of hand, for this might further alienate disillusioned Labour supporters, encouraging them to believe that Labour was insensitive to their problems. The Wilson government, therefore, resorted in the late 1960s to that favourite expedient of a harassed administration, a Royal Commission. This would contain any demand from devolutionists in the party to meet the nationalist threat with radical new measures. Indeed, by the time the Royal Commission reported, it might be that the nationalist threat would have disappeared in which case its findings could be quietly pigeonholed. It seemed, therefore, that nothing would be lost by playing for time.

The decision to set up the Commission was taken in the autumn of 1968, but its members were not actually appointed until April of the following year. The terms of reference of the Commission were extremely wide-ranging, and the government's levity was shown by the fact that it did not seek to co-ordinate the work of the Commission with the work of the Redcliffe–Maud Commission on Local Government in England, nor with that of the Wheatley Commission on Local Government in Scotland, both of which reported in 1969. Yet the proposals of these two Commissions, and especially those of Wheatley, were bound to impinge upon devolution.

The Royal Commission on the Constitution was beset by difficulties. Its chairman was Sir Geoffrey, later Lord Crowther, a former editor of *The Economist*, but he died suddenly in April 1972, and was replaced by Lord Kilbrandon, a Scottish judge. Three other members resigned from the Commission during its deliberations. The Commission reported in October 1973, but its Report was not unanimous, and was accompanied by a Memorandum of Dissent signed by Lord Crowther-Hunt, a Labour peer and Fellow of Exeter College, Oxford, and by Professor Alan Peacock, professor of economics at the University of York and an adherent of the free-market school of economics.

The Report and the Memorandum of Dissent differed not so much on specific proposals as on the interpretation of the very wide-ranging terms of reference given to the Commission which required it to 'examine the present functions of the central legislature and government in relation to the several countries, nations, and regions of the United Kingdom', and to consider 'having regard . . . to the interests of the prosperity of Our people under the Crown whether any changes are desirable in those functions or otherwise in present constitutional and economic relationships'. This, as the Memorandum of Dissent pointed out, meant 'that virtually every aspect of the central legislature and government is subject to our scrutiny . . . Indeed, only if we recommend the abolition of the Monarchy would we be in conflict with our terms of reference.'[8] The signatories of the main Report, however, took the view that 'the main intention behind our appointment was that we should investigate the case for transferring or devolving responsibility for the exercise of government functions from Parliament and the central government to new institutions of government in the various countries and regions of the United Kingdom'.[9] The Report, therefore, might be more accurately described as a report on devolution rather than on the Constitution, and the Commissioners who signed it were perhaps guilty of assuming that devolution was the only plausible response to the dissatisfactions with government which they found.

The Memorandum of Dissent, on the other hand, interpreted the terms of reference far more widely, and produced a far-reaching scheme of constitutional reform, involving not just devolution, but also the reform of Parliament and of the political parties. Broadly, it recommended that Britain adopt the German model of federal government; but there were various nuances of that model which escaped the authors of the Memorandum, who devoted insufficient thought to the problems involved in transposing a system of government from one country to another which had different historical traditions and methods of law-making.

It has been said that Royal Commissions are not suitable bodies to evaluate controversial proposals for change, since they are likely to be composed of representatives of different outlooks, unwilling to thrash out their differences in order to reach positive agreement on what should be done. Instead, they are likely to compromise in a report which will not only be 'vague, general, ambiguous,' but which 'perhaps even expresses conflicting views in different corners'.[10] Such a description is certainly applicable to the Report of the Royal

Commission on the Constitution, a diffuse and long-winded document in which it is difficult to disentangle the essential arguments. Indeed, the division between the signatories of the Report and the Memorandum of Dissent is itself misleading, since the signatories, even of the Report, were divided. They were in fact able to agree on very little. All, however, rejected separatism; and also federalism, to which they gave less space than separatism, on the somewhat inadequate grounds of 'very little demand ... and people who know the system well tend to advise against it ... if government in the United Kingdom is to meet the present-day needs of the people it is necessary for the undivided sovereignty of Parliament to be maintained.'[11] The signatories all supported a directly elected assembly for Scotland—although they disagreed on whether it should have legislative, executive, or advisory powers. The Commission was, however, unanimous in recommending that elections to any devolved assemblies that were set up should be by the single transferable-vote method of proportional representation rather than by the first-past-the-post system.

The real division between the Commissioners cut across that between the signatories of the Report and the Memorandum of Dissent. The division was in fact threefold, between nationalists, regionalists, and sceptics.

The nationalists, who comprised six members of the Commission, were not in favour of independence for Scotland and Wales, but believed that they deserved special treatment on the grounds of nationhood. They therefore recommended devolution for Scotland and Wales, but were opposed to directly elected regional assemblies for England. This group included all five of the Commissioners from Scotland, Wales, and Northern Ireland, including the Chairman, Lord Kilbrandon, but only one English Commissioner.[12]

The regionalists comprised Lord Crowther-Hunt and Professor Peacock, the two signatories of the Memorandum of Dissent, and Lord Foot and Sir James Steel, who indicated their views by means of footnotes to the Report. All four believed that the causes of dissatisfaction with government were common to all parts of Britain, even if, in the absence of nationalist parties, they could not be so easily expressed in England as in Scotland and Wales.[13] They insisted also, as a basic constitutional principle, that devolution must be based upon equality of political rights, and that the claims of Scotland and Wales to separate nationality did not, in the words of the Memorandum of Dissent, 'entitle the people in Scotland and Wales to be better governed or to have more participation in the handling of their own affairs than is offered to the people of Yorkshire or Lancashire'. Indeed, for Professor Peacock, the principle of equality of rights was 'not only an important matter of principle, but also a reasonable prediction of what would be politically acceptable in the long run'. For, without equality of rights, 'there would no longer be any reality to the concept of the practical unity of the United Kingdom'.[14] The regionalists favoured, therefore, devolution, not only for Scotland and Wales, but also for the English regions, so giving to Scotland and Wales nothing which was to be denied to England. They believed that all of these assemblies should possess executive, but not legislative powers.

There were, however, two obvious difficulties with this position. The first is that many, if not most, of the English regions did not want devolution, while it seemed that Scotland did. The second was that it did not take sufficient account of the special features of Scottish legislation which resulted from the existence of a separate legal system. The Crowther-Hunt and Peacock scheme would have led to the absurdity that, after devolution, Scottish laws would still have been made by Westminster, continuing to legislate for an alien legal system, while in Edinburgh, Scottish ministers, familiar with the Scottish legal system, would not be able to legislate for it.

Significantly, the four members of this group all had strong regional ties and none of them hailed from London or the south-east. Lord Crowther-Hunt, although an Oxford academic, had been born in the north of England, while Professor Peacock had spent much of his academic life at the University of York. Sir James Steel was an industrialist from the north-east concerned lest Scotland gain advantages through devolution denied to his own area, and Lord Foot was a prominent solicitor living in the south-west. There was only one Commissioner with a personal background in the north of England who did not share the regionalist position.

The third group, the sceptics, consisted of Sir David Renton, Conservative MP for Huntingdon, whose roots lay in East Anglia and the south-east, Nancy Trenaman, a former civil servant and Principal of St Anne's College, Oxford, and Harry Street, professor of law at Manchester University. They were entirely against devolution to Wales, favouring only a Welsh Council with deliberative and advisory powers, but two of them—Mrs Trenaman and Professor Street— thought that there was a case for legislative devolution to Scotland; although Nancy Trenaman was later to retract her support for devolution in Scotland, and to argue that the issue at stake was solely whether or not Scotland wished to remain in the United Kingdom.[15] Sir David Renton favoured a Scottish assembly with primarily deliberative powers.[16]

Professor Street and Nancy Trenaman were the only two members of the Commission to favour different treatment for Scotland and Wales. No member of the Commission proposed the precise mix of legislative devolution to Scotland and executive devolution to Wales which was to form the basis of the devolution proposals both of the 1974–9 Labour government and the 1997 government.

It is not surprising that, faced with so wide a range of differing views whose significance was concealed rather than brought out by the form of the Report, most MPs greeted its publication with bafflement and even mirth. The Report appeared in October 1973, shortly after the Yom Kippur War in the Middle East, and at a time when there seemed to be a serious threat to Britain's oil supplies. It seemed, therefore, quite irrelevant. The Report was debated briefly in the Commons. Both government and opposition promised to consider its findings carefully, but it was then forgotten. Neither the Labour nor the Conservative manifestos for the February 1974 election, fought on the issue of the miners' strike and Edward Heath's question—who governs: the government or the miners?—made any proposals for devolution.

When, however, devolution once more became a serious issue, the Commission's Report came to take on a new significance. MPs and opinion-formers remembered not the careful qualifications, but the main message, which was taken as being in favour of directly elected assemblies in Scotland and Wales. The fact that the Commission's members recommended no less than three different types of assembly was less noticed. The majority of members of the Commission, moreover, had taken the view 'that it is not necessary to have a uniform system of government in all parts of Great Britain'.[17] It seemed, therefore, that the Commission had shown that devolution to Scotland and Wales was possible without major constitutional consequences in England and without breaking up the United Kingdom. The nationalists on the Commission had not considered the implications for England of their proposals, and in particular the problem of the role and number of Scottish and Welsh MPs in Westminster after devolution—the problem of representation which had so baffled Gladstone nearly ninety years earlier. The Commission indeed contented itself with the following anodyne reflection:

We have, for example, noted the thorny problem of the representation of Scotland and Wales at Westminster if they alone were to have legislative assemblies of their own; the difficulties are not, however, in the view of most of us so great as to make legislative devolution to Scotland and Wales impracticable unless it is extended to England.[18]

It was not until the proposals for devolution were debated in Parliament that these implications were noticed. But by then it was too late to do anything about them, as the government had become committed to its policy, and it used the Commission as authority for not coming to terms with the problem. In 1977, Francis Pym, the Conservative spokesman on devolution, asked Michael Foot, Leader of the House:

Will the right honourable Gentleman explain why there is no mention of, let alone any solution to, the single most contentious problem to arise in our debates on the bill; that is, the role and the number of Members of Parliament representing the Scottish and Welsh constituencies? . . . Why is it that, in spite of the Government's recognition of the profound implications upon England of their devolution proposals, they have failed after nearly a year of consideration to put before the House their conclusions in relation to England?

Foot replied:

The right honourable Gentleman said that the most contentious question to arise in our earlier debates was that of representation in this House and the form that that representation should take. I am sure that by this time the right honourable Gentleman must have studied the Kilbrandon Report, which came to the same conclusion as we reached on the major in-and-out question which has sometimes been advocated. We have taken that conclusion into account.[19]

This view—that devolution to Scotland and Wales would not entail repercussions in England—was the legacy of the Royal Commission of the Constitution, and it was to colour thinking on devolution for many years to come.

III

Following the result of the general election of February 1974, devolution returned rapidly on to the political agenda. The result of that election is shown in the Table 6.1.

Harold Wilson took office as Prime Minister of a minority Labour government, seventeen seats short of a majority, in circumstances such that a second general election could not be long delayed. Meanwhile, Wilson desperately needed the support of the nine nationalist MPs as well as the fourteen Liberals who were strongly committed to devolution. The Labour manifesto had contained no reference to devolution, yet in the Queen's Speech it was announced that the government would 'initiate discussions in

Table 6.1 General election results, February 1974

	Seats
Labour	301
Conservatives	297
Liberals	14
United Ulster Unionist Council	11
SNP	7
Plaid Cymru	2
SDLP	1
Others	2

Scotland and Wales on the Report of the Royal Commission on the Constitution, and will bring forward proposals for consideration'. But, in reply to an interjection from Winnie Ewing, leader of the SNP, Wilson, in the debate on the Queen's Speech, went further, declaring that 'Of course we shall publish a White Paper *and a bill*'.[20]

With another election in the offing, time was short. A consultative document, *Devolution within the United Kingdom: Some Alternatives for Discussion*, setting out the various options proposed by the Royal Commission, was published on 3 June 1974. Comments were invited from the public, but the deadline was 30 June. The summer months were spent in ensuring that the Labour Party in Scotland came out in support of devolution, and on 17 September 1974, three weeks before polling day, the government published a White Paper, *Democracy and Devolution: Proposals for Scotland and Wales* (Cmnd. 5732).

This White Paper laid out various decisions of principle with regard to devolution. They were as follows:

1. There would be directly elected assemblies in Scotland and Wales.
2. The Scottish Assembly would have legislative powers, the Welsh Assembly only executive powers.
3. The assemblies would be elected by the first-past-the-post system.
4. The assemblies would be financed by a block grant allocated by Parliament. There would be no devolution of revenue-raising powers.
5. There would be no reduction in the number of Scottish or Welsh MPs at Westminster.
6. The offices of Secretary of State for Scotland and Wales would remain, and the office-holders would continue to sit in the Cabinet.
7. Devolution in England would be postponed for further consideration.

These 'decisions of principle' had been hurriedly formulated. They were determined more by the fear of electoral losses to the SNP than by any particular conviction of the merits of devolution. Senior

ministers were either sceptical or definitely opposed. At a ministerial meeting in July 1974, Roy Jenkins, the Home Secretary, despair-
ing of the levity with which the issue was being treated, burst out,
'You cannot break up the United Kingdom in order to win a few seats
in an election.'[21] After the last draft of the White Paper had been
agreed in Cabinet, Harold Wilson issued his benediction, 'And God
help all who sail in her'. Civil servants were, according to Barbara
Castle, 'deeply alarmed at the whole exercise'.[22]

Nevertheless, through all the long debates on devolution, the government never departed from its hurriedly formulated 'decisions of
principle'. They formed the basis of the Scotland and Wales Acts of
1978. In the 1998 Scotland Act and Government of Wales Act, the
Blair government at last departed from the principles, but in a very
limited way: it abandoned the third principle and marginally altered
the fourth—since a small tax-varying power was proposed for
Scotland, and the fifth—since provision was made for a reduction in
the number of Scottish MPs to be returned to Parliament. With regard
to the seventh principle, on English devolution, although no specific
proposals were presented, provision was made for devolution to the
regions if and when there was a demand for it. On the whole, however, it is the similarities and not the differences which are remarkable when comparing the legislation of 1978 with that of 1998.
Decisions made hastily in the 1970s were thus fundamentally to
determine the shape of devolution in the 1990s.

Following the October 1974 general election, in which Labour
gained an overall majority of three, a further White Paper, *Our
Changing Democracy: Devolution to Scotland and Wales*, (Cmnd.
6348) was published in November 1975, turning the general principles of devolution into detailed proposals. This White Paper put
forward a minimalist conception of devolution circumscribing the
proposed assemblies with seemingly powerful restraints to prevent
them undermining the policy of the British government. In addition, the government declared that it would not devolve major economic and industrial powers or matters related to energy or agriculture.

The government also decided that, although Scotland and Wales
were to be offered quite different types of devolution, it was, in the

words of Michael Foot, Leader of the House of Commons, 'logical that the matter should be dealt with in the same bill'.[23] The Scotland and Wales Bill was given its second reading in the Commons on 13 December 1976, by which time James Callaghan had replaced Harold Wilson as Prime Minister. In introducing the bill, Callaghan declared that it would promote 'a new settlement among the nations that constitute the United Kingdom'.[24]

The bill passed its second reading comfortably by 294 votes to 249, a government majority of forty-five. But there was a considerable amount of cross-voting amongst MPs from the major parties. On the Labour side, ten MPs voted against the bill, while forty-five abstained or were paired. On the Conservative side, five MPs voted for the bill and forty-two abstained or were paired, including the former Prime Minister Edward Heath.

The composition of the majority on second reading was ominous and showed that the bill would not enjoy an easy passage through the Commons. For the government, if it were to succeed, would need to obtain a majority for a guillotine motion during the committee stage of the bill. Otherwise it would be filibustered to death by its opponents. But, on a guillotine motion, the Conservative dissidents, having made the point that they favoured devolution in principle, would rejoin their party, while the Labour dissidents were mainly irreconcilables whom it would be difficult to win back. Equally ominous was the attitude of the Liberals on whose support the government was relying. For David Steel, the Liberal leader, made it clear that his party was voting for the second reading only on the understanding that the bill would be fundamentally amended in committee, so as to provide for proportional representation in elections to the assemblies and the devolution of revenue-raising powers. Concessions to the Liberals, however, and in particular proportional representation, would make devolution even more unpalatable to Labour back-benchers, whose commitment to devolution was already only lukewarm. The government seemed caught in a revolving-door situation. It decided, therefore, to offer a political concession to Labour dissidents, in the form of referendums on devolution.

One of the reasons for introducing the devolution proposals in a bill covering both countries had been to disarm Welsh Labour opponents of devolution, who would not then be able to oppose devolution in Wales without also opposing devolution in Scotland, where it was thought to be essential to overcome the threat of the SNP. The Welsh dissidents, led by Leo Abse, MP for Pontypool, sought to circumvent this tactic by putting down an amendment proposing that the implementation of the bill be made subject to referendums in Scotland and Wales.

The case in principle for referendums was that they would test the government's argument that there was a powerful popular demand for devolution in Scotland and Wales. Moreover, if devolution were to fail, it would be better for it to be rejected by the Scots and Welsh themselves, rather than by the House of Commons. For if an over-whelmingly English-dominated Parliament rejected devolution, the nationalists would undoubtedly be granted an extra grievance to help stoke their campaign for independence. But the referendum had a tactical point also, for it would enable the Welsh dissidents to support the bill in Parliament, but then argue against devolution in the refer-endum campaign in Wales.

It was at first thought that the Abse amendment could not be selected for debate at the committee stage of the bill on the grounds that it was unconstitutional. For, in the words of the nineteenth edition of *Erskine May*, published in 1976: 'Amendments to a bill proposing that . . . the provisions of a bill should be subject to a ref-erendum, have been ruled out of order as proposing changes in leg-islative procedure which would be contrary to constitutional prac-tice.'[25] The chair, however, declared that it would admit the Abse amendment, since it ruled that the European Community referendum had created a precedent. That referendum, however, had not been introduced as an amendment to an already published bill.

By the time the second reading debate of the Scotland and Wales Bill had begun, the Abse amendment had attracted eighty signa-tures. The government therefore decided to accept the amendment in committee; and, on 10 February 1977, it introduced a referendum clause amidst scenes of some procedural chaos. For a number of back-benchers bitterly objected to what they saw as a tactical manoeuvre by which a referendum was being introduced as a new clause on an already published bill in order to overcome resistance to it. By this time, the view was widespread that the government had lost its way. John Mackintosh, MP for Berwick and East Lothian, a fervent supporter of devolution, declared that the Scotland and Wales Bill was so bad that if the referendum result was Yes, the 'appalling difficulties' inherent in the bill 'could . . . endanger the unity of the country'. He continued:

Seldom have I seen the House or the Government in quite such a mess or in such difficulties as we are in over this bill . . . What has happened is that this house does not contain a majority for this bill. As a person who has supported devolution for twenty years, I would rather see this house have the courage of its convictions and reject this bill. It should be thrown out and the electorate should make their views known at a General Election, so that the government can come back with a better bill at a later stage.[26]

At this stage, only three clauses and the new referendum clause had been debated in a bill of 115 clauses. Debate on such important matters as the powers of the assemblies, the reserve powers of the Secretaries of State, and the financial provisions had not yet begun. The government therefore proposed an allocation-of-time motion— a guillotine—without which the bill could not be passed. It was, however, unable to attract its own dissidents back to the fold, nor keep the support of dissident Conservatives, while eleven of the thirteen Liberals now decided to vote against the government. Thus the only supporters of the bill outside the Labour Party were now the nationalists. In David Steel's words: 'The whole exercise started as a ploy to keep the nationalist wolves from the door, but the government find they have ended up in bed with them. The government have as their non-Labour supporters only those people in the House who know that the bill will not work and hope that it will not'.[27]

At 10 pm on 22 February 1977, the guillotine motion was defeated by 312 votes to 283. Twenty-two Labour MPs voted against the motion and twenty-three abstained. The Scotland and Wales Bill was in effect dead. It was the first defeat for any major item of government legislation since 1969, when the previous Labour government had been bogged down in committee on its bill to reform the House of Lords, and had been forced to abandon its plans. But abandonment of House of Lords reform had not endangered the survival of the government, for that government enjoyed a large majority in the Commons. Abandonment of devolution, however, did threaten the survival of the Callaghan government which was in a minority in the House of Commons by February 1977. It depended therefore on the support of the minority parties. With opinion polls seeming to show that the SNP was now the leading party in Scotland and had the support of 36 per cent of the electorate, the nationalist parties withdrew their support from the government in an attempt to precipitate a general election. The government, therefore, needed the support of the Liberals to survive. But part of the price of that support would be a new and improved devolution bill.

IV

The government's response to the defeat of the Scotland and Wales Bill was to propose all-party talks to resurrect devolution. The Conservatives agreed to talks, but wanted them to consider 'proposals for the better government of Scotland and Wales within the United Kingdom, including . . . the Scotland and Wales Bill and federalism'. The government, however, indicated that it was only prepared to discuss its own legislation. That ended any prospect of talks with the Conservatives.

But in March 1977 Labour agreed to a parliamentary pact with the Liberals, the terms of which included negotiations to produce better legislation on devolution. Yet the Liberals failed to secure either of their two main aims—proportional representation and revenue-raising powers for the assemblies. The government offered a free vote on the electoral system, but this, predictably, led to its defeat in the Commons. The government remained adamant against revenue-raising powers, and indeed any concessions on this issue would have antagonized English back-benchers, making it even more difficult to pass the legislation through the Commons. So the Liberals had to accept devolution without proportional representation and devolution without revenue-raising powers, the alternative being no devolution at all.

In fact, the main difference between the first devolution exercise and the second was the division into two of the Scotland and Wales

Bill. Michael Foot, who on 18 January 1977 had declared that there was a logical case for dealing with devolution in one bill, argued in July that 'the House would welcome the separate consideration of what are dissimilar proposals'.[28] This was, ironically, unwelcome to the Liberal Party's Machinery of Government panel which believed it 'a major tactical blunder ... bound to endanger the Welsh bill'; and if the Welsh bill were lost, this 'would completely scupper any chance of pressing the case for a measure of regional government in England. A Scottish assembly would be seen as *sui generis* and not inviting parallels elsewhere.'[29] The separation of Wales from Scotland seemed to put the Liberal idea of federalism even further into the remote distance. The Liberals, all the same, had no option but to support the resurrected Scotland and Wales bills unless they wished to force an election at a time when by-election results and survey evidence indicated that they would lose many of their seats.

The Scotland and Wales bills were given second readings in the Commons on 14 and 15 November 1977 respectively, and then immediately guillotined after second reading. The success of these guillotine motions was due not only to the accretion of Liberal support, but also to the return of Labour dissidents. Of the forty-five who had abstained or voted against the guillotine on the Scotland and Wales Bill, only sixteen were still prepared to withhold their support.

It was not that there had been significant Labour conversions to the cause of devolution. Rather, the consequences of the defeat of the first bill and the realization that the government could be driven from office if devolution were to be defeated for a second time, persuaded doubters to conform. Besides, there was always the possibility, especially in Wales that the bills could be defeated at the referendum stage. Eric Heffer, the left-wing Labour MP for Liverpool, Walton, rationalized his support for the bills in these terms:

I am in favour of sustaining the government. Therefore if I do vote for the government it will not be because I agree with the proposals, but merely to help sustain it. I have not become converted to devolution. I think it is unnecessary and a great mistake, and if the proposals are accepted, could lead to the break-up of the United Kingdom and ultimately of the Labour movement. If the bills do go through I shall offer my services to those in the Labour and trade union movements in Scotland and Wales who oppose the proposals and speak and campaign in the referendums against the legislation. I hope that at that stage the people will vote the proposals down.[30]

In a speech at Bexhill on 25 November, Enoch Powell referred to this tactic as:

without precedent in the long history of Parliament . . . that members openly and publicly declaring themselves opposed to the legislation and bringing forward in debate what seemed to them cogent reasons why it must prove disastrous, voted nevertheless for the legislation and for a guillotine, with the express intention that after a minimum of debate the bill should be submitted to a referendum of the electorate in which they would hope and strive to secure its rejection.

The referendum was becoming, in the words of one constitutional authority, 'the Pontius Pilate of British politics', enabling MPs to vote for a bill while washing their hands of it.[31] There can be little doubt that, in free votes, the Scotland and Wales bills would not have passed the Commons.

Even so the bills were passed with a small number of amendments. Two of them, however, were of fundamental constitutional importance, including one which was to prove fatal to devolution in Scotland.

The first amendment of constitutional importance which became part of the bill had been proposed in the House of Lords by Lord Ferrers, a Conservative front-bench spokesman on devolution. It was rejected in the Commons on the casting vote of the Speaker, but returned again by the Lords, and eventually, when it came back for a second time to the Commons, carried by one vote against the advice of the government. The Ferrers amendment, which became section 66 of the Scotland Act, provided that if any Commons vote on a matter devolved to Scotland were passed through the votes of Scottish MPs, an Order could be laid before the House requiring a second vote to be taken two weeks after the first. The purpose of the amendment was to deal with the question, which had baffled Gladstone, of whether MPs from a devolved area, in this case Scotland, could after devolution continue to vote on domestic affairs for England, Wales, and Northern Ireland, when English, Welsh, and Northern Irish MPs would no longer be able to vote on Scottish domestic affairs. The Ferrers amendment may thus 'be regarded as a specific type of "in-and-out" clause'.[32] For its implication was that pressure would be exerted upon Scottish MPs not to participate in the second vote, held two weeks after the first. Then the House of Commons would become, for part of its life, an assembly for England, Wales, and Northern Ireland only. This was a change with profound consequences for the future of British government, especially when, as in 1964 or October 1974, a government depended upon Scottish MPs for its majority. In such a situation, ministers responsible for matters such as education and health which had been devolved to Scotland, would have found that their majority in the Commons had disappeared. There would then be a bifurcated executive, one majority when all MPs were voting, and another majority, of a different political colour, when the Scottish MPs were absent. It is not easy to imagine how effective Cabinet government could continue under such circumstances.

V

The second amendment of major significance to the Scotland and Wales bills was the so-called 40 per cent rule, requiring 40 per cent of the registered electorate to support devolution for it to be implemented. This was inserted into the bill against the wishes of the government by a Labour MP, George Cunningham, an expatriate Scot, who sat for Islington South and Finsbury. The genesis and constitutional status of this provision are of great interest and indeed it has some claim to be regarded as the most important back-bench initiative in British politics since the war.

Clause 82(2) of the Scotland Bill which provided for a referendum, declared: 'If it appears to the Secretary of State, having regard to the answers given in a referendum and all other circumstances, that this Act should not be brought into effect, he may lay before Parliament the draft of an Order in Council providing for its repeal.'

This clause gave the Secretary of State considerable discretion in interpreting the result of a referendum. Yet the argument for the referendum was that it would test the case that devolution met a powerful demand in Scotland. Would that case be vindicated by a narrow majority on a low turnout—or should a stiffer test be required?

The Cunningham amendment required a repeal order to be laid before Parliament if fewer than 40 per cent of Scottish electors voted Yes. Its rationale was stated by another Labour back-bench opponent of devolution, Bruce Douglas-Mann, who, however, favoured a 33⅓ per cent threshold.

I regard this amendment as absolutely central to the support I give to the bill. I abstained on second reading of the Scotland and Wales bill and I voted against the timetable motion for that bill. By the end of the summer, I had come to the conclusion that if—it is a large 'if'—a substantial majority of the people of Scotland were determined on this measure, it was not for English members to defeat it.33

George Cunningham added the powerful argument that devolution was, in effect, an irreversible constitutional change. In many countries with codified constitutions, there was some special method of validating such constitutional changes. Britain, Cunningham argued, ought not to make such a change without convincing evidence that it was sought by the people of Scotland.

The amendment, to the surprise of the government, was carried, ironically, on Burns night, 25 January 1978, by 166 votes to 151. The Conservative opposition front bench abstained, but a number of Conservatives voted in favour, while four Conservatives, led by Edward Heath, voted against. The amendment could not have been passed without at least the tacit support of Labour back-benchers, who refused to vote it down. Many Labour MPs had become profoundly indifferent to devolution, which seemed to be clogging the parliamentary timetable, while some Labour MPs 'who had been voting with the government, in a bored and listless way . . . were actually convinced or converted by George's speech which was a massive piece of advocacy'.34 The government attempted at the report stage of the Scotland Bill to delete the amendment, but this time the Conservatives turned out in force to support it, and the motion to delete the amendment was defeated by 298 votes to 243. The fact that the Cunningham amendment was resisted by supporters of devolution showed that their confidence in the strength of the pressures for devolution in Scotland was not as strong as it appeared. But those who supported the amendment also displayed less than total confidence in their case—for they seemed to be conceding that devolution in Scotland would not be defeated on a straight referendum vote.

VI

The Cunningham amendment, which became section 85(2) of the Scotland Act, declared: 'If it appears to the Secretary of State that less than 40 per cent of the persons entitled to vote in the referendum have voted "yes" . . . he shall lay before Parliament the draft of an Order in Council for the repeal of this Act.' A similar provision was added to the Wales Act.

The amendment was widely seen as a device to prevent devolution. But it could not of itself achieve that aim. Had support in Scotland been sufficient to overcome the 40 per cent hurdle, devolution would have occurred. Parliament had accepted, perhaps grudgingly, that if Scotland wanted devolution, she could have devolution. What the amendment achieved was to ensure that Scotland did not have devolution in the *absence* of strong support for it. That support could be shown either by a high turnout or by large majority for a Yes vote.

The Cunningham amendment subtly combined two separate requirements: first, that a minimum percentage of the electorate should turn out to vote; and second, that there should be considerable support for devolution if the legislation were to come into force. The lower the turnout, the higher the majority that would be needed. In the unlikely event of an 80 per cent turnout, a majority of one would be sufficient. If the turnout were to be 70 per cent, a 57 per cent Yes vote would be needed, while if the turnout were only 60 per cent, a 67 per cent Yes vote would be required.

The amendment, however, was advisory and not mandatory. It required the Secretary of State only to lay a repeal order before Parliament if the Yes vote was less than 40 per cent. Parliament could, however, vote down the repeal order; and it would undoubtedly have done so if, for example, the outcome had been, say, 39 per cent Yes and 25 per cent No. Thus, as George Cunningham appreciated, the amendment did not 'decide whether devolution takes place or not, but only whether the matter goes back before Parliament in the event of an inconclusive referendum result'.35

A crucial problem with the amendment, however, was that the electoral register was not accurate enough to enable the definitive number of all those who might conceivably be 'entitled to vote' to be calculated. It was not in fact designed for that purpose, but for the very different purpose of *including* all those entitled to vote. The register might very well contain names which ought not to have been included and who would be unlikely to vote. The electoral registration officer for the Lothian Regional Council declared that 'in so far as the register may contain names that ought not to have been included, this is the result of deliberate policy'.36 Moreover, errors and omissions in the register meant that it would be far from being completely accurate. In addition, hospital patients and the seriously disabled or ill, while entitled to postal or proxy votes, might well not claim them, while those who had moved home after the qualifying date for the register in October 1978 would find it difficult to vote in a referendum held in March 1979.

The government, however, took the view that the amendment bound it to discount the votes only of those not legally entitled to vote; it could not also discount the votes of those unable to vote, or very unlikely to vote. The government, therefore, made a discount for four categories. These were, with the numbers in Scotland:

1. Those on the electoral register, but below the age of 18 on 1 March 1979—49,802.
2. Those who had died between October 1978 and March 1979—26,400.
3. Students and student nurses living away from home but in Scotland and registered both at their home and at their college or hospital address—11,800.
4. Prisoners legally disbarred from voting, but registered at their home address—2,000.

The total discount, then, amounted to 90,002. It is, however, possible to suggest that a deduction of a further 535,226 voters could be justified to take account of errors in the electoral register, hospital patients, the seriously disabled, those ill at home, and removals.37

With the figure of 535,226 added to the government's figure of 90,002, the target for a 40 per cent Yes vote would have been reduced from 1,498,845 to 1,284,754 votes, only 31,252 more than the actual Yes vote in the referendum. Supporters of devolution, therefore, could complain that they were being handicapped by over 200,000 votes—the difference between the two targets.

The referendums on devolution were held on 1 March 1979. In Wales, devolution suffered a massive defeat:

Yes	243,048	20.2%
No	956,330	79.8%

The turnout was 58.8%.

In Scotland, however, the result was a narrow victory for devolution, on a turnout of 62.9 per cent:

Yes	1,253,502	51.6% of those voting: 32.85% of the electorate
No	1,230,937	48.5% of those voting: 30.78% of the electorate

This result destroyed the credibility of devolution. It had been pressed in Parliament on the ground that there was a surge of popular demand for it in Scotland, but the outcome of the referendum entirely undermined that claim. Not only was the Yes vote well below 40 per cent, but the closeness in the popular vote and the fact that the Yes majority was concentrated entirely in the central regions of Scotland, the Highlands, and the Western Isles, made it impossible for the government to implement the Scotland Act.

The Callaghan government, in a minority position in the House of Commons and so dependent on nationalist and Liberal support, strove manfully to avoid defeat, hoping that it could persuade the Commons to vote down the repeal order, a tactic which came to be known as the Frankenstein solution. According to ex-Prime Minister Harold Wilson, 'There had been some hope in the Cabinet that, having laid the repeal Order, their own supporters would vote the other way and keep devolution alive. But strenuous inquiries by the Government Whips revealed that some forty or so Government back-benchers would join the Conservatives in killing devolution.'[38]

When it was seen that the government could not implement devolution, the SNP put down a no-confidence motion. The Conservative opposition then put down its own motion of no confidence, and on 28 March, it was carried by one vote, the first time such a vote had been carried since the defeat of Ramsay MacDonald's first Labour government in 1924. The Liberals voted against the government as did the SNP, which declared that Labour MPs preferred Margaret Thatcher in Downing Street to a Scottish assembly in Edinburgh. Plaid Cymru, however, continued to support the government. It was thus devolution and not the industrial and economic troubles of the 'Winter of Discontent' of 1978–9 that was the immediate cause of the collapse of the government, and which was to inaugurate eighteen years of Conservative rule.

The new Conservative government, elected in May 1979, repealed the Scotland and Wales Acts in June 1979. The repeal of the Wales Act was passed by 191 votes to 8, and the repeal of the Scotland Act by 301 votes to 206, but of the Scottish MPs, 43 voted against repeal and 19 in favour with 9 absent. Devolution, which had probably never enjoyed a majority in the House of Commons, was now off the legislative agenda. Scotland had, all the same, voted for it, by however narrow a margin, while the vote on the repeal order showed that her representatives in the Commons remained committed to it.

VII

The devolution referendums had been held at the worst possible time for the Callaghan government, shortly after the 'Winter of Discontent', when Labour's standing in the polls was very low. Nevertheless, the policy had originally been put forward not because it was an essential part of Labour's ideology, but because it was believed that the Scots and the Welsh wanted it. By the time the proposals came to referendum, however, there was considerable disenchantment with institutional reform, the recent reorganization of

local government in Scotland and Wales being seen as a costly failure. Devolution, moreover, might require a further reorganization of
local government, since the two-tier local government structure set
up in the early 1970s would not co-exist easily with the new assemblies. Indeed the new local authorities in Scotland and Wales were to
survive for fewer than two decades, being replaced by unitary authorities in 1996. Paradoxically, the establishment of these new unitary
authorities by the Conservatives removed a major obstacle to devolution.

In 1979, however, it was argued that devolution would introduce
yet another layer of administration on top of two tiers of local government, and this would mean higher costs and more bureaucracy.
The argument that the assemblies would make government more
accountable fell on stony ground, since there was as much suspicion
of politicians as of officials. Many indeed feared that a Scottish
assembly would replicate the weaknesses of local government in
Scotland in that it would be dominated by machine politicians of the
Labour Party which would, under the first-past-the-post system, normally be in control of it.

In Wales, similar anxieties were expressed with regard to the
Labour machine in south Wales. The chairman of the Clwyd 'No'
Campaign argued in 1979 that: 'People in South Wales are very
charming, but as a crowd they are loud and coarse. We do not want
to be governed by Cardiff. The Assembly will be permanently dominated by Labour. It will be a dictatorship.'[39] Other opponents of
devolution used the contrary argument, that the Assembly would be
dominated by a Welsh-speaking clique from the north and the west.
The Welsh legislation, moreover, was criticized even by those who
had helped draw it up as muddled and confused. Lord Crowther-
Hunt, who had been a minister of state working on devolution, told
a Labour Party rally two days before the referendum that the Wales
Act was 'a dog's breakfast', and so badly drafted that 'it must
amount to sabotage by the drafters in London', although he still
invited the Welsh to vote for it.[40] It is not surprising, perhaps, that his
invitation was declined.

The Labour Party was divided on devolution and appeared to lack
enthusiasm for it. In Wales, indeed, the majority of constituency

Labour parties were opposed, while in Scotland, the most eloquent spokesman on the Labour side was an opponent of devolution, Tam Dalyell. His 'Labour Vote No' campaign may well have led some to believe that there was official Labour support for a No vote. The only real enthusiasts for devolution were the nationalists, but this served to deter Yes voters, since it fuelled fears that the assemblies would prove a stepping-stone to separation.

The Conservatives, in their eagerness to defeat the devolution proposals of the Callaghan government, had argued that the referendum in Scotland was a specific one, on the particular proposals put forward by the government, rather than a vote on the principle of devolution. Lord Home, the former Prime Minister, argued that the Scotland Act was flawed, but could be replaced by something more workable, and that, therefore, a No vote need not imply any disloyalty to the principle of devolution. 'A "No" vote does not mean the devolution question will be buried', declared Margaret Thatcher the day before the referendum, a promise which may have persuaded Scottish Conservatives not to vote Yes.[41] Once the Scotland Act was repealed, however, devolution was indeed buried, and the administrations of Margaret Thatcher and John Major, which governed Britain between 1979 and 1997, ensured that it was not resurrected. The defeat of devolution in 1979 was thus to prove a turning-point not only in Scottish, but also in British history. For, instead of beginning the task of dispersing power, Britain took a different path, moving, under the Conservatives, towards a more uniform and inflexible system of government, and one which accentuated the geographical and social conflicts between different parts of the country.

Throughout the period of opposition, however, Labour continued to support devolution, its commitment growing stronger as the years passed. Thus, while its belief in devolution had been hesitant in the 1970s, by 1997 it had become one of the main items on Labour's programme. Paradoxically, the defeat of devolution, far from destroying what had seemed a merely tenuous commitment, served instead to reinvigorate it. The explanation is not difficult to find. Devolution had been pressed by its advocates as a means by which the distinctive voice of Scotland and Wales could be expressed through government. But it seemed unnecessary during the 1974–9 period because the voices of Scotland and Wales were already being heard by a government so dependent on Scotland and Wales for its majority. When, however, in 1979, 1983, 1987, and 1992, England voted for the Conservatives, Scotland and Wales remained loyal to Labour (Tables 6.2, 6.3).

There had never been so prolonged a period of geographically one-sided government in Britain in the twentieth century. After 1987, the government was supported by fewer than one-seventh of Scottish MPs and fewer than a quarter of Welsh MPs. The Conservatives gained a large overall majority with the votes of less than a quarter of the Scots, and around three-tenths of the Welsh. Thus Scotland and Wales, instead of following England by swinging to the Right, were developing a specifically Scottish and Welsh consciousness of their own. This consciousness would prove incompatible with hitherto-accepted constitutional arrangements for governing Scotland and Wales.

Table 6.2 Scottish results in the elections of 1979, 1983, 1987, and 1992

		Seats	% of votes
1979	Conservatives	22	31.4
	Labour	44	41.6
	Liberals	3	9.0
	SNP	2	17.3
1983	Conservatives	21	28.4
	Labour	41	35.1
	Alliance	8	24.5
	SNP	2	11.8
1987	Conservatives	10	24.0
	Labour	50	42.4
	Alliance	9	19.2
	SNP	3	14.0
1992	Conservatives	11	25.7
	Labour	49	39.0
	Liberal Democrats	9	13.1
	SNP	3	21.5

Table 6.3 Welsh results in the elections of 1979, 1983, 1987, and 1992

		Seats	% of votes
1979	Conservatives	11	32.7
	Labour	22	48.6
	Liberals	1	12.8
	Plaid Cymru	2	8.1
1983	Conservatives	14	31.0
	Labour	20	37.5
	Alliance	2	23.2
	Plaid Cymru	2	7.8
1987	Conservatives	8	29.6
	Labour	24	45.1
	Alliance	3	17.9
	Plaid Cymru	3	7.3
1992	Conservatives	6	28.6
	Labour	27	49.5
	Liberal Democrats	1	12.4
	Plaid Cymru	4	8.8

The situation might conceivably have proved politically manage-
able had the Conservatives displayed the sensitivity to Scottish opinion of the Churchill or Macmillan governments of the 1950s, but it
was made more intractable by the attitudes of Margaret Thatcher, an
instinctive assimilationist, who saw little need to maintain the conventions of the union state. The Union with Scotland, she was to
write in her memoirs, was 'inevitably dominated by England by reason of its greater population. The Scots, being an historic nation with
a proud past, will inevitably resent some expressions of this fact from
time to time.' Margaret Thatcher saw Scotland as an outpost of the
dependency culture which she was determined to extirpate, while the
'very structure' of the Scottish Office 'added a layer of bureaucracy,
standing in the way of the reforms which were paying such dividends
in England'.[42] This outlook heralded the end of the 'dual polity'
which had dominated territorial relations since at least the 1920s, 'a
state of affairs in which national and local politics were largely
divorced from each other', and which had allowed Scotland and

Wales a significant degree of autonomy whatever the political colour of the government in London.[43]

The Thatcher government's policies of competitive individualism were resented both in Scotland and Wales, where they were seen as undermining traditional values of community solidarity; and policies such as privatization and opting out from local authority control had little resonance there. But resented above all was the community charge, the poll tax, introduced into Scotland in 1989, a year before it was introduced in England and Wales. The Scottish Office, significantly, seems to have been 'excluded from all forums engaged with the detailed work of the review until it became de facto policy'.[44] The new tax gave a considerable fillip to the SNP which urged non-payment, and indeed levels of non-payment in Scotland were higher than in any other part of the country. But, more generally, the fiasco of the poll tax seemed to prove to the Scots and Welsh that, in rejecting devolution, they had surrendered themselves to a government which cared little for their interests. Only devolution, so it seemed, could protect Scotland and Wales against future outbursts of Thatcherism.

In Wales, Labour did not renew its proposals for devolution until the late 1980s. When it did so, it kept devolution as an internal party issue, and did not seek to involve other parties in its work. In Scotland, however, the process was more complex. On the first anniversary of the devolution referendum, 1 March 1980, an all-party Campaign for a Scottish Assembly was established to renew the battle. It seemed to be making little headway, however, until, in 1988, it appointed a Constitutional Steering Committee which issued a Claim of Right for Scotland and called for the establishment of a Scottish Constitutional Convention which could draw up proposals for the reform of Scotland's government. A Convention was duly established in 1989, and declared that sovereignty in Scotland lay with the Scottish people and not with Westminster. Labour and the Liberal Democrats agreed to participate in the Convention, but the Conservatives refused, as did the SNP, which declared that it could support only a directly elected convention prepared to draw up a constitution for an independent Scotland.

The aim of the Convention was to translate what seemed like

widespread support for devolution into concrete proposals for legislation, for there seemed no other constitutional way by which Scots could have their demands recognized. Devolution was not a high priority at Westminster, even for Labour, and there were fears that a Labour government might not be willing to prepare new devolution legislation only to see it once again destroyed by hostile English back-bench MPs, as had occurred in 1977 with the Scotland and Wales Bill. Since Scottish issues were subsidiary to United Kingdom matters, there seemed no way in which the Scots could make known their support for devolution other than by voting for the SNP, and that would be regarded as a vote for separation. There was, therefore, a gap in the Scottish representative system. The Convention was intended to fill that gap. Its role was to draw up a specific scheme which could then be adopted by an incoming government sympathetic to devolution; and also to promote its chosen scheme.

Although not elected, the Convention comprised a large slice of Scottish opinion, not only Labour and Liberal Democrat MPs, but also trade unions, representatives of local government, the churches, and other representative bodies. The Convention produced two reports, the first, in 1990, *Towards Scotland's Parliament*, and the second, in 1995, entitled *Scotland's Parliament, Scotland's Right*. These reports laid out a scheme for devolution which was to form the basis of the Scotland Act in 1998. The most significant innovation was the agreement between Labour and the Liberal Democrats that the Scottish Parliament should be elected by the additional-member system of proportional representation. Labour appreciated that if it wanted to win support for devolution outside the party, that was the price which had to be paid. The Liberal Democrats, in turn, appreciated that Labour would never accept their favourite nostrum, the single transferable vote, and were prepared to compromise on another system. The outcome showed what could be achieved by co-operation between parties and perhaps prefigured the more general consultative arrangements on constitutional matters developed by the Blair government after 1997.[45]

The Convention did not, however, devote sufficient consideration to many of the other problems which had bedevilled devolution in the 1970s, in particular the relationship between a Scottish

Parliament and local government, the West Lothian Question, and, more generally, the future relationship between Edinburgh and London after devolution. The Convention would have liked to propose the devolution of revenue-raising powers to the Scottish Parliament, but was dissuaded from doing so by the Labour leadership, frightened of any apparent commitment to higher taxes. Moreover, just because the Convention's reports seemed, and no doubt were, supported by the bulk of Scottish opinion, it became difficult in 1997 for either the Blair government or Members of Parliament to suggest alternative proposals. Thus, although the Convention was to succeed in pre-empting English parliamentary hostility to devolution, it did so at the cost of also pre-empting serious scrutiny of the devolution legislation. There were no parallel debates on devolution in England.

The Convention's first report was produced in 1990 during the period of Neil Kinnock's leadership of the Labour Party. Kinnock had, as we have seen, been an opponent of devolution in the 1970s, but now agreed to support it. John Smith, who replaced Kinnock in 1992, had become a far more enthusiastic devolutionist, but Tony Blair, who succeeded Smith after the latter's untimely death in 1994, was more aware of the difficulties involved in getting so complex and controversial a constitutional measure through Parliament. In June 1996, therefore, he insisted that there be referendums on devolution in Scotland and Wales and that these be held before legislation was introduced into Parliament, rather than afterwards, as in 1979; and he also insisted that the Scots be asked not one question, but two: not simply whether they wanted a parliament but also whether that parliament should have income tax-varying powers. Blair was much criticized in Scotland and Wales for insisting on referendums, oddly perhaps, since the signatories of the Claim of Right, having celebrated the sovereignty of the Scottish people, now seemed to want to prevent the Scots from actually exercising it. Blair's tactic, however, was to succeed in disarming English back-bench parliamentary criticism of devolution; and it can be seen, in retrospect, that it was one of the factors ensuring that devolution would at last actually come to fruition.

Labour won a landslide victory in the general election of 1 May 1997 and, following the passage of a Referendum (Scotland and

Wales) Act, referendums were duly held. The Scottish referendum was held on 11 September 1997, two questions being asked on separate ballot papers. There was a 60.2 per cent turnout, as compared with a turnout of 62.9 per cent in 1979.The result in Scotland was a decisive victory for devolution and for tax-varying powers.

I agree that there should be a Scottish Parliament

   1,775,045   74.3%

I do not agree that there should be a Scottish Parliament

   614,000   25.7%

I agree that a Scottish Parliament should have tax-varying powers

   1,512,889   63.5%

I do not agree that a Scottish Parliament should have tax-varying powers

   870,263   36.0%

The proportion of the electorate voting Yes in 1997 was 44.7 per cent for a Scottish Parliament and 38.1 per cent for tax-varying powers. Thus, if a 40 per cent rule had been in operation, the Scottish Parliament would have been approved but without tax-varying powers.

The referendum in Wales was held on 18 September 1997, a week after the Scottish referendum, so that Welsh opinion might be influenced by a favourable result in Scotland. That might indeed have swayed the outcome, since the result was a very narrow victory for devolution by less than 7,000 votes out of over a million cast, on a turnout of just over 50 per cent.

I agree that there should be a Welsh Assembly

   559,419   50.1%

I do not agree that there should be a Welsh Assembly

   552,698   49.9%

The referendum was won through an alliance between Welsh-speaking Wales, the heartland of the north-west, and the industrial Wales of the valleys, the former coalfield areas. It seemed, by comparison with the 1979 result, to show that Welsh identity was becoming less divisive and that a sense of Welshness was growing irrespective of language, a sense of Welshness which may be more deep-seated than social analysts have noticed. Remarkably, the distribution of voting within Wales almost exactly replicated the political geography of the reign of Edward I over seven centuries earlier. The areas which he had succeeded in conquering—English Wales—voted No; while the rest of Wales voted Yes.[46] Thus, although narrow, the majority in Wales did reflect a real consciousness of Welshness, a consciousness which, no doubt, the Welsh National Assembly will strengthen and intensify.

Legislating for Devolution
The Constitutional Problems

The British Constitution presumes more boldly than any other the good faith of those who work it.

(W. E. Gladstone)

The basic structure

The Scotland Bill and the Government of Wales Bill were introduced into Parliament in 1997. They were the tenth major measures of devolution to have been introduced by governments since 1886. Eight of the previous ten had failed. The 1886 and 1893 Government of Ireland Bills never reached the statute-book. The 1912 bill reached the statute-book in 1914, but was suspended on the outbreak of the war. The 1920 bill also reached the statute-book but was implemented only in Northern Ireland. Devolution as provided by the Northern Ireland Constitution Act of 1973 lasted for just five months in 1974; and, under the Northern Ireland Act of 1982, for just four years. The 1976 Scotland and Wales Bill had been withdrawn after the government had failed to secure its guillotine motion. The Scotland and Wales Acts of 1978 had been repealed in 1979 after failing to win sufficient support in referendums. In 1998, by contrast, with devolution to Scotland and Wales having been endorsed in referendums *before* being introduced into Parliament, the legislation reached the statute-book without difficulty.

All previous devolution measures, except for the Government of Ireland Act of 1920, which replaced the Act of 1914, and the Acts of 1973 and 1982, were introduced in hung parliaments where the government of the day was dependent upon nationalist votes, either the Irish nationalists, as in 1886, 1893, and 1912, or the Scottish nationalists, as in 1976 and 1978. There are good reasons for believing that devolution legislation would not have been introduced had these governments not been so dependent. The 1997 Labour government, by contrast, was quite independent of nationalist votes. Far from there being a hung parliament, the government had a majority of 177 seats, the largest majority that Westminster has seen since 1935. The government, therefore, was free to introduce devolution and to shape the legislation as it thought best, rather than having to respond to outside pressures. Precisely because it enjoyed so large a majority, however, and because devolution had already been endorsed in the referendums, the legislation was little scrutinized in the House of Commons. Indeed, many of the key clauses were not discussed in committee.

The legislation received much closer scrutiny in the House of Lords, where all of the major clauses were discussed. But the Lords too were bound by the outcome of the referendum and also by the Salisbury Convention, which dictated that they could not reject or even amend in principle a measure which had been in the government's election manifesto. Thus, while the debates in the Lords highlighted many of the difficulties of devolution, they did not result in the legislation being altered to any significant degree. For all practical purposes, the Scotland and Government of Wales bills reached the statute-book in the same shape and form as when they were introduced into the Commons.

*

The Scotland Act provides in section 1 for the establishment of a Scottish Parliament. Section 28 provides that this parliament may make laws within its area of competence; subsection 7 declares that 'This section does not affect the power of the Parliament of the United Kingdom to make laws for Scotland'. This subsection succinctly lays out the central constitutional principle underlying devolution. It rejects both separatism, under which the Parliament of the United Kingdom would no longer have power to legislate for Scotland at all; and federalism under which the Parliament of the United Kingdom would have power to legislate for Scotland only in certain defined areas, other areas becoming the entire responsibility of the Scottish Parliament. The Act thus, in theory at least, preserves parliamentary supremacy, and Westminster can, if it wishes, continue to legislate on matters devolved to Scotland.

Devolution is not intended to affect the unity of the state or the form of government in the rest of the United Kingdom. The provisions of the Scotland Act, therefore, contain safeguards to ensure that the Scottish Parliament does not abuse its powers. The first is the supremacy of Westminster, reaffirmed in section 28 (7). The second consists of provisions limiting the legislative powers of the Scottish Parliament to domestic matters, and preventing it, in virtue of section 35 (1) (b), from legislating on such domestic matters so as to influence the administration of matters reserved to Westminster in a manner harmful to the public interest. The third consists of the limitation of the revenue-raising powers of the parliament to a variation of not more than 3 per cent in the basic rate of income tax from that determined for the rest of the United Kingdom by Westminster.

The Scotland Act provides for a Scottish Parliament directly elected by the additional-member system of proportional representation, similar to that used in Germany, and consisting of a total of 129 members. Seventy-three of these members will be elected from the seventy-two single-member parliamentary constituencies, with Orkney and Shetland being split to make two constituencies. The remaining fifty-six members will be elected proportionally, seven each in the eight regional constituencies used until 1999 for elections to the European Parliament.

There is to be a separate Scottish Executive led by a First Minister, and comprising other ministers appointed by the First Minister, together with two law officers, a Lord Advocate and a Solicitor-General for Scotland. The First Minister is to be appointed by the Queen following election by the Scottish Parliament. The Parliament will have a fixed term of four years. It can be dissolved, under the provisions of section 3, and an extraordinary general election held, only if a two-thirds majority of the Parliament as a whole votes for it, or if the Parliament is unable to nominate a First Minister within a period of 28 days. If it is dissolved, however, the general election that would have occurred at the end of the four-year period still takes place, unless such a poll is held within six months of a previously scheduled election. Thus, for example, if the first Scottish Parliament, elected in May 1999, were to be dissolved in May 2001, the general election in May 2003 would still be held. If, however, the first Scottish Parliament were to be dissolved in December 2002, the election of May 2003 would no longer be held, and the next election would be in December 2006.

By contrast with the abortive Scotland Act of 1978, the Scotland Act of 1998 lists, in schedule 5, the reserved, not the devolved, functions. Reserved functions are those which must be carried out at United Kingdom level, such as foreign affairs and defence, and those where significant anomalies are unacceptable for other reasons. The main reserved functions are:

(*a*) The Constitution, including the Crown, the succession to the Crown, the Parliament of the United Kingdom, and the Union of Scotland and England.

(*b*) Foreign affairs and the European Union.

(*c*) The civil service.

(*d*) Defence.

(*e*) Fiscal, economic, and monetary policy—although local taxes funding local authority expenditure, for example the council tax and non-domestic rates, are not reserved.

(*f*) The currency, financial services, and financial markets.

(*g*) Elections and the franchise for local government elections. Otherwise, however, local government elections are not reserved.

(*h*) Immigration and nationality.

(*i*) National security.

(*j*) Emergency powers.

(*k*) Extradition.

(*l*) Competition and import and export control.

(*m*) Telecommunications and the Post Office.

(*n*) The bulk of energy policy.

(*o*) Certain essentials of transport policy.

(*p*) The bulk of social security policy.

(*q*) Employment, industrial relations, and health and safety.

(*r*) Abortion.

(*s*) Broadcasting.

Anything not specifically reserved lies within the legislative competence of the Scottish Parliament, which will have power to legislate over a broad range of Scottish domestic affairs, and in particular, over home affairs, the legal system, local government, housing, agriculture, health, social, educational, and environmental policy.

The bulk of the funding for the Parliament will be derived from a block grant paid annually by the Secretary of State, but the Scottish Parliament will, as noted above, have the power to vary the basic rate of income tax in Scotland by up to 3 per cent of the rate in the rest of the United Kingdom. Moreover, since the Parliament will be responsible for the financing of local authorities, it will have the power to secure revenue for itself by withholding revenue-support grant from local authorities. The Parliament could moreover, if it so wished, abolish the council tax in Scotland, replacing it with another form of local taxation, and it could, if it so wished, return the power to fix the non-domestic rate, the uniform business rate, to local authorities. It could also abolish the capping of local authorities.

The Scottish Parliament and the Scottish Executive will, by contrast with the 1978 Act, enjoy a direct relationship with the Crown. Legislation passed by the Scottish Parliament will not need to go to the Secretary of State for approval, apart from the special circumstances associated with section 35 of the Act and mentioned below. Otherwise, the Secretary of State, again by contrast with the 1978 Act, is to have no governor-general functions and will not act as an intermediary between the Scottish Parliament and the Queen.

The Scotland Act contains provisions to ensure that the Scottish Parliament does not overstep its powers. First, the Presiding Officer of the Parliament must assure himself that any proposed legislation lies within its powers. This provision could easily prove controversial. It would be perfectly possible for the Presiding Officer to take the view that a proposed bill is *ultra vires*, while the majority in the Parliament takes a different view. It is not clear what would happen in the case of such a disagreement. The courts, clearly, could not give a verdict on whether proposed legislation was *ultra vires* or not, until it had actually been passed by the Parliament. Possibly, however, the courts might be asked for an advisory opinion in such a situation. Nevertheless, this provision could easily lead to conflict between the Presiding Officer and the Scottish Executive and Parliament.

Second, the Act provides that the Presiding Officer shall submit bills for the royal assent only after four weeks have elapsed following the passage of a bill. During this four-week period, the Scottish law officers may refer a bill or part of a bill to the Judicial

Committee of the Privy Council for a decision as to whether it lies within the legislative competence of the Scottish Parliament. The purpose of this provision is to ensure that the Queen is not offered conflicting advice, the Presiding Officer of the Scottish Parliament advising her to give the royal assent, but the British government advising her to reject it because it believes that it lies outwith the powers of the Scottish Parliament. The Act prevents such a situation arising since the Advocate General, a new Scottish law officer, would have secured a judicial verdict before the bill is submitted to the Queen. Nevertheless, this provision puts the courts and the Judicial Committee of the Privy Council in the position of deciding a question of *vires* in the abstract rather than in the context of a concrete case, without which there may be an incomplete understanding of the facts. Any opinion is bound to be in large part hypothetical, since it would be given before the Act had come into operation and without any real evidence as to the effect of the legislation.

The third provision ensuring that the Scottish Parliament does not overstep its powers is that of post-assent judicial review. An Act of the Scottish Parliament will be in the same position as the decisions of any other statutory body in that its legislation can be reviewed by the courts. Anyone with a *locus standi* may therefore challenge Scottish legislation in the ordinary courts, although the ultimate authority on the interpretation of the Act is to be the Judicial Committee of the Privy Council. There is thus both pre-assent and post-assent review. But to determine the validity, as opposed to the construction, of primary legislation within the United Kingdom will be a novel function for a British court—always excepting the Northern Ireland experience—and it will mean that an Act of the Scottish Parliament will be law only in so far as a court has ruled that it is valid, or if it has not yet been challenged. However, the Scottish Office Minister for Home Affairs and Devolution, Henry McLeish, has given as his opinion that 'the overwhelming majority of issues will be resolved in very early stages'.[1]

The Judicial Committee of the Privy Council will come to assume the function of a constitutional court for devolution issues. It is in fact rare for common-law countries to have a separate constitutional court since, under such jurisdictions, constitutional issues can arise from all kinds of litigation, often as side issues. These matters, therefore, are generally dealt with, in common-law countries, by the ordinary courts. The Judicial Committee is the final court of appeal for British dependent territories and for those independent Commonwealth countries which chose to retain this particular avenue of appeal on attaining independence. It does not deal with domestic matters other than appeals from the Channel Islands and the Isle of Man, some church matters and appeals, and appeals from the disciplinary and health committees of the medical and allied professions. It was, however, chosen as the final court of appeal rather than the House of Lords, which does not hear appeals from Scottish courts in criminal cases. For the House of Lords is a constituent part of the United Kingdom legislature, presided over by a member of the British government, the Lord Chancellor. It would not perhaps be the body best placed to adjudicate questions which may raise the issue of the relative competence of Westminster *vis-à-vis* the Scottish Parliament; for the British government might itself be a possible party to such a dispute. Moreover, the Appellate Committee of the House of Lords has a majority of English judges, while the composition of the Judicial Committee is more flexible, being open to any judge who is a member of the Privy Council and holds or has held high judicial office within the Commonwealth. It will thus be much easier to ensure that there are sufficient Scottish judges on the Judicial Committee than it is in the House of Lords. The Minister for Home Affairs and Devolution, Henry McLeish, has indicated that the government 'expect cases to be considered by five of the 12 Lords of Appeal in Ordinary and we would expect the two Scottish Lords of Appeal to be members of the Judicial Committee to consider devolution *vires* cases.'[2] It is to be hoped, however, that there are not too many occasions on which the two Scottish judges declare an Act of the Scottish Parliament *intra vires*, while the three non-Scottish judges declare it to be *ultra vires*. For, even though the judges will have acted in a perfectly professional manner, such a division would provide powerful ammunition for those in Scotland who sought to create conflict between Westminster and Edinburgh. The precise membership for any hearing of the Judicial Committee will in practice be determined by the senior Law Lord. It is perhaps surprising that there is no provision regulating the constitution of the Committee for hearings that may arise from the terms of the Scotland Act. For a constitutional court, which is what the Judicial Committee will in effect become, needs a stable membership, with the same set of judges considering the various cases which raise issues of *vires*, not a different membership for different cases. Since, moreover, many people are not particularly aware of the role of the Judicial Committee, it may take some time for its decisions to yield the same legitimacy as those of constitutional courts in federal countries.

Fourth, and finally, under section 35, a Secretary of State may issue an Order prohibiting the Presiding Officer of the Scottish Parliament from submitting a bill for royal assent if he has reasonable grounds for believing that it would be incompatible with Britain's international obligations, including defence and security obligations, the nature and extent of these obligations being matters for the government to determine; or if, although the bill lies within the legislative competence of the Scottish Parliament, it nevertheless would have an adverse effect on some reserved matter. A Secretary of State's use of this power will in general be subject to the negative-resolution procedure of both Houses of Parliament, and will no doubt, like other delegated legislation, be reviewable by the courts. The purpose of this provision is to ensure that the Scottish Parliament does not use its powers in an unacceptable manner. For example, a Scottish Parliament dominated by unilateralists might decide to build a housing estate near a military airfield, so rendering the airfield inoperable. That would no doubt be thought by a Secretary of State for Scotland to be unacceptable as affecting the operation of a reserved matter, namely defence.

This provision also ensures that the Queen is not offered conflicting advice. The Secretary of State, if he believes that the Queen ought not to sign a bill of the Scottish Parliament, when he has specific grounds for that belief in terms of section 35, may prohibit the Presiding Officer of that parliament from submitting the bill in question to the Queen. Thus this provision and the provision for pre-assent review ensure that the Queen will not be put in the position of appearing to have to arbitrate between the British government and the Scottish Executive. All disputes ought to have been resolved by the time a Scottish bill is passed to the Queen for the royal assent.

Even so, a situation in which a bill has been allowed to go through all of its stages in the Scottish Parliament and is then declared to be unacceptable by the Secretary of State under section 35, is likely to arouse considerable animosity in Edinburgh. The hope must be, therefore, that intermediate political and administrative mechanisms such as the Joint Ministerial Committee (see p. 284) will resolve problems amicably before section 35 has to be brought into play.

*

The Government of Wales Act differs fundamentally from the Scotland Act in that it proposes a novel form of devolution, one hitherto untried in the United Kingdom. It confers executive but not primary legislative functions on a National Assembly for Wales—not a parliament as with Scotland. The assembly will have the power, transferred from ministers, primarily the Secretary of State for Wales, to make subordinate legislation in areas within its competence. The Government of Wales Act, by contrast with the Scotland Act, specifies, in schedule 2, fields in which the Secretary of State must consider whether functions are to be transferred. These include:

(*a*) Agriculture and fisheries.
(*b*) Culture.
(*c*) Economic development.
(*d*) Education and training.
(*e*) The environment.
(*f*) Health.
(*g*) Highways.
(*h*) Housing.
(*i*) Industry.
(*j*) Local government.
(*k*) Social services.
(*l*) Sport.
(*m*) Tourism.
(*n*) Town and country planning.
(*o*) Transport.

(*p*) Water.
(*q*) The Welsh language.

The courts have the power to determine whether the Assembly has acted within its powers, with the final court of appeal being the Judicial Committee of the Privy Council.

The National Assembly also has the power under section 27 to transfer to itself the functions of the health authorities in Wales, and then, if it so wishes, to abolish them. It may do the same, under section 28, with various Welsh nominated bodies specified in schedule 4. This comes near to giving the National Assembly legislative competence. Under section 113 (1) of the Act, the Assembly is required to prepare a scheme setting out how it proposes 'to sustain and promote local government in Wales'; and it is required also to establish a Partnership Council for Wales, with advisory powers, consisting of members of the Assembly and members of Welsh local authorities.

The Act provides for a National Assembly of sixty members, to be directly elected by the same system of proportional representation as the Scottish Parliament. Forty of the members are to be elected in the single-member parliamentary constituencies of Wales by first past the post, and the remaining twenty will be elected proportionally, four each from the five regional European parliamentary constituencies in Wales.

The Act requires the Assembly to elect a First Secretary and also to establish committees which must reflect the party balance in the Assembly. Section 56 of the Act requires the Assembly to establish an executive committee comprising the First Secretary and Assembly Secretaries. The model seems at first sight to be broadly of the local government committee type, with the executive committee corresponding to the Leader's Committee of a local authority, single party in nature, and the locus of political direction. This system was valued as a protection for minority parties. However, in the Commons, these minority parties urged a Cabinet system. Moreover, in its programme for the regeneration of local government, the government proposed that local authorities be allowed and indeed encouraged to adopt alternative models of internal management to remedy weaknesses in the traditional committee model which has dominated local government since the 1835 Municipal Corporations Act.3 It would have been absurd if the government had declared that the committee model was unsuitable for local government, but required for the Welsh National Assembly. Therefore, the then Secretary of State for Wales, Ron Davies, tabled new clauses to the Government of Wales bill, giving the First Secretary rather than the subject committees the power to appoint Assembly Secretaries, and allowing the Assembly to delegate its functions. He indicated that he would not in fact approve any standing orders for the Assembly which did not allow for delegation of functions to the executive committee, and that a two-thirds vote would then be needed to alter the standing orders. Thus the Assembly will in practice operate a Cabinet-type system, with the executive committee being appointed by the First Secretary.

The Assembly will, by contrast with Westminster, but analogously to many local authorities, sit for a fixed four-year term, and, by contrast with Scotland, there is no possibility of early dissolution; moreover, and again by contrast with Scotland, the Assembly will have no revenue-raising powers.

Scotland and Wales are to retain their existing representation at Westminster. But section 86 of the Scotland Act amends the rule in the Parliamentary Constituencies Act of 1986 which provides that Scotland is to have no fewer than seventy-one parliamentary constituencies. It also provides for the Boundary Commission for Scotland, in the next full review of Scottish parliamentary constituencies, which will in fact not occur before 2003, to use an electoral quota for Scotland which is the same as the electoral quota for England, rather than, as now, an electoral quota for Scotland which is lower than the quota for England. Thus provision is made for Scottish over-representation to be ended, and for her to be represented in proportion to population on the same basis as England. That would mean, in practice, that instead of returning seventy-two members to Westminster, as at present, Scotland would return around fifty-nine MPs. There is no similar provision for Wales, it being thought, no doubt, that there is no case for a reduction because responsibility for primary legislation for Wales remains with Westminster.

There is to be no separate Scottish or Welsh civil service and the offices of Secretary of State for Scotland and for Wales are to remain. Their role, however, will be very different from what they have been in the past.

The Scottish Secretary will lose all of his departmental functions. He will survive solely as the link-man between the Scottish Parliament and the Cabinet. In the words of paragraph 4.12 of the White Paper, *Scotland's Parliament* (Cm. 3658, 1997):

Once the Scottish Parliament is in being, and the Scottish Executive established, the responsibilities of the Secretary of State for Scotland will change. The focus will be on promoting communication between the Scottish Parliament and Executive and between the UK Parliament and Government on matters of mutual interest; and on representing Scottish interests in reserved areas.

These, however, are the sorts of functions which between 1921 and 1972 were performed for Northern Ireland not by its own Secretary of State, but by the Home Secretary. For, so the Royal Commission on the Constitution believed, under such circumstances, 'there would in the ordinary course be little for a Secretary of State to do when devolution was working smoothly.' The Commission went on to say that:

Retention of the office of Secretary of State for Scotland with a separate department for Scottish affairs would then be difficult to justify. The principal spokesman for Scotland would be the head of the Scottish Government, and it would detract from his status if there were also to be a Secretary of State for Scotland in the United Kingdom Parliament.[4]

It will be difficult for the Scottish Secretary to speak at Westminster on domestic Scottish affairs when he no longer has statutory responsibility for them, and when policy is formulated and enacted by the Scottish Parliament. Under these circumstances, the power of the Scottish Secretary might well, as one critic of devolution forecast, 'be amputated, and an amputated limb is discarded and soon forgotten'.[5]

The Welsh Secretary will retain responsibility for primary legislation for Wales and a small team of civil servants, but powers of implementation will pass to the Assembly. The Secretary of State's task will be to represent government to the Assembly and the Assembly to government. As with the Scottish Secretary, however, problems may arise when the Secretary of State and the majority in the Assembly belong to different parties. There will then be disputes about who—the Secretary of State or the majority on the devolved body—is the real representative of Wales.

It must, moreover, remain open to question whether the Welsh Secretary retains sufficient responsibilities to justify a separate place in the Cabinet—without executive responsibilities or a budget, he might well come to be ignored; and also whether England will continue to tolerate territorial ministers for areas which have their own directly elected bodies. Significantly, the Conservatives, who secured no representation in either Scotland or Wales in the 1997 general election, did not appoint Shadow Secretaries for Scotland or Wales in the 1997 Parliament. It may be that the posts of Secretary of State for Scotland and for Wales will become merged with that of a minister for the regions so as to create a single territorial minister in the Cabinet. Such a figure would be more likely to be a senior figure in the government than the Secretaries of State for Scotland and Wales, and would, therefore, have greater weight in Cabinet discussions. An alternative would be to subsume the territorial responsibilities with those of the Home Secretary, who was responsible for Northern Ireland matters until 1972, and for Welsh matters between 1951 and 1957. A solution of this kind for the representation of areas with devolved bodies in the Cabinet was recommended by the Royal Commission on the Constitution.[6]

Government formation and dissolution

In Scotland, devolution seems, at first sight, to create a simulacrum of Westminster in Edinburgh. There are, however, two important dissimilarities, since, first, the provisions for the formation of the executive and the dissolution of Parliament differ from those at Westminster; and second, the electoral system is different.

In Northern Ireland, between 1921 and 1972, the sovereign's duties of choosing a government and agreeing to a request for the dissolution of parliament were carried out by the Governor, who acted as the sovereign's representative. Such a solution was thought unsuitable for Scotland, since a Governor would be a non-elected official who would seem to have little to do other than carry out a few ceremonial functions. Under the abortive Scotland Act of 1978, these functions would have been undertaken not by a Governor, but by the Secretary of State for Scotland. This provision gave rise to much criticism, since the Secretary of State is of course a member of the British government, and might well belong to a different party from that of the majority in the Scottish Parliament. It would have been difficult for him to act both as a party politician and also as a constitutional arbiter.

Under the Scotland Act of 1998, neither of these precedents has been followed. The Scottish Parliament and Executive will have their own direct relationships with the Crown, as occurred in Northern Ireland. The Secretary of State for Scotland will not be an intermediary, as he would have been under the provisions of the Scotland Act of 1978. Under the 1998 Act, the relationships between the Scottish Parliament and Executive and the Crown will be mediated by the Presiding Officer of the Scottish Parliament, an elected person, rather than by a Governor. It will be the Presiding Officer of the Scottish Parliament who carries out the sovereign's functions in Scotland. It will be he who, under section 46 (4), will recommend to the Queen the appointment of a particular First Minister after the Scottish Parliament has nominated one of its members to undertake that position; and it will be he, not the First Minister, who will, under the provisions of section 3, seek a dissolution, when the appropriate circumstances obtain. This is an entirely novel arrangement in Britain, and the role of the Presiding Officer in Scotland may well come to resemble that of the Speaker in Sweden, who has taken over the sovereign's constitutional prerogatives there since the time of the new Swedish Constitution, the Instrument of Government, in 1974. On the Continent indeed, the Speaker tends to be an active party member with direct involvement in the organization of parliamentary business, while the British and Commonwealth conceptions of the Speaker imply a strictly impartial presiding officer. It is this Continental conception which is being introduced in Scotland, and it is possible that if it is successful there, it will be used by some as an argument for the Westminster Speaker being given a similar role to that of the Presiding Officer in the exercise of the sovereign's prerogatives. However, the new functions proposed for the Presiding Officer in Scotland make it more rather than less necessary that he or she should be strictly impartial.

Relationships between the Scottish Parliament and the Scottish Executive will be quite different from those between Westminster and the United Kingdom government. For the processes of government-formation and the dissolution of parliament are bound to be more complex in a fixed-term parliament which is elected by proportional representation than in a parliament such as Westminster elected under the first-past-the-post system where a Prime Minister can normally obtain a dissolution at a moment of his own choosing.

It is difficult therefore to understand the rationale for the government's contention in para. 2.6 of the White Paper, *Scotland's Parliament*, Cm. 3658, that 'The relationship between the Scottish Executive and the Scottish Parliament will be similar to the relationship between the UK Government and the UK Parliament.' For one almost certain consequence of proportional representation is that no single party will enjoy a majority in the Scottish Parliament. The last popular majority in Scotland was achieved by the Conservatives in 1955, when they gained just over 50 per cent of the Scottish vote. Labour, by contrast, has never achieved a majority of the vote in Scotland. The last popular majority in the United Kingdom as a whole was achieved by the National government in 1935.

If, as is likely, there is no overall majority in the Scottish Parliament, it may not be immediately obvious after the election who should be the First Minister. Such a situation occurs rarely at Westminster, since the first-past-the-post system normally produces an overall majority for one party. On only three occasions since 1918 has it not done so—after the general elections of December 1923, 1929, and February 1974. When a hung parliament occurs, the sovereign invites someone, normally a party leader, to form a government. Thus, in the hung parliaments after the general elections of 1923 and 1929, George V asked Ramsay MacDonald to form a government, while in March 1974, Elizabeth II asked Harold Wilson to form a government. The sovereign may enjoy a genuine discretion in such situations. The Scotland Act, by contrast, makes the Queen's appointment of a First Minister purely formal, since it is the Scottish Parliament, not the sovereign, which chooses the First Minister, and, by sections 45 and 46 of the Act, Parliament's recommendation is conveyed to the Queen by the Presiding Officer.

In a parliament without a single-party majority, it is always possible for political alignments to change within the course of a parliament. Thus, the first Scottish Executive in 1999 might well be a coalition between Labour and a minority party in Scotland—either the Liberal Democrats or the SNP. That minority party might then decide to leave the coalition after, say, two years, on account of policy differences. The Labour First Minister might then be tempted to dissolve the Parliament for tactical reasons. In consequence, proportional representation combined with a First Minister's right of dissolution could lead to frequent and possibly destabilizing general elections. With a fixed-term parliament, by contrast, Labour, in the situation described above, would not be able to dissolve and would have to seek an alternative combination if it was to carry on governing in Scotland. The defect of a fixed-term parliament, however, is that it could lead to deadlock if it proves impossible to form a government able to command the confidence of parliament. The provisions in the Scotland Act seek to steer between the Scylla of frequent dissolutions and the Charybdis of deadlock. They comprise the second difference between Scottish Parliament–Executive relations and Westminster–UK government relations.

Westminster is a maximum-term parliament which can, under normal conditions, be dissolved by the Prime Minister at a moment of his choosing. It is only under very rare circumstances, as in 1924 or 1979, that a Prime Minister, commanding only a minority in the House of Commons, is forced to go to the country at a time not of his own choosing, following defeat in a vote of confidence. That is a consequence, in large part, of the first-past-the-post electoral system which converts a minority of the votes in the country into a majority in the House of Commons.

The Scottish Parliament, by contrast, will be not a maximum-term parliament, but a four-year fixed-term parliament. There are,

however, two circumstances in which there can be an early dissolution: when a two-thirds majority of the Parliament votes for it, or
when the Parliament fails, after twenty-eight days, to choose a First
Minister. This second provision is designed to avoid the deadlock
which could otherwise occur when a First Minister has lost the support of the Parliament, but there is no alternative government which
enjoys Parliament's confidence, and no two-thirds majority to dissolve. However, even when either of these contingencies occurs, it
is not, as in Westminster, the leader of the government, but the
Presiding Officer of the Parliament, who asks the Queen for a dissolution. The rationale behind this provision in the Scotland Act is
that it is Parliament and not the executive which decides that there
ought to be a dissolution and that the fixed-term rule should be
breached. It is for this reason that it is the chair of the Parliament,
acting, it is hoped, impartially, and not the head of the Executive,
the First Minister, who seeks the dissolution. Thus decisions on the
timing of the election are removed from the control of the leader of
the government. Moreover, the Presiding Officer seems to have no
discretion as to when to seek a dissolution. He can do so only under
very precisely formulated rules.

The requirement for dissolution is placed at two-thirds rather than
a majority of the Parliament so as to prevent a First Minister, in command of a majority, from stage-managing a dissolution at a moment
of his choosing by instructing his supporters to vote for it. But a First
Minister in command of a majority in the Scottish Parliament might
be able to stage-manage a dissolution in another way. For he could
instruct his followers who, *ex hypothesi*, are in the majority, to support a vote of no confidence; or simply resign. The majority can then
ensure that no alternative administration is chosen within the period
of twenty-eight days. In those circumstances, the Presiding Officer is
required to seek a dissolution from the Queen. It seems that, in this
way, a First Minister could *always* stage-manage a dissolution. It is
not clear whether such a situation was envisaged by those who
framed the Scotland Act. Nor is such stage-management a merely
theoretical possibility. It is precisely what Willy Brandt and Helmut
Kohl did under a similar provision in Germany in 1972 and 1983
respectively. On both occasions, the Chancellor sought to dissolve

the Bundestag at a favourable moment and therefore asked his supporters to ensure that a vote of no confidence was passed. In Scotland, admittedly, by contrast with Germany, a dissolution, unless held within six months of the general election, does not obviate the need for the ordinary general election which takes place at the end of the four-year cycle; and this provision lessens the attraction of a stage-managed dissolution. Moreover, a stage-managed election would take place in the full glare of publicity and would risk incurring the displeasure of the electorate. Nevertheless, under the Westminster system, the sovereign can prevent any abuse of the right to dissolution by refusing to grant one. Under the provisions of the Scotland Act, it seems that she has no such power. This could mean that one very real defence against an abuse of the rights of parliament is lost.

*

The Welsh Assembly, by contrast with the Scottish Parliament, is to be a fixed-term body with no provision for dissolution. The case for this arrangement is that the Assembly, in its original form, would have been like a local authority, based on the committee structure and with no separate executive. But, as we have seen, the then Secretary of State for Wales declared that he would not approve any standing orders for the Assembly that do not provide for the delegation of powers from the committees to the Executive Committee, so that the Assembly will operate under a *de facto* Cabinet system.

The danger of not providing for dissolution is that of a deadlock in the Assembly. Like the Scottish Parliament, the Assembly will be elected by proportional representation. It would be perfectly possible for a change of political alignments in mid-term to deprive a particular administration in the Assembly of its majority, without any alternative administration being possible. Such a situation might have arisen, even under the first-past-the-post electoral system, at Westminster, after the election of February 1974, when, it could be argued, it was only the possibility and the threat of a further dissolution which prevented a paralysis of government.

Moreover, the Welsh Assembly is not intended to be a mere local authority. It is the National Assembly for Wales. As such, it needs strong leadership. One criticism of the committee system in local government, indeed, is that it does not yield such strong leadership. That, no doubt, is why the Secretary of State for Wales has proposed artificially to create a Cabinet system in Wales. But the executive committee may well be handicapped by its inability to dissolve. Indeed the fixed-term provision conflicts with the *raison d'être* of the National Assembly, and will make it more difficult for the Assembly to provide effective leadership in Wales.

The electoral system

The elections held in May 1999 for the Scottish Parliament and the Welsh National Assembly were the first to be held on the mainland by any proportional representation system since the abolition of the university seats in 1950. Until 1999, moreover, all proportional representation elections in the United Kingdom, with the exception of the election for the Northern Ireland Forum in 1996, where a list system was used, have been held by the single-transferable vote method of proportional representation. That, indeed, has been the method advocated by the Liberal Party, which supported proportional representation from 1922, and its successor party, the Liberal Democrats. It is also the method which was unanimously recommended by the Royal Commission on the Constitution for elections to any devolved bodies. Elections to the Scottish Parliament and Welsh National Assembly, however, are to be by an additional-member system, a system very similar to, although not exactly the same as, that used in Germany and in New Zealand since that country abandoned the first-past-the-post system in 1996.

In Scotland, the proposal for proportional representation derived, as we have seen, from the Scottish Constitutional Convention, from negotiations between Labour and the Liberal Democrats. Its effect, however, ironically, will be to benefit the parties which did not participate in the Convention—the Conservatives and the SNP.

Labour appreciated that proportional representation was the price which it had to pay for agreement with the Liberal Democrats. Nor was Labour unwilling to pay that price. The party was aware that one of the reasons why the Scotland Act of 1978 had failed to gain a sufficient majority in the 1979 referendum was the fear that, in a four-party system, Labour, representing just the central belt of Scotland, might gain an overall majority on just over 35 per cent of the vote; or, alternatively, that the SNP might gain an overall majority on just over 35 per cent of the vote and use that majority to claim that the Scottish people had given a mandate for independence. Under proportional representation, by contrast, the SNP would need to win 50 per cent of the vote to claim a mandate. Thus, while first past the post offered the prospect of a majority for Labour or the SNP, proportional representation offered the prospect of a majority for the union. But if Labour was prepared to accept proportional representation, it was not prepared to accept the single transferable-vote method. Labour has always been sceptical of this method, which involves intra-party competition, because it would publicly expose divisions within the party, both between Left and Right and between Old Labour and New. Moreover, Labour has traditionally been attached to the single-member constituency, an attachment that may well be shared by many Scottish voters. If, therefore, Labour would have to accept proportional representation to secure an agreement with the Liberal Democrats, the Liberal Democrats would, in turn, have to abandon their favoured system, the single transferable vote, to secure agreement with Labour. This they were prepared to do, and the additional-member system, therefore, became the compromise endorsed by the Convention.

In Wales, as in Scotland, the failure to adopt proportional representation may have been a contributory factor in the heavy defeat of devolution in 1979. For, under first past the post, the Assembly would, almost certainly, have been run by the Labour machine in south Wales. Proportional representation, on the other hand, offered some chance of overcoming the spatial and linguistic divide which had doomed prospects for devolution in Wales ever since the failure of *Cymru Fydd* in the 1890s.

The additional-member system, however, came about in a different way in Wales from Scotland, for there had been no cross-party Welsh Convention. This was so for two reasons. The first is that Labour has always been stronger and more self-confident in Wales than it has been in Scotland—between 1945 and 1970, indeed, it won over 50 per cent of the vote in Wales at every general election—and the separatist threat was much weaker. The second reason is that

Labour in Wales was more internally divided over devolution than Labour in Scotland. For in Wales many Labour MPs remained as sceptical about devolution as they had been in 1979. Thus, in Wales, by contrast with Scotland, policy on devolution was made by an internal party commission, which recommended retention of the first-past-the-post system. In 1995, the Welsh Labour Conference also declared for first past the post, contrary to the wishes of the Shadow Secretary of State for Wales, Ron Davies, and the party leader, Tony Blair. But Blair and Davies asked the Welsh party to think again, and in 1996 it duly did so, agreeing at last to accept proportional representation.

Under the additional-member system, each elector has two votes, one for a constituency member, the other for a party list. Constituency elections take place as under the first-past-the-post system. Votes for the party list are then used to elect additional members so as to secure a proportional outcome. Those who are to become additional members will be decided upon by the party concerned. If, say, three candidates are elected as additional members, then the top three candidates on the list are elected as additional members. Voters are not allowed to alter the order of the lists as determined by the parties.

The working of the additional-member system may be illustrated by the example shown in the table, taken from the notes on clauses to the Scotland bill, published by the Scottish Office in January 1998. The example is based on the North East of Scotland European parliamentary constituency. It is assumed that electors would cast their regional votes for the constituency candidate whom they voted for in the general election of 1997. Independent candidates and parties other than Labour, the Liberal Democrats, the SNP and the Conservatives are excluded.

The number of votes cast for each party list is first divided by the number of constituency members of the Scottish Parliament plus one. The use of this divisor is known as the d'Hondt method. There are also various alternative divisors. Under the d'Hondt method, however, Labour, which has won five constituency seats has its vote divided by 6. Then the party with the highest vote gains the first regional seat. In this case, it is the Conservatives. For the second to

Table 7.1 Voting in the North-East of Scotland European parliamentary constituency: the additional-member system

NE Scotland	Labour	Lib Dem	SNP	Conservative	Result
Party vote	113,021	69,164	95,493	82,079	-
Constituency members of the Scottish Parliament	5	2	2	0	-
1st additional member	18,837	23,055	31,831	82,079	Con.
2nd additional member	18,837	23,055	31,831	41,040	Con.
3rd additional member	18,837	23,055	31,831	27,360	SNP
4th additional member	18,837	23,055	23,873	27,360	Con.
5th additional member	18,837	23,055	23,873	20,520	SNP
6th additional member	18,837	23,055	19,099	20,520	LibDem
7th additional member	18,837	17,291	19,099	20,520	Con.
Additional members	0	1	2	4	
Total representation in NE Scotland	5	3	4	4	

the seventh seats, the same calculations are carried out, but party-list seats gained are included. Thus, on the second round, the Conservative figure is divided, not by 1 but by 2; and then, on the third round, after it has won two list seats, by 3. The final regional seat was won on 20,520 votes, which is around 5.7 per cent of the total vote.

That is the implicit threshold in this constituency, i.e. the hurdle which a party or indeed an independent candidate has to overcome to win a seat. Any party or independent candidate failing to win 5.7 per cent of the vote will not win a seat.

The working of the additional-member system in Scotland and Wales is slightly different from its working in Germany and New Zealand. In those countries, an equal number of members are elected from the list and from the constituencies. In Scotland and Wales, however, fewer members are elected from the list than from the constituencies. In Scotland, there will be 73 constituency members and 56 list members, a ratio of 57 to 43. In Wales, there will be 40 constituency members and 20 list members, a ratio of 60 to 40. The outcome in Scotland, therefore, is likely to be somewhat more proportional than in Wales, where the implicit threshold will be around 8 per cent. The Labour Party, however, is stronger in Wales than it is in Scotland, and so it would seem that Wales deserves more, not less, proportionality than Scotland. It is indeed not immediately apparent why the degree of proportionality should be different for elections to the two devolved bodies.

In Germany and New Zealand, proportionality is at *national* level, and subject to an explicit threshold. In Scotland and Wales, by contrast, there is no explicit threshold, but proportionality is at the level of the regional Euro-constituencies and not at the level of Scotland and Wales as a whole, and there will be no explicit threshold. The system as used in Scotland and Wales does, however, as we have seen, yield an implicit threshold.

The additional-member system is likely to increase the number of women elected to the Scottish Parliament and the Welsh Assembly. There is good evidence that it is more difficult for women to secure nomination in single-member constituencies, since constituency associations will tend to choose a 'safe' candidate who often turns out to be white, middle-aged, and male. Under the additional-member system, by contrast, a party would be wise to seek a more balanced ticket. Since the list will contain a large number of names, the absence of a due proportion of women will cause offence and narrow the appeal of the party. For, whereas under a single-member constituency system, it is the *presence* of a candidate who deviates from the male norm which is noticed, in a party-list system, it is the *absence* of a female candidate, the failure to present a balanced ticket, that would be noticed and made the subject of adverse comment. Under the German electoral system, as we have seen, 50 per cent of the candidates are elected by single-member constituencies and 50 per cent through party lists. Between 1949 and 1994, 790 women were elected to the Bundestag. Of these, no fewer than 605 were elected from the list, and only 185 from the constituencies.

The additional-member system has the further advantage that it enables the voter to indicate which coalition he or she favours. The voter can do this by, for example, supporting Labour on the constituency vote and, say, the Liberal Democrats on the list vote. This would indicate that the voter supported a Labour–Liberal Democrat coalition. A list vote for the SNP, by contrast, would indicate that the voter favoured a Labour–SNP coalition. In Germany, the Free Democrats, who have not won a constituency seat since 1957, once used as an election slogan: 'A FIRST-class decision; your SECOND vote for a THIRD force.' Signalling a coalition in this way limits the power of the party leaders. It prevents them from constructing, in proverbial smoke-filled rooms, coalitions which do not correspond with the wishes of voters. On the other hand, the additional-member system does not ensure such an outcome. For example, in the first New Zealand election held under this system, in 1996, the New Zealand First party held the balance of power between Labour and the National Party. The New Zealand First Party had seemed close to Labour, and the distribution of its constituency votes were more strongly Labour than National. Nevertheless, after eight weeks of negotiations, the New Zealand Party decided to ally itself with the National Party, and these two parties together formed the new government.

The additional-member system creates two kinds of MP—constituency members and list members. Before becoming a Welsh Office minister, the Labour MP Peter Hain had attacked the system on these grounds, saying that 'The Additional Member System (AMS) favoured by most PR advocates in the Labour Party would mean two classes of MP: some constituency-based, the others constituency free-loaders chosen from lists and without any constituency responsibilities.'[7] In 1993, the Plant Report, established by the Labour Party to consider various alternative electoral systems, argued:

It would be wrong to have two classes of members in the Commons—those who represent constituencies and those who do not. There would be a danger that the latter would still be less directly accountable; and there would be differences in workload with non-constituency members relieved of constituency casework. This could also mean the latter would be less in touch with the day-to-day concerns of the electors.[8]

The working party conceded, however, that there were compensating advantages to the system.

In Germany, there is no difference in status between the two kinds of MPs; once in the Bundestag they perform similar functions. But that is in large part due to the special circumstances of German federalism. For, in Germany, constituency work is the responsibility not of members of the Bundestag, but of local councillors and members of the Landtage—regional parliaments. Members of the Bundestag, unlike elected representatives in Britain, are not expected to involve themselves in constituency work. In Scotland and Wales, by contrast, the constituency representatives will presumably be expected to undertake such work. Therefore a difference in status between the two kinds of member might well arise. Moreover, if the figures for the 1997 election were to be replicated in the first elections to the Scottish Parliament, most of the additional members would be Conservatives who gained no seats despite winning 17.5 per cent of the vote; and Scottish Nationalists who gained only six of the seventy-two Scottish seats despite winning 22.1 per cent—over one-fifth—of the Scottish vote. In Wales, the extra seats would go to Conservatives, who won no seats despite winning 19.6 per cent of the vote; and to Liberal Democrats who won only two out of the forty Welsh seats despite winning 12.5 per cent—nearly one-eighth—of the Welsh vote. Thus the Labour members of the Scottish Parliament and the Welsh Assembly are likely to bear the brunt of the constituency work, while the other parties will be able to devote their time to scrutiny of legislation. The difference in function between the two types of member might come to be very marked. On the other hand, it is perfectly possible that the regional-list MPs come to take on constituency functions for those in the constituencies who voted for minority parties. This could lead to more effective representation since electors would be able to choose who to go to for constituency service, rather than, as now, being restricted to a single MP whose outlook may be alien to them.

In Scotland and Wales, as in Germany and New Zealand, the lists will be closed lists; the order will be decided by the party and the voter will not be able to alter it. This contrasts with the situation in many other west European countries, for example Belgium and Switzerland, where the voter can either alter or determine the order of the list. Under the closed list, party nomination to a high place on the list will normally prove sufficient to secure election. In the illustrative example above, all of the Conservatives seats in NE Scotland are from the list. The Conservative members of the Scottish Parliament from NE Scotland, therefore, will be chosen by the party apparatus, not by the voters. They will not have presented themselves to the voter, who will not be able to remove them. In the 1997 general election, the voters in Tatton *were* able to remove Neil Hamilton, even though he had been nominated as the Conservative candidate in what would normally be a safe Conservative seat. With a closed list, however, Hamilton, if put in a high enough position, would be irremovable by the voter.

The main virtue of the additional-member system is that it will secure a more proportional outcome than first past the post, although, in the form adopted in Scotland and Wales, not a wholly proportional outcome. Its central weakness is one that it shares with first past the post. It deprives the voter, except in marginal seats, of any choice of candidate. It is in danger of giving too much power to the party machine at the expense of the ordinary voter. This may have important consequences for devolution. Much of the work of the Scottish Parliament and the Welsh Assembly will involve negotiations with the United Kingdom government. These could well prove to be negotiations between different branches of the Labour Party machine, in London, Edinburgh, and Cardiff. Members of the Scottish Parliament and the Welsh Assembly might, as a result of the electoral system, be a little too eager to support the party leadership so that they can be renominated to a high position on the party list. Thus the electoral system will tend to the strengthening of the devolved executives at the expense of the legislatures. The additional-member system, especially when accompanied by a closed list, operates against the values of devolution and democratic accountability which require the transference of power away from Westminster to Edinburgh and Cardiff. It could easily lead to the recentralization of power through the party machines. If that happens, the ideal of devolution will come to be undermined by the realities of the modern political party machine.

The West Lothian Question

The West Lothian Question was named after Tam Dalyell, who was MP for West Lothian when devolution was debated at Westminster in the 1970s. The question asks whether it is justifiable for Scottish MPs, after devolution, to continue to be able to vote for English domestic affairs when non-Scottish MPs will no longer be able to vote on Scottish domestic affairs. Scottish MPs would be able to vote on the arts in Alnwick, but English MPs would not be able to vote on the arts in Armadale, West Lothian. Scottish MPs would be able to vote on local government reform in London, but English MPs would not be able to vote on local government reform in Linlithgow. Scottish MPs would be able to vote on schools in Sheffield, but English MPs would not be able to vote on schools in South Queensferry. In this situation, policy on English domestic affairs might be decided by the balance of Scottish MPs although English MPs had lost the practical opportunity of voting on Scottish domestic affairs. This situation would have occurred, for example, in 1964 or October 1974 when, without Scottish MPs, Labour would not have enjoyed a majority in the House of Commons.

Would it, moreover, be appropriate, after devolution, for a Scottish MP to become a minister in a British government exercising functions which, in Scotland, were the responsibility of the Scottish Parliament? On 16 February 1992, Robin Cook, as Shadow Secretary of State for Health, said in the BBC television programme *On the Record* that it would not. 'Once we have a Scottish parliament handling health affairs,' Cook added, 'it would not be possible for me to continue as Minister of Health, administering health in England.' Cook was, admittedly, disowned by the then Labour leader, Neil Kinnock. Nevertheless, during the years when Northern Ireland enjoyed devolution, no Northern Ireland MP occupied a Cabinet post involving responsibility for matters devolved to the Northern Ireland Parliament.

The West Lothian Question was pursued with much pertinacity by Tam Dalyell in the 1970s. Francis Pym, the Conservative spokesman on devolution, then called it 'the single most contentious problem to arise in our debates',[9] while, in a speech on St Andrew's Day in 1995, Michael Forsyth referred to it as 'the Bermuda triangle of devolution'. During the committee stage of the first devolution bill, the Scotland and Wales Bill, in February 1977, Tam Dalyell declared: 'The point cannot be made too often.' To which the Minister of State at the Privy Council Office, John Smith, who was in charge of the bill, replied: 'Yes, it can.'[10]

The West Lothian Question draws attention to a constitutional and political imbalance arising from asymmetrical devolution in an otherwise unitary state. It asks: after devolution, how ought Scotland to be represented in the House of Commons? This is the same question which, as we have seen, baffled Gladstone in the nineteenth century. Indeed, one constitutional authority has written that only 'those with short memories called this the "West Lothian Question" '.[11]

There is only one logical answer to the West Lothian Question, but it is politically unrealistic: it is for Britain to implement legislative devolution all round, so becoming a thoroughgoing federal state. But there is no demand for legislative federalism in England. Even if English regional assemblies were eventually to come about—and that at the present time hardly seems likely—they would almost certainly not be given legislative powers. Their powers would be much more like those of the Welsh Assembly than those of the Scottish Parliament, and statutory responsibility for English legislation would, therefore, remain with Westminster.

It might perhaps prove possible for England to mitigate the effects of the West Lothian Question by adopting special parliamentary arrangements such as an English Grand Committee, composed only of English MPs, to consider English legislation. There is indeed a Standing Committee on Regional Affairs in the Commons, formed in 1975, in anticipation of devolution to Scotland and Wales. This Committee comprises all the MPs for English constituencies, together with five additional members. It met between 1975 and 1978 to debate various regional matters. It has not, however, met since 1978, and indeed, if all 529 English MPs were to attend, it would be a somewhat cumbrous body, hardly equipped for parliamentary committee work; but in any case it is the House of Commons, not the Grand Committee, which actually votes on legislation. Moreover, such special parliamentary arrangements for England would not overcome the problem which would arise when, as in 1964 or October 1974, the political majority in England differed from that in the United Kingdom as a whole. The West Lothian Question cannot, therefore, be answered by special parliamentary arrangements for one part of the country.[12]

The other proposed answers to the West Lothian Question are as inadequate today as they were over a hundred years ago when Gladstone first proposed them. It would obviously be absurd to exclude Scottish MPs altogether from Westminster while Parliament remains responsible for reserved matters. Under the Scotland Act, all taxation for Scotland, unless Scotland uses its very limited tax-varying power, continues to be imposed by Westminster. It would be unjust for Scotland to be taxed by Westminster without being represented there.

Two further answers to the West Lothian Question are to cut the powers of the Scottish members by allowing them to vote only on Scottish matters, or to cut the numbers.

Cutting the powers of the Scottish members would be to revert to the 'in and out' solution which Gladstone proposed in 1893 and then abandoned. The Ferrers amendment, section 66 of the 1978 Scotland Act, was also, as we have seen, an example of an 'in and out' clause. In Northern Ireland, as noted in Chapter 3, Harold Wilson, when the Labour government enjoyed a majority of only two in 1965, sought to deter MPs from the province from interfering in British domestic affairs. On that occasion, the Conservatives insisted that MPs from Northern Ireland should exercise the same rights as every other Member of Parliament. Peter Thorneycroft, the Conservative Shadow Home Secretary, spoke as follows:

The honourable Member for Manchester, Blackley [Paul Rose], argued that honourable Members representing Northern Ireland seats should not have the right to talk about very much in the House of Commons except Northern Ireland. We have heard some rather loose talk of that kind from some other quarters on the Government side from time to time. I hope that the Joint Under-Secretary will make it absolutely clear that that kind of nonsense does not form any part of the Government's thinking, that every Member of the House of Commons is equal with every other Member of the House of Commons, and that all of us will speak on all subjects, subject always to keeping within the bounds of order.[13]

An 'in and out' solution is almost certainly unworkable for two reasons. The first is that it puts the onus on the Speaker, who would have to decide on contentious bills whether or not they were purely Scottish bills. 'I am afraid', Gladstone told Lord Rosebery when the latter proposed the 'in and out' solution in 1886, 'that the Speakership would hardly bear the weight of your proposal.'[14] The difficulty would be all the greater now since, under the Barnett formula (see next section), an increase in expenditure on a domestic service, such as education in England, would have consequential effects on the total of Scotland's block grant, and therefore on the total of public expenditure in Scotland. In addition, of course, increases in expenditure on English domestic affairs would involve an increase in taxes throughout the United Kingdom. As the Royal Commission on the Constitution noticed:

Ability to vote could not depend simply on whether the matter at issue related to a reserved or transferred subject. Any issue in Westminster involving expenditure of public money is of concern to all parts of the United Kingdom since it may directly affect the level of taxation and indirectly influence the level of a region's own expenditure.[15]

It is questionable, therefore, whether there are any specifically 'English' domestic issues in the sense of issues which have no consequential effects in Scotland and Wales

The fundamental reason, however, why the 'in and out' solution is constitutionally impossible is that, when party majorities in Scotland

and the United Kingdom were different, as in 1964 or February 1974, it would bifurcate the executive. The government in London, Labour in each case, would lack a majority on English domestic affairs when the Scottish MPs withdrew. There would thus be a Labour government on foreign affairs and defence, but a Conservative government when the Scottish MPs were absent, on health and education. It is not easy to see how effective government could continue under such circumstances.

It has been suggested that such situations would be highly infrequent, since it has only been in the short parliaments of 1964–6 and March–October 1974 that a non-Conservative government has faced a Conservative majority of English MPs, and 'these short parliaments did not inflict major legislative changes on a bitterly hostile electorate'.[16]

The chances of such an outcome occurring again are, however, greater than this argument suggests. This is because the gap between the number of seats gained by Labour and by the Conservatives in Scotland has increased enormously in recent years. In 1950, the two parties won an equal number of seats in Scotland; but in 1987 Labour won forty more seats than the Conservatives, and in 1992 thirty-nine more. In 1997, Labour won fifty-six seats in Scotland and the Conservatives none. Thus the chances of a Conservative majority in England being outvoted by a Labour majority in Scotland must be much greater now than they have been in the past, unless there is a substantial reversal in political trends in Scotland.

The alternative approach, of cutting the number of Scottish MPs, still leaves open the possibility of a majority of Scottish MPs of a different colour from the majority in the rest of the United Kingdom determining the domestic affairs of England; but of course it lessens the likelihood of such an outcome actually occurring; and cutting the numbers can be justified on other grounds as a means of remedying the over-representation of Scotland at Westminster.[17]

Scotland's over-representation has been defended by Neil MacCormick on the basis of 'reasonable assurance for minority countries . . . Since a whole country [in 1707] was being incorporated into a larger, there was special reason to ensure that its interests could not be ignored or belittled. There was also concern about unfair discrimination against the interests of a minority with a long prior history of conflict with the new majority'.[18] The Royal Commission on the Constitution, similarly, put forward the argument that:

the maintenance of the representation of Scotland and Wales at their present levels would be justified by their separate national status. England already has a preponderance of representation in Parliament compared with the smaller nations. To base representation simply on the basis of counting heads is to ignore the important nationality factor. Moreover, there are ample precedents, for example, in international organisations and in the second chambers of many federal countries, for giving to smaller states a greater representation than would be justified by their populations.[19]

Yet Scotland has been over-represented, not since 1707, but only since 1922. Scottish over-representation is not, therefore, a result of the Treaty of Union, which did no more than guarantee Scotland forty-five seats in the House of Commons. The over-representation is rather a result of the successful use of bargaining power by the Scots and Welsh and it has no constitutional status at all.[20]

Moreover, the Royal Commission on the Constitution did not believe that Scottish over-representation would continue to be justified after legislative devolution. For, after all, the Scottish Parliament is likely to provide at least as good a 'reasonable assurance', to use MacCormick's words, that Scotland's interests will be respected, as over-representation at Westminster. The Royal Commission therefore recommended that any area of the country which enjoyed legislative devolution should have its representation at Westminster reduced. That is the approach which the government has adopted in the Scotland Act. It decided, however, not to reduce the representation of Wales, which will thus enjoy the twin benefits of over-representation and executive devolution. Over-representation may perhaps be seen by the Welsh as compensation for the absence of legislative devolution. To the English, however, it may seem over-compensation.

If the West Lothian Question cannot be answered, a second question poses itself. Is the imbalance of representation an acceptable anomaly or a fatal weakness in the attempt to institute asymmetrical devolution in an otherwise unitary state?

It is noticeable that, on the Continent, anomalies of the type represented by the West Lothian Question have in fact been accommodated without difficulty. In Denmark, the Faeroe Islands and Greenland both have their own parliaments and both are outside the European Union, of which Denmark remains a member state. In Portugal, the two island areas—Madeira and the Azores—enjoy devolution while mainland Portugal remains a unitary state. In France, Italy, and Spain, there has been devolution across the country as a whole but it has been asymmetric, with some regions enjoying greater powers than others. In France, Corsica and the overseas territories have special status. In Italy, there are fifteen ordinary regions with no exclusive legislative powers at all, but five special regions—Valle d'Aosta, Trentino–Alto–Adige, Fruili–Venezia–Giulia, Sardinia, and Sicily—with exclusive legislative powers in economic, social, and cultural matters. The five special regions, moreover, were set up in 1948, twenty-two years before the other regions were established. In Spain, seven of the seventeen 'autonomous communities'—Andalusia, the Canaries, Catalonia, Euskadi (the Basque country), Galicia, Navarre, and Valencia—have a greater degree of autonomy than other areas, with power over their own health and education services; some of them also run their own police forces. Yet there is no 'West Madeira Question' nor any 'West Sardinian Question', nor any 'West Catalonian Question', in these countries. In France and Portugal, this is because the consequences of asymmetry are minimal, the regions in Portugal being geographically isolated and containing only 5 per cent of the Portugese population. In Italy and Spain, however, the consequences of asymmetrical devolution are by no means minimal, and yet devolution has proved perfectly workable. There seems no reason why the same should not prove true in Britain also.

The West Lothian Question, moreover, would be less likely to come into play were there to be a change in the electoral system for the House of Commons to one of proportional representation. For Labour's strength in Scotland is in part a product of the first-past-the-post system.

The 1997 general election results in Scotland are shown in Table 7.2. Under a strictly proportional system, however, the seats would have been distributed quite differently (Table 7.3).

Table 7.2 General election results, Scotland, 1997

	Seats	% of vote
Labour	56	45.6
Conservative	0	17.5
Liberal Democrats	10	13.0
SNP	6	22.1
Others	0	1.9

Table 7.3 Distribution of seats under a proportional-representation system

	Seats
Labour	33
Conservative	13
Liberal Democrats	10
SNP	16

The chances of Scottish Labour MPs making the difference between a Conservative and a Labour government at Westminster would be much reduced, although not of course eliminated. If that is so, then non-Scottish MPs need not regret the loss of their power to discuss and scrutinize Scottish legislation; for, as we have seen, even under the pre-devolution arrangements, Scottish legislation was largely the province of Scottish members. Hardly any non-Scottish MPs took much interest in it, and any who did were likely to be regarded by Scottish MPs as intruders. Thus, English MPs have little interest in Scottish domestic affairs, while England's dominant position in the United Kingdom means that there are hardly any wholly 'English' domestic issues of no concern to MPs from Scotland and Wales. In a sense, then, the West Lothian Question is falsely posed.

Nevertheless, the question raises in an acute form the issue of whether it is possible to devolve to one part of an otherwise unitary state. The answer rests on a political judgement as to whether it is better to accept the risks of asymmetry in preference to the alternative risk of fuelling support for Scottish separatism by denying devolution. The unionists take their stand on a symmetrical constitution. The devolutionists can point to the long history of Britain's relations with Ireland as well as experience on the Continent in countries such as Italy and Spain, and they can argue that this experience yields the following answer to the West Lothian Question: where the will to conciliate is present, special treatment may, by containing centrifugal impulses, help to preserve the unity of a country when the urge to symmetry would destroy it. That at least must be the premiss on which the policy of devolution is based.

However, devolution will alter the role of Westminster very radically, by introducing the spirit of federalism into its deliberations. Before devolution, every Member of Parliament was responsible for scrutinizing both the domestic and the non-domestic affairs of every part of the United Kingdom. After devolution, by contrast, MPs will normally play no role at all in legislating for the domestic affairs of Northern Ireland or Scotland, nor in scrutinizing secondary legislation for Wales. Only with respect to England will MPs continue to enjoy the power which, until now, they have enjoyed for the whole of the United Kingdom. Westminster, from being a parliament for both the domestic and the non-domestic affairs of the whole of the United Kingdom, is transformed into a domestic parliament for England, part of a domestic parliament for Wales, and a federal parliament for Northern Ireland and Scotland. The West Lothian Question, then, draws attention to the fact that devolution will transform Westminster into the quasi-federal parliament of a quasi-federal state.

Financing devolution

Finance is the spinal cord of devolution, for it is the financial arrangements which will largely determine the degree of autonomy enjoyed by the devolved administrations; the financial settlement, therefore, will exert a dominant influence on whether the aims of devolution are sustained or frustrated.

Post-war experience has not augured well for supposing that the financing of devolution would necessarily be consistent with the policy aim of dispersing power away from Whitehall to Edinburgh and Cardiff. For, over the past fifty years, the allocation of functions to public authorities and the pattern of public finance have come increasingly to be divorced from each other. The result has been that finance has frequently frustrated, and rarely sustained, broader policy aims.

The 1980s saw a progressive weakening of local autonomy which went along with a weakening in the tax-base of local authorities. In 1979, under the rating system, local authorities raised around 40 per cent of their revenue locally. The Royal Commission on the Constitution declared in 1973, at a time when 60 per cent of local revenue came from the centre, that 'This degree of financial dependence on the centre is generally considered to be unhealthy.'[21] The council tax, however, accounts for an even smaller proportion of local government revenue—around 20 per cent in most authorities. Local autonomy has suffered because local revenue has been insufficiently buoyant to accommodate the expansion of public services. This has been of some comfort to central government, seeking to control the totality of public expenditure, and fearful that local authorities will refuse to comply with government requests for restraint. From this point of view, the revenue-raising power of local authorities may be seen as a loophole in the system for controlling public expenditure. Even so, governments have been hesitant about abolishing local tax-raising powers entirely, for fear, perhaps, of totally extinguishing local autonomy.

Two fundamental factors have been responsible for the increasing drift to the centre. The first is that distribution according to relative need is the cardinal feature of the UK system of allocating public expenditure. Resources are distributed not according to geography, but according to need. The danger, then, of any devolution of the taxing power is that it will enable the richer parts of the country to benefit at the expense of those less well favoured. According to Sir George Godber, a former Chief Medical Officer at the Department of Health and Social Security:

Anyone familiar with the pattern of development of local authority health services before 1948 ... knows well that the wealth of an authority has a direct bearing on the quality of the service provided. This was not the sole factor, but it was in my belief, the most important. A county like Surrey, for instance, was able to recruit doctors for its public health services in the 1930s much more easily than a county borough like, say, Bootle, for the simple reason that it offered £600 a year as compared with £500 a year, which was the minimum negotiated rate.[22]

It was indeed because they feared that devolution would lead to the allocation of public resources on the basis of geography and political clout, rather than need, that left-wing MPs such as Eric Heffer and Neil Kinnock were so opposed to devolution in the 1970s. They took the view that only central government could determine the relative degree of deprivation in different parts of the country, and that those living in Glasgow, for example, should not get a better deal than those living in Liverpool, simply because Glasgow was a part of the country with an elected assembly which could put political pressures upon Westminster and Whitehall.

In a debate on tax-raising powers for the Scottish and Welsh Assemblies in January 1978, Neil Kinnock declared in the Commons:

We shall be introducing into all political considerations an argument that has barely figured at all in British political dialogues and discussions. There has barely been a vote to be gained in this country, except among nationalist paranoiacs, throughout the time that we have had the modern pluralistic, parliamentary, elected democracy, on the basis of where a candidate comes from or the immediate interests he is trying to serve. We have had divisions on a class basis, but not on a geographic or nationalistic basis.[23]

The philosophy that the allocation of public expenditure should be determined on the basis of need and that only central government is in a position to be able to secure the equitable distribution of public resources on the basis of need, still exerts a powerful hold on politicians of both left and right, and also upon the civil service, and in particular the Treasury.

The second fundamental factor militating against the devolution of tax-raising powers is that central government's approach to finance must always be different from that of local authorities or devolved administrations. Local or devolved bodies need revenue to finance their expenditure plans; central government by contrast is responsible for stabilizing the economy, controlling borrowing and holding down the burden of taxation to sharpen incentives in the private sector. The Treasury's fear has always been that the dispersal of revenue-raising powers will make economic management more difficult. For the larger the amount of public expenditure which lies outside the direct control of the government, the greater the scope for evading measures of macroeconomic control. The governments of Margaret Thatcher and John Major, for example, found their attempts at public expenditure control hampered by left-wing local authorities which refused to comply with government requests, and instead of cutting expenditure, sought to raise extra revenue locally in order to finance a higher level of services than the government thought desirable. It was largely for this reason that Margaret Thatcher's government assumed, in the Rates Act of 1984, powers to cap the rates, i.e. impose maximum rate levels on local authorities. This principle of capping was continued with the community charge—the poll tax—and also the council tax which has replaced it. Capping was a constitutional innovation in that, for the first time, government was telling individual local authorities how much revenue they could raise locally. In opposition, Labour opposed rate-capping, but the Labour government elected in 1997 had not, by 1999, surrendered the bulk of its capping powers. How much more difficult it would be for governments to carry out their macroeconomic policies successfully if they were confronted, not only with recalcitrant local authorities, but also with powerful devolved bodies with their own revenue-raising powers, bodies with much more political weight than local authorities, and therefore better able to resist government requests for restraint.

British governments in the post-war period have believed that macroeconomic stabilization policy requires them to control not only the global totals of expenditure, but also the balance between public and private spending, which could of course be altered through decisions taken by the devolved bodies. It was for these reasons that

Labour governments, both in the 1970s and in the 1990s, decided not to devolve substantial tax-raising powers to Scotland or Wales.

The Welsh Assembly, as defined in the Government of Wales Act of 1998, is to have no revenue-raising powers at all, but the Scottish Parliament will have the power to vary the basic rate of income tax by 3p in the pound. This was first suggested by the Scottish Convention which was unable to be more radical because it feared giving the opponents of devolution and of Labour an opportunity to gain a propaganda victory with attacks on a new 'tartan tax'.

The tax-varying power is in fact minimal. It gives the Scottish Parliament control over £450m.—index-linked—out of a total Scottish Office budget of £14.6bn. It is difficult, however, to imagine this power being used except to *raise* taxes. For, if it is used to lower taxes, then expenditure on public services in Scotland would have to be cut. The British government would then reduce the overall level of resources passed to the Scottish Parliament in the block grant.[24] Tony Blair has promised that Labour, if it forms the Executive in Scotland, will not raise taxes during the first Scottish Parliament; as Lord Sewel, a Parliamentary Under-Secretary at the Scottish Office, declared during the devolution debates, 'there is a world of difference between having a power and exercising that power through a policy'.[25] Thus, for practical purposes, the Scottish Parliament will be entirely dependent on Westminster for its financing.

The Scottish Parliament and the Welsh National Assembly do, however, enjoy a hidden power to tax, by withholding finance from local government and keeping it for their own use. For the block funds which the devolved bodies receive include an element taking account of the need to provide revenue support grant to local authorities. Almost 40 per cent of Scotland's annual block of £14.6bn.— £5.2bn.—goes to finance local authority expenditure, with around £1.2bn. of Scottish local authority expenditure being financed from the council tax. But it is for the Scottish Parliament to decide, after consultation with local authorities, whether to distribute £5.2bn rather than a higher sum or a lower one. The Welsh Assembly has a similar power. That is part of the essential discretion of the devolved bodies to reorder priorities in devolved spending. But the result is that Scottish and Welsh local authorities will be seeking funds from the devolved bodies, which may well wish to earmark them for their own purposes. There is thus an inbuilt conflict of interest between local authorities and the devolved bodies, which will have their own views of the appropriate mix of local expenditure in Scotland and Wales, and will, no doubt, seek to ensure influence over how available moneys are spent. Were the devolved bodies to withhold finance from local authorities, the latter would of course need to raise the level of council tax very considerably to maintain services, given the high proportion of their income which derives from central grants.

Alternatively, or in addition, the Scottish Parliament, though not the Welsh Assembly, could return the levying of the uniform business rate to local government and reduce the amount which it gave to local authorities. Local authorities would have to raise either the council tax or the non-domestic rate to maintain services. Thus the Parliament would be able to secure revenue of its own while it would be local authorities which incurred the odium.

Another way in which the Scottish Parliament, but not the Welsh National Assembly, could enjoy a hidden power to tax would be by keeping for itself the income raised from the business rate. This is at present equalized in England and Scotland, although 10 per cent lower in Wales. Previous Conservative governments have pledged that these levels would remain. These pledges, however, cannot bind the Scottish Parliament, since local government finance is a devolved matter.

It may be argued that this hidden tax-raising power is not an innovation in that, before devolution, the Secretary of State could, if he so chose, withhold money from Scottish or Welsh local authorities. Responsibility for the determination of local government funding must, after all, be located somewhere. After devolution, this power will be located not with a member of the Cabinet, but in a body that is specifically accountable to the Scottish or Welsh people. This may be regarded as a democratic advance.

What is clear, however, is that the hidden tax-raising power is capable of securing far more revenue for the devolved bodies than raising income tax in Scotland by 3p in the pound. But if there were to be too rapid a rise in local authority expenditure, then the government would act. Paragraph 7.27 of the White Paper, *Scotland's Government*, Cm. 3658, declares:

Should self-financed expenditure [by Scottish local authorities] start to rise steeply, [and] . . . if growth relative to England were excessive and were such as to threaten targets of the United Kingdom economy . . . it would be open to the United Kingdom government to take the excess into account in considering the level of their support for expenditure in Scotland.

The justification for this would be that the financial policy of Scottish local authorities would be entrenching upon macroeconomic policy, which is a reserved and not a devolved matter.

Nevertheless, the arrangements for the financing of the Scottish Parliament and Welsh Assembly are hardly compatible with the dispersal of power that devolution is intended to achieve. If local authority autonomy is secured by the power to raise local taxation, however small a portion of local revenue is actually comprised by local taxation, it seems odd that bodies intended to represent the people of Scotland and Wales should not be given a similar power. The Welsh Assembly which is to have no revenue-raising powers at all is in a worse position than parish and community councils in England and Wales which can precept on councils, and raise revenue from fees and charges.

The central criticism of the financial arrangements is that they divorce the power to raise money from the power to spend it. That these two powers should be in the same hands has long been thought of as a fundamental tenet of responsible government. In its report to the Cabinet in 1912, the Committee on Irish Finance, the Primrose Committee, set up to consider the financial relationships between Britain and Ireland after Home Rule, claimed that it was:

a first principle of sound government that the same authority that has the spending of revenue should also have the burthen, and not infrequently the odium of raising that revenue. That one should have the unpopular duty of providing the same, and another the privilege of expending them, is a division of labour that leads to disaster.[26]

Over sixty years later, the Layfield Committee on Local Government Finance echoed this sentiment when it declared: 'whoever is responsible for spending money should also be responsible for raising it so that the amount of expenditure is subject to democratic control'.[27] In Scotland and Wales, with the responsibilities separated, the danger will always be that the Scottish and Welsh executives claim credit for improvements in services while blaming their problems upon the parsimony of London. As Lord Vaizey said in the debates on the 1978 Scotland Act: 'Nobody in his senses would say, "I am standing on the basis of switching expenditure from housing to hospital services." That is what the Government want him to say, but he will not say it. What he will say is that he will come to Westminster and say that he wants to change the formula.'[28]

The devolved administrations may thus take on the character of pressure groups focused on London rather than responsible political bodies. Moreover, the pressure-group relationship is bound to be an unstable one. For the demand for improved public services in Scotland and Wales is almost infinite. Whenever the standard of roads or hospitals or schools in Scotland or Wales is held to be inadequate, London will be blamed. Deficiencies in public services in Scotland and Wales will be attributed less to the devolved administrations in Scotland and Wales than to the niggardliness of London in refusing to adopt a more generous formula for distributing grant. The SNP and Plaid Cymru will benefit the most from this instability. For they alone will not be constrained by wider UK party loyalties in bidding for funds from London. A Labour administration in Edinburgh or Cardiff would be under some pressure from a Labour government in London not to damage national economic policy by overspending. Conservatives would not wish to appear profligate when one of the Conservative Party's main policies is tight control of public spending. The SNP and Plaid Cymru, however, will be continually seeking to prove that it is only the parsimony of the British government which is preventing them from improving services.

Moreover, the devolved administrations may have fewer incentives to economize when they are not raising their own funds. Devolved administrations would be much more likely to spend moneys which they receive from central government than moneys that they had to raise themselves. The only financial initiative, however, which the devolved administrations seem able to take is to suggest that the government alter the formula for distributing grant, and then blame London if it does not do so. Thus failure to devolve revenue-raising powers will fundamentally affect the working of the devolved administrations.

The arrangements for distributing grant to Scotland and Wales after devolution will continue to be based on the Barnett formula, developed in 1978, and named after Joel Barnett, then Chief Secretary of the Treasury. The formula has been in operation since 1980, but the principles behind it were not set out in public until December 1997 in a written answer by Alistair Darling, Chief Secretary to the Treasury.[29]

The formula is based on the population of the different territories comprising the United Kingdom. It is designed to deal with changes—whether increments or decrements—in comparable public expenditure. The formula was originally 85 : 10 : 5—that is, for every marginal £85 on comparable public expenditure on English services equivalent to those in the Scottish/Welsh block, the Scottish block automatically received £10, and the Welsh £5. The formula was extended to Northern Ireland, which received an extra £2.75 when comparable expenditure in Great Britain on services that in Northern Ireland were within the block increased by £100.

The Barnett formula has been much misunderstood. In the second reading debate in the Lords on the Government of Wales Bill, Lord Callaghan, the former Prime Minister, reminisced, declaring that the formula added 'something which was fairly rational onto something which was completely irrational'.[30] The rational element is the formula for marginal changes in public expenditure; what Lord Callaghan referred to as the irrational element is the base, the overall level of public expenditure. The Barnett formula, then, is *not* designed to deal with the overall level, which was inherited when the formula was introduced, reflecting past negotiations and historic, rough and ready estimates of the needs of the different parts of the United Kingdom.

The formula entails that public expenditure in Scotland, Wales, and Northern Ireland is driven by the level of public expenditure in England, since it is the change in the English level, agreed by English departmental ministers in Cabinet, which determines the sum available to other parts of the United Kingdom.

The formula originally gave Scotland 11.76 per cent of any change in English spending and Wales 5.88 per cent. It was, however, recalibrated in 1992, following the 1991 census, to reflect

Scotland's smaller share of the population. The new ratios were 85.7 : 9.14 : 5.16, and, on the new formula, Scotland gained just 10.66 per cent of changes in comparable English expenditure, while the Welsh share went up to 6.02 per cent. Northern Ireland's share went up to 2.87 per cent of changes in comparable expenditure in Great Britain.

The Barnett formula was developed in 1978 when devolution to Scotland appeared likely. Its purpose was to avoid an annual squabble for funds between the Treasury and the executive of the proposed Scottish assembly. In the eighteen years prior to 1979, Scotland and Wales seemed to have gained considerably in terms of relative public expenditure per head. The formula was intended to help secure territorial justice by preventing further relative gains on the part of Scotland and Wales, and indeed by producing convergence in levels of funding per head. Whether it would in fact produce convergence depended upon two factors: first, the rate of growth of comparable spending in England—the faster the rise in spending in England, the more rapid the convergence; and second, the relative stability of population relativities within the United Kingdom—were the Scottish population to decline relatively, as has in fact happened, that would tend to offset the convergence effect.

Scottish Office ministers were content to accept the Barnett formula in the late 1970s, perhaps because they foresaw that Britain was entering a period of financial retrenchment, when Scotland's position might come under threat. Scotland, as we have seen, has benefited considerably, since at least the time of Thomas Johnston, by having a minister of her own who could press for her needs to be recognized. That era, however, appeared to be coming to an end in the late 1970s.

In 1980, in the Select Committee on Scottish Affairs, Donald Dewar asked the then Conservative Secretary of State for Scotland, George Younger, whether the basis for the Scottish Office's acceptance of the Barnett formula was 'What we have we hold'. Younger's reply was: 'Yes'. A Scottish Office official elaborated on this: 'I think it was calculated that the arrangement was advantageous because public expenditure control was getting tighter and more complex and that the days of table-thumping were ceasing to have their effect. This was the consideration that was borne in mind in accepting this arrangement.'[31]

The Barnett formula, it has been suggested, 'introduces a quasi-federal funding arrangement, which guarantees to Scotland and Wales a fixed proportion of the spending allocated to England, while preserving any historical advantages'.[32] It provides, parallel to the Scottish, Welsh, and Northern Ireland Offices, a mechanism for the determination of expenditure on territorial rather than functional grounds. Had the formula not been in existence, the Conservative governments of the 1980s, whose electoral basis of support lay in southern England, might otherwise have shifted expenditure from Scotland and Wales to England. Moreover, the Barnett formula freed the Scottish and Welsh Secretaries of State from annual negotiations with the Treasury and gave them the freedom to switch expenditure between services. Once the block for Scotland and Wales had been determined, the Secretaries of State were free to adopt the spending mix they thought appropriate for their territories regardless of the approach adopted by English departmental ministers. They were allowed to adopt a territorial rather than a functional approach to public expenditure. This meant that when, for example, in the 1980s Sir Keith Joseph, as Education Secretary, refused to seek higher spending on education, George Younger and Malcolm Rifkind, as Scottish Secretaries, were able to switch money from other pro grammes into education to meet what they saw as Scotland's own particular needs.

The Barnett formula succeeded, to some extent, in protecting Scotland from expenditure cuts in the 1980s and 1990s, since, without it, cuts in the Scottish block might have been more severe, on account of alleged 'over-provision' in Scotland. But the formula does not seem to have achieved convergence between Scotland and England. The reason for this is that the two factors on which the operation of the formula depended have worked to prevent convergence. For there was retrenchment in public spending in the 1980s and 1990s, and the Scottish population declined.

Since the 1970s, the distribution of public spending between different parts of the United Kingdom has become much more explicit. This has led to criticism, primarily in England, suggesting that the higher share of per capita identifiable expenditure in Scotland is, of its very nature, unjust, and that it ought to be reduced or ended following devolution. Such expenditure would not, however, be unjust if it reflected Scotland's greater needs as compared with those of England; and it would in any case be quite wrong to exclude Scotland from the national needs-assessment process simply because she had voted for devolution. The question, however, is whether the higher share of per capita identifiable expenditure in Scotland does in fact wholly reflect Scotland's needs.

The difficulty in answering this question is that there is no scientific or objective way of determining needs. The Barnett formula never claimed to be anything more than a very rough and ready approach but it has so far proved politically acceptable to British governments, whether Conservative or Labour. The formula was designed to secure a convergence in expenditure ratios by ensuring that changes in expenditure were determined by the extant population ratios. The ratios are to be recalibrated regularly to take account of population changes, but not to take account of changing needs as one part of the United Kingdom becomes relatively richer or relatively poorer than another. It could, of course, be argued that because the formula has failed to lead to convergence between Scotland and England, it ought to be altered to England's advantage; on the other hand, it seems that the position of Wales has worsened since the formula was adopted, because Wales, in the words of a Welsh Office official, now

has the lowest level of GDP per head of any region in Great Britain, 18 per cent below England, the lowest level of personal disposable income of any region, 17 per cent below England; the level of economic activity in Wales is only above Merseyside and North East, average earnings in Wales second lowest in Great Britain, 11 per cent below England. Wales has the highest proportion of population with limited long-standing illness in the United Kingdom, and of those figures, GDP per head, average earnings, economic activity rates and household income proportionate to England have all actually gone backwards since the 1970s.[33]

As part of the preparation for devolution, the Treasury carried out a needs-assessment survey, which was published after the Scotland and Wales Acts were repealed in December 1979. It concluded that, using data for 1976-7, the relative amounts of expenditure per capita

Table 7.4 Relative expenditure per capita for devolved services (per capita public expenditure 1976–7 at 1978 survey prices, expressed as a percentage of expenditure in England)

	England	Scotland	Wales	Northern Ireland
A. Per capita public expenditure	100	122	106	135
B. Relative needs	100	116	109	131
Relation of expenditure to needs		+6	−3	+4

Source: HM Treasury, *Needs Assessment Study Report*, para. 6.5, HMSO, 1979

required to provide the same range and level of service as in England for devolved services were as indicated in Table 7.4.

The Barnett formula was not, however, adjusted to take account of this assessment. Nor has any similar needs assessment been carried out since 1979. Indeed, part of the reason for adopting and retaining the Barnett formula was to *avoid* highly contentious annual arguments in Cabinet concerning the 'true' needs of Scotland and Wales. The reason why no further needs assessment has been carried out is clear: if such an assessment were to suggest that the Barnett formula ought to be altered to Scotland's disadvantage, there would be a political outcry in Scotland; and it would be argued, perfectly correctly, that needs assessment cannot be a scientific activity. The Scots would suggest that there were special factors which the needs assessment had not taken into account, or to which it had given insufficient weight. Indeed, referring to the 1979 Needs Assessment exercise, George Younger, as Secretary of State for Scotland, told the Select Committee on Scottish Affairs in 1980: 'My opinion is that the bases upon which the study was made are unproven and therefore I regard it as an interesting document but not as a definitive document.'[34]

The Welsh, on the other hand, might well feel that a new needs assessment is imperative so as to allow the formula to be changed to their advantage. Indeed the House of Commons Welsh Affairs Committee in its First Report of 1997–8 on 'The Impact of the Government's Devolution Proposals on Economic Development and Local Government in Wales', argued that the needs assessment should be brought up to date. The Treasury Committee, a majority of whose members represented English constituencies, in its report on the Barnett Formula, agreed.35 English Members of Parliament, many of whom are somewhat sceptical of devolution, could well face requests from their constituents, especially in the north-east and the north-west, to ensure that Scotland does not benefit at the expense of underprivileged regions in England. During the preparatory phase of campaigning for nomination as Labour candidate for mayor of London, Ken Livingstone, the former leader of the GLC, argued that territorial justice required some of Scotland's money to be diverted to London. On 15 April 1998, the *Scottish Mirror* replied, on its front page, 'You want £2bn. from Scotland? Get Lost! Fury over cash demand from man who would be Mayor of London'.36 That may be just a foretaste of what is to come.

It was because of such possibilities that the Royal Commission on the Constitution argued against a formula approach, declaring that:

In view of the practice which has been built up for the detailed measurement of needs, service by service, it is very doubtful whether an arbitrary formula, resulting in a fixed grant for any five year period, would be acceptable or indeed workable. It would be necessary to construct a more flexible system which, whilst retaining the block grant idea, would include a fairly sensitive measurement of marginal needs, probably every year.37

The Barnett formula will be transformed, after devolution, 'from a mechanism *internal* to government to one used for regulating the transfer of money *between* tiers of government'.38 In theory, it could be altered by ministerial discretion. In practice, it will be difficult to alter it to the disadvantage of the Scots or the Welsh. For it would be politically difficult if not impossible for central government, having decided to established devolved bodies in Scotland and Wales, to apply a more detailed needs assessment, such as the standard spending assessments which apply to local authority expenditure in England, to these bodies. This might give them *less* discretion than the Secretaries of State had enjoyed, and would hardly be compatible with a policy of devolution which implies a dispersal rather than a recentralization of power. Moreover, removing the excess in Scotland would yield England only a minuscule benefit. One authority has calculated that 'If the Treasury analysis [of the excess of Scottish public spending over needs in 1979] was precise (which it is not), it would imply *at most* a reduction in Scottish spending compared with the UK average of £800m. If this were made available to the English population, it would amount to around £17 per capita, a minimal impact.'[39] The problem of underprivileged English regions, then, might be seen as one for England to solve through altering the allocation of public expenditure to regions within England rather than by redistributing from Scotland to England.

The government has proposed, therefore, that, apart from annual recalibrations of the formula to meet changing population relativities, any changes to the formula would, in Alistair Darling's words, 'need to be preceded by an in-depth study of relative spending requirements and would be the subject of full consultation between the devolved administrations and the United Kingdom Government'.[40]

Although the devolved administrations will be *consulted*, changes could nevertheless, in theory at least, be made without their *consent*, since Westminster remains sovereign. Thus the devolved administrations will not enjoy a formal veto power over alterations in the formula. In practice, however, these bodies, representing the people of Scotland and Wales, may well have what amounts to a veto power, since it would take a brave government to face the outcry and loss of electoral support that would ensue as a result of changing the formula to the disadvantage of Scotland or Wales. This will especially be the case during the inaugural period of the devolved administrations, when altering the formula could easily be seen as an attempt to punish Scotland for having voted for devolution. Moreover, it can be argued that devolution was supported in the referendum on the understanding that the existing grant and formula arrangements would continue as outlined in the White Paper. To suggest that the Scottish Parliament should begin by cutting its services, an inevitable consequence of altering the formula to Scotland's disadvantage, would yield a propaganda gift to the SNP; and yet, the purpose of devolution was to contain separatism, not to encourage it. In practice, therefore, Westminster will probably decide on a quiet life and let sleeping dogs lie.

A further weakness of the formula approach, however, is that expenditure in Scotland and Wales comes to be determined by expenditure in England. The point was made in relation to the Goschen formula which, between 1888 and 1957, determined Scotland's public expenditure as eleven-eightieths of that of England, by R. Munro-Ferguson, a Liberal MP, who told the Commons in 1912: 'Scotland is simply tied to the tail of England, and she is denied all initiative. She becomes the dumping ground for some equivalent grant when expenditure is undertaken in England for some purpose that in Scotland is practically uncalled for.'[41]

Such a position is inevitable with a formula arrangement, given the discrepancy in population sizes between England and Scotland. With expenditure in Scotland driven by expenditure in England, an additional £85 in England yields an extra £10 in Scotland and £5 in Wales. With a formula driven by Scotland, however, extra Scottish expenditure of £10 would yield an extra £85 in England and £5 in Wales. The multipliers are 17.65 per cent and 900 per cent respectively. As one authority has commented: 'No UK Treasury could ever be unaware of this asymmetry: equivalent provision for Scotland involves a modest increment over the English cost, whereas equivalent provision for England would involve a huge budgetary cost.'[42] Thus it is expenditure in England which will determine the levels of Scottish and Welsh expenditure. In particular, the funds available to the devolved bodies will depend upon the skills of English spending ministers in such departments as education and health in protecting their budgets, both against the Treasury, and against ministries dealing with reserved matters such as foreign affairs and defence. Were a Conservative government in London, for example, sharply to raise the defence budget and cut the education budget in compensation, that would clearly entail a drastic cut by means of the Barnett formula in the moneys available to Scotland and Wales. The powers of the devolved bodies would in those circumstances be limited. All they could decide is where to make cuts. Or suppose that a future

Conservative government decided to introduce tax incentives for private health insurance, reduce spending on the NHS, and cut income tax. That would lead automatically, under the Barnett formula, to a cut in the additions to the block grant for Scotland and Wales. Yet the devolved bodies in Scotland and Wales might well not wish to follow Conservative policy by reducing NHS spending.43

The implication of devolution is that there can be a good justification for differences in public expenditure patterns between Scotland, Wales, and England. In Scotland there is already less middle-class exit from the National Health Service, and less use of private facilities than in England, while students stay at school for a shorter period and spend longer at university than students in England or Wales. The Scottish Executive might well wish to build on these divergences to develop distinctively Scottish policies in health and education. But the more expenditure patterns come to differ from those in England, the more arbitrary the formula may appear, and the more incentive there will be for the devolved administrations to press for alterations in the formula on the ground that the different pattern of expenditure justifies more money. Thus the formula approach seems to contradict the very purpose of devolution.

Labour governments, both in the 1970s and 1990s, in deciding not to devolve major revenue-raising powers to the devolved bodies, drew on the distinction which the Royal Commission on the Constitution had made between a revenue basis for financing the devolved institutions and an expenditure basis for financing them.

Under a revenue basis, a devolved government is given certain taxation powers and certain fixed sources of revenue and is obliged to finance services out of the income which these sources produce. Under such a system, the main determinant of the total amount spent by a devolved government is the taxation decisions which it takes. That, as we have seen, was the basis of finance in Northern Ireland under the Government of Ireland Act of 1920.

Under an expenditure basis, by contrast, the expenditure requirements of the devolved government are decided, and it is then provided with the income to meet its requirements. Under such a system, the main determinant of the total amount spent by a devolved government is the resources provided for it by the centre. The system of finance in Northern Ireland, as we have seen, began on a revenue basis but came in practice to operate on an expenditure basis.

The Royal Commission on the Constitution believed that an expenditure basis was preferable to a revenue basis on the ground that only an expenditure basis was compatible with the distribution of public resources on the basis of need. The case of Northern Ireland was also adduced to show that an expenditure basis was to be preferred.[44] A revenue basis would mean that the public expenditure of each devolved part of the country would, so the Commission argued, depend upon its resources, not upon its needs.

If that argument were correct, however, it would also be an argument against local authorities being given revenue-raising powers. Yet such powers are not thought to be incompatible with the equitable distribution of public expenditure, provided that they are supplemented by an equalization element. So also, it would be perfectly possible for the devolved administrations to be financed on a revenue basis, but for this to be supplemented by an equalization element. The failure, indeed, of the Northern Ireland system of finance derived not from its being established on a revenue basis, but from the absence of such an equalization element. The Northern Ireland government did not agitate for such an element, since, as we saw in Chapter 3, its central concern was to maintain parity with the rest of the United Kingdom, to follow expenditure patterns elsewhere rather than to diverge from them. The Scottish and Welsh administrations will be under no equivalent temptation.

The right approach towards financing the devolved administrations would have been to ensure that as much as possible of their revenue came from transferred taxes and from local shares of reserved taxes, together with an equalization element. Of course, there would be an inevitable element of subjectivity about the size of the equalization element, precisely because it is not possible to discover an objective criterion for Scottish or Welsh needs. Nevertheless, since the equalization element would be a far smaller element of Scottish revenue than the block grant which will finance the whole of the Scottish Parliament—with the minimal exception of the tax-varying power—and the Welsh Assembly, it would not be so controversial. The debate in Scotland and Wales would not then turn so continuously on the parsimony of London and on the question of which party in Edinburgh or Cardiff would be best able to squeeze more money out of the British government.

A second-best alternative would have been a system of assigned taxes such as that in operation in Germany. The vast majority of regional finance in Belgium, Portugal, and Spain also derives from assigned revenues. Such a system would not have yielded tax-raising powers to the devolved administrations, and would not have made them as accountable to their electorates as would a revenue-based system. But it would at least have given them an entitlement to revenues, in place of the relationship of dependence which the Scotland Act and the Government of Wales Act will create. In Germany, this entitlement is crucially dependent upon the part which the *Länder* are able to play in the process of determining how much they receive from the federal government through the participation of their governments in the upper house, the Bundesrat; and there is of course no equivalent to the Bundesrat in Britain. Even in Germany, however, the *Länder* are arguing that they should have their own tax-raising powers.

The devolved administrations in Britain will enjoy no constitutional protection similar to that of the *Länder* in Germany. In a unitary state, the Cabinet is the forum within which the territorial division of public expenditure is decided. There is, however, a definite need for some other forum at which territorial financial questions can be discussed and at which both the British government and the devolved administrations can be represented. The Royal Commission on the Constitution suggested that a nominated National Exchequer Board, on the model of the Exchequer Board for Northern Ireland under the 1920 Government of Ireland Act, also composed of nominated members, be established. But a nominated body could not be allowed to take *decisions* on the territorial distribution of public moneys. For, as we have seen, these decisions depend upon essentially political judgements. So an Exchequer Board, if one were to be established, should enjoy only advisory and not executive or arbitral functions; it should be a body which collects information and applies expertise, such as the Commonwealth Grants Commission in Australia, rather than a body enjoying the power of decision.

We may conclude, however, by reiterating that the financial provisions constitute the weakest element in the devolution legislation. Not only do they represent a centralist solution, but they may also give rise to instability and conflict in the relationships between the devolved administrations and Westminster. Paradoxically, a less centralist solution, devolving revenue-raising powers to the devolved bodies, would be more likely to bind them into the United Kingdom than a solution which denies the devolved bodies the financial responsibilities that should naturally accompany their powers. Nevertheless, if devolution is indeed to prove a process and not an event, it is reasonable to hope that the financial provisions mark the beginning and not the end of the debate on the financing of the devolved administrations. That debate will only have been concluded when financial arrangements are put in place which serve to sustain rather than to frustrate the fundamental purpose of devolution— the dispersal of power.

The Welsh model

The Government of Wales Act provides not legislative devolution but executive devolution, the devolution of secondary legislation and other executive powers. The rationale for this has never been wholly clear. The Royal Commission on the Constitution believed that, in both Scotland and Wales, there were large numbers 'who wish their distinctive national identities to be recognised in the system of government in some way short of separation', and that 'In these two countries the centralisation of politics and government in London is resented more than it is in England.'45 From this, it would seem to follow that Scotland and Wales should receive common treatment on grounds of nationhood. It would be odd to suggest that the Scottish identity was that of a primary legislation nation, while the Welsh identity was only that of a secondary legislation nation. There were, as we have seen, only two members of the Commission—Professor Street and Mrs Trenaman—who favoured different treatment for Scotland and Wales, and Mrs Trenaman was later to withdraw her support for devolution entirely. Only four members of the Commission—Lord Foot and Sir James Steel, as well as the two signatories of the Memorandum of Dissent, Lord Crowther-Hunt and Professor Peacock—favoured executive devolution for Wales, but these four favoured executive devolution for Scotland also.

Labour governments in the 1970s and 1990s, however, were impressed, and perhaps over-impressed, as were Professor Street and Mrs Trenaman, by the case for special treatment for Scotland on the grounds of her separate legal system. Indeed, it seemed, in the 1990s, that Labour regarded only Scotland as a nation. The White Paper, *Scotland's Parliament*, Cm. 3658, 1997, begins with a resounding declaration by the Prime Minister, 'Scotland is a proud historic nation in the United Kingdom'. But the White Paper, *A Voice for Wales*, Cm. 3718, 1997, contains no such declaration. Instead, the foreword by the then Welsh Secretary, Ron Davies, declares that 'The referendum offers the people of Wales a new beginning, *alongside other successful economic regions* of Europe' (my italics). Scotland, then, is a nation, Wales a region. The model of devolution proposed for Wales is indeed more suitable for a region than a nation. The consequence, however, is that, of all the bodies represented in the British–Irish Council created by the Belfast Agreement—the Republic of Ireland, the United Kingdom, the Isle of Man and the Channel Islands, and the devolved bodies of Scotland, Wales, and Northern Ireland—only the Welsh Assembly will be without primary legislative powers.

Executive devolution may appear at first sight as merely a weaker variant of legislative devolution. The Welsh Assembly will have no power to pass primary legislation, but only secondary legislation, responsibility for primary legislation remaining with Westminster. Secondary legislation involves orders, rules, and regulations which fill in the details of the framework set out in the primary legislation, the Act of Parliament. Executive devolution, however, is not so much a weaker form of devolution than legislative, but a quite different one, which introduces into Britain a wholly new and as yet untried structure of governmental relationships. For, while the Scotland Act introduces a form of quasi-federalism into British government, the Government of Wales Act provides for a form of regionalism.

Legislative devolution involves a *transfer* of powers, executive devolution involves a *division* of powers at present united in the hands of ministers as well as a transfer of powers. It is possible broadly to ascertain the precise functions of a parliament such as the Scottish Parliament with legislative powers by inspecting the provisions of the relevant legislation, in this case the Scotland Act. With the Welsh National Assembly, by contrast, its functions depend not only on the provisions of the Government of Wales Act, but also upon the way in which legislation for Wales is drawn up by the government and the degree of discretion which central government thinks it right to confer upon the Assembly. For there is, in Britain at least, no clear dividing line between policy-making and administration, and thus no basis of principle for determining whether a particular matter falls under primary legislation, in which case it ought to be retained, or secondary legislation, in which case it ought to be devolved.

Legislative devolution involves a decision as to whether or not to transfer responsibility for a particular function, for example education. Executive devolution involves a second decision—*how much* decision-making power should be transferred. This requires an answer to the prior question of how primary legislation ought to be drafted. If it is drafted loosely, then there will be greater scope for the Welsh Assembly than if it is drafted more tightly. If, for example, an Act were to provide that 'Provision may be made for Wales by Order as the Assembly sees fit', that would yield considerable autonomy to the Assembly. If, however, it were to provide that 'Provision for Wales shall be by Order by the Assembly in like manner as for England in this Act', the Assembly would have very little autonomy. A Conservative government at Westminster, faced with a politically hostile Welsh Assembly, might well have been tempted to legislate in this manner on some controversial policy initiative of the 1980s such as, for example, the introduction of grant-maintained schools, the sale of council houses, or the poll tax, so as to prevent the Assembly from frustrating its policies.

It is often suggested that devolution would have spared Wales the poll tax. But the National Assembly would have had to introduce it since it was, of course, provided by primary legislation. Moreover, the bill, as drafted, allowed little scope for discretion in the secondary legislation. The most that the Welsh Assembly might have been able to achieve would have been the variation of the bands so that the tax approached a little more closely to a local income tax. Of course, it might be argued that, had the Assembly been in existence at that time, this would have induced a spirit of greater co-operation from central government. It is difficult, however, to imagine Margaret Thatcher's government allowing a Welsh Assembly to evade what she regarded as a vital part of her policy. Indeed, with a Welsh Assembly in existence, Margaret Thatcher might well have drawn up the poll-tax legislation not more loosely but more tightly, depriving the Assembly of the opportunity even of varying the bands. It is important, therefore, not to exaggerate what devolution can be expected to achieve.

Executive devolution involves dividing powers which have hitherto been united and creating a new layer of government to administer a portion of them. There is of course nothing novel in creating bodies with subordinate powers in Britain. Indeed, local authorities are such bodies. But there is no general guidance available on the appropriate division of powers between central government and a devolved body to which powers of ministers are to be transferred, and no general rule as to whether a particular function should or should not be transferred. Moreover, because there is no clear basis of distinction between policy-making and administration, then, to quote the Royal Commission on the Constitution, the division of functions: 'would not be capable of simple definition. . . . The division would be an arbitrary one in that the range of powers conferred on the assemblies would depend upon a political judgement of the extent of the control it was necessary to retain at the centre'.[46]

In Britain, legislative and executive powers have, until now, been so closely fused that, to quote again from the Royal Commission on the Constitution, 'the division between them is not a precise one, and under the present arrangements they are not clearly separated'.[47] In the past, legislation does not seem to have been guided by any clear principles. The dividing line seems rather to have been drawn for reasons of convenience. As the Permanent Secretary at the Welsh Office, Rachel Lomax, declared in a speech to the Institute of Welsh Affairs on 7 November 1997, 'The Secretary of State's present powers have accumulated piecemeal over a long period of time, and the distinction between matters that are dealt with in primary and secondary legislation has reflected pragmatic considerations as much as principle.'

The reason for this is that the distinction between primary and secondary legislation was never intended to provide the basis for a division of powers between different elected bodies. Instead, primary and secondary legislation have been regarded as part of a single process. Therefore, with regard to existing legislation, the Welsh Assembly could easily find that its powers were of uneven scope and depth since there would be no reason why the division between primary and secondary legislation in one policy area, for example, health, should match the division in another, for example, education. If that were so, the initial powers of the Assembly would have no clear rationale and an integrated approach to policy-making would become impossible.

Powers are to be transferred to the National Assembly in two ways. First, under section 22 of the Government of Wales Act, functions of a minister of the Crown can be transferred by Order in Council, subject to an affirmative resolution in both Houses. The Welsh Office has published a draft Transfer Order which give the Assembly powers to make subordinate legislation. The government's intention is that virtually all of the executive powers currently exercised by the Secretary of State should be so transferred.

Second, functions can be conferred directly on the Assembly by primary legislation. Sections 27 and 28 of the Government of Wales Act, for example, confer directly on the Assembly powers to reform the Welsh health authorities and other Welsh public bodies. This is of particular importance since one of the arguments for Welsh devolution has been that too many governmental functions are carried out by *ad hoc* bodies of various sorts—quangos. Sections 27 and 28 provide for the amendment of primary legislation by means of secondary legislation—known as a Henry VIII power—and, in effect, they give the Welsh Assembly a power of primary legislation.

Once the existing functions of the Secretary of State have been conferred upon the Assembly in the first Transfer Order, there are two methods of giving the Assembly additional functions: first, by further Transfer Orders, to effect transfers of existing executive powers exercised by other ministers *vis-à-vis* Wales; and, second, by means of new primary legislation conferring new functions and powers on the Assembly directly. In paragraph 3.39 of the White Paper, *A Voice for Wales*, Cm. 3718, 1997, it is said that: 'The Government will consider, in drafting each Bill that it introduces into Parliament, which of the new powers it contains should be exercised by the Assembly. This could include giving the Assembly responsibility for bringing the Bill's provisions into force in Wales.'

This means that future bills dealing with matters covered by the fields within which the Assembly exercises responsibility will be, in a sense, devolution bills in that they will sct out the limits within which secondary legislation can take place; and, given the possibility of further transfers of powers from other ministers to the National Assembly, devolution will, as the former Secretary of State for Wales Ron Davies often insisted, be not an event but a process.[48] Tax-varying powers, however, since these are not powers given to ministers, would require primary legislation. The powers of the Welsh National Assembly, then, might be very different after, say, ten years from what they are when the Assembly begins its work.

Thus executive devolution, devolution of a 'horizontal' type, is not just a weaker form than legislative devolution, devolution of a 'vertical' type, but a wholly different kind of animal and it raises problems which have not hitherto been confronted in the British political system. If executive devolution is to prove effective, two fundamental problems will need to be resolved.

First, primary legislation for Wales will have to be drawn up more loosely than primary legislation for England, so as to give scope to the Assembly, without giving too great a discretion to ministers in charge of English departments. This means that future statutes will have to be framed differently for England and for Wales. For, if they were to be framed similarly, either they would be very loosely drawn both for England and for Wales, in which case the Assembly would have considerable scope but English ministers would be given too wide a discretion; or, alternatively, if the legislative framework were drawn up equally tightly for England and Wales, the Welsh Assembly would find that its powers over secondary legislation did not amount to very much.

Second, principles must be devised to regulate the dividing line between primary and secondary legislation. Such principles have been developed in Germany, whose federal system is based primarily on the division of executive rather than legislative powers, although the *Länder* do have some legislative powers. In Germany there is a system of administrative law which 'displays a relatively high degree of coherence and homogeneity' so that 'it is possible . . . to achieve a consistency of principles . . . which is unattainable within the traditions of pragmatic positivism which have shaped both the common law and the statutory public law in Britain'.49 Whereas in Britain, statutes generally confer duties on local authorities and other public bodies and controlling and supervising powers on ministers, in Germany they are normally drafted in general declaratory terms. They provide only the framework of policy, leaving a good deal of initiative to the *Länder* in implementation. But the discretionary powers of government have to be exercised in accordance with general constitutional principles or they will be challenged in the courts. An approach of this kind, however, would involve fundamental changes in our notions of public law and in such constitutional doctrines as the responsibility of ministers to Parliament.

Because this framework is so unfamiliar in Britain, it will be difficult to attain some basis of principle for the transfer of powers, a basis of principle which could be used to regulate future legislation for Wales. The ideal would be a convention or published concordat regulating what can be dealt with by primary legislation for Wales and what by secondary, so that primary legislation affecting Wales becomes more permissive, laying down only very broad general objectives instead of providing also the details.

Even if this is done, however, the Welsh Assembly would not be the final authority on the policies for which it is responsible, for Westminster still retains control of all primary legislation for Wales. Moreover, many devolved functions involve the supervision of services delivered by local authorities, and the Assembly is required to set up a Partnership Council with local government which will be empowered to make representations to the Assembly on matters affecting local government. No doubt this Council will have as one of its tasks the drawing-up of conventions governing the respective spheres of the Assembly and local authorities in the government of Wales. Nevertheless policies involving, for example, education or the social services will have to proceed through three layers of government—central government, the Welsh Assembly, and Welsh local authorities. This could lead to a confused system of government with no clear lines of demarcation between the different layers.

It may become more difficult, after devolution, for the government to draw up primary legislation for Wales, since it will have lost contact with Welsh local authorities actually delivering services, such contact being mediated by the Assembly. Deprived of this contact and of feedback, the Secretary of State for Wales may well find himself less well informed about the needs of Wales. His weight in Cabinet will also be less since he will have lost his executive powers, while officials preparing Welsh legislation will no longer be responsible for its implementation in Wales.

The Assembly will, of course, be in a better position to appreciate Welsh needs; but, because it has no primary legislative powers, it will have to rely upon close co-operation with the Secretary of State for Wales to promote legislation. In Germany, the *Länder* are in a much stronger position in this regard since their role is constitutionally guaranteed through the representation of their governments in the federal upper house, the Bundesrat. Matters affecting the rights of the *Länder* require the consent of the Bundesrat as well as the lower house, the Bundestag, and so the governments of the *Länder* can veto legislation if they believe that its consequences would be deleterious for them.

Under section 31 of the Government of Wales Act, the Secretary of State is required to consult with the Assembly on the government's programme, 'as appears to him to be appropriate'. But there is no requirement to consult on every bill. The Secretary of State may refuse to do so if he 'considers that there are considerations relating to the bill which make it inappropriate for him to do so'. Of course, the Secretary of State might well belong to a different party from that of the majority in the Assembly. Under those circumstances, there might be two contradictory voices speaking for Wales, the Secretary of State and the First Secretary of the Assembly. If there is conflict, it would prove difficult for the Assembly to gain influence over government legislation, but equally difficult for the government to enforce its policies for Wales over the head of a politically hostile National Assembly. What is certain is that consultation and co-operation cannot be taken for granted. Even so, under the pre-devolutionary dispensation, Welsh Office ministers and officials consulted with their colleagues in Whitehall and served on teams drawing up legislation when Welsh interests so demanded. It is not clear whether the Assembly will be able, similarly, to examine policy proposals which are in the process of formulation by ministers. For this to happen, the Secretary of State would have to be prepared to engage in a genuine dialogue with the Assembly, representing both the government to the Assembly and the Assembly to the government. He would have to be prepared, for example, to put forward amendments to draft government legislation to his colleagues even if he were not wholly convinced of their merits. All this implies a new and untried set of relationships in British government.

Nevertheless, the hope must be that, in the words of a Cabinet paper written in 1975 in preparation for the abortive Wales Act of 1978:

the Assembly's views will carry more weight than those of most other bodies. First, the Assembly will represent the people of Wales and will speak with a virtually unique political authority on matters affecting the Principality. Second, the Assembly will be responsible for the implementation of legislation on devolved matters in Wales; it will know the situation 'on the ground' and will speak with knowledge on proposals relating to that situation. In reality, therefore, the Assembly's *influence* on legislation could be substantial.[50]

The Assembly is likely to be a powerful pressure-group on primary legislation as it affects Wales. It is likely, under favourable circumstances, to be a more powerful pressure-group on government than the Secretary of State for Wales has been in the past. The Assembly will also yield more detailed scrutiny, openness, and public participation in the making of secondary legislation than occurs at Westminster. Moreover, it will be possible to amend secondary legislation for Wales in the Assembly, while at Westminster, by contrast, secondary legislation must be either accepted or rejected and no amendment is possible.

It is clear that the effectiveness of devolution in Wales, executive devolution, relies, even more than legislative devolution, upon co-operation between the Assembly and central government. Where instead of co-operation there is an adversarial relationship, as might have occurred during the period of John Redwood's Secretaryship of State between 1993 and 1995, had there been an Assembly in existence at that time, the Assembly would find itself in the invidious position of being required to implement legislation with which it fundamentally disagreed, and with which, *ex hypothesi*, the majority in Wales also disagreed. Such an adversarial relationship can by no means be excluded. Indeed, since 1868, apart from the war years, the political complexion of the government in power has been different from that of the majority in Wales for around two-thirds of the time.

In Germany, by contrast, the country from which the idea of executive devolution is derived, political relationships, even between members of opposing parties, are often co-operative and consensual rather than adversarial. Moreover, the division of powers in the federal system is buttressed by a constitutional court which ensures that the demarcation lines are observed. In Britain, there is, of course, no such constitutional court and there is no way in which Westminster could bind itself to observe those principles regulating the division between primary and secondary legislation which happened to be drawn up by a particular government at a particular time.

In order to meet this problem, the government has proposed that there be a series of non-statutory concordats defining the working relationship of officials with Whitehall departments. The concordats will be published and will create what Lord Falconer, as Solicitor-General, called 'a legitimate expectation of consultation'.[51] They will, however, not be enforceable in the courts, although if an individual is damaged by the breach of a concordat, it may be that the breach can be raised in court proceedings. The idea of the concordat is an innovation in British constitutional life, since it imposes a self-denying ordinance upon government, limiting its power to legislate.

Welsh devolution, if it is to succeed, will require a considerable alteration in our constitutional habits. Not only will it require governments to accept principles which limit their power; it will require government and the Welsh Assembly to share power, to co-operate, rather than indulge in adversarial relationships. It will require what the Royal Commission on the Constitution called 'a new style of thinking, positively favourable to devolution and based on co-operation rather than the exercise of central authority'.[52] It will require, in short, a very radical change in our whole political culture.

The English dimension

England is hardly mentioned in the devolution legislation, and yet England is, in many respects, the key to the success of devolution. This is because any devolution settlement has to be acceptable not just to the Scots and the Welsh but also to the English, who return 529 of the 659 Members of Parliament to Westminster and who constitute 85 per cent of the population of the United Kingdom. The success of devolution will depend in large part upon whether English opinion believes it to be a fair and equitable settlement.

There may, at first sight, seem to be no reason why devolution to Scotland and Wales should have any consequences for England at all. Devolution, after all, involves the transfer of power over only Scottish and Welsh domestic matters, and the legislation provides that the central instruments of economic management, together with all major economic and industrial powers, remain with Westminster. Moreover, the government will continue to be responsible for the nationwide allocation of resources throughout the United Kingdom on the basis of need. Devolution, then, seems restricted to those matters which primarily affect those living in Scotland and Wales, and which can be administered separately without deleterious consequences on those living in England. The Long Title of the Scotland Act refers to its providing for 'the establishment of a Scottish Parliament and Administration and other changes in the government of Scotland'; the Long Title of the Government of Wales Act refers to its purpose as being 'To establish and make provision about the National Assembly for Wales'. They make no reference to the fact that they are making very radical changes to the government of the United Kingdom as a whole. They therefore imply that the establishment of a Scottish Parliament and a Welsh Assembly will not prejudice the interests of England.

Devolution, however, will accentuate an already existing constitutional imbalance in favour of Scotland and Wales. They already have their own Secretaries of State pressing their case at Cabinet level; they are over-represented in the House of Commons by comparison with England; and there is a good case for arguing that Scotland at least benefits more from public spending than those English regions whose GDP per head is lower. After devolution, Scotland and Wales will have control over local government spending on devolved services; they will have freedom to establish their own expenditure priorities; they will enjoy an advantage through their powerful political status in bidding for industry, and very possibly a greater opportunity of putting their case directly to the European Union. Above all, they, but not the English regions, will be able to negotiate with the government on any revisions of the Barnett formula or the assessment of needs; and this may well give them what amounts to a veto on changes deleterious to their interests. The Scottish Parliament and the Welsh Assembly are thus likely to enjoy very considerable political power and influence.

Those living in the more underprivileged English regions, such as the north-east or the north-west, may already regard themselves as second-class because they have no territorial ministers able to argue their case in Cabinet. After devolution, they may come to believe that they are third-class, since they have no assemblies either. It is by no means clear that a constitutional imbalance which has been broadly acceptable until now will continue to be acceptable after devolution. It is misleading, then, to regard devolution simply as a process by which the Scots and the Welsh manage their own domestic affairs. The Scottish Parliament and the Welsh Assembly may well be able to use their influence to ensure that they achieve an even greater share of resources than they obtain at present. If that occurs, it is likely to be the less well-off regions of England which will suffer. It will be difficult for the English regions, lacking representation in the Cabinet and without assemblies of their own, to counter this influence. In this way, the *constitutional* imbalance accentuated by devolution could lead to a serious *economic* imbalance favourable to Scotland and Wales, but unfavourable to the less privileged English regions. One consequence of this imbalance might be the generation of powerful regional lobbies in England. Whether that happens or not, the consent, or at the very least the acquiescence, of England is essential to the success of devolution.

In his poem 'The Secret People' G. K. Chesterton wrote, 'Smile at us, pay us, pass us, but do not quite forget; for we are the people of England that never have spoken yet.' England has not yet spoken because, constitutionally, England does not exist. 'England', it has been said, 'is a state of mind, not a consciously organised political institution'.53 There has been no English parliament since 1536. There is no English Office comparable to the Scottish, Welsh, or Northern Ireland Offices, the 'English' ministers being so only because their non-English functions have been hived off to the territorial departments. The 'English' legal system comprises both England and Wales. The Treaty of Union which the Scots claim to have agreed with the 'English' in 1707 was in fact agreed with the English state, which then comprised both the English and the Welsh people.

England has long been the stumbling-block for supporters of devolution. For England, since the time of the union with Scotland in 1707, has resisted integration, while remaining unsympathetic to federalism. It is the supposedly unified and homogeneous nature of England which has in large part been responsible for the preservation of the unitary state. It is largely for this reason that England has not until now sought devolution. Until she does, governments have taken the view that she ought not to have devolution thrust upon her. In 1977, when the Scotland and Wales bill was under consideration by Parliament, Michael Foot declared that 'The Government do not propose to initiate any major constitutional change in England until there is evidence of much more extensive support for it.' 54 That remains the position of the Labour government elected in 1997. There could be no justification for requiring England to accept devolution against her wishes just because there has been devolution to Scotland and Wales. To force devolution upon England, far from assuaging resentment against Scotland and Wales, could well intensify it.

In February 1998, however, the Conservative leader, William Hague, called for changes to be made in the government of England, following devolution to Scotland and Wales. He put forward as suggestions an English Grand Committee or an English parliament. There is in fact, as we have seen, provision in the standing orders of the House of Commons for a Standing Committee on Regional Affairs, a kind of English Grand Committee. But that Committee has not met since 1978 for the very good reason that it proved to be nothing more than a cumbrous talking-shop.

In January 1998, the Eurosceptic Conservative back-bencher Teresa Gorman moved a private member's bill calling for a referendum on Hague's other proposal, an English parliament. The main purpose of such a parliament would be to resolve the West Lothian Question. Yet it would be pointless to 'resolve' it by a massive upheaval in England unless that were also desired for other reasons, and unless it served to make government more effective. An English parliament, however, would yield a form of 'Home Rule All Round' which would be highly unbalanced in population terms. Indeed, an English parliament could hardly avoid becoming a real rival to Westminster. As the Royal Commission on the Constitution warned,

A federation consisting of four units—England, Scotland, Wales, and Northern Ireland—would be so unbalanced as to be unworkable. It would be dominated by the overwhelming political importance and wealth of England. The English Parliament would rival the United Kingdom federal Parliament; and in the federal Parliament itself the representation of England could hardly be scaled down in such a way as to enable it to be outvoted by Scotland, Wales and Northern Ireland, together representing less than one-fifth of the population. A United Kingdom federation of four countries, with a federal Parliament and provincial Parliaments in the four national capitals, is therefore not a realistic proposition.[55]

Moreover, an English parliament would do nothing to remove the problems of over-centralization and lack of democratic accountability which comprise the dynamic behind devolution. Were an English parliament to be set up, there would still be a need to disperse power within England. So an English parliament, while it might resolve the West Lothian Question, would not resolve the problem to which devolution is the answer. Devolution in England, therefore, if it is to serve the same ends as devolution in Scotland and Wales, must be devolution to the English regions, not to an English parliament. It is no doubt for this reason that, in the preface to the White Paper, *Scotland's Parliament*, Cm. 3658, Tony Blair indicates that his government's 'comprehensive programme of constitutional reform' involves as well as 'a Scottish Parliament and a Welsh Assembly' 'more accountability in the regions of England'. 'The Union', the document goes on to say, 'will be strengthened by recognising the claims of Scotland, Wales and the regions with strong identities of their own'.

There are, however, no ministers for the English regions as there are ministers for Scotland and Wales and, by contrast with the Scottish and Welsh Offices, the regions are not directly represented in the Cabinet. The Labour government elected in 1997, however, established a new Department of the Environment, Transport and the Regions; and, since 1994, there have been Government Offices for the Regions, which bring together the regional offices of the Departments of the Environment, Transport, and the Regions, Trade and Industry, and the Training, Enterprise and Education Directorate of the Department for Education and Employment. These Offices administer or advise on programmes such as housing, urban regeneration projects, and training and education budgets. They provide a single point of contact with central government for local businesses and councils whose bids for money for economic development and urban regeneration are submitted via the Government Offices, as are bids for industrial aid and moneys from the European Union regional and social funds.

The establishment of these Offices in the regions involved a further change of great importance for the debate on devolution, in that it marked a step towards the establishment of common regional boundaries in place of the previous unsystematic arrangements. When John Gummer, the Conservative Environment Secretary, commended the

Government Offices for the Regions to the House of Commons, he declared: 'For the first time, there will be coterminous regions for the Departments, and that is the vital change. It has always seemed ridiculous to me that different departments had different regions. That made any sort of planning almost impossible.'[56]

Admittedly, there is still considerable variation between the boundaries of the Government Offices, and those of agencies, established under the 'Next Steps' programme, and non-departmental public bodies, even those run by the departments brought together in the Government Offices for the Regions. Major executive agencies within departments participating in the Government Offices, for example the Highways Agency, have an established regional structure with boundaries differing quite markedly from those of the Regional Offices. In addition, the regional boundaries of the NHS also differ from those of the Government Offices. Moreover, by no means all of the regional functions of government are carried out through the Offices. Regional functions in health and education as well as the regional functions of the Home Office, for example, do not operate through the Government Offices. One authority has discovered nearly a hundred different regional structures ranging from the six regional crime squads covering England and Wales to the nine Bee Health Inspection regions of the Ministry of Agriculture, Fisheries and Food.[57]

It would be wrong to regard these regional institutions as comprising a regional layer of government. Many of them are regional outposts of central government, a structure still primarily determined in England by functional rather than territorial considerations and one whose features are influenced as much by administrative convenience and historical accident as by any deliberate policy of regionalism. Regional institutions are highly fragmented, comprising as they do a jumble of heterogeneous bodies with quite varying functions and no clear pattern. Nor do most regional institutions enjoy policy-making functions, being primarily concerned with the administration of policy decided in Whitehall and the casework flowing from it. They administer nationally determined policies, which are not necessarily suitable for regional devolution. It is a fallacy, therefore, to suppose that because a function is carried out in a region, it is a function suitable for regional devolution.

Moreover, unlike local authorities, regional institutions do not in the main provide services, but rather distribute resources and grants to local authorities and other bodies. Thus, if the functions of the Government Offices for the Regions were to be transferred to directly elected regional assemblies, the powers of these assemblies would be largely concerned with the distribution of resources to local government. They would then be very tempted to establish tighter supervision over local government. If that happened, devolution would centralize government, not decentralize it. The existence of regional institutions cannot, therefore, be used as a conclusive argument for regional devolution in England.

Moreover, regional devolution in England would almost certainly require further reorganization of local government. England, unlike Scotland or Wales, still has a predominantly two-tier structure of local government outside London. Devolution was made easier in Scotland and Wales because local authorities had already been reorganized and unitary authorities established there. In England, by contrast, there was no legislation providing for reorganization; instead a Local Government Commission was set up to consult with local opinion. This Commission failed to discover any consensus for reorganization and, in consequence, thirty-four of the thirty-nine shire counties in England retain a two-tier system of local government. There is indeed no standard region with wholly unitary local government outside London. To impose regional assemblies on a two-tier system of local government is hardly feasible. 'One thing we are clear about in England,' Jack Straw declared as Shadow Home Secretary in 1995; 'you cannot establish regional assemblies as well as having shire counties and districts underneath them'.[58] Regional assemblies, then, would mean the end of county government in England, and the regions would replace the counties. Thus regional government in England would require a further reorganization of local government which practically no one wants. Reorganization, moreover, would probably mean that some of the functions of the upper tier of local government, the counties, would be transferred, not to the lower tier of local government, the districts, but to the regions. It would be natural to propose a new division of functions such that personal services—education and social services, for example—remained with local authorities, while strategic services, such as planning, transport, economic development, and European liaison, were transferred upwards to regional level. That would be seen as a threat by local government and as contrary to the purpose of devolution, which is to disperse power.

The fundamental difficulty with devolution to the English regions, however, is that there is so little demand for it. It is for this reason that English regionalism has been called 'the dog that never barked'.59 Devolution in England has to confront the problem that the regions are in large degree simply ghosts. For regional institutions to be effective, there would need to be a much stronger sense of regional awareness, similar to the sense of Scottish or Welsh awareness. At present, a sense of regional awareness does exist in those regions most distant from London, the north-east and the north-west, and perhaps also in the south-west, where geographical remoteness from Westminster co-exists with a feeling of economic disadvantage. It is possible that regional institutions could increase that sense of regional awareness, just as the Welsh Office seems to have increased Welsh awareness, but it cannot yet be said that there is a regional consciousness sufficiently strong to sustain directly elected regional institutions with powers devolved from central government.

In the 1970s, proposals for devolution to Scotland and Wales did, it is true, stimulate regional feeling in England, especially in the north of England. But that feeling was primarily directed at preventing devolution. There was little spontaneous demand for regional assemblies, and indeed the demand for such assemblies would probably not have been put forward at all had the Labour government not proposed devolution for Scotland and Wales. With devolution a *fait accompli*, however, it may be that the strategy of those who feel that their interests have been deleteriously affected will alter, and they might seek to establish regional assemblies in England in order to counter the greater political weight of Scotland and Wales. In November 1997, in what may prove a portent, a Declaration for the North appeared, calling for a regional assembly. It was signed by the majority of Labour MPs in the north-east, the region's four MEPs, and by much of the Labour establishment in the region. Pressure for a northern assembly may well increase once the Scottish Parliament is in operation.

Developments in Europe may also contribute to regional awareness, although, as the next section shows, the significance of these developments should not be overestimated. The European Union is very far from being a Europe of the Regions, and it would require radical changes in the policies of the member states to create it. Nevertheless, in order to improve their position in bidding for European Union funds, local authorities have begun to organize themselves on a regional level. The whole of England is now covered by regional associations of local authorities, and there is thus an embryonic bottom-up regionalism, to match the top-down regionalism of the Government Offices. The 1999 European Parliament elections in Britain may also serve to strengthen regional feeling, for they are to be conducted by proportional representation based on regional lists. Thus the regions, for the first time, might become political units in their own right.

The Labour government elected in 1997 faced the same problem as its predecessor in the 1970s. It was instinctively sympathetic to regional devolution in England, but felt unable to proceed in the absence of clear indicators of support for it. The government therefore decided to adopt an evolutionary approach. In 1997 it issued a White Paper, *Building Partnerships for Prosperity*, Cm. 3814, which proposed the establishment of regional development agencies, and also indirectly elected regional chambers chosen primarily from local authorities. These chambers, according to para. 1.7 of the White Paper, 'may be a first step towards greater devolution in England'. In the House of Commons, John Prescott, the Secretary of State for the Environment, Transport and the Regions, declared: 'We are committed to moving, with the consent of local people, to directly elected regional government in England. That complements devolution in Scotland and Wales and the creation of a Greater London Assembly. Demand for directly elected regional government varies across England, and it would be wrong to envisage a uniform approach at this stage'.[60] The White Paper expresses the hope, however, that the creation of regional development agencies 'will help to foster a sense of regional identity and develop a regional capability. In time, this may lead to further transfers of functions and responsibilities to regional structures' (p. 52). Nevertheless, devolution to the regions is unlikely in the 1997 Parliament. Richard Caborn, the Minister for Regions, Regeneration and Planning, told the Environment, Transport and Regional Affairs Committee of the House of Commons, that people in the regions would 'be given the opportunity . . . to make them [the chambers] directly elected at a time after the next general election'.[61]

The essence of the programme for devolution in England is that it will be granted to any region which seeks it; at the same time a region which does not seek devolution will not be able to prevent any other region from embracing it. Devolution in England, however, is to be subject to a threefold test to ensure that there is real popular demand for it. First, there must be a plan for devolution drawn up and approved by the regional chamber, indicating that it is supported by the majority of local authorities in the region. Second, the plan must be approved by Parliament, with the Secretary of State being required to consult the opposition parties before giving it his own approval. Third, there must be clear evidence of popular support, probably including a referendum. Thus, in contrast to the 1970s, when Labour, despite having promised regional government in opposition, delivered nothing, in the 1990s the party proposes a staged approach which perhaps offers a greater chance of success.

This staged approach, or rolling devolution as it is often called, is similar to that adopted in Spain after the death of Franco in 1975 and the return to democratic government. In Spain, a distinction was made between the so-called historic communities—Catalonia and the Basque country—corresponding perhaps to Scotland and Wales, and the other regions where the demand for devolution seemed less pressing. The new democratic government legislated immediately for devolution to Catalonia and the Basque country, and waited until a popular demand for devolution was expressed elsewhere. Thus, as with the United Kingdom, devolution was not introduced at the same time for every region of the country, but only if and when there was a demand for it. The hope was that the success of devolution in the historic communities would lead to a demand for devolution elsewhere; and that, indeed, was what occurred. Moreover, and again there is a parallel in the United Kingdom, devolution was asymmetrical, with Catalonia, the Basque country, and five other regions being given greater responsibilities than the remaining ten regions. The principle of rolling devolution adopted by the Labour government offers the best hope of constructing a practical devolution policy for the whole of the United Kingdom, one which addresses the fact that the different nations and regions of the country seek devolution, if at all, with very different degrees of intensity.

In one part of England, however, London, a quite different route has been taken. For, instead of a regional authority in London, there is to be a directly elected mayor and a city-wide local authority. Whereas the leaders of the Scottish and Welsh devolved bodies are to be chosen by the devolved bodies themselves, the mayor of London is to be directly elected. This gives him or her a powerful popular mandate, but he or she will enjoy comparatively few powers. Indeed, there is to be no devolution of central government powers to London at all, not even powers over secondary legislation. The mayor will have no health, training, further education, or economic regeneration functions and, by contrast with the Welsh Assembly, he or she will have no powers over land-use or development control. It is the Secretary of State for the Environment, Transport and the Regions, not the mayor, who will remain the final appeal on planning matters; and the mayor, unlike the Welsh Assembly, will have no block grant from Whitehall. Although the London authority will be the largest local authority in the country, the mayor will have to rely, like a county council, on precepting the lower tier of local government, and also upon predominantly fixed grants from central government. Most government funds will in fact still be channelled through the London boroughs. Nor will the mayor have the power of the Welsh Assembly to place various public bodies—quangos—under his or her authority, or even to abolish them if he or she so wishes. All he or she will be able to do is to make appointments to them. The role of the authority will be primarily one of scrutiny.

Thus the London mayor and authority will be part of a weak upper tier of local government rather than an embryonic regional authority. The mayor's lack of powers, by contrast with those of the Welsh Assembly, will make it more likely that he or she will interfere with the service-delivery responsibilities of other local authorities, just as the GLC, enjoying only a few functional responsibilities, sought to encroach on the powers of the London boroughs. In providing for a mayor and an authority in London, therefore, the government took a conscious decision against devolution. The concept of a directly elected mayor is quite opposed to that of power-sharing executives in Scotland and Wales, chosen by bodies elected by proportional representation.

The government's proposals for the regeneration of local government, moreover, envisage mayors in other large cities where there is demand. Such mayors would constitute a powerful institutional force against devolution to the regions since regional assemblies would be likely to detract from their authority. Moreover, mayors might claim that it is they who are the true spokespersons for their regions. A mayor of Newcastle, for example, might well claim to be the spokesperson for the north-east, while a mayor of Liverpool might claim a similar role in the north-west. The new assertiveness of the cities would make it more difficult to implement the programme for regional assemblies. Thus the proposals for local government reform, like the policies adopted for London, cut across those for regionalism. Perhaps they will prove a substitute for it.

The development of regional government in England, therefore, remains highly problematic. Were it ever to occur, however, it could have profound effects upon the political system. For the fundamental purpose of elected regional authorities would be to allow for divergences of policy. There would be no point in creating regional assemblies simply to replicate national policies at regional level. Regionalism, therefore, would make for much greater policy diversity. This could well serve to loosen and diversify party structures, so that locality would come to act as a counterweight to the disciplines of the national political parties. Policy would no longer be wholly determined at Westminster by a centralized and disciplined party, but would come to have a much greater local and regional input. Were there to be a fragmentation of the party system along these lines, this could reinforce regional diversity, and territory might once again come to be a crucial factor in politics as it was in the years before 1914. Moreover, while regional devolution would not resolve the West Lothian Question, except in the unlikely event of regional authorities being given legislative powers, it might help to reduce its political salience. For if Scottish MPs were to continue to legislate in detail on the domestic affairs of, for example, the north-east of England, that would only be because the north-east of England had chosen not to take advantage of an offer of devolution, less devolution than that granted to Scotland, but substantial all the same.

Were regional devolution in England to occur, we would have embarked on a process of rolling devolution which could turn Britain into a quasi-federal state, still asymmetrical, but with a rough balance of power between Scotland, Wales, and the English regions. Perhaps the government's proposals for the regions will lead the country in the direction, slowly, almost by stealth, step by step towards a quasi-federal Britain. If this occurred, it would be characteristic of constitutional reform in Britain in that it develops not through any explicit acceptance of a new principle, but by means of piecemeal reforms to meet concrete needs. If a quasi-federal Britain comes about in this way, it will be, perhaps, an excellent illustration of the Hegelian notion of the Cunning of Reason.

The European dimension

The European Union is based in part on the premiss that the nation state is no longer necessarily the best unit for carrying out certain functions of government, which may be better conducted at supranational level. It would be natural, then, to believe that some of the functions of the state are best carried out at *subnational* level. Europe involves power-sharing with other member states, devolution the sharing of power within a single member state. Europe and devolution, therefore, represent twin challenges to the traditional role of the state.[62] For this reason, in many of the member states of the European Union, there is an alliance between Europhiles and decentralizers. That is certainly the case in Britain where many, although by no means all, of those who support closer European integration also support devolution. Conversely, many Eurosceptics are also hostile to devolution, believing as they do that power should remain with the nation state.

Two developments in the Maastricht Treaty of 1991 seemed to give the devolutionist cause added strength. The first was the creation, under Article 198a–c of the Treaty, of the Committee of the Regions. The second was the introduction of the doctrine of subsidiarity under Article 3b. These developments, however, are unlikely to have more than a symbolic effect on relations in Britain between Westminster and the devolved bodies.

The Committee of the Regions is a body with purely consultative powers, but it does institutionalize the role of the regions implying as it does that the construction of European Union requires the contribution of subnational as well as national governments. The Committee indeed seeks to organize the participation of subnational bodies in the decision-making processes of the European Community. These bodies are likely to press the case for the regions at European level. Indeed, the German *Länder* wanted the Committee to be a second chamber of the European Parliament and the leader of the government of the Catalan autonomous region in Spain, Jordi Pujol, has echoed this call. Such a transformation, however, if it ever occurs, lies a very long way in the future.

The significance of the Committee of the Regions should not be exaggerated. Its establishment is very far from bringing about a Europe of the Regions. For the Committee comprises representatives of local authorities as well as regions. The British representatives are entirely local councillors appointed by the government, although in future the devolved bodies are likely to be represented on it. Only Austria, Germany, Italy, and Spain send a majority of representatives from the regions, as opposed to local authorities, to the Committee. Were England to have a regional layer of government, no doubt regional representatives would be included on the Committee. Yet, precisely because the Committee is composed of representatives from bodies whose constitutional status differs widely, it is difficult to envisage it enjoying, for the foreseeable future, more than consultative powers.

The principle of subsidiarity in the Maastricht Treaty requires that decisions should, as far as possible, be taken at the lowest level of government. This principle applies, however, only to relationships between member states and the European Union. It does not apply to relationships between governments and subnational governments. Indeed, the European Union has no jurisdiction over such relationships, and it would probably be regarded as an intrusion if it did. For the freedom of each member state to decide upon the division of powers which it thinks appropriate might well be considered part of the very meaning of subsidiarity.

European regional policy has, since 1988, brought the regions directly into the European Union decision-making process, in the bidding for regional funds. But this does not in practice seem to have increased the political power of the regions. Although the regions do, it is true, establish bilateral relationships through the regional directorate-general of the European Commission, it is nevertheless the member states which lay down the guidelines for regional policy. In Britain, the exigencies of negotiating in and with the European institutions have served to strengthen rather than weaken the lead role of the Department of Trade and Industry.

This is because the institutions of the European Union, far from transcending member states, work through them.[63] The Union is primarily an arena within which the member states bargain, rather than an arrangement for superseding them. Thus, whatever the internal political arrangements of a country, whether it is federal or unitary, the European Union holds member states liable for their obligations under European Community law. Europe has, therefore, despite the subsidiarity principle, undoubtedly exercised a centralizing effect both on relationships between central and local government and on relationships between central government and subnational layers.

The Committee of the Regions and the principle of subsidiarity do not alter this basic constitutional position, that the conduct of relations with the European Union remains the responsibility of member states. Precisely because it is the governments of member states which are liable for European Union obligations, it must remain for these governments to determine their nature and extent. Moreover, each member state, in negotiations within the Council of Ministers, must put forward a common negotiating position and that position must be put forward by a united delegation. There can be no question of a regional unit negotiating independently with Brussels or acting in opposition to its national government, whether that region lies in a federal relationship with its government or is merely devolved.

It is important all the same for regional and subnational voices to be heard in Brussels. If they are unstructured, as is the case in Britain, then regional interests may not be given the weight they deserve. In Britain, the regions are at a disadvantage as compared with the *Länder* in Germany, where there is a constitutionally defined means of determining regional priorities.

Before devolution, the interests of Scotland and Wales were represented by the Secretaries of State for Scotland and Wales, and the Secretary of State for Scotland was specifically charged with ensuring that policy-making in the European Union took account of the special features of the Scottish legal system. After devolution, however, responsibility for a number of areas of European Community legislation, and in particular agriculture and fisheries, will be in the hands of the devolved bodies. In theory, the Scottish Executive will have full responsibility for agriculture and fisheries, while the Welsh Executive will have partial responsibility for them. Policy in these areas, however, is determined primarily in Brussels. Yet there is no statutory requirement that the devolved bodies be involved in negotiation with Brussels. Thus, while the Scottish ministers who will be responsible to the Scottish Parliament for agriculture and fisheries will have no statutory right to be part of the negotiating process and can be overruled by ministers in the British government, ministers in the British government who are responsible for negotiating will not be responsible to the Scottish Parliament. There is thus a disjunction between the constitutional position of the devolved bodies and their actual powers, which could cause disillusionment in Scotland and Wales when it comes to be appreciated that there is a countervailing force to devolution in the form of the European Union.

In this area, as in so many others, devolution will work successfully only if there is close and effective liaison between the government and the devolved executives. The government proposes that ministers and secretaries of the devolved bodies should be involved, as part of the British negotiating team, when matters of Scottish or Welsh concern are being considered. Ministers from the devolved executives might even be able to speak, with the agreement of the lead minister, for the United Kingdom in the Council of Ministers. Scotland and Wales would then become the only subnational units in the European Union with individual access to the Council of

Ministers, since subnational access in Austria, Belgium, and Germany is by common representatives putting forward collective subnational positions. Access to the Council of Ministers by subnational units has become possible in virtue of the revised Article 146 of the Treaty of European Union, agreed at Maastricht, which declares that 'The Council [of Ministers] shall consist of a representative of each member state at Ministerial level, authorized to commit the government of that member state'. This Article was put in to persuade the governments of the German *Länder*, represented in the Bundesrat, to accept the Maastricht Treaty. In fact, however, Article 146 does not offer subnational governments much, merely the right to be a mouthpiece for the position of a member state which they may have played but a small role in formulating. Moreover, since the votes of a member state in the Council of Ministers cannot be split, subnational units must agree a common position with the government of their member state. Thus the devolved executives might, by agreement, speak for the United Kingdom, but they would be doing so as representatives of the UK government, not as representatives of Scotland or Wales.

Involvement by the devolved executives, then, will be subject to their accepting the agreed United Kingdom position which they may or may not have helped to formulate. The devolved executives will not be able to put forward a specifically Scottish or Welsh position which is not also the position of the British government; and it is because the United Kingdom must put forward an agreed position to the Council, which is that of the British government, and because Britain is not becoming a federal state, that Scottish and Welsh executives cannot have a *right* of representation at the Council. They will be invited only if they are prepared to accept the agreed negotiating position of the government. In the words of the White Paper, *Scotland's Parliament*, Cm. 3658, 1997, para. 5.12, 'Provided the Scottish Executive is willing to work in that spirit of collaboration and trust, there will be an integrated process which builds upon the benefits of the current role of the Scottish Office within government.'

The devolved executives will, moreover, be bound by the conventions of confidentiality and collective responsibility which apply to the Cabinet, 'without which', to quote the White Paper again, 'it would be impossible to maintain such close working relationships' (para. 5.4). Thus the devolved bodies do not even enjoy a right of consultation. They will be consulted only if they are prepared to accept the conventions which go with consultation. Moreover, the devolved bodies will also be bound by the confidentiality of meetings of the Council of Ministers.

Thus, whatever role the devolved executives play, they will still be bound by government decisions. Formally, then, devolution will not increase the powers of Scotland and Wales nor alter their constitutional status *vis-à-vis* Europe. Subnational units of government can only be separately represented in Brussels on the Council for a matter for which they enjoy exclusive competence; these, except for language in Belgium, and education in Germany, are generally of a minor kind. But, given that, in Britain, Parliament remains constitutionally supreme, there is *no* matter on which the Scottish Parliament or Welsh Assembly will enjoy exclusive competence.

This, of course, could give rise to problems for Scottish and Welsh interests in Europe. The danger is that Scotland and Wales come to be excluded from the negotiations and the forums in which the vital decisions are made; and that, even when they are admitted, this will be only on sufferance. It is, moreover, difficult to influence a process when one is not part of the give and take of Cabinet discussion. A dispute between, for example, the interests of agriculture in Scotland and East Anglia might be arbitrated, not in negotiations between government and the Scottish Executive, but in Cabinet, a forum in which Scottish interests will be weaker, because the Secretary of State for Scotland no longer enjoys executive functions. If the Scottish or Welsh executives were tempted to publicize their disagreements with the British government, the penalty could be exclusion from the negotiating and decision-making process entirely.

It was to avoid problems of this kind that in Germany the Bundesrat insisted, as a condition of accepting the Maastricht Treaty, on a new Article 23 in the Basic Law, the German constitution, to protect the rights of the *Länder*. This article guarantees the *Länder*, acting collectively through the Bundesrat, involvement in any European Union matters affecting them. A nominated representative from the Bundesrat, moreover, has the right of representation in the German delegation in the Council when a matter of exclusive competence to the *Länder* is being considered, such as culture or the arts. But, even so, there must still be an agreed member-state position in the Council, since the representative of the *Länder* is committing the German government, not just the *Länder*. It is, however, easier for the German *Länder* to secure involvement in the governmental decision-making process than it would be in Britain, for two reasons. First, there are sixteen *Länder* of equal constitutional status covering the whole country, rather than asymmetrical devolution with bodies of very different constitutional status covering just a small part of the country; and second, there is so much more compromise and consensus between the German parties, and the system of government is coalitional at both federal and land level. This makes it possible for there to be members of opposing parties in the German national delegation so that representatives of the *Länder* can become in effect national representatives. It is by no means so clear that such a congenial result could occur in Britain. It is not easy to envisage an SNP executive in Edinburgh, for example, working happily as part of a national delegation with a Labour or Conservative government in London; nor to envisage a Labour administration in Edinburgh working successfully with a Conservative government in London.[64]

It may seem, then, that the position of Scotland and Wales could well be weakened after devolution, and that they will be cut off from the process of decision-making in London, and therefore find that their influence on the process of deciding the United Kingdom position in the Council of Ministers is reduced. Such a judgement, however, may overestimate the influence of the Scottish and Welsh Offices on the pre-devolution decision-making process. On European matters, these Offices have not often taken independent initiatives. Moreover, the Scottish and Welsh Secretaries of State are not frequent attenders at the Council of Ministers. In the years between 1992 and 1996, for example, Scottish Office ministers attended very few meetings:

1992: attended 8 meetings out of 125.
1993: 8 out of 125.
1994: 6 out of 125.
1995: 7 out of 83.
1996: 15 out of 84.[65]

It can be argued, then, that Scotland and Wales will gain rather than lose, since the devolved bodies could prove to be powerful pressure groups influencing both Whitehall and Brussels. They will, in particular, be able to influence the European Commission, which in practice sets the agenda for the European Union. In addition, the devolved administrations will almost certainly open offices in Brussels, which will enable them to bang on doors and lobby more effectively. It is possible that Scotland and Wales will gain more through this pressure-group activity than they will lose through having their European interests represented by the Scottish and Welsh Secretaries. As in so many other areas, devolution is a trade-off and it will not be possible for many years to come to see whether it works for or against Scottish and Welsh interests.

*

Devolution is a transfer of powers. It seems to imply the removal of powers from a superior layer of government to a lower layer of government. It seems to create new independent layers of government. Yet, in reality, it creates not independent but new interdependent layers. As with Europe, so with the financial settlement: devolution will work successfully only if there are interlocking arrangements between central government and the devolved administrations. Such arrangements would also be helpful in ensuring that primary legislation relating to Wales is confined to broad and major questions of policy so that the scope of the Welsh Assembly is not unnecessarily diminished. The Welsh model of devolution, even more obviously than the Scottish, creates interdependence between two layers of government. Indeed, in the modern world, it is hardly possible in any democracy to maintain a rigid line of demarcation between different levels of government. That is why, in most modern federal states, 'dual federalism', of two layers of government each with its own carefully defined sphere of action, has been replaced by 'co-operative federalism', marked by an interdependent relationship between the federal government and the provinces. Devolution, too, if it works successfully will establish not independent, but interdependent bodies in Scotland and Wales, and it will require co-operation and reciprocity between the devolved executives and central government.

Interlocking arrangements generally play an important role in federal systems of government. In Canada, for example, the interlocking principle is given effect through interministerial conferences between representatives of the federal government and the provinces. In Germany, there are regular intergovernmental meetings between ministers and officials of the federal and land governments. In addition, of course, the Bundesrat is itself a powerful instrument of co-ordination.

In the 1978 devolution legislation, no provision was made for such interlocking institutions; nor was any provision made in the actual legislation in 1997. During the House of Lords debates on the Scotland bill, however, a government minister, Baroness Ramsay of Cartvale, made an important announcement:

The Government intend that there should be standing arrangements for the devolved administrations to be involved by the UK Government at ministerial level when they consider reserved matters which impinge on devolved responsibilities. It is envisaged that this would be achieved through the establishment of a joint ministerial committee of which the UK Government and the devolved administrations would be members. The joint ministerial committee will be an entirely consultative body, supported by a committee of officials and a joint secretariat. . . . Where there is agreement between the parties that it should do so, the JMC could also discuss the treatment of devolved matters in the different parts of the UK.[66]

The proposed joint ministerial committee provides institutional recognition of the fact that devolution creates a situation of interdependence rather than a separation of powers. Germany, however, has developed the interlocking principle much further through her second chamber, by means of which the *Länder*, through the representation of their governments in the Bundesrat, are enabled to participate, as of right, in national policy-making. The Bundesrat also provides a countervailing pressure to the natural processes of centralization which affect all governments, whether of the Left or of the Right. As we have seen, the Bundesrat played an important role during the negotiations for the Maastricht Treaty in ensuring that the centralizing tendencies of the European Union were counteracted by the forces of subnational governments. In Britain, co-operation is likely to be greater when the same parties are in office in London,

Edinburgh, and Cardiff, than where there is party conflict. Germany, with its coalitional system, is less troubled with this problem, and there has never been a time when all *Länder* governments have been headed by the same party or parties, although the Bundesrat has on occasion had a different majority from the lower house.

Pressures from subnational government for formal representation at the centre are likely to increase following devolution. Already, in March 1998, the Scottish TUC called for a Scottish seat on the Bank of England's monetary policy committee. This led the Conservatives, no doubt mischievously, to propose an amendment to the Scotland Bill, which was passed in the Lords, but rejected by the Commons, giving the Scottish First Minister power to nominate a representative to this committee.

The most valuable way of creating a forum for subnational interests, however, would be to follow the German model by giving the devolved governments formal access to the legislative process in a reformed second chamber. With reform of the House of Lords currently under consideration, it would be natural to suggest the creation of a second chamber similar to the Bundesrat to replace the present upper house of hereditary and nominated peers. That would be one way of ensuring that the second chamber in Britain gained democratic legitimacy while at the same time basing it on a principle of representation different from that of the Commons.

All such interlocking arrangements, however, raise difficult problems of political accountability which have nowhere been fully resolved. Interlocking means that more decisions are reached through bargaining, at one remove from the electorate, who will find it difficult to pinpoint responsibility. This makes it easier to pass the buck and avoid accountability for unpopular decisions. In the German federal system, there is so much sharing and overlapping of functions that it is difficult for the voter to determine who is responsible for what. Where power is interdependent, to whom is it accountable?

The structure of government in Scotland and Wales, and indeed in the United Kingdom as a whole, is bound to become more complex after devolution. If devolution is to be successful, it will require the construction of new political relationships of tact and harmony between those working in different levels of government, and from different political parties. Devolution requires, and may conceivably help create, new relationships of consensus and co-operation. It will have very profound consequences not only for the government of Scotland and Wales, but for the whole of the United Kingdom.

Conclusion
Federal Devolution

A federal state is a political contrivance intended to reconcile national unity
and power with the maintenance of 'state rights'.

(A. V. Dicey, The Law of the Constitution)

I

When the Scottish parliament voted for union with England, so dis-
solving itself, the Scottish Lord Chancellor, the Earl of Seafield,
wryly declared, 'There's ane end of ane auld sang.' The setting-up of
the Scottish Parliament and the Welsh Assembly mark the start of a
new song. They seem to imply that the United Kingdom is becoming
a union of nations, each with its own identity and institutions, rather
than as the English have often seen it, according to the Royal Commission on the Constitution, 'one nation representing different kinds
of people'.[1]

Constitutionally, devolution is a mere delegation of power from a
superior political body to an inferior. Politically, however, devolution
places a powerful weapon in the hands of the Scots and the Welsh;
and, just as one cannot be sure that a weapon will always be used
only for the specified purposes for which it may have been intended,
so also one cannot predict the use which the Scots and the Welsh will
make of devolution. For the devolved bodies will represent areas of
the United Kingdom with long histories of national identity and
pride. It will be the reaction of these attitudes upon the new institutions which will determine their path of development. The impact of
the Scottish Parliament and the Welsh Assembly will thus depend far
more on political and indeed psychological factors than on constitutional ones. To form an estimate of the consequences of devolution,
therefore, we must peer beyond the formal arrangements in order to
penetrate the realities which lie beneath.

The White Paper, *Scotland's Parliament*, Cm. 3648, states the constitutional position after devolution. It retains, however, a traditional constitutional vocabulary, proclaiming in stern Diceyan tones in paragraph 42 that 'The United Kingdom Parliament is and will remain sovereign in all matters', while section 28 (7) of the Scotland Act announces that 'This section', which provides for the Scottish Parliament to make laws, 'does not affect the power of the Parliament of the United Kingdom to make laws for Scotland.' So also the 1978 Scotland Bill contained as its first clause an assertion that it did not affect Parliament's 'supreme authority to make laws for the United Kingdom or any part of it'. MPs, however, threw out the clause and it did not form part of the Scotland Act. Were they not displaying a better grasp of the political realities than the government? For what can it mean to reiterate the traditional vocabulary of the Constitution and assert supremacy when such wide legislative powers are being devolved to another directly elected body?

Constitutionally, the Scottish Parliament will clearly be subordinate. Politically, however, it will be anything but subordinate. For the Scotland Act creates a new locus of political power. Its most important power will be one not mentioned in the Act at all, that of representing the people of Scotland. The basic premiss of devolution, after all, is that there is a separate political will in Scotland. The First Minister in Scotland will be seen as an executant of that political will, backed as he or she will be by a popular majority in Scotland. It will be the First Minister who will claim the right to speak for Scotland, and claim that he or she has more right to do so than Westminster MPs or the Secretary of State who will have been denuded of his powers, and who, in any case, may represent a party unable to command a majority in Scotland. In practice, therefore, the First Minister in Scotland is likely to be seen as the real leader of Scottish opinion; he or she is likely to be seen as the Prime Minister of Scotland.

It will thus not be easy to bring into play the constitutional restraints in the Scotland Act. For it would be difficult to imagine an issue more likely to unite Scottish opinion than a conflict between the Scottish Parliament and a remote, London-based government. Even if London were to get its way in the end, this would probably be at the cost of considerable political disaffection and loss of support. In practice, therefore, Westminster will find it extremely difficult to exercise its much-vaunted supremacy.

Section 75 of the 1920 Government of Ireland Act offered a far more ringing declaration of supremacy than is to be found in the 1998 Scotland Act: 'Notwithstanding the establishment of the Parliament of Northern Ireland—or anything contained in this Act, the supreme authority of the Parliament of the United Kingdom shall remain unaffected and undiminished over all persons, matters and things in Northern Ireland and every part thereof.'

Yet we have seen in Chapter 3 how difficult it was for Westminster to exercise its supremacy over Northern Ireland. Indeed, on one of the only two occasions when the Lord Lieutenant seriously considered exercising his reserve powers to withhold assent to proposed legislation from Northern Ireland, abolishing proportional representation in local government in the province, he was met by a threat of resignation from the government of Northern Ireland and was compelled to give way. If Westminster found itself incapable of exercising its supremacy over the Northern Ireland Parliament, how much more difficult its task will be *vis-à-vis* Scotland. For Northern Ireland did not see herself as a separate nation within the United Kingdom, nor had she sought devolution. Therefore she had every incentive to avoid conflict with the British government. The Scottish Parliament will have no such incentive. It will speak, moreover, not for an artificially created province in danger of being extruded from the United Kingdom against its wishes, but, as the Scots conceive themselves to be, a nation. For Scotland has, as we have seen, a history of statehood and a national tradition embodied in concrete and ever-present institutional form. Independence is therefore a very real option for her, which it never was for Northern Ireland.

We have seen that the White Paper *Scotland's Parliament* insisted that supremacy remained with Westminster. Many Scots, however, and by no means only those who vote for the SNP, take the view that if Scotland is a nation, it enjoys an inherent right to self-determination. That indeed was the position of the *Claim of Right*, the foundation document of the Scottish Constitutional Convention. The *Claim of Right* was, as Neil MacCormick has noticed, as categorical as the White Paper, 'but in an opposite sense'.[2] It declared: 'We, gathered as the Scottish Constitutional Convention, do hereby acknowledge the sovereign right of the Scottish people to determine the form of Government suited to their needs'. Sovereignty, on this view, lies with the Scottish people not with Westminster, a claim perhaps implicitly accepted by Labour, which, both in 1979 and 1997, restricted the vote in the devolution referendum to electors registered in Scotland.

In the Government of Ireland Act of 1920, the supremacy of Parliament was preserved not only by section 75, but also by section 6 and section 12 of the Act, allowing the Governor to withhold assent to Northern Ireland legislation. This led K. C. Wheare in his classic text *Federal Government*3 to deny that Northern Ireland lay in a federal relationship with Westminster. In practice, however, as we have seen, the Government of Ireland Act did create a quasi-federal relationship between the parliament of Northern Ireland and Westminster, and the canons of interpretation adopted by the courts when dealing with the legislative competence of the Northern Ireland Parliament came to be very similar to those applied in federal systems. In the leading case *Gallagher* v. *Lynn*, for example, Lord Atkin declared (emphasis added):

These questions affecting limitation on the legislative powers of subordinate parliaments *or the distribution of powers between parliaments in a federal system* are now familiar, and I do not propose to cite the whole range of authority which has largely arisen in discussion of the powers of Canadian Parliaments.4

The relationship between Scotland and Westminster, like that between Northern Ireland and Westminster, will also come to be quasi-federal. Wheare in *Federal Government* finds the distinguishing mark of federalism to lie in a constitutionally guaranteed division of powers between co-ordinate and independent levels of government. Clearly neither the Scottish Parliament nor the Welsh Assembly will enjoy such a constitutional guarantee. But the division of powers in Scotland, and to some extent Wales, will be guaranteed in a different way, by the support of their people against any attempt by Westminster to vindicate its supremacy.

If the new arrangements work as intended, the Scottish Parliament will be the supreme authority over Scottish domestic affairs. 'As happened in Northern Ireland', Lord Sewel, a Scottish Office minister, told Parliament, ' . . . we would expect a convention to be established that Westminster would not normally legislate with regard to devolved matters in Scotland without the consent of the Scottish Parliament.'5 The normal convention will be that Westminster ceases to legislate for Scotland, or to intervene in her domestic affairs. The devolution of powers to the Scottish Parliament is likely to be accompanied, as it was with Northern Ireland, by the removal of ministerial responsibility for Scottish domestic affairs from Westminster. No doubt the convention will be adopted as it was in Northern Ireland that questions about Scottish domestic affairs can no longer be asked at Westminster since there is no minister responsible for them. If so, then it will hardly be possible for Westminster to continue to legislate for Scottish domestic affairs when there cannot be that continuous scrutiny and calling to account of ministers which is the hallmark of ministerial responsibility. It is difficult to see how Westminster could continue to legislate for the domestic affairs of Scotland when it will no longer be debating them and no longer holding ministers to account for them.

It is then in constitutional theory alone that full legislative power remains with Westminster. It is in constitutional theory alone that the supremacy of Parliament is preserved. For power devolved, far from being power retained, will be power transferred; and it will not be possible to recover that power except under pathological circumstances, such as those of Northern Ireland after 1968. Thus the relationship between Westminster and Edinburgh will be quasi-federal in normal times and unitary only in crisis times. For the formal assertion of parliamentary supremacy will become empty when it is no longer accompanied by a real political supremacy.

In Scotland then, the supremacy of Parliament will bear a very different and attenuated meaning after the setting-up of her parliament. It will certainly not mean the supremacy over 'all persons, matters and things' of the 1920 Government of Ireland Act. For Westminster, instead of enjoying a regular and continuous exercise of supremacy, will possess merely a nebulous right of supervision over this parliament. Political authority, however, depends upon its regular and continuous exercise; it is not the mere incursion of legislative authority once every ten, fifteen, or twenty years. In these circumstances, the assertion of supremacy becomes, in Enoch Powell's words, 'so empty that it could eventually be given effect only by what would in reality be a revolutionary act'.[6] Thus Westminster's supremacy in Scotland, which was once a real power to make laws affecting Scotland's domestic affairs, will become merely the power to supervise *another* legislative body which will make laws over a wide area of public policy.

In relation to the Scottish Parliament the supremacy of Westminster is thus likely to bear a highly attenuated meaning. It will probably mean no more than:

(*a*) The more or less theoretical right to legislate on Scotland's domestic affairs against the wishes of the Scottish Parliament, something never done in Northern Ireland; and

(*b*) The right to abolish the Scottish Parliament. It is, however, by contrast with the experience of Northern Ireland, difficult to see this happening against the wishes of the Scottish Parliament and people, especially as the Scottish Parliament, unlike the Northern Ireland Parliament established by the Government of Ireland Act in 1920, has been validated by a referendum. It would be difficult to abolish it without another referendum in Scotland.

It will not even be easy for Westminster unilaterally to alter the devolution settlement to Scotland's disadvantage. There is perhaps a case, as was argued in Chapter 7, for revising the needs assessment determining the size of the block fund going to Scotland, which, so it is alleged, is unduly favourable to Scotland. It will, however, be much more difficult to do this, with a Scottish Parliament in existence, than it was before. For, although the provisions of the Scotland Act can in theory be altered by a simple Act of Parliament at Westminster, it would in practice be very difficult to do so on a matter which the Scots regard as affecting their interests without the consent of the Scottish Parliament. Thus, in practice, the supreme body with the power to alter the provisions of the Scotland Act will be not Westminster alone, but Westminster together with the Scottish Parliament. In so far as any major amendment of the Scotland Act is concerned, Westminster will have lost its supremacy.

Dicey declared that one of the characteristics of the sovereignty of

Parliament was that there was no distinction between fundamental and ordinary laws. The Scotland Act, however, might come to enjoy just such a fundamental character. For it will not in practice be alterable in the same way as other legislation.

Thus the Scotland Act, although nominally an Act providing, as its Long Title declares, for 'changes in the government of Scotland', creates in reality a new Constitution for Britain as a whole. This is because it does more than devolve powers. It *divides* the power to legislate for Scotland between Westminster and Edinburgh, creating a quasi-federal relationship between the two parliaments. Moreover, as in a federal system, the operation of the Scotland Act will continually raise questions about the limits of authority of both Edinburgh and Westminster. A constitution which divides powers requires therefore a court to police the division. The Scotland Act provides for this also in that the division of powers will be adjudicated by the Judicial Committee of the Privy Council, which will come to assume the role of a constitutional court on devolution matters.

Of course, the Judicial Committee will be able to pronounce only on Scottish and not on Westminster legislation. It will be able to declare that a Scottish statute is repugnant to the constitution, i.e. that it contravenes the Scotland Act, but not that an Act of the Westminster Parliament is repugnant to it, since the supremacy of Parliament is in theory preserved. Nevertheless, if the Judicial Committee decides a dispute in Scotland's favour, it would be difficult for Westminster to legislate for Scotland on that matter when the Judicial Committee had ruled that it lay within the scope of Scotland's transferred powers. The decisions of the Judicial Committee, therefore, may well have the consequence that the prerogatives of Westminster are diminished. If that happens, Westminster will lose yet another of the characteristics of a supreme parliament, the right to make any laws it wishes. For both Westminster and the Scottish Parliament will have come to depend upon the Judicial Committee for the protection of their sphere of action, a condition characteristic of federal systems of government.

It is, moreover, worth noticing that the whole concept of the supremacy of Parliament is shakier now than it was when the

Government of Ireland Act was passed in 1920. This is because Britain is now a member of the European Union and Westminster seems, in consequence, voluntarily to have abrogated its sovereignty. Indeed, the *Factortame* cases have shown that judges will refuse to apply UK legislation which contravenes European Community law.[7] Although of course the transfer of legislative powers to Scotland is quite different from the transfer of powers to the European Union, because Community law has direct effect in the United Kingdom, nevertheless it is not impossible to imagine a future phase of judicial activism whereby judges would refuse to allow provisions of the Scotland Act, which they might come to regard as fundamental constitutional legislation, to be impliedly repealed by Westminster. What is certain is that parliamentary supremacy no longer possesses the clarity and firmness which it enjoyed when the Government of Ireland Act was passed in 1920.

In his *Introduction to the Study of the Law of the Constitution*, Dicey detected 'three leading characteristics of completely developed federalism—the supremacy of the constitution—the distribution among bodies with limited and co-ordinate authority of the different powers of government—the authority of the courts to act as interpreters of the constitution.'[8] The Scotland Act not only in effect distributes powers. It also introduces a judicial element into the determination of that distribution. It provides therefore for an enacted constitution establishing a quasi-federal system of government and in effect a constitutional court to interpret the distribution of powers. Moreover, the Scotland Act will in effect supersede the supremacy of Parliament, since Parliament will not in practice be able to alter its provisions without the consent of the Scottish Parliament. It would be difficult to imagine a more profound constitutional revolution in the government of the United Kingdom.

II

Dicey believed that a federal system, in order to be successful, requires 'a very peculiar state of sentiment among the inhabitants of the countries which it is proposed to unite. They must desire union, and must not desire unity. If there be no desire to unite, there is clearly no basis for federalism.'9 This 'peculiar state of sentiment' will also be needed if the quasi-federal arrangement established by the Scotland Act is to prove workable. The sense of common feeling will have to prevail over the sentiment of states' rights. Indeed, because it creates governmental relationships of some complexity, quasi-federalism probably requires a *greater* sense of loyalty to the whole, to the United Kingdom, than is necessary in a unitary state.

Will the new constitutional settlement preserve the unity of the United Kingdom; or will it prove a springboard for separatism? In the debate on the White Paper on Wales in the House of Commons, a senior Welsh Labour back-bencher, Donald Anderson, declared that devolution was the beginning of a 'mystery tour' whose final destination was unclear. 'I recall', Anderson went on, 'the fine story of a Welsh mystery tour by bus from Cwmrhydyceirw in my constituency. There was a sweep about where the tour would end, and it is said that the driver won. The people of Wales are driving this mystery tour. They will decide the pace and the direction'.10 The same is true in Scotland. It will be the people of Scotland who will decide whether devolution yields a stable settlement, or whether it proves but a staging-post on the way either to federalism or separatism.

Some of the demands which have fuelled support for devolution in Scotland and Wales have been economic in nature. Resentment against London stems from a feeling that Westminster and Whitehall have ignored Scotland's economic problems. Yet few economic powers are being devolved. This could lead to disillusion when the exaggerated claims made by supporters of devolution are contrasted with the realities. Critics would then argue that devolution had given Scotland the power to deal with matters on which there was comparatively little discontent, while denying them the power to deal with matters on which there was a great deal of discontent. If there is no rapid improvement in public services in Scotland, the Scottish Parliament could become a focus for discontent. Then, devolution would weaken the Union. The contrast between the powerful electoral base and legitimacy of the Scottish

Parliament and its comparatively limited powers could thus fuel separatism.

Devolution to Scotland, where nationalism is stronger than it is in Wales, may thus, by providing legitimacy for Scottish national claims, stimulate the demand for independence. It is sometimes, however, suggested that devolution will, in these circumstances, have *caused* separatism—the slippery-slope argument—but that is misleading. For it implies that the Scots will somehow find themselves independent without having sought to be so.

The constitutional hurdle to be overcome before Scotland becomes independent remains the same after devolution as it was before. Independence requires that the Scots return a majority of SNP MPs to Westminster. Parliament would not, as it did with the Irish, resist the wish of the Scottish people for independence, but it would ensure that independence was in fact Scotland's settled demand by holding a referendum. Separation, therefore, could come about with minimal disturbance, but it would hardly be possible for it to occur through inadvertence on the part of the Scottish people. It is unlikely to happen by accident.

It may seem, from the argument in the preceding chapter, that an independent Scotland would be worse off economically than it is today. Indeed, Ian Lang, the then Secretary of State for Scotland, declared in 1995 that an independent Scotland would have to raise income tax by 19p in the pound to maintain public services at their current level.[11] Yet a country seeking independence tends to find that it is economically feasible. Nations struggling to be free have rarely been deterred by the constraints of economics.

It does not follow, however, that devolution will in fact lead to break-up. A more benign scenario is possible. In Spain, Belgium, Italy, and France, devolution has led not to break-up but to power-sharing. In Catalonia and the Basque country, it has weakened the demand for independence, not strengthened it. The main nationalist parties there no longer seek independence, while electoral support for parties campaigning for separation has declined. Devolution in Britain could well have the same effect, defusing the demand for independence, isolating extremists, and strengthening rather than weakening those powerful forces holding the United Kingdom together. The leitmotif of the twentieth century has, admittedly, been nationalism. But that of the twenty-first century could well prove to be power-sharing.

III

Separatism, then, is by no means the necessary or even the most likely outcome of devolution to Scotland. The nationalist parties may find that they have achieved not independence, but rather a dispersal of power to Scotland and Wales, the greatest reversal of the trend to centralization in government for many years. Many of the supporters of the nationalist parties indeed have sought not separation, but the humanization of the state through a reduction in the scale of government. If they succeed, then the economic and technological developments whose tendency has been to make men and women more and more alike will have found themselves checked by political pressures—the search for identity and the urge to participate. It was Rousseau who was the first to understand that these emotional needs demand satisfaction if men and women are to lead truly fulfilling lives. 'Mankind has lost its home,' Franz Kafka told his friend Gustav Janouch. 'Men always strive for what they do not have. The technical advances which are common to all nations strip them more and more of their national characteristics. Therefore they become nationalist. Modern nationalism is a defensive movement against the crude encroachments of civilisation.'[12] The demand that government be made more responsive and less remote, that its scale be smaller, may be seen as the reassertion of a human imperative against the dominant economic and technological forces of the age.

If there are these powerful centrifugal forces at work in Britain today, it might well be that the best way to strengthen national unity is to give way to them a little, the better to disarm them. Then those deep underlying causes which make for unity can be allowed to operate without arousing antagonism or disenchantment.

Political science has been much concerned with the key question of how political societies are held together. To that question, the traditional British answer has been to concentrate responsibility and political authority in one undivided central parliament. But the case that centralization makes for national unity is something that needs to be argued for and not simply asserted. This book has attempted to show that an alternative answer is possible—that a society may be held together through what Gladstone called a 'recognition of the distinctive qualities of the separate parts of great countries'.[13] If that answer is correct, then devolution will strengthen the United Kingdom, not weaken it.

Notes

Chapter 1. The Making of the United Kingdom

[1] L. J. Sharpe, 'The United Kingdom: The Disjointed Meso', in L. J. Sharpe (ed.), *The Rise of Meso Government in Europe* (Sage, 1993), 290.

[2] Richard Rose, *Understanding the United Kingdom* (Longman, 1982), 37.

[3] James Campbell, 'Observations on English Government from the Tenth to the Twelfth Century', *Transactions of the Royal Historical Society*, 25 (1975), 52.

[4] Conrad Russell, 'Composite Monarchies in Early Modern Europe: The British and Irish Examples', in Alexander Grant and Keith Stringer (eds.), *Uniting the Kingdom: The Making of British History* (Routledge, 1995), 146.

[5] Cited by Bernard Crick, 'The English and the British', in Crick (ed.), *National Identities: The Constitution of the United Kingdom* (Blackwell, 1991), 100.

[6] John Davies, *A History of Wales* (Penguin, 1993), 232.

[7] Edmund Burke, speech on conciliation with the colonies, 22 Mar. 1775, in Burke, *Speeches and Letters on American Affairs* (Everyman edn., 1961), 115.

[8] Cited in H. R. Trevor-Roper, *From Counter-Reformation to Glorious Revolution* (Secker and Warburg, 1992), 289.

[9] W. S. McKechnie, 'The Constitutional Necessity for the Union of 1707', *Scottish Historical Review*, 5 (1908), 55.

[10] J. D. Mackie, *A History of Scotland* (Penguin, 1969), 8–9.

[11] G. S. Pryde, *The Treaty of Union* (Nelson, 1950), 21.

[12] R. S. Rait, *The Parliaments of Scotland* (MacLehose and Jackson, 1924), 9.

[13] Pryde, *The Treaty of Union*, 37.

[14] William Ferguson, 'The Making of the Treaty of Union, 1707', *Scottish Historical Review*, 43 (1964), 110.

[15] T. C. Smout, 'The Road to Union', in G. Holmes (ed.), *Britain after the Glorious Revolution* (Macmillan, 1969), 191.

[16] Pryde, *The Treaty of Union*, 48–9.

[17] Cited in Sir R. Coupland, *Welsh and Scottish Nationalism: A Study* (Collins, 1954), 109.

[18] McKechnie, 'The Constitutional Necessity for the Union of 1707', 60.

[19] For a detailed analysis, see Colin Munro, 'The Union of 1707 and the British Constitution', 87–109, in P. S. Hodge (ed.), *Scotland and the Union* (Edinburgh University Press, 1998).

[20] Ibid. 97–8.

[21] A. V. Dicey and R. S. Rait, *Thoughts on the Union between England and Scotland* (Macmillan, 1920), 253.

22 Stein Rokkan and Derek Urwin, 'Introduction: Centres and Peripheries in Western Europe', in Rokkan and Urwin (eds.), *The Politics of Territorial Identity: Studies in European Regionalism* (Sage, 1982), 11.

23 G. C. Bolton, *The Passing of the Irish Act of Union: A Study in Parliamentary Politics* (Oxford University Press, 1966), remains the best account.

24 A. V. Dicey, *England's Case against Home Rule (1886)* (Richmond Publishing Co., 1973), 191.

25 House of Commons Debates, 4th series, vol. 7, col. 215, 9 Aug. 1892.

Chapter 2. Irish Home Rule

1 Gladstone Papers: May 1886, BL Add. MS 44772, f. 82.

2 John Redmond, 'Historical and Political Addresses, 1883–1897', Dublin, 1898, cited in Grenfell Morton, *Home Rule and the Irish Question* (Longman, 1980), 87–8.

3 Gladstone Papers: BL Add. MS 44631.

4 A. G. Gardiner, *Life of Sir William Harcourt* (Constable, 1923), i. 497.

5 Gladstone Papers: BL Add. MS 44772, ff. 58–60 and House of Commons Debates, 3rd series, vol. 304, col. 1043, 8 Apr. 1886.

6 Ibid; BL Add. MS 44672, f. 95.

7 House of Commons Debates, 3rd series, vol. 304, col. 1082, 8 Apr. 1886.

8 A. W. Hutton and H. J. Cohen (eds.), *The Speeches and Public Addresses of the Right Hon. W. E. Gladstone, M.P.* (Methuen,1894), ix, 1886–8. Speech on Welsh and Irish Nationality at Swansea, 4 June 1887, p. 226.

9 Gladstone, *Special Aspects of the Irish Question* (John Murray, 1892), 133.

10 House of Commons Debates, 3rd series, vol. 304, col. 1081.

11 Ibid., cols. 1544–5, 13 Apr. 1886.

12 Speech on American Taxation in *Speeches and Letters on American Affairs* (Everyman edn., 1961), 59–60.

13 Gladstone Papers, Notes for Speeches, 8 Apr. 1886, BL Add. MS. 44672, f. 21.

14 *Special Aspects of the Irish Question*, 218–19.

15 House of Commons Debates, 3rd series, vol. 304, col. 585, 10 May 1886.

16 Gladstone Papers, BL Add. MS 44772, ff. 131–2.

17 *Special Aspects of the Irish Question*, 47.

18 Memorandum to the Queen, Mar. 1886: Gladstone Papers, BL Add. MS 44772, ff. 64–5.

19 *Special Aspects of the Irish Question*, 47, 49.

20 Gladstone to Peel, 17 Oct. 1841, BL Add. MS 40469, f. 20.

21 Gladstone Papers, BL Add. MS 44672, f. 122.

22 Lord Thring, 'Home Rule and Imperial Unity', in *Contemporary Review*, 51 (1887), 315. Lord Thring was chief parliamentary draftsman on the 1886 bill.

23 Gladstone Papers, BL Add. MS 44772, f. 51.

24 Ibid., f. 103.

25 Gladstone to the Queen, 2 Apr. 1886, PRO CAB 41/20/13.

26 Gladstone Papers, BL Add. MS 44255, f. 178.

27 L. P. Curtis, jun., *Anglo-Saxons and Celts: A Study of Anti-Irish Prejudice in Victorian England* (New York University Press, 1968), 103.

[28] Quoted in A. B. Cooke and J. R. Vincent, *The Governing Passion* (Harvester Press, 1974), 419.

[29] Gladstone Papers, Notes for Speech, 8 Apr. 1886, BL Add. MS 44672, f. 27.

[30] House of Commons Debates, 3rd series, vol. 304, col. 1055, 8 Apr. 1886.

[31] Ibid., col. 1056.

[32] Gladstone Papers, 8 Apr. 1886. Add. MS 44672, f. 27

[33] Ibid., MS 44772, ff. 47—8.

[34] Granville to Hartington, 20 Dec. 1885, cited in Lord Edmond Fitzmaurice, *Life of Earl Granville* (Longmans Green, 1905), ii. 468.

[35] Speech at Newcastle, 22 Apr. 1886, quoted in A. V. Dicey, *A Leap in the Dark* (John Murray, 1893), 43.

[36] Gladstone Papers, 8 Apr. 1886, BL Add. MS 44672, f. 28.

[37] Ibid., 5 May 1886, MS 44772, ff. 103–4.

[38] Lord Thring, 'Ireland's Alternative', in James Bryce (ed.), *A Handbook of Home Rule* (Macmillan, 1887), 204.

[39] Gladstone Papers, MS 44772, f. 101.

[40] Ibid., MS 44771, f. 81.

[41] W. R. Anson, 'The Government of Ireland Bill and the Sovereignty of Parliament', *Law Quarterly Review*, 2 (1886), 442.

[42] Quoted in F. S. L. Lyons, *Charles Stewart Parnell* (Collins,1977), 449.

[43] Ibid. 451

[44] Memorandum by the Committee of the Irish Parliamentary Party on the Contribution by Ireland to Imperial Charges, 13 Jan. 1893, p. 9. PRO CAB 37/33. no. 7.

[45] Report of Committee on Irish Finance (Primrose Committee), Cd. 6153, 1912, p. 11.

[46] E. W. Hamilton, Finance brief. 17 July 1893, Harcourt MS Bodleian Library, Box 160, f. 277.

[47] Hamilton Diary, 14 Jan. 1893, BL Add. MS 48659, f. 81, and 20 Mar. 1893, 48660, f. 19.

[48] Childers to Gladstone, 18 Mar. 1886, Gladstone Papers, BL Add. MS 44132, f. 227.

[49] Dicey, *A Leap in the Dark*, 107.

[50] Memorandum by the Chancellor of the Exchequer on the financial arrangements proposed in the Government of Ireland Bill, 16 Jan. 1893, p. 4. PRO CAB 37/33, no. 4, f. 4.

[51] Harcourt to Ripon, 19 Jan. 1893, quoted in D. R. Brooks, 'Gladstone's Fourth Ministry, 1892–94. Policies and Personalities', Ph.D. thesis (Cambridge University, 1975), 99.

[52] PRO CAB 37/108, no. 132, p. 18.

[53] Harcourt to Gladstone, 15 Feb. 1893, BL Add. MS 44203 f. 52.

[54] Harcourt MS, Box 160 f. 97.

[55] Primrose Committee, Cd. 6153, 1912, p. 26.

[56] House of Commons Debates, 4th series, vol. 16, cols. 1504–7, 30 Aug. 1893.

[57] Cited in H. Montgomery Hyde, *Carson* (Constable, 1974), 116.

[58] House of Commons Debates, 4th series, vol. 10, col. 1629, 6 Apr. 1893.

[59] Cd. 6153, 1912, p. 22.

[60] Quoted in J. E. Kendle, 'The Round Table Movement and "Home Rule All Round" ', *Historical Journal*, 11 (1968), 338.

[61] House of Commons Debates, 5th series, vol. 116, col. 1930, 3 June 1919.

[62] Ibid., col. 1898.

63 Patricia Jalland, 'United Kingdom Devolution 1910–14: Political Panacea or Tactical Diversion?', *English Historical Review*, 94 (1979), 765–7; House of Commons Debates, 5th series, vol. 36, col. 1043, 11Apr. 1912.

64 W. F. Monypenny and G. E. Buckle, *The Life of Benjamin Disraeli, Earl of Beaconsfield* (John Murray, 1920), vi. 510.

65 House of Commons Debates, 3rd series, vol. 36, col. 1205, 8 Apr. 1886.

66 House of Commons Debates, 3rd series, vol. 36, col. 1143, 7 June 1886.

67 Cited in John D. Fair, *British Interparty Conferences: A Study of the Procedure of Conciliation in British Politics, 1867–1921* (Oxford University Press, 1980), 229.

68 Report of a Joint Deputation from the Houses of Parliament to the Prime Minister on Federal Devolution, 26 June 1918, cited in Fair, *British Interparty Conferences*, 229.

69 Cited in R. J. Lawrence, *The Government of Northern Ireland* (Oxford University Press, 1965), 188.

70 A. V. Dicey, *England's Case Against Home Rule*, (Richmond Publishing Co. Ltd., 1973), 178.

71 A. V. Dicey, *Letters on Unionist Delusions* (Macmillan, 1889), 34–5.

72 Viscount Ullswater, *A Speaker's Commentaries* (Edward Arnold, 1925), ii. 269–70.

73 Conference on Devolution: Letter from Mr Speaker to the Prime Minister, Cmd. 692, p. 6.

74 Cited in John Kendle, *Ireland and the Federal Solution: The Debate over the United Kingdom Constitution, 1870–1921* (McGill, Queen's University, Kingston, Ontario, 1989), 222.

75 Letter from Mr Speaker, 38.

76 House of Lords Debates, vol. 33, col. 526, 5 Mar. 1919.

77 Ullswater, *A Speaker's Commentaries*, ii. 271.

78 Salisbury to Rev. M. MacColl, 12 Apr. 1889 in G. W. E. Russell (ed.), *Malcolm MacColl: Memoirs and Correspondence* (Smith, Elder, 1914), 137.

79 J. E. Cairnes, 'Fragments on Ireland', in *Political Essays* (Macmillan, 1873), 198.

80 Nicholas Mansergh, *The Government of Northern Ireland: A Study in Devolution* (Allen and Unwin, 1936) 16.

81 BL Add. MS 44772, f. 74.

82 House of Commons Debates, 3rd series, vol. 36, col. 1240, 7 June 1886.

83 Paul Bew, *C. S. Parnell* (Gill and Macmillan, 1980), 70.

84 Cited in H. C. G. Matthew, *Gladstone Diaries* (Oxford University Press, 1994), xiii. 126.

85 Kenneth Rose, *King George V* (Weidenfeld and Nicolson, 1983), 242.

Chapter 3. Northern Ireland

1 John Morrill, 'The British Problem c1534–1707', in Brendan Bradshaw and John Morrill (eds.), *The British Problem, c1534—1707: State Formation in the Atlantic Archipelago*, (Macmillan, 1996), 10

2 Oliver MacDonagh, *States of Mind: A Study of Anglo-Irish Conflict 1780—1980* (Allen and Unwin, 1983), 19–20.

3 House of Commons Debates, 3rd series, vol. 34, col. 1200, 8 Apr. 1886.

4 House of Commons Debates, 3rd series, vol. 15, col. 259. 6 Feb. 1833.

[5] Lewis Harcourt Diary, Harcourt Mss, Bodleian Library, Box 378, f46, 29 Mar. 1886.

[6] Mansergh, *The Government of Northern Ireland*, 93.

[7] Cited in Michael Laffan, *The Partition of Ireland, 1911–1925* (Dundalgan Press, 1983), 33.

[8] Ibid. 36.

[9] House of Commons Debates, 5th series, vol. 39, col. 773, 11 June 1912.

[10] House of Commons Debates, 5th series, vol. 59, col. 934, 9 Mar. 1914.

[11] Letter from Lloyd George to Bonar Law, 2 Nov. 1918, Lloyd George papers, House of Lords Record Office, F/68/1.

[12] House of Commons Debates, 5th series, vol. 123, col. 1198, 22 Dec. 1919.

[13] Eamon Dyas, *Federalism, Northern Ireland and the 1920 Government of Ireland Act* (Institute for Representative Government, Belfast, 1920), 25.

[14] Cabinet Committee on Ireland, 1919–20, 1st Report, 4 Nov. 1919, p. 5. PRO CAB 27/68.

[15] Cited in St John Ervine, *Craigavon: Ulsterman* (Allen and Unwin, 1949), 444.

[16] Cited in John Kendle, *Walter Long, Ireland and the Union, 1905–1920* (McGill, Queen's University Press, Montreal, 1992), 183. Emphasis added.

[17] House of Commons Debates, 5th series, vol. 127, cols. 928–9, 29 Mar. 1920.

[18] Cited in Nicholas Mansergh, 'The Influence of the Past', in David Watt (ed.), *The Constitution of Northern Ireland: Problems and Prospects* (Heinemann, 1981), 12.

[19] Thomas Jones, *Whitehall Diary*, iii. *1918–25* (Oxford University Press, 1971), 128, 130.

[20] Quoted in Ronan Fanning, 'Britain, Ireland and the end of the Union', in Lord Blake (ed.), *Ireland after the Union* (Oxford University Press, 1989), 116.

[21] House of Commons Debates, 5th series, vol. 127, cols. 990–1, 29 Mar. 1920.

[22] Jones, *Whitehall Diary*, iii. 131.

[23] Ibid. iii. 161.

[24] H. H. Asquith, *Memories and Reflections, 1852–1927* (Cassell, 1928), ii. 192.

[25] House of Commons Debates, 5th series, vol. 129, cols. 1279–80, 18 May 1920.

[26] Ibid., cols. 1289–90.

[27] *Correspondence between His Majesty's Government and the Prime Minister of Northern Ireland*, letter from Sir James Craig to Lloyd George, 11 Nov. 1921, p. 5.

[28] Mansergh, *The Government of Northern Ireland*, 236–7.

[29] House of Commons Debates, 5th series, vol. 127, cols. 989–90, 29 Mar. 1920.

[30] R. J. Lawrence, *The Government of Northern Ireland: Public Finance and Public Services* (Oxford University Press, 1965), 181.

[31] House of Commons Debates, 5th series, vol. 711, cols. 1560–2, 6 May 1965.

[32] F. H. Newark, 'The Law and the Constitution', in Thomas Wilson (ed.), *Ulster Under Home Rule* (Oxford University Press, 1955), 31.

[33] See e.g. the 5th edn. (London University Press, 1959), 157.

[34] House of Commons Debates, 5th series, vol. 63, cols. 1624–5, 3 May 1923.

[35] House of Commons Debates, 5th series, vol. 707, cols. 79–80, 22 Feb. 1965.

[36] House of Commons Debates, 5th series, vol. 698, col. 1151, 14 July 1964.

[37] House of Commons Debates, 5th series, vol. 718, cols. 45–6, 58, 26 Oct. 1965.

[38] Paul Rose, *Backbencher's Dilemma* (Frederick Muller, 1981), 179.

[39] House of Commons Debates, 5th series, vol. 751, col. 1686, 25 Oct. 1967.

[40] Standing Advisory Committee on Human Rights, *The Protection of Human Rights in Northern Ireland* (HMSO, 1977), para. 2:11.

41 Tom Hadden and Paddy Hillyard, *Justice in Northern Ireland: A Study in Social Confidence* (The Cobden Trust, 1973), 11.

42 Jonathan Bardon, *A History of Ulster* (Blackstaff Press, 1992), 499.

43 Meeting of the British co-signatories of the Irish Treaty, 7 Sept. 1922, PRO CAB 43/1.

44 Quoted in Paul Arthur, 'Devolution as Administrative Convenience: A Case Study of Northern Ireland', *Parliamentary Affairs*, 30 (1977), 98. See, more generally, Patrick Buckland, *The Factory of Grievances: Devolved Government in Northern Ireland, 1921–39* (Gill and Macmillan, 1979), 268–75. This book, based largely on Northern Ireland government archives, presents a powerful case against the devolution experiment in the province; also P. Buckland, 'Who Governed Northern Ireland? The Royal Assent and the Local Government Bill, 1922', *Irish Jurist*, 15 (1980).

45 Brigid Hadfield, *The Constitution of Northern Ireland* (SLS, Belfast, 1989), 36.

46 Harry Calvert, *Constitutional Law in Northern Ireland: A Study in Regional Government* (Stevens, 1968), 87–9. This book contains the best account of the constitutional relationships between Westminster and Belfast before the troubles.

47 Disturbances in Northern Ireland, Report of the Cameron Commission, Cmnd. 532, Belfast, paras. 229, 138, and 139.

48 Quoted in Laffan, *The Partition of Ireland*, 114.

49 Quoted in Buckland, *The Factory of Grievances*, 236.

50 Mansergh, *The Government of Northern Ireland*, 138.

51 Cornelius O'Leary, 'Northern Ireland, 1921–1929: A Failed Consociational Experiment', in Dennis Kavanagh (ed.), *Electoral Politics* (Oxford University Press, 1992), 254, 253.

52 Mansergh, *The Government of Northern Ireland*, 143.

53 Thomas Hennessey, *A History of Northern Ireland, 1920–1996* (Macmillan 1997), 54–5.

54 Bardon, *A History of Ulster*, 511.

55 Cameron Report, Cmnd. 532, Belfast, para. 229(a)(6).

56 Colin Coulter, 'Direct Rule and the Ulster Middle Classes', in Richard English and Graham S. Walker, *Unionism in Modern Ireland* (Macmillan, 1996), 169–70.

57 James Loughlin, *Ulster Unionism and British National Identity since 1885* (Pinter, 1995), 173.

58 James Callaghan, *A House Divided: The Dilemma of Northern Ireland* (Collins, 1973), 1. See also Kenneth O. Morgan, *Callaghan: A Life* (Oxford University Press, 1997), 347.

59 Terence O'Neill, *The Autobiography of Terence O'Neill* (Faber, 1972), 146.

60 PRO CAB 24/137. CP 4081.

61 Quoted in R. J. Lawrence, 'Devolution Reconsidered', *Political Studies*, 4 (1956), 8 n.

62 Ibid.

63 House of Commons Debates, 5th series, vol. 335, cols. 1708–9, 12 May 1938.

64 Lawrence, *The Government of Northern Ireland*, 70.

65 Cmnd. 5460, para. 1304.

66 *The Autobiography of Terence O'Neill*, 39.

67 Cmnd 5460, para. 1307.

68 *Minutes of Evidence*, (HMSO, 1971), iii, para. 19.

69 Martin Wallace, 'Home Rule in Northern Ireland: Anomalies of Devolution', *Northern Ireland Legal Quarterly*, 18 (1967), 161.

[70] Richard Crossman, *Diaries of a Cabinet Minister* (Hamish Hamilton and Jonathan Cape, 1977), iii. 187.

[71] *Minutes of Evidence*, (HMSO, 1971), iii. 176.

[72] Lawrence, *The Government of Northern Ireland*, 143.

[73] F. H. Newark, 'Some Developments in Northern Ireland Since 1921', *Northern Ireland Legal Quarterly*, 23 (1972), 96.

[74] *Minutes of Evidence*, iii, para. 245.

[75] Ibid.

[76] Garret FitzGerald, *Towards a New Ireland* (Charles Knight, 1972), 77.

[77] Terence O'Neill, *Ulster at the Crossroads* (Faber, 1969), 81.

[78] Cited in Derek Birrell and Alan Murie, *Policy and Government in Northern Ireland: Lessons of Devolution* (Gill and Macmillan, 1980), 148, 380. This book offers a fine, albeit critical, analysis of the Stormont regime.

[79] *Minutes of Evidence* (HMSO, 1971), iii, para. 27.

[80] Cmnd. 5460, para. 1256.

[81] Ibid., paras. 150, 151.

[82] *Minutes of Evidence*, iii, 71.

[83] Lawrence, *The Government of Northern Ireland*, 75.

[84] D. P. Barritt and Charles Carter, *The Northern Ireland Problem: A Study in Group Relations* (2nd edn., Oxford University Press, 1972), 112.

[85] Quoted in Martin Wallace, *Northern Ireland: 50 Years of Self-Government* (David and Charles, 1971), 52.

[86] See M. N. Hayes, 'Some Aspects of Local Government in Northern Ireland', in Edwin Rhodes (ed.), *Public Administration in Northern Ireland* (Magee University College, Londonderry, 1967), esp. 88–97.

[87] Callaghan, *A House Divided*, 66.

[88] The structure of government at the beginning of direct rule is described by Lord Windlesham, one of the first Ministers of State for Northern Ireland, in 'Ministers in Ulster: The Machinery of Direct Rule', *Public Administration*, 51 (1973), 261–72, reprinted in his book, *Politics in Practice* (Jonathan Cape, 1975), ch. 5.

[89] Cmnd. 7110, 1978.

[90] James Prior, *A Question of Balance* (Hamish Hamilton, 1986), 191.

[91] House of Commons Debates, 6th series, vol. 23, col. 479, 10 May 1982.

[92] Prior, *A Question of Balance*, 182.

[93] Quoted in David Blomfield and Maeve Lankford, 'From Whitewash to Mayhem: The State of the Secretary in Northern Ireland', in Peter Catterall and Sean McDougall (eds.), *The Northern Ireland Question in British Politics* (Macmillan, 1996), 148.

[94] Prior, *A Question of Balance*, 194.

[95] Letter from Professor J. H. Whyte to Clerk Assistant of the Northern Ireland Assembly, 19 Sept. 1984, in Northern Ireland Assembly, Second Report from the Devolution Report Committee (HMSO, 1985), vol. ii, NIA 182–II.

[96] Cornelius O'Leary, Sydney Elliott, and R. A. Wilford, *The Northern Ireland Assembly 1982–1986: A Constitutional Experiment* (C. Hurst, London, 1988).

[97] Ibid., p. v.

[98] The Belfast Agreement: An Agreement Reached at the Multi-Party Talks on Northern Ireland, Cm. 3883, 1998.

[99] Dail Debates, 21 Apr. 1998, col. 1028.

[100] This analysis of the Belfast Agreement owes a great deal to Brendan O'Leary, *The British–Irish Agreement: Power-Sharing Plus* (Constitution Unit, London), 1998.

Chapter 4. Scotland

[1] Hardwicke to Kames, 17 Oct. 1754, quoted in Philip C. Yorke, *Life and Correspondence of Philip Yorke, Earl of Hardwicke, Lord High Chancellor of Great Britain* (Cambridge University Press, 1913), i. 623.

[2] Quoted in Arthur Midwinter, Michael Keating, and James Mitchell, *Politics and Public Policy in Scotland* (Macmillan, 1991), 52.

[3] House of Commons Debates, 3rd series, vol. 304, col. 252, 13 Apr. 1886.

[4] H. J. Hanham, 'The Creation of the Scottish Office, 1881–87', *Juridical Review* (1965), 229.

[5] Report of Royal Commission on Scottish Affairs, Cmd. 9212, 1954, para. 13.

[6] Lord Morrison of Lambeth, *Herbert Morrison: An Autobiography* (Odhams, 1960), 199.

[7] J. M. Ross, *The Secretary of State for Scotland and the Scottish Office* (Studies in Public Policy, 87; Centre for Studies in Public Policy, Strathclyde University, 1981), 9.

[8] William Miller, *The End of British Politics? Scots and English Political Behaviour in the Seventies* (Oxford University Press, 1981), 10.

[9] Crossman, *Diaries of a Cabinet Minister*, iii. 48

[10] House of Commons Debates, 6th series, 29 Nov. 1995, vol. 267, col. 1234.

[11] Lord Kilbrandon, 'A Background to Constitutional Reform', Presidential Address to Holdsworth Club, University of Birmingham, 1975, 19.

[12] Scottish Home Rule Association, 'Statement of Scotland's Claim for Home Rule' (Edinburgh, 1888), 5, 10–11.

[13] In one Belgian election, the *Front Democratic des Francophones*, a party representing the French-speaking population of Brussels, gained a higher percentage of the vote in Brussels.

[14] Peter G. J. Pulzer, *Political Representation and Elections in Britain* (Allen and Unwin, 1967), 98.

[15] David Butler and Donald Stokes, *Political Change in Britain* (Penguin edition, 1971), 189.

[16] Ian Budge and D. W. Urwin, *Scottish Political Behaviour* (Longmans, 1966), 134.

[17] William L. Miller with Bo Särlvik, Ivor Crewe, and Jim Alt, 'The Connection between SNP Voting and the Demand for Scottish Self-Government', *European Journal of Political Research*, 5 (1977), 99.

[18] W. Miller, J. Brand, and M. Jordan, *Oil and the Scottish Voter*, SSRC, North Sea Oil Panel Occasional Paper, No. 2 (London, 1980), 5.

[19] John Vincent, 'What Kind of Third Party?', *New Society*, 26 Jan. 1967.

[20] John Vincent, *The Formation of the Liberal Party, 1857–1868* (Constable, 1966).

[21] James Kellas, *The Scottish Political System* (2nd edn., Cambridge University Press, 1975), 210 n.

[22] Vincent, 'What Kind of Third Party?'. See also Ken Young, 'Orpington and the Liberal Revival', in Chris Cook and John Ramsden (eds.), *By-elections in British Politics* (UCL Press, 1997).

[23] R. Coupland, *Welsh and Scottish Nationalism* (Collins, 1954), 246.

[24] J. G. Lockhart, *Life of Sir Walter Scott* (C. A. & W. Galignani & Co., 1838), i. 299.

[25] Crossman, *Diaries of a Cabinet Minister*, ii. 1976, 550–1.

[26] *Scotland's Government*, The Report of the Scottish Constitutional Committee (Edinburgh, 1970), 62.

[27] *Scotland's Government*, preface, p. v.

[28] Ibid. 65, 41.

[29] Quoted in J. P. Mackintosh, 'The Report of the Royal Commission on the Constitution, 1969–73', *Political Quarterly* (1974), 116.

[30] Margaret Thatcher, *The Path to Power* (Collins, 1995), 322.

[31] K. O. Morgan, *Wales in British Politics* (University of Wales Press, revised edn., 1970), 199.

[32] Tom Johnston, *Memories* (Collins, 1952), 69.

[33] Quoted in Michael J. Keating, 'Nationalism in the Scottish Labour Movement, 1914–74', unpublished paper prepared for the Political Studies Association Conference, Aberystwyth, 1977, p. 17.

[34] Quoted in William Ferguson, *Scotland from 1689 to the Present* (Oliver and Boyd, 1968), 388.

[35] Cited in Miller, *The End of British Politics?*, 21.

[36] R. Rhodes James (ed.), *Winston S. Churchill: His Complete Speeches, 1897–1963*, viii. *1950–63* (Chelsea House, New York, 1974), 7936–7, election address, 14 Feb. 1950.

[37] George Pottinger, *The Secretary of State for Scotland 1926–1976: Fifty Years of the Scottish Office* (Scottish Academic Press, 1979), 106, 102.

[38] Royal Commission on the Constitution, *Minutes of Evidence*, iv (HMSO, Edinburgh, 1971), paras. 70, 126.

[39] Crossman, *Diaries of a Cabinet Minister*, iii. 106.

[40] H. M. Drucker, *Breakaway: The Scottish Labour Party* (Edinburgh University Students Publications Bureau, 1978), 28.

[41] Tam Dalyell, *Devolution: The End of Britain?* (Jonathan Cape, 1977), 106.

[42] Drucker, *Breakaway*, 29.

Chapter 5. Wales

[1] Quoted in Coupland, *Welsh and Scottish Nationalism*, 48.

[2] Quoted in Kenneth O. Morgan, *Wales in British Politics* (revised edn., University of Wales Press, 1970), 65.

[3] Tom Nairn, 'Scotland and Wales: Notes on Nationalist Pre-History', *Planet*, 34 (Nov. 1976), 8.

[4] Engels, *The Magyar Struggle* (1849), quoted by Harvie, *Scotland and Nationalism*, 26.

[5] Henry Pelling, *The Social Geography of British Elections, 1885–1910* (Macmillan, 1967), 369, 415–16.

[6] J. Vyrnwy Morgan, *The Philosophy of Welsh History* (John Lane, 1914), 154.

[7] W. Llewelyn Williams, *Young Wales Movement: Cymru Fydd: Its Aims and Objects* (Roberts Bros., 1894), 3.

[8] Morgan, *Wales in British Politics*, 164.

[9] Quoted in J. Graham Jones, 'Michael Davitt, Lloyd George, and T. E. Ellis: The Welsh Experience, 1886', *Welsh History Review*, 18 (1997), 481.

10 The quotations in this and the preceding para. are from Morgan, *Wales in British Politics*, 107, 231.

11 Quoted in Neville Masterman, *The Forerunner: The Dilemma of Tom Ellis* (C. Davies, 1973), 256. See also, for this episode, Emyr W. Williams, 'Liberalism in Wales and the Politics of Welsh Home Rule, 1886–1910', *Bulletin of the Board of Celtic Studies*, 37 (1990).

12 K. O. Morgan, 'The Welsh in English Politics, 1868–1982', in R. R. Davies *et. al.* (eds.), *Welsh Society and Nationhood* (University of Wales Press, 1984), 239.

13 Coupland, *Welsh and Scottish Nationalism*, 199.

14 Morgan, *Wales in British Politics*, 306–7.

15 K. O. Morgan, 'Introduction' to *Lloyd George: Family Letters, 1885–1936* (University of Wales Press and Oxford University Press, 1973), 8.

16 Henry Pelling, *Popular Politics and Society in Late Victorian Britain* (Macmillan, 1968), 112–13.

17 Quoted in Ioan Bowen Rees, *The Welsh Political Tradition* (Plaid Cymru, 1975), 14.

18 Royal Commission on the Constitution, Report, para. 349.

19 House of Commons Debates, 5th series, vol. 403, col. 2312, 10 Oct. 1944.

20 House of Commons Debates, 5th series, vol. 428, col. 405, 28 Oct. 1946.

21 Kenneth O. Morgan, *Rebirth of a Nation, Wales 1880–1980* (University of Wales Press and Oxford University Press, 1981), 376.

22 Alan Butt Philip, *The Welsh Question* (University of Wales Press, 1975), 316.

23 Reprinted as 'The Fate of the Language', *Planet*, 4 (Feb.–Mar. 1971), 26–7.

24 Gwynfor Evans, *Plaid Cymru and Wales* (Llyfrau'r Dryw, 1950), 17.

25 Quoted in Butt Philip, *The Welsh Question*, 186.

26 Philip N. Rawkins, 'Minority Nationalism and the Advanced Industrial State: A Case-Study of Contemporary Wales', Ph. D. thesis (Toronto University, 1975), 368.

27 Gwynfor Evans, *Wales Can Win* (C. Davies, 1973), 124.

28 David McKie, *Guardian*, 20 July 1968.

29 P. J. Randall, 'The Development of Administrative Decentralisation in Wales, from the establishment of the Welsh Department of Education in 1907 to the creation of the post of Secretary of State for Wales in October 1964', M.Sc. Econ. thesis (University of Wales, 1969), 58.

30 Notes for the President of the Board of Education, 'What the Welsh Department has done for Wales since its creation, 29 November 1909', quoted in Randall, 'The Development of Administrative Decentralisation', 51.

31 W. J. Braithwaite, *Lloyd George's Ambulance Wagon* (Methuen, 1957), 222.

32 Randall, 'The Development of Administrative Decentralisation', 72.

33 Sir Henry Bunbury, 'Introduction' to Braithwaite, *Lloyd George's Ambulance Wagon*, 31.

34 Quoted in Randall, 'The Development of Administrative Decentralisation', 101.

35 James Griffiths, *Pages from Memory* (Dent, 1969), 161.

36 Morgan, *Rebirth of a Nation*, 379.

37 House of Commons Debates, 5th series, vol. 702, cols. 624, 627, 19 Nov. 1964.

38 House of Commons Debates, 5th series, vol. 697, col. 755, 25 June 1964.

39 Royal Commission on the Constitution, *Minutes of Evidence* (HMSO, 1971), i, para. 14.

[40] Crossman, *Diaries of a Cabinet Minister*, ii. 344.

[41] *Western Mail*, 19 Jan. 1968.

[42] Crossman, *Diaries of a Cabinet Minister*, ii. 771.

[43] *Western Mail*, 24 Mar. 1972.

[44] 'How Local Government?' *Planet*, 31 (Mar. 1976), 8.

[45] House of Commons, Standing Committee D, 1971–2, vol. v, cols. 2914, 2890, 16 Mar. 1972.

[46] Quoted in John Osmond, *Creative Conflict*: *The Politics of Welsh Devolution* (Routledge and Kegan Paul, 1977), 142, 143.

[47] Osmond, *Creative Conflict*, 149.

Chapter 6. Devolution: Challenge, Defeat, and Renewal

[1] Ross McKibbin, *The Evolution of the Labour Party, 1910–1924*, (Oxford University Press, 1974), 241–2.

[2] Kenneth O. Morgan, *Labour People*: *Hardie to Kinnock* (Oxford University Press, revised edn., 1992), 32.

[3] Hugh Seton-Watson, *Nations and States* (Methuen, 1977), 445.

[4] House of Commons Debates, 5th series, vol. 885, col. 1031, 3 Feb. 1975.

[5] House of Commons Debates, 5th series, vol. 922, col. 1369, 13 Dec. 1976.

[6] Ibid.

[7] Michael Steed, 'The Core-Periphery Dimension of British Politics', *Political Geography Quarterly*, 5 (1986), pp. S91–S103; and Vernon Bogdanor and William Field, 'Lessons of History: Core and Periphery in British Electoral Behaviour: 1910–1992', *Electoral Studies*, 12 (1993), 203–24.

[8] Cmnd. 5460–1, para. 1.

[9] Cmnd. 5460, para. 13.

[10] Jenifer Hart, 'Some Reflections on the Report of the Royal Commission on the Police', *Public Law* (1963), 303.

[11] Cmnd. 5460, paras. 498, 539.

[12] Ibid., para. 1123.

[13] Ibid., paras. 1108, 1123, 1189, and 1192.

[14] Cmnd. 4360–1, para. 129, p. x and para. 126.

[15] In *The Times*, 8 Oct. 1976.

[16] Cmnd. 5460, paras. 1123, 1182, 1186.

[17] Ibid., para. 1217.

[18] Ibid., para. 1111.

[19] House of Commons Debates, 5th series, vol. 936, col. 316, 26 July 1977.

[20] House of Commons Debates, 5th series, vol. 870, col. 84, 12 Mar. 1974, emphasis added.

[21] Edmund Dell, *A Hard Pounding*: *Politics and Economic Crisis, 1974–76* (Oxford University Press, 1991), 51.

[22] Barbara Castle, *The Castle Diaries, 1974–76* (Weidenfeld and Nicolson, 1980), 179, 497.

[23] House of Commons Debates, 5th series, vol. 924, col. 221, 18 Jan. 1977.

[24] House of Commons Debates, 5th series, vol. 922, col. 992, 13 Dec. 1976.

[25] Sir David Lidderdale (ed.), *Erskine May's Treatise on the Law, Privileges, Proceedings and Usage of Parliament* (19th edn., Butterworth & Co., 1976), 523.

26 House of Commons Debates, 5th series, vol. 925, cols. 1715–16, 10 Feb. 1977.

27 House of Commons Debates, 5th series, vol. 926, col. 1273, 22 Feb. 1977.

28 House of Commons Debates, 5th series, vol. 936, col. 313, 26 July 1977.

29 The Government's Devolution Plans: A Note of Dissent from the United Kingdom Liberal Party's Machinery of Government Policy Panel, Autumn 1977.

30 *Guardian*, 14 Nov. 1977.

31 S. E. Finer (ed.), *Adversary Politics and Electoral Reform* (Anthony Wigram, 1975), 18.

32 Brigid Hadfield, 'Scotland's Parliament: A Northern Ireland Perspective on the White Paper', *Public Law* (1997), 668 n.

33 House of Commons Debates, 5th series, vol. 942, col. 1462, 25 Jan. 1978.

34 Letter from the late Ian Mikardo, MP, to the author, 15 Sept. 1979.

35 George Cunningham, 'The Case for the 40 per cent Test', *Scotsman*, 1 Feb. 1978.

36 J. S. Gardner, Electoral Registration Officer, Lothian Region, Letter to the *Scotsman*, 'Purpose of the Electoral Register', 26 Feb. 1979.

37 This calculation represents the author's view of the maximum possible number of deductions. It is based on the research of David Butler and Colm O'Muircheartaigh, reported in *The Economist* on 19 Feb. 1979, and an article, 'The Two Registers', in the *Scotsman* on 12 Feb. 1979. The argument for the calculation is given in Vernon Bogdanor, 'The 40 per cent Rule' in *Parliamentary Affairs* (1980), 249–63, reprinted in Vernon Bogdanor, *Politics and the Constitution, Essays on British Government* (Dartmouth, 1996), 227–41.

38 Harold Wilson, *Final Term* (Weidenfeld and Nicolson and Michael Joseph, 1979), 213 n.

39 David Foulkes, J. Barry Jones, and R. A. Wilford (eds.), *The Welsh Veto: The Wales Act 1978 and the Referendum* (University of Wales Press, 1983), 125.

40 Ibid. 134.

41 The *Scotsman*, 15 Feb. 1979, and William L. Miller, *The End of British Politics? Scots and English Political Behaviour in the Seventies* (Oxford University Press, 1981), 249.

42 Margaret Thatcher, *The Downing Street Years* (HarperCollins, 1993), 624, 619.

43 Jim Bulpitt, *Territory and Power in the United Kingdom: An Interpretation* (Manchester University Press, 1983), 235.

44 David Butler, Andrew Adonis, and Tony Travers, *Failure in British Government: The Politics of the Poll Tax* (Oxford University Press, 1994), 195.

45 Kenyon Wright, *The People Say Yes: The Making of Scotland's Parliament* (Argyll Publishing, 1997), is an account of the genesis of the Convention and of its work by one of its two co-chairmen.

46 I owe this point to Patrick Wormald.

Chapter 7. Legislating for Devolution: The Constitutional Problems

1 Scottish Affairs Committee, 1 July 1998, HC 460–II, Qu. 328.

2 Ibid., Qu. 325.

3 See the White Paper, *Modern Local Government: In Touch with the People*, Cm. 4014, 1998, ch. 3, 'New Political Structures'.

4 Cmnd. 5460, 1973, para. 819.

5 George Pottinger, *The Secretaries of State for Scotland 1926–76: Fifty Years of the Scottish Office* (Scottish Academic Press, 1979), 197.

6 Cmnd. 5460, para. 820.

7 Peter Hain, 'Selling the System: The Alternative Vote', in Gareth Smyth (ed.), *Refreshing the Parts* (Lawrence and Wishart, 1992), 47.

8 *Report on the Electoral System* (Labour Party, 1993), 23.

9 House of Commons Debates, 5th series, vol. 936, col. 316, 26 July 1977.

10 House of Commons Debates, 5th series, vol. 925, col. 262, 1 Feb. 1977.

11 Brigid Hadfield, *The Constitution of Northern Ireland*, (SLS, Belfast, 1989), 89.

12 See R. L. Borthwick, 'When the Short Cut may be a Blind Alley: The Standing Committee on Regional Affairs', *Parliamentary Affairs*, 38 (1978), 201–9.

13 House of Commons Debates, 5th series, vol. 178, cols. 96–7, 26 Oct. 1965.

14 H. C. G. Matthew, *The Gladstone Diaries* (Oxford University Press, 1990), xi. 542, entry for 28 Apr. 1886.

15 Cmnd. 5460, para. 813.

16 Professor William Miller, in a letter to the *Scotsman*, 23 Jan. 1995, cited in *Scotland's Parliament: Fundamentals for a New Scotland Act* (Constitution Unit, 1996), 109.

17 See Iain McLean, 'The Representation of Scotland and Wales in the House of Commons', *Political Quarterly*, 66 (1995), 250–8.

18 Neil MacCormick, 'The English Constitution, the British State and the Scottish Assembly', *Scottish Affairs: Understanding Constitutional Change* (1998), 131.

19 Cmnd. 5460, para. 815.

20 See McLean, 'The Representation of Scotland and Wales', 250-8.

21 Cmnd. 5460, 1973, para. 659.

22 Sir George Godber, 'Regional Devolution and the National Health Service', in Edward Craven (ed.), *Regional Devolution and Social Policy* (Macmillan, 1975), 77.

23 House of Commons Debates, 5th series, vol. 941, col. 1540, 10 Jan. 1978.

24 See the remarks of Lord Sewel, a Parliamentary Under-Secretary at the Scottish Office, in House of Lords Debates, vol. 581, col. 150, 1 July 1997.

25 Ibid.

26 PRO CAB 27/108. No. 132, 36.

27 Committee on Local Government Finance, Cmnd. 6453, 1976, ch. 15, p. 283, para. 2.

28 House of Lords Debates, vol. 391, col. 330, 3 May 1978.

29 House of Commons Debates, sixth series, vol. 302, Written Answers, cols. 510–13, 9 Dec. 1997.

30 House of Lords Debates , vol. 588, col. 1055, 21 Apr. 1998.

31 Select Committee on Scottish Affairs, *Minutes of Evidence*, 7 July 1980, HC 689, 1979–80, Qu. 50.

32 James Kellas, 'The Scottish and Welsh Offices as Territorial Managers', *Regional and Federal Studies*, 8 (1998), 96.

33 David Richards, Principal Finance Officer, Welsh Office, giving evidence to the House of Commons, Treasury Committee, on *The Barnett Formula*, HC 341, 1997, Qu. 198.

34 Select Committee on Scottish Affairs, *Minutes of Evidence*, Qu. 32.

35 HC 329, 1997–8, para. 90; HC 341, 1997–8, para. 11.

36 I owe this reference to David Heald.

37 Cmnd. 5460, para. 669.
38 David Heald and Neil Geaughan, 'The Fiscal Arrangements for Devolution', to be published in J. McCarthy and D. Newlands (eds.), *Devolution in the United Kingdom* (Gower, 1999).
39 Treasury Committee, *The Barnett Formula*, HC 341, Memorandum by Arthur Midwinter, 31.
40 House of Commons Debates, sixth series, vol. 302, Written Answers, col. 513, 9 Dec. 1997.
41 Cited by David Heald, 'Formula-Based Territorial Public Expenditure in the United Kingdom', *Aberdeen Papers in Accountancy, Finance and Management* (1992), 57. Munro-Ferguson was later, as Lord Novar, to become, between 1922 and 1924, Conservative Secretary for Scotland.
42 Ibid.
43 Robert Hazell and Paul Jervis, *Devolution and Health* (Nuffield Trust Series, No. 3, 1998), 68.
44 Cmnd. 5460, paras. 649–56 and 1314. The Memorandum of Dissent, on the other hand, came out in favour of devolved taxes. See paras. 262–76 and appendices A and B of Cmnd. 5460–1.
45 Cmnd. 5460, para. 1100.
46 Ibid., para. 829.
47 Ibid., para. 828.
48 See e.g. House of Commons Debates, 6th series, vol. 302, col. 677, 8 Dec. 1997.
49 Royal Commission on the Constitution: Research Papers, Nevil Johnson, 'Federalism and Decentralisation in Germany', para. 6.
50 Extract from a Cabinet paper written in 1975, entitled 'The Role of the Welsh Assembly in Primary Legislation', quoted in John Osmond, *Creative Conflict* (Routledge and Kegan Paul, 1977), 153.
51 House of Lords Debates, vol. 588, col. 1132, 21 Apr. 1998.
52 Cmnd. 5460, para. 282.
53 Richard Rose, *Understanding the United Kingdom*, 29.
54 House of Commons, 5th series, vol. 939, Written Answers, col. 108, 15 Nov. 1977.
55 Cmnd. 5460, para. 531.
56 House of Commons Debates, 6th series, vol. 231, col. 524, 4 Nov. 1993.
57 Brian Hogwood, *Mapping the Regions: Boundaries, Coordination and Government*, Report to the Joseph Rowntree Foundation (1996).
58 Quoted in John Mawson, 'The English Regional Debate: Towards Regional Governance or Government?', in Jonathan Bradbury and John Mawson (eds.), *British Regionalism and Devolution: The Challenges of State Reform and European Integration* (Jessica Kingsley, 1997), 186.
59 Christopher Harvie, 'English Regionalism: The Dog that Never Barked', in Bernard Crick (ed.), *National Identities: The Constitution of the United Kingdom* (Blackwell, 1991), 105.
60 House of Commons Debates, 6th series, vol. 302, col. 359, 3 Dec. 1997.
61 Environment, Transport and Regional Affairs Committee, Regional Development Agencies, HC 415, 1997–8, Qu. 561.
62 Michael Keating, 'The Continental Meso: Regions in the European Community', in Sharpe (ed.), *The Rise of Meso Government in Europe*, 296.
63 Ibid. 306.
64 There is a valuable account of the role of the *Länder* by Hans-Georg Gerstenlauer

in his chapter 'German Laender and the European Community', in Barry Jones and Michael Keating (eds.), *The European Union and the Regions* (Oxford University Press, 1995).

65 Figures cited by Alex Salmond, leader of the SNP, House of Commons Debates, 6th series, vol. 304, col. 63, 12 Jan. 1998.

66 House of Lords Debates, vol. 592, col. 1488, 28 July 1998.

Chapter 8. Conclusion: Federal Devolution

1 Cmnd. 5460, para. 331.

2 Neil MacCormick, 'The English Constitution, the British State and the Scottish Anomaly', *Scottish Affairs* (1998), 142.

3 K. C. Wheare, *Federal Government* (4th edn., Oxford University Press, 1963).

4 [1937] AC 863. Emphasis added.

5 House of Lords Debates, 21 July 1998, col. 791.

6 House of Commons Debates, 5th series, vol. 924, col. 458, 19 Jan. 1977.

7 *R* v. *Secretary of State for Transport ex parte Factortame Ltd.* [1990] 2 AC 85; *R* v. *Secretary of State for Transport ex parte Factortame Ltd. (No. 2)* [1991] 1 AC 603; and *R* v. *Secretary of State for Transport ex parte Factortame Ltd. (No. 3)* [1991] 2 Lloyd's Rep 648.

8 *The Law of the Constitution*, 144.

9 Ibid.

10 House of Commons Debates, 6th series, vol. 298, col. 1164, 25 July 1997.

11 David Heald, Neil Geaughan, and David Robb, 'Financial Arrangements for UK Devolution', *Regional and Federal Studies*, 8 (1998), 35.

12 Gustav Janouch, *Conversations with Kafka* (2nd edn., André Deutsch, 1971), 175.

13 Speech at Swansea, 4 June 1887, in A. W. Hutton and H. J. Cohen (eds.), *The Speeches and Public Addresses of the Right Hon. W. E. Gladstone*, ix. *1886–1888* (Methuen, 1894), 225.

Suggestions for Further Reading

These suggestions make no pretence at being comprehensive. They comprise only those books and articles which proved most useful in preparing *Devolution in the United Kingdom*.

The Making of the United Kingdom

Aylmer, G. E., 'The Peculiarities of the British State', *Journal of Historical Sociology*, 3 (1990).

Bolton, G. C., *The Passing of the Irish Act of Union: A Study in Parliamentary Politics* (Oxford University Press, 1966).

Bradshaw, Brendan, and Morrill, John (eds.), *The British Problem c1534–1707: State Formation in the Atlantic Archipelago* (Macmillan, 1996).

—— and Roberts, Peter (eds.), *British Consciousness and Identity: The Making of Britain, 1533–1707* (Cambridge University Press, 1998).

Campbell, James, Observations on English Government from the Tenth to the Twelfth Century, *Transactions of the Royal Historical Society*, 25 (1975).

—— John, Eric, Wormald, Patrick, and Addyman, P. V. (eds.), *The Anglo-Saxons* (Phaidon, 1982).

Coupland, Sir R., *Welsh and Scottish Nationalism: A Study* (Collins, 1954).

Evans, Neil (ed.), *National Identity in the British Isles* (Coleg Harlech, 1989).

Grant, Alexander, and Stringer, Keith (eds.), *Uniting the Kingdom? The Making of British History* (Routledge, 1995).

Hodge, P. S. (ed.), *Scotland and the Union* (Edinburgh University Press, 1998).

Loyn, H. R., *The Making of the English Nation from the Anglo-Saxons to Edward I* (Thames and Hudson, 1991).

Mason, Roger (ed.), *Scotland and England 1286–1815* (John Donald, Edinburgh, 1987).

Robertson, John (ed.), *A Union for Empire: Political Thought and the British Union of 1707* (Cambridge University Press, 1995).

Russell, Conrad, 'John Bull's Other Nations', *Times Literary Supplement*, 12 March 1993.

Stafford, Pauline, *Unification and Conquest: A Political History of England in the Tenth and Eleventh Centuries* (Edward Arnold, 1989).

Thomas, Keith, 'The United Kingdom', in Raymond Grew (ed.), *Crises of Political Development in Europe and the US* (Princeton University Press, 1978).

Urwin, Derek, 'Territorial Structures and Political Development: The United Kingdom', in Stein Rokkan and Derek W. Urwin (eds.), *The Politics of Territorial Identity: Studies in European Regionalism* (Sage, 1982).

Williams, Glanmor, *Recovery, Reorientation and Reformation: Wales c.1415–1642* (Oxford University Press, 1987).

Wormald, Patrick, 'Engla Lond: The Making of an Allegiance', *Journal of Historical Sociology*, 7 (1994).

—— 'On Second Thoughts: The Making of England', *History Today*, 44 (1994).

Irish Home Rule

Dicey, A. V., *England's Case against Home Rule* (1886) (Richmond Publishing Co. Ltd., 1973).

—— *Letters on Unionist Delusions* (Macmillan, 1889).

—— *A Leap in the Dark* (John Murray, 1893).

—— *A Fool's Paradise* (John Murray, 1912).

Gladstone, W. E., *Special Aspects of the Irish Question* (John Murray, 1892).

Hammond, J. L., *Gladstone and the Irish Nation* (revised edn., Cass, 1964).

Jalland, Patricia, 'United Kingdom Devolution 1910–14: Political Panacea or Tactical Diversion?', *English Historical Review*, 94 (1979).

Loughlin, James, *Gladstone, Home Rule and the Ulster Question, 1882–93* (Gill and Macmillan, 1986).

Mansergh, Nicholas, *The Irish Question, 1840–1921* (George Allen and Unwin, 1965).

Northern Ireland

Bardon, Jonathan, *A History of Ulster* (Blackstaff Press, 1992).

Birrell, Derek, and Murie, Alan, *Policy and Government in Northern Ireland: Lessons of Devolution* (Gill and Macmillan, 1980).

Buckland, Patrick, *Ulster Unionism and the Origins of Northern Ireland, 1886–1922* (Gill and Macmillan, 1973).

——*The Factory of Grievances: Devolved Government in Northern Ireland, 1921–39* (Gill and Macmillan, 1979).

Calvert, Harry, *Constitutional Law in Northern Ireland: A Study in Regional Government* (Stevens, 1968).

Dyas, Eamon, *Federalism, Northern Ireland and the 1920 Government of Ireland Act* (Institute for Representative Government, Belfast, 1988).

Hadfield, Brigid, *The Constitution of Northern Ireland* (SLS, Belfast, 1989).

Hennessey, Thomas, *A History of Northern Ireland, 1920–1996* (Macmillan, 1997).

Laffan, Michael, *The Partition of Ireland, 1911–1925* (Dundalgan Press, 1983).

Lawrence, R. J., *The Government of Northern Ireland: Public Finance and Public Services 1921–1964* (Oxford University Press, 1965).

Mansergh, Nicholas, *The Government of Northern Ireland: A Study in Devolution* (George Allen and Unwin, 1936).

—— *The Unresolved Question: The Anglo-Irish Settlement and its Undoing* (Yale University Press, 1991).

—— *Nationalism and Independence*: *Selected Irish Papers* (Cork University Press, 1997).

O'Leary, Brendan, *The British–Irish Agreement*: *Power-Sharing Plus* (Constitution Unit, London, 1998).

The Belfast Agreement: An Agreement Reached at the Multi-Party Talks on Northern Ireland, Cm. 3883, 1998.

Scotland

Bochel, John, Denver, David, and Macartney, Alan (eds.), *The Referendum Experience*: *Scotland 1979* (Aberdeen University Press, 1981).

Devine, T. M., and Finlay, R. J. (eds.), *Scotland in the Twentieth Century* (Edinburgh University Press, 1996).

Dicey, A. V., and Rait, R. S., *Thoughts on the Union Between England and Scotland* (Macmillan, 1920).

Finlay, Richard J., *A Partnership for Good? Scottish Politics and the Union since 1880* (John Donald, 1997).

Harvie, Christopher, *Scotland and Nationalism* (2nd edn., Routledge, 1994).

—— *No Gods and Precious Few Heroes*: *Twentieth-Century Scotland* (Edinburgh University Press, 3rd edn., 1998).

Levack, Brian P., *The Formation of the British State*: *England, Scotland, and the Union 1603–1707* (Oxford University Press, 1987).

McKechnie, W. S., 'The Constitutional Necessity for the Union of 1707', *Scottish Historical Review*, 5 (1908).

Miller, W., Brand, J., and Jordan, M., *Oil and the Scottish Voter* (SSRC, North Sea Oil Panel Occasional Paper No. 2, 1980).

James Mitchell, *Conservatives and the Union*: *A Study of Conservative Party Attitudes to Scotland* (Edinburgh University Press, 1990).

—— *Strategies for Self-Government*: *The Campaigns for a Scottish Parliament* (Polygon, Eden, 1996).

Wright, Kenyon, *The People Say Yes: The Making of Scotland's Parliament* (Argyll Publishing, 1997).

Wales

Butt Philip, A., *The Welsh Question*: *Nationalism in Welsh Politics, 1945–1970* (University of Wales Press, 1975).

Davies, John, *A History of Wales* (Penguin, 1993).

Foulkes, David, Jones, Barry J., and Wilford, R. A. (eds.), *The Welsh Veto*: *The Wales Act 1978 and the Referendum* (University of Wales Press, 1983).

Morgan, Kenneth O., *Wales in British Politics 1868–1922* (University of Wales Press, revised edn., 1970).

—— *Rebirth of a Nation, Wales 1880–1980* (Oxford University Press and University of Wales Press, 1981).

Osmond, John, *Creative Conflict*: *The Politics of Welsh Devolution* (Routledge and Kegan Paul, 1977).

Williams, Emyr W., 'Liberalism in Wales and the Politics of Welsh Home Rule, 1886–1910', *Bulletin of the Board of Celtic Studies*, 37 (1990).

The contemporary debate

Official documents

Royal Commission on the Constitution, Cmnd. 5460, and Memorandum of Dissent, Cmnd. 5460–I, 1973.

White Paper, *Scotland's Parliament*, Cm. 3658, 1997.

White Paper, *A Voice for Wales*: *The Government's Proposals for a Welsh Assembly*, Cm. 3718, 1997.

Treasury Committee, 2nd Report, *The Barnett Formula*, HC 341, 1997.

Books and articles

Bates, T. StJ. N. (ed.), *Devolution to Scotland*: *The Legal Aspects* (T. and T. Clark, 1997).

Bogdanor, Vernon, and Field, William, 'Lessons of History: Core and Periphery in British Electoral Behaviour: 1910–1992', *Electoral Studies*, 12 (1993).

Bradbury, Jonathan, and Mawson, John (eds.), *British Regionalism and Devolution: The Challenges of State Reform and European Integration* (Jessica Kingsley Publishers, 1997).

Bulpitt, Jim, *Territory and Power in the United Kingdom: An Interpretation* (Manchester University Press, 1983).

Crick, Bernard (ed.), *National Identities: The Constitution of the United Kingdom* (Blackwell, 1991).

Dalyell, Tam, *Devolution: The End of Britain?* (Cape, 1977).

Hadfield, Brigid, 'Scotland's Parliament: A Northern Ireland Perspective on the White Paper', *Public Law* (1997).

Hazell, Robert, and Jervis, Paul, *Devolution and Health* (Nuffield Trust Series, No. 3; 1998).

Heald, David, *Financing a Scottish Parliament: Options for Debate* (Scottish Foundation for Economic Research, Discussion Paper No. 1; July 1990).

—— *Formula-Based Territorial Public Expenditure in the United Kingdom* (Aberdeen Papers in Accountancy, Finance and Management; 1992),

Hogwood, Brian W., and Keating, Michael, *Regional Government in England* (Oxford University Press, 1982).

Hope of Craighead, Lord, *Working with the Scottish Parliament: Judicial Aspects of Devolution* (Hume Occasional Papers, No. 54; David Hume Institute, Edinburgh, 1998).

Jones, Barry, and Keating, Michael, *The European Union and the Regions* (Oxford University Press, 1995).

Jones, Timothy H., 'Scottish Devolution and Demarcation Disputes', *Public Law* (1997).

Keating, Michael, and Bleiman, David, *Labour and Scottish Nationalism* (Macmillan, 1979).

MacCormick, Neil, 'The English Constitution, the British State and the Scottish Anomaly', *Scottish Affairs* (1998).

Madgwick, Peter, and Rose, Richard (eds.), *The Territorial Dimension in United Kingdom Politics* (Macmillan, 1982).

Norton, Philip (ed.), *The Consequences of Devolution* (King-Hall Paper No. 6; Hansard Society for Parliamentary Government, 1998).

Rose, Richard, *Understanding the United Kingdom* (Longman, 1982).

Sharpe, L. J. (ed.), *The Rise of Meso Government in Europe* (Sage, 1993).

Steed, Michael, 'The Core-Periphery Dimension of British Politics', *Political Geography Quarterly*, 5 (1986).

Tindale, Stephen (ed.), *The State and the Nations* (Institute for Public Policy Research, 1996).

Tomkins, Adam, *Devolution and the English Constitution* (Key Haven, 1998).

Index

MORE OXFORD PAPERBACKS

This book is just one of nearly 1000 Oxford Paperbacks currently in print. If you would like details of other Oxford Paperbacks, including titles in the World's Classics, Oxford Reference, Oxford Books, OPUS, Past Masters, Oxford Authors, and Oxford Shakespeare series, please write to:

UK and Europe: Oxford Paperbacks Publicity Manager, Arts and Reference Publicity Department, Oxford University Press, Walton Street, Oxford OX2 6DP.

Customers in UK and Europe will find Oxford Paperbacks available in all good bookshops. But in case of difficulty please send orders to the Cash-with-Order Department, Oxford University Press Distribution Services, Saxon Way West, Corby, Northants NN18 9ES. Tel: 01536 741519; Fax: 01536 746337. Please send a cheque for the total cost of the books, plus £1.75 postage and packing for orders under £20; £2.75 for orders over £20. Customers outside the UK should add 10% of the cost of the books for postage and packing.

USA: Oxford Paperbacks Marketing Manager, Oxford University Press, Inc., 200 Madison Avenue, New York, N.Y. 10016.

Canada: Trade Department, Oxford University Press, 70 Wynford Drive, Don Mills, Ontario M3C 1J9.

Australia: Trade Marketing Manager, Oxford University Press, G.P.O. Box 2784Y, Melbourne 3001, Victoria.

South Africa: Oxford University Press, P.O. Box 1141, Cape Town 8000.

A Very Short Introduction

POLITICS

Kenneth Minogue

Since politics is both complex and controversial it is easy to miss the wood for the trees. In this Very Short Introduction Kenneth Minogue has brought the many dimensions of politics into a single focus: he discusses both the everyday grind of democracy and the attraction of grand ideals such as freedom and justice.

'Kenneth Minogue is a very lively stylist who does not distort difficult ideas.'
Maurice Cranston

'a dazzling but unpretentious display of great scholarship and humane reflection'
Professor Neil O'Sullivan, University of Hull

'Minogue is an admirable choice for showing us the nuts and bolts of the subject.'
Nicholas Lezard, *Guardian*

'This is a fascinating book which sketches, in a very short space, one view of the nature of politics . . . the reader is challenged, provoked and stimulated by Minogue's trenchant views.'
Talking Politics

A Very Short Introduction

BUDDHISM

Damien Keown

'Karma can be either good or bad. Buddhists speak of good karma as "merit", and much effort is expended in acquiring it. Some picture it as a kind of spiritual capital—like money in a bank account—whereby credit is built up as the deposit on a heavenly rebirth.'

This Very Short Introduction introduces the reader both to the teachings of the Buddha and to the integration of Buddhism into daily life. What are the distinctive features of Buddhism? Who was the Buddha, and what are his teachings? How has Buddhist thought developed over the centuries, and how can contemporary dilemmas be faced from a Buddhist perspective?

'Damien Keown's book is a readable and wonderfully lucid introduction to one of mankind's most beautiful, profound, and compelling systems of wisdom. The rise of the East makes understanding and learning from Buddhism, a living doctrine, more urgent than ever before. Keown's impressive powers of explanation help us to come to terms with a vital contemporary reality.'
Bryan Appleyard

A Very Short Introduction

CLASSICS

Mary Beard and John Henderson

This *Very Short Introduction* to Classics links a haunting temple on a lonely mountainside to the glory of ancient Greece and the grandeur of Rome, and to Classics within modern culture—from Jefferson and Byron to Asterix and Ben-Hur.

'This little book should be in the hands of every student, and every tourist to the lands of the ancient world . . . a splendid piece of work'
Peter Wiseman
Author of *Talking to Virgil*

'an eminently readable and useful guide to many of the modern debates enlivening the field . . . the most up-to-date and accessible introduction available'
Edith Hall
Author of *Inventing the Barbarian*

'lively and up-to-date . . . it shows classics as a living enterprise, not a warehouse of relics'
New Statesman and Society

'nobody could fail to be informed and entertained—the accent of the book is provocative and stimulating'
Times Literary Supplement

ARCHAEOLOGY

Paul Bahn

'Archaeology starts, really, at the point when the first recognizable 'artefacts' appear—on current evidence, that was in East Africa about 2.5 million years ago—and stretches right up to the present day. What you threw in the garbage yesterday, no matter how useless, disgusting, or potentially embarrassing, has now become part of the recent archaeological record.'

This Very Short Introduction reflects the enduring popularity of archaeology—a subject which appeals as a pastime, career, and academic discipline, encompasses the whole globe, and surveys 2.5 million years. From deserts to jungles, from deep caves to mountain-tops, from pebble tools to satellite photographs, from excavation to abstract theory, archaeology interacts with nearly every other discipline in its attempts to reconstruct the past.

'very lively indeed and remarkably perceptive . . . a quite brilliant and level-headed look at the curious world of archaeology'
Professor Barry Cunliffe,
University of Oxford

OXFORD BOOKS

THE NEW OXFORD BOOK OF IRISH VERSE

Edited, with Translations, by Thomas Kinsella

Verse in Irish, especially from the early and medieval periods, has long been felt to be the preserve of linguists and specialists, while Anglo-Irish poetry is usually seen as an adjunct to the English tradition. This original anthology approaches the Irish poetic tradition as a unity and presents a relationship between two major bodies of poetry that reflects a shared and painful history.

'the first coherent attempt to present the entire range of Irish poetry in both languages to an English-speaking readership' *Irish Times*

'a very satisfying and moving introduction to Irish poetry' *Listener*

THE OXFORD AUTHORS
SAMUEL TAYLOR COLERIDGE
Edited by H. J. Jackson

Samuel Taylor Coleridge, poet, critic, and radical thinker, exerted an enormous influence over contemporaries as different as Wordsworth, Southey, and Lamb. He was also a dedicated reformer, and set out to use his reputation as a public speaker and literary philosopher to change the course of English thought.

This collection represents the best of Coleridge's poetry from every period of his life, particularly his prolific early years, which produced *The Rime of the Ancient Mariner*, *Christabel*, and *Kubla Khan*. The central section of the book is devoted to his most significant critical work, *Biographia Literaria*, and reproduces it in full. It provides a vital background for both the poetry section which precedes it and for the shorter prose works which follow.

THE OXFORD AUTHORS

SAMUEL JOHNSON

Edited by Donald Greene

Samuel Johnson the 'personality' is well known to most readers—perhaps too well known, for, as Edmund Wilson wrote, 'That Johnson really was one of the best English writers of his time, that he deserved his great reputation, is a fact that we are likely to lose sight of.' This volume tries to correct this state of affairs by providing a selection from Johnson's manifold writings that includes not only his more familiar pieces, but a substantial sampling of less well-known prose dealing with political, historical, legal, theological, even bibliographical matters, and of his shorter poetry, letters and journals. In it the reader will find not only a superb mastery of the English language, but, as Johnson said of Bacon, 'the observations of a strong mind operating on life'.

THE OXFORD AUTHORS

JOHN DRYDEN

Edited by Keith Walker

Keith Walker's selection from the extensive works of Dryden admirably supports the perception that he was the leading writer of his day. In his brisk, illuminating introduction, Dr Walker draws attention to the links between the cultural and political context in which Dryden was writing and the works he produced.

The major poetry and prose works appear in full, and special emphasis has been placed on Dryden's classical translations, his safest means of expression as a Catholic in the London of William of Orange. His versions of Homer, Horace, and Ovid are reproduced in full. There are also substantial selections from his Virgil, Juvenal, and other classical writers.

THE OXFORD AUTHORS

JOHN KEATS

Edited by Elizabeth Cook

This volume contains a full selection of Keats's poetry and prose works including *Endymion* in its entirety, the Odes, 'Lamia', and both versions of 'Hyperion'. The poetry is presented in order of composition illustrating the staggering speed with which Keats's work matured. Further valuable insight into his creative process is given by reproducing, in their original form, a number of poems that were not published in his lifetime. A large proportion of the prose section is devoted to Keats's letters, considered among the most remarkable ever written. They provide not only the best biographical detail available, but are also invaluable in shedding light on his poetry.

THE OXFORD AUTHORS
JOHN MILTON

Edited by Stephen Orgel and Jonathan Goldberg

Milton's influence on English poetry and criticism has been incalculable, and his best-known works, *Paradise Lost, Paradise Regained*, and *Samson Agonistes* form a natural mainstay for this freshly edited and modernized selection of his writings. All the English and Italian verse, and most of the Latin and Greek, is included, as is a generous selection of his major prose works. The poems are arranged in order of publication, essential in enabling the reader to understand the progress of Milton's career in relation to the political and religious upheavals of his time.

THE OXFORD AUTHORS

WILLIAM WORDSWORTH

Edited by Stephen Gill

Over the course of his long life Wordsworth revised and altered his earlier works considerably, and readers today are often familiar only with these last revised versions. This edition is particularly important in that it presents the poems in order of composition and in a textual form as near as possible to their earliest completed state. This is invaluable for those interested in tracing the development of Wordsworth's art, and also gives the modern reader the opportunity to share something of the experience of Wordsworth's contemporaries such as Keats, Shelley, Hazlitt, and Lamb who would have read the poems when they were first published.